THE AXE AND THE THRONE

Bounds of Redemption, Book 1

M. D. IREMAN

Published by JayHenge Publishing KB

eBook ASIN: B00OKZIEGI
ISBN: 1523483229
ISBN-13: 978-1523483228

PUBLISHING HISTORY
Character Art Paperback / January 2016
Market Paperback / February 2015
Paperback Edition / December 2014
eBook Edition / October 2014

Cover Illustration by Pablo Fernández Angulo
Character Art by Brandon Leach

DEDICATION

To my wife.

ACKNOWLEDGMENTS

My sincerest thanks to my editor, Jessica Augustsson, who was instrumental in the alchemy that turned a manuscript into something more; to my readers, whose enthusiasm has been heartening; and to the fantasy writers with truly inspired tales involving more than an orphaned hero destined to save the world. And perhaps to the few who are able to retell that story so well that it is still a joy to read.

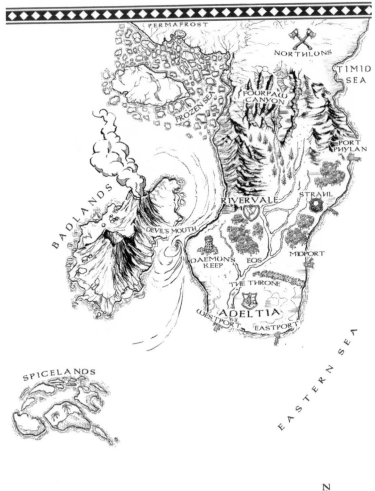

PERMAFROST

NORTHLONS

TIMID SEA

FOURPAW CANYON

FROZEN SEA

PORT PHYLAN

BADLANDS

DEVIL'S MOUTH

RIVERVALE

STRAHL

DAEMON'S KEEP

EOS

MIDPORT

THE THRONE

ADELTIA

WESTPORT   EASTPORT

EASTERN SEA

SPICELANDS

His height in thickness is the stone
That guards from eyes a man's design,
And though I watch his actions all,
Hear every tale, see every wrong,
Were I to damn him 'fore his end,
It would be I who need atone.

-Nameless Gazer

TALLOS

W*here are your friends?* Tallos wondered, growing restless. These were the first two Northmen Tallos had ever laid eyes on, and he was quite sure they'd not come alone. They clung to the side of a bluff high above, unmoving.

Tallos's attempt to swallow was met with little success. His woolen tongue clung to the roof of his mouth, yet his palms were so slick with sweat he feared he'd be unable to grasp his bow when the need arose to use it—when the other Northmen showed themselves in an attempt to save the two above. *This moisture would serve me better were it in my mouth,* Tallos thought, wiping his hands again upon the legs of his trousers with slow, deliberate motion.

He and Lia, his hunting partner and most trusted companion, were no strangers to these northern forests. Normally he would not feel so exposed, confident in his ability to hide his lank frame amongst the brush, but today they'd brought others with them from the village. Tallos glanced at them now, the anxious boys who had followed him and Lia, all foolishly hoping for a chance to kill a Northman. They squirmed and fidgeted in their poorly chosen spots of concealment, looking more like bait than an ambush.

At least there is one here I can trust, Tallos reassured himself. He stroked the hair upon Lia's head to give her comfort. Though he did his best not to think of it, it was impossible not to note just how coarse those hairs had become with age. She crouched beside her master, eyeing him with affection, awaiting his command with eager patience.

They had remained in that same spot hearing the same somber song from an unrelenting sparrow for an hour, perhaps two. Time had an interesting effect on his fear, first causing it to heighten as his anticipation built. Then, as the hours passed with no action, he mellowed. His mind wandered, going mostly to thoughts of his wife. Two days' travel south, safe in their small home of their small village, he imagined her busying herself drying meats to keep her mind from belaboring the danger he faced. But it was impossible to think of Leona and not be reminded of the state in which he'd left her. *I will return to you and earn your forgiveness*, thought Tallos. *That I promise.*

✦ *Two Days Prior* ✦

"They're already dead." One of the many men that had gathered in the village center voiced his opinion on the matter at hand. "Northmen don't take prisoners. They take the dignity of wives and the purity of daughters, forcing the fathers to watch. Then they kill them all. Your boys are dead, Erik."

The man's assertions were met with a mixture of grumbling that sounded mainly of solemn agreement.

"Northmen have never been seen in our finger of the canyon," came a younger, less decided voice. "And perhaps this will be the only time they're seen if we bring the fight to them. I have no wish to have my throat slit while I sleep."

"We're farmers, not warriors. What chance do we stand?"

"The boy spoke of only four…"

"And you believed him? The boy was white with fear. Couldn't tell up from down by the look of him."

Tallos had noticed the same. Erik's boy was near dumb with terror when he'd stumbled home without his two older brothers. "They were four," was all he muttered in between his spastic sobbing inhalations.

"Enough." Greyson's command cut through the chatter, hushing the crowd. As the town elder and tacit leader, he was the final authority in disputes such as these. "Your boys had no reason to be wandering north. You've been told as much before."

The father of the boys wore desperation on his usually amiable face. Erik was not just Tallos's neighbor. Tallos had called the big bastard friend since childhood, been present for the births of all four of his children, and could not help but feel somewhat responsible for the peril now faced by his two eldest sons.

"They are but four, and we have over twenty able-bodied men and half again as many dogs," Erik contested. But Greyson was not alone in vocalizing disapproval of the notion.

"It is not our way to go looking for trouble," said one of Greyson's supporters.

"We'd not be looking for trouble," said a different man. "We'd be looking for his sons. And we'd be looking to send a message that our canyon is not to be raided."

Tallos saw the division clearly. The older men with sense opposed the action, and the young men with swollen pride wished to puff out their chests, safe in the knowledge that the chance of any rescue being mounted was slim. In any case, Tallos was inclined to agree with the elders. His trips with Lia in the North were difficult enough when the two were by themselves. With a group of unseasoned woodsmen—farmers' boys with delusions of heroism—the results of an encounter with even four Northmen would be ugly.

"Tallos, tell them we can do such a thing," begged a young cousin of Erik's. "You know the North better than any."

"He's the reason those boys are there in the first place," grumbled a man hidden in the back.

To hear it voiced made Tallos's chest tense with inescapable blame. All three of Erik's boys idolized him, unduly. They made their hatred for farming known when put to the task, voicing their desire to hunt like their uncle Tallos rather than labor in the soil for the small, deformed produce grown on their father's farm. As a compromise, Erik let his boys go north to practice hunting with their bows, so long as the three stayed together. He did this against the advice of all, Tallos included.

Forgive me, Erik, Tallos thought as he looked at his friend, *but I warned you this may happen*. Be it brawl or town meeting, Tallos could always depend on the man's support. That he could not give his own in return this day would be a source of shame for years to come.

"The Northluns are more than simply dangerous," Tallos began. "Any attempt we'd make would—"

"It is a fool's errand," interrupted Greyson. "As head of the town council I *forbid* it."

Tallos returned Greyson's chiding look with a scowl of his own. *How is it you can be so cross even when we are in agreement?*

"They are my boys, and I will be damned if I am not going after them." Erik's voice was strong and set, but his glistening eyes betrayed the uncertainty and fear amidst his determination.

"You were damned when you let your boys go up there in the first place." Greyson seethed with indignation. "Perhaps if you were more a father to those blood-betting bastards and imposed some discipline, they would not be off in the woods pretending to be your better." The elder hurled the insult with enough force to hit all that heard it in the gut, Tallos most of all.

Tallos envisioned removing his blade and slicing the old man from ear to ear—blood gushing, horrified looks on the faces of the gathered men. Had he actually done such a thing, he would no doubt see nothing but red the moment the blade made contact with skin. It happened to him when he hunted, as soon as his arrow was loosed. He would awake from his blood-visioned trance to an unsavory scene: a deep gash in the deer's neck where he had finished it with his knife and Lia lapping the blood off his hands, tail wagging as she saw he'd returned to his senses. It must have been some latent mechanism of self-protection which sheltered him from the gory reality of killing.

The only red he saw now, however, was on Erik. His friend's fiery mane looked less bright compared with his face, now turned the color of his beetroots. It was likely all Erik could do not to throttle Greyson, who had already begun to walk away.

"If any of you leave on this hopeless task, you will not be welcomed back," Greyson shouted over a shoulder. "This whole town will be in danger if you take men with you to go after those disobedient brats, who'd run straight back into the Northluns the first chance they got."

On this Tallos did not fully agree. Their town was in a canyon valley bordered on the east and west by massive cliffs. Climbing these was unthinkable, and a fall from the top would give one plenty of time to ponder their foolishness before making a sudden and final impact. The way north was quite narrow, and it would be impossible for the Northmen to pass by them and their dogs undetected to endanger the town.

Tallos saw the futility pooling in Erik's eyes, ready to spill over.

"We will gather those men who are willing and leave at once," Tallos yelled, hoping Greyson was still close enough to hear his defiance. Foolish though it was, he knew it would not be hard to find more like Erik's sons, eager to follow him to the Northluns—at the very least for some attempt at revenge. He was unsure of how many would live to make the trip back home, however.

⊷≻⊷

A branch snapping as if underfoot brought Tallos's mind back into focus. One of the boys of his group had adjusted his position and now cringed in horror as if he had cost them all their lives. Tallos felt his own face relax from the scowl it bore with a twinge of guilt. He knew most of his anger lay within himself, for he had allowed his thoughts to wander far too long.

The mist had begun to clear. Tallos usually loved the mist; it both smelled and tasted of the freshest mana and reminded him of his mother, who claimed the mist was mana itself. But now the tiny, floating bits of water only served to help conceal the likely Northman ambush.

"We should move," said Jegson, one of the more aggressive young men of the group. He was a nephew of Erik's wife Megan, and he had a knack for speaking just before Tallos, and too loudly at that. "We've been staring at them for half a day."

"Lower your voice," Tallos whispered, not for the first time.

Tallos glanced upward again at the two figures that clung to the craggy bluff. It did not appear as though they'd moved since they were spotted earlier that morning. Tallos had had their group progress in slow creeps, stopping for hours at a time to listen for danger. He believed they'd avoided detection, but to trek around to the top in broad daylight would make them easy targets for any Northmen waiting above.

"We could be up there killing them by now." Though no others voiced it, Tallos guessed Jegson was not alone in his impatience. "They're Northmen. *Savages.* That is no trap, and if they were going to attempt rescue they would have done so by now. Those rock-locked men were left to die."

"Quiet, boy." It was perhaps the first thing Erik had said since the town meeting, though he looked the same as he had when they left—like he had been sentenced to death and was eager to get it done with. He would follow Tallos to the underworld and showed no sign of second-guessing his strategy, but Tallos knew he must be in turmoil with the waiting.

Tallos surveyed his men and animals for signs that they'd be unable to wait another hour for the daylight's dimming. Of the six men who had come with Tallos and Erik, each had brought one or more dogs, and Jegson, grandson to wealthy breeders, had insisted on bringing three. Almost in unison, the dogs began to sniff at the air, a scent Tallos could not yet detect.

"They smell them," said Jegson, finally whispering. "The Northmen are near."

Tallos did not judge the boy for the fear now present in his voice, though Jegson's assertion was wrong. Tallos caught the scent; it was simply smoke, and that the wind came from the south made it mean very little. Lia looked at Tallos in a way that implied she understood her master's frustration with their ill-trained companions.

"It is just smoke." Tallos saw the relief in his men when they heard his words. "We move when the Dawnstar crests the trees and we can walk in the shadows." Even the dogs seemed to relax as if knowing that they did not have to sit there indefinitely.

As Tallos's thoughts began once again to drift, a tumult of snapping twigs and branches broke the quiet. The sound rushed at them from the distance, bouncing off the canyon walls, growing louder at an impossible rate. Whatever made that noise traveled faster than any Northman—faster than any creature Tallos knew—and it would soon be upon them.

LEONA
Many Years Ago

"Where do you think you're off to, girl?"

The gruff and unexpected voice sent a jolt through her body. Leona had been gathering her things quietly in the hopes of delaying this confrontation. Without turning to face her father, she answered. "I am going to Emie's for a night or two."

"You think I'm a fool?"

It was another question that would be best answered with a lie. Instead, Leona continued pressing her things into the hempen sack that still smelled of mold and potatoes, determined to fit her every belonging of worth inside the single bag.

"Answer me when I speak to you," her father demanded.

"Yes," Leona shouted at him. "You *must* be a fool to think I will remain here with you and mother, washing away other people's filth, in a cold so fierce the cloth threatens to freeze, along with my hands, in the washbasin." Try as she had to explain to him the benefits of having the basin inside the home rather than in the adjoining shed—the one he liked to pretend was plenty warm—her father would not allow it, fearful of a few soapy splashes on the plank floors he was so proud of.

"It is honest work that you should be thankful for."

"And I would be," Leona snapped, "if the money earned from my chores went to anything of value."

Her father took a step forward. He had a new anger in his voice. "Do you think it is easy to keep you and your mother warm and fed during the winter?"

"I think it would be easier if you did not waste all we had warming your own belly with drink."

He grabbed her by the wrist, jerking her away from the wooden box that served as her clothes chest. "You don't think I know where you're off to? With that Northman's bastard? It's bad enough that you were born with those ears you must hide. How do you expect to ever find a

husband of worth when everyone knows what a little whore you are?"
The familiar smell of mead was on his breath.

The air around Leona felt charged with energy, and the faintest
breeze blew, within the confines of her small room, pulling her hair
forward. "Release me," she warned, feeling oddly in control.

Her father made a sound of disgust and let her go.

"If you think I have any intention of marrying some old man who
owns a kennel then you must truly think me a whore." Leona shoved her
last bits of cloth into the bag angrily. "And Tallos's father came from
Rivervale."

"Is that what he told you?" grunted her father. "His parentage is the
least of your problems. That boy cannot put a roof over your head. He's
no carpenter."

She looked at the man before her, the miserable thing that he had
become. White and black stubble covered a face her mother said was
once fine, now turned to the perpetual frown of self-pity. "And when
was the last time you built anything out of wood other than a fire,
Father?"

Her father looked at her with such contempt she feared she may have
pushed him too far. "I am warning you, girl. If you leave here, do *not*
come back."

◁═╬═▷

A mile downstream, where the two sour oaks grew together into one,
Leona waited. The air that played with her long brown hair was crisp and
carried with it the smell of fallen leaves, and the trickling of the brook
was ever changing like the notes of a subtle song sung just for her. She
waited with an anticipation that put a discomfort in her belly and a
longing like hot coals in her chest as her odd ears twitched, straining to
listen for the sound of his approach.

They came here often just to be alone, spending endless hours
wading in the cold clear waters where the brook became deeper and
more still. They searched for rare rocks that hid their patterns when dry
but were brilliantly ornate when wet, keeping the choice ones for their
collection. And as the Dawnstar peeked at them through the leaves, they
lay together, naked on the soft beds of moss, finding that they were
strangely warm in spite of the climate.

She was not supposed to wander so far from the town… No one
was. There were dangers. Savages who sometimes raided villages like
hers, taking what they pleased. But those were Northmen, and she was to
the south. Tallos had told her there was no real danger in the southern
valleys—that the elders were old fools too scared to leave their farms and
kennels. And she had cause to believe him.

Leona thought she heard a sound in the distance, the crackling of dry
leaves underfoot, perhaps. Her heartbeat quickened, and she held her

breath to better hear. No other sounds followed, however.

"Tallos?" she called after waiting as long as her suspense would allow. She hoped he would be within earshot, though in truth she was probably still early. She had left in a hurry, spurred by her father's ire, setting off before she should have. Leona twirled the ring of crude metal Tallos had shaped for her around her finger, both out of nervousness and to remind herself that it still remained.

The weight of eyes fell upon her, and she scanned her surroundings for movement. A dark figure approached from the east, moving with purpose like a lynx shadowing prey. He was a tall man, leaning forward as he stalked. He had a bow in one hand, arrow nocked, ready to draw. With his other hand he put a finger to his lips. It was Tallos.

As he continued forward with stealth, Leona remained silent. She now heard in the distance what he must have already noticed—a far-off cry or whimper. She thought she'd heard it before, but it had been so faint she had convinced herself it was only the keening of the wind. That he heard it too, however, meant it was real. Whatever was making the noise might be in danger, or at least attracting it. She did not have Tallos's knowledge of the woods, and if he was being cautious, it was for good reason.

He motioned for her to remain where she was as he continued past. She wanted nothing more than to run to him and seek comfort—to hide behind him as he flushed out whatever dangers hid in the distance—but she trusted his judgment and remained where she was. Tree upon tree wove their way in between them as he went, and within a few minutes he was out of sight.

You mustn't leave me like this, she thought. The brook no longer sang to her—it was merely noise that kept her from hearing him, and the wind was no longer refreshing—it only burned her eyes, causing them to moisten. She waited now, as he wanted her to, but it would not be long before the wind stung her to the point that tears may fall.

"Leona," she heard him yell. "Come quickly!"

She dropped her hempen sack and ran toward his call, dirtying her dress in the mud of the riverbank. It was not like him to sound so distressed. He was always in control of any situation placed before him. Tallos shared the courage of the very mountain god he so revered.

She found him crouched at the water's edge facing away from her, and though she could hear the whimpering clearly now, she could not see what made it. She hurried to Tallos's side to aid him.

In his lap was a young pup, soaked through and covered in splotches with mud as if it had been playing along the bank. Looking much like a wolf but with floppy ears and a thicker snout, it appeared quite healthy as it jumped and licked at Tallos's face with vigor.

"What is this you've found?"

"It looks to be some sort of dog," Tallos replied. She would have punched him had she not been so relieved.

"I nearly died of fright. You should have let me come with you."

Leona thought at first the poor pup had been sent down the creek to die or had climbed its way to freedom out of the disgusting conditions found in some nearby village kennels, but she saw the guilty smirk on Tallos's face and the leather in his hand and knew at once the true nature of this chance discovery.

"You *bought* it?"

A puppy was quite a luxury to a young couple such that they were, and it would have cost him nearly all his worth to make the purchase. She begged his hazel eyes for truth while admiring the handsome lines of his face.

Tallos handed her the muddy pup, allowing it to finish the job of ruining her only good dress, but she was beyond caring. Any gift from Tallos was worth more than a hundred silly dresses. She pressed the filthy puppy's shivering body into hers to share in her warmth and to dry its coat on her cloth, but Leona found she could not help but wet the creature more with her tears.

"It seems we have a daughter," said Tallos, beaming confidence. "Now to make some sons."

TITON SON OF TITON
Years Ago

Titon, the firstborn of two brothers, bore an unfortunate name. His mother had chosen to call him after his father and leader of their clan, Titon son of Small Gryn. Titon's father was a great man—a giant among Galatai. His presence was such that he towered over all other men, even those few of greater height. He made the walls and frames of normal architecture appear to bend way as he passed, lest they be crushed in his wake. And when his father was near, Titon was able to take some small comfort in knowing that, for the time being, he was not the only one who felt small.

Titon did all he could to better himself—to be more like his namesake. He ate to the point of pain at every meal and washed it down with two cups of goat's milk in expectation of growing larger. He lifted and pressed stones above his head in his free time with the aim of getting stronger. He taught himself to read and studied the meaning of the words in their collection of pilfered books in the hopes of becoming wiser. But he eventually became all too aware that his father would forever look down at him. Even if Titon son of Small Gryn lived long enough to be shrunken and hunched, he would still likely dwarf Titon son of Titon—both in stature and accomplishment.

"A kiss for the one whose arrow flies truest."

Stunned near to disbelief, Titon looked to the speaker. It was Red. Considered prettier than most girls her age due to her straight, bright-red hair, Titon knew he was not her only admirer. She made no effort to hide the glee in her announcement, and Titon allowed himself to briefly entertain the idea that she might be so excited because she knew he was the one most like to win.

The contest of skill was open to all the handful of boys present in the woods. The other boys shot their arrows, some missing the intended target entirely, the closest still a hand's length away. Decker, Titon's younger brother, loosed his arrow which struck a mere finger's width from the center. His pride in the shot showed on his face. At fifty paces it was a fine accomplishment for even a trained Galatai archer. But Titon had a confidence and coolness that the larger boys like his brother lacked—at least when Titon had a bow in his hand. His smaller size seemed to make him more dexterous, and he took to archery as does a goat to spring buds. Having grown tired of shooting the fungus stumps and such chosen by boys his age, he made games of picking a tiny spec within the target and trying to eliminate it completely with the tip of his arrow. Because of this, few realized his true mastery of the weapon.

Titon nocked and let sail his projectile with a half draw in a gentle arc. It lodged in beside Decker's arrow, squeezing itself between it and the bull's-eye. Titon smiled at his accomplishment, then blushed remembering what he'd won. The giggling from the other girls who had come with Red did not comfort him any.

"Axes!" cried Decker, roaring as though he was already a man. "Any boy can shoot a bow. The way you barely pull yours back, you'd never kill anything anyhow. We will throw axes to see who wins."

Titon's eyes went, along with all the others', to Red for her response.

"Very well. A kiss and maybe more for the winner."

Something in the way she spoke reminded Titon of her mother—but that was no bad thing. Kilandra was revered the clan over for her beauty. She walked with a fascinating sway in her hips and clad herself in far less than the other women, who dressed with concern only for the cold. Red's dress was modest, but she stood out among her peers more than even her mother with her scarlet glow.

"You throw first this time," insisted Decker.

Titon, engrossed in a momentary reverie of what "more" might entail, was at a loss for words. He nodded and removed the light axe from his belt and spun it in his hand. He faced a tree fifteen paces away with an obvious rounded knot that could serve as the target. Titon was proficient enough with axes when it came to accuracy, but axe throwing took more than that. It required an intuitive feel for how much power one had to put into rotation so that it would arrive blade first in a target of arbitrary distance. Some simply learned to throw an axe at a specific amount of paces, but a true axe thrower needed to master the nuances that would allow him to make use of the weapon in actual combat.

Titon did as his father instructed, which was to envision the axe in his mind, spinning through the air, the lead edge landing perfectly in its mark. Titon found it easier to see things in his mind with his eyes closed—much to his father's annoyance—so closed they were as he threw, and closed they remained as he heard the "thunk" of the blade biting into wood, followed by a gasp from Red.

Titon never discovered whether her gasp was due to his accomplishment or because she bore witness to the event that followed. Later he learned that Decker, probably convinced that Titon had tried to make him look foolish, swung with all his rage, smashing Titon's face with his fist.

The memory of the events leading up to that punch might one day fade, but Titon knew he would always remember, with crystal clarity, the expression on Red's face as she roused him. Strands of her hair clung to her wet cheeks, darkening its normal red to an exquisite chestnut. On her face, stripped of its usual mask of fake confidence worn attempting to match the expressions of her licentious mother, he saw for the first time an expression of her own invention. It was not compassion in her eyes, it was fear—fear for her own wellbeing. He was well aware that she was desperately afraid of being held responsible and punished for what had transpired, but it only served to magnify his infatuation. Something carnal and primitive stirred inside him as he looked into those frightened eyes, something that wanted both to conquer and to protect, to subjugate and to shelter. He wanted her to be completely his—to remain unsullied by so much as the thought of another laying claim to her.

She wrapped her arms around him. Titon would have been elated had it not been for the realization that he'd wet himself while unconscious. He clumsily pushed her away and tried to run off. A wave of nausea and dizziness hit him, causing him to stumble to his side where he flopped like a fish a few times. He continued his escape from the scene, but it seemed he could not escape the prison of embarrassment, as his only mode of transport was to crawl on all fours due to lack of balance. He thought he heard one of the boys say, "He peed," but could not be certain. He was certain, however, that the crotch of his trousers was wet enough for all to see, that he stunk of piss, and that tears were flowing freely down his cheeks. Finally able to clamber to his feet, he ran off on wobbly legs.

DECKER
Years Ago

Decker's shame cut him like an axe to the gut. He had not meant to hurt his brother. More than that, he felt sick with the shared ache of Titon's embarrassment. But Decker's regret was not fully empathetic. He had envisioned finally besting his brother at either archery or axes and wooing Red. Instead, he had earned her scorn.

"You big dumb oaf!" she had yelled at him after Titon fled. "Now we are all like to be punished." She collapsed melodramatically, sobbing as her female retinue surrounded and tried to calm her.

It was his own fault, thought Decker. *If he had beaten me without such a show, I would not have struck him in anger.* It became easier to shift some of the blame to Titon whose ostentatious performance had humiliated him. *Two lucky shots and this cunt of a whore is impressed?* Their father often spoke ill of the cunts of whores, and though Decker did not know precisely what they were, he was now sure Red was liable to be one. *Titon can have her and her damn firehead.*

The image of his brother crawling away with the piss soaked through the ass of his trousers still plagued him, however. How could Titon ever be respected among the other boys now? How could he ever take their father's place as head of the clan?

Their father must have pondered the same questions as he learned of what had occurred.

Decker mentally prepared himself for the beating—the punishment often threatened, but now finally earned. He was determined to withstand it with honor. He would not cry out in pain or cringe in fear of the blows; he would seek the void as he was taught, and he would absorb the punishment with only courage, as was expected of a Galatai child being disciplined. But his punishment did not yet come.

Instead, Titon son of Small Gryn took Decker and his brother to the southern side of a nearby mountaintop overlooking a valley of moss-covered stone and scraggy pine. He sat down with them and spoke softly, softly at least for the man that he was.

"Beyond the trees and the clouds and the rocks to the south there are evil men. Men that would like to destroy you and your brother, your father and your mother."

Decker saw his brother smile at the delivery. To hear a giant, serious man such as their father accidentally stumble into a silly rhyme sounding like the songs of dancing girls was amusing, but the humor was lost to them both when their father noticed that smile as well.

"Listen to me, you mischievous bastard. You will not like what you hear next." Decker did not think their father had understood the reason for his brother's momentary expression. That he was no longer the sole object of his father's wrath brought Decker no relief. His father glowered at little Titon who looked down and blinked rapidly.

"These men take the noblest of creatures from the forest and chain them to trees." Titon's voice rumbled through Decker like thunder. "They torture and torment them and turn them against each other. They feed them the flesh of their dead and dying fellow man. They turn them into slaves and demons."

They'd both heard these stories before and seen the plunder brought back from raids on the Dogmen villages, but neither had ever actually seen a Dogman. Decker knew from the tales that they were usually scrawny men with hair cut crudely short. The Dogmen and their homes reeked like animals as they often allowed their demonic companions to share the same roof—sometimes going so far as to have them sleep beside them in the same bed.

"Have you ever seen a wolf attack a man except to defend their young? Have you ever seen a wolf steal a goat except in the most desperate times? No!" Titon slammed his fist into the earth. "They run in packs and hunt deer as do we. They eat rabbits and berries as do we. They call to each other when lost. They clean each other's wounds. They are as great and noble as Galatai."

His father's voice softened, but only just. "It is a vile thing those creatures they become when deprived of food and freedom. Snarling demons that hate all men, most of all their tormentor, the one that gives them just enough flesh to survive, just enough flesh to be a slave."

The three of them sat in silence for a time, his father looking into the mists below the cliffs, his brother still looking down at his hands, clearly hurt.

Their father had never exactly been cruel to either of them, but Decker could not shake the feeling of guilt he had for being the presumed favorite. Seeing his brother so scorned—when he'd done nothing wrong—seemed more than unfair. It would have been kinder to them both, had their father simply beaten Decker as he'd first expected.

"We are like the wolves, and they are like us in many ways," continued their father. "And like them we fight among ourselves. Not the cowardly biting of the hindquarters of an unsuspecting brother…"

Decker could feel his father's scowl though neither was turned toward the other. He welcomed the weight of it, eager to share in his brother's burden.

"…But a fight to determine who is best fit to lead. Just like wolves, men need leaders. *Strong, powerful* leaders that others will follow without question."

Their father's emphasis on strong and powerful was yet another blow against Titon. Decker's brother was quick, dexterous, and cunning, but strong and powerful he was not. Decker felt his face contort to a scowl of his own as his anger grew. *This is not right, Father,* he thought.

"There will come a time when the two of you, my wolf pups, will *need* to fight. Yesterday was not the time, nor was that over anything of importance from what I could tell. Some tart of a girl, I'd wager. You will need to fight to determine who will lead our clan, our pack, against the Dogmen. To see them crushed and driven from the land. Certainly no easy task, as they look like men but breed like rabbits. Each time we raid there seems to be more of them, yet always farther south and with less food."

The thought of succeeding his father ahead of his brother had never crossed Decker's mind. He may have been larger than Titon, but his brother was irksomely smart and better with both bow and axe. Decker rarely bested his brother in training, and when he did it never truly felt deserved. This new idea that they would one day fight to determine who would lead turned Decker's stomach. He looked to his brother, but Titon still stared at his hands.

"Each year it grows colder. Each year the frost lasts longer. It used to be that these lands were lush for half the year, but the goats have little to eat now. Some do not agree, but it is known among those wise that we will need to move south in time. We must go to those lands where rabbits and berries are plentiful and cleanse them of Dogmen. We must take the forests of the valleys for our own."

Decker could not control the fire in his chest, and the single droplet he saw hit his brother's thumb almost drove him to madness. *I will not fight you,* Decker promised in silence. *You are the elder brother. The right to lead is yours.*

"To defeat the Wolfsbane and defend the land from southern armies, we will need to unite the clans," their father went on. "I cannot do as such, for I have made too many enemies among them in my time. But someone must. If we are to survive, someone must. A leader of the pack. A *strong* and *powerful* leader."

TALLOS

Tallos drew an arrow and fumbled trying to nock it when a massive thud reverberated through the ground, ending the noise of crashing branches. Their group sat petrified in the silence that followed, even the dogs—such a noise was not made by the footfalls of any prey dogs could hunt. Even Tallos, who now knew the sound had to be from something having fallen from the bluff, was gripped with the childish vision of a giant cyclops charging and slamming a mighty fist into the ground, spurring him to run. But if Northmen above were pushing boulders off the edge of the cliff, it was likely in the hopes of prodding them to run so they could be picked off by arrow fire.

"One's gone," shouted Jegson. Tallos wanted to backhand the boy for being so loud, but it seemed he had come to the correct conclusion before the others. "The fecking Northman's dead!"

Indeed, it appeared there was one less dark shape clinging to the bluff above.

"Keep quiet," Tallos said between teeth clenched in anger, "and move slowly to where he fell."

It was a rather tiny Northman from the looks of him, but Tallos reasoned they came in all sizes. The body was face down, pressed into the ground, bent and smashed in unnatural angles.

"He's dead all right," said Jegson, quietly but with plenty of mirth. His dogs were the first to the body, sniffing hungrily, snarling and snapping at each other as if competing over the carcass.

Three dogs were two too many...perhaps three too many if they were fed the flesh of men. The accusation was never spoken aloud, but there were some who wondered how Megan's parents kept their dogs from starving during times of famine when even their own household members fell dead from malnourishment. Watching Jegson's dogs so eager to get to the body brought a wave of sickness to Tallos and likely to the others as well.

Tallos glanced at Lia, feeling somewhat guilty that he was looking to see if she shared in the other dogs' excitement. Seeing her first human corpse, however, had had a much different effect on the old girl. She looked distressed, as if she knew something the others did not.

Jegson pulled his dogs back violently, unsheathed his dagger, then plunged it into the Northman's back with a triumphant laugh. Tallos was about to scruff the boy when Lia lunged ahead of him, grabbing Jegson's knife hand by the wrist and shaking back and forth.

"Lia, no," Tallos shouted, running to grab her before Jegson's dogs, still frozen from the shock of it, realized they could easily take her. Lia had never bitten a person before, but Tallos had no time to contemplate what had driven her to attack an ally.

Lia released the boy as Tallos approached, but her agitation was far from finished. She remained close to Tallos's knees, still bristling, as Jegson's own dogs began to circle them.

"I'm bleeding!" Jegson had an incredulous look that soon turned to outrage. "I'll have your mut—"

He was interrupted by a familiar crashing through the trees above, followed by a heavy thud. The second body fell only paces away from them, hitting the ground legs first and folding back onto itself at the knees and waist. Crumpled like a ragdoll, the cracked head oozed blood onto the soft, green moss below.

The eyes of the body were wide open, yet the mouth or some hole in the skin was making a noise like air leaking from a bellows. Tallos was given to a moment of fear at the thought that this Northman might still be alive and able to harm them, but it was not so. This was another body, but one too small to be a raiding Northman. Tallos thought he recognized the puny man, but the skin on his face was so badly bitten by frost that its gross red and black colors masked the likeness.

Erik fell to his knees and began to heave up his dried meat and berries. He was the first of the men to recognize the bodies were those of John and Jarl, his two eldest sons.

KEETHRO

"I do not have the mind of a warrior, as I am just a woman. Perhaps you can explain to me then, why we remain huddled in our homes with winter approaching while the Dogmen and their treasures lie to the south, ripe for the taking."

Keethro looked down at his curving forearm, its muscles rippling as he clenched his fist, knuckles cracking—a ritualistic reminder to himself of who he was. He was Keethro son of Leif, second in status among his people only to Titon, and second to none with an axe. He was the man whose affections young women had clamored for above all others in his youth. And his affections he did give to them, one after the other. *If only those days had never ended*, he mused.

Yet for all his raids on the Dogmen, all the bloodshed with rival clans, and all his prowess with women, it seemed he fought most of his battles within the pine walls of this bedroom.

"You still follow that big fool. He was a great man once perhaps, but he now sits in his home with his simple wife while we starve year after year." Kilandra's words threatened to ignite his fury, and she spoke them with full knowledge of this. Keethro let the wave of heat pass over him before speaking.

"I warn you—not for the first time—do not speak that way of Titon or his wife, even in private. It only serves to undermine my plans to one day lead our clan, united with the others, not only to raid the South but to take it for our own." Keethro replied with the coolness of a man poised for violence. He had long since grown tired of this argument.

"Your *plans*? I thought I married a man of action. What good are your *plans* to me now? I sit here in squalor, eating the same dried old leathery goat, hoping that one day a *true* leader from another clan will come and unite us. I see no hope of it from any man in our own."

This was her nature. Her emasculating words had no effect on his pride; he'd heard worse from her before. And by now her motives were transparent: to test and provoke. He was not particularly fond of her methods, but he played along nonetheless. The end result of this charade was not without its benefits.

He looked at his irate and beautiful wife. Her near thirty years and bearing of their child had seen no ill-effect on her appearance. If anything they had merely intensified her vibrant defiance that he still found so alluring. Her hair was of the deepest brown but had in it streaks of violet, artfully applied with dye from tinder berries. Her eyes were large and obstinate, the type lesser men would find challenging to gaze into for fear of the embarrassment of having been caught staring at a woman above their station. Her tight-fitting furs squeezed the frame of her body in a manner which roused him.

But whereas he could find no flaw in her appearance, he found, it seemed, less and less to appreciate otherwise. He had won her with his looks, his charms, and his wits, but none could ever hope to tame so wild a spirit. She stood with her shoulders tall and did not have the look of a woman claimed, nor did she dress it. It was certainly not common among Galatai women to have the inner sides of their breasts bare during winter, and though it irked him, he was not fool enough to try to shame her into covering herself. "A supple grip holds twice as strong," his father had taught him. Keethro found this to apply to many things, women most of all. He knew she dressed as she did not only as an exercise of her own pride, but as a subtle if not subconscious test for him as well. A woman who knows her lover fears her leaving is far more inclined to do so. Keethro had seen it time and again in his youth. More often than not, he had been the one for whom the women had left.

Keethro scruffed his wife by the hair and held her in place as the two exchanged glowers. Then he kissed her forcefully.

This was the game they played. She would provoke him, and he would answer as expected with a certain violence. But as he held her down and took her, he could not help but be distracted by a recurring concern. He watched her hair of deepest brown, once tinged of faux blue but now of violet, as it bounced around her shoulders and down her gracile back, and wondered how it was that their daughter, in her youth, had come to have hair of such brilliant red.

LEONA

Several days had passed since she'd pleaded with her husband not to leave.

"Old and stubborn, though he is, Greyson is right. You are a wise and practical man. Do not let your loyalty to your friend force you to seek what you know is not there."

"Leave it to you, my wife, to insult me with compliments," Tallos snapped back at her. He was on edge. Though she did not believe him to think of Erik's boys as sons—troublesome nephews perhaps at best— she knew they saw him as a father, a thing that must weigh heavy on his conscience. More than that, Tallos would not want to let down Erik. Erik was a silly lout of a man, but in a village small as theirs, one was lucky to have such an honest friend. It was in vain that she attempted to sway Tallos to reason, but she was unable to stop herself from trying.

"Tallos, the boys are dead. Northmen do not take prisoners, you have said so yourself. They steal goats, rape girls, and slaughter all that lives, be it man, woman, child, or pup. They are savages, and our home could be in their path. Would you leave us unprotected?"

"The Three be damned, Leona, you try my patience. You call me wise yet think me fool enough to leave you vulnerable?" Tallos finished tying off his bundle of dried meats with a violent tug on the bindings. "The cliffs protect you east and west. To the south is Rivervale in all its lawful glory. I am headed north through the narrow canyon between the cliffs. Should the Northmen be headed south they'll not escape my eyes nor my ears. I am not one to leave my wife in danger." With that he gathered his remaining supplies from the kitchen table and left with Lia quick at his heels.

Leona knew his words to be spoken in truth, but the truth was twisted in a way in which to justify foolishness. It was not like them to fight. Though they had been frustrated with their inability to forge a family of their own, she never feared it lessening their bond. She had eventually grown content with their fate and even wondered in secret if it had not been a blessing that they should have only each other and Lia. She would never speak as such to Tallos, for she knew he wanted sons. His lack of a father made him wish to have children who he could give the strength and guidance to that he had gone without. But what Leona saw in other households did not convince her that children were the root of happiness. Too often she saw couples united in love transform into bickering adversaries as they fought over the methods and responsibilities required to rear their children. They competed against each other for their children's affections and lived in constant fear for their safety. Worse still, they wore their greater love for their children over that of their spouse like a badge of honor—a thing Leona saw no more honor in than proudly proclaiming to have a favored child. It did not seem a joyful life, and Erik's missing children only solidified her belief.

By contrast, their beloved dog, in all of the twelve years they'd had her, had brought them nothing but joy. Leona watched as Lia's tail disappeared out of the door, a sinking feeling in her stomach that it would be the last time she would see it. Though it was not right to think such things. Tallos hunted alone in the Northluns every month without incident.

Leona picked up a broom and began sweeping the floor that needed no cleaning, a task that failed to distract her from her worry. She hurried out the door to see if Tallos was still in view, but his long woodsman's strides had already put him beyond a point where she could quickly catch up to him. She did not wish to be seen slowing their departure and have others think of her to blame when their mission failed as she knew it would. She just hoped they would return safe—she hoped specifically that Tallos and Lia returned safe. *The others be damned for this whole mess. Those boys had no business being in the Northluns in the first place.*

In spite of her thoughts, she resolved to speak with Greyson the next day. She would beg him to send more men to help the few that went with Tallos. She might be able to convince him, as they both thought it was a foolish task, but sometimes a foolish task can be that which unites a village.

◒═◍═◓

With each passing day, Leona felt worse for the way she had argued with Tallos before he'd left, wishing she could go back and simply support him in his decision. She pictured him walking along the steep scree-covered slopes of the Northluns. It was no place to be when your mind was elsewhere, concerned over petty squabbles. *Forgive me and return home and unharmed,* she thought, willing to endure her discomfort for as many days as necessary so long as he returned.

The Dawnstar bathed her with late-morning rays as she sat at the table in their home's main room, storing the meats she had smoked to dry perfection. This batch would have to last them through the winter that was already threatening to take hold, so it was essential she take every precaution with its preservation. In each of the open jars, she placed a tea sock filled with iron shavings tied off with cotton twine. With clean hands, she then placed as much meat as she could inside, without disturbing the sock or breaking the meat apart. "I prefer venison jerky," Tallos had teased her the previous year, "to venison flakes." It had easily been their best winter together, and they had both been in good spirits. The iron sock idea Tallos had come up with—seeing how mold seemed averse to growing on rusted metal—had kept their meat preserves edible far longer than either expected, and Leona looked forward to another winter where they would have plenty to both share and barter.

As she secured the lid on one of the jars, she thought she saw movement out the window. Her heart raced with excitement and anxiety. He had heard her thoughts and returned. She cupped her hands to the hazy glass, peering out and straining to see. Much to her amazement, several hilltops away in the far distance, she saw the unmistakable figures of men returning home—more than had originally set out. *Tallos, you brave fool, you even found Erik's boys,* she marveled. *I should have never doubted you.*

TALLOS

Little was said after discovering the identity of the bodies fallen from the mountainside, but it was obvious their mission for rescue and vengeance had ended. All that was left was to bundle the twisted remains of the boys and make their way back.

Heads hung low, Tallos's party retraced their steps with humble footfalls. Even the birds that would ordinarily trill at the presence of anything larger than an acorn seemed somber and silent as the procession of men made their way through the forest.

Tallos's stomach was laden with stones of sickening regret, yet he did not feel half as bad as his friend looked. After his violent heaving and sobbing, Erik had become unthinking, his movements lifeless and mechanical. He stared ahead, not speaking to anyone—not that any tried—looking a man with no reason left to exist.

How many hours had they sat and watched the boys as they clung desperately for life, and all of it under Tallos's command? The despair Tallos felt for the loss of the boys was eclipsed only by the guilt of being responsible for the decision that had caused it. Had they circled around to drop rocks on them as Jegson had suggested, they would have recognized and been able to rescue the youngsters before their fall. *What kind of man are you?* Tallos asked himself, further sickened by the self-serving wish that they had never gone searching in the first place.

With Lia picking her steps carefully and looking at her master with worry, Tallos crunched heedlessly through the deadfall. The noise they now made while walking was inconsequential. Tallos almost wished for a Northman attack on his party, an outlet through which he could vent his frustration, but he knew he would not be so lucky.

He was left instead with distasteful visions of what his life would be upon their return. All would know what happened, and everyone would whisper that it could have been avoided had Tallos not have been so cowardly. Greyson's sneers would be insufferable, and Jegson would tell tales to those who would listen of how he fought Tallos's order, how he begged and pleaded that they "charge 'round the bluff" and kill or rescue whoever clung to the rock. Yet all of that would pale in comparison to having to face Erik day in and day out. Erik, the one Tallos had known from childhood and would back him no matter the encounter, Erik who had been hurt already by his boys' admiration of Tallos, Erik who sat patiently, obeying his command to wait for a full day while his boys clung to a mountainside, only to watch them fall to a gruesome death.

Tallos resigned himself to the notion that he, Leona, and Lia would simply have to leave. They would pack their belongings and find a new village somewhere farther south—maybe travel all the way to Rivervale. But even his thoughts of Leona were tainted with regret and self-reproach. The way in which he'd left her was unacceptable. He could not recall another time when he'd departed without saying his farewells and with a promise of his safe return. *It was a mistake I shall not repeat. This I promise you, Leona.* He estimated it would be another night before they reached the village, one more agonizing night in the hell of the Northluns, a place he vowed he'd never return.

His thoughts of Leona were interrupted as several of his party stopped walking, the rest soon following suit. When they were all motionless, he could hear what had caused their alarm. Encroaching sounds: the plodding stride of someone's careless approach.

Tallos's chest felt as though it were collapsing, overwhelmed by the mistake of having wished to be attacked. He bent at the knees and tried to will himself to invisibility. Lia was by his side, as always, poised to protect him against whatever threat may appear.

The noises grew louder. How something could make so much racket walking through dried leaves and not yet be visible, Tallos could not understand. Bears were not like to be out this season, and he could think of nothing else that would advance with so little worry of attracting attention. And then he saw it.

The solitary figure that approached them was a sickly old man. His white hair bounced with his ungainly steps as he trudged through terrain unkind to his spindly legs. It seemed a wonder his frail frame could endure the punishment of those steps without breaking as the man continued forth with no regard for his own wellbeing.

The figure neared, and familiarity gave way to recognition. It was Greyson. He looked as though he was wont to commit murder, but in fairness that was his usual expression. He must have formed a party of reinforcements to save face with the villagers, becoming separated at some point during the trek. It was all too easy to lose sight of others among the trees and elevation changes, and without a strong sense of hearing, one could find himself lost even after stepping away to piss.

Greyson continued onward, moving toward them without words but with purpose—purpose and pure hatred burning in his eyes.

TITON SON OF SMALL GRYN
Years Ago

"Get your wooden axes, and come with me." Titon son of Small Gryn barked the order at his two sons.

It had not been a particularly pleasant day for him. Another raid sent south by his clansmen, led by Keethro, had been unable to find any inhabited Dogmen villages prior to the need to turn back. That news alone had been enough to put Titon in an unfriendly mood, but far worse was what Keethro had told him about the men. "They grumble and complain that you are not there to lead them," Keethro had said. "When I fail in finding a village it is you they wrongfully blame. And I must admit, they are not alone in their desire to see you lead them once again. I am not able to push them far enough. They will not follow me beyond the point at which return is impossible without success." Titon was not pleased by his friend's confession, and the two men had not parted on the best of terms.

"But we just started eating," Decker moaned.

His boys were tall with pride, having returned from their first hunting trip that was both unsupervised and successful. Animals in these parts were skittish and scarce, and that little Titon had managed to skewer a tree rat with an arrow was indeed an accomplishment. The boys had made a meal of it by combining the skinned animal with tinder berries, boiling it to oblivion, and had just begun to enjoy their first tastes of the tangy mush spooned up with bits of hard bread.

"Then finish it quick and get your axes."

Titon waited outside while his sons shoveled down their meal, recalling his own such moment of triumph. He and Keethro had snuck out at a younger age, and Keethro took the head off a rabbit with a throwing axe. Finding that the rabbit was tied to a tree, kept alive by a neighbor for a later date, had not discouraged them enough to keep from roasting it and savoring every morsel.

Moments later, the boys trudged out of the house, mouths stained fuchsia and looking sick. The three made their way to the usual spot in the woods, well out of earshot of their mother, not that she was like to hear them.

"Let's see if you weaklings remembered anything from our last attempt at this," Titon taunted. "Ten paces apart."

His two sons could not have been any more dissimilar in appearance. Whereas small-framed Titon's dark, handsome features took after neither parent, Decker was a brute, pale eyed like his mother and red and freckled like his father. There was no mistaking which son had been born on the waning moon and which on the waxing. To make matters worse for his eldest, little Titon had been born during the worst winter their clan had ever endured. So dire was the famine that all their goats had to be killed and eaten, and when the meat was gone, he and Elise chewed on the remaining leather until their gums bled. Elise's breast went dry, but she did not allow their son to perish. She kept him alive by the sustenance of her tears, as they were all that was plentiful.

The boys faced each other, neither wishing to begin, just making feints as if about to throw or charge in for a swing. Their axes were made of a lightweight wood and suitable for both throwing and swinging, though not particularly great for either. Being struck was nonetheless quite painful.

"Come on! Fight already," Titon yelled.

Decker was the first to action. He ran forward a few steps as if to charge, then lobbed his axe at Titon. Titon easily avoided the tumbling weapon, closed the distance, and swung at Decker's neck, not making any contact of consequence.

"Is there something wrong with your arm?" Titon asked his elder son with muffled rage. It seemed there was an unspoken agreement between the two not to strike with full force, which was detrimental to their learning proper technique.

"The point is mine, Father. He has lost his axe, and I struck his neck," Titon replied, irresolute.

"You don't fight for points. This is not some southern game. You are training to protect your family. Now hit him! How else will he learn?" *How have I raised these boys to be so feeble? They will die on their first Dogman raid if they do not learn to swing with some fecking force.*

Titon struck Decker with a partial-strength blow to the shoulder.

"By the Mountain's tits! That was pathetic," Titon cried at them. "Try again, let's go… Hurry up."

The boys squared off again, and again it was Decker who acted first, charging at his brother. Decker already outweighed Titon by a small margin, but Titon's extra experience and dexterity more than made up the difference. Titon ducked the attack and jabbed at Decker's stomach. The force of the blow was multiplied by Decker's forward momentum, causing him to double over and reel in pain. Shortly thereafter, he emptied the contents of his stomach onto the snow. The result was a pile of blood-red, half-chewed meat and berries.

Little Titon was wide eyed and staring at the mess, which truth be told looked not much different than a pile of entrails. All the efforts of their first hunt, the fun of which had already been stolen by the interruption of training and their father's mood, now lay on the ground, wasted. *It is a small price for them to pay*, Titon told himself, stemming his own guilty frustration.

"I am sorry," Titon said to his brother, prompting a growl from his father.

"The Dogmen will not be sorry when they spill your brother's guts, and that is what is like to happen if you two keep fighting like southern princesses. My father would have made me eat the food you just wasted, Decker, but you two are far too prissy for that. Pick up your axes, and fight right this time before I get angry."

Decker had tears in his eyes and a face twisted with rage. This time Decker charged his brother with an added war cry. Titon stepped to the side, and Decker went past. The only good strike open was to the back of the head, and Titon took it, but carefully. His cautious attack was too slow and only grazed his brother. While Titon was realizing his mistake, Decker turned and threw his axe, smashing his brother in the face. Some blood started to trickle from Titon's now-swelling upper lip.

That's more like it, Decker.

"Not fair," said little Titon with a slight lisp, his lip causing him trouble.

"Not fair? What kind of Dogmen bitches did I raise? You swing like a girl, and you get killed like a girl. Decker won that. Now go again."

Decker retrieved his axe and the boys walked to their positions, both visibly angry.

"Maybe this time, Titon, you can pretend you are fighting to defend someone you care about since your family's safety means so little to you. Perhaps you can fight for Keethro's little slut, Red." *That ought to get him.*

And it did. This time when Decker threw his axe, Titon parried it, closed distance, and clobbered him on the skull. It was not enough to break the skin, but a swollen lump formed on Decker's head as he writhed around in pain, crying in spite of his efforts.

"I guess that is what it takes to finally get you to fight like a man," said the son of Small Gryn.

Little Titon's face was ashen as he stared at his squirming brother. The sound of his brother wailing, the blood-red splotch in the snow, the insult to Red, and the shame of being goaded into hurting his younger brother must have all been too much. He screamed and flung his axe at his father with force. Titon did not react quite in time, and the axe struck his arm first, continuing its rotation to smash him in the eye.

"You little shit!" he yelled as he tried to chase after his defiant son, but he could not see well enough to do so effectively. Titon ran off and had weaved out of sight amongst the trees within moments. If events occurred the same as they had in the past, little Titon would spend the night in the cold and come back later the next day as if nothing had happened, and neither would speak of it.

Titon rubbed his throbbing eye and sat in the snow for a bit to regain his bearings. Then he picked up the training axes, gave Decker, who was no longer crying, a pat on the back and began to walk him home.

On their way back, a satisfied smile formed on Titon's face. *The boy can throw an axe.*

LEONA

Leona plucked a leaf from the mint plant on the windowsill, popped it in her mouth, and sprinted to the bedroom. Standing at her clothes chest, she began to brush her hair, her face feeling flushed as memories surfaced of the countless times she'd similarly prepared to meet with Tallos as a young girl.

Her life with her parents had consisted each day of toiling to eek out a meager existence and battling the never-relenting foes of thirst, hunger, and the cold—a thing made evermore difficult by her father's love of mead. Leona had resigned herself, as per her mother's instruction, to be content with what little they had, to take refuge in the fact that Northmen had not yet come to kill them, and to find a husband, preferably an old and established dog breeder or distiller who would better support her. Then Tallos had come, upending all her mother's best-laid plans.

Tallos, it seemed, knew no fear. He traveled to areas that no other men dared and more often than not came back with skins, meat, and stories of vistas of great beauty. What other boys bragged of planning, Tallos was busy doing, and doing far from poorly. The cozy home in which she and Tallos now lived was built by his hands and hers. He had shown her they could accomplish through will, trial, and his endless pool of resourcefulness, whatever it was they sought.

Leona looked at her reflection in the palm-sized square of silvered glass, the only such piece they owned, and traced the lines on her face with a finger. *Damn you for making me smile so deeply*, she cursed her husband, sending an unpleasant twinge up her back at the thought that the gods may have heard her and mistaken her intent.

She had taken his gods, the Mighty Three. Tallos did not know his father, but he knew the man did not follow the Faith, the predominant religion of the Fourpaw villagers. Tallos's mother had told him of his father's gods: the River, the Mountain, and the Dawnstar. Knowing little more than their names, Tallos worshipped them in his own way. Leona believed that his worship was not out of true belief but rather in reverence to his father, who was—by his mother's account, at least—a good man, and Leona was happy to worship them in kind.

Prosperous though they were in their own way, Leona's thoughts slipped to years past, during an unrelenting string of harsh winters. Many villagers had succumbed to starvation or cold. Tallos had been faced with the burden of not only supporting their own family of three bodies and eight legs but that of helping his friend Erik and his wife and new son. All of them grew gaunt, but none so much as Tallos. She'd begged him to save more for himself, but he insisted that she and Lia remain as well fed as he could manage. Erik, Megan, and their child were taken in by Megan's parents in a neighboring village, dog breeders with enough wealth and provisions saved for such times. Leona did not know whether Tallos would have survived otherwise. Toward the end, he and Lia grew scarily thin, and with Tallos fearing for Lia's safety he had begun to make her, with great difficulty, remain home when he went to hunt. During one such outing, Lia escaped while Leona had fought gusts of wind at the door. She cried as she confessed to Tallos upon his return how her stupidity had cost Lia her life. "Lia is wild in her heart, and with so little to eat she was like to leave at some point," Tallos had said. "Though it is cold, she may be better off on her own. Do not fear for her. She will find food and shelter," he promised.

Two days later Lia returned to them, skinny as ever, with a well and dead fox in her mouth. She dropped the fox on the floor, wagged her tail and licked at their faces. It was the only time Leona had seen Tallos cry. He wept quietly and embraced his companion. They made a stew of the fox, bones and all, of which Lia received the wolf's share. Tallos never again went hunting without Lia and often gave her the freedom to roam distant and catch extra game on his longer trips.

Leona abandoned her brush and silvered glass, less interested now with the state of her appearance and more anxious about the state of her husband. She ran out her bedroom and through the front door. Beaming with energy, she scanned the faces of the men who'd just crested the nearest hill, eager to find her husband's.

Numbness consumed her arms and legs. Her vision blurred and doubled as she lost the ability to focus. Sound was replaced with a gentle ringing, which bled into a blanket of silence. The fact that the faces of the tall men approaching were those of strangers was less concerning to her than the reality that Tallos was not among them. A faraway voice from another time spoke to her, reminding her of what she knew to do in such an instance. They had planned for it together when building their home, she and Tallos. "If a raiding party should crest the ridge, or even a group of men you simply do not recognize, regardless of their dress, weaponry, or potential intentions, regardless of whether I am among them, you are to run. Run into the house as if to hide, then straight out of the rear door which we have built for this purpose and bar it from the outside. Do not hesitate, do not think, just run. Run south beyond the point at which we met Lia. Run and do not stop until you can no longer lift a foot. Follow the river as far as you can travel. I will find you."

She tried to twirl the ring on her finger, but the motion impossible without the feeling in her limbs. She was paralyzed, unable to move except at perhaps an implausibly slow rate of speed as if in a nightmare. *He is dead.*

TALLOS

It was not the first time Tallos had seen his friend gravely wounded. Erik had no knack for climbing, but with Tallos as his only friend, he had no options but to follow or be left alone. When they were young, Erik had fallen when a loose root chosen as a handhold gave way. Sliced to ribbons, blood streaming down his face, and with a broken leg, Erik would have died where he lay had Tallos not dragged him miles back to their village. But the thick blood now spurting from the hole in Erik's neck stripped Tallos of his usual composure.

Still carrying the remains of his eldest son, Erik had been unable to avoid the attack that came. Greyson had approached the encumbered giant, looking hateful as he always did, and with unforeseen rage, he plunged a knife to the hilt into Erik's neck.

As Erik collapsed to the ground, Tallos's own body felt weightless. The tall pines around him began to spin, surrounding him in an ever-shrinking prison. His disembodied feeling of drifting, as if to sleep, was blanketed by a grim reality: Erik's wound was fatal.

The barking of dogs and shouting of men came from all directions. Greyson was the only one who seemed to be screaming anything of any sense, though the most Tallos could make out was "You fools!" and "Hope they kill every one of you!"

Tallos dropped the body of Erik's other boy and ran to help. Lia remained close to her master's side, her tail stiff, anxiously awaiting instruction on how to help.

"Put it down," Tallos shouted at Greyson, much in the way he would to Lia when she grabbed something she should not. Greyson did not seem to hear his words, continuing to charge toward the next closest man in a clear effort to end their lives. There was no demented mirth in his actions; Greyson slashed at each target with every ounce of his desperate spite.

Tallos glanced at Erik. Lying on his back, blood pulsing between his fingers at his neck, Erik gasped for air like a dying fish. His eyes were wide with panic when they found Tallos's and pleaded for help, but there was nothing Tallos could do to comfort his friend until Greyson was no longer a threat.

A handful of the young men in their company had begun to circle Greyson, but most had scattered to a safer distance. Some had bows in hand, but none had weapons at the ready. *Had this been a coordinated attack by Northmen, we would all be dead.*

"Put down the—"

Tallos's second request was cut short as an object flew end over end out of the nearby trees, lodging itself in the back of Greyson's skull. The impact pushed his frail frame forward, where he toppled headfirst onto the stony ground and lay motionless.

Knowing they should have been able to subdue the old man without the need for more bloodshed, Tallos breathed deeply to shout at whichever fool had thrown the object, Jegson he guessed. But before he could, a guttural war cry filled the air—a deep, fearsome noise. None of the men in his party could have made such a sound. *Northmen.*

Tallos had never considered himself a coward. In fact, he had resolved to never again take the path of caution over that of action after what it had so recently cost him, but with Erik moments from death, his other men so sprawled and ineffectual, and faced with the prospect of his own mortality, Tallos's instincts screamed for him to run. Later he could dwell on whether running was indeed a path of action, and later he could hash out the hypocrisy of wishing for a valiant fight with Northmen only to flee when they appeared, but he had no time for rationalizations. He would run, hopefully faster than all the fools who had followed him and Erik to what would be an early death.

He glanced once more at Erik, if only to nod him a farewell. His foolhardy friend had brought himself to a knee and was motioning with his free hand for Tallos to leave.

"Lia, with me." Tallos turned away just as a dozen or more men with long, shaggy manes charged out from behind the brush. Carrying only his bow, arrows, and a knife, he ran. He weaved purposefully through the trees as he went, hoping any axes or arrows sent his way would hit a trunk behind him instead of lodging itself in his head or back. Although he could feel phantom projectiles splitting his skin and cracking his bone, as far as he could tell he was yet uninjured. He did not dare look back, but the thought of those wide-eyed men giving chase drove him on at a speed that was itself dangerous on such craggy terrain.

Lia kept up with him. He could hear her heavy footfalls and panting beside him. For her this was not a difficult speed, but it was equally dangerous due to the jagged rocks. *Be careful, girl,* he pleaded in thought.

His progress came to a sudden stop when he found himself staring up from the bottom of a cliff not unlike the one that Erik's boys had clung to. Climbing it was not an option. Tallos figured he'd been running for a few minutes, enough to gain some distance from where the fight had begun. He had no way of telling if he'd been followed. His racing heart bade him keep running, to trace south without stopping, but given the narrowness of the canyon he would no doubt be heard when the fighting ceased. Against his instincts, he decided to sit with his back to the cliff and wait.

With an arrow nocked and ready, he strained to listen for any who had pursued him, finding it exceedingly difficult. In addition to Lia's panting and the sound of his own labored breathing, Tallos felt as if his skull had been stuffed full with cotton, and his heartbeat was unending thunder in his ears.

"Shhh, quiet, girl," he said in a hushed voice to have some of the distraction diminished, and Lia began to pant a bit more softly.

The lichen at his back was moist and began to soak through his shirt as he pressed his body hard against the rocks of the cliff, as if doing so might put greater distance between him and the unseen threat. It only served to give him a chill.

A distant rustle of leaves caught his attention, but the sound stopped as soon as it had come. Tallos adjusted his position to face the exact direction of the noise and waited. "Good girl," he mouthed as Lia mimicked her master with silence.

Near as frightening as a Northman having followed him would be one of the men from his own party crashing through the bushes, breathless, making enough noise to attract all the North. He wondered if he would be forced to silence such a man with an arrow—a thing he never would have considered if not for the frantic nature of his overwrought mind. *If it is Jegson, I will shoot.*

Through the thick fog of fear clouding his thinking, he envisioned Leona. His reminiscence of her was immediately corrupted, recalling how shameful their last exchange had been. Tallos's resolve hardened to that of steel, and he gnashed his teeth. *I will not die before seeing Leona and making right the way in which I left her. I will shoot any man who approaches, even Erik healed back to health.*

Before Tallos could pass final judgment on his most recent thoughts, a figure charged from the woods where he faced. The man was tall and heavy, running at full speed with tangled hair bouncing behind him. Neither the thick furs that clad him nor the weapons dangling from his waist seemed to abate his reckless dash.

Tallos drew and loosed an arrow—an easy shot at that distance under normal circumstances, but shooting a man intent on splitting his head was not something he had experience with. In his rush to fire he pulled the shot right. He watched in horror as the arrow sailed off, missing its mark by over half a foot. Now close enough to be clearly seen as a

Northman, the runner showed no intention of slowing, and his axe was poised as if to throw once in range.

Tallos readied himself to jump left or right the moment the axe was thrown, hoping the man would not wait until it was too close to dodge. But it was Lia who acted first, snarling and bolting toward the attacker. The relief of realizing he had help turned to dread as the Northman threw his axe instead at Lia. She made no effort to avoid the tumbling weapon, which sliced her along the back, not affecting the speed of her assault. Tallos sprinted behind her with his knife in hand.

Lia reached the Northman first and dug her teeth into his arm, shaking her head violently. Tallos was not far behind, expecting at any moment for his vision to go red like when finishing a deer. He saw with crystal clarity, however, the edge of his knife bite first into the hand and then into the neck of the flailing man. The Northman continued to fight with surprising strength as the blood gushed out of him, and Tallos stabbed him repeatedly in the chest and stomach. Finally, the man curled up, only trying to shield himself, then ceased to move altogether.

Lia seemed to know instinctively that the man was dead but remained close to the kill. "Over here, Lia," called Tallos, not wanting her near the corpse for some reason. His heart pounded, and he could see now his hands were shaking and felt oddly cold. There was no time for worry, however; he could check for wounds later. He was more concerned about the potential for other Northmen to follow, and he led Lia back to their original place of ambush to wait.

Minutes of silence passed followed by distant yelling as one Northman continued to call the name of another without answer.

In time, the yelling stopped and Tallos heard nothing more, but he watched in the same direction without making any movement of his own. Blood rushed back into his fingers bringing with it the relief of knowing their cold had not been from an injury, but he still feared death as much as ever. Tallos focused on the spot from which the man had come with unwavering intensity. *This time I must not miss.*

They waited for the better half of an hour but did not hear any more signs of life. Tallos looked again at the Northman's corpse. *Leknar*, he thought, recalling the name that had been yelled. *Could that be the name of this man I have killed?* He tried to imagine such a man having a family of his own, a wife awaiting a return that would never come, but he felt only hatred. This man did not belong here, and his fate was deserved.

From the corner of his eye Tallos noticed Lia move. She remained beside him, but apparently too tired to squat at the ready, she had laid down on her side with a whine.

"Quiet, Lia," he said with anger and frustration in his voice. She could easily have drawn more attackers with her noise. He spared a glance in her direction and was sickened to see her covered in blood. It did not appear to be the darkened caking blood of a wound sealed or from the Northman. The blood was thin and bright red.

"Stay, girl. You're all right," he said, more to convince himself than her, as he went to examine her for wounds, encumbered with worry. The gash across her back from the thrown axe was dark and scabbed and did not look life threatening. "You're all right," he repeated as he moved her around gently to try to find where the fresh blood was coming from.

He saw what appeared to be a deep wound in her side that continued to bleed. The Northman must have had a knife and managed to stab her while she clung to his other arm, keeping the man from attacking Tallos. Tallos knew immediately it was serious. It had to be sealed or she would bleed to death, and to do so he must get her home where he could find hot coals in the fire. Not thinking quite clearly, he cut a piece of his shirtsleeve off and tried to push it against the wound. He sliced off a larger piece and tied it around her to keep it pressed firmly and slow the bleeding. His makeshift bandage was already soaked red when he stood up and tried to gain his bearings.

"Come on, girl," he said. He would have preferred to wait longer, but Lia needed help as soon as possible. She looked up at him with mournful eyes but did not move. "Come on. Let's go home," Tallos pleaded. She stood and tried to move but fell down again with a yelp. *Gods of the River, the Mountain, and the Dawnstar, you took my friend and his sons, but you will not take her.*

Tallos threw all his gear on the ground that he did not need— everything except the knife at his belt. "I am going to pick you up," he said to her and bent down to do so. He managed to lift her, intending to put her across his shoulders, but as she whined in protest he realized it would be too painful for her due to her injuries. He would have to carry her in his arms which would be far more difficult.

Tallos did his best to cradle her in front of him. She whimpered at first, but he could see she understood he was only trying to help, just as she did when he'd need to pull a thorn from her paw. He imagined the pain of a thorn must pale in comparison to her current suffering, however.

Determining that he was on the eastern cliffs, he estimated it would be six or so more miles south to reach his home. That was when the realization swept him. The Northmen had come from the south.

THE SPURNED
Many Years Ago

"I would let you die." The words came from the silhouette of a man in the doorway just as something heavy flopped onto the dirt floor in front of her. "...But the Faith does not allow it."

"I am sorry," she cried. "Wait!" But the blinding rectangle of light folded in upon itself until gone—and with it, another day's worth of hope.

She crawled toward where the object had fallen and found it with her fingers. The top was warm and slick, the rest covered with fine dirt that had already turned to muddy paste. *At least it is fresh*, she thought as she wiped her fingers on her clothing and attempted to rub clean a portion of the raw meat.

The words were cruel but comforting. In the dark she was not afraid—not afraid of death at least. It was the tedium that was killing her. Day after day of no contact, no interaction, nothing to do save make mounds of dirt and knock them down again. It wore on her like a mortal disease. It was good to hear a voice, regardless of what was said.

She was alone in here, just her and her bucket, and there was not much joy to be gleaned from a bucket full of your own leavings. He would only take the bucket once a week, and by then it was near full. Each time the metal pail was swapped for a new one, she would use it to dig. She dug in the same spot by the rear wall, and each day she would get a little deeper through the near frozen ground. When she could hold back no longer, she'd be forced to use her bucket for its intended purpose and push all the dirt and rock back into its proper place. What he would do if he saw that she attempted escape, she did not venture to guess—she only knew it would not be good.

A scraping noise came from the door causing her to snap to attention. Dropping her meat to the ground, she raced to the door, and pressed her ear against it.

"Mother?" she whispered. "Is that you?"

Eternities passed as she waited for a reply. Sometimes she thought she heard weeping, but not today.

"Tell Father I did not mean to do it...and it will never happen again. Tell him it was an accident. Please."

She pushed her ear harder against the cold wood, hearing nothing but her own breathing and heartbeat. After a while her ear began to ache, so she cupped her hands around it and listened that way.

"I will always use a flint, Mother. I promise. It was just so cold, and we were in a hurry. I did not mean to stray from the Faith. I am sorry for what I did."

Her heart jumped as she felt a bump through the door. Someone had leaned against it or pushed away from it—she could not tell.

"Mother?"

She waited. Her muscles hurt from squatting the way she was for so long, but she endured.

"How is Enka?" she pleaded. "Did her sickness pass? Just scratch the door once if she has gotten better."

She listened for the scratch that never came. As her muscles began to cramp and burn she was forced to sit, her back against the door. Crying did her no good. She had abandoned it after several weeks of wasted tears, but the anguish of desolation never went. *I would rather die than live like this forever.*

"She is dead."

Her mother's voice was so unexpected she believed it to have been imagined, but then it continued.

"Enka has gone, and I intend to follow. Know that it was your doing. Goodbye, Elise."

ELISE

Seated in her rocking chair, propped up with pillows, Elise stared out the window of her family's thatch-roofed home. Through the glass, a snowy valley could be seen. It stretched between mountains and was traversed by a stream that flowed gently past the house. So high were they in the mountains that when the rains fell the stream did not flood, but countless miles away it grew into a rushing river larger than imagining. Titon claimed their creek at the top of the world was the start of the mightiest river of the land. The Eos, he said, was so wide that a man could not swim across it, so plentiful that a fish could be speared by an arrow shot without aim, and that grasses grew along the banks so thick that goats could grow fat and produce milk year-round. All this was fantasy, she knew, yet in her heart she somehow believed him to be speaking truth. For all the years they had spent together, she had never known him to tell a lie.

Everything she had she owed to Titon, a giant, fearsome, dangerous man, a man whose axe had taken countless heads—heads of foes and heads of friends—but never of those undeserving. He was the most rare and noble of men. He was the stone that formed her hearth. *And I do not deserve him.*

TITON SON OF SMALL GRYN

He saw her there by the window, gaze transfixed on a single point in the distance, eyes never straying, rocking chair never moving. He marveled at how she had so well retained her beauty. Her stark-white hair cascading past her shoulders to her waist caught the light and shone with health in spite of her frailty.

"Ellie," Titon said to his wife. To his men he spoke with booming authority that commanded respect, but to her he spoke gently. "Our two sons give me a pride I fear might anger the gods. Our youngest has grown with a speed I have never before seen. He has but fourteen years, and he may best me in strength before another two. He is a wolf among men and is yet still a boy.

"But Titon, the one the Mist Spirits tried to steal from us, the one we feared might never walk or learn to speak, his skill with bow and axe is without equal. Everything I show him, he knows before the lesson is done. He knew words on paper better than I, or even you, and that was before we thought to teach him. Every task I give him, he completes in some way of his own invention that takes half as long and is done twice better. If only I could task him with growing another head in height, he'd lead our clans into the South, steal the Eos itself and bring it back."

Elise did not move or respond. Titon paced while he spoke, his wife continuing to gaze out the window without answer. He stroked his thick auburn beard as was his habit while thinking.

"What god was it that you took to bed while I was out hunting to make such a lad?" It was a joke Titon had the habit of repeating, one of many jokes he told as if for the first time, but none seemed to annoy her as much as this one. "Ah, it is just a jest. Do not be angry with me, Ellie. ...But if you wish to rise and strike me, I would not be angry with you."

He looked to his wife. He studied her for the smallest sign of motion, willing her to retaliate. *Get up,* he pleaded. *Please.* Minutes passed, yet she refused to move. He wiped at his eyes, breathed deeply, and hardened his face.

"The others will not follow him. They do not respect his size, and they fear his wits. Nothing can be done about it. We Galatai are a stubborn lot, though, are we not? I do not know how a pretty southern girl like you can put up with the likes of us."

Titon stopped his pacing before the wall where his two-handed axe hung, hesitated, then removed it from its perch. Attempting to put his mind from the task, he examined the blade. It had seen more sharpening than use since his wife had stilled. It should have no trouble with her delicate neck.

It was the axe he'd used to kill many men, among them her father. By his sixteenth year, Titon was leading parties of Galatai south to raid the Dogmen villages. These were not just raids for food or supplies, these were raids fueled by hatred. Titon had come to despise Dogmen in earnest by what he'd borne witness to. Wolves and dogs tied to trees, beaten, starved, made to fight each other for scraps, all for the men's amusement—these were a people worth wiping from the land. The raping was also justified as far as Titon was concerned, though he no longer partook. The women certainly were not any less guilty than the men, and in fact most kennels were maintained by the *fairer* sex. The Dogmen's women were certainly pleasant enough to the eye, looking about the same as Galatai, if slightly shorter and more buxom. Titon's father had taught him that to rape a woman was to kill her soul, and to kill a man's soul one had merely to rape his woman. Titon had long ago vowed not to spare any Dogmen souls, and when he still led raids, his men had been happy to oblige.

There *were* limits to their debauchery, however. It was forbidden to take a Dogman as prisoner, be they man or woman. Galatai put chain to neither man nor wolf.

Whereas the Galatai's persecution of the Dogmen was checked by certain restraints, it would seem in contrast the Dogmen's impropriety had no bounds. On occasion, during raids in the cold winter months, Titon found the dogs chewing on the frozen remains of piles of starved children and perished elders. It was true that digging a grave during the winter was ten times as hard, but one could thaw the ground somewhat with a fire or at the very least place the body under a pile of river rocks. Titon's father said it was the true measure of a man whether he buried his fallen during the dead of winter, and as such Titon had always dug an even deeper hole in the frozen earth for his dead brothers, to show proper respect.

Almost equally offensive was that so few of the Dogmen fought to protect themselves. All Galatai, even the girls, were taught to use a bow and throwing axe at a young age and were expected to use them to defend their homes. These Dogmen had at most only one of every ten men take to weapon to defend what was theirs while the rest cowered inside. Titon found it beyond disgraceful.

Elise's father was one that hid, and he hid more than himself. After finding the man trembling in a corner, begging for his life, Titon, as he often did, began first to destroy his fancy home. It was not enough to kill these evil men. They had to also know that all they had was being ruined.

Her father was a rich man with a large home. Dogmen considered those who bred demon-dogs to be most valuable, and kennel owners tended to have the most wealth. Her father must have had over five-dozen dogs crammed into a small shed overrun with piles of shit and reeking of death from the stillborn pups left to rot or be eaten.

As Titon used Elise's father's head as a battering ram to remove some walls, he broke through to a hidden room. Large houses held large secrets he had learned, and this was not the first such room he had discovered within Dogmen homes. Titon let out a monstrous roar of laughter, eager to see what treasure was within. The room did not smell of gems and coins, however. It had the familiar stench of piss and shit like the kennels. In the center of the room he saw a girl on all fours, dressed in loose rags, chained to a spike in the ground as a dog or wolf might be. But Titon saw only wolf in this girl as she snarled and growled and snapped at him in defiance when he approached. She was a few years younger than he, and her long messy hair was as white as the fur of a Storm Wolf—save for the dirt in it.

The girl was wild and Titon could not conceive of a way to subdue her without the same disgraceful bindings used by the Dogmen, so he simply broke her chains and hoisted her to a shoulder, allowing her to claw and bite him until she tired. She had a fiercer stamina than expected, and she gave him some of his better scars that day, as well as removing part of an ear. Galatai wore their scars proudly, however, and ears were just fodder for frostbite the way Titon saw it.

"The feck are you doing with that Dogman bitch? You can't take any prisoners. Everyone knows that." Edgur was five years Titon's senior and clearly resented being under the leadership of the younger man.

Among Galatai, one either followed his leader or killed and replaced him, but one did not speak to him as if he was a child. This was not the first time Edgur had been insubordinate either. Titon once found him bludgeoning dogs to death after Titon had given explicit orders that dogs were not to be killed without him present. Putting down the dogs was the hardest part of raiding for Titon, and though he saw the remnants of wolf in their eyes, he knew that once turned they could never be wolf again. Nevertheless, it was a duty he did not stray from. The dogs Edgur was killing were chained inside kennels and no threat to the men, but he was beating the life from them just the same and taking great pleasure in doing so. It was all Titon could do not to kill Edgur then, but he settled for a severe reprimand, hoping the shame would sort the man.

"This is no Dogman. Her mane is white as the Storm Wolf's coat—a sign from the Mighty Three perhaps. She was chained by the Dogmen much like a wolf would be. Do you see any chains on her now? She is not my prisoner, but she is mine." Titon replied with all the authority of a clan leader despite his age.

"Does a Storm Wolf roll around in its own shit? Her mane is about as white as my arse after I've made a pile with nothing to wipe. That don't bother me though, she's fair enough. Let her down. We'll give her a ride, slit her throat, and be on our way then."

Edgur was like to be expecting a chuckle from the other men, but a silence hung among those present. Even the squirming girl on Titon's shoulder seemed to quiet.

"You would seek to rape the woman your leader just laid claim to?" Titon glowered at Edgur in a way that meant he had no means of escape, not with an answer nor an apology.

A moment passed as the blood drained from Edgur's face, and he chuckled nervously. Titon's glare remained fixed on the man, but Edgur soon lowered his eyes, turned as if he were walking away, then grabbed for the axe at his belt. "I challenge you—"

His scream was interrupted by Titon's own axe making a wet sound as it split Edgur's skull, landing between the nose and left eye, planted firmly. The throw was quite difficult given Titon's cargo, but Titon rarely botched an axe throw—not when it mattered.

"Do any others wish to challenge Titon son of Small Gryn for the right to lead?" He posed the question with the woman still on his shoulder, vulnerable to attack but without fear. There were no such volunteers, nor did anyone else take issue with Titon's claim to the wolf woman. The action cost him more than Edgur, though. It made him many enemies among the leaders of other Galatai clans who believed he had broken a sacred law.

Titon squeezed the soft leathern bindings of his axe. *Ellie, what would you have me do? I fear your wish would be for me to speak to you softly, long into the night. To tell you how strong our boys have grown and how I still care for you. To hold your hand as we watch our last setting of the Dawnstar, then end your eternal purgatory.*

Titon stared at the old axe in his hands as its image began to blur. *But I cannot.*

And so Titon did the same as he had near every night for so many painful years. He sat with his wife in the small home he'd built for them by the creek at the top of the world. He talked to her long into the night as he held her hand, and they watched the Dawnstar disappear behind the mountains far to the west.

DECKER

Side by side Decker and his brother stood, knee deep in the thick snow, before an assemblage of other young men and boys. *Today we take our first steps toward glory,* thought Decker, eyeing those that may be lucky enough to accompany them.

Enough had gathered that the need for words had become pressing. Decker looked toward Titon, hoping he would address the crowd—this was after all a plan of Titon's sole invention.

Decker had continued to grow both in stature and spirit. Though not yet fifteen, he was near his father's equal. He only wished the same could be said for his older brother. Although not a weakling for his age, Titon was still a runt by Galatai standards. Had Titon a different name and different brother, perhaps it would not have been so embarrassingly blatant, but the two brothers, when standing abreast, made a pair hard not to comment on—a comment more wisely made in silence to oneself.

"Hello, men." Decker recognized his brother's words as a thing their father often said to silence his men, but they failed to carry the same authority as when the son of Small Gryn spoke them. Many in the group continued to talk among themselves.

"My brother Decker and I have summoned you here to…" Titon struggled for words while speaking over the chatter. Brilliance and book knowledge, Titon had in abundance, but neither seemed to serve him now, not with this rowdy bunch in attendance. "We have summoned you here to go south with us. South to slay Dogmen and bring home their provisions for our families."

"What do you know of the South, boy?" asked a faceless voice from the rear of the group.

Titon was visibly taken aback by the question. He had witnessed the many times his father's men had cheered and raised axes at the mere mention of heading south. He clearly was not prepared to be met with skepticism or apprehension.

Decker watched Titon from the corner of an eye, but mostly he tried to read the faces of those before them. Things looked bleak, as the few who had shown Titon any courtesy at all with their silence still nodded in agreement with the question put forth. He allowed his brother to continue, hoping his wits would see him through this ordeal.

"I know my father used to lead men such as us to the South," said Titon. "Each time he had returned, it was with victuals to last for months and stories of the battles with those Dogmen brave enough to take up arms and die with some modicum of honor." He now had more power behind his words. Titon always spoke proudly of their father...in public.

"Aye, but you are not your father." This time the voice was not faceless. It was Arron, the son of the clan's tanner. "You can keep your victuals and modicums. I don't think they will help us to kill Dogmen." Arron was fifteen, same as Titon, and was a bit over-serious for his age— something that may have come from years of being teased for smelling like soured piss, the hallmark of his father's profession.

Decker saw where this was headed. He did not have his brother's intellect, but he had a better understanding of the way men acted in packs. And this pack was about to turn on a leader deemed unfit to lead. The results for Titon would be embarrassing at best, violent at worst. The young men grunted their approvals of Arron's objection.

"Enough!" Decker's booming voice silenced the grunts. "My brother offers you glory in battle and you quibble over his words? Winter approaches, and we are not ready. We need the Dogmen's mutton and cheese that the older men have been unable to acquire. Who here wishes to suffer through another winter with an empty belly?"

The usual raiding parties had been met with poor results as of late. After the tiring and dangerous descent snaking through scree-covered bluffs to where the Dogmen villages previously sat, the real task of finding the Dogmen began. The villages they came upon were either abandoned or sacked, and where the villages were deserted no greenery grew. The Dogmen, it seemed, used some sort of poison to spoil the land, making it difficult for the raiders to advance southward with nothing to forage or hunt along the way, and returning empty handed from raids was fast becoming the norm. That the son of Small Gryn no longer led the raids was a cause for great concern among the elders. But their father had not left their mother's side for more than a day since she'd taken ill, and he'd remained in power all these years due only to the overwhelming respect he commanded. *The time has come for a son of the son of Small Gryn to lead*, thought Decker.

Some of the boys not yet old enough to attend the raids voiced their approval of Decker's speech, though it was like to have more to do with their awe of Decker than the content of his argument.

Arron had not been swayed. "The older men have experience raiding these Dogmen, and most of us have never so much as seen one. What makes you think we will succeed where the others have failed?"

Decker smirked and looked toward his older brother. The stiffness in Titon's body seemed to have gone, encouraged by the fact that the men were now asking a question he knew how to answer. It was Titon who had conceived of the unconventional strategy that would allow them to attack Dogmen villages much farther to the south. It was Titon who had first needed to convince his younger brother that the strategy had merit, and of that Decker was thoroughly convinced.

Decker turned to Arron, staring him down. "They did not have a Titon."

CASSEN

"Grace, prosperity, health, and wealth." Cassen sat at his vanity, staring into its oval of silvered glass as he repeated his morning affirmation. He scowled at the plump-bodied reflection and moved his face closer until their two noses almost touched, then pinched a bit of raised, reddened skin on his cheek with a look of contempt. "But not clarity of complexion." His expression shifted theatrically to sadness, and he pouted with his twin visage, comforted by the thought that he did not suffer alone.

Into Cassen's outstretched hand, a servant boy placed a small glass container. Cassen noted with a feeling of accomplishment the fear on the servant's face, seen unbeknownst to the boy in his reflection. With a finger Cassen dabbed a bit of the minty cream upon his blemish, refreshed by both the scent and coolness of it.

Layer upon layer of long silk flowed around Cassen as he stood, enough to adorn a palatial suite with curtaining. He may have felt light and airy under such delicate fabric, but the appearance was anything but…and it was something of which he was well aware. Nonetheless, his servants were acquainted with his propensity to lash out and strike them when the need arose, a fact evidenced by how quickly the fair-skinned boy moved to retrieve the glass of ointment from Cassen's bent-wrist hand.

"Now run along, my little—"

Cassen's attempt to dismiss his two boy servants was interrupted by the crack of shattered glass. In his haste, the one boy must have lost hold of the container. Its contents now seeped into the plush carpet beneath Cassen's feet.

Cassen nudged his head toward the far corner of the room, and both boys darted there.

"Down them," Cassen commanded. He saw from the edge of his vision the reluctant motion of both boys obeying, lowering their trousers, but he only saw the glint of pale cheeks on one. Cassen was more concerned by the puddle of ointment, which was beginning to change from greenish white to reddish brown due to the leaching of the carpet's pigments. *That piece is surely ruined,* Cassen sighed to himself, not at all happy that he would be tasked with replacing it.

A saunter brought Cassen to the same corner where the boys stood, faced away from him. He positioned himself purposefully close to the one whose ass remained hidden—close enough for the boy to feel Cassen's breathe in his hair.

"Pull them down," Cassen said gently. This boy must not have suffered this punishment before, or was demonstrating some rebellion to being penalized for the other's mistake. "Or I'll do it myself."

After a moment, the boy acquiesced, causing Cassen to shake his head in disappointment. It was so hard to find one with any spirit.

Cassen returned to his vanity, sat, then peeked back at the trembling boys. The sight almost caused him to snort, but he caught himself. The absurdity of having two boys—who were each old enough to be chasing girls—baring their backsides at his request, as though it should please him, was nearly too much to take.

"And don't you dare move," Cassen seethed at them, only partially needing to fake his anger on account of the carpet.

Confident that neither of their noses would leave the corner, Cassen allowed his demeanor to shift. He exhaled a deep breath through loose lips and let his body relax as he sunk back into his chair.

So many years you have allowed to pass without advancement. Cassen looked again upon his disappointing reflection, unsure of whether he should continue his deserved berating or instead remind himself how near at hand change was to come. Determining that both acts were a form of wasteful self-indulgence, he decided instead to evaluate once again whom it was most responsible for impeding his ascent—whom it was that would soon be trampled by the assault Cassen had invited upon the kingdom.

Cassen was the *Duchess* of Eastport, and as such, answered only to King Lyell of House Red Rivers, ruler of Rivervale and Adeltia. By custom he should have answered also to the King's First, Derudin the Wise—*Derudin the Charlatan*—but Cassen had managed to escape the need to so much as speak with the old wizard in a way in which only he could.

Cassen's insistence on being addressed as *Duchess* was particularly disagreeable to the elder Derudin. Years past, in a High Council meeting, after Derudin had referred to Cassen as *Duke*, Cassen interrupted the advisor's speech about whatever it was and corrected him. Derudin could have simply grunted his disapproval and continued, as was his wont, but had instead proclaimed, "I am Derudin, born of Erober, tempered in the fiery mouth of a mountain broken by dragon's breath. Over one hundred years ago, I alone crossed the Devil's Mouth. I and all other men with reverence for the Ancient Laws will call a man by a man's title and no other."

"My dear Derudin," Cassen had said with a coy look. "I never thought you so brazen as to hatch a scheme to get me to remove my underclothes for you with so many witnesses. I am quite sure I would not match the definition of what you nor your *Ancient Laws* consider a man." Cassen did not need to shift his gaze to know the looks on the faces of the other council members would have mostly been those of poorly concealed amusement. A bit of fear may have been mixed in as well— fear of what Derudin the Wise might do in reprisal. A conflagration that would fill the room perhaps, scorching all in attendance to death merely to be rid of the fat man and his silks. Cassen had no such fear, however. He'd dealt with worse men—far worse. Derudin did not frighten him, nor did he believe there to be any truth to the tales of his ability to conjure lightning or flames, or that he could do any form of magic save for amusing children and dolts with some sleight of hand. Derudin was a fraud, a man elevated to greatness by wizardly garb and a white beard, a man not so different from himself if he were to be quite honest. *But not as clever, not by half.*

No fireballs had erupted, and Derudin simply left the room without further words. Since both men curried great favor with the king, Lyell decreed that they would attend alternating council meetings except when dictated by extenuating circumstances. But Cassen had no trouble finding reasons to attend the majority of meetings. His command over Eastport meant he controlled a handsome portion of the kingdom's income, and there were always problems of great import when it came to the kingdom's coin. Gradually, Derudin attended fewer and fewer meetings of the High Council until he was no longer expected to appear at all. He remained the King's First and still had the king's ear and trust, but it was well known that commoners joked, if Derudin was the First, Cassen must surely be the queen.

A gentle knock sounded on Cassen's door, followed by a servant boy announcing with what he probably thought was distinguished inflection, "Young Lady Amalee here to see you, Duchess."

The boy's voice was like vomit in Cassen's ears. He could tell from the sound of it exactly where in Eastport this new addition to his staff was from—a shithole in the northeastern section of the city sheltered to darkness by the King's Arm, the Wall to End All Wars.

"She may enter," Cassen said.

Cassen watched via his mirror the young girl who walked in, old enough to have flowered but not so old as to be called a woman. She was dressed in commoner's clothes and had the fresh, enticing look of a girl who belonged to a neighbor and was off limits due to social decorum, age, or both. The boy servant, who had noticed the other two in the corner, quickly shut the door behind her, sealing her inside with Cassen as he turned to face her with steepled fingers. *I will have to remember to replace that boy.*

The girl held her wrist at her stomach while staring at her feet, avoiding eye contact. Cassen looked her up and down, examining her as one might a horse, sans the touching.

She then performed what must have been a nervous attempt at a curtsey, appearing to Cassen more like she was about to piss on and ruin yet another carpet. *I will find a home for this one*, he thought, *but she will first require some work...as do they all.* He glanced once more at the bare-assed boys, gaining some satisfaction in the knowledge that the girls were much more quickly trained.

"Turn," he commanded. The girl hesitantly did as requested. Not much in the breasts, but the firm, plump buttocks made up for it, he decided. *A loving home indeed.*

"What is your name, young one? Your *real* name."

"Amalee Stonesmith," she squeaked.

The speed with which he was able to reach her and smack her on the face seemed to startle her more than that of being struck. Tears welled in her eyes and began cascading over her bottom lids, but she did not sob or turn away.

"Your name is *Lady* Amalee. You have no other name. You have no common house name."

Cassen embraced the girl, and then the sobbing began. It was a soft and practiced embrace, like that of a mother to her daughter—for that was his role to play in this charade.

"Your name has not changed much, but I would rather you not consider it changed at all. Know that you have always been a lady. You will forever act as a lady should. It is true, you will be a servant to whatever master I can find for you, but you must erase from your mind the notion that you were ever less than what you now are, a *lady*." Cassen paused and raised the girl's chin with his hand. "Remember that, my lady daughter, and I will keep you always safe and well cared for."

ETHEL
Years Ago

"Wyverns," said Ethel.

Ethel studied Master Annan for any clue that she was making some headway. The old woman stared at Ethel with her usual aloof curiosity, seated behind a desk absurdly large for so small a person. Above her teacher loomed a bookshelf half again as tall as any man, armored with the spines of countless texts, all seemingly selected for their dry content. *Perhaps not as dry as her hair*, thought Ethel, unable to keep from glancing on occasion at the woman's solitary grey braid that reached to the floor, sweeping up dust whenever she turned her head. "Wyverns?" her teacher asked.

Having forced herself from bed earlier than was usual, Ethel thought she had accomplished the hardest task of her day. She was wrong. The overwhelming feeling of being pulled to sea by outward flowing tides fought her will, but she forced herself to remain calm, remembering to whom she was speaking. Had she needed to, Ethel could probably convince Master Annan that it was not even a day of learning, that the old woman had mixed up the days of the week as she was prone to do, and that she had come to teach a class that would remain empty. But Ethel had no need to confuse the woman. She wanted only to convince her of an undeniable truth: that the book she'd brought was worthy of being added to the curriculum.

"Wyverns," Ethel confirmed with a nod. *A family of wyverns*, Ethel added, albeit only in thought. The intrigue of wyverns was as good a selling point as any, and sure to interest her fellow students. That, combined with it being so large a text, was sure to impress her old master, and for once the class would get to read something that would engross them. They might even thank Ethel for having recommended it, though perhaps that was a stretch.

Master Annan looked at her askew. "This is a class of literature, child.

Wyverns are the subject of...science, I believe. You should give this book to Master..." She trailed off, lost in thought. It could have afforded Ethel a few minutes to think, but Ethel had already decided how to convince her master of the true merit of her submission.

"But Master Annan, look how *big* it is."

Master Annan broke from her trance and did as she was told; she looked at the book in her hands. As if prompted by the realization that it was indeed very large, she let it fall to her desk, sending bits of dust flying from the surface.

"It *is* heavy," she conceded, giving Ethel hope that she had pursued the correct avenue of persuasion.

Her master retrieved a ruler from the top drawer of her desk and used it to measure the book's thickness. As Master Annan's eyes widened, Ethel could not control her growing smile.

"It is over three fingers," she said, setting the ruler down on her desk.

"So we can read it in class?"

Master Annan slid the book toward Ethel, now disinterested. "I am afraid not. We seldom read texts larger than one finger's width."

Ethel's heart sank.

"And it is difficult enough to get your classmates to read those," added Master Annan with frustration in her voice.

The sound of chairs being dragged along the floor alerted Ethel to the presence of her peers. No one ever arrived early, meaning class would be starting shortly as the wave of children flooded the room. Ethel acknowledged her master's implicit dismissal with a curt nod and brought the book to her seat.

Wyverns? It is big? She chided herself for having so poorly explained why the book was of both substance and merit, though it made little difference. Her father was always right about these things. "Your master already has a list of texts, and more importantly, copies for the students," he'd explained after she brought up her plan at last night's supper. "Pay no mind to Alther," her mother had said. "You do as you wish, as a princess is entitled." Ethel hated how rude her mother always was to him, and worse, how she always called him Alther, even when speaking *of* him to her and Stephon. "I see no harm in trying," her father agreed, his pleasantness undaunted by her mother's ornery tone. "But remember, even if your master agrees and adds it to her list, your classmates may not enjoy it near so much as you. Even you might not have loved it, had you read it for the first time in class. It is our nature to dislike the things we are forced to do," his assertion earning him a glare from her mother. Ethel had found that difficult to accept, believing she would love the story in either case. "Now eat your beans," her father had concluded with a grin.

Giggling in the back of the classroom drew Ethel's sudden attention.

She was not blind to the ugly irony that giggling, a thing that should be welcomed by a girl her age, was instead a cause for anxiety. It seemed the only person who could giggle in her presence without Ethel worrying that she was being made a fool of was Griffin, but he was a year older than she and did not attend the same classes.

As she glanced back from her seat in the front of the classroom, Ethel saw the cause for the excitement. Matthus, one of the more clownish children, had something stuffed under his shirt. Ethel quickly turned forward, hoping none had noticed that she had looked, but more so, hoping she was not to be the object of their antics. Though her mother assured her she would grow out of it, claiming she, too, had been a plump child, Ethel had become increasingly self-conscious of her portly cheeks and rounded belly.

"Have a seat," said Master Annan to the children in the rear. "Class is to begin soon."

"He's too big to sit," cried one of the boys, provoking some chortles from the other students.

"What is the matter now?" As expected, their master was quite oblivious to the prank being played.

"It's my swollen belly," said Matthus.

"Oh, Matthus, did you eat something you should not have?" Master Annan had honest concern in her voice.

Ethel prepared herself for the coming joke about him having overindulged in sweets. At the start of the year, when invited to share something about themselves, Ethel had made the mistake of telling the class her favorite activity was eating pastries with her best friend Griffin. It had been a source of ridicule ever since.

"No, Master Annan…" Matthus spoke with emotion. "A babe grows in my belly."

The tension that had been building in Ethel's body released all at once. He apparently was not making fun of anyone in particular today, just messing about in a random attempt to provoke laughter and delay their lessons—a task in which he was succeeding. Ethel turned in her desk, further relieved to see every student was looking at Matthus.

"But that is only half the problem," he continued.

"Be quick with it, Matthus. We must begin the day's lessons."

Matthus grinned with devious intent, a look that put Ethel ill at ease. "The real trouble is…" His gaze shifted, and with it went the eyes of every student. They whipped to Ethel, each eager stare falling on her like a scourge's lash. "I have no clue who the father is."

The room filled with the raucous laughter of each and every student, some covering their mouths, succeeding only in spraying their hands with mirth, others just openly howling. All, that is, except for Ethel, who turned slowly in her seat to again face forward. That the other children had begun to understand what her being the princess's bastard truly meant was not a welcome evolution in their ability to torment her.

She opened the largest book on her desk, one about wyverns, and held her face as close to it as possible for one to believe she might be reading as opposed to hiding. It was too late to keep from crying, but she could at least keep them from seeing it.

It was for the best that Master Annan had refused to add this book to the curriculum. The others did not deserve it.

TALLOS

Nearly dead with exhaustion from a night spent walking in the moonlight, straining to see, Tallos staggered through the harsh landscape like a man possessed. His every step was labored as he fought to maintain the concentration required to prevent a fall that would harm his precious cargo. He'd found that it was easier to carry the bloody bundle of fur that lay across his arms if he reached with his hands toward the collar of his shirt and took hold. So it was with a collar stretched halfway down his chest that Tallos stumbled toward home, hoping desperately to find the fire still lit.

As he trudged, he'd had more time to think than was wanted. He recalled a story his mother had told him when he was a child. She had died when he was young, but he remembered her well. She spoke of a cursed man, Nekasr. Everywhere this man went, everyone this man knew, and everything this man touched, eventually withered and died. It did not happen immediately, she said. Nekasr did not believe in curses, and every time misfortune befell him, he would move to another place, making new friends, and sometimes even starting a family. Each time Nekasr would grow to find himself contented, so much so that he would forget all that he and those he'd loved had suffered in his past lives. And it was then, just as memory forgave, that the gods sought to remind. The God of the River would flood his home and drown his livestock, the God of the Mountain would crush his loved ones with landslides and boulders, and the God of the Dawnstar would bring forth brilliant rays of early light to illuminate the destruction in all its glory. Nekasr always survived, unscathed, so that he could witness it all without distraction. The Mighty Three, his mother said, did not like a man who forgot that all he had was precious, all he had was fragile, and all he had could be taken away. A man is not a god, and a man who foolishly sought to gain and protect a godly amount of happiness would reap a godly amount of misery and despair in its stead.

"Stay with me, girl," he spoke to his limp companion that lay across his arms. Each step must have been torture for Lia as the wound in her side was twisted and stretched. Tallos had thought many times about stopping and making a fire so that he could scorch her wound shut the best way he knew how, but having dropped his bags prior to running, he no longer had the necessary implements to make one quickly enough to justify not heading straight home. Nor did he have a needle with which to stitch her shut; their only needle was kept in a box on the clothes chest. *Would it even be enough at this point,* he worried, looking at her dangling head.

"Lia," he said to her with a whispered shout, and her head moved toward him somewhat, enough to make weak eye contact for a moment. "Good girl, we are almost there."

But he could not look down at her without seeing just how soaked his shirt was with her blood. It had climbed and spread throughout his clothing, infusing every fiber with its metallic-smelling crimson.

He had determined during his trek home that he had not sustained any injuries, which only served to make him feel more guilty about the multiple wounds now sapping the life from Lia. His sleepless mind chased tangents at a frenzied pace, refusing to allow him to plan the series of tasks he would have to perform in order to patch Lia and catch up to his wife.

Leona.

Fear ripped through him as he considered what he may find upon coming to their home. He imagined approaching the wooden steps that led up to the door. Leona had carved his name on the topmost step, a thing he'd weakly protested out of embarrassment. "Stomp your feet and cover it with dirt as you walk in, then, so you will not cover the floors instead," she'd said, somewhat hurt. Not wanting to sully the carving she must have spent hours on, Tallos had always stomped his feet on the two preceding steps.

Those memories would not preclude his thoughts of doom. He imagined that topmost step caked with mud—mud from a Northman's boot. The door slowly creaked open in his mind, revealing a scene of utter destruction. The items of the house were strewn about as if wild animals had been trapped inside. The air was pungent with the smell of sweat from dirty, desperate men. A trail of clothing, Leona's clothing or the remnants of them, led to the door of their bedroom. Torn strips of her delicate blue dress lay on the floor, covered with spots of blood that had flowed from her nose. Her undergarments peeked from beneath the partially closed door, and as it swung open, Tallos could see the scene in all its brutality.

He shook his head violently as if to be rid of the images and bring himself back to alertness. It took all his effort to be able to focus.

Gods, let there be embers with which to make a fire. And see that Leona is safe, alone in the southern woods.

"There will be a fire, girl," Tallos said. "It will hurt, but we will get you better."

Lia whimpered in what sounded like weak approval. *She likes me talking to her,* thought Tallos.

"You remember helping to build that giant stove don't you? All those stones we moved?" Lia was not content merely accompanying Tallos on his errands. She loved to help him pull the sled whether it was piled with wood or stone or iron.

"It will go for almost two days with a full load of wood in it. That was your idea to make it only burn a few logs on one side while others dropped down one by one?" Lia's tail may have wagged, but it was hard to tell.

"We will have to work quickly when we do get home. We do not want your mother alone in the woods for long or she'll get lost. I will have to leave you after you are patched up and go look for her, but I won't be gone for long. Don't worry."

Tallos was more concerned about leaving Lia at home alone than going after Leona. His wife would be easy enough for him to track once she hit the muddy riverbank, but Lia might hurt herself if she tried to follow when he was away.

"You have to promise to wait for us though," Tallos continued. "I will leave you with enough food and water that you will have no excuses for doing otherwise."

He thought it best not to tell Lia what his plans were then, after they came back for her; she was no city dog. But once Lia was healthy enough to walk, they would all head south again, possibly as far as Rivervale. Leona was content in their home in the woods, but he knew she might wish, even if she did not admit it, not even to herself, to visit the city, to see the sights and taste the foods. Tallos could take up a trade easily enough. Things would be difficult at first, but he would be able to make enough coin to support them if any man could.

His home came into view in the distance, and as he feared, no smoke rose from the small flue. He resisted the urge to run, as it would only cause more pain for Lia, and walked the remaining way with anxiety burning in his every bone, spurring him to move faster.

His name was clear to see on the top step; there was no more dirt on them than usual, and the front door was closed. Tallos struggled for a moment with the latch, finding it unlocked, and was greeted with a sight not far from what he'd expected. The home had been completely tossed. He was relieved, though, to see no blood, nor a trail of clothing, heading toward their bedroom door.

He gently placed Lia down near the hearth, which was warm but no longer contained flame or ember. Before starting the fire, however,

Tallos ran to their bedroom and swung open the door, eyes focused to see any horror splayed out before him, should it be there. Relief washed over him as he saw only the same ransacked mess that greeted him in the main room. It gutted him to see the stones he and Leona had collected at the river strewn aimlessly around the room, along with the clothing from their drawers, but he reminded himself it was of little consequence so long as his wife had escaped to safety. The bed had been overturned and some of the flooring ripped out, but Tallos was not a rich enough man to have anything hidden beneath.

He returned to the main room and was troubled to realize his flint that normally rested upon the hearth's mantle was nowhere to be seen. It was a common item of little worth, but he felt the loss of it horribly. Without it, starting a fire became a skill at which he was not thoroughly adept.

Fecking Northmen! Tallos flung some debris across the room in a rage, cursing his luck.

Deciding to search the rest of his home for the flint in the case they had merely thrown it down elsewhere, Tallos made his way into the kitchen. And there he stopped.

Standing in the doorway, Tallos's head swam with dizzy regret. This was the room where he had last seen Leona, the room in which she'd begged him not to leave. He remembered it clearly: his anger, his unkind words in response to her questioning his wisdom, and his leaving her, sad and alone.

Bent over the wooden table of the kitchen, skirts torn, was Leona's lifeless body.

TITON SON OF TITON

I will do it, Titon told himself, struggling to take control of his fickle will. *Today I must finally ask her for a kiss.*

His eyes were to the ground as he crunched through the hardened snow. No longer was it the soft powdery stuff that had covered them to a knee the previous day, when he and Decker had rallied the other young men. They were to set off on their raid first thing next morning, and Titon still had not completed the packing necessary before he could depart—the very chore he instructed the others to have completed no later than the Dawnstar's setting. Yet he was out here, alone, hours from his home as the sky showed signs of darkening, doing what exactly, he could not recall for the moment.

Keep your eyes sharp, he commanded himself, realizing he had been walking without focus. All this wandering would be for nothing if he managed to pass by the object of his search. Titon backtracked until he saw ground that he thought looked familiar, then retraced his previous steps with bitter determination.

He had debated it thoroughly: whether or not he should first ask for her permission. The more he thought about it, the more the advice he had overheard seemed contemptible. The act of pressing one's mouth, uninvited, against another's would be an irrevocable violation. He could not imagine a more thrilling sensation, though; that of making contact with her tender lips, but the thought of her response made him cringe in trepidation. Would her doe-like eyes fill with fright as he touched her? Would they show disgust? *Rage?* She had matured in a way that was almost intimidating. With each passing year, her hair had grown darker. The vibrant red of her youth had transformed into a deep auburn, so deep in fact that the red was near imperceptible. That flame which once crowned her remained elsewhere, Titon feared. Dormant. Those faultless eyes of shadowy blue could erupt to fire, perhaps, if she were truly offended.

He had not known her to act as such, however. The melodramatic ways of her youth had been replaced with mellow bashfulness. Her entourage of peers had gone as well. One girl, Maridith, who had followed Red always, mimicking her every action as though it would make her closer her equal, had turned to an adversary. Maridith wished so desperately for some way to demean her, but she had trouble in that regard. Her intimations that Red was loose like her mother Kilandra bore no weight. The other girls were reluctant to defend or attack either girl, and the boys had never managed to be more than friendly with Red. When Maridith attempted to tease her, Red had no retort, and Titon did not enjoy watching her endure the other girl's falsehoods in silence. When Maridith proclaimed that Red was a trollop just like her mother, and that she pleased boys in secret at the wading pool, Titon had responded that such accusations would not preclude the fact that Maridith's father was accused of the very same thing—which of course he wasn't. The braying laughter elicited from all those boys in earshot was enough, however, to silence Red's heckler for the time being. The discomfort Titon felt from sullying a man's name undeservedly was wholly negated by the thankful smile he got from Red the next day.

Every twig that poked through the snow caught Titon's attention, but none were the shadows of the stalk for which he looked. Every fleck of dirt upon the dull white drew Titon's eye, but none were the fragile anthers of the blossom he sought. He had only ever seen two snow lilies before, and the chances of him finding one such flower in just a single day's search were shrinking with the Dawnstar's descent toward the horizon.

All the realm's songs and poems: worth less a single kiss, the words returned to him. He had read it in a Dogman book, one he had very much enjoyed. A southern knight had managed to steal a king's wife in that story, and it was Titon's aim to be at least half as chivalrous and charming as he. In doing so, Titon had begun to write small verses of praise for Red, and he left them for her, anonymous. It was rare, though, for a Galatai to be very well read, and rarer still to be well written, so he was quite sure she would be able to guess from where the notes had come. He only hoped she noticed how the words were formed not only to be flattering, but to end with similar sounds, like those in a song. *She notices,* he reassured himself. *And she appreciates it.* They both were quiet people, and he imagined Red must spend much of her time studying Dogman books, just as he did.

Titon's breath left him as he caught sight of it. It was tall enough to shame him for being less than tall himself, and it was almost perfect enough to be worthy of its intended recipient. Seven dark anthers stood atop angel hair filaments, enveloped by six achromatic petals. Where all other flowers had stems of green, this had a stem and three leaves of glintless white. He hesitated only a moment before he plucked it from the ground, able to pinch it off where it left the snow as to sever it from its darker base. A rush of courage buoyed him as he made his way back to his clan's territory, where he would finally do what he had wanted to for so long. *I will kiss her.*

The trees to Titon's left and right were tantalizingly straight, he could not help but notice, and they had an almost uniform thickness from their base up to two men's height. They were ideal for the construction of a home—one he had already been planning in his mind. He made note of the area as he hurried through, knowing he would return here at some point, hopefully not alone. The cabin of his visions had room enough for two.

His haste got the better of him when he reached his destination, and Titon's knuckles rapped on the door of Red's home before they should have. Expecting Kilandra to be the one to answer, he planned to talk to the woman mindlessly about his coming raid, simultaneously coming up with words he should have already prepared for Red. As the door creaked open, he began to worry that it may be her father, Keethro, who would greet him. It was known that Titon was planning a raid meant to accomplish that which Keethro's raids had failed. It was not likely to make the man friendly. Titon bowed his head in worry that he was soon to be nose to nose with their clan's second most fearsome warrior.

Titon's spirits were lifted as he saw that the leather-covered feet of the person at the door could not be Keethro's, and he raised his head with a confident smile.

His confidence left him when he saw Red standing before him.

"Hello," she greeted him kindly.

"Red," he heard himself speak her name as though he was the knight from his novel. Then he became bolstered further, remembering that he had gallant plans to confirm to her. "In the morning, we depart for the Dogmen villages. I wanted to say my farewells in case I do not return."

Titon did not truly fear the prospect of not returning—not because it was totally improbable, but simply because he hadn't had the time yet to give it much thought. What he did fear, however, was that silence was beginning to linger for too long. Red did not appear as though she was prepared to answer him. The only motion she made was with her fingers, fiddling with the side of her skirt. She looked rather uncomfortable, and the more Titon considered it, the more foolish it seemed for him to need to say farewells to a girl he'd barely spoken to until now.

"I have for you two gifts," Titon broke the lull with words sure to please her.

"Oh?" she said, seeming at least interested. "What are they?"

From behind his back, Titon produced the lily. Not at all wilted, it stood as proud as it had when he first plucked it from the snow. After they had both stared at it for a while, Titon pushed his hand forward for her to take it, just as she reached out as well. Their hands collided in an awkward manner, making him fear she might think he'd done so on purpose just to touch her. Nonetheless, she managed to take hold of the flower, and she clasped it in front of the furs which lined the top of her woolen gown.

"It is very beautiful," she said, though she examined the flower more like someone who had been told they must.

Titon considered telling her that he felt the same about her. He tried with all his might to determine if that was the sort of thing that a charming southern knight would ever say, or only write out on paper.

"What is the second?" Red asked, probably after another lengthy silence had occurred.

"The second is for you to determine," said Titon, feeling a bit better to have a chunk of guaranteed conversation to follow. "As you know, it is ever difficult to bring things of value back from the Dogmen, and we must first think to bring that which will help us through the winter. But I would also like to secure for you a gift of conquest. I ask that you would tell me what might please you most for me to return with and bestow upon you."

Red made an unexpectedly wry face, as if she was having difficulty determining an answer or had not even understood his question. It was only then Titon considered just how much he was speaking like the Southman he meant to emulate, rather than a Galatai about to raid Dogmen. It had taken him some time to fully understand the meanings of all their different words and phrases himself, and Red was likely suffering the same.

"Jewelry," she finally blurted.

Her answer restored his spirits. Jewelry was not the sort of gift exchanged between mere friends. "Very well," he told her, hoping she would notice his self-assuredness. "I will acquire for you all the jewelry I can find in the homes of the richest, fattest Dogmen."

Titon thought he noticed the faintest blush spread to her cheeks as she pulled her lips in and bit them for a moment. When her mouth returned to normal, Titon remembered his vow. Every feature of her face was so delicate, he no longer worried about her dormant flame catching light. He only hoped that he might be lucky enough to make contact with her small, rounded nose with his own when he leaned in to kiss her. But first, he must request her permission.

His lips parted, ready to speak the words that—in his fantasies—she longed to hear.

He mumbled goodnight, he turned on his heel, and he left.

CRELLA

Crella felt her pulse throbbing in her temples as her eyes went to the bosom of the woman at her doorstep. The suckling infant did little to cover the flesh of her single bared breast, a taunting specimen of ample rounded perfection.

"It is your husband's, m'lady," repeated the woman, nudging the infant upward. "And I cannot afford—"

"I *assure* you, you are mistaken." Crella showed her a wan smile and spoke calmly. "My husband has no need for the services of whores."

As she closed the door on her scowling visitor, Crella was forced to confront the falsity of her words. There may not have been a married man in the kingdom more in need of such services than Alther—but that would be no excuse, had he made use of them. A flash of vengeance entered her thoughts, of her standing above her bloodied husband as he lay in bed, a dagger through his chest. To kill a man for infidelity when no love was had for him in the first place was a bit spiteful, she reasoned, but they *had* born a child together. And after all these years of mock marriage, whoring may finally be one iniquity too many.

Crella swung the door back open and saw the woman was already many paces away.

"Young woman," she called out to her, not happy to have to shout so loudly and cause a scene. "Please, return and join me for some tea."

The woman looked irked as she strutted back, not thankful to soon be sharing a drink with a noblewoman as she should have been. Crella let her in and showed her to a small table set for two, then left her there with her infant who had begun to cry.

A mask of feigned serenity covered her face as Crella strode toward Alther's quarters. She knew she would find no evidence of impropriety there, but still she wished to clear her mind of the images of harlot's clothing strewn about. *The whore can wait,* she told herself. *At the very least, until the babe has shushed.*

The room she entered was in disarray. There was a pillow dirtied and askew on a chair, the drapes lacked symmetry in the way in which they were drawn, and worst of all, a thin layer of dust had started to gather on the armoire. Hard to detect by the untrained eye perhaps, but Crella could see undeniably that dust was beginning to take.

With the aid of a purposefully deep breath, Crella attempted to lessen her frustration. Had her husband truly been responsible for the multitude of pregnant and nursing women that visited their door, he would not have committed the act here. Nonetheless, the predictable sight before her was not pleasing to witness. *Aunt Adella would have had her servants impaled for this disgrace. Perhaps her husband as well, should she have had one.* But Crella was not her aunt, nor was Crella the queen.

Alther was like to have recently sat in the chair to finish lacing his boots, peered out the drapes to check the weather, and not allowed a servant entrance for a dusting in well over a day—and it was just this lack of concern for her wishes that infuriated Crella. Alther had left to do the one thing she detested most as well. She'd begged him to stop on countless occasions, but hunting was in the blood of the men of House Red Rivers. *It is a vile Northman tradition, the killing of wild animals for sport.* Alther now knew, at least, to keep his distance from her when he returned from such activities. Crella would not tolerate the scent of dead animal anywhere around her.

Alther was no Northman in truth; the temperate climate of Rivervale could scarcely be considered northerly. Adeltian nobility, still bitter after having surrendered their kingdom, enjoyed labeling Rivervalians as such as a means of reproach. Puerile though it may be, Crella reminded herself that she had surrendered more than just a kingdom.

Crella called for her staff of two, and they soon appeared before her.

"How is it that I have come to discover the conditions of these quarters without also finding you doing what is necessary to remedy them?" she demanded.

Crella noted the honest worry in the eyes of the two old women, but she did not soften her own countenance. To be any less than dutifully firm, even with these two, would be an error. "Show an ounce of weakness to one, and all will take from you a pound," Aunt Adella had told her. It was a lesson Crella did not truly grasp until nearly all had been taken from her.

The two servants dragged themselves inside as quickly as their decrepit bones could manage and began to haphazardly wander about the room, shifting things in and out of place, trying to both look busy and guess what details Crella wanted attended to.

"The pillow, please."

The elder of the two servants returned to the chair and righted the pillow, brushed it with a lint comb and righted it once more, still failing in her effort to ensure exact placement. Crella sucked at her teeth as if it was all she could do to not discipline the crone for having performed the task improperly but was letting it pass to demonstrate her leniency.

These hags are simply not up to the task. It was true, a younger staff with keener eyes and more dexterous wrists would have seen the room cleaned twice as quickly and to a higher level of perfection. She had witnessed it firsthand while visiting her friend. Nora, married to a successful spice merchant, had her palatial estate cared for by a staff of three *lady servants.* Those dove-like girls flew around with fastidiousness, making sure every corner was cleaned, every pillow turned, every inch of fine fabric free of stray hair and lint. To say it irked Crella that the wife of a merchant would have a domicile better cared for than the princess and spouse of the heir to the throne would be an understatement. She and Alther could easily afford the young servants, but there were other complications Crella sought to avoid. She did not like the idea of such creatures buzzing around her husband. One did not have an eye as keen as Crella's without spotting more than just motes of dust and asymmetry. She saw the way men peered at the lovely birds from the corners of their eyes like wolves in a henhouse. *Rabid wolves in a chickhouse, more the like.*

But there was more to it than the potential for her husband to stray. Gibes aside, Alther's Rivervalian lineage made him more trustworthy than the Adeltian men Crella had come to know since the end of the war. The whore's baby who could still be heard screaming from down the hall was *not* Alther's. The women who had appeared at her doorstep time and again were sent by another, Crella believed—possibly even the king. It was not enough that Lyell had stolen her kingdom, killed her aunt, and forced her to marry his son; he sought to demoralize and degrade her without end.

Just as she did not believe Alther to partake in whoring, she did not truly fear that he would take a lady servant to bed. *What difference would it make, should you see him peering at them?* It was a conversation she'd had with herself already. *You do not love the man.* Nonetheless, the thought of seeing in his eyes that he desired another was not a welcome one. Crella could read a man by his eyes, and Alther's hid very little.

She could not so easily read a *duchess,* however. Crella had nothing but contempt for Cassen, the pasty Duchess of Eastport. His every feature, from his grossly short-cropped hair to his pastel silken slippers, turned her stomach for reasons she could not fully define. Hiring lady servants meant having to meet with Cassen to select the workers and discuss the terms, and she had no desire to speak to let alone do business with him. Cassen had served as an apprentice to Crella's late uncle, Calder, the former Duke of Eastport. It was a time of which she would rather not be reminded.

It was certainly not customary for a duke or duchess to be involved in what was tantamount to running a high-end maid service; however, Cassen was certainly not a duchess bound by common custom. It was a bit of a mystery to all as to why he would continue in the lowly business of servant management, but none could argue with the quality of his product. His lady servants were the best trained, fastest working, most obedient of servants. They were also the most expensive. They shared nothing in common, it seemed, with their ostentatious proprietor. They were paragons of civility and were renowned throughout the kingdom for pleasing—most of all—their masters' wives with their demure nature and tireless work.

But I would be their master, she thought, *not Alther. How nice it would be to have some daughterly company in the home.* Crella had felt the absence of her daughter more than she had expected since Ethel left to attend school in the Adeltian Throne. Headstrong though she was, Ethel had at least begun to dress and act the part of a lady, giving her mother some reprieve. Crella would have much preferred that Ethel had joined her in embroidery, but with Ethel's living room chair empty at nights, there was no denying how much Crella wished to have her daughter there with some book in her lap. *A lady servant is no replacement for a daughter,* she conceded sullenly.

The wailing of the distant infant grew to untenable levels, and Crella decided she would just send the whore away. She glanced around Alther's room a final time, watching as one of the women fought her own curved spine in an attempt to reach under the bed. *Such a shame,* Crella thought in surrender, *but I must simply endure this imperfection.*

And yet the next day, Crella found herself being escorted by one of Cassen's many boy servants to his grand chamber's door. She could not live with the state of her home any longer and required professional services...*for my sanity,* she reasoned.

"Her Majesty Princess Crella to see you," said the boy after three fast and gentle knocks. Cassen was predisposed to addressing people with titles above their station, something he must have trained his boys to do as well. It was flattery to some, but others more rightly took offense. At best it was delivered with playful mischief, but Crella knew it to be a tool used to put off-balance and provoke—and she would be neither.

"Your Grace, you honor me." With the words, Cassen performed a nimble curtsey in spite of his corpulence. He was covered by his usual silks, wrapped around him in some haphazard fashion. His jowls were weak and saggy, but his face appeared thinner in person than memory served. *Perhaps he is ill.*

"Please," said Crella, already uncomfortable in his presence. She glanced around the room, noting with disgust the garish décor: candles everywhere, velveteen upholstery, silvered glass framed by thick wood, carved and gilded. "I am here against my better judgment to employ some of your ladies."

"Ah yes." Cassen stood before her, his face aglow. He was not put off in the least by her quip. "But I must insist you understand that it is I alone who *employ* my ladies, I who house and protect them. They perform their services from the moment the Dawnstar first ascends in the east until it disappears to the west." Cassen raised a finger. "They return under strict curfew in spite of any commands to the contrary. You and yours may be their master for a time, but I will forever be their employer, their guardian…their mother."

"All of that is fine," Crella responded tersely, already wanting this conversation over. "As one would expect of someone in my position, I am quite busy with no time to discuss every intricacy of your…*business*." Crella did have a tea sipping scheduled with Nora for later that night, and she was eager to share the news that she would no longer be at the mercy of her two elderly servants. More so, she needed to be out of this room which stunk of perfume and tallow. "I wish to hire your ladies for their services and with haste. If that is too much to ask I will find services elsewhere."

Cassen appeared to have found this most amusing, letting out a silent giggle with raised shoulders. "Oh, Your Majesty must not mean the women of Shal'sezar! They will remain in your company overnight if that is what you and your *husband* desire, but I must insist, if cleanliness is what you seek you must look elsewhere. And I do believe there is little where else to look."

Crella felt the heat building under her skin. *This pig of a man insults me to my face. Why the king allows him to remain in power is beyond my comprehension.* Though his insults were indirect, the intention seemed not. She sought to calm herself in the way her husband always suggested. Alther did not respond to her tantrums like most men—in kind with rage of their own, or worse yet with the back of a hand. He would show a stolid smile and tell her that in times of rage one should seek the void. She never had allowed him to know she ever took this advice, and receiving it only angered her further. But she now sought to clear her mind and let her muscles relax, finding she was able to better retain her composure.

"Duchess Cassen, I have no wish to trade insinuations and insults as it is neither becoming nor entertaining. I will see your lady servants for selection or be on my way."

Cassen studied her so intently it made her wish to shy away. "My sincerest of apologies, Princess Crella. I meant no disrespect. A mother is ever so protective of her daughters. You must understand." Cassen clapped his hands twice and a long procession of lady servants streamed waiflike into the room. "These are among the ladies in training not yet assigned to masters. As you must know, payment begins immediately, yet there is a lengthy period of waiting between selection and the completion of training, after which services can begin. I wish that I could have before you fully-trained ladies from which to select; however, it seems demand far outstrips the supply, and it is all I can do to find, train, and house enough ladies for this small corner of the kingdom."

Crella braced herself for the hatred she would surely feel toward these girls when she laid eyes upon them. A few were very young, but most had surely flowered. They were all so innocent and naïve, like a row of frightened deer staring politely downward—not at their own feet, which would be rude, but aimed at the knees of those who would command them. *Already quite well trained, it would appear.* These were not *ladies*, in her opinion; these were obedient girls. The hatred she thought she would feel was not present, yet she still felt Cassen's use of the term lady to describe them quite disrespectful to true ladies.

There did not appear to be a pattern in the way the girls were assorted, but for some reason Crella found herself inclined to choose the three on the far left. They had decidedly more daughterly qualities as opposed to the neighbor-girl look that could more easily turn a man to lust.

"I will have these three," Crella motioned with cascading fingers.

"Three!" Cassen said with mock surprise. "Your estate must be *very* dirty."

Crella ignored the slight. "When can they begin?"

"For Her Majesty I can have these ladies ready in oh, say, three short months. I remind you they receive quite thorough training."

This was another seemingly deliberate slight. Nora received her lady servants in no more than several weeks. Crella refused to give Cassen the satisfaction of having thought she was annoyed.

"Very well. I suppose we are finished here then?"

"Oh, I am afraid not quite yet," said Cassen, twirling a stray silk at his hip with his finger. "There is still the issue of the deposit…"

TITON SON OF SMALL GRYN

The pungent scent of onion greens wafted through their home. Goat meat boiled with potatoes and the stalks of onions was Elise's favorite dish, and so he prepared it for her, hoping his offering might lessen the blow of what he must let her know.

Unbeknownst to his clansmen, Titon had become somewhat of a master of the pot since his wife had fallen ill. It had been a challenge of his to try to recreate his and her favorite dishes, the ones she used to make for him when he returned from hunting or raiding. He had hoped that the smells of those dishes might bring her back to sound mind, but to no avail. Nevertheless, as in all things, once he put himself to task he never tired of his effort.

He ladled some stew into a large bowl and sat by his wife as she gazed out her window. He burned his lips and tongue on the hot broth, just as he always had when returning from conquest, too ravenous to wait for it to cool, savoring the familiarity of it. Fire, it seemed to him, burned much more gently than did the cold.

When it had cooled to a point where it was safe for his wife, he began to slowly tip spoonfuls into her mouth. After a while, her body would involuntarily swallow, an action he had seen enough by now to believe it was not painful.

"Good, is it not?" he asked, half expecting an answer given the perfection to which he had prepared it.

"My Storm Wolf, I have good news. Our boys now lead a raid south to slaughter countless Dogmen and bring back food to last through the winter. Others may doubt them, the old and the timid who have failed before them, but I know they will succeed." Titon searched her face for some change in expression, finding none. "I see some part of us in each of them, all the better parts or so it would seem."

The chair Titon sat on groaned in protest as he shifted his weight. The discomfort he now felt had nothing to do with the hard seat.

"I need to tell you something else that I hope you will understand," he continued. "I am leaving for a while. How long, I cannot say. I have no way of knowing how far I will need to travel. Those lands to the south where the rivers flow like oceans and the goats grow fat as pigs, they are said to have healers—healers with potions, elixirs, and magic able to cure any ailment." Titon fed her another spoonful and waited for her to swallow. "I do not believe in magic, the stuff of children's tales, but I believe I can convince any such healer to inform me of his methods and ingredients. I can be quite persuasive."

Titon had planned this trip for some time and had given it plenty of thought—certainly enough to realize the obstacles he'd face would be many. Southern men were not like to take well to a giant of a man such that he was, but that only concerned him to the extent that it would make finding her remedy more difficult. Though his people and those to the south looked little different, his size and dialect would reveal him for what he was, a Northman, and his scars would betray him as a Galatai warrior.

"Do not fear for your care. I have arranged for some of Ulfor's girls to tend to your needs and comforts. Just do not be too mean to the poor girls. You can have quite the temper," he gibed.

More troubling than the dangers of the journey itself was how Titon imagined his sons might react upon returning to find him gone. He did not like the thought of leaving while they were off, but it was the best way to ensure they would not follow him. Whichever of the two took his place while he was away, Titon had decided that that son would remain as clan leader even upon his return... Should he return.

"I am taking Keethro with me." Titon answered the question his wife could not ask. He placed the empty bowl on the ground and sat in silence, trying to come to terms with his feelings on the matter.

He is a good man, thought Titon, wishing for that to be the end of his unrest.

He had known Keethro as long as he'd known anyone. Keethro was Titon's most respected and trusted friend, and the one to whom Titon had turned to keep the clan fed when Titon could no longer lead the raids. *But will he agree to come?*

Titon had put off the asking due to his concern that he might be refused. Keethro was a cautious man, or at least he'd become one, and a trip farther south than any had attempted, to find an elixir that may not exist, was not like to interest him. *I am still his leader, and I will command him if need be.*

But the thought of ordering his friend to partake on a potentially futile and deadly quest was an ugly one. Fifteen years ago Keethro would have gone gladly, but things were different now. *His harlot is what changed him*, thought Titon.

It went without saying that Kilandra had been pressuring Keethro to usurp control of their clan during Titon's decade of decline. Titon knew—likely better than even Keethro—just how hungry she was for power. *How much poison has that woman infected him with? Can I trust a man whose motives may no longer square with my own?*

Leaving without Keethro was out of the question. Titon had never truly feared Keethro challenging him for leadership, but in his absence that might change. The idea that Keethro may fight Titon's sons for the right to lead revolted him. Though it would not be a true betrayal, as these were the ways of their people, it still felt as such—perhaps only because he knew it would be Kilandra's ambition that caused the needless death of one or both of his sons. Neither would be any match for Keethro, not yet. They lacked his veteran's maturity. *You would take my son's from me? Because of that succubus?*

The snapping of wood brought Titon back into focus. In his hand he held the right arm of his chair, now detached from its base. He looked at his wife guiltily, but she was far from accusing.

Keethro would come. That was simply the end of it. It made no sense to worry over scenarios that would not be. Even so, Titon was not free from misgivings when it came to leaving his sons behind.

To each of his boys and to the best of his ability, Titon had written a letter. To Decker he wrote of his pride in the man that he had become. He reminded him that the clans needed a leader who could unite them to conquer the Dogmen, take their lands, and build a defense against the other southern men who were liable to attack in retaliation. Titon was confident Decker would find his way to greatness with or without his further guidance.

His letter to his elder son was of a different nature. Throughout young Titon's upbringing, Titon had been careful not to show how he favored the boy for fear that it would complicate matters when Decker inevitably seized the right to be the clan's next leader. And though he'd kept it hidden, Titon was awestruck by his firstborn's intelligence and wit as well as his prowess with axe and bow. He feared the boy had no idea of this, which was something he aimed to remedy in his letter. Given the likelihood that he might not return from his trip to the South, it was of great consequence.

> Titon, I see in you the same soul of a Storm Wolf I saw in your mother, that which made me break from our customs and protect her as one of our own. Decker is a good lad and a man other men will follow into battle without question, but you are a far rarer breed. It is true, you are not the son I always wanted, you are one better. Please watch over and protect your brother and mother while I search for her cure. They will need your help and your guidance.

The sealed letters lay on the table where the boys were sure to find them when they came to check on their mother. *With the reading of my words, they will understand my leaving*, Titon resolved.

"Ellie," Titon said to his wife with stony determination, "my promise to you is this: I will go to the South with Keethro. I will find the remedy to your ailment. You will awaken from your slumber, and we will be together again as a man and woman should." He looked into her unmoving eyes and half imagined they showed an uncharacteristic wetness. "And I will kill every man, woman, and child that stands in my way."

THE SIREN
Many Years Ago

Kilandra had been stalking him for several miles, the man she would seduce, stopping in kind when he checked his traps. The soft crunch of snow beneath her rabbit-skin boots required that she keep her distance, lest she be heard before they were safely alone.

Her prey was formidable in every regard. The shadow he cast was monstrous, and all men seemed fearful to be within it. Though still a young man, he was the leader of their people, a tenacious leader. That he had taken control of their clan was perhaps the only reason they all yet lived. He led raids farther south than any before him, bringing back food to help see them through winters plagued by famine.

There was no doubt in her mind that the interest he no longer showed her was due only to strength of will, but that did not ease the flutter in her belly. Ever since he had returned with his stolen bride, he'd no longer looked at Kilandra in the same way. Truth be told, he barely looked at her at all, for if he had, his eyes would no doubt suffer the drop-anchored weight that pulled all men's gazes downward, some stopping awkwardly at her chest, but most following the full length of her before turning to the side as if the entire motion had been some means of looking elsewhere.

And she was well aware of what they saw in that fleeting glance. Hours of each day were allotted to the study of her own form. "Just as a warrior must know his blade, so should a woman know herself," her mother had taught her, and Kilandra had been forged of the finest steel. No other woman had features that bested her own, none at least that she had seen...save perhaps Kysa's dainty knees and ankles—a meager gain not worth the flesh of hips and chest it cost the girl. It was loathsome what little regard the other women had for their appearance. None so much as brushed their mane, it seemed, let alone labored over it as Kilandra did. Her brown hair, dark as obsidian, shone with the faint cobalt luster of the poisonous privet berries she used to tint it, and when haloed by the white fur of her hood, her locks were quite striking. Framing a face of devilish innocence, it was no wonder men could not resist knowing what form of figure stood beneath, nor was it that some found it impossible to tear eyes from the bare flesh of her breasts that peeked from beneath her bodice.

With some difficulty she was able to place her feet within the tracks he had left behind. *Best to be limber for what is to come*, she mused, without any flush of embarrassment. Her thoughts may have been forward, but her tactics were not. She knew a man fell harder upon hunted prey, and though following a man through the snow was hardly coy, her methods upon her discovery would be abashed and subtle. And she had made no mistake with her timing. The man's wife had been swollen with a babe in her womb for months, assuring his violent need for release. No Galatai man would bed a pregnant woman for fear of rubbing members with his future son—in this thinking there was no dissension.

The shiver that ran from the backs of her knees to the nape of her neck was not from the cold. She had long since become accustomed to exposing skin to the late autumn nip without discomfort, but there was no remedy for the elation of enticing an unfamiliar touch. The man she'd left behind, the one she called husband, may have been the most coveted of men, due to his sculpted form, dark features, and eyes of indomitable blue, but the man she stalked had no equal in authority.

Kilandra wrapped her arms around herself and quickened her pace. *Perhaps there is no need to travel farther*, she reasoned. *Perhaps the threat of being caught in misconduct would only serve to heighten the thrill.* It was a foolish means of rationalizing her impatience, she knew, but her hastened stride continued until she halted with sudden alarm.

He had stopped as well, his head turned to the side, not checking a trap. If he was to see her coming from so far away she feared it may make her appear desperate. And to a man of confidence there was nothing less arousing than a desperate woman, another of her mother's lessons.

She remained motionless, hoping he could not see her from his periphery, the true danger of her task now becoming apparent. Had he been any other man it would not be so, but he was no stranger to her husband. The two men were closest friends, further complicating this affair. Warmth flooded her body as she contemplated her mistake. Forcing herself to remain calm, she inhaled slow and deep, filling her lungs with the brisk chill. It would not do to arrive wet with the sweat of worry.

The distant man remained motionless, as if listening. Her legs, caught midstride, ached and begged her to fall flat to her stomach, but the motion would draw his hunter's eye. With her hood drawn tight, hiding her hair, she would be near invisible in her furs of all white. She waited, reminding herself that it was she who was the hunter, a thought that was difficult to accept until he had once again turned his head forward, resuming his gait. She let him gain more distance before continuing her advance—this quest must not be botched by zeal.

With her dread turning again to craving, she allowed her imagination to take flight. Whether he would yield to his basest desires was not what enthralled her, for she had every confidence in her ability to ensure that was the case. It was what he would do when, after having just begun their transgression, she suddenly rebuffed—that was what caused her heart to quiver. How would a man such as he respond to her rejection, her insistence that her intent was misinterpreted, her struggle to be free from his grasp? How would a man who answers to none respond when denied his fruit, the price of which was already paid by the taint of impropriety? She had her suspicions, consistent with her desires: that with hands of steel he would force her compliance. But if this was to be done properly, she would not know with certainty for yet another mile.

KEETHRO

Keethro swung his axe with rancor. The viscous blood of his victim clung to the well-worn head of his weapon as he continued his assault. Swing after swing, Keethro's wrath only built as the corpse of his fallen foe stubbornly refused to break way.

Petrified, those he would kill next looked on in silent horror. Droplets of sweat pooled on his brow, falling with some of the fiercer blows into the deep wound he had carved. Then, with a final stroke, Keethro's blade bit into the center of the wooden cadaver, breaking it into two manageable pieces.

He turned and flung his axe at the next tree. Botching the release, his axe flew downward into the knee-high snow as Keethro squeezed his eyelids closed with the force of his embarrassment. No matter how he practiced, he simply could not throw an axe—not with his left. He could shave the wings off a dragonfly in flight with his right, however.

His sled piled high with half a day's work, Keethro made his way back to his home. Iron pine, with its thick crimson sap impossible to remove from the skin and heartwood hard as stone, was the bane of many men. Difficult that it was to fell, it provided more than enough heat to be worth the added labor. This trip would be Keethro's last, having gathered enough to warm his home, largest of the clan, through the coming winter.

Keethro stopped as he saw what awaited him. He removed a flask from inside his furs and took a swig of the sour alcohol. The figure in the distance, that beguiling siren he called wife, standing upon the balcony built by his own hand, was no doubt scowling though he was too far away to tell. Keethro resumed his march into the awaiting ambush.

"You would leave your wife and daughter to starve in the cold of winter?"

It was as charming a greeting as he could have expected, but it did not warrant a response. He began to move armfuls of the firewood to the neat stack under the balcony. For the winter they had food enough for three stored—plenty, considering it would only need to support the lesser two.

"While you go seek the warm beds of southern whores?" Kilandra snarled.

It is a wonder we need wood at all given her fiery rage, he thought.

Keethro was not one to suffer discomposure from a woman's scorn. After facing the likes of hardened warriors from other clans, screaming and spitting in his face, eager to feed him his own entrails, and always emerging the victor, Keethro had no mind to be brought to anger. "I believe in the dead of winter even the beds of southern whores can be cold."

He turned to face her as she flew down the steps of the balcony. The sight of her—her sultry defiance that begged him to overpower her, to force her surrender—was enough to turn his own pine to iron, but he was resolved to thwart her advances. He allowed her to slap him once across the face. Her second strike, he caught.

"You must put an end to this foolishness and kill him! Kill him and we—" Keethro's unyielding grip was around his wife's throat, silencing her. He glowered his warning, letting her know this was not to be one of their games.

"Talk like that will get us both killed," he said through clenched teeth. *With her harlot's body came a harlot's mind. Perhaps I will see if southern beds creak in much the same way northern beds do, and bring back a young maiden kissed by dawnlight.* "You would announce to the whole clan my intentions? Now how do you expect me to return on the next moon, alone, with a tale of how clumsy Titon tripped and fell from a cliff?"

Keethro had no desire to go south with Titon, nor did he feel any real obligation to do so. The friend and brother in battle that Titon once was had long since disappeared, replaced by a man consumed by the hopeless revival of his slumbered wife. This voyage, apart from having no chance of success, was like to cost Keethro his life, or—should he somehow manage to survive—his marriage. Keethro was more concerned of the damage that would be dealt to his name if he returned to find Kilandra had strayed. "The mighty Keethro," they would taunt, "handsomest of all Galatai, but unable to keep a woman in his own bed." The source of his inadequacies would be implied, and he would end up killing many a drunken brother in his own drunken retaliation. It was not acceptable. He would not spend countless months in search of a cure that did not exist only to return to a life in ruin. *Better to kill the one brother than the many.*

"I promise you this," she said after released. "If you do not return far sooner than that, you will find I am no longer waiting." She spoke with all the venom she could spit, but Keethro heard in her voice her sincerity—and *that*, he could not forgive her.

He walked away, leaving Kilandra standing beside the still-loaded sled. *May the next fool be more tolerant of your nature.*

Sweet dry air filled his lungs as he stepped foot into his home. The raw timbers of its sturdy pine framing supported its impressive ceilings and large rooms. In stark contrast to the warmth of his home was the cold countenance of his teary-eyed daughter seated at the kitchen table. If not for the faint glow of auburn in her hair, he would have believed she was every bit his daughter with her dark blue eyes so matching his own.

He leaned to kiss her on the head before he left.

"I hate you!" Her verbal assault was accompanied by a knuckled punch to his chin. "I pray you do not come back this time," she yelled over her shoulder as she ran to her room.

Keethro was a warrior and knew little of raising a girl, and his mastery of seduction did not translate to fatherhood. His reputation only seemed to cause Red to despise him as she grew older and understood more of what the stories about him meant. Nor was it any help that her mother saw fit to poison her mind with her own beliefs about the cruelty and duplicity of men—all men. *Or perhaps Red simply loathes me because she too suspects the truth.*

Keethro never doubted Kilandra would bed a man of higher position, given the chance, and there was but one. Keethro believed that a man should hold his woman responsible for infidelity, since believing otherwise would have made him quite the hypocrite. However, in the case that the man also claimed to be your friend, it was unforgivable of both parties. *He will confess with his dying breaths. I'll make sure of it.*

Keethro hoisted his readied supplies onto his back and set out for the journey with his best and only friend—the one he sought to kill.

THE MIDWIFE
Many Years Ago

A banging on her door had awoken Janin from slumber. It was not unusual for her to be called upon in the dead of night, but the urgency with which her summoners had insisted she come worried her greatly. By Peace's grace there had been no miscarriages or stillbirths since the Rivervalians overran their kingdom. *What will they do to me,* she wondered, *when I fail to deliver one of their own?*

As they rushed to an undisclosed residence, Janin prayed in silence. The near panicked men who'd roused her now compelled her to move at a pace that had her almost tripping on her skirts. Given the direction they led her, they could be headed to the estate of any number of noble houses. If forced to guess, as it seemed she was, she would have assumed it was the young princess who was in need of her services—the one whom she had helped through a pregnancy just two years prior, back when the queen sat the throne and Crella was still the *very* young princess…and unmarried, at that. Crella had come to term a week ago by Janin's best estimate, and she visited the girl daily.

She was eager to confirm her suspicion, but her mutes for escorts refused to tell her to where they were headed on account of an archaic tradition. Commoners were not to be told who'd summoned them. This was not the first time she had been troubled by this predicament, but the nobles always seemed to forget to give special instruction to forgo such idiocy in, of all times, those of emergency.

"It is important I know beforehand so that I may best prepare myself to tend to the needs of my patient. If you will not speak her name then at the very least give me some sign that my assumption that I have been called to care for the young Lady Crella is correct."

One of the half dozen men escorting her made a noise somewhere between a grunt and a cough. It was not uncommon for these men to make such noises for no apparent reason, but she believed the glare from the noisemaker's commander to be proof enough that it was the sign she'd requested.

Freed from her burden of not knowing what to expect, Janin became aware of the oppressive heat. Even during the night, the summers of Adeltia felt little different than leaning over a pot of boiling water. She glanced around, hoping to not be alone in her discomfort, but she could not discern any of her escorts' expressions, let alone any beads of sweat.

Their lanterns directed the light downwards, and the only visible detail of interest was the authoritative crest of the Protectors of the Realm that glimmered upon all their chests. Known more commonly as The Guard, these men foreswore their allegiance to any kingdom and were bestowed a duty of service first and foremost to the realm. *First and foremost to the king who pays their wages,* Janin thought, disgusted that they now bent to the will of their Rivervalian conqueror.

As they neared their destination, Janin could hear muffled moans of pain and suffering coming from inside the home. It was, as expected, the home of Crella and her new husband.

Crella looked to be in great distress, but perhaps not so much as did the young father. It was the first time Janin had been in the same room with Alther, the son of Adeltia's new king, and she was surprised by his vulnerability. He knelt at Crella's bedside, looking eager to hold a hand she would not give him, his face pale with apparent concern for his wife and unborn child. The sweat on his brow was unlikely to be from the heat. Janin was relieved to be inside this home cooled by means beyond her comprehension.

"My lady," Janin addressed the princess. Despite her pregnancy and current state of misery, Crella remained quite stunning. The glow from several sconces shone on her golden hair which fell in waves, and lit the delicate features of her face that one would expect and desire in royalty. "You must tell me what ails you, and please, be precise in your detail."

The princess's emerald eyes flashed annoyance. "What ails me is that this pregnancy has gone on for long enough."

Janin noted the young woman's ferocity with heartache. She was an entirely different patient than she had been two years prior, but Janin did not judge her for it. *To have endured what she has...*

"It is time for it to be over with. I will not suffer another night of back spasms and utter discomfort."

"My lady, are your spasms in your back or your belly?" Janin asked with the utmost respect. She knew how to deal with highborn in distress. She was direct but humble and obedient.

"Have you become deaf or merely stupid? Did I not just tell you it was my back that spasms?" Crella turned to her husband. "Must I repeat my every utterance to this fool while your heir grows cold and dies in my womb? I warn you now—I will *not* be made to suffer another pregnancy." The venom that came from such young lips would have been shocking to Janin had she not heard much the same during her other recent visits.

"Apologies, my lady. I had to be sure. It has great bearing on the child's delivery. Please, sit back and try to rest. I must have a look." Janin turned first to the few of her escort who yet lingered. "I would ask that all gentlemen leave the room." There was no need for the princess to suffer any undue embarrassment during delivery, the entire process of which was decidedly unladylike.

"I would wish to stay and comfort my wife from her bedside, if there would be no ill-effect on the child." Alther was a fair-looking man, not notably strong in chest or chin but neither weak. He was several years Crella's senior with a rich head of short brown hair and a thick beard to match. The prince looked to the midwife for response as a son does to a mother.

"Just do as she says and leave." Crella waved her hand toward the door. Her pain must have subsided considerably—had it truly been there to start—as she was no longer concentrated on drawing attention to her discomfort.

"It would not harm the child in any way if you remained, but please do not stray from her side if you choose to stay, my lord," Janin responded, shuffling the remaining men out of the room.

Janin was predisposed to disliking the nobility she served, and certainly bore no love for Alther's father and the war he'd waged on her people, but Alther seemed a man of honest compassion. She almost pitied him for the rudeness of his wife, though the princess was far above his station in appearance. "Seek a mate above yourself and be forever beholden," her grandmother had always told her, and thus Janin remained unmarried.

"Yes, please stay." Crella's tone had softened, but only for the moment. "I may need you to spur this midwife with the back of your hand should she fail to deliver this baby with haste."

Janin examined the princess quickly and was not surprised by what she saw. "My lady, I beg your forgiveness, but you are not meant to have this baby tonight." She did her best to not vex the highborn as it would only make things worse. "Things have not progressed to that stage. It could be another week or more, in fairness."

The princess sat up, placing her hands upon the top of her swollen stomach and glowering at Janin from between her own legs. "I *will* have this baby tonight—the one you said would come a week past. The only question that remains is whether you will deliver it or I will be forced to push it from my belly by strength of hand. Should it be the latter, I assure you I will be *delivering* your head shortly thereafter to whichever lowborn is in your closest acquaintance."

She believed Crella to be speaking the truth, for if there was one thing highborn learned at an early age, it was the importance of following through on a threat. Janin bowed her head and turned toward the husband. His look of worry bade her do as his wife demanded.

"I will do as you command, my lady. Though I would not recommend we induce for yet another week, I do not feel that doing so now would be of much harm to the child. We must have a horseman fetch a tonic that is necessary to hasten the process, and you will hold in your arms your child by midmorning." Alther still wore a look of concern, but it seemed both he and Janin were of like mind in knowing that there would be no bending of Crella's iron will.

Seven hours later, the wailing of the princess was replaced with the wailing of a very small, very frail-looking infant. He was nevertheless crying with great strength—a good sign of health. The new father was the first to reach for the swaddled infant.

"He sounds so strong and hearty. My wife, you have given me the greatest of gifts, a son. I think we should name him Leofwin after my father's father. He was a great and noble king."

His wife reached out her arms, and he gave her their new child. She looked at the babe and haughtily proclaimed, "We will not name him after some wretched Northman. We will name him after my beloved brother who died as a young boy to the sweating sickness. His name will be Stephon."

ALTHER

Dusk fell upon the wooden tiles of the rooftops causing the specks of sap to glow as if self-illuminated. It was the mightiest city in the mightiest of kingdoms—the kingdom his father had taken when Alther was a boy not much older than his own son now was. Adeltia spread out before him as he gazed from the castle walls of its capital city, taking a reticent pride in the fact that it was Rivervale's banners that now hung from every turret of the distant outer walls, boasting the sigil of many tributaries converging into the mighty Eos. He recalled not his first trip to this kingdom, but his first trip here as a conqueror. *How differently I then envisioned my life would be, helping to rule this kingdom.*

Alther looked to his son beside him and exhaled, knowing it was a mistake to have brought him. Stephon stood tall for his age of fifteen in his high-collared leathern tunic, his tournament foil kept proudly at his belt. He had his father's spry frame and his mother's bright golden hair, prized among Adeltians, but where Crella's was long and wavy, his was short with tight ringlets. He cast his aristocratic gaze into the distance, admiring the view of what would one day be his kingdom. Alther imagined Stephon must be having the same thoughts of glory and grandeur he himself had imagined as a young man. *I have seen little of either since becoming a joyless custodian of that which these walls protect.*

The two resumed their stroll along the wall walk, hearing what sounded to be children at play below. Had Alther been told two decades prior that his father would be allowing children in the courtyards, a place where knights should be swinging swords and hurling insults, sharpening steel against steel and mind against mind, Alther would have considered it madness. But King Lyell had seemed to have softened over the years, at least in terms of military preparedness. Having conquered all the civilized lands of consequence on their continent, the apparent need for such military strength and readiness dwindled.

Alther had been raised during the height of his father's zeal and could still feel the blows from the intense training. "An angry opponent is an easy opponent," his father would say. "Revel in the joy of taunting your foe to the point of him defeating himself, and then you will know *true* victory, for a sharp mind can cut even an armored man to the quick." However, it was Alther who found himself to be the one provoked to anger, always losing to the larger, nimbler, and more experienced swordsmen his father put before him. He learned to endure the abuse with detachment, as any whines or wincing only furthered the length and severity of his training. And he had become a fine swordsman, even by his father's measure, able to withstand the barrages of slices, thrusts, and insults all aimed at fresh wounds and tender flesh. But Alther had learned, above all, that no matter how much he trained, there would always be a good many better swordsmen. It was a lesson he did not think his father had intended to teach.

"Grab the pig-wizard's cape," cried one of the courtyard boys below. "Come on, show us a trick!"

Alther peered over the parapet to see four tall boys surrounding a fifth who was small only in height. The pig-wizard, as they called him, had the shape of a ham in truth, though this ham had upon its back a violet cape of a renowned Adeltian house. The boy may have been royalty, but it made no difference to the four surrounding him, who in all fairness were likely just as royal given their access to the courtyards.

"Why is your tail draped about your neck and not sprouting from your ass, pig-wizard?"

"Careful, he might turn you into a toad or something."

"I'd be more afraid of him farting a fireball!"

The children laughed at the stout one in the middle and began their assault. The one closest grabbed the boy by his cape, jerking him backwards so that he fell on his ass. He turned and got to his feet slowly only to have a different boy pull him down hard again upon his backside. By the third time, they had dragged him far enough that he nearly smashed his head upon the stone forming the perimeter of the gardens.

"That is enough," Alther called down to them blandly. They quickly dispersed when they realized they had an audience. The tortured boy continued to cry, not seeming to have heard Alther's intervention. He stood up, dragged the top of his arm all the way down to the finger across his snotty nose, brushed off his cape, and limped off.

"That was poorly done, Father." Stephon spoke as if lecturing a servant. "A man must learn his place." He then turned and resumed his noble saunter, his lesson having been concluded.

Half his blood is mine, thought Alther as he trailed Stephon toward the king's chambers, *but it seems he is pure Adeltian, in truth.*

⚔

Alther and his son entered his father's study and proceeded down the long entryway that led to the seated king. Aside from the grand desk and ornate topographical carvings on the walls, it was a simple room with simple furnishings. His father preferred to do his work of import within the comforts of this room adjacent to his bedchambers. It had none of the regality of the massive throne room, which saw little use by Lyell, but the nature of the study lent it an air of muffled secrecy. A man could enter a room such as this, never exit, and none would be the wiser. *I must maintain composure and show discipline so that I may walk out the same way I walked in.* Alther did not truly fear his father killing him, but it never hurt to be scrupulous.

"Ah, my son and his," said Lyell as he looked up from the pile of papers on his desk. "Come to tell me of the wealth and riches they have secured for my kingdom, no doubt." Lyell was by all accounts an old king, yet he had the look of a man that retained enough strength from his youth to gladly throttle a man should the need arise. His skin sagged slightly around the eyes, but his short and cleanly cropped beard of thick white hair and his penetrating stare made him a formidable presence. Alther was much the younger reflection of his father, with darker hair, firmer skin, and a more lithesome build, but where his father was all steely resolve, Alther was troubled apprehension—a fact he was especially cognizant of when in his father's presence.

"I am afraid not, Father." Alther knew he must look how he felt, sour and melancholy, the way he always felt when having to report his failure to his father. *I was trained to wield swords and lead men into battle, not to manage the finances of a foreign land where all despise me and plot to ensure my downfall.* "The merchants of the Spicelands have once again increased the price for transporting pepper and poppy. Worse yet, the price of salt has increased tenfold without cause, and they report supplies of juniper and corian—"

"No need to list every spice in the cook's kitchen, my boy," interrupted the king. Alther had carefully planned this speech, ensuring that it would detail the multitude of obstacles that stood in the way of him meeting his own modest goals, which were but a fraction of his father's lofty requests.

"Yes, Your Grace. What I mean to say, in short, is that Westport will not be producing the, ehm, amount of revenue for the Throne that we had anticipated. The amount we had agreed upon, I mean to say." Alther spoke meekly and stumbled with his words.

He immediately regretted calling his father by the formal title for a ruler as he knew it was like to only incite the man to anger. "I am your father and your king," he had reminded Alther in the past, "and there is nothing unduly graceful about either."

The king returned his gaze to his papers and let out a sigh of displeasure. He then allowed silence to linger as he was prone to do. It was far easier for Alther to endure his father's discourtesy when alone, but Stephon had been adamant about getting a chance to show his newly acquired prowess for politics to his grandfather.

"Perhaps you could explain to me, Alther, how it is that Westport, the richer of the sister cities before we took the Throne, the richest city in all the realm, has now come to be evermore poorer while Eastport's incomes grow with fervor?" Lyell still looked down at his papers.

Alther was prepared to trade ill words in regard to the merchants but was not ready to answer any questions of substance as to his continued failure. He had been so engrossed with his own finances that he had little time devoted toward righting the problems with his city's income. Crella spent more than he wished on unnecessary luxuries, but the true source of his troubles came from using his own money to help pad and conceal the disastrous state of his city's lack of revenue. That was a solution, however, that could not continue; he had nearly consumed all his own once substantial monetary reserves. *If left to the devices of my lovely wife and these merchants I shall be a pauper and worse yet, an embarrassment to my father.*

"Your Gr—." Alther caught himself and began anew with a deep breath, cursing his father for having had him trained in Adeltian customs only to later discourage their use. "Father, it has been difficult to maintain order in the city. The Adeltian people resent my rule more than that of Cassen's, as I am an outsider, and he is not. The conditions near the docks are poor, and sailors I hear prefer the cleaner bars and brothels of Eastport in spite of the extra distance. They fear the waters near the Devil's Mouth as well and favor the more southerly route." Alther thought it best not to mention the demon ships the sailors claimed to have been attacked by. Even Alther knew they were pirates at most.

The king pinched the bridge of his nose and grimaced. "Did I not pay to have you schooled and tutored as a boy? Did none of those tutors show you a map? The Devil's Mouth is of no threat to sailors on their way to Westport, and the conditions of the waters have not changed since our seizing power." Lyell turned his attention to Alther now. He wore a look of disappointment that only a father can give a son after assigning him a task that he was right to fear was beyond his capabilities. "Had it occurred to you, my son, that your governing of Westport might be somewhat hindered by your residing in Eastport?"

It had occurred to Alther, and his father had brought it up on several occasions already. Westport was a city devoted wholly to trade and had no castles or structures built specifically for royalty. Alther had been unable to find in Westport a place regal enough for his highborn wife, and Crella forbade him under threat of public humiliation to live under a separate roof. "If you cannot secure an estate for your family that meets the standards of what should be provided for the wife and son of the *heir to the throne,* you are certainly free to find a smaller such home where you alone can stay. Just know that upon your return I will have let a number of gentleman into my bedchambers commensurate with my estimate of the amount of whores and trollops you have debased while away," she had informed him. *Would that I could please both my father and wife… I fear it an insurmountable goal.*

"I am afraid I have been unable, as of yet, to find a residence beseeming my good wife." In Alther's befuddled state he had at last given his father the true reason for his remaining in Eastport, a fact he had been careful to conceal for fear of ridicule.

"Ha! Did you hear that, Derudin? My noble son, the heir to the throne who shall one day inherit the kingdoms of both Rivervale and Adeltia, is unable to manage his own household—let alone the once thriving city of Westport." The king appeared to be genuinely amused by the fact.

Alther flinched, less at the words from his father—for he had endured far worse from him—and more from the realization that Derudin was present in the room. His father's sage advisor stood just to the side of the desk in fact, if not a little to the rear, where he always stood. It was unsettling how the old man was able to remain hidden in plain sight or even stand motionless for so long at his age. Derudin made no sound or gesture in response, but his acknowledgment of the king's sentiment appeared somehow implicit.

"That Adeltian bitch has surely been your downfall, my boy," the king concluded.

Stephon was visibly taken aback by the remark about his mother. Alther exchanged a glance with his son imploring him not to challenge his grandfather's assertion.

"Is there something you wanted to add, young prince?" goaded Lyell.

Alther prayed that his son was not so stupid as to react in anger towards his king. He knew the boy was protective of his mother and quick to defend her and her Adeltian lineage.

"If I may be so bold, Your Grace," began Stephon. Alther winced at the mistake repeated by his son, but Stephon was overly fond of proper Adeltian titles and customs and would not have heard instruction to the contrary. "It would seem to me that a raising of taxes is in order." Stephon addressed the king with a profound confidence. He held his pointed chin high and managed to rid his face of his usual smirk in order to look quite stately.

Alther was relieved that Stephon had not fallen into one trap, yet cringed as he saw he had merely stumbled into another. If there was one thing Lyell disdained, it was receiving advice from a source of ignorance.

"Oh yes, yes! We'll raise the levies! Why had you not thought of that, Alther? This one has a nose for politics." The king's feint was convincing enough to earn a proud smile of accomplishment on the young prince's face. *Bringing the boy was a mistake, as I feared it would be*, thought Alther.

"And what would we do if the peasants threatened revolt?" asked Lyell with surprising believability.

"Father—" Alther tried to intervene, but he was silenced with a hand gesture from the king.

Stephon shot a quick look of spite in Alther's direction for attempting to steal his moment of glory, then he whipped out his foil and executed some fancy thrusts into an invisible foe, accompanied with all the elaborate footwork of a trained fencer. "I'd have a mind to run through a few such peons so that the rest may be taught a lesson. ...It is an act of justice I am quite familiar with dispensing, as it so happens."

It was true. At the age of thirteen, Stephon had pleaded with Alther to allow him a "stroll among the commoners" as he had put it. Alther thought that perhaps it might ground the boy to see how others lived and acquiesced against better judgment. The ill-fated decision resulted in Stephon killing a supposed robber who was no more than ten years of age. The bread thief turned out to be the son of the very merchant whose wares Stephon was so valiantly protecting. The woman had made the mistake of shouting "thief" at her child when he attempted to run off with an early supper, but ran into Stephon's pointed steel instead. It was a difficult matter to conceal the truth from the public, involving first the bribery of the boy's parents and then the taking of their other son as a vassal in hopes that fear for his safety would keep them quiet. The truth was hidden from Stephon as well, Crella not wishing to plague her son's conscience with a deed misdone. But Stephon's friends had let him know about the rumors circulating that the boy killed was indeed the son of the baker, to which Stephon replied unabashedly, "A thief is a thief."

"Guards, seize the boy and see him to the dungeons. He shall be executed on the morrow for raising weapon against his king." Lyell's tone was as if he was ordering his usual meal with which to break his fast.

"Father!" Alther cried out in desperation. He was immediately unsure of whether he was more afraid of losing his son or his wife's reprisal. That his father would go through with this action was within his character, yet simultaneously unthinkable.

Stephon stood there, mouth agape, foil still dangling in his hand, as two armored guards seized him under the arms and began dragging him back down the long entryway. The king returned to his papers, entirely disinterested with the scene before him.

The wide-eyed blinking confusion Alther saw on Stephon's face was justified. The boy deserved to be chastised; it was only now that Alther realized it had been his hope, bringing Stephon here, that his father *would* have severely scolded him. All of Alther's advice to his son fell on ears of stone, and he required a lesson from someone whom he might truly fear. But surely Stephon had not earned a night in the wretched prison where he could suffer unknown depravities, and certainly he had not earned an execution. Alther waited as long as he could for his father to reveal his bluff.

Alther dropped to a knee, beseeching. "You mustn't!"

At last it seemed Lyell had been stirred to real emotion. "You dare command me? Your father? Your *king*?" The words exploded out of him and reverberated throughout the room. The guards dragging Stephon paused to hear whether their king required more urgent action, and Alther likewise lowered his head in obedience. His father's words continued to echo.

Papers still in his hand, Lyell peered at the dumbstruck Stephon. "Your beheading will be a mercy, little boy. Have you ever seen a man killed by impalement? Or by a mage's fire? I would not have blamed Derudin if he'd turned you into a pile of smoldering ash where you stood."

Lyell seemed to shift into a yet angrier state, dropping his papers to his desk and placing his palms on its surface. "Raise the levies you say? Your father has already done as much—twice now, I believe. He drives all the business he can away from his ports and to the East."

This is my fault, not Stephon's, Alther realized. Had his city of Westport spiraled into poverty on its own, perhaps it would not have been so humiliating, but Cassen's rule over Eastport had been so successful it was hard to even comprehend. Lyell, who would have drowned Alther had he ever shown the effeminate proclivities of Cassen, may now have come to wish the eunuch over his own son as an a heir.

"Worse yet," the king went on, "the levies are but a pittance of our kingdom's income. The wolf's share is made through the spice trade that we alone control, and your father has managed to allow his merchants to repeatedly increase the cost of shipment to his ports, which, if I am not mistaken, are the same distance by sea from the Spicelands as have they always been.

"It is perhaps my greatest regret…" Lyell looked for a moment at Alther before returning his glare to Stephon. "…That Adella managed to throw herself from atop her tower before I could capture her. She would have made a fine prop to unite our two peoples, the river and the delta. Not to mention a fine addition to the comforts of my bedchambers."

Stephon looked like he might piss himself at any moment when Alther stole a glance at him, but at least he appeared willing to weather this speech in silence.

"We had agreed before the war, *Queen* Adella and I, that your father and Crella would be married. There would be peace between our kingdoms eternal, without need of the silly wall. But when Adella got a look at your father, she changed her mind; said her little niece was far too fair for a 'Northerner' such as him. That cunt. Too fair for the likes of *my* son? Crella? That slut of a girl with her bastard daughter and the audacity still to call herself a princess?" Lyell raised his voice, turning again to Alther. "I took this kingdom to preserve our family's honor, to preserve *your* honor."

Alther remained as he was, not meeting his father's stare. The recollection of those past events was not pleasant, nor was the fact that Alther seemed to always take the full burden of a blame that was not his. What his father neglected to mention was that Crella had first been promised to Alther's older brother. Edwin was easily the more comely of the two, taller and with the boyish features that girls of Crella's age seemed to prefer, and that he was the realm's best horseman only added to his charms. Upon learning that his father intended to marry him to the foreign princess, however, Edwin renounced his claim as heir, thus eliminating the possibility that Adella would allow the marriage to take place. It was a crucial part of the scandal that Lyell seemed happy to forget, instead harping on her later rejection of Alther. Lyell's fury at Edwin waned over time, the two reconciled, and he gifted him lordship of Strahl, a port city far north of Eastport. Alther remained heir to a throne he neither wanted, nor was originally intended to receive.

"Perhaps I was wrong to have given Crella to you after the war," Lyell continued, "in the hope that it would help you regain respect and allow you to garner the support of the Adeltians that you now so poorly rule. Young though she was, she would have made a fine addition to my bedchambers as well." The king grunted. "Perhaps it is not too late for that, should you continue to disappoint me."

The silence that remained after that threat was uncomfortable, but Alther was still more concerned about his son. He looked back at him, seeing him now gaping at what the king had just said. It was only then Alther realized he should probably be more angry with his father—that his father *wanted* him to be. He prepared a grimace, but lost it when he saw a hint of smirk on the king's face.

"Release the boy," Lyell commanded his guards, and they complied with haste. Stephon stood there dumbfounded until he finally dropped his foil to the ground as if he were afraid the action of sheathing it might earn him a second sentencing.

"You think I fear a boy with a stick?" Lyell gestured with his wrist, mocking the fencing maneuvers. "Let this be a lesson on how quickly your life can come to an end out of ignorance. You may have slain a baker's boy, but faced with a hundred such boys, you would be overrun with your eyes clawed out. Which is surely what would happen in time, were the city placed under such oblivious governance."

The insult seemed to sober the prideful boy. He made no move to pick up his foil, but he frowned, smoothed his tunic, and walked cautiously back to his father's side. Relief should have returned to Alther as well, but it did not.

"As your king, I command you, Alther, to take your insolent child and Adeltian bitch with you to live in Westport where you belong.

Should you fail to fix the state of the city, I will make good on my promise to take from you your responsibilities. *All* your responsibilities."

Only then did his father's threat to take Alther's wife as his own fully impress, causing Alther to stand and confront his father. Crella had been forced to marry Alther, forced to conceive his child, and Alther had been disgustingly complicit, always unable to defy his father's mandates. The prospect of his father forcing *himself* as well upon Crella was more than Alther would allow. He felt his lips curl back. He felt rebellion build from his stomach to his throat, ready to burst from his mouth.

Alther swung with speed, connecting the back of his hand with Stephon's jaw for the first time in the boy's life. From the corner of an eye, he had seen his headstrong child opening his mouth in anger, about to make some dangerous objection.

As Stephon fell to the ground clutching his face in pain, so did Alther drop again to one knee before his king. "As you command, Father."

DECKER

This would be a lonely place to die, thought Decker, wondering if one could even be buried here.

There were no bushes or shrubs, no greenery at all save the occasional spiny weed, and the only trees in sight were solitary pines with more dead branches than needles. No birds sang, and no tree rats protested their presence. The scree and small rocks they were accustomed to had been replaced by boulders so immense a shadow cast could eclipse their entire party, and the foggy mist that clung to their ankles only added to the ominous nature of this cold, desolate land.

Decker and his brother had led their party on a southwestern march for several days, the trip thus far uneventful. The terrain was more easily navigated than the more direct southerly route would have been, but as this was the first raid for the majority of the men, there was no appreciation for the difference. Some began to grow dour, muttering under their breath about their various discomforts.

He and Titon continued to push the pace. It was important that they did not exhaust their supplies before reaching the Dogmen, and unbeknownst to the other men, Titon had predicted they would have hit their first landmark by now. If they did not find it by nightfall they may have made a grievous error.

"Titon," Decker began. There was no privacy, but when keeping their voices low they were able to speak without much of their conversation being heard. The men were like to assume they were just discussing some minutiae of battle strategy, and being the young fools that they were—eager for battle and assuming certain victory—they had visibly bored of Titon's tactical musings. "You should take the first woman."

Decker looked at his older brother to see if he understood, but Titon had on the same expressionless mask he'd worn since having awoken that morning.

"Or at the very least, the first bitch attractive enough to rouse you to action," Decker added. *Of all you must accomplish on this epic raid, this should be by far the easiest.* He shot Titon a brotherly grin to make him feel as though they were both of like mind and equal experience.

But they were not. It was known that Decker, in spite of his age, had already shared a bed with several women from their clan. Decker did not need to boast of it either. When it came to talking among themselves about their carnal mischiefs, the girls of the North were no different from those of the South, ill-reputed for their gossipy nature. Inexperienced girls with no reference of comparison soon spread tales of Decker's more prominent characteristics, earning him both respect and lighthearted ridicule from the other young men.

"Of course. Yes." When Titon finally spoke it was as if it had been his plan all along.

As with most things related to virility, Titon lagged behind him. He had not yet been with a woman as far as Decker knew, though Titon certainly made it obvious enough that he would not turn down the opportunity, so long as it was with Red. Decker wondered if Titon had a notion that remaining chaste until he won her affections would make their eventual encounter that much more meaningful to her, and he hoped for Titon's sake that he did not. Aware of Titon's infatuation, Decker made it a point to stay away from Red, who to her credit, at least did not share the lascivious reputation of her mother. He did this solely out of respect for his brother. Decker no longer believed Red to be a cunt of a whore. It had been impossible to deny the dark-haired beauty she'd become.

"I shall bestride the first bitch that I find appealing."

Decker winced at his brother's words. *And stop speaking like that.*

Whereas most Galatai had little use for books taken from the Dogmen except as trophies, Titon would have his nose in one at every opportunity—even during the nightfall camps of this journey, further distancing himself from the men. It made little sense to Decker, having never found the humor or wisdom the elders claimed hid between their many pages. His several attempts to enjoy Titon's favorites had resulted in the same mind-numbing boredom he was accustomed to when forced to read by their father.

"Do you know if it is customary to do…as such…with an audience?" Titon's voice had been lowered to such an extent that it was hard to make out his words.

Decker could not help but laugh, then wish he hadn't. "I am sure that some do, but I know that I will be taking my women behind closed doors. The things I will do to them might be unsettling, even to the older men in our company." It took Titon longer than it should have to respond to Decker's joke with appropriate laughter. *Some things cannot be learned from books.*

"How 'bout a rest?" The sour voice belonged to Galinn, a lank boy of similar age to Decker. "I'm hungry, and my knees ache from walking atop boulders all day."

"Aye," chimed in Galinn's elder cousin, Griss. "We're overdue for a stop. We don't even walk toward the Dogmen. What's the hurry?" Griss's every word seemed spat with lye.

"It is crucial we maintain our pace," Titon yelled back to them, not slowing his stride.

"We'd walk faster after a rest," argued Griss.

Decker and Titon exchanged glances and shook their heads in disbelief.

We should not have let him come, thought Decker. Griss was irritable and grubby for his age, a thing forgiven by most only because his mother had lost her husband in a raid just prior to Griss's birth. Decker had suggested to Titon that they not take him, but Titon had pointed out that refusing him would mean they would also lose Galinn, one whose axe they could use. Decker had begrudgingly conceded.

"Yeah, just a short rest," agreed Galinn.

"If your knees hurt, walk softer. If you hunger, then eat," said Decker. "And give your scraps to Griss. He prefers the leavings of others." The comment elicited some chuckles from the group, all knowing Decker spoke of Anna.

"You act like you were the son of the Mountain," Griss snapped. "But your father is the reason I'm forced to come with a group of boys. To do what *men* should have done months ago."

"Funny that the *men* did not think you fit to join them on their raids," Decker said.

"No funnier than your father having gone as stupid as your mother." Both Titon and Decker slowed to a walk at Griss's mention of their mother. "How is it that he can still call himself leader and not lead a single raid? He's become an elder, but without any of their wisdom. He's like an old woman. You're not the son of a—"

"My father took food off our plates during winters and gave it to you and your ugly mother," Decker yelled, having turned to face his adversary. "To your family of vultures."

"Food we threw to our goats!" Griss raged. "You think we'd eat your trash?"

"Do you give Anna to the goats as well? You don't just eat my trash. You call it wife."

Filled with the satisfaction of having delivered a mortal blow with words—a thing Decker was not known for doing—he still hoped Griss would escalate the fight to combat. Decker had never killed a man, nor had he ever wanted to as much as he did now, but his father would not forgive him for killing a brother without just cause. The laughter Decker thought he'd earned never came, though. The men were still and silent, all eyes on Griss.

Griss eventually responded, but only with the most bitter of grins. Then he turned and walked to the back of the group, taking with him not only Galinn, but all Decker's exultation.

"Let's move," Decker said to the group which was eager to oblige.

More and more boulders passed underfoot, all with no hint that this landscape would ever change. *I should not have said that*, Decker realized after he'd cooled. It would be Anna who would suffer when Griss returned, and Decker had already been the cause of enough pain for the girl. If there was a more difficult thing a man could do than explain to a girl how she'd taken a simple coupling to mean more than it did, Decker did not yet know of it. Building the courage to make clear her misunderstanding was hard enough, but watching the girl's glee turn to anguish had devastated him far worse than any punishment he'd suffered at the hands of his father.

As doubt that this trip would become anything but an exercise in starvation crept in, a distant sound drew Decker's attention. The men exchanged looks of concern as they too noticed the foreboding wail that continued to grow in strength.

"Is that what I think it is?" Decker asked, but his brother only shrugged and walked faster.

What had first appeared to be no more than a violent wind sounded more like a giant beast breathing with rage and hurling boulders at the side of a mountain. Titans and dragons were the stuff of children's tales, but the will of some of the men looked to waver as the noise built without end.

Decker gave a great guffaw and taunted, "You call yourselves Galatai warriors? Look how you tremble at the most welcome of greetings." It was enough to keep them moving.

Finally, Decker and Titon came to a highpoint that gave them view of what they had been hoping so desperately to see. Immense waves carrying white boulders of ice barraged the rocky cliffs that made up the shore. The dark blue sea stretched out endlessly, packed with the jagged caps of snow-covered bergs. The other men stared in amazement when they reached the two brothers and shared in the vista.

"There it is, Titon, as you said it would be." Decker slapped his brother on the back, sharing in the triumph. "The Frozen Sea!"

CASSEN

A single tallow candle burned, casting a faint but steady light upon the suite. Arms of intricate wrought iron suspended linen drapes over grandiose windows, the glass of which gleamed like obsidian against the black of night. Centered in the room was an enormous bed, standing near chest height and covered in dozens of pillows positioned with care, not a single astray.

Cassen was stirred from his slumber, unsure if he had been awoken by a noise or mere fitfulness. Suspecting the former, he threw off his blankets and pushed them, along with the small floor mat he'd been sleeping upon, underneath the bed. His suspicion proved correct.

"Apologies, Duchess. Some ladies here to see you." The servant boy spoke loudly from beyond the door, considering the hour. Cassen nodded to himself with contentment. *A smart enough boy to place greater weight upon my instruction than upon his fear of disturbing me.*

Cassen began draping himself in silks with considerable dexterity—he was no stranger to the task. Only when he had built up a large enough mass of the finery about him did he reply. "They may enter."

In walked three of his lady servants. Two clearly tended to the needs of the third whose head was buried in her hands as she wept. Cassen directed them to a small curved sofa where they sat the crying girl. *This looks promising.*

"You may leave us." Cassen waved off the two girls who had brought her. One began to leave, but the other was not so quick to action.

"Is there something else?" he asked Annora, the one who loitered. She was one of his Spiceland girls, made clear enough by her wavy brown hair and olive skin. Her face was stronger than most of the girls Cassen employed, but she was still quite striking in her beauty. Truth be told, she was one of his favorites in terms of appearance. *This one tempts me above the others.*

"If it pleases you, we would like to stay. We may be of some assistance in comforting her, Duchess." Annora made the request with the utmost courtesy, yet it was a dangerous border to be pushing after having been dismissed. *She is ever so forward.*

Cassen gave her a coy frown. "You know I dislike it when you call me that. I am a duchess, to be sure, but I am foremost your mother and protector."

"Yes, Mother," replied Annora. She bowed her head in reverence.

Cassen pretended to ponder it for a time as he studied his brazen lady. *I do wonder how I only noted her appearance during her training and not her spirit. I suppose I am, after all, a man.* Although amused by the thought, he did not allow it to change his countenance.

"Yes, the two of you may stay. But…" he said with a serious furrow of the brow, "do not speak of this lest your sisters think I favor some over the others."

The relief visible on Annora's face caught him off guard, despite his high standard when it came to the appreciation of body language and expressions. It was clearly relief not for herself but for her friend, at whom she now gazed with a look between pity and sympathy. *This one surprises me, it seems, with her every action. Perhaps I am losing my touch… Or perhaps I am merely infatuated.* Again he kept his amusement hidden.

Cassen shifted his attentions to Annora's friend who had sobered to formality in his presence. "Now, what is it that ails you, my lady daughter?"

The girl broke again into tears. Cassen, expecting no different, was quick to embrace her. As the two sat upon the sofa he comforted her, stroking her hair gently as he turned his attention to the remaining girls. *Perhaps we can expedite this normally lengthy process.*

"It was her patron," Annora said, anticipating Cassen's request for an explanation.

At last she says something thoroughly predictable.

"He has mistreated her in the gravest of fashions," she concluded.

Oh, heavens no! Cassen's sardonic and silent humor allowed him to survive the normal drudgery of this routine, but he found he was enjoying himself more than usual. It was progressing quickly, and he was becoming somewhat enamored with this Spiceland girl—in his own way.

"Remind me again, who is her patron?" Cassen was confident in the response, but better to be sure. He knew his girls well, but they all tended to look the same when they came in bawling and eyes puffed.

"Master Warin, Mother."

With Cassen's newfound feelings for Annora it seemed more disconcerting than usual to be called by his requested title. The name revealed, however, was as he had hoped. Warin was a man who under normal circumstances could have never afforded the luxury of a lady servant. As the Master of The Guard he held a position of great power and even had a seat on the High Council, but all members of The Guard were paid very little for their services. It was Cassen who had suggested to Master Warin that he, and more specifically of course his wife, could benefit from such services, and that the costs were not near so much as the nobles aggrandized. Cassen had, out of sheer benevolence no less, lowered his rates substantially so they would indeed be within the master's means. Since then, Warin and his wife had been quite pleased with the services rendered by all reports.

"And he *forced* himself upon her?" Cassen asked as if the proposition was unthinkable. Annora and the other standing girl both nodded while the third, Ryiah, a girl Cassen had acquired from a poor family in Westport for a pittance, continued to sob and shake in Cassen's arms.

"This troubles me greatly. I bear no burden of greater precedence than that of keeping all my daughters safe. This violation must not go unpunished." He extended the crying girl before him, and she stopped sobbing momentarily to hear his words. "I need you to be strong and understand what must be done in order to right this wrong. The politics of rank and nobility are complicated and perverse. If we were to accuse him of such an action it would merely be the word of a servant, lady that she may be, versus that of the highest ranking member of The Guard, the supposed Protectors of the Realm. I could not testify in support of your claims by rule of hearsay, as I did not bear witness."

Ryiah looked as if she was about to sob again, but Cassen squeezed her arms to shush her and regain her attention. "Listen to me carefully. We will have our justice. Any man evil enough to commit such an act has secrets—secrets that would likely destroy him if they came to light. You must tell me everything you hear during your service that you think is of import, and much of what you think is not. Secrets are power, my daughters, and if you give me the power I will see that he is punished. So that he can never do such a thing again to you or anyone else." Cassen concluded his performance by brushing some damp hair out of Ryiah's face and nodded a signal for the two girls to take the newly quieted one back to her quarters.

They moved to obey, but as the girl had been brought to her feet, Annora's dark brown eyes fixed on Cassen. "Mother, what would you have Ryiah do if her master tries again to…dishonor her?"

Girls rarely asked this question. It was assumed that they must continue to endure the abuse until secrets enough were obtained to corrupt the perpetrator. Sometimes the abuse would stop after Cassen approached the man, as he always did, and asked for favors in return for keeping the matter quiet; however, this was the exception and not the rule. It was of no real consequence to Cassen, so long as the man continued to be beholden to his demands for favors.

Cassen lowered his head in faux shame. "I cannot begin to imagine being myself in such a horrid circumstance. I see no alternative to that which has been previously done that would not invite violence and unduly endanger her, my daughter." Practiced though he was in the art, it almost hurt Cassen to tell this lie. He himself *had* been faced with a similar circumstance when he was younger, and much to his credit he thought, had not reacted in the way he now suggested. "I can only beg her to be strong and keep ears open to the secrets that may be her salvation."

It was clear to see how this answer troubled Annora, and Ryiah had taken again to tearing. Annora voiced her concern. "Mother, but there is an alternative. I apologize for not having told you, but I too was assaulted some time ago."

Cassen scoured his memory to determine whom she must be speaking of. It could only be Emrel, an Adeltian wine merchant who was patron to Annora still. Cassen certainly had expected results from having planted her there within short time, but when they never came, it slipped his mind as there were no pressing favors needed from the man.

"When his wife was away with her friends touring the gardens he tried to grab at me and force off my clothes. It is ill-becoming of a lady, but I am not ashamed to say I bit him to the point of bleeding and kicked him hard between his legs." The Spiceland accent she tried so hard to suppress intensified as she recounted the tale. "He cried out in pain, and let me be. I am now more careful when alone in his presence, but he has never since tried to attack me. Could Ryiah not do the same?"

Cassen stared blank-faced at Annora for a moment before answering with the inconclusiveness of the politician that he was, but he was moved by her formerly unexposed strength and beauty. *A lady after my own loveless heart.*

ETHEL
Years Ago

"Ethel, you have barely touched your meal."

Ethel peered at the glistening hunk of bone and meat upon her plate. What was the point? Every bite she took drove her that much further from the appearance she wished to have. How it was that her mother could eat seemingly whatever she fancied, never to gain an ounce, was puzzling and above all unjust. Ethel had never desired to meet her birth father for any reason but to punch him in what must have been his enormous gut—a thank you for what he'd passed down to her. And it was evermore reason to wish Alther had been her real father. The lissome frame he'd passed to Stephon could have been her own, had her mother simply waited for a proper husband. Whatever had possessed her to play the part of harlot at such a young age, Ethel could not guess, nor could she ever recall having seen that side of her mother.

"If you are trying to starve yourself into a slender figure, I assure you, that is not a proper way to do it. Do as I, and eat a bit of all that is served, stopping *before* you've had your fill. Then, if you must, allow yourself just a taste of dessert—that is your biggest issue. Perhaps skip dessert altogether if you don't have the control—"

"Mother, enough!" Ethel had heard this speech so many times she could repeat it verbatim, and each time she heard it only made her want to do the opposite that much more. And doing so was worth it, but not for the look of anger on her mother's face when Ethel labored theatrically to consume the final bite of yellow cake, declared her fullness, then kindly asked a servant for a second. No, it was her father's reaction that made her repeat the performance. Watching him struggle to hide his amusement was reward enough for any action, no matter what it may cost her.

"You should listen to Mother," said Stephon.

Should I? she lashed at him satirically in thought. Quarreling with her brother had become a pastime, but she tried to avoid doing so at supper as it turned her father somber. Even now he had a look on his face that pleaded that she not engage her brother.

"Thank you, Stephon. Now that I have your input, I do believe I will finally heed Mother's words."

Stephon nodded his approval while chewing the last of his second or third serving of braised oxtail, a meat so rich it coated her teeth with a disgusting film. *Yes, Stephon, by all means—I'll take advice from a boy who could eat nothing but butter and see no ill-effect.* It mystified her—not her brother's eating habits as that seemed to be the norm for boys his age—but his intelligence. Most often he would seem the dullest of knives, unable to slice through the supple irony she served him. But other times he astounded her, coming to conclusions that seemed so far from his reach, if not her own, that she made a note to analyze even his most foolish assertions in the off chance he'd stumbled blindly onto some elusory truth.

"Good," continued Stephon, seemingly unaffected by her sarcasm as usual. "It would be a great shame for you to stop eating, given that you lost your only other friend so recently."

He delivered the words with such utter lack of emotion Ethel paused to look at him, trying to discern whether he was truly attempting to hurt her or merely stating a fact. Stephon did not smirk, or smile. He did not even look to her for response. He had engaged a servant, asking for another plate.

Had Griffin told the other boys? It was one thing for him to have crushed her, but it would be another for him to revel in it with others. She had to know, but she had to proceed carefully so Stephon would not know she was hurt or angry.

"*What* is *that* supposed to mean?"

Not only had she failed in self-restraint, she feared she now scowled at Stephon in the very way her mother scowled at her father—a reviling look that Ethel had resolved never to imitate.

Stephon looked at her, seeming perplexed by the fury he'd stirred.

"I just assumed the way you've been locking yourself in your room lately instead of sneaking off to the buttery with him that he'd finally told you he can't be seen with you anymore. It was bound to happen. Everyone made fun of him for it." Stephon's plate of cake had arrived and was placed in front of him. He picked up his fork and stuffed a third of the slice into his mouth without a care.

Ethel had fantasized about running off—to where exactly she did not know. The realm seemed so small, or at least the portion of it that had the potential to be pleasant. She'd never wanted to run off quite so badly as she did now, however. In her books there was no end to the places she could escape to, the only problem being she always had to return. She would leave for good though, some day. Alone if she had to, but she would not remain here. It was unthinkable.

"I hope you choke on that cake and die." Ethel no longer cared if she scowled like her mother. "The day the realm is passed to you will be a day mourned by all." With that, Ethel pushed from the table and stormed off to her room, ignoring her mother's chiding.

ALTHER
Years Ago

"Leave me be!"

It was a response to be expected.

"It is me," Alther said. "May I come in?"

Alther thought he had given her enough of an opportunity to stew that she may be amenable to some distraction. She did not answer his question, and he waited there some time before he heard the door unlock.

The room always shocked him, looking more as if it belonged to a crazed librarian than a princess. As a boy he had spent little time in his room, certainly not enough to have amassed such a collection of books, placed in seemingly random piles. *Perhaps her birth father had been a curator,* he had mused to himself. Alther had made a game when she was younger of having her close her eyes while he read the title of one of her books, challenging her to find it within the chaos. She always did, though.

"Thank you," he said, pulling the chair from her writing desk to sit upon.

How can I even be of any comfort to her? he wondered. Perhaps sitting there was enough. He did not think asking her about Griffin would do any good.

"Why must we stay here?" Ethel asked.

"This is our home."

"No, it's not," she said. "Your home is in Rivervale, and a family goes where the father belongs. That *is* where we belong."

"We belong where the king commands us. *My* father. And I tell you, Rivervale is no better a place than here."

"You lie."

He was not offended by her accusation. Had he been in her position he would most likely feel the same, or at the very least wish it to be true—that there was a city to where she could go and be accepted. But if she thought Rivervale was such a place, she was painfully mistaken. If the Adeltian bastard princess was scorned in Adeltia, it would be far worse in

Rivervale. Her only chance of peace was to go unrecognized, and that was not a thing he could provide for her.

"I wish I was lying," he said. "Rivervale is like any other kingdom. That it is a bit poorer than this kingdom does not make it better."

"I'd rather be poor."

"I claimed the same when I was a young prince. Do you think I'm lying about that as well? One thing I have come to know with certainty, however, is that any amount you wish to trade places with a common child, that child wishes to trade places with you far worse. And which do you think truly has the right of it?"

He took her sullen silence to indicate her having understood his meaning.

"Why are boys so cruel?" she asked after a silence.

Alther exhaled, giving himself time to think.

"I honestly do not think your brother wishes to aggravate you with the things he says. He merely blurts out what is on his mind. Stephon lacks something when it comes to seeing things from another's perspective."

"Not him, Father," Ethel said meekly. "Griffin."

"He's an idiot. What more explanation is necessary?"

"He is *not* an idiot, though."

"He is a dullard with no equal, and if he were my own I would see him shamed for such foolishness."

He could see Ethel was not satisfied with his sentiment.

"Would it make you feel better to know all boys his age make similar mistakes?" Alther asked, not expecting an answer. "I do not think we are born with empathy. We learn it only after we have felt the hurt that we've inflicted on another."

"How is that supposed to make me feel any better?"

Perhaps it shouldn't, he admitted.

"There was a girl when I was young—back when I lived in Rivervale, mind you, the place of fairytales." He beamed her a grin, causing Ethel to blush. "She was ridiculed mercilessly, for what reason I cannot even say other than she dressed a bit matronly. She lived with her grandparents, I believe, who must have been somewhat impoverished." Alther closed his eyes, rubbing his temples to massage the details back to memory. "After a while she disappeared."

"She disappeared?"

"I don't mean she really went missing. She was still there, but people had stopped going out of their way to pick on her. Nobody noticed her so much. Oh, her name was Beth—not that that did her any favors either." Alther took a moment to regret having said that. The name Ethel did not exactly conjure images of youth and grace. "One day she came dressed completely different. *Completely.* She had on a knee-length dress, her hair was done up in some special way, she looked…" Alther saw the face Ethel was giving him, realizing he'd let the story get away from him. "She looked very *pretty*. I knew it was her from the start, but my friend, a far more handsome lad than I, was caught unawares by her transformation. He stopped mid-sentence as he spoke to me to gaze at her, and even went so far as to chase her down and touch her arm. He introduced himself in some boneheaded way that made most girls blush, but her…it made her face light up. I do not know how to describe it, but she came alive for the first time when she saw his interest was sincere…"

Why am I telling her this? It was too late; he was beyond committed. There were plenty of witnesses that day, but he had never repeated the story, nor did he want to hear it told aloud in its entirety now that he had reawakened his disgust.

Ethel insisted with a look that he continue.

"And so I laughed like a fool and said, 'That's Beth, you idiot.' Everyone joined me in laughter except the two of them. He was stupefied, but she was crushed. I will never forget her face."

"Well, what happened?" Ethel prodded.

"I felt horrible."

"No! What happened to Beth?"

Alther cleared his throat, still envisioning her run away in the shame he'd caused her. Had he simply announced her in some respectable fashion rather than seizing the opportunity to win a chuckle at her expense… "She did not return to classes for several days, and when she did, she was her old self again, if not worse. She never made eye contact with anyone, let alone me."

"Well, where is she now?"

Alther knew where she was, should she still be alive. She was no ugly girl, that much was true. And like many pretty girls unable to attract a husband, she soon took up the trade that paid best. How many revolting men had she had to endure inside her thanks to Alther's foolish outburst? He had snuffed out not only a light but a life with his laughter, and he would never forgive himself.

"She married an older man and they have some children," he lied.

"I don't care for older men," said Ethel.

"No, you misunderstand. I am not comparing you to her. You are… You are a *princess* and she was just some poor girl you claimed to want to trade places with. But the point is that all boys make grave errors. Griffin will come to realize that, and if he does not, then I was right that he is an idiot."

The two sat in silence. The scent of old papers and bindings gave the room a tranquil feel where quiet thought was welcome.

"What's Mother's excuse?"

The question caught Alther off guard.

"Her excuse?"

"Yes. Young boys are cruel because they're stupid you said. What about her?"

"Your mother is not cruel to you. She merely wants—"

"What's best for me?" Ethel interrupted with an accusatory tone.

"What she thinks is best would be a better way to put it," said Alther.

"That's not even what I was asking though. Why is she so cruel to *you*?"

Being forced to marry a man has that effect, he thought. But even that did not fully explain it. Alther had numerous noble acquaintances with wives compelled to marry for one reason or another who'd come to love them, or at least respect them enough to be civil. *She is cruel because she finds me unworthy and appalling*, he admitted to himself, *as she always has and always will.*

"I have told you before that people are inclined to resent being told what to do," said Alther. "Your mother is no exception."

"But you do not tell her to do *anything*," objected Ethel. "You let her make every decision."

It was for the most part true. Alther scanned his mind for instances where he had actually been firm with his wife and found few of any real consequence.

"I did not let her make you get rid of this." Alther gestured about the room. "This massive collection of yours. I made sure you were allowed to ride the palfrey your grandfather gave you. I made sure you were allowed to wear what you wished. I have had my share of victories." He delivered the words playfully.

"I'm allowed to wear what I wish only when inside our home," she corrected, but she had not been immune to his playfulness and cracked a smile of her own. Then she became serious.

"Would you think less of me if I did as Mother suggests? If I dressed like her, sipped tea, and acted...proper?"

Alther gave a chuckling snort. "Your mother is a good woman. I would not recommend you emulate her every mannerism, but I have no doubt you can tell the good from the bad. Do not ever think that you should do opposite of her in order to please me. I love both you and your mother, and that will not change, whether you wear trousers and ride horses, or wear skirts and embroider. You must do whatever it is you desire to do, and never be afraid to change one way or the other."

Ethel turned away from him. If there was one thing he hated to see, it was his daughter tearful.

"Plus," he added, "it might be fun to see her face if you came to supper in a dress and sipped your tea like one of her aristocrat friends. She might be so shocked as to demand you go back to your room and change into something *less* decent."

Her giggle was the outcome he'd hoped for, and it gave him a pride he seldom achieved. In this foreign land of sweltering heat, hubris, and pretentiousness, Ethel was a lovely oddity. Yet as he looked at his adopted daughter, Alther could not help but wonder: if she had not been born a bastard, if she had not been a pariah among her peers, would she still be the exemplar of innocence? Or would she be the typical Adeltian princess and despise him every bit as much as her mother and the rest?

KEETHRO

They had been three days at sea on the eighth day of what Titon believed would be their epic journey. Keethro still had other plans.

It had taken four days of fast-paced travel to reach the eastern coast, passing many Galatai clans along the way who wished them well and restocked their supplies. A full day was then spent on the construction of their modest sea vessel, using a design similar to ones they had built together in their youth, with the addition of a large square sail. It had a pointed bow that would cut through water and a rudder. Together, these would make straight travel over long distances a simple task. The wood they used was light and buoyant, allowing for the many leaks they would have, given their quick construction. Perhaps most importantly, it had enough room for them both to crouch beneath a slanted piece of thatching that would shelter them from any weather; if one were to die on these waters it would likely be from exposure, not from capsizing. The boat came together faster than they'd expected, and they shared pride in their accomplishment before hoisting her into the calm waters of the Timid Sea.

"You took an arrow, did you not?" asked Titon, looking content. Keethro did not remember the Dogman battle Titon recalled with the same fondness.

"Caught it in the meat of the thigh," said Keethro. *A reminder of the danger I find when following you.*

"It was a fine battle, considering the foe," Titon reminisced. "A good surprise at least to have them raise weapons for once."

Keethro snorted. "Yes, I was quite pleased as I limped home over the scree." *You have a strange notion of what makes for pleasant surprises*, thought Keethro.

"Ha," Titon cried. "You may have limped to the barrow. We took turns dragging your dead weight home while you drank and cursed your luck."

Keethro could not help but laugh at himself as the faint memory came back to him. He turned his gaze toward the coastline. The jagged points of intraversible mountains reached to the sky.

"What else was there?" Titon asked. A silence hung while the two of them tried to remember any story worth reciting.

"Gunnar's goats," Keethro recalled aloud, feeling the grin that formed on his face.

Titon laughed loudly in response. "That dumb bastard with the pretty young wife—and the even prettier goats!" Titon slapped his thigh. "Every time we dressed a goat of his in one of your sister's skirts, he'd become even more furious. Just couldn't let it be. Even bothered the elders about it, not that they cared. That poor bastard."

"Aye," said Keethro.

"You were a clumsy oaf back then, though. How many times did you get snagged on his fence, forced to muck the goat houses by his woman?" Titon asked.

"Just once."

"No, you damn fool," said Titon shaking his head. "I remember it well. You must have been caught near half a dozen times. You would get snagged on the same loose wire and wear the same shaggy coat time and again, despite my telling you better."

"Aye, I was caught maybe five or six times. But of those times I only shoveled goat shit once, and of those times I was only truly a clumsy fool once," Keethro replied, still wearing his grin, allowing Titon to put together the pieces.

But Titon just looked at him skeptically with half a frown, imploring explanation.

"Young, yes, and pretty as well, his wife was eager to find me punishments that were, well, more *rigorous*."

Hearing that, Titon burst into a roar of laughter. It was a decent story to be sure, but given their circumstances, everything seemed half again as funny as it ought to be, giddy with the prospect of adventure.

"Perhaps her husband truly did prefer his goats then if she was so eager to jump in the sack with the likes of your ugly arse," said Titon. The mock insult was enough to bring Keethro back to the present, where he was again sailing with a man he intended to kill rather than a friend with whom he intended to find the far corners of the realm. "But you did always have a few secrets when it came to women."

The breeze here was not strong enough to ripple their sail, and for some moments all that could be heard was the gentle, infrequent splash of a new wave against the prow of their boat.

"Aye, but I never did stray from Kilandra's bed." It was a lie, but it was as good a trick as any for Keethro to try to catch Titon in a lie of his own. "Did you?" *Did you ever stray* into *Kilandra's bed?* Keethro prodded in thought.

"Stray from Ellie?" Titon was fiddling with some splintered wood on the handle of the rudder, his gaze having broken from Keethro. "Never. Not even with a Dogman bitch I intended to kill." Titon's eyes met Keethro's again. "You do not want to draw the anger of a Storm Wolf. One might suffer less godly wrath after pissing on the River."

Not even once, old friend? Keethro left the question unasked.

"What about that boy…Dicun?" asked Titon. "Everyone whispers that he is your bastard, and he certainly looks it."

It was no small charge, to be a bastard among their people. Should a Galatai woman give birth to a child that was not her husband's, the man would have the right—if not the responsibility—to snuff that child. But the father of the one Titon spoke of died before the truth could be revealed—during a Dogman raid Keethro well remembered. *He was a decent man*, Keethro recalled with some remorse, but he had not once regretted his action that spared the boy.

"Perhaps he is mine. He is a handsome lad," Keethro reluctantly agreed. "I only claimed to have not strayed from Kilandra's bed. I never claimed not to have brought someone else into it."

Titon laughed like a drunken warrior after a triumphant raid, and Keethro joined him with feigned candor as the wind pushed them farther southward.

◦◦◦◦◦

The sea journey came to an end upon reaching Port Phylan. Though no Galatai were known to have traveled so far south, they were well aware of the existence of this city, often doing trade with its people. Phylan seafarers' unconventional sails allowed them to travel northwards on the Timid Sea in spite of the invariably southward winds, and they would often bring jewelry and glass to the northern coasts in exchange for leather, furs, and Dogman plunder.

"I suppose one night in our own clothes will do little harm," said Titon. They had tied their humble vessel—which looked truly woeful in the face of the many Phylan ships—to a rotting piling of a dock that was barely holding together. Keethro would have complained, but the boat could drift off for all he cared. It would be of no use for sailing north again. "The shops look to all be closed in any case. Some food and a night's rest then? We'll find some southern dress in the morning."

The shops Titon spoke of were squeezed in so close together that they could have each shared walls. Where they fought for space on the ground, they grew larger above, their second stories protruding over the road of timbers beneath.

"Aye," agreed Keethro, though he was not happy to be seen here as a Northman. "I barely slept a wink on that boat."

They came to an obvious inn, the only place with some bustle within it. It not the cleanest looking establishment, but neither were Keethro and Titon the cleanest of patrons. His Grace's Hole, as dubbed by its signage, had a rowdy crowd gathered in the first floor's eating and drinking area. The smell of sweat and spilt ale fought the scent of water and lye as they entered. They were then consumed by the dark, uninviting atmosphere of a place frequented only by locals.

"Barkeep," cried Titon upon finding a pair of empty stools. "We will take your heartiest meal and two strong meads. Both meads are for me, though. My friend here prefers the rich flavor of pickled milk."

It seemed as if everyone in the place was eyeballing them, but Keethro had expected little different.

"Make that a strong mead for me as well," said Keethro, unoffended by Titon's hackneyed gibe. "I'm feeling oddly daring tonight."

Failing to appreciate the humor, the barkeep was at least kind enough to oblige them in their request after seeing their coin. They were served their drinks and some house stew. To their surprise the food was quite impressive: a hot mash of chicken and beef, potatoes and carrots, sage and thyme, nearly overflowing the wooden bowls in which it was served. They also received some warm crusty bread that had a light coating of flour still on the surface as if it had been made in a hurry. A generous mound of honeyed butter melted in the middle of each split loaf, steam rising from the gap. Bread was not a staple in the Northluns where there was no land suitable for grain, and it was a welcome treat whenever they had the chance to trade for or steal some.

Titon raised his mug. "To two brothers, once again spitting in the eye of destiny and charging south for glory!" Keethro raised his mug in kind, no longer caring so much if they made a scene, and the two men downed their drink and devoured their food.

The drinking did not end there, however. The shadowy, dank conditions of the lively place seemed to darken and become yet more raucous as they continued their sudden quest to empty the bar of all its mead. There had probably been several dozen patrons there to start, but now only a few clusters remained. As Keethro glanced around, he no longer met stares of men, but could not be removed of the feeling that all of the turned eyes he saw had just been aimed at his back.

One ray of light was seen by Keethro amidst the gloomy sea. A barmaid who had been tending tables looked in his direction, and he was quick to ensure she noticed he was looking back. Her homely smile was warm and engaging, and her plaits of hair on either shoulder gave her a look of innocence unbefitting her surroundings. *If there are often girls like this in shitholes such as these, I might enjoy these southern lands.*

Upon looking to his left to brag to Titon that he might soon be absent for a while, he saw his big companion face down on the bar, snoring. Keethro gave his full attention to the woman who approached.

"Your friend all right?" she asked.

"I am afraid he is dead," Keethro replied.

"Dead?" she spoke as though he wouldn't have been the first but was still dubious. "Isn't he breathing?"

"Nay, he is good and dead. I am quite sure of it. He pissed in a river this morning, and now he has drowned himself accidentally in his cup. Happens all the time to Northerners like us." There was no point in trying to pretend they were from anywhere but the North in their current state of dress.

The perplexed look on the girl's face let Keethro know all his drunken humor had been lost on her. *She is dull, but I'd likely still be a maid if I had always let that stop me.* He changed tactics and showed her a warm smile, which she was happy to mirror.

Keethro was accustomed to winning hearts with little effort, but this one seemed willing to melt faster than the honeyed butter. Perhaps being a foreigner here was the reason, or perhaps the women here lacked the same restraints as those of the North, but it was not long before he and the barmaid were headed upstairs. She led him to a bedroom where she quickly slipped into a cozy-looking bed. Then she began to throw her clothing out from under the blankets one piece at a time. Keethro rushed to undress, first kicking off his shoes. As he removed a leg from his trousers, the door to the bedroom swung open again with an unpleasant creak.

Three men strode in, all with knives in hand, and closed the door behind them. Keethro had a knife of his own, but it was on the belt of his trousers that were now on the floor with one of his legs still through them. Any move he made to get it would no doubt result in all three of the men jumping him with their own blades.

"Here's how this'll work," said the leader of the men. He was large, top-heavy, and appeared as though he had not bathed for several weeks on account of some principle—the type of man whose own shit was happy to be free of. "You strip naked, hand over all your money and clothing, and we don't cut either of your heads off." The downward nod the man included let Keethro know that both the heads in question were his own.

Possible scenarios raced through Keethro's sobering mind. He thought about screaming to Titon for help, which he would not hear. He thought of charging the men with his trousers half on and killing them all—a difficult task without being mortally wounded himself. He thought of trying to slam through the weak wooden floor to make a dashing exit, but that would be unlikely even if his boots had still been on. He even thought of killing the girl who had lured him here before the men killed him. He could do that easily enough, but it did not meet all his desired criteria.

"Do I have your word, as gentlemen, that I will at least get my time in the sheets with her after I've done as you ask?" Keethro inquired.

The leader's smile of mock amusement showed he was not impressed. "We'll see how funny you are with your cock in your mouth." He and the other two men began to spread and advance. They had done this before, and Keethro now imagined he remembered seeing blood stains on the floorboards when he'd entered the room.

A violent crash sounded as the door burst open in two vertical pieces, showering the room with splinters of wood. By the time Keethro could gather what was happening, Titon had already picked up a chair, smashed it over the head of one of the men, and was using the two wooden legs that remained in his hands to beat the life out of another.

Keethro grabbed the bed cover and attempted to fling it like a net over the third man. The clump of cloth hit him in the face, but it was Titon's distraction that gave Keethro the opportunity to snatch his knife and follow up with an attack. The slash severed both skin and muscle of the man's upward forearm, who then lunged at Keethro as if not even wounded. Keethro was reacting slower than expected, and the man's blade might have caught him if it had been thrust with any skill, but Keethro avoided it in time and plunged his own knife deep under the man's chin. Titon continued thumping his two adversaries until there were surely three corpses in total—and some puddles of blood that would serve to produce yet more stains on the warped floorboards.

There was also a very plain-looking naked woman trying with desperation to cover the loose flesh of her sagging breasts that Keethro had remembered being presented so differently when she still wore cloth.

"I'm sorry," she whimpered repeatedly.

Keethro snorted contempt at the girl for whom he felt no pity. "These men killed each other fighting over who would first share your bed tonight, right?"

The girl just stared at Keethro, not seeming to understand. It made no difference; all would know what truly happened regardless of what she said.

Titon motioned for Keethro to put on his trousers so they could leave before having to deal with the mess they'd just made.

CASSEN

Cassen sat at his desk, opening, signing, and sealing his various accords. Every scratch of his quill upon parchment followed by a globule of vermilion-tinted beeswax, then pressed into the shape of his insignia, secured another moon's worth of lucrative trade. Tiresome as the task was, it was far better than hauling around pots of piss—a thing he reminded himself of when calling for the boy who fetched his chamber pot.

He heard the sound of approaching footsteps, the precursor to the familiar rap at the door.

I must get out of this room, he thought. *Perhaps whatever lady this is will get to take a stroll with her mother in the gardens.* Cassen wiped his quill clean of ink, placed it to rest, and waited.

"His Majesty the Prince to see you, Duchess," the boy servant from behind the door soon called.

"Send him in." Cassen turned in his seat to face his guest, somewhat perturbed. As intriguing as a visit from Alther was, it deterred his plans of enjoying some dawnlight. The thought of walking together with Alther, however, arm in arm through a forest of flowers, brought an honest smile on Cassen's face. It only remained for a moment.

"My young prince," Cassen exclaimed. "What a pleasant surprise." The unexpectedness of the person who appeared caused Cassen a lapse in concentration, and he forgot to address Stephon by an appropriately inflated title.

Did his mother put him up to this? Cassen wondered. *An envoy to beg a refund of her deposit perhaps?* The coinage received from Crella's messenger yet remained under his bed. Its value to him had doubled when Cassen heard whispers of the king's command for Alther and his family to move to Westport, where his lady servants could not follow. Still, he would have gladly given it all back to have seen Crella's reaction upon hearing the news herself.

"Please, have a seat wherever you like." Cassen motioned toward the small sofa and chaise longue, both upholstered to look as though they might have been pilfered from a princess's suite. His furniture was specifically designed to make his male visitors uncomfortable and less inclined to judicious thought. It often had the same effect on women as well.

"I…" The prince glanced around the room, his high collar almost restricting the motion. "I believe I will stand."

"Very well. How can I be of service to His Majesty?" Cassen inquired.

"Please. You may dispense with formalities when speaking with me," said Stephon. Whether he meant to be congenial or disdainful was hard to tell.

"As you wish, Prince Stephon."

"Stephon will do."

"Yes, I suppose it will."

The prince shot him an incredulous look but quickly replaced it with one of faux pleasantness. *My sardonic tongue will get me in to trouble some day*, Cassen chided himself.

"You must be wondering what has brought me here," the prince said, attempting to look dispassionate.

"I am." It was perhaps the first truth Cassen had spoken all day.

"As you may or may not be aware, His Grace the King has ordered my family to take up residence in Westport."

"Oh, I had not heard… When will you be leaving?"

"I do not intend to." The prince lifted his chin slightly in demonstration of his defiance.

"Ah, I see. Have you made your wishes known to your parents?" Cassen still could not see where this was headed.

"I am not a child, Duchess Cassen." The prince struggled with Cassen's title. "…In no way am I a child." He then flashed what he must have thought to be a charming smile—the type of audacious smirk an overconfident prince might show a lady he hoped to bed. *He couldn't possibly…*

Cassen was well practiced at suppressing laughter, but this was too much even for him. He quickly moved his hand to his face and tried to turn what would have been an unbridled guffaw into an embarrassed-looking giggle. Cassen was quite sure that the prince only had interest in the fairer sex and that these advances, if that was indeed what they were, were only a ploy. To what end exactly he could not guess, but he could certainly attempt to determine the authenticity of the prince's forwardness. *A little test perhaps.*

Cassen floated in his silks from the desk to the curved sofa, sat down on one side and patted the seat beside him, smiling coquettishly. The flash of horror on the prince's face lasted only a moment, but it revealed what Cassen had already surmised.

Stephon had the presence of mind to blush and feign bashfulness to delay and let his mind process the situation. He reluctantly acquiesced and sat across from Cassen, though leaning somewhat farther away than an actual suitor might have. *You pompous little ass. Now to make him think he has accomplished the task.*

"Prin— ...Stephon, you most certainly are no child, and I apologize for the implication. I want you to know that I think of you as an...ally." Cassen reached out and touched the prince's hands with his. To his credit Stephon did not pull back in revulsion, though it probably took every fiber in his being to avoid so. "But how can I assist you in staying in Eastport? Surely you have some plan?"

"Everyone is aware that you have my grandfather's ear." Stephon spoke quickly. "Perhaps if you told him it was necessary for me to remain in Eastport for some reason."

Cassen mulled it over. "As an apprentice of mine perhaps." As Cassen said the words he shot a flirtatious smile at the prince. *I should be careful not to push him too far. All men have their limits. I of all should know.*

"Yes, perhaps. I suppose it would be good for me to learn the ways of *successful* city management." Cassen saw no fakery in the boy's jab at his father.

"Hmmm..." Cassen pretended to weigh his options, though the choice was clear. Both Crella and Alther would be appalled by the prospect of their son in his clutches, which was reward enough for any trouble the boy caused him. "Consider it done, then," he promised Stephon, his newest pet.

The satisfaction showed on the prince's face. It bothered Cassen that this boy thought he had managed to manipulate him, but it would only serve to make Stephon easier to manipulate, himself. He gestured with a palm that Stephon could leave, and Stephon stood.

"You will make a fine apprentice, I think," Cassen said warmly. *You shall indeed.*

DERUDIN

Alone in the king's study, Derudin and Lyell performed their nightly ritual. After a servant had brought the king his evening meal, he and Derudin would speak in earnest of the happenings of the kingdom and how best to manage the intricacies therein. Tonight it was one of the king's favorites: crisply roasted pheasant, first marinated in beer, served with a hot chutney of butter-fried gooseberries, sausage, and sage.

"You are a fool, Derudin," said the king. Derudin tried to think back on all the kings and leaders he had advised in the past hundred years. Had it truly been only a hundred years since crossing the Devil's Mouth? It seemed more like a thousand. He believed, in any case, that the man seated before him, sucking his fingers of the fatty juices from a meal that smelled of heaven, was among the better of those kings.

"There are men who forgo the pleasures of sex," continued Lyell. "Fool men of foolish religions, I say, but I can, in a perverse sort of way, understand their restraint. Coitus makes a man weak, truth be told. Makes his head not work in the way it ought. Like a hungry hunter. Nevertheless, you are a man. I have seen you take to bread and water as we all do. And every night I have brought for you a meal that is, well, befitting a king. And every night you abstain. I think perhaps you have a lunacy exceeding that of those of celibacy. Ha!" The king had been amused by his unintended poetry and rewarded himself with another mouthful of food.

"A mage's conductance comes from focus and is amplified by continence, my king." Derudin was always content to recite an Ancient Law and took pride in being recognized for the supreme restraint he exhibited—the meal did look and smell delicious.

The king licked his fingers, pushed his plate piled with bones aside, and took a long swig of wine from his wooden goblet. Then he leaned forward and dragged Derudin's plate close, digging his fingers in and once again covering them with bits of food and grease. *Nor do I think you would wish to be denied your second plate.*

"So tell me." Lyell paused and swallowed the food that fought his speaking. It would have amused Derudin, watching this man, with a beard of pure white so meticulously groomed, do everything in his power to cover his face instead with chutney. But the reports Derudin must share left no room in his mind for humor. "What news of the kingdom tonight?"

"Some troubling things, my king."

"There always are. I'll hear them just the same."

"It would appear our friend Duke Veront has taken to calling himself a lord."

This bothered the king enough that he hesitated a moment before stuffing another finger full into his mouth. "Never trust a man who eats with knife and fork," he once told Derudin, "for such a man must think that having clean hands at supper will somehow keep them cleaner after having betrayed your trust." Derudin thought it a wise observation.

"That rapacious fool." The king gesticulated with a pheasant bone. "Had I a better alternative for Rivervalian rule, I would have chosen as such. He is too thin and hungry. But even so, a king's throne makes a duke feel lordly and a lord feel kingly. It will not be long before we are at each other's throats."

"We should be able to easily defend against any threat he poses, should he turn against us, given our twenty thousand men to his ten and the richness of these lands." Derudin was stating a fact that they both knew, but even to himself his voice lacked reassurance. He had advised the king to remain at the Adeltian Throne after the victory, a decision he had been second guessing for some time now.

"Aye, but I hope it does not come to that. Half of his men are those that took Adeltia. Good men—I'd remember their faces if I saw them today. They would not march against their true king and leader." Lyell took another sip of wine, and his face soured. "The man is a fool if he tries to overreach his power…" The king's grip on his cup tightened as his expression darkened further. "I should crush him now and be done with it. Damn him!"

"I would advise against it, my king. We can remain passive, collecting the income he still sends to us as commanded. If the payment stops, we will know his intention, and we can move to have him eliminated. We have many allies in Rivervale who will see it done." Derudin had already thought the matter through. Assassination was not a tool he advised lightly, but it was a fitting punishment for what would be such blatant and treasonous betrayal, should Veront rebel.

"You speak as if Rivervale is not my kingdom. They are my *subjects*, not my allies. But yes, that is the wisest course of action. A dirty business though, killing a man in the bed he sleeps. Mind you it is *my* bed that he sleeps in. What else?"

Derudin perused the room before speaking. The maps carved of wood on the walls showed him the realm, and the troubles they faced came from all directions, as well as from within. "I have it on good authority, my king, that some among the Adeltian nobility seek to conspire against the throne." *As have they ever, though I fear these plots to be more dangerous than before.*

"I have beaten the fools into submission while keeping them well fed, rich, and seemingly in good spirits. On what authority do you make this claim?" The king had finally reached the limits of his stomach and pushed Derudin's half-eaten plate of pheasant away.

"Firsthand authority, my king." *And I know Cassen to be involved as well, but I must not implicate the king's favored Duke, the magician of coin, without tangible evidence, lest I draw suspicions of pettiness.*

"Very well. You have never led me astray with your gazings. See to it that all potential conspirators have as many ears close to them as possible. I would like to pull this weed at the root this time." The king finished off his second goblet and slammed it back down on the table as if to drive home the thought. He enjoyed his wine but was not given to overconsumption as his father had been, another quality Derudin respected. "Any good news?" the king asked in jest.

Derudin paused to contemplate what he was to report, fearing it would not be taken seriously. *But I feel it is more serious than one might presume.*

"There are accounts, my king, of ships to the south. From enough sources that I feel it worthy of mentioning."

"My good man, you are not a sailor. When two ships at sea spot each other, one will naturally be more southerly than the other and may report it as such. What of it?"

Derudin did his best not to take offense at what his king had said. Derudin's trip across the Devil's Mouth may have taken place before Lyell could form memories, but he well knew the tale. The sudden thought that the king may doubt the veracity of the story gave Derudin a rare anger toward his leader, and he fought to keep it from his voice.

"These are not reported to be ships of our own, nor ships of the Spicelanders. They report goliath ships of four masts and square sails, always too far for more detail to be seen. I fear them to be warships from an unknown people." Derudin chose his words wisely—a *forgotten* people would have been a more accurate description but would have also invited ridicule.

"Ships with square sails are of little concern to me. I know a thing or two about sea travel, and any people yet to perfect the sail and be able to tack into the wind are sure to be primitives and no threat to our kingdom. But I would like to see these new people, should they exist."

"As would I, however, I do not think these ships should be overlooked. Even primitive ships can carry an army in favorable winds."

Derudin knew enough about ships to know the king was wrong in his assertion about sail shape. He also knew enough about kings not to contradict him.

Lyell looked toward Derudin with sincerity. "Derudin, I respect your judgment, but a king must weigh his decisions so that we do not spread resources so thin attending to every potential threat that we have none left for those of true merit. Though I often cede to your knowledge, if I always did as such it would be you who ruled the kingdom and not I. Keep me abreast of any developments in the southern seas, but I do not wish to build a southern fleet merely to fend off ghost ships."

"As you wish, my king," Derudin conceded, their discussion having come to a close. *To rule the kingdom myself? How curious that the idea never crossed my mind.* Derudin's inward smile beamed. He had a very good reason as to why he would never seek to rule. *The Ancient Laws can be a cruel mistress.*

ALTHER

"Fifty thousand marks?" Alther repeated the amount to emphasize its absurdity. He felt his face contorting to an uncharacteristic expression of indignation.

"It is a *deposit*," Crella explained as if to a child, "covering the first of five years' service for three such ladies."

How it was that she remained most enticing when she was at her most cavalier he did not know, but each time he pondered it, he could not escape recalling his first glimpse of her.

Crella was the object of raunchy jokes among Rivervalian boys. The Adeltian Tart, they called her, not yet ripened but already with a babe. Her bedchamber was a royal bordello, they said, and for a few silvers anyone could be prince for a night. The girl Alther had expected to meet on his trip to Adeltia was a younger version of any of the whores that worked the docks along the Eos: a loose-fitting dress, messy hair, crooked teeth, and a desperate smile devoid of all dignity. What he had actually seen was the opposite entirely. Her form-fitting bodice betrayed her slender curves, a modest bosom balanced by a delicate waist. Her hair was a perfect waterfall of loose golden curls, and the prideful look of derision she gave him let him know that it made no difference if he had all the silver in the realm—he could never hope to have her.

"And I will be quick to relieve the old crones currently under my employ," she continued, "once their replacements have proven themselves."

Alther trailed his wife as she went from one piece of furniture to the next, seemingly determined to rearrange every object in their home. So little had changed, it seemed, since he'd first seen her. In spite of their marriage and the child they'd had, to her, he was still the lustful boy chasing after the unattainable princess.

"That does not lessen the amount. You will speak with Cassen, explain your lack of need for the services, and apologize for the miscommunication." *This time she goes too far. God of the Mountain, give me strength not to act in anger.*

"I will do no such thing." Crella turned to face him, fastidious in her rebuke. "How dare you even suggest it? The wife of the heir to the throne and future queen will not be seen groveling to some lowborn upstart. Most certainly not one of Cassen's persuasions."

"Then take care that no one sees it." Alther could feel the tension in his jaw building, his teeth threatening to shatter. He had not yet revealed to Crella the king's order that they change their place of residence, but Alther anticipated her response. They could not disobey the king, but Crella would seek every avenue of escape from this reality, and at Alther's expense. In his desperation, Alther envisioned how his father might handle this situation, then cringed at the thought.

"I refuse to live in squalor. A cobbler's wife would not put up with such insolent servants nor such an impertinent husband. This residence requires the services of three lady servants, and that is the end of it." Crella, quite confident in having won the debate, returned to her task of looking busy doing nothing to dismiss her husband.

As she leaned to reach for items on the rear of the sideboard, he was reminded of how often she refused his advances: to the point that he no longer made them. In their near sixteen years of marriage he'd be surprised if they had been intimate so many times. "You reek of your putrid hunt," she would tell him, months after his last excursion. The dress she now wore may have been the very one he'd first seen her in, she had remained so gracile. And he could have her now if he so chose, tearing fine cloth from flesh. Even the defunct Adeltian law had a version of the Rivervalian Husband's Right, allowing a man to take that which his wife did not willingly provide. But after their wedding night, when neither truly had a say, he had never forced her to do anything she did not wish to. And although today would inevitably be a first in that regard, he resolved only to compel her to again do as their king had commanded.

"Aye, this home may require such services, for I believe I spotted a bit of dust gathering on the crystal chandelier... The one in the never-used dining hall." He allowed her a moment to puzzle over his change in tone, but she only ignored him. "But I am afraid we will not be residing here for much longer." Alther's words had in them all the coolness he could muster.

Crella had no interest in playing his game and continued with her faux tidying, muttering something under her breath about the absurdity of having to do a servant's work. The fragrance wafting from the candles she repositioned was putrid in its strength: a funereal bouquet of flowers, powders, and wax that clung to the lungs—scents she knew he despised. He had told her before how they caused him headaches and sternutation. That she insisted they be placed in the anteroom, making it unavoidable for him not to whiff them upon every arrival, reminded him of her spitefulness.

"We leave for Westport in three days by decree of our king. The arrangements have already been made." Alther finished the statement and found he was oddly eager to see his wife's reaction. *She did not choose me as husband, but she will obey and acknowledge me as one when presented with no alternative.*

He had not predicted her fury.

"You *coward*," she turned and yelled. "You dare hide behind your father's edict like a little boy? You shame us all with your incompetence and above all your impotence!" With her final words she came at him as if to slap him.

Alther's unassuming nature hid from many his true prowess with that of halberd or sword and shield. He had endured, in his youth, the countless hours of training with real steel expected of Rivervalian nobility—training that would make Adeltian boys shudder at the thought. Alther still had the scars and the skills to show for it, though neither served him much purpose with his current surroundings. Alther caught his wife's wrist with one hand and struck her cheek with the back of his other. He immediately regretted not the strike, but the force with which he threw it, fearing it was too much for her delicate frame. His blow, it seemed, was if anything too weak. She screamed and swung her free hand clenched in a fist at his face. He caught her other wrist and attempted to subdue her, yelling in kind. "Stop," he pleaded, but the moment her struggle finally ceased he felt something crash against the back of his skull.

KEETHRO

"I thought I was dead," Keethro admitted. "And I thought you were dead asleep."

He and Titon had a fire built in the woods of the rocky foothills several miles south of Phylan. Having taken some clothing off the bodies of those they'd killed, they no longer looked so much like outsiders. Their new coats smelled of old sweat and fresh piss, but they were both too charged from the battle and too tired from so many days without proper rest to care.

"It takes more than that cider they call mead to put me down," said Titon. "I saw you eyeing that ugly barmaid and knew there was going to be trouble. I figured better sooner than later, should I truly fall asleep."

"Was she indeed ugly…aside from the sagging flesh?"

Titon rubbed his jaw with a look somewhere between concern and humor.

"Perhaps I have been too many days in travel," said Keethro. *On a voyage I did not wish to take,* he reminded himself.

"More likely too many cups of southern cider. But you never could handle your drink." Titon spoke in his usual gibing manner. "It has been like old times though, has it not?"

"Aye," Keethro replied truthfully. "It has." There was joy to be had in accompanying Titon in his recklessness, and there was spitefulness to be had in the fact that there had been nothing of the sort since Titon's wife fell ill. They were too old now to properly enjoy such meaningless exploits. They had accomplished nothing so far, except getting farther from safety. *I must do what I originally intended or die out here like a fool. Tonight has only confirmed that.* Bile rose in his throat at the thought, and he was thankful for the lingering effects of his earlier drinking.

They sat in silence for a good while, both poking at the fire for no apparent reason. Keethro wondered what it was that kept Titon awake. They had been so long without sleep, and Keethro had an unsavory task to complete that he would rather get over with as quickly as possible.

"How are you and Red?" Titon asked.

"My daughter?" Keethro gave it a moment's thought. It was not a topic of conversation he had expected from Titon. "She hates me. When she was very young we were close, perhaps, but no longer, not since she's grown." It seemed there should be more reason to it than that. He could not recall ever being mean or vindictive toward the girl. "I suppose she is simply too much her mother. And I am done with that woman." He'd known it for some time now, but to say it aloud was relieving.

"A shame to have a child that does not understand you," said Titon, seeming to purposefully avoid conversation about Kilandra. He threw another log onto the fire, sending embers floating into the air only to die moments later. "It is the same with Titon."

"He is a good lad, I've seen. Fierce with an axe, and smart as any from what I hear."

"Smarter," said Titon. "I am a fool and a coward though. I told him in a letter before departing what I should have told him long ago, eye to eye." A jolt of shame shot through Keethro, and he became uncomfortably warm. "As much as I wish to return with a remedy for my wife, I wish equally to return and see my sons, to know they have been successful on their raid, and to let them see the pride they give me."

Keethro stared into the fire, letting it burn into his vision as punishment for previous misconduct. *It was a cruel and stupid thing to have stolen*, he thought, disgusted with himself.

"Then we will see it done, my friend." Keethro said, hearing his words but troubled by their lack of sincerity.

"Aye," said Titon, probably nodding. "Good night, brother."

Keethro fought to stay awake until he heard Titon snoring, this time in earnest he hoped. His mind had been plagued with doubt during what felt like an eternity waiting for those snores. The finality of what he must do weighed on him like a mountain. Whether it was due to his lack of sleep or his rediscovered affection for his friend of old, he did not know, but he found himself wavering in his resolve to go through with his original plan.

He studied Titon, the mammoth that he was, the chest beneath his beard rising and falling with each breath. How many times had Titon saved him and he saved Titon in scuffles such as earlier that night? He could not recall. *When I sink the blade into your neck, will you awaken in time to know it was me? And with you gone, what will remain?*

Keethro had no desire to hurt this man who he was now realizing was perhaps his only source of happiness left. *But I have already caused damage with my misplaced spite that I cannot mend*, he thought with regret. He turned around to rummage through the bag he had been leaning upon, checking periodically to make sure Titon was still asleep. His throat tightened as he found what he searched for. *You fool, do not do this.* But he saw no other options.

Keethro approached the fire with deliberate steps. "I am sorry, my friend. You deserved a better brother than I," he whispered under his breath.

Upon the fire he placed the two letters he'd swiped from Titon's home before they departed, watching them wither and burn. It was bad enough that he had not thought to write a letter of his own to Red, but that he had cost Titon what would most likely be his last farewell to his sons was far worse. As the wind picked up the final remnants of Titon's words, now turned to ash, Keethro's insides twisted and shriveled.

Now I must see this journey through and get you home alive. It was the only way he could think to rectify what he had done. *Or at the very least, die a fool for trying.*

CRELLA

Crella stood, dumbfounded, looking at her husband who lay unconscious on the floor of their anteroom. Pieces of a large vase were scattered around him on the porcelain tile. Blood slowly pooled from the broken skin on his head.

He was no Sir Stormblade, the dashing knight fawned over by all Adeltian girls prior to the war. He was overcautious and spiritless. Yet when held up against the other Rivervalian invaders, when held up against the men—Adeltian or otherwise—who remained alive after those of true principle had been lost in combat, Alther was perhaps the least offensive. Fault him though she may for his timidity, she could hardly have wished in earnest for him to be a more assertive man.

"What were you thinking?" Crella demanded under her breath.

Lank and noble, her son stood before her. Her unyielding nature toward Alther had seen its way even into the heredity of their only offspring, as the young prince was almost her twin in appearance.

"I was thinking of your safety. I—"

"This could be seen as *treason*," she interrupted. Things had escalated with such immediacy she had no time to think. Moving to Westport suddenly seemed like it would not have been much trouble at all.

"He was going to kill you," Stephon replied, much too loud, as though he wanted others to overhear him.

"Lower your voice." Crella shushed him with her angry command.

Stephon's assertion was so absurd it might have been funny under different circumstances. Alther had struck her with less force than an actor would an actress in a play. Her rage when she counterattacked was more directed toward how long it had taken her to awake some sort of spark in the heartless man—a thing she hoped could be redirected toward the king.

The only one with the potential for death now was Alther, and forced to contemplate a life without him, she realized this man did not deserve the fate she'd secretly prayed would befall him since they had been married. What she blamed him for most was the very thing she was guilty of herself. Where she had no capability, Alther had no will to rebel against their king. That Alther had taken her baseborn daughter, Ethel, as his own and kept her safe from harm should have been reason enough for Crella's appreciation, an appreciation she only now regretted having never shown.

She knelt at her fallen husband's side and was relieved to hear his breathing was regular. The bleeding from beneath his hair was significant, however.

"He was not going to kill me," she scolded her son as she rose and faced him. *Though that may be the story of necessity*, she admitted to herself.

Crella knew her son to be hot tempered and defensive of her, but she had never expected him to be witless enough to strike the heir to the throne. She thought she'd raised him with more sense than that.

"Now what can we do about this?" Crella posed the question to herself. She fought back the worry that was consuming her from the inside. *I must be strong for Stephon's sake.*

"Is he dead?" Stephon asked.

"No, his chest still rises and falls with strength."

"Should we kill him?"

Crella slapped her son across the face for his idiocy. Stephon recoiled in confusion.

"He is your *father!*" Crella felt as though the world she had constructed had shattered along with the vase that struck her husband. All of the posturing, all of the effort to always look composed and act in a way that would not draw the ire of these Rivervalian invaders, but also not allow them to think that they could do with her as they pleased—all of it was being undone by one action, made by the one she strove most to protect. "I will say that it was a burglar or a jealous woman or some like." A moment's reflection revealed she much preferred the former. "We will hide you until this misunderstanding is resolved."

"Mother, that is foolish."

It did seem an outlandish story, but less plausible things had happened within the walls of the kingdom, and she could think of no alternative.

"Just do as I say," she said.

"Cassen trusts me. I will go seek his aid." Stephon boasted as if she would be impressed that he had made Cassen an ally.

"Absolutely *not.*" The thought that he would seek Cassen's assistance over hers nearly drove her to slap him again. "Cassen is the king's vile pet, and you have just struck the king's son. Have some sense. Cassen will only use this to his own advantage and to our detriment."

Crella paced, the hem of her dress catching pieces of the broken vase, making a scratching noise on the tile that threatened to wake Alther. She forced herself to stand still.

"I have friends who bear no love for Alther or his father, Adeltian nobles who are still rich and powerful. I will send you to them for safekeeping."

Stephon frowned, still not grasping the seriousness of the situation. It seemed he was still thinking only of the punishment that would come from his father when he should have been concerned far more about the king. Lyell would not tolerate the half Adeltian prince striking Alther, no matter the story.

"I do not wish to go live with those I do not know." Stephon rubbed his brow as if exhausted by this unnecessary exercise.

Crella scowled at him. "How many people do you know in the dungeons? You will be living with them and for much longer if you do not obey me and do so with haste."

At the mention of the dungeons Stephon's demeanor changed. His face became more serious.

"Pack some things. It must look as though you had been staying with them since yesterday. Make a note of anyone who may have seen you here today—I will need to know. I will write a letter for you to bring to my friends, and you will travel to them in secret as soon as can be arranged. Now hurry!"

Stephon snorted the last of his defiance and obeyed.

DERUDIN

"Focus, Toblin, focus."

A stout boy of eight years stood at the front of the class facing away from the other students. He was focused intently on a candle. It floated on the surface of the water in a glass bowl atop an old wooden table. Beyond the table was a massive hearth with a fire ablaze. Beads of sweat formed on the boy's brow as he trembled. His luxurious violet cape with yellow embroidery, which he never was without, swayed with his efforts.

"Do not strain. Use neither muscle nor strength. Only seek to guide the power from one source to the other, you the conduit." Derudin encouraged without allowing his expression to change from that of complete stoicism. *This boy does not belong.*

He knew Toblin had little chance of achieving this menial task. The boy simply had no natural focus. But his parents had influence, and with it they had insisted he be trained in the ways of a mage. Most of Derudin's class was filled with those whose parents had enrolled them in an effort of last resort, desiring to see their children rise from mediocrity. No visions were required to know this boy would never heft a sword with any grace, and unfortunately, the same could be said for his potential for magecraft. In decades past, Derudin may have rejected the boy outright, but in these times he was lucky to be able to fill half the seats of his small classroom, even with the butts of non-potentials. Interest and faith in the abilities of mages had diminished greatly over the years, and so too had there been a decline in those with the natural predisposition for conductance. Of his seven apprentices, only two had any true natural focus that he knew of, and they lacked promise in other areas.

Finally, Toblin let out a pathetic whimper and allowed his body to relax. His eyes turned downward with dejection, away from the unaltered wick of the candle.

"A noble attempt, young Toblin," lied Derudin. "Let us try to determine the cause of your failure so that your next shall result in brilliant flame."

Derudin floated in his robes toward the table—a mere trick of the eye due to proper starch levels in its grey fabric, but in a world where magic was all but absent, even simple artifice was a powerful tool in achieving respect without wasted effort. Derudin's days of performing parlor tricks to convince nonbelievers were long and gone, however. He had the ear of the king, won by years of sound guidance preceding the conquering of the Adeltian Kingdom, and that was currently all that concerned him.

Derudin submerged a sealed glass tube containing a grey liquid into the water and waited patiently, as did the six apprentices in attendance.

"Two and a half degrees," Derudin announced. "A fair amount of power to have transferred over the course of several minutes, albeit to the wrong destination. You may sit."

Toblin waddled back to his chair, cape swinging, and sat with the others. There were two rows, each of eight chairs, with no table or surface in front upon which to write. Derudin told new apprentices that any lesson they sought to remember should be stored in their minds and not upon paper. Mindlessly transcribing words, he found, was a good way to ensure the writer had no time to discern their meaning. Nor was there much to remember, in fact. Of the countless Ancient Laws, only the first three pertained specifically to mages.

"And who would like to try next?" Derudin did not need to look up to know whose fingers would be raised. As he added cold cellar water to the bowl to equalize its temperature with that of the surrounding air, he envisioned what he would see when he turned to face them. Sture and Signy, he predicted, would both have their index fingers raised as high as they could stretch them to show their over-enthusiastic zeal for demonstrating their talents. Both could light a candle within a few moments, and both were eager to show that they could do it more quickly than the other. The same noble blood coursed through the veins of the two cousins, each twelve years of age. They looked more like mirrored siblings than cousins, both with their bright blonde hair and air of authority—learned from their noble parents no doubt. Neither was particularly impressive, in Derudin's opinion, but they at least had focus, which was more than he could say for the remainder of the students. In Derudin's day, a child of twelve would be expected to be able to call lightning—not that any actually met those expectations. *Save for one*, Derudin remembered with unabashed pride.

"Flow the heat from the hearth into your eyes and throughout your body. Let it fill your veins or lungs or stomach. The path each mage uses is different, but it must flow both in and out again, directed to your intended target… *Directly* to your target. Focus is the goal of this exercise as it takes very little power to light a wick." Derudin let his gaze linger on the pewter pot that held the cellar water. The engravings were impressive, but it was the condensation that captivated him. With the fire burning, the warm Adeltian fall felt more like the mouth of a volcano. *A dip in the Rivervalian springs would do these old bones well,* he thought, but that was not to be.

Turning to face the class, Derudin saw that both Signy and Sture had their fingers raised as far as possible without separating from the hand.

"A mage is a conduit of power, nothing more, nothing less. This is the first of the Ancient Laws. You are not the creator of the power, only that through which it flows. Remembering, no, *understanding* this will help you maintain focus." Derudin had certainly said as much before, complete with his self-correction, but repetition was the only tool he seemed to have left at his disposal.

An odd flicker caught his eye as Derudin moved to accept Signy's request. He shifted his gaze toward the end of the front row where the girl in the plain dress sat. Nine or ten years in age, she had attended classes for over a month now, never having volunteered for an exercise. Since Derudin was not in the habit of forcing such things upon a student, he had never seen her demonstrate her abilities in any way. She was a peculiar thing to him, with her stark-white hair which reached just past her shoulders and was worn always down, never up in the way most girls were doing lately. But fashion, it seemed, was another thing she did not exercise, as her clothing appeared oddly plain even to a man who wore nothing but grey robes. Her index finger was slightly raised, her hand still resting upon her lap.

"You may stand and attempt to light the candle," Derudin told the white-haired girl. He was not in the habit of acquiring names of students until they showed some form of ability, or at least failed enough that he felt compelled to regardless.

She rose and walked toward the table.

"Have no fear of drawing too much power from the fire in the hearth. If you transfer more than the candle can contain, the water will absorb the rest. You can only draw that which you can dispense—you mustn't worry about excess energy being left in your body and burning you to ash. That happens very rarely."

Some of the children laughed quietly at Derudin's humor. *Perhaps that joke was not appropriate before her first demonstration.*

"Just focus on the smallest bit of fiber at the very top of the wick, not the full breadth of it. And do not be discouraged when nothing happens at first. No one is expected to light a candle on their first attempt." Feeling a bit guilty for having caused her peers to laugh, Derudin attempted to ease her mind more than he was apt to on a pupil's first effort.

The girl faced the candle, but Derudin could see her eyes were closed. It was common for some to close their eyes to achieve better focus, but he figured it was more like to be due to her embarrassment. He could not tell if she attempted anything, but after a moment a few bubbles came out of the water, a thing noticed by all.

"She projected a fart into the water!" While Derudin tried to make sense of it himself, Sture had been the first to wager a guess.

The five seated children burst into laughter, especially Toblin who seemed to be relieved that there would be a new person for his classmates to harass instead of him.

"Silence." Derudin did not need to speak loudly to get their full attention, and the laughter ceased. "You have done well, though I believe you have managed to boil some water rather than light the candle. In any case, it was a fine first attempt. Please have a seat."

The young girl, now thoroughly humiliated, returned to her seat. Tears looked as though they would burst forth at any moment.

"Boiling water is perhaps more difficult than lighting a wick," Derudin explained. "In fact, it is quite more difficult when attempting to boil but a small portion in such a large bowl. What is your name, young apprentice?"

The girl took a moment to calm herself, and Derudin remained busy with his thermometer so she would know she had the time.

"Eaira," she finally responded.

"Well, Eaira, you have a good deal of natural focus. And what is more, you showed incredible restraint in taking so long before demonstrating your natural gifts. Sture, would you be so kind as to remind us what the second of the Ancient Laws is?"

Sture looked befuddled at first but regained his composure as he stood, reciting the second law with his usual authority. "A mage's conductance comes from focus and is amplified by continence."

"Before you sit, let everyone know exactly what that means."

Sture's look of confusion quickly returned, and his eyes wandered around the room as if looking for the answer.

"It means," said Derudin, "that without both focus and continence, or, in simpler terms, concentration and self-restraint, you will not be able to transfer power effectively. One is born with focus, but restraint must be practiced. Some of you probably saw it as a weakness that it took Eaira a month to finally do an exercise, and you could not be more mistaken. Restraint should be practiced in all things if you are to truly be a mage."

Derudin glanced at his thermometer to see how much heat had been transferred into water, but the level of the grey liquid inside refused to budge. *That is odd*, he thought. Even practiced mages would have transferred some heat into the surrounding water. He then spotted water pooling around the bottom of the glass bowl and looked toward the pewter pot to see if the condensation had run from the sides, but it had not. He noticed, instead, a tiny trickle of water leaking down the back of the glass bowl itself, out of what must have been a pin-sized hole. His attention snapped toward Eaira.

"But even with extreme restraint, a mage is useless without natural focus," Derudin continued speaking calmly in an effort to quell the odd sensation in his gut. "The Dawnstar radiates more power than we could possibly fathom, but because it does so in all directions, devoid of focus, we can bathe in its rays for hours with no more ill-effect than some reddening of the skin. A true mage must have the ability to direct power toward the smallest of targets, in the smallest of rays." He looked at Eaira and gave her half a smile as he noticed her spirits had been lifted. *I now have a theory as to why you always wear your hair down.*

TITON SON OF TITON

So filled with exhilarant warmth, Titon had been unable to feel the sting of the cold, salty spray off the Frozen Sea. In all of Titon's fifteen years, he could not remember a time in which he'd felt more accomplished, and he was not alone in that feeling—at least for the duration of their coastal travel. The spirits of the men had all lifted upon reaching the fabled shores, realizing they were not to be clobbered to death by boulder-hurling giants.

Galatai believed they had no reason to come west due to the lack of greenery along this coast and the unfishable nature of the violent, icy waters. It was thought, as previous journeys had demonstrated, that nothing lived here that would make the voyage worthwhile, and it seemed as though that thinking may have been correct. As they walked south across these massive mountains, the tops of which were made flat by some unexplained force, there were no signs of life. No crabs scurried into the cracks of the rocks, no gnats pestered their eyes, no gulls called from the sky...not even snow survived on the boulders, darkened with wetness and bereft of powder.

The men got their first taste of battle, however, in the most unexpected fashion. They'd come upon an enormously rotund creature that resembled an old mustached man with widespread eyes, flippers for limbs and two huge teeth, each near half a man in length. The beast was no match for their bows and axes and came to a quick, albeit gruesome, death. The men were elated to find the fat and meat they butchered was quite edible, and the few who protested at first, claiming that it might be cannibalistic to eat such a creature, came around soon after they smelled the fat sizzling over the fires.

With full bellies and enough meat left to last well over a week, they turned east. Titon led them inland after he'd determined they'd followed the sea southward for long enough. He'd calculated the distance based on the hours spent traveling and their paces per hour, but with a stick shoved into a crack in the stony ground and some thoughtful looks, Titon pretended to glean cryptic knowledge from the Dawnstar based on the shadow cast. *Let them think me a mage. What could be the harm?* Having read about magecraft, Titon was convinced it was nonsense, but he thought the men in their party were like to be the type to believe in such foolishness.

"How much farther do you think?" Decker asked him. The two were at their usual place at the front of the pack.

"I cannot say for sure." Titon did not meet his brother's gaze, instead looking forward. "As I have mentioned, there is no way of knowing how far the flat rock spans between the Frozen Sea and the canyon that is home to the Dogmen. We are the first to travel this way."

"Yes, but you must have some idea. We have been walking east for several days now. We are not lost are we?"

"Of course not," said Titon tersely. *Of course we are lost. I just told you, no one has ever traveled these plateaus.*

Titon had given up using the term "plateau" as it only seemed to incite mockery. It was becoming increasingly vexing to Titon that the knowledge he had gained from his study of Dogmen books, the ingenuity he had used to devise a method for them to descend the cliffs—the very essence of that which made this raid possible—was the object of constant ridicule. Now that they headed inland and were faced with another journey of indeterminate length, the thrill of having found the Frozen Sea was sapped from him by the childish impatience of those around him. *I expected as much from the others, but not from you, Decker.*

"We are only a few days' travel from the canyons," Titon said, hoping it would be true. "I am quite sure of it."

"Fair enough," Decker responded. "I think we all just miss the flat stones of the frozen coast. The way here is quite rocky."

Titon snorted, shook his head, and fell back so he would no longer have to speak to his brother. He had no desire to explain to him how stupid it was to be complaining that one part of the journey—the part they should all be thanking him for—was easier than the rest.

It was only a day later when they reached the promised canyons, but peering over the cliff's edge put new worry in Titon. It was a sight that no doubt would have been awing had they been able to see anything but a bottomless river of fast-moving mist. The normally pleasant scent of rain that hung in the damp air seemed to forebode them somehow drowning in the thick, swirling vapors.

All ridicule ended, for the moment, as Titon instructed the men on how to use the rope system he had invented. It would allow them, in theory, to be safely lowered, one at a time, to the canyon floor. Many men had died attempting similar descents in the gorges of their homeland, but that was due mainly to the inability of the man being lowered to communicate with those lowering him. The screaming winds, loose rocks, and unknown depth of the descent were also much to blame.

Titon's three-rope system, one harnessed to the man to be lowered by those above, one static that the man could climb down under his own power, and the third thin line for communication, made the very difficult task quite possible in his estimate.

"I will go first," said Decker, securing the harness rope to himself. "Titon, you will need to stay at the top as long as possible to make sure these fools understand your complex system."

There is nothing complex about it, Titon thought in annoyance, but he knew Decker to be right. The boys they called peers had a glazed-over look in their eyes when Titon had first explained it, and their only hope of learning was by repeated example.

"I suppose if it supports your weight it will support anyone," Titon admitted. "Remember, if you run out of rope or simply cannot descend farther, it is five quick tugs, and we will hoist you back up. If you give five tugs and the rope is slack, we will assume you have made it to the bottom."

"Yes, I remember. Make sure those that will remain know the system well enough by the time you must descend so that they do not cost us our only working mind." Decker glared at the four. "You hear that Griss, Galinn, Hallon, and Dicun? I know your names, and if you drop my brother you'd best jump after him. It will be a better death than the one you will suffer at my hands." Decker looked as if he meant it, and even Titon felt the chill induced by his brother's words.

Those Decker had addressed nodded their understanding, Griss doing so with a smirk.

"Good," said Decker. "I'll see you four in a week or so. As for the rest of you… I'll see you at the bottom."

Decker disappeared over the edge with mirth on his face, and his descent continued as planned without complication. It seemed the only communication Titon felt through the thin line was one tug, urging them to keep lowering him. Knowing Decker, he was probably pushing himself with his legs, recklessly swinging as far from the cliff face as possible, growing bored with the methodical rate at which they lowered him. Titon had no plans of allowing the men to increase that rate, however. After what seemed like an hour, but was probably less than a quarter, Titon felt two quick tugs.

"Halt!" Titon had given the command in a panic, having momentarily forgotten what the signal actually meant.

"The harness rope is slack," said Dicun, one of the three lowering Decker. Titon had intended for those who were to remain at top be both the first and last to handle the ropes, therefore giving them plenty of practice while also allowing them time to rest before it was Titon's turn. "Should we take in the remainder?"

"No," Titon said with more harshness than he intended. "He gave two tugs meaning to wait and only that."

They waited for a moment, then Titon thought he felt three tugs. As Decker had descended, the tugs became far less precise. They felt like long stretches that blended into each other.

"More slack...I think. It was three tugs."

"You want us to give more slack or not?" growled Griss.

"Yes, give him about a man's length of slack," said Titon, and the three on the harness line complied.

"He has tugged thrice again. More slack, another man in length. He must be on a tricky ledge." Titon now hoped the bottom would not be so much farther that multiple quick tugs became indiscernible—that, and they were running short on rope.

Several minutes passed with no communication from Decker and no motion on any of the ropes.

"Did he fall?" asked Griss.

"Of course not," Titon snapped. "The rope would have gone taut." *Ignorant fool.* Even so Titon, found himself picturing a short drop to a lower ledge incapacitating his brother or separating him from the communication line.

As Titon was about to ask the men to bring tension on the harness rope in hopes of eliciting some response from Decker, he felt an unmistakable five tugs on the line.

"Five tugs. He has either made it or needs to come back up. Slowly take in the slack until you feel tension."

Dicun, Griss, and Galinn retrieved the rope gradually, but since no tension was felt for some time, they sped to haul the empty harness. It was too soon to celebrate, however, not knowing for sure that Decker had made the bottom.

"Arron and everyone else who goes after him, remember to hold tension on the communication and the static...er...the *climbing* rope after you descend so that the harness rope does not upset their placement," Titon instructed, realizing now that that may become an issue. Arron was next in turn to go down, decided unanimously. "And do slow tugs, not rapid ones. They tend to blend in to each other at a distance."

Arron and the others nodded.

"The feck is that?" Galinn was the man lowest of the three pulling the harness rope back up, and the first to spot the blood red color.

Attached to the harness was a bundle of flowers.

"That bastard wanted the slack so he could give us a gift from the bottom," Titon cried with relief.

The men cheered, but Titon knew it was for Decker and not for the victory of his rope system. Decker simply had a way with these men that befuddled him, but even he had to admit the bouquet was a welcome surprise that would put the men at ease, or at least embarrass them to the point of feigning it when it came time for their descents.

They repeated the procedure with Arron, without issue—other than the updraft wafting his aroma to their nostrils. Several bags of weapons and supplies were then lowered, followed by the remaining men. Some required time to rest halfway down, signaled by two tugs, and the rest made it to the bottom just as Decker had. Then Titon was alone with the four that would remain.

"Time for His Royalness to go," snickered Griss, Galinn and Hallon joining him with smirks of their own. "Don't slip on any loose rocks now."

Titon was suddenly grateful for Decker's previous threat. He thought of reminding them of it, but decided against it as it would make him look a weakling.

"Just remember all the signals," Titon said, "and we will all return home with the glory of victory. Pray I make it safely as well, as I may be the only one who knows the route home."

Griss gave him a mocking look. "We're to trace the canyon northeast from here to meet you where it flattens. From there it'd be more northeast to get home… We'd make it just fine without you." Griss beamed at him.

Titon returned Griss's stupid grin. "You sure about that?" he asked, quite sure that they would starve in the Dogmen wastes if that route was taken, especially without a successful raid.

"The Mountain's strength and the River's deftness be with you on your raids," said Dicun. "We will wait for you up canyon and help you to carry the plunder, brother."

"Aye." Titon was happy to at least have one man atop who did not want to see him dead. He tried to ignore both Griss and the knots in his stomach while he lowered himself over the edge.

The hardest part of passing the edge of the cliff to begin his descent was done, but no longer spurred by the faces of his peers, Titon found himself gripped with an uncertainty that bordered on terror. He gave two hurried tugs on the thin line, justifying the cowardly action to himself as merely a test of the response time of those above. His progress halted, and he could hear their laughter above.

The wind and the cold had only increased as each man had been lowered, and it grew dark as well. Gusts of air whipped up the mists from below, moistening his skin and freezing him to the point of sharp pain. He was already concerned about retaining full and proper use of his hands and knew he was better off descending with quickness. One tug later and he was once more being lowered, into the throat of the mist eager to swallow him, making it impossible to see even the rock wall just beneath his feet.

Titon panicked again as he realized there was no longer any tension on his harness line. He cursed the men above in his mind, too scared to make any actual sound, and attempted to concentrate on a way to survive. All his weight was now supported by his hands and legs wrapped around the static line. If they had released the harness line he would need to slide down the static line the remainder of the way, and he had barely gone any distance at all. He would run out of strength and die unless he slid painfully fast. He refused to slide down, however, fearing the rope burns, and started to lower himself carefully under the power of his arms. He was then stricken with the realization that if they wanted him dead— and they must if they had released the harness line—they would now be cutting the static line. Titon pictured what must be unfolding above: Dicun subdued by Galinn as Griss sawed strand by strand with a knife through the thick rope, Hallon merely looking on in horror. Titon loosened his grip, determined to slide down as fast as possible.

The jolt he received as his momentary plunge was halted by his harness shocked him.

You fool, he thought to himself. They had done as instructed and stopped feeding the harness line due to lack of tension as Titon clung to the static line so forcefully in his fright that he'd ceased descent. *I must put my trust in them and place weight upon my harness or I will not have the strength to reach the bottom.* He did as his thoughts commanded but kept his mind sharp in case he had to grab hold and stop a sudden fall. *And thank you, Dicun*, he added, in the case that Dicun's threats were all that kept Griss from treachery.

A rock came up beneath him without warning and bent Titon's ankle in an odd way. He jerked in shock as the jolt of pain shot up his leg. It immediately began to throb, but Titon could tell it was not broken. It was only a sprain. Such a minor thing would not have bothered him much on land, but every injury, no matter how small, seemed to foretell disaster at this height. Titon wondered if all the men had hit that very rock and injured themselves as such, then pictured Decker shoving himself away from the cliffside and enjoying every moment of his conquest. *Only an imbecile could take pleasure in this*, he reasoned with himself, secretly wishing for some of Decker's witless confidence.

More craggy ledges tried to break his legs, the rope began to eat as his skin of his hands, and the moisture in the air dampened him to the point of freezing, but after what felt like an endless ordeal, Titon heard hollering from below. The men had seen him as the mist gave way at the bottom and yelled in celebration. They were no doubt eager to begin what now had the potential to be the greatest raid their people had seen since the times when his father, Titon son of Small Gryn, still led them.

ALTHER

"And I would never awaken?" Alther asked.

"Those afflicted with slumberskull are doomed to a life of foul dreams." The elderly mender roughly placed his fingers about Alther's head while he spoke. "Or so we assume, since none awaken." A stab of pain went through Alther as the man pressed a bruised part of his scalp. "Please, be still."

"He was a madman," Alther overheard Crella say to the handful of members of The Guard in the other room. "He ripped the necklace off and struck me... Yes, his hand... Then he absconded—he ran... No, I did not recognize... Well, I suppose it could have been... I do not know all of the estate staff..."

"There are no signs of fracture," said the mender. "But you did suffer a good blow. You'll need to listen and remember my instruction—"

"Crella," Alther called to his wife.

"You should not raise your voice or exert yourself in any way," scolded the mender.

Crella entered the living area hurriedly. In addition to some minor bruising, she had a worry upon her face that was almost believable. "Will he be all right?" she asked of the mender.

"I was just explaining to your husband that he must remain awake for a full day, no less. I will have a tea brought that will aid in the task. A bitter tea, but it should be sipped regularly. Also..."

Enduring bitterness is a task I am adept at, thought Alther as the mender rattled on for several minutes.

"The tea," Crella said, "would there be any harm in my sharing in it?"

Alther found Crella's explanation of what had occurred—far fetched as it was—more plausible than the idea that she meant to stay up with him out of selfless concern. Alther had awoken after what she said was the better part of an hour, surrounded by guards. Her pearls were strewn about the floor, and she was overly distraught, repeating often how unfortunate it was that Stephon had so recently departed to stay with some of her friends, as he surely would have slain the assailant.

"It would do no harm," said the mender.

Hours later when the commotion had subsided and the two of them were left alone, she explained.

"I did not want them assigning you some little tart to stay with you all through the night."

Crella sat across from him in their living room, her cup approaching her lips and the plate in her hand unfortunately obstructing the view of her bust. *Had I ever told her that was my favorite of her dresses?* he wondered, admiring how the thin fabric revealed form without baring skin.

"No, I suppose not," Alther replied, a devious smile growing on his face. "For all your flaws, you never had an issue keeping me roused."

Something about having been told by a mender that he might never wake had given Alther new license. Should this be his last conscious night, he had no intentions of spending it in fear of his wife's rejections. After her charade with the questioners, in stark contrast with her current look of concern that appeared somehow honest, Crella no longer seemed so much the imposing Adeltian princess that he had always known. *She is perhaps as vulnerable as any other.*

"I am afraid you have had your wits knocked from your head. That is no way to speak to a lady." Crella took a hastened sip of her tea, clearly bothered. "And of what flaws exactly do you speak?"

"Oh, I would not wish to name them all. We are only to remain awake for one full day," he said, wondering in amazement why he'd never taken this tack before.

She blushed with anger. "I would slap you if not for your recent trauma. You have no right—"

He stood dismissively to interrupt. "I believe the heir to the throne can speak to his wife in any way he pleases. You forget your place."

"I am an Adeltian princess. Daughter of King Adellos II."

"That you are. But he is dead, and so is your aunt. It is my father, King of Rivervale, who now sits atop the throne. And without me you are just another pretty Adeltian girl. Have I not treated you well? And treated your daughter as if she were my own?"

It was incontrovertible that he had. Ethel was just a toddler when they were married, and Alther played the part of father well despite the embarrassment it caused and advice from his father to the contrary. Ethel, now nearly eighteen, lived in the Adeltian Throne where she attended a school for manners with other debutantes, all paid for by Alther.

"I would still be every bit as highborn as I always was," Crella said with certitude, but she changed the subject so quickly that it let Alther know his point had been made. "And you will be happy to know that after this incident with the bedlamite who stole my pearls and nearly killed you, I no longer have any desire to live here in Eastport. It simply is not safe."

Alther was surprised to hear her say as such but was also fully ready for her explanation of how she must return to the Throne to be closer to Ethel or something of that nature.

"And provided we can find somewhat decent accommodations in Westport, I will be willing to make the sacrifice," she finished.

This was not the Crella Alther knew. *What is it you are hiding?*

"Of course," he replied, unable to think of what else to say as he gazed out the window.

"Then there is the issue of the lady servants," said Crella.

"Do not worry about them." Alther walked back to his seat. "I will speak with Cassen personally and see the matter resolved."

Crella simply nodded. He knew she bore no love for the man. She only ever spoke poorly of him.

"While we are being completely honest with each other, there is one other thing I would like to ask you, my dear wife." Alther stared at her with all his newfound confidence, enjoying this unfamiliar role. "How is it that Stephon and I had broken our fast together this morning if he was with your friends?"

The blood visibly drained from Crella's face. *So it was Stephon. I'll need to have a talk with that boy.* Alther had not actually eaten with his son that morning, and having tricked his wife only further swelled his confidence. He could understand why his son had struck him. Alther had borne witness to fights between his own mother and father as a child. He knew what it was like to wish to intervene, though, of course, he never had. If Stephon had walked in at the wrong time and seen them grappling, he could have thought Alther posed a true threat to his mother's safety and acted to stop it. *Better a vase than a foil.*

After some time Crella finally responded. "You must be mistaken. You have suffered a bad blow to the head, and your recollection is askew."

"Yes, that must be. However…" Alther went completely serious. "It is important that none of the estate staff be wrongly accused of this crime. I will not stand for an innocent suffering punishment when the real malefactor yet roams. Do you understand my meaning?"

"Very well," said Crella, turning her head away, resigned.

Alther took the opportunity to study her nape's slender curve, as it met with her strong yet feminine jaw. She was truly beautiful, in spite of her manner, and he now felt he had a greater grasp on how best to deal with—if not finally conquer—her.

If a broken vase is the price of her amenability, perhaps I shall be buying her more flowers. The thought made him grin. It was the most Alther had smiled in his recent memory. He sipped his tea, enjoying both his new contentment and the lovely sight before him.

TITON SON OF SMALL GRYN

"So where exactly are we headed?"

It had been several days since their scuffle at the inn, and Titon had noticed a marked improvement in his friend's demeanor. Keethro seemed more eager to get in a few gibes of his own on Titon, and they were gladly received.

"South." Titon's response coincided with his march.

The terrain had changed as they headed out of foothills and into rolling plains. The ground was so flat and dry it was unnatural, and the path they walked was straight enough to see for miles down its barren length. On either side of them the vegetation varied between patches of thick spruce forest and open stretches of nothing but tall grass.

"Do you perhaps have a particular kingdom you would wish to see along the way?" Keethro asked in good humor.

Together they knew about the lands to the south what every Galatai knew, which was very little. They knew they shared the continent with at least two great kingdoms, one that was said to be of the rivers and the other of a great delta at the foot of the Eos.

"I would hope to find the kingdom of the delta, but I will settle for the kingdom of the rivers if we come across it first. It makes no difference to me where we find the proper elixirs, so long as we find them."

"Would it be too soon to ask for help finding such places?" Titon did not need to look at Keethro to know he'd posed the question with a jovial expression.

They had their reasons for not yet seeking aid in direction. The farther north they were, the more likely the people were to be frightened of Northmen, yet toward the south, Titon's appearance would be more of an oddity than an immediate threat. They also simply did not wish to look foolish. More specifically, Titon did not wish to look foolish. Keethro had wanted to ask someone for guidance for some time now, not that they'd had many such opportunities.

"No, I suppose not. We will ask the next traveler we see."

"Ha," replied Keethro. "Fair enough."

Since having left Phylan they had seen only one other pair of travelers. It looked to be a man and a child, but they did not get close enough to see. Titon and Keethro had separated from the trail by several miles while the two went past. Better to have fewer people see where they were headed in case word got out about a handsome man and a giant having killed some thugs in a dirty inn.

He would not let Keethro see, but Titon himself was growing impatient. Capable though they were at hunting and foraging for food, Titon would have preferred the expedience of simply buying some. Their coin purses, heavy-laden from years of raiding Dogmen, were of little use in these lifeless plains. Titon estimated the near three hundred and fifty marks they had started with would keep them fed for a few months, if not years. Some reassurance that they were headed toward an inhabited location would have been welcome, as the path they traveled gave no such indication.

Hours later, the Dawnstar's glow turned the plains of tall grass to a sea of gold.

"Our goats would grow fat in such a place," said Keethro.

"Hmph…" Titon stopped to look around. "So would we. Winter is taking root, yet there is snow only on the fingers of the pines."

Keethro continued down the path a ways but stopped as well, turning to face him. "Perhaps a fourth god exists in these lands, a god of fire who warms the very ground."

Titon scowled with honest anger. Keethro was never one to show much respect for the Mighty Three, and Titon was no fan of his blasphemy. *You'll condemn us both with such speech.*

Keethro apologized quickly. "A foolish thing to say and said in jest. There are surely only three, and we will need their support if we are to brave this path without dying of boredom."

Having received no response, Keethro dropped all jocularity and raised his hands in innocence, but Titon's attention had been drawn elsewhere. "I meant no disres—"

"Do you see that?" Titon pointed past Keethro into the distance.

"What kind of beast is that?" asked Keethro.

The two men stared down the road at silhouettes they could not identify. There were no animals in the North that would give a pair of armed Galatai warriors cause to run and hide, but these were larger than a full-grown elk, and their antlers moved as if alive, pointing toward them. By the time they realized the silhouettes were those of men upon beasts it was obvious they too had been spotted.

"We should hide in the grass. These are not men I would seek direction from," said Keethro.

"It is too late for that. If they mean us harm they will pursue us." Titon resumed moving forward to meet them, hoping for the best.

"Halt." The man atop his horse spoke with authority. Though there were none in the Northluns, Titon knew of horses and had realized what they were upon getting close enough to see their manes.

Keethro and Titon obeyed. *Perhaps halt is a common greeting in the South,* Titon seethed to himself, *but I do not like this man's tone.*

"Hello, men," said Titon, his voice making the horses uneasy. There were three riders, armed with spears. Their horses were adorned with fabric bearing an identical scene of the Dawnstar rising above grassy plains, its rays emanating in all directions.

"Who goes there?" asked the same man.

Titon looked at Keethro who shrugged.

"We are headed to the kingdom of the delta." Titon hoped his response would answer the man's question.

"I don't have time for games. Who the feck are you?"

"I am Titon son of Small Gryn—who the feck are *you*?" Titon roared back. He was not used to being treated like an impotent fool, nor did he have any intention of forming such an acquaintance.

"I'm the law out here, you common shit. Now throw down your arms or I'll stick you like the giant boar you are." The man raised his spear as if ready to strike, and his two companions did the same.

Titon suddenly wished he had brought his axes. Both he and Keethro had left them behind for fear of attracting too much unwanted attention. A hunting bow and knives were all the weaponry they had, but Titon figured they would have some spears soon enough the way this was headed. He was more concerned about the horses than the men. *I wonder if they bite.*

Titon yelled and charged, driving his shoulder into the chest of the lead man's horse. He had intended to grab the spear and fend off the horse, but rather than biting a chunk out of Titon's neck, the horse reared, sending its rider crashing to the ground with such violence that he was not like to be of any threat for the moment.

The second man, a boy no older than Titon's sons, urged his animal forward, shouting something about the light. Titon retrieved the fallen man's spear in time to parry the boy's attack, at which point his senseless yelling turned into girlish shrieks. An arrow had sprouted from his eye, and Titon wasted no time finishing him with a spear through his soft leathern tunic.

The third man was already galloping away from them on his horse. Titon stumbled for his bow but had lost his arrows in the commotion. Keethro looked to be gauging the wind as he took his time aiming at the fast-riding man, finally loosing an arrow. The metal of the sharpened tip flickered as it spun, catching the Dawnstar's low rays. The arrow arced downward, finding a home far to the right of its intended target in some distant grass. Keethro shrugged as Titon stared at him in disbelief.

"I'm better with axes," said Keethro.

"You shot that one right in the eye."

"I was aiming for his chest," said Keethro with enough candor to be believed.

Watching the man gallop into the setting Dawnstar, no doubt going to raise a small army, Titon had to laugh.

The man who was thrown off the horse, the mouthy one, was still alive, wheezing noisily. Titon approached him and put the spearpoint to his neck as he lay on his back.

"Who is your king?" Titon demanded.

The man looked confused. "You are?"

Keethro chuckled, but Titon was already losing patience. "What kingdom are you from, and who rules it?"

"I am from Castle Strahl…" Titon pushed the spear hard against his neck to get him to hurry. "We are part of Kingdom Rivervale where Duke Veront sits. But King Lyell rules both kingdoms from the Adeltian Throne. He is king."

It sounded a bit too complicated to be believable, and Titon was afraid the man was trying to make a fool of him.

"Where will I find elixirs?" Titon asked him.

"Elixirs?"

Titon was at his wit's end and plunged his spear through the man's bowels. He screamed out in pain and pleaded for Titon not to kill him.

"Where would I go if I wanted to have you healed?" he asked the man.

"A mender, please, take me to a mender!"

"*Where,* you damn fool?" Titon cried in anger.

"Strahl!"

"What direction?" Titon asked, eager to finally be getting some useful information.

The man pointed toward where he and his friends had come, the same way Titon and Keethro had already been traveling.

Titon drove the spear through the man's skull with a crunch. "We go to Strahl."

ETHEL

It was a night eagerly anticipated, a night to be celebrated and cherished by all. All except Ethel, of course.

A myriad of candles, each with their own silken shade, cast a faint glow from their crystalline perches high above. Below were dark wood floors, waxed and polished to a gleaming shine, the marks and scuffs from the small army required to light the chandeliers having been erased.

Standing atop the floor, dressed in pastel shades, were the finest and most reputable debutantes of the Adeltian Throne, and thus the Adeltian Kingdom. Scattered among them were the men, some equally young and some much older, who courted them. Unobtrusive music wove through the ballroom, created by a small orchestra tucked away in a sounding corner, and tables were adorned with Adeltian and Rivervalian delicacies that were as much art to the eye as to the tongue. There were cherries, first marinated in Spiceland rum, then filled with thick cream and coated in dark chocolate; there were sugary cookies flavored with mint and citrus, in the shape of the petals of the orange blossom; and there were hundred-layer pastries, shaped as shells that protected a mildly sweet cheese within as an oyster guards a pearl.

Extravagant balls such as these took place with some frequency; however, this particular event was in celebration of Mazelina, a girl Ethel knew well. The two looked quite similar, truth be told. Both had long hair of dark golden waves that glimmered even in the dimmest light, facial features denoting that of elegance and status, and long slender frames. They could have been mistaken for mirrored siblings if not for their two blatant dissimilarities. Whereas Ethel stood of average height for a woman, Mazelina stood a head taller. Whereas Ethel's cheeks had natural lines, Mazelina's had pronounced dimpling. Both height and dimpling were said to be renowned qualities in a young woman, and early on Ethel had envied those very features possessed by her rival that she herself was without. But as time progressed, Ethel found herself politely refusing some suitors of quality, all far too old for her to have ever found attractive, whereas the only suitors Mazelina had to decline until today were so far beneath her station that it was somewhat of an insult that they had even thought to pursue her.

It was, in fact, rather embarrassing for a girl to reach her eighteenth year and have a ball thrown in her honor. Though the initial intent of such a celebration was to show a young lady in her best light and at the ripest age in the hopes of attracting a mate, it was now perceived more as a final act of desperation, one in which the girl would often settle for an older man, as the most sought-after girls all had suitors begging for their hand no later than age sixteen. But Mazelina, refusing to be rid of her heel-raising footwear, towered over most of the men in attendance and yet seemed unable to garner interest from any but the shortest and least comely. Ethel almost pitied her, but reminded herself that their differences were not just in appearance. Mazelina was a girl of quick temper and slow wit, traits no man much admired.

A pair of girls walked Ethel's way, almost as if they planned to speak to her. Their path veered from Ethel's lonely corner, however, keeping at a safe distance, smirking at her as they passed. Ethel smirked back only on the inside and made no effort to remember their names as she once did. Her lust for spiteful vengeance on her peers had long since died.

A hush fell over the crowd as members of The Guard entered, their presence possibly signifying some emergency. Ethel scanned the room and noticed pairs of guards had appeared at regular intervals along the second story's inner balcony as well. Her mother had told Ethel more than once how it had been members of The Guard who had delivered her to their Rivervalian conquerors, having quickly changed allegiances once the kingdom had fallen. *That cannot be the case now*, Ethel said to herself, attempting to calm her beating heart. *There is no one who would threaten our kingdom.*

The cause for their presence was made known when Lyell entered the ballroom. The king had come to only a handful of these events since taking the throne sixteen years past, and each time he had forgone the usual fanfare of trumpets. Since he was without a queen it was expected that he would have attended more regularly until he found a new wife to sit beside him. To most of the girls, the lack of flourish and infrequency of his appearances seemed to add a certain mystique to the elderly man of power. It was not so with Ethel. To her he would always be the loathsome grandfather-by-marriage who despised her.

Any pity Ethel had for Mazelina quickly vanished. Having the king show at one's ball was a great honor, raising the girl's status and increasing competition among suitors. The thought of the king choosing to favor a girl who looked so similar to Ethel herself left her feeling somewhat unsettled and dirty. As the king disappeared into the crowd of young ladies, Ethel hoped it would be the last she saw of the man that night.

Ethel's gaze passed over the remainder of the room. Clusters of people stood together, no fewer than three to a group. She knew all the girls, having attended lessons with them, and most of the boys, if only by reputation. It was not that Ethel was entirely without friends; she had several hundred friends, confidantes from her youth, gathered together on trays atop the tables. It seemed a cruel matter that the delicacy tables were the only place she could loiter within a crowd without causing the other guests to disperse for fear of being associated with her—the very place she would allow herself only a single trip and for just a taste. It was not out of necessity that she practiced this discipline. As her mother had promised, Ethel had slimmed as she grew taller, though without any change in habit—tonight she had planned her usual two slices of yellow cake accompanied with frozen milk. But the chiding of her youth yet remained, in spite of her figure. *I will not give them the pleasure*, she told herself, looking about the room at her many detractors, though the chocolate-covered cherries bade her come and keep them company.

Having caught a glimpse of Griffin, Ethel turned her eyes downward. With her youthful plumpness no longer able to be blamed, it was perhaps even more cruel that he still refused to acknowledge her presence. That he had ascended social rank and gained popularity so rapidly after disowning her only worsened the hurt. As whatever girl Griffin currently favored passed Ethel in the hall, smiling repugnantly, it was little respite to know she would be able to mirror that smile if she wished, after Griffin had moved on to the next girl.

Another renowned guest was making his entrance known, distracting Ethel from her solitary plight. The wealthy middle-aged man rarely missed a ball but was never seen, nor expected to be seen, pursuing any of the young women. Surrounded by several of his own ladies, Cassen strode in with all the ostentatiousness that one would expect from the Duchess of Eastport.

It would seem both the king and queen are in attendance tonight. Ethel tittered in silence at the blasphemy of her thoughts and studied the demure girls accompanying Cassen. All three were of or below average height and petitely built, but while two had the fair skin common among Adeltians, the other had an olive-colored complexion that Ethel found intriguing.

Ethel had little need for the typical services a lady servant would provide, yet she had long dreamed of having one such lady to fill a more desperate void. Seeming to read her thoughts, Cassen turned her way, and it was not long before he, in all his silks and glory, was upon her.

CASSEN

"Good evening, Lady Ethel," said Cassen.

Ethel performed a diminutive but elegant curtsey. "Duchess Cassen, how pleasant to see you again."

Cassen studied her face. *You hide your hatred for me better than your mother.*

"I hope my presence is not scaring off too many potential suitors, but my taste for the exquisite makes it difficult for me to avoid going straight for the most radiant diamond when I see it." Cassen found there was no better way to win the trust of a young highborn girl than with embellished compliments, but in this case it was almost sincere.

"If I did not know better, I would assume you were pursuing my hand in marriage, if not at the very least a dance," said Ethel.

"No, I am afraid I am not built properly for either of those tasks," Cassen said with a false simper. "The best I can do is drape myself with silks and hope their buoyant grace will somehow distract from my lack thereof." Ethel did not seem to find his self-deprecation as humorous as most noble girls, always eager to consort in some form of derogation. "So do tell me, why is it that you, in all your loveliness, stand here alone, bereft of any suitors bearing proper equipment?"

"I had pegged you for a smarter man, Cassen. It no doubt has something to do with my birth parents, the details of which escape my mind at the moment. Was it on my mother's side or the side of my father? I can never quite remember."

Ethel's ditzy girl charade was entertaining to Cassen despite the fact that she referred to him as a man. *The ones who see me as a man are the ones that must be watched the closest.*

"Then they are fools. Had I a son, I would instruct him to pursue you to the edges of the realm." Cassen made a dismissive gesture with his hand toward a group of young men who loitered in a corner.

"It makes no difference to me. Most of them are arrogant fools that I would have no interest in."

Now there is a lie.

"Ah, but arrogant confidence is more oft rewarded with success than is humble indecision." Cassen hoped to get her to disagree on account of principle.

"Fultaer?"

"I beg your pardon?" Cassen asked, somewhat in disbelief.

"Are you in the habit of quoting others to impress young girls at such events?" Ethel's own confidence was near off-putting.

"I did not know young girls were taught philosophy in schools of manners."

"Young girls can read books the same as old men."

"And do you agree with that which I have plagiarized?" *You can remember the words, but can you comprehend them?*

Ethel's response was delayed as she surveyed the room. "It certainly looks as though it is the most arrogant and cocksure of the men, both young and old, that woo my fellow debutantes."

Ethel suddenly looked as radiant as the diamond he had originally accused her of being. *I will make you an ally, or at the very least I will keep you contained.*

"How perceptive you are, my young lady. And please forgive my rudeness for not having yet introduced my own ladies. With me tonight are the young ladies Amalee, Mollie, and Annora."

The three lady servants curtsied in turn when their names were said. *Now to convince you that you need one. And to think, if I am successful, how it will anger your mother. Perhaps she will break another vase atop Alther's head.* Cassen's pleased expression was more for the thought than for his pride in his ladies' graceful display.

"I am honored," Ethel said to the ladies. "It is known throughout the kingdom how coveted your services are. It is much to the Throne's detriment that such services are only available in Eastport." Ethel had dropped her sardonic tone, pleasing Cassen to know she may be speaking with honesty.

"Yes, that is normally the case, as it is known that the ladies must return to my care and protection shortly after dark. But it is not without precedent that a lady servant could remain in the service of a fellow lady of nobility, provided she were living in the absence of men." *Would that interest our little friendless bookworm?*

"It would have to be Annora." Ethel seemed to shock even herself with her forwardness as Cassen observed she moved to put her hand over her mouth and stopped mid-gesture.

How did I know one diamond would seek the other?

"I am afraid that most likely cannot be arranged." Cassen delivered the words with feigned reluctance. "Annora currently has a patron, you see."

"It must be her," said Ethel, this time with conviction. She may not be like most of the debutantes here, but Cassen knew stubbornness was bred into all highborn girls.

"You put me in a terrible spot." Cassen did his best to look troubled. "I will see what I can do—as a favor to you and your family—but I cannot make any promises. All I ask in return is that you put in a good word for me with your mother. I fear she despises me without cause, and I am powerless to correct it."

"I will," said Ethel. "That I promise you."

"Very well. Annora must return with me tonight, but you two can dawdle in the meantime."

Ethel did another quick curtsey and motioned for her new servant friend to come join her. Annora looked to Cassen, and he nodded his approval. Cassen watched what he believed to be the second and third most beautiful gems of the kingdom make their way toward the delicacy tables.

TITON SON OF TITON

A thick crust of frost blanketing the fallen leaves made silent travel near impossible as they approached the Dogman village. Snow clung to the western side of the many slender guardians, some birch and the other a type of oak that grew oddly straight and tall. The trees would have formed a natural barrier had they been any closer together. Large webs, gilded in ice and absent spiders, hung ominously between the trees.

"Never attack Dogmen at night," Titon's father had told him. "They are so weak and pathetic that you are more like to suffer casualties caused by your own men striking each other in the darkness than of a Dogman managing to fight back. And their demon-dogs can see in total darkness."

Titon wondered how true those words were—any of them. This village did not appear as though it was built by weaklings or idiots. The construction of their homes was sound, and their efficient use of the land for crops impressed him. He had heard so many stories about the impotence of these people that he now feared it may have all been bluster; there was certainly no shortage of it among his people, he was learning.

He had with him just over twenty men, and while a few such as Decker may have justified counting as double, the potential existed for as many as forty men to be in this village, strong after a good night's rest and just now preparing to go outside for a hard day's work. By contrast his people had barely slept, kept up by the giddiness of the prospect of drawing their first Dogman blood.

"Remember, men," whispered Titon, "Keep your range. Do not close on an armed Dogman when you can kill him from afar."

"Yes," said Decker. "Listen to my brother. I may not need your help killing these Dogmen, but I will need you all to help carry back the plunder, so try and stay alive."

The men gave a hushed chuckle, putting Titon on edge with the unnecessary noise. *None of this feels right*, he thought. *I merely wish for it to be over.*

"We creep upon them until detected," Titon further instructed. "Only then do we charge or make a sound. Do not enter a home without a partner to watch your back, and do not turn your back on an occupied home from which someone could spring and attack you."

The group nodded in anxious approval, and they all began to creep forward. With a growing sickness in his gut, Titon wondered if perhaps it would have been a better tactic for the leaders to stay toward the rear so that he could more easily direct the assault and call out orders if need be, but it was too late for that.

They fanned out with crunching footsteps that would wake the dead, and surrounded the first several homes. Titon had predicted they would have been detected already. That they had not been made his nerves build to the point of trembling. The sound of a door being smashed released his tension, replaced by anger at his men for defying orders.

He had expected to hear the sound of husky war cries associated with battle, but what he heard was far different. His own men had remained silent, and the air was filled with the horrific shrieks of those they attacked. The men, women, and children all sounded equally hysterical as they screamed, not for help or to alert their fellow villagers, but with no apparent justification other than to grate their attackers with such caustic noise that they might end their lives sooner. And indeed it seemed to be working.

One by one the shrieks heard from those in the nearer homes were silenced. Decker burst through the door of the home he and Titon were upon, revealing within it a man, a woman, and a crone, all standing and in their undergarments with hands extended in front of them as if to fend off blows. The woman wasted no time taking to shrieking, and the man fell backward onto the bed they shared, cowering. Decker was upon them. He threw a small axe, which smashed the man in the head with the blunt end, and followed up with his large axe to cleave the Dogman near in half. Decker then went for the woman, who was about as attractive as her husband was brave, and took off her head. The older woman had managed to arm herself with a knife and, to her credit, moved toward Decker as if to stab him. Titon flung his axe. It embedded itself in the side of her head, killing her instantly.

Titon stared at the picture of gore before them. The younger woman's headless corpse spurted blood from the neck as it had fallen backwards against the wall. The man who had been sliced from the left of his neck to his right hip had organs, blood, and feces spilling out onto his bed. The old woman he himself had killed was crumpled on the floor, his axe still in her skull.

"Get your axe. We move," said Decker.

Titon complied. As he pulled his axe from the feeble old woman, the only of the three to effect any form of offense, he wondered if indeed his father had spoke truly about these people. It was hard for Titon to imagine even his comatose mother putting up less of a fight than did the man of this home.

After stepping outside the safety of the wooden walls, Titon felt the twinges one had when fearful that at any moment a projectile may come and strike him. These Dogmen, now undoubtedly alerted to their presence, would have bows, though Titon had yet to see sign of any such threat. A well-placed arrow could spell the end for even a beast such as Decker. Titon's men ignored his rule of only breaking into homes with partners, as the bloodthirsty among them who had missed out on the first homes were eager to ensure they got their kills. It would be embarrassing for any of them to have to admit they had not managed to help in the battle, and Galatai did not lie about their headcounts. Members of their party darted off alone after the few men and women who chose to flee on foot rather than barricade themselves inside. Others chopped through doors that had been locked and fortified, sending splinters flying with blows from their axes.

Titon spotted a broad-shouldered Dogman who appeared to be putting up a fight. The man had a knife in one hand and a pitchfork in the other, and had already dodged or deflected a few poorly-thrown axes. The Dogman flung his knife, barely missing his attacker, a boy Titon recognized from the back as Arron. Titon lobbed an axe at the man from thirty paces away, hoping that he would not move much during the time it would take to arrive. The man moved left, then right again, and Titon's axe sliced into his shoulder causing him to drop his pitchfork and grasp at his wound. Arron was on the man at once with his heavy axe, a weapon that had proven surprisingly ineffective versus the length of the pitchfork, and finished him off with a blow that split his skull. Arron gave Titon a thankful nod.

"Titon," called Decker from nearby. He was poised to break into the closest home but had waited for Titon's attention.

The rest of the battle proceeded with little difference. Every door they broke down hid only cowards. The most difficult part was catching those villagers who fled their homes, but so few chose to do so that it was possible they may have managed to kill every inhabitant. Any that had escaped their grasp would likely die of exposure.

"The first of many victories, brother," Decker said with conquest. Through the battle Decker had never left his side—a thing Titon found surprising. He'd expected Decker would want to brag of having killed as many men as possible.

Titon cleared his throat to ensure his words would not come out squeaky. "Are there any wounded?"

There came no replies.

"Are there any still hungry?" shouted Decker. The cries of affirmation that returned his question were overwhelming.

As he surveyed the men, Titon was surprised to find that none had wounds worse than small cuts or deep bites probably suffered upon engaging in carnal combat with the Dogmen women.

Never before having seen a person killed by a thrown axe, Titon had often wondered how destructive such an attack would be. Now that he had his answer, his mind was not at ease. The sound of his axe cracking into the brittle skull of the old woman remained in his ears, and he was unable to replace it with thoughts of the throw that may have saved Arron from injury.

"Titon, over here," yelled Decker with elation in his voice.

It was what they had come for. They'd broken into what must have been a very rich man's cellar. There was more food than Titon could recall ever having seen stored in a single location. This slaughter had not been without purpose. The survival of his people through the coming winter was now ensured.

❦

"Four days of raiding and you have not yet taken a woman," said Decker.

Both Titon and his brother had blood spattered upon their clothes and carried bags full of meats, cheeses, and vegetables. Their side entrance into the canyon landed them into the richest Dogmen farms imaginable—rich in provisions, at least. Titon had still not found any of the jewelry or gems he sought that would allow him to keep his promise to Red. There were not even many of the demon-dogs their parents had told them stories of, and the ones that they had come across did not seem to Titon much like demons. It was mainly goats and pigs, farms and farmers, and none particularly good at defending what they had. Only one of their crew had been slain so far, and that was due to infighting over a wheel of cheese.

"But neither have I. I believe only the most desperate among us have. These Dogmen bitches are far uglier than I could have imagined!" Decker barked with laughter to drive home his point.

Even Titon had to chuckle at the observation, though he did not believe it to be true—at least not the part about Decker having taken no women as of yet. Unlovely though they may have been, Titon had seen Decker exiting a home with the need to retie his trousers, something rarely required after standard combat.

"Do you enjoy this, brother? The killing?" Titon asked.

"Eh. It is little more than slaughtering livestock," said Decker with a shrug. "The only difference is we eat their supplies and not their flesh."

Titon had found killing Dogmen to be crude and unsavory work, but nonetheless, it was empowering knowing how easy it was to take from these men all they had. The harsh training their father had put Decker and him through seemed to have more purpose now that he saw the results of those who went without such preparation.

"That does not mean I would not enjoy killing, should I find a man worthy of my axe," added Decker.

With these words still echoing, the brothers crested a hill, and saw in the distance a solitary woman standing outside a small home. As a hawk can see a mouse from beyond a mile, so can a man see a woman who is of proper form and proportion. All of the men stopped and took notice that the figure in the distance did not share the same hunched back, oversized hips, or any other of the traits that seemed to plague the women in this region. From the corner of his eye, Titon could see Decker give him a nod, the meaning of which was clear. Titon did not expect himself to have been so quick to action, but he found he was sprinting toward the woman, hoping her face was as comely as her silhouette. Toward his rear he could hear his brother yelling, "To the victor, the spoils!" along with the hoots of the other men.

As he closed upon her, she did not flee. Her mind appeared to be trapped elsewhere, and she did not even seem to notice him nor look in his direction.

Perhaps she is simple. Not that it mattered. He would have his way with her just the same and think of Red all the while. It was the compromise he'd come up with to maintain an ideal of faith to her while still doing what was expected of him as a leader of men.

He was quite relieved to see she was indeed beautiful. She was perhaps of a mother's age but certainly had a maiden's figure. Her long brown hair was cared for every bit as well as Red's, and her face had the glow of youth. Her eyes, however, carried in them an incredible depth of sadness. Somehow he knew that look, and it turned his stomach.

He grabbed her by the hair and dragged her inside. Titon then went from room to room in search of some sign of wealth. A woman as fair as this was sure to have some jewelry.

The home had a strong fire burning in the large stone hearth but reeked of demon-dogs. This was a home of those who slept with their foul creatures beside them, but the animals were nowhere to be seen. The mantles and shelves were cluttered with knickknacks, mostly ordinary stones that gave Titon a sinking feeling. These Dogmen were a strange people to put the prettiest among them in a tiny home adorned with worthless rocks, but he put the thought aside and bore down on the task at hand.

The woman struggled now, but slowly and weakly as a person might do while dreaming. He put her face closer to his so he could look upon her and stir himself to action, but the utter despondency he saw in her eyes again sickened him in spite of her lovely features. In a rage he threw her, face down, upon a small table in what looked to be the home's kitchen. He could feel her firm form trapped beneath him, and he became more than ready for what must be done. He readjusted his grip on her hair, exposing her neck and ears, and yanked her head back with violence.

An image appeared in Titon's mind, one most unsettling given the circumstances: his mother's face, young and smiling. With outstretched arms she bade her new toddler approach her. Decker crawled to their mother through the lush grass of summer where he paused, lifted a knee, and stood. With bumbling steps, and undaunted by their father's roar of laughter, Decker slogged his way toward their mother, the breeze pulling at her hair. Titon flinched as if caught in mischief when his mother's eyes then darted toward him, accusingly. And there her final conscious gaze lingered, captivated by some unknown force, unwilling or unable to glance at Decker as he reached her.

An overwhelming feeling of abhorrence flooded Titon as he returned to the present, his focus again on the woman he had pinned to the table.

Her ears, those small, slightly-pointed ears, the look of dejection in her eyes, the near-catatonic state, they were all so familiar because they were identical to the features of his own mother. They did not share the same face, nor color of hair, but the similarities they bore were unmistakable. Without thinking, Titon removed his knife and opened her neck with a single slice. *Like you should have done years ago, Father.*

Blood fountained out her wounded throat and upon the wooden floor. The house seemed to be growing smaller, trapping Titon inside. Scant relief came moments later when he saw that she had succumbed, but Titon still felt just as eager to be gone from this home.

He ransacked the few rooms of the house, hoping to find a hidden compartment or lockbox, but the most valuable item in the entire structure seemed to be a near worthless flint. Forced to check the woman's body as a last resort, he found only an ill-fitting ring of crude metal on her finger. *Perhaps Red will be touched by the sentiment,* he thought. A ring of metal was after all a difficult thing to make and was only given by a man to a woman if he intended to bed no others. Crude that it may have been, it was obvious someone had spent many hours toiling to shape its pattern. It was better, he supposed, than coming back empty-handed.

The men made noise outside now, and they would surely wish to go through the belongings themselves to see if Titon had left anything of value. Titon tore the woman's skirts to give the appearance of what had been expected. Then he put on his best fake grin of accomplishment and walked out of the home to be greeted by the half-taunting, half-cheering men to whom he felt no kinship. *If this is all the glory of victory,* he thought, *I should surely hope to never taste defeat.*

TALLOS

Tallos knew little of his father's faith to which he had tried to be true, only what his mother had told him. He knew that one should not piss in a river, one should not sleep through the rising of the Dawnstar, and one must bury the bodies of the dead so they can return to the Mountain. He had obeyed all these laws of the three gods of his father. In return, they had taken from him everything.

Seemingly without effort, Tallos had also abided by all the tenets of the Faith, the religion of his fellow villagers: one should be kind and giving to one's fellow man, one should be clean of mind and body, one should maintain monogamy and faithfulness to one's spouse, and one must never eat nor burn the flesh of man. There were others, but these were the core beliefs shared by all villagers…and often abided the least by those who proclaimed themselves to be most pious.

And so he watched as the home he built with his wife and shared with his faithful companion began to burn. Great clouds of black smoke billowed as the tar packed between the logs caught fire, filling the sky with the taint of his hatred while he remembered what he had found within.

Why she was still inside when he had returned, he did not know. The door in the kitchen, the one that led to a narrow vine-covered pathway, able to be barred from the outside, remained unbroken. The front door had also not been broken or dislodged in any way. *You let them inside?* Tallos thought, unable to understand. *What were you thinking?*

His despair had turned to fury as he'd sat with her on the blood-covered floor, squeezing her cold body in his arms. He would never forgive himself for having left her, but he wondered if he could forgive her for not having done what together they had so carefully planned. He sought more reasons to justify his anger towards her, or at least to explain what to him made no sense. The house was in disarray, but the table he found her on still had objects upon it. *Did you not even fight your attackers?* Tallos's rage overtook him. *Did you enjoy it, you whore?*

Tallos shook his head violently as he rid himself of his spiteful thoughts. He shamed himself and apologized to his wife in his arms for even having momentarily had them. The men who attacked their village were savages; they had likely ambushed her while outside, and they had surely killed her before raping her—he desperately hoped that was the case. It was known to occur. Sobbing uncontrollably, he clutched her body tight against his own. *I am sorry,* he told her again and again, realizing no amount of sorries could ever atone. *I am the one to blame.* Leona had all but begged him not to leave, and he'd answered her pleas with frustration and anger. He thought of how she had looked the day he left, the last image of her that he would forever keep. Even when angry with him, she still somehow gave him her backing. The same aura that had surrounded her as a young washwoman had never diminished over their many years together. Now it had been debased and snuffed out in the cruelest way imaginable. He thought of how she blushed when he had tricked her into baring her breast during a dip in the brook, the trust in her eyes when she unpacked her belongings in their first tiny hut, having left her family, and the work and pride they'd shared upon completing their current home. He thought also of when he brought her to meet Lia at the muddy riverbank. The memories tore at him.

Flames leapt to the roof where they danced defiantly, consuming in an instant the thatching that Leona had woven so perfectly as to always keep them dry, even during the worst of storms. The roof collapsed, sending an explosion of embers into the air that drifted with demonic grace. They would be burning now, Leona and Lia. It hurt him to know, but he embraced the pain. He needed their memory erased for his sanity. He needed to burn it out of the world and out of himself, but it would not yet let him be.

As he had sat on the kitchen floor with Leona, he'd heard a faint cry, and, for a moment, he had let himself believe it could be his wife. Putting her at arm's length, searching for some sign of hope, all he saw was the same lifeless corpse with the smiling wound on its neck. It was no longer the wife he had loved. It was a laughing husk, a horrible reminder of what he'd had and what he'd thrown away, but he was as gentle with her body as if she were merely unconscious as he laid her down, not wanting to leave her. Hearing the cry again, he sunk yet deeper.

He found Lia lying in front of the hearth as he had left her. She was saturated in blood, some dry and some still sticky wet. The bandage he had made for her was not adequate to staunch the flow. The trickle had all but ceased only due to her now having so little left to lose. Without the strength left to lift her head, her eyes begged him to fix her. Clinging to life, she looked confused as to why he had waited so long to pull the thorn from her paw, to give her relief. There was nothing he could do to save her, however. She was far worse than he had expected. Even with a flint and quick fire his efforts likely would have resulted only in lengthening her torment. He had only to end her suffering or watch her slowly die, and having had made a promise to himself to never again avoid the path of action, he removed the knife from his belt. But as he saw the dull luster of his small blade, he could not help but imagine it to be little different than the one used to kill Leona. He could not cut Lia's throat. Loss of blood did not kill as quickly as one might think. It would simply cause her more pain.

"I am sorry, girl," he'd sobbed with tears in his eyes. He stroked her head where she had no wounds, trying to comfort her as he put his head beside hers. But she had lacked the strength to lick his face. "I'm going to help you."

Lia's breaths came rapid and labored as she foolishly fought to stay alive so that he could save her. Unable to bear allowing her to hurt any longer, he hoisted the iron kettle from the hearth above his head, wishing she'd look away, though she did not. He peered into her sad, confused eyes one final time. Images of her as a pup dirtying Leona's dress on their first meeting barraged him. The horrific injustice too much to bear, he'd screamed out with rage and fury when the deed was done, hoping it would stir the very gods that had forsaken him.

Tallos turned away from the house and the horrible memories sealed inside. With outstretched arms he backed closer toward the inferno. Heat surged from the source and scorched his naked skin, causing it to redden. The fine hairs on his arms were the first to be singed to nothingness, filling the air with an acrid stench. Leaning his head back, he allowed all the hair remaining atop his head to shrivel and smoke, until his scalp was seared, as was the rest of his back, his legs, and the tops of his arms. He moved closer still as flames licked at him, causing his skin to broil and blister. He remained there, listening to the hissing of the boiling fluid as his blisters burst open. Unable to wash out the agony and suffering he had endured with tears, he welcomed the cleansing pain, his only respite, as his vision turned to red.

THE ISLAND GIRL
Years Ago

"She's Cassen's property."

Annora pressed her ear to the dank wood of the door, desperate to hear more of the conversation that would determine her fate.

"So she is," came the voice of the viler man. "And even more reason for us to have a taste. I'd give her a lesson in obedience that cockless daint is unable to teach."

As best Annora could tell, they'd been sailing for no more than three days, yet the green crystal seas and white powder beaches of her people's islands seemed forever distant. These foreign men spoke with a coarse accent tinged with menace. And when they had stared at her prior to cramming her into this closet that now served as her cabin, she felt their eyes defiling her.

How have you been so foolish to arrive here? she demanded of herself. Annora had always wished to leave her home, to be free from her father's rage and her mother's ambivalence. Now, however, she found herself longing to be sheltered by them—not the parents she had always known them to be, but the generous, pleasant people they had transformed into months earlier. It was a front, she knew, yet she'd allowed herself to enjoy those weeks leading up to the event, her father showering her with gifts and her mother smiling with pride. *What did you expect would happen when you disgraced them so horribly? That your life would return to normal?*

Not allowing her ear to part from the door, Annora felt around in the darkness for anything sharp. It would be little good as a weapon against the countless men aboard this ship, but she could use a piece of glass or rusty nail on herself, dragging it from eye to lip just as she should have done before. It would have precluded her from having to become one of the many wives had by their island king, and with far less shame brought to her family than the method she had chosen in its stead. She feared, though, even a horrific scar may not be enough to prevent these foreigners from the acts their leers promised.

"You think all he teaches them is how to tidy things? It makes no difference, though. If his cargo is touched, Cassen will bar this ship from Eastport. Then the captain will have us both keelhauled—until barnacles have stripped us of flesh."

Annora almost started as she felt the door bow inward, creaking against the weight of a man. Far closer than she ever wished to be, she could hear his breathing now, but she did not retreat from her place at the door.

"No one has to know," he said, near a whisper.

The other man made an angry noise. "I've heard enough. There are others for you to toy with. Leave this one be, or we'll both pay the price."

As the parting man's footsteps faded, Annora was left alone with the wheezy breather, her door still bearing his weight.

"But those ones have no life left in their eyes." The man spoke with a sullen honesty that served to worsen Annora's nausea and worry.

The sharp sound of splintering wood shot through the door, causing the hairs upon her arms to stand. He was only picking stray slivers from the surface of the door, she realized, but each tiny piece removed meant he was that much closer to undressing her. She remained deathly still, knowing that any movement she made now he would feel through the slim barrier.

"What is your name, girl?" The words came as if he knew she was close.

Her first instinct was to ignore him, to pretend she was asleep or unable to hear him. He would soon bore of this game and let her be.

"I know you can—"

"My name is Annora," she interrupted, startling even herself with the strength of her defiance. "What is *your* name?"

He chuckled before he answered. "My name is Pyke. You will know it well by the time we cross the sea."

"I will remember it," she said, summoning what remained of her courage. "And when we reach Adeltia, I will have Cassen punish you if you touch another person aboard this ship." She did not know this Cassen, but that the men appeared to fear him seemed her only leverage.

Pyke was silent for a good while before letting loose a guffaw that threatened to break down her door.

"You little tart," he said. "I will have to save you for last." She felt his weight shift away from the door, then return. "But I *will* have you."

The cries and whimpers that came from the compartment beside her own soon after he left let Annora know just how little he thought of her threat. *I should have just pretended to be asleep,* she lamented, fearful that the one next to her may be suffering more due to her audaciousness.

Her searching in the dark continued, hastened by hatred. She dragged her hands over the floor, flinching each time another splinter penetrated her skin. There was nothing more than wooden planks, damp rope, and stale mops, however. Then her hand fell upon something so familiar that it felt wrong for it to be here. She rubbed her fingers over its cold surface, feeling each of its many crenulations once and again.

It was no great feat to find one perfect half of a seashell on the coast of her former island, but to find one here gave her a sudden rush of achievement—until she remembered what she had planned to use it for. The top edge of it felt purposefully sharp, as if the previous captive had spent endless hours making it so. It would cut through flesh easily enough, either Pyke's or her own. It would not cut deep enough to end a man's life, however, and an image of his face came to her, embroiled with a mix of rage and glee, thankful that she'd given him a reason to hurt her even more. If she was to use this weapon, it could not be on him.

The cries from her neighbor had ended, though they refused to leave her mind. *A wound to my face will neither stop this man,* she confessed to herself. With the shell clasped tightly in her hands she pressed the serrated edge against her chest, fearing the pain that would come, fearing that such an act may cost her her life, but mostly fearing that she lacked the courage to go through with it.

ANNORA

"He is a disgusting old man. I will *not*," came the voice of a girl.

"He is mature and wealthy," said a man. "You are being unreasonable."

The fight between what sounded to be a father and daughter coming from outside the carriage was a familiar one, and the longer Annora eavesdropped, the less she found it an entertaining distraction.

"How *long* can he make us wait in here?" asked Mollie.

As long as he likes, Annora thought. Mollie may have been a fellow lady servant, but she had the look and haughty mannerism, at least when not in Cassen's presence, of Adeltian nobility.

Annora simply shrugged and Amalee shrugged in kind. It did not seem right to complain about being stuck in a carriage, waiting to be the guests of an event that most girls, even highborn, would give anything to attend.

"At least we have food and drink," said Amalee as she helped herself to another of the thin cookies that Annora had found to be grossly sweet.

"I have to use the privy…" said Mollie.

"Perhaps, then, you should put down your glass." Annora had watched Mollie drink the sour punch with such a thirst she wondered if she had ever tasted anything but water. Annora's suggestion earned her a look of annoyance.

"What is he *doing* anyhow?" said Mollie. "The ball started hours ago, and we wait out here like idiots."

"I am sure *Mother* has her reasons," said Amalee.

Mollie sneered. "The only thing he's a mother to is lies," she spat. "I think I know by now the look in a man's eyes when he wants more than he's being given."

"You are being vulgar. Don't talk that way," said Amalee. "Mother treats us all like daughters."

Mollie snorted and rolled her eyes. "Tell her, Annora. I see the way he looks at you. I am sure you two have shared more than secrets."

It was a loathsome thought. Cassen had a nimble way with words that allowed him to speak deceitfully without lying, but thankfully, he had never shown any of the other characteristics Mollie was claiming she saw in him.

"For so knowledgeable a girl, it is surprising you do not know why Cassen delays us," Annora said.

Mollie showed mock boredom before she spoke. "Oh, please. The Spiceland girl will teach me about the importance of arriving late to events? I shudder at the thought of what would pass for an event on your savage islands."

This may have been the first trip to the Adeltian Throne for the other two girls, but Annora, who had accompanied Cassen on several occasions already, knew enough to realize the ball was not their main reason for being here. "Savage though I may be," she said, making a conscious effort to keep her accent from flaring, "I would not be foolish enough to attempt to teach you anything."

Mollie rolled her eyes again. "I never called you a savage."

She hadn't, Annora realized, but the reference to her islands as savage was perhaps more hurtful due to the truth of it. The life Annora had known across the Western Sea seemed barbaric now by comparison to what she had come to know in Adeltia, but that did not change the reality that, here, she was a slave.

"How much of what your patron discusses with his friends do you overhear?" Annora challenged the impudent girl.

"Plenty," said Mollie. "Too much. It is tedious. I do what I can *not* to listen."

It was difficult to take this girl seriously. Mollie's patron was a powerful merchant who worked closely with Emrel, Annora's own patron. Annora knew both men to be entrenched in plots of subversion.

"And you know nothing about their plots of treason?" asked Annora, keeping her voice low.

Mollie's eyes went wide with fear, and Annora would have savored the victory had the girl's eyes remained fixed on Annora. That was not the case, as Mollie looked over Annora's shoulder toward the carriage window.

"Mother," said Mollie, her tone having changed completely. "We were just speaking fondly of you."

Annora did not even have the strength to scowl at the girl, instead using what little vitality that remained to will that Mollie was only playing a trick on her. Amalee, who faced the same as Mollie, did not betray any emotion other than her usual doe-like awe.

"Is it time for us to depart, Mother?" said Mollie. She then broke into a fit of giggling, allowing the blood to return to Annora's face.

Just to be sure, Annora looked over her shoulder. Seeing no one behind her, she shifted her position so that she no longer faced Mollie, and had a view of the window out of her periphery.

"You scare too easily," said Mollie, still tittering.

Go ahead and laugh until you piss yourself, thought Annora. She was done speaking for the night. For Cassen to have walked upon them gossiping like women in the laundry would have been bad enough, but had Cassen overheard their conversation it would have been unforgivable. Annora did not divulge much of what she gleaned from her patron to Cassen, in spite of her implicit duty to do so. Escape from servitude was her main concern, and she had not yet determined if Cassen's knowing of the impending plots would help to that end.

❧

"Come, my doves," Cassen had said upon finally returning. "You must accompany your mother as I flutter around those of dignity."

The three of them did their best to hide their excitement as Cassen had instructed, a thing far easier for Annora as her night had already been all but ruined. Her mood was soon forgotten, however, as she was calmed by soothing music and enchanted by the beautiful sights—of those sights Annora found her gaze lingered on several of the young men. Light featured and thin, Adeltian men were not those she would consider paragons of attractiveness, yet they had a certain elegance about them, dressed in their high-collared suits.

Cassen had gone straight toward one of the prettier girls in attendance who stood oddly apart. She looked to Annora to be as snooty as the rest of the highborn girls she'd had the privilege of meeting, and her initial assessment seemed to be correct. As Cassen and the girl conversed, however, Annora was impressed, if not shocked, by the way she fenced with him. Most were either fearful or disgusted by Cassen, but this Lady Ethel was not afraid to trade witticisms with the man.

As the conversation turned in the most unexpected of directions, Annora knew both Mollie and Amalee would be salivating at the prospect of being chosen by Ethel. Looking so different from the people of Adeltia and already having a patron, Annora was sure she stood no chance of becoming this girl's personal servant, and when Ethel chose her by name, she did not know if she should be elated or scared. Annora had grown accustomed to the life she knew in Eastport, and eager though she may have been to flee from it, she was wise enough to realize this would be no true escape. Nonetheless, she found herself delighted— if only for knowing how jealous Mollie must have been—as she was led off, arm-in-arm, by this bold-spoken highborn.

Just as they had gone a far enough distance for them to speak in private, they were interrupted. Annora immediately bowed in reverence when she noticed they were in the company of His Grace the King, fearful that somehow the man might be able to tell she'd so recently uttered the word treason. Ethel's impropriety seemed without bound as she stood stiff legged, acknowledging the regally dressed king with only a nod as one might a person of equal status.

"Good evening," said Lyell. He did not look to be a man suited for such events, but he was doing well in hiding any discomfort.

"Grandfather," said Ethel.

Are Adeltian ladies supposed to refer to the king as their grandfather? Annora thought it best to keep her eyes down and mouth shut, as was often the case.

"You must not call me that, Ethel. We share no blood relation. …Though I did almost marry your mother… She is a pretty thing, that one," he finished, now looking off into the distance.

"Yes, she is. Thank you," replied Ethel. It was clear to Annora that Ethel was not enjoying this encounter. Any elevation to her status gained by speaking with the king, who apparently truly was her grandfather, if only by marriage, was not worth the discomfort it appeared to be causing her.

The king snapped his attention back to Ethel and studied her head to toe in a way far from grandfatherly. "As have you become." Lyell cleared his throat. "I hope I am not too forward in asking you for a dance." Before having finished the request, he'd already begun to take Ethel by the hand, leading her to the center of the ballroom, away from Annora.

Annora stood alone and watched as Ethel did her best to conceal her displeasure while dancing with the elderly ruler. Annora saw other girls pointing with disbelief at the dancing pair, some actually appearing jealous while others snickered. Despite his old age and matching demeanor, the king moved with the grace of a man who, even if having no love for the act, was familiar and adept at performing the motions.

Annora wondered if sharing her secret of what to whisper in a king's ear to repel him would help Ethel, but given Ethel's existing relationship with the man it was not likely. In any case, she and Ethel would have much to speak about when they were finally alone. They already had more in common than Annora would have ever guessed, and they were yet to trade words.

DECKER

Having not encountered the expected Dogman wastelands as they traveled north, Titon had explained they must be in a finger of the canyon so far to the west that it was yet to be raided. Nonetheless, the terrain had changed drastically as they went, forcing the men to recognize just how much time Titon had saved them via the route along the flat cliffs of the western shore.

Rocks and deadfall littered the uneven ground making travel slow and dangerous, especially so with all the plunder dragged and carried. Decker warned the men that any clumsy enough to break an ankle would have to limp home without aid, as they would not slow their pace for a single man. It was not long before one among them challenged him on that claim.

"You are lucky it was just a sprain and not a break," Decker told Tryg, a boy of eleven years whose foot had found a hidden hole. "Else you would be feeding the vultures." *Else you would have made me a liar,* Decker admitted to himself, believing his father would have done the same. The men took turns supporting the weight of the hobbled boy as he limped along. In spite of his injury, it was not the boy who had slowed their pace. It was the grey-haired Dogman who called himself Greyson.

They had acquired him at the last village where he'd begged them to spare him. It was not something any had a mind to do until he explained he only wished to live long enough to have vengeance on the "fools who left their village unprotected" as he put it. The band of Dogmen Greyson sought apparently had gone looking for a fight, and with Titon indifferent, Decker made the decision to allow this man his revenge—so long as he led them directly to these Dogmen who might give them their first real skirmish.

"Slay the mad one first. I will not have the stories say we let an old, crazed Dogman do our killing for us." Decker got a good bout of laughter from the men prior to them charging in to annihilate the group of Dogmen they'd been led to, but not before one of their axes found its way into Greyson's skull.

"Mountain's tits!" Decker shouted in frustration. "These were the bravest Dogmen?" This was the last battle they would likely have on their way home, and it was not one to be remembered. The Dogmen and their demonic companions scattered like frightened pests. At Decker's feet was the only Dogman still to draw breath, although not easily. He was a large man with hair as fiery as Red's when she was younger. He almost looked as if he could be Galatai. *Perhaps this one would have fought.* It was a shame that this was the man Greyson had chosen to wound with his cowardly assault. Had he been any other Dogman, Decker would have let him suffer, but the way this man clung to both life and hatred was respectable. Decker rewarded him with an end to his agony.

The red Dogman aside, these were a sad and pathetic people. There was no heroism in having defeated them in battle. Titon must have felt the same, as he did not even bother to make chase when the cravens fled. He had not seemed himself since having taken the pretty woman at the previous village, and Decker suspected it had not gone as Titon had hoped. Some of the Dogmen women were quite strong, and Decker had almost been stabbed by one from the same village. *Perhaps Titon caught a knee with his manhood.*

After picking through the corpses' belongings and finding only a few knives and bows worth keeping, Decker checked to see if any of their men were missing.

"Where is Leknar?" Decker asked, shocked by the possibility of having lost such a capable, if not foolhardy, man. He received nothing but dumb looks in return.

"Leknar!" Decker's shout echoed against the rocks and faded without response.

"Perhaps he's lost," said Arron.

"He must be," said Decker. "He's too strong to have been killed by any of these weaklings." Decker drew a mighty breath. "Leknar!"

Decker did not wish to have his brother's raid stained with so needless a casualty, but neither did he wish to wander aimlessly in the canyon in search of a fool. As disgusting as it was to have possibly lost a man to mere disorientation, Leknar—aside from Griss—the man Decker least cared for of their group. Remembering that Leknar had also been responsible for their only other death, having axed a brother over a cheese wheel, Decker lost all will to draw out this search any longer.

"If Leknar fails to meet up with us north with the others, I say his cheese goes to Titon!" Decker had hoped to raise the mood with his declaration, but when the men laughed instead of cheering, Titon shot him a look of sour reproach. *Perhaps I could have worded that better.*

"Will we head for the shore after we meet up with them?" asked Arron.

The question had been directed at Decker, and he deferred to his brother with a questioning glance.

"I suppose."

"Good." Decker met his brother's melancholy with cheer, hoping it might affect him. "The flat tops will make dragging these supplies far easier, and it only makes sense to return the same way we came—through Titon's path of glory."

❦

Though it took longer than expected, their group reached the coastline as victors. The Frozen Sea, the very sound of which had once put fear in their chests, now welcomed them with adulation.

Heavy-laden though they were with quantities of both meat and cheese, they had very little in the way of treasures. Decker had snagged a broken piece of silvered glass and some of the men had taken metal cooking utensils with shoddy engraving, but they found no precious metals or gems. It did not bother Decker any. His main concern was seeing his clan through the winter, and this would do that and more. Titon, however, had the look of a man defeated.

"You do not seem pleased with your raid," Decker said.

He and Titon had been walking in silence for what felt like ages as Decker gave Titon time to overcome whatever it was that dejected him.

Titon shrugged his shoulders as his only response. His continued mood puzzled Decker. They had just led the most successful raid in as long as he could remember, and Titon had orchestrated the entire incursion. His brother said little or nothing when they ate together, he did not join the men in song, and the one person among them Titon did speak to was an outcast himself. *Nearly three weeks away from the tannery and Arron still smells like piss*, Decker mused in amazement. Decker did not know how Titon could endure the assault on the nostrils that a lengthy conversation with Arron must entail and was afraid the stench might somehow infect his brother in kind.

"It will take time for the men to see you as their leader."

"I am not their leader," replied Titon, still looking down. "Our fool of a father has been wrong about a great many things, but he was right about this. These men will not follow me. Nor do I wish to lead them."

Decker tried to make sense of what he'd heard. Everyone wished to lead. *For such a smart man, Titon speaks much nonsense.* "Given time—"

"No," Titon said, cutting him off. "And it makes little difference. This raid went well, but it will only force the Dogmen farther south. *Given time*, we won't be able to reach the Dogmen villages even via descending the cliffs." It seemed as if Titon emphasized his words in a way to make Decker feel as stupid as possible.

Titon was always right and this was like to be no exception, but Decker had grown tired of trying to console a man who should be overjoyed with accomplishment. Decker decided he would prefer to drop behind and speak with men that he knew would be in higher spirits. *If you continue this way, Titon, none will follow you. A cynical leader inspires no belief.*

ALTHER

In spite of conditions frigid enough to have made a similar trip via carriage an uncomfortable affair, Alther had warmed to the point of becoming wet with sweat while riding his silver-grey palfrey. In stark contrast with Rivervale, the kingdom of Adeltia saw no snow even at the height of winter, but the humidity remained year round, ensuring discomfort.

I must take Crella and Ethel to Rivervale to see their first snow, Alther resolved. Why it had not occurred to him before was puzzling. *I should take Stephon as well, if he will come.* But he knew better. It was too late for Stephon to form the types of memories Alther recalled with fondness, those of King Leofwin upon a black steed kicking up puffs of white powder. His grandfather had made a point to visit his family weekly—a tradition Alther wished Lyell had continued.

The mender would not approve of him exerting himself just a day after having suffered the blow to his head, but he could not remember last having felt more robust, and there was no faster means of travel. *Perhaps it was something in that tea*, he thought, amused. That might also explain his wife's behavior. It had been years since he could remember actually having enjoyed a night with her, if indeed he ever had. But the two of them turned giddy as the night went on, sipping their tea and becoming blithesome in their overtired state.

It was certainly the first time he had seduced her. Their previous fornications had been out of the necessity to consummate their marriage and produce an heir, but this was different. She yielded to him with grace, and for a night he was her equal. He would not forget it, nor would he allow himself to change back to the Alther whom his wife scorned and pitied.

His pace varied between a smooth ambling gait and a full-on exhilarating gallop as he made his way toward the Throne. Alther did not push his horse hard for long, but he took great pleasure in the short bursts of speed along the more favorable terrain. *I will insist that Crella finally learn to ride.* Riding was common enough among Adeltians, but it was not cherished in quite the way it was in Rivervale. Crella had always been opposed to learning, not wishing to dirty anything she owned, or to "stink as a foul beast," and the old Alther would have known better than to press her. *In Westport I will buy her a mature palomino palfrey, with a good temperament and golden mane to match her own. She will learn to ride it or sleep in the stables until she does.* Alther knew he'd never have the spine to demand such a thing of her, but the thought still brought a smile to his face as he galloped the final quarter mile.

The Dawnstar was still high in the western sky as Alther strode with purpose toward his father's chambers. The trip that normally would have taken at least two hours by carriage had taken him well under one—a welcome gain, as he was eager to speak with his father and clear up the matter involving his assailant. It was always best to be honest with the man. Lyell had spies everywhere and would respond very poorly to being misled. Alther expected his father would give him the right to punish Stephon with the method of his choosing, though Lyell would likely have some harsh suggestions of his own. *I might even consider them this time.* The thought of his estate staff being interrogated also weighed heavily upon Alther, and he wanted it immediately halted.

"Stop!"

Alther had nearly crossed the wall walk to reach the turret that housed his father's chambers when he heard the shout. He did not need to look, for he knew it was not directed toward him; it was the pleading voice of the same caped child he and Stephon had seen tormented on a prior visit. Alther found himself reveling in his rage—a feeling he would have previously restrained. Below him he knew he was like to see the same four boys torturing the helpless one they had aptly dubbed the pig-wizard. He was angry at the boy for not defending himself, he was angry at the bullies for continuing their assault after having once been warned, and he was angry at himself for having been more often on the side of those doing the bullying in his youth.

As he looked into the courtyards, the scene he saw beneath him was close to what he had expected, although there were only three of the four aggressors from the previous encounter. Two of them held the smaller one in place by his arms as he knelt before a stone saucer where the birds bathed. The third was on the other side of the saucer, facing Alther, the glee on his face clear to see. Alther strained to remember his own bullying, assuring himself that he had never borne quite such an exalted expression. Alther had never been the ringleader, and his participation was merely a means of keeping from being targeted himself, or so he rationalized.

"Come on, don't pig-wizards like slop?" The lead aggressor forced the boy's face into the water of the birdbath, thick with the brown of decaying leaves and the white and black of bird droppings. Only after quite some time did he allow the boy's head out of the mess, then looking at his victim with scorn.

"Why are you not eating any? I will drown you if need be, but the pig-wizard will eat some slop tonight!"

The two holding the boy's arms snickered as the ringleader forced his head into the sludge again, holding him down longer this time. Alther wished to intervene, but he had no desire to merely run the boys off as he had the first time, only to have them return to torture the child on another night.

He envisioned training the child. He could put a sword in his hand, as Lyell had his own, and show him what it took to have the strength to wield it. It would require months of hard work, perhaps years, but the fat on the ham would slowly render, and the meat would firm around the bone. Alther tried to picture what the child would look like after years of training, but all he could imagine was the same hapless, chubby face upon another's body, still wearing the ludicrous cape of royal violet with yellow embroidery. It would be of no use. The child would never be a swordsman, and even if he were, a sword is not a tool that lends itself to defense against bullies.

The boy's head jerked out of the saucer as it was finally released. After a few coughs he sobbed, "I'm eating it," and he must have been as all three of the others burst into laughter.

The familiar laughter turned Alther's blood to froth, and he gripped at the wall, his knuckles going white. The memory surfaced, the one he had suppressed in hopes that it would never return. But it did, and often, and with it came the rush of blood to every inch of his skin: his elder brother and hero, Edwin, upon his knees, humiliated beyond repair. How boys seemed to be born with the instinctive ability to degrade each other so thoroughly was beyond comprehension. Had Alther promptly left, Edwin may not have seen him, and he would not have seen in Edwin's eyes the look of shame that to this day haunted him.

A piece of stone broke free in his right hand, and without thinking Alther hurled it at the leader of the boys, half expecting it to not even reach. The large chunk of rock tumbled through the air, landing with a sickening thud onto the skull of one of the other laughing boys. Alther had time to see the boy's body crumple to the ground before he ducked behind the wall and waited for the others' cries to alert the guards.

His drenched clothing clung to his body as his skin alternated between sickly hot and cold. If he had maimed or killed the boy, the fact that they had been taking part in some childhood bullying would be no excuse. Even a prince could rot in a dungeon if his father did not see fit to conceal the incident. *And why should he?* thought Alther. *Westport would be better off in the hands of another.*

Moments passed, and no cries were heard, just hasty footfalls. So badly he wished to peak over the wall to see if the boy struck by the rock had run off or was lying there dead, but he could not risk it. With his heartbeat pulsing in his head, Alther crawled along the walkway until he knew he would be out of sight from anyone in the courtyards. Then he stood and paced back to his horse, looking as calm as his nerves would allow while passing the several guards.

I just killed a child, Alther confessed to himself when he was safely outside the castle walls. Astride his tired horse, he trotted slowly back to Eastport, shivering from the cold and trying to weigh his danger. The guards might wonder how his trip to the castle had been so short lived, but they were not likely to report such activity. Alther should have continued in to meet with his father as if nothing had happened, though turning back now did not seem prudent. Ultimately it should not matter. Even when the boy's death was investigated, it was hard to imagine being named as a suspect. The other boys would likely bear the blame, deservedly so. All of the tormentors of that poor caped boy could be sentenced to impalement for all he cared. Alther's greatest regret was that he would not be able to speak to his father that night and clear up the matter of his own brat. *I brought one Stephon into the realm. That I might have just removed one may be my absolution.* He then jumped off his mount and began heaving. His horse shied and whinnied, attempting to flee, as Alther sprayed all the contents of his stomach onto the ground.

ANNORA

"Where are your things?"

It was the third time she had been asked that same question, and Annora had grown tired of answering.

After the ball, but before Annora could exchange any words of substance with her new friend, Cassen had insisted Annora return with him to Eastport where she was to retrieve her belongings. In truth it seemed he only wanted to instruct her on her responsibilities when she was away—a reminder that her new life with Ethel would not be without strings.

Cassen had been the first to ask.

"All my belongings are inside." Annora indicated the small muslin bag containing her entire wardrobe. As Cassen dictated his lady servants dress only in silk, the few dresses, skirts, and bodices she owned took up little space, the bulk of the bag filled instead with her cotton underthings and nightdress.

"I have no doubt that will change shortly, as the young princess will likely shower you with gifts. Do *not* allow her to buy your trust." Cassen looked more serious than Annora could remember.

"I will not, Mother."

"No, I would not think that you would. You are perhaps the best suited of my daughters for this task. And you understand the most important gift that, as your mother, I have provided and will continue to provide when you are away. *Safety.*"

Freedom would be a far greater gift, thought Annora, but as usual, her snarky quip lost its poignancy as she recalled the truth behind his words. She could still hear with clarity the revolting sounds of joyous molestation that had come from the cabin beside her on her sea voyage to Adeltia. *Had I not been Cassen's property, I would not have arrived the same girl I'd departed as*, she reminded herself.

"Yes, Mother," Annora responded.

"Take note of any and all turmoil concerning Ethel and her family. It will serve me to know such things. And I will expect you to learn a great deal more than you have from Emrel, seeing as you will be paired with a far more willing source of information."

Annora nodded her understanding, already uneasy at the prospect of spying on the girl she was meant to befriend.

"Oh and one last thing," said Cassen. "If young Lady Ethel is so forward as to try and play with you…under the covers." Cassen raised his brow. "Refuse her if you must, but please, do not *bite* her—at least not so hard as you did your last patron."

As Annora rode alone in the carriage, her bag on her lap—not placed in the back as the young porter had suggested—she felt oddly displaced. She'd never been especially close with any of her fellow lady servants, but what little attachment she had made with them now tugged at her. She did not miss any one girl in particular, but the force of their collective pull made her stomach queasy. *You claim to want freedom*, she scolded herself, *you can survive a ride alone in a carriage.*

In spite of her trepidation, the trip that led her to the door of Ethel's dormitory seemed a short one.

"These are all of my things," said Annora in annoyance, optimistic, at least, that this would be the last time she would have to answer this question. She kept her eyes downcast courteously as she spoke to her new mistress.

"You may look at me," said Ethel. "…I would prefer it," she added as Annora had been slow to comply.

Annora raised her eyes to see the blushed face of the same pretty girl she remembered from the candlelit ball, but the natural light that came through the glassed ceilings of the hallway lit Ethel's lonely face with more detail. Had Annora not known better, she would have thought the girl had colored in concern for having embarrassed her. The sincerity in Ethel's large eyes was a sight seldom seen in highborn and, for whatever reason, spurred Annora to chide herself for already acting like the spoiled friend of a princess in her previous annoyance.

"We must unpack your things to see what you are lacking," said Ethel. "So that we may remedy it."

The haste by which Cassen's prediction had come true was amusing, but Annora made sure it did not show on her face. "You are most kind, but I can do with very little. I am here to serve your needs, not to burden you."

Something about Ethel's smile made Annora feel as though she were witnessing a rare and cherishable occurrence. "Well, I *need* to get you some appropriate dresses. I have arranged for you to attend my classes with me."

❧

Annora had been surprised by the quaintness of the room she was to share with Ethel. Though it was easily large enough for the two of them, the modest room had little in the way of suggesting its occupant was daughter to the heir. The walls were adorned with thick flocked paper of a raised floral pattern, blossoms of pinkish taupe trimmed in white. The curtains, too, were of a fine make, but the window frames were old and weathered, the paint cracking, and the two small beds were no more than thin mattresses on stout wooden frames.

The heir's adopted *daughter*, Annora reminded herself. There seemed the potential for misstep in every spoken word due to Ethel's intricate family structure, and Annora's carefulness to avoid insult manifested itself in her remaining mostly silent.

"We will have to see a mender," Ethel teased. "We are in need of a tonic to loosen your tongue."

Annora smiled and nodded as her response. There was no malice in her words. In fact, it seemed Ethel spoke out of a new nervousness. The hour they'd spent unpacking Annora's things and looking through Ethel's prized possessions—most of them dreary-sounding books—had gone by quickly. They were now headed to eat, something Annora was quite thankful for. Her appetite had come to her in force after receiving such a warm welcome from Ethel, putting her at ease, and she was eager to sample the castle's delicacies.

"Beautiful, isn't it?"

It took a moment for her to realize Ethel spoke of the glass ceilings Annora's upward glance had lingered upon. The light came through in pastel pink and dark blue, the clear midday light transformed to those of the setting Dawnstar. It was made even more impressive by the fact that the glass itself was not flat but curved to form a dome that ran the length of each hallway.

"How do they color the glass?" Annora wondered aloud, regretting having asked such a childish question.

"I do not know. Berries perhaps," said Ethel with a shrug, though her expression did not lack interest. "Our lessons do not teach us things of relevance. Mostly they are instructions on how to better attract noble men of worth. And yet the girls who do poorest in class tend to garner the most attention."

"How do you do?" asked Annora. "In your classes," she was quick to specify.

"I do very well in my classes," said Ethel with a snicker. "And in turn do rather poorly elsewhere."

Annora would not have believed her had she not seen how alone Ethel was at the ball, and she was not about to contradict her by pointing out that she had been pursued by the king.

As if on cue, a group of three young men made their way toward her and Ethel from the opposite end of the hall. Of various heights and builds, all three of them appeared confident and strong in their own way—a disarming revelation as Annora realized she could not remember the last time she had considered being courted by anyone other than a disgusting old man whose advances she would do everything in her power to reject. As they neared, Annora had difficulty determining whether their shared strut was exaggerated or if that was indeed how young men, slender in waist, broad in shoulder, and strong of hip, actually walked.

Each of them either smirked with confidence or raised a brow as they walked past, bursting to laughter shortly thereafter.

"What was that about?" Annora asked.

"Just fool boys," said Ethel. "And they should not even be in here."

There were no boys in the dining hall they eventually came to, yet it was difficult for Annora to believe so much noise could be created by only ladies-in-training. Rows of wooden tables with simple chairs spanned the length of the room, tables that looked oddly bare to Annora with no cloth, plates, or cutlery arranged upon them. Their only contents were tall shaded candles, placed at regular intervals and unlit.

She followed Ethel to stand in line at the head of the room where large chafing dishes, some steaming and others spotted on the outside with condensation, sat upon the few tables that were clothed.

"Not what you were expecting?" asked Ethel.

Indeed it was not, but Annora merely shrugged. The suppers served by Cassen when the lady servants returned in the evening were nothing like this. Their plates were brought to them by boy servants, a single course, but artfully prepared. Flowers, candles, a glass of wine, water in a cellar-chilled stein, a fork, a spoon, two knives, butter, and bread was present in front of each seat.

"They say it is to instill humility. ...Ah, this is my favorite." Ethel placed a large spoonful of stew on her metal plate. Annora was surprised, half expecting Ethel, dainty as she was, to eat no more than vegetables. Mirroring Ethel, Annora filled her plate with the same portions of food. The meaty stew, a piece of soft yellow bread, half a spoon of lumpy, buttery potatoes, and a full spoon of loose corn that she hoped was sweet.

"This way," said Ethel after they had retrieved their cutlery.

Having noticed Ethel's demeanor had gone from eagerness to stoicism and her pace had quickened, Annora surveyed the room to see that nearly everyone was looking at them—more specifically at her.

Annora did not think herself one to be intimidated, especially not by pompous highborn girls, but the weight of so many eyes was oppressive. She walked with Ethel, wishing she was not moving so fast, as it only served to make them appear more diffident. Nonetheless, Annora wore what she believed was an expression of confidence and kept in stride. At seventeen she was older than most of these girls, and she was not about to be baited to blunder.

Her poise was not having the intended effect, however, as many of the girls who stared at her gave way to poorly concealed laughter. How it was that she felt less secure in a room full of harmless girls than she had in the home of a would-be rapist, Annora could not explain, but she was desperate to be seated, preferably far from the oglers.

"Be careful," said Ethel, looking worried, but her words made little sense, and Annora's head felt wrapped in wool.

Ethel finally sat down near the end of the dining hall, Annora content to sit beside her.

"I will get us some water and napkins," said Ethel.

"I'll come with you." Annora had no desire to face that walk again, but she also did not wish to show any sign of weakness. When Ethel's eyes went to her chest, Annora felt a surge of heat flood her. She looked down as well to see the line of brown stew sauce that had stained her dress. Annora had believed the girls stared and laughed because she was the only one in silk, all others dressed in simple cotton, but she must have been clutching her plate tight to her chest, ignorant to the fact that she was ruining her most expensive garment. Annora nodded.

Ethel had only just left her, yet it felt as though Annora had been sitting alone for an eternity. *This is idiotic*, she told herself. *I am not a blushing girl in need of support.* She believed herself to have calmed after forcing a deep breath, but true relief only came when she saw Ethel returned with a comforting look on her face

"We have all done it. The plates are so shallow. I'm an imbecile for not warning you." Ethel dipped a cloth napkin in her glass of water and handed it to Annora.

In time, the stain was reduced to a mild blotch, difficult to see without knowing it was there, but the dress was still ruined.

"Now you cannot protest when I insist you get more clothes."

"I suppose you are right," Annora agreed, realizing she was thankful for Ethel's ability to find a reason to somehow celebrate misfortune. Remembering how the girl had sparred with Cassen, however, Annora resolved to not underestimate her.

Annora put a piece of the bread in her mouth, determined to start pleasant conversation when her chewing was done. "Do you see your parents often?" Annora forced herself to ask upon realizing she had swallowed the bread, too busy thinking of what to say to have made note of the taste.

"No. Not as often as I would like. My mother comes to visit about once a month, my father as often as every week. Whenever he is summoned to the Throne."

Annora assumed she was speaking of Alther. There was no cordial way of gaining clarification on the matter.

"What was life like in the Spicelands. Do you remember it well?" asked Ethel.

This was not a topic Annora wished to discuss, especially not in public, but they were so far down the table that none were near enough to eavesdrop.

"I am sure it is little different than what you have heard." Annora did not believe that to truly be the case, but it seemed more polite than accusing her mistress of ignorance.

"I have books that say your people are savages, that they fight naked with each other using wooden spears, and marry hundreds of wives."

Annora finished a mouthful of corn, delightfully sweet as she'd hoped. "Do your books speak of any people other than your own that are *not* savages?"

Ethel paused to think, then smiled. "You have a point, but I still wish to hear the truth."

"Our men can be savage, and they fight with spears, as do the men of this kingdom if I am not mistaken. But not in the nude…not unless it is very hot."

Annora feigned seriousness for a moment, then showed a trace of a grin causing Ethel to almost spit out her water.

Having recovered, Ethel pursued further. "Do they really marry so many wives?"

The way in which she asked let Annora know how abhorrent the prospect was to Ethel. *What would you think of me if you knew I once wished to be one of those wives?* "Our kings marry many."

Annora put a blind spoonful of food in her mouth. It was her adversary, the stew, which was actually quite good. The meat was tender and the broth was rich with flavor. She could not say for sure if she would ever have the courage to get it again, nor anything with such potential to spill over the edges of these plates.

Ethel's eyes widened in astonishment. "I did not believe it when I read it. Hundreds even?"

"I am sure on some island there is a king with near a hundred wives."

Ethel shook her head, disapproving, and Annora felt strangely offended. "And your kings, do they not share beds with many women? Is it less offensive that they do not call them wives?"

A sickening wave of self-reproach immediately swept Annora. It might have been a perfectly appropriate question, had Ethel's grandfather not been the king. Annora could scarcely believe she had been goaded into such a gaffe during harmless conversation.

"I am sorry," Annora said before Ethel could respond, looking downward and finding her appetite had left her.

"You should be," said Ethel. "But only for apologizing. And you are right. Our kings are little different it would seem. I am naïve for having believed otherwise."

They sat unspeaking for a good while, both picking at their food but not eating much. Annora broke the silence, answering questions that Ethel surely would have liked to ask. She had no desire to, but it did not feel right, already being so indebted to someone she had just met and was supposed to serve.

"I was thirteen when my father sold me to Cassen."

Ethel looked dismayed. "*Sold* you?"

"I do not know what else you would call it. My father received a heavy purse, and I was shipped here with no say in the matter."

It was Ethel's turn to be apologetic, but she did so without words.

"It was possibly for the best. Cassen treats us like daughters, that much is true. I have a better life here."

Ethel nodded in solidarity and did not press her further, nor did Annora offer more explanation. It had not been her intent to gain Ethel's pity, and having done so made her feel somehow dishonest. Truth be told, she pitied Ethel. Her complete lack of friends was evident at this point. Annora could not help but wonder how difficult these meals must have been for her, forced to come here without companionship, sitting alone at the end of a table as far from the stares and teasing as she could get. Dining here with a friend was hard enough.

"Your father may have done such a thing, but you are not Cassen's property. Slavery is forbidden in these lands, and no man can own a woman."

No, thought Annora. *Nor can naivety be cured during a single meal.* She smiled in thanks at the sentiment.

KEETHRO

Titon's actions reminded Keethro why he had originally planned to murder the man. After killing the two riders who claimed to be lawmen, Titon had insisted on continuing on their path directly to Strahl.

"Titon, let's be rational." Keethro did not think Titon a fool, but his friend certainly had it in him at times to be foolish. He would have preferred to have waited longer before making this entreaty, giving Titon time to calm from combat, but Strahl could be mere miles away.

"He said there were *menders* in Strahl. Do you think he was lying?"

"No, I am quite sure he was being honest," said Keethro, recalling the agony of the man screaming with the spear in his guts.

"Then we go to Strahl." Titon was not being argumentative; he simply stated what he believed to be the obvious course of action. *The man is blinded by focus.*

"And what do you expect we will see in Strahl, other than the inside of a dungeon?"

Titon took some time to think about what Keethro had asked, seeming at last to grasp his meaning. "Aye, we may have to fight more of these weakling bastards, but what of it? We will cut them down as they ride these tame beasts." Titon slapped the shoulder of the horse they had captured, and it gave a frightened snort.

"That is the problem. You know no fear. We have been made soft and overconfident by years of fighting the impotent Dogmen." Titon scowled at him as he spoke, but Keethro did not allow it to derail him. "You know it to be true. Do not expect these people to be dumb enough to continue to send groups of only three men with spears to attack us. If they are wise enough to make the elixirs we seek, they will be capable of killing two men, no matter how strong. They will send archers, and we will be skewered with arrows from afar. What good will it do Elise when we die on this road?"

His words must have resonated. Titon's pace slowed, and he had a thoughtful look on his face. Truth be told, Titon was one of the smarter men Keethro had known, but he could become so engrossed with a task that it was difficult to make him see anything but a straight line toward its achievement. "What would you have us do then?"

Keethro had already determined what they should do but took some time to best choose his words. They continued their slowed pace as they took in their surroundings. These fields and forests must have teemed with life, all of which was shrewd enough to remain well and clear of the path. The parched sands under their feet, still impressed with the prints of the horses from the very men they had slain, seemed to thirst for blood. The only sounds came from the wind in the grass and the angry calls of the circling birds, annoyed by Keethro and Titon's endurance. *I will not have this barren path be the place in which my bones are left to bake in the rays of the Dawnstar, flesh eaten by foul vultures.*

"I say we break from this trail of certain death and head west. We bring the horse with us and eat it when we grow hungry. We could have enough meat to reach the Frozen Sea if need be. Once we hit mountains or the fabled Eos, we head south again, and we do it in such a way as to kill as few people as possible. We are supposed to be Southmen now, and we need to play the part." Keethro observed Titon's frown of thought.

"Hrmph," was Titon's eventual response.

"We will hopefully miss Strahl and end up in the kingdom of the river or the delta, both of which are more likely to have the elixirs we need. Neither of us had even heard of this Strahl. It may be no more than a Dogman village in comparison to the mighty kingdoms—a village with horses instead of dogs and many men with spears."

Titon stopped where he stood and looked to the west. The birds, noticing his lack of motion, began to caw more loudly in anticipation of Titon's response, as if they knew his decision would affect them in kind.

"Very well," he agreed as relief flooded Keethro. "We head west, but for no more than seven days. Then we go south until we find the kingdom of the delta."

Two days later the men were many miles west of the trail Keethro would just as soon have forgotten. Travel in the plains was little different than walking a path, and Keethro was thankful of the short stretches through forest for the shade it gave from the Dawnstar's blinding rays.

"Venison," said Titon, then he sniffed at the horse's side again. "They do not smell as bad as I would have imagined, and they certainly do not inspire fear. They must be good for something. Probably delicious."

For the entire duration, Titon had speculated as to what the horse might taste like, alternating between beef, venison, and mutton. It did not bother Keethro; he too was rather curious, and it had kept his friend's spirits high despite not marching straight for their destination.

The torment of not knowing finally became too much for Titon, and they slaughtered and butchered the animal in a way to best preserve its meat. It took two more days to smoke the horse's hocks, and Titon agreed that the time spent doing so would not count toward the seven days of westerly travel.

"What do you think?" Keethro asked him.

Titon was chewing on some of the more tender meat from along the horse's back. They had seasoned it with salt—which they were running low on—and quickly seared it over the wood fire. "Beef," he said. "I can hardly tell the difference." He sounded a little disappointed the horse did not have a more exotic flavor.

For several more days they traveled due west. They'd had little trouble finding water. Every day now they had come to a new river they were forced to wade across—each larger in size than the last—until finally they found themselves on the eastern bank of a truly large, deep river. Wading across would be impossible, and swimming would soak their horsemeat, making it go rancid.

"Another boat?" Keethro asked.

"It must be the only way," said Titon. "I never thought I would see a river so large. Even a raft would scrape the bottom of our brooks and go nowhere, but you could fit five boats with sails and rudders across the breadth of this giant." The two men took a moment to stare in amazement. Though if this was the Eos, it was far smaller than the stories told.

"It would not make sense to build a boat upon every river we hit, and it will be too heavy to bring with us after crossing. Perhaps we should simply let it take us south." Keethro spoke the words hoping they were far enough west to be clear of Strahl. A river this large would surely lead them to some town or city.

"Agreed. We'll head south, stopping only to piss among the trees. It would be foolish, indeed, to anger the God of the River upon so mighty a stretch." Titon was a rather superstitious man, but Keethro did not fault him for this precaution. Even though he had no belief in the Mighty Three, dangling one's member over the deep, dark waters of this river would be frightening enough, simply not knowing what might jump out and try to remove it.

"Aye. Let us make a craft worthy of this godly river."

ETHEL

Hedge after hedge whirred past to her left and right, yet Ethel felt as if her near-frantic stride was getting her no closer to her destination. "We are so late," she worried aloud.

Had they been headed anywhere else—to a morning class or to meet with her mother or father—it would not have mattered. To upset a king with tardiness, however, was a mistake best never made. There was no need to remind Annora, either; she had been present for the ridiculous events that had caused their delay.

"Should we have brought a gift of some sort?" Ethel asked Annora as they continued their hurried pace. Annora shrugged with her eyes. Ethel's Spiceland servant knew less than she of the customs and etiquette surrounding a private meal with the king. It seemed rather silly, too, that Ethel should concern herself now with worry over decorum. It had been her original intention to arrive to this dinner looking a mess. She purposefully had not brushed her hair since waking and had worn her most threadbare outfit, which was sure to disappoint King Lyell. The childishness of her spiteful plan was only made clear to her as she glanced into her silvered glass a final time before setting out. In a panic, Ethel had raced to correct her condition. She tugged at her knotted hair with a comb—too tangled for a brush—and sent Annora to fetch a suitable dress. Ever since the dance, the whispers among the highborn were that Lyell meant to marry Ethel. Unthinkable as that was, it had been foolish to believe that Lyell would have simply lost an interest in her—were it there to start—if she had shown up to this dinner looking like a pauper. He would have canceled the event and rescheduled another, which would have started with him already angry over the first.

For all her efforts rushing to correct her appearance so as to not draw the ire of the king, Ethel knew he would now be offended regardless. Kings did not wait patiently for anything, and she would have no excuse for why he'd had to.

Perhaps it was the season, or just the weather, but the sky looming behind the castle was oddly dark and angry. This supper was meant to have been enjoyed during the Dawnstar's setting, but the Dawnstar was no longer in sight. The dreary twilight rays dwindling beyond the western horizon only seemed to light Ethel's way to doom. She was at first relieved that the portcullis guards escorted them without further delay, but Ethel thought she detected worry on one of their faces. *I must be more tactful when dealing with the king,* Ethel determined. *Discouraging his advances will not be as simple as if he were some persistent boy.*

They walked up stairways and along the tops of walls, giving sight to the majesty of the Adeltian Kingdom, but Ethel focused only on what she would say when Lyell soon glared at her. Her lateness was not her only offense. She had been summoned to attend alone, yet she had brought Annora with her. Lyell would be pleased by neither.

As the doors to the king's study swung open, Ethel found herself slightly relieved. She had pictured from her memory this room having a more intimate setting. She feared she would be forced to sit so near him that she might smell his old man's breath. The table she saw as she walked down the lengthy room was a massive one, however. Additionally comforting, the king was not alone. He sat at the table's head, opposite the room's entrance. Seated to his right were a man and a woman. Most unexpected, though, was the king's demeanor. Even from this distance, she could tell he was cheery—not brooding over her late arrival as she'd anticipated. He gestured to the pair beside him, while his chest bounced with the chuckles of honest amusement.

Ethel's momentary lightheartedness was dispelled with the closing of the doors behind her. There would be no escape now until the dinner was done—a dinner that had the potential to ruin her life, should Lyell decide she was fit to be his queen. In spite of that, she had trouble hating the man she saw at the far end of the table as her legs carried her forward; he looked so exuberant, young even—at least for one of a grandfather's age. He was dressed more like an Adeltian nobleman would be, in a regal tunic of obsidian leather, which contrasted with his hair and beard of perfect white almost fashionably. Maybe it was his drinking that made him so jovial—not that Ethel cared at all for drunkenness—but he appeared to be enjoying himself without having acquired any of the detachedness that came from excessive consumption. There was something to be admired in this king. But love him, she certainly never would.

"Ethel," said Lyell blithely when he noticed her approach. "Have a seat." He motioned to his left where a single setting had been prepared. Ethel was happy to see it was no closer to the king than was the seat of the other woman in attendance. "You brought your serving girl?"

Ethel was so discomposed that she had all but forgotten about Annora, who trailed behind her.

"We have plenty of minions here already to serve us, I assure you." The king spoke the words just as a modest-dressed man topped off his goblet.

Lyell had no malice in his voice, but Ethel took offense, nonetheless.

"She is my friend," Ethel asserted.

The king looked amused, glancing first at the other two guests before speaking. "You see this man here?" he said, motioning to the one who had filled his cup and now stood behind him. Ethel looked at him, troubled. She knew the expression on his face. It was the very look her adopted father, Alther, wore when gravely concerned over displeasing his father, the king—a look she hated to see on him.

"*He* is my friend," Lyell went on. "But I am the king, and he is a servant. So he stands with a bottle in his hand, and we sit and eat and drink."

It was hard to tell if Lyell was only attempting to be humorous, or if he was insisting that Annora would not be given a seat at the table. In either case, Ethel felt a smoldering in her chest she thought only her brother had the capability of inciting. She did her best to remain composed; she did not want her coming retort to sound overly contentious. Ethel further diffused the situation by looking kindly at the other guests. The woman had the light hair and mannerisms of Adeltian nobility, and was only somewhat older than Ethel. The man, however, was clearly of Rivervale. His long brown hair and muscled jaw made him out to be a knight, yet his clothing seemed too stately for that. That he looked like a brawny version of Alther made her wonder if he was in fact Edwin, Lyell's other son, but the wrinkles that formed as he smiled at her showed him to simply be too old for that.

"Your friend," Ethel challenged the king politely, "what is his name?"

"Jarrod," the king answered immediately and with confidence— letting Ethel know her intention of proving there was no honest friendship had failed. He then peered over his shoulder at the serving man, who had an anxious look about him. "James," Lyell corrected himself, squinting his eyes as if to better see him. "No, no. John," the king finally settled on.

If Lyell wanted the servant to confirm that one of his guesses had been correct, he did not. He stood quite still, the only motion coming from the lump in his throat as he swallowed.

"Something with a J, though, no?" the king wheedled.

The man's eyes stayed forward, looking at no one, but his head shook once back and forth, ever so slightly.

King Lyell exploded into laughter, slapping himself once on the thigh with delight. The other man at the table had a bit of a laugh as well, and the woman appeared to force herself to join in with a courtly smile.

"You see," the king said, not at all put off by the fact that Ethel's point had been proven. "That is why he has no seat!"

Ethel gave him a moment to subdue himself before she spoke. "This is Annora," she said, presenting her friend as though she were every bit as highborn as the rest of them. "*She* is my friend, and she requires a place at the table."

Lyell acquiesced without resistance, signaling some other servants with a nod of his head. "Go fetch a setting for the servant girl," he told them. "There is, of course, plenty to eat," he said to Ethel with a smile that reminded her of Stephon. "Both of you, then, have a seat, please." He motioned again for Ethel to take the place at his left. It was a good two paces' distance from him, yet it still felt awkwardly close.

He is your grandfather only by marriage, she told herself. Ethel had already determined that she would sooner die than share a bed with him, but if she could make herself less uncomfortable, she knew she would be able to think more clearly. The other plan she had construed—the one not involving ragged clothing—came back to her. It was the way in which she would cause Lyell to lose any attraction to her without her intention being obvious. It was a rather simple plan, really. The majority of what she was taught at the Adeltian School of High Manners—much to her chagrin—was the way in which a lady should act in order to be most appealing to her suitors. It became quite effortless for Ethel to excel in her classes, for she had learned an easy trick. It seemed the *proper* way of acting could be achieved merely by doing the very opposite of her true impulse: to act disinterested when actually charmed, to appear pleased when offended, to remain flirtatious with those in whom she had no interest, and so on. Thus, she had concluded, it should be equally effortless for her to dissuade the king's advances, merely by acting exactly in the way she was naturally inclined.

Ethel motioned for Annora to sit, but did not yet do so herself.

"Sir," said Ethel, attempting to gain the attention of the servant whose name Lyell could not recall. She endeavored to speak to him without using any of the typical demeaning titles. So far, however, Ethel was successful in commanding the attention of everyone in the room, save the one to whom she called. The king and both guests stared at her questioningly before turning in their seats toward the man.

"Cupbearer," Ethel said, deciding that would be less derogatory than calling him servant. He immediately began moving in Ethel's direction, no doubt expecting she wished for a drink, but she stopped him with a gesture. "Please," said Ethel, smiling kindly at him in an attempt to put him at ease. "I believe it is time we all learned your name."

Ethel did not care for the way in which the matter of the servant's name had been dismissed, as though it never mattered in the first place. *Perhaps if the king truly knew his name, he might be inclined to treat him like an actual person,* she mused.

The servant, who Ethel could now see must have been part Spicelander, part Adeltian, appeared to quake. His light brown hair which fell just below the ears remained still while his face trembled. It was as if he was trying to look at both Ethel and the king simultaneously, so that he would offend neither, and it made Ethel sick to know she was the cause of his anxiety.

"Go on," urged the king impatiently. "Tell us your name already."

"Ya-Ya-Yallendulaliel," the man stuttered.

Dead silence followed the man's name. Even Ethel had trouble digesting what he had said, wondering if he stuttered naturally or out of fright, and even if perhaps the proper pronunciation of his foreign-sounding name required as such.

The king broke the silence with the sort of disbelieving snorts that preceded laughter. "Sir Yallendulaliel," he said with enthusiasm, turning to face his guests again, "of House Cupbearer!"

The servant cast a momentary look of both offense and hurt Ethel's way before returning to his place against the wall, and Ethel felt her ears burn hot as they were prone to when she was embarrassed. The king and his guests—even the woman—were consumed by guffaws, both men doubling over from the severity of it.

Ethel turned to Annora, praying she too was not laughing. Her Spiceland friend gave her a somber, consolatory look, which did nothing to alleviate Ethel's discomfiture. Ethel wanted support, not sympathy, but it was foolish to think Annora could provide her such a thing. She was yet another powerless servant.

"Well," said King Lyell, still not fully composed, "that simple name should be easy enough for me to remember." Then, after a few more chuckles, "Sit, sit."

Only then did Ethel realize she was the lone member of the dinner party still standing, and she did what she could to remain ladylike, though she felt more like fleeing. She smoothed her silken skirts first in the front and then the back—as she was taught—before taking her seat. *Lest I wrinkle my dress,* she thought to herself sardonically, slightly disgusted by her propensity to resort to her ill-guided training when flustered.

"Drinks," the king commanded. Ethel was happy to see a new servant appear with a platter of goblets. She decided she would take a cup, but not once bring it to her lips, so that it would remain completely full. Thirsty though she was, Ethel did not want to face the cupbearer again.

"You share the former queen's compassion," Lyell said to her, complimentarily.

It was hard to accept his flattery, sincere as it may have been, with his iniquitous laughter still echoing in her ears.

"Alther's mother?" Ethel baited him, cutting him off as soon as he went to answer. "Or the queen you threw from the Throne's tower? *My grandmother.*"

Ethel saw from the corner of her eye the woman in attendance draw her hand to her mouth, but she stayed focused on the king. Lyell was unreadable at first. The pleasantness from his request for her to sit was gone, but he was otherwise indifferent.

"No one threw that woman—"

The low, bitter voice of the male Rivervalian guest went hushed when the king raised his hand just an inch from the table.

Lyell gazed at Ethel intently, scrutinizing her. "I can see you share much of the late Queen Adella's zeal as well—an admirable trait. She was your mother's aunt, though. Not your grandmother."

Ethel felt a hand upon her leg. It was Annora, and it was probably meant more as a plea to stop fighting with the king than as a means of comfort.

"But, no. I spoke of Alther's mother," said Lyell. For the moment he sounded fondly reminiscent. "She was a good woman. Such a tender heart." His demeanor changed as he continued. "Alther took after her too much, I am afraid."

The charge that Alther was too tenderhearted bothered her. *My father is no such thing,* Ethel thought to herself, attempting to win the argument in silence for her own sake. It took all her willpower not to say it aloud, since repeating it to herself was not having the intended effect. She just kept picturing Alther at his worst, looking sad and helpless when his good nature was taken advantage of by all those around him.

"Alther is not a man of war," Ethel stated simply.

The king, who had until now seemed amused by Ethel's belligerence, scowled at her. It made her feel as though she was in the presence of a dangerous and unpredictable animal, and she was about to be trampled for crossing its path.

Motion surrounded the table, causing Ethel to fear that perhaps Lyell had managed to secretly summon his guards to escort Ethel to a dirty cell. Rather than arrest her, however, the five men besieged the table with bowls of soup, one placed in front of each guest. Ethel hid from the king's glare by looking at the dish, which appeared to be mostly cream and potatoes.

"You say that as though it was laudable."

Ethel envied the servants, who retreated to safety as the king spoke. He did not sound as angry as he had looked, but he was far from amiable. She would have answered him in the affirmative, but she had lost her desire to protract this battle. She kept quiet for now and picked up her spoon.

"Go on, taste it," the king urged, no longer sounding antagonistic. "We have waited long enough to eat."

Ethel was happy for the change of subject, even if it meant the king was reminded of how late she had arrived. The spoonful she placed in her mouth was unexpectedly flavorsome. What looked like a simple cream broth was actually rather complex, first tasting of the green herbs which topped it, then of rich, buttery cream, earthy potatoes, and finally something completely foreign. Ethel had to chew the little chunks of meat vigorously, which she did not mind. It made the dish quite hearty.

"These clams must be from the west," said the Rivervalian man.

"Aye," said the king. "Stolen from the Devil's Mouth."

She had tasted clams before, but never in a soup. Ethel did not remember being too fond of them, yet her tastes when it came to the bounties of the sea seemed to change by the day.

"You do not care for men of war, then?" asked Lyell after they'd all had some time to fill their bellies, resuming the discussion which Ethel had hoped was over.

"No, I do not," Ethel responded, seeing no way out of this other than the truth. "Nor do most women, I would think."

The Rivervalian man got a chuckle out of her statement, but the king merely nodded before raising another spoonful of soup to his mouth. When his spoon hit the bowl again, it sounded empty. How he had managed to devour the entire thing so fast, Ethel could hardly imagine.

Lyell picked up his napkin, blew his nose into it, and returned it to the table. He then took in a slow breath and let it out. "So," he said dispassionately, as though his attention was only half consumed by the conversation, "you prefer men of peace?"

Ethel felt as though she was the one being baited now, and she lost what appetite she had left. She placed her spoon in her half-eaten soup and slid the bowl forward. A servant quickly retrieved it.

"I could only ever see myself with such a man," Ethel responded.

Again the king nodded, but Ethel found no comfort in his agreeability.

"I do not know what it is they teach the young women who attend your school of manners. Whatever it is, you do not seem to have taken to it the same way your peers have."

Ethel knew she had begun to frown, but seemed powerless to prevent it.

"I mean it as no insult," Lyell went on. He looked upon her now. It was an entitled gaze which made her even more uneasy. "Many people gossip, I realize, about why it has taken me so long to find a new queen. I wonder if those people have taken note of the stock of women available." The king cleared his throat and shook his head, indicating he was again being misunderstood. "It is not that they are unlovely—quite the contrary. They are all quite beautiful, quite young, quite…supple."

Ethel mirrored the action of the other Adeltian woman in attendance;

they both brought their napkins to their face. Ethel could only assume she, too, did so to hide any inadvertent looks of revulsion.

Lyell noticed, but he continued, uncaring. "But they all share a similar failing—each and every one of those young women who seem to have the desire, if not the potential, to be the next queen. They feign coyness for a while, so artless and transparent. But any man of experience can see: they are all so *eager*. Eager to agree, eager to indulge, eager to please. It seems, more often than not, I find them naked and purring, long before even the clams have been served."

Behind the napkin which obscured her face, Ethel gaped. Were she to remind herself again that this man was not her grandfather, it would do nothing to calm her throbbing pulse. She would rather the guards reappear and drag her to a cell than endure the rest of this lurid speech. Annora's hand, which must have been on her leg this whole time, slid slowly and apologetically away.

"Truthfully, I admire you, Ethel. You are not a shrew, not a weakling, not a strumpet. You have somehow avoided those common pitfalls of the other women your age." The king took a swig of wine before he continued. "And again, truthfully, I think you will come to admire me. There was a war, long ago—a war I started out of necessity and ended with victory. It was regretful how many good men had to die because of it, but it saw the realm—for the first time in its history—unified. Just as a scythe is required to cut the wheat which is used to make the most delicate bread, so is a sword required to establish the incontestable rule that allows for peace and order. So, I would tell those who label me a man of war: yes. I am proud to call myself as such." He beamed at her with intensity. "But I would also put to them this question: what would you call the man responsible for the greatest stretch of warless tranquility the realm has ever known, other than a man—an *exemplar*—of peace?"

CRELLA

"Crella, how pleasing to see you again."

Crella had waited at the door while a pair of lady servants fetched the man of the estate. He was dressed in the richest of cloth; a thick velvet in deep hues of royal blue and purple constructed his doublet and matching trousers. Crella found herself wondering how someone would be able to keep from sweating under such extravagant and unnecessary luxury, but quickly scolded herself for thinking the way her husband would. *I am a highborn Adeltian. Of that I must not forget.*

A glance around the anteroom made her almost cringe at the gaudy display of opulence. Pleated fabric covered walls framed with molding bound in tooled leather, above which the ceiling portrayed idyllic scenes engraved into hardwood. *The room feels not unlike a coffin,* she thought, also noticing that the pleasant outdoor chill had been replaced by a stuffy heat.

It was a mystery to her how these Adeltian nobles seemed to live so much more lavishly than her, when it was she who married the conqueror, and they who were the conquered. Crella had no misgivings about King Lyell. He was a cruel and terrible man who had thrown her aunt from the heights of the Throne, but as she stared at the display before her, she could not help but wonder why it was that he did not take for himself all that she saw. *Lyell is either the most astute or idiotic of conquerors to have allowed the Adeltian nobles to retain so much of their wealth.*

"How long has it been since we last saw each other?" the man continued.

He was Lord Junton. Although stripped of his title after Lyell's conquest, those of the Adeltian elite still appreciated the former viscount as such.

"Far too long," Crella said, unconvinced by her own words. She had never really known the man, just spoken with him briefly at banquets and the like, but he had reached out to her several times to extend friendship over the past decade, an offer she had neither rejected nor accepted. He had an air to him similar to Cassen which bothered her. *Surely that which offends me in him is not that which I project myself.* She tried to put the troubling notion out of her mind. Her husband had had her second-guessing herself ever since the unexpected night they'd shared with the tea.

"I pray your husband is recovering well?" Junton motioned for her to walk beside him as they made their way down a corridor. He was a gaunt man with skin aged beyond his years. Though by no means attractive, plenty a young maiden had swooned over him due to his wealth and presumed power.

"Yes, he is a resilient man," Crella said. "And your wife, Lady Beyla. Is she well?"

Crella had expected to meet Beyla at the door of their home, as it was Adeltian custom to be first welcomed by the lady of an estate. Crella remembered her to have been a young woman of great beauty years prior, when she had married the far older Junton, and Crella was eager to see if time had been kind to her.

"That she is." Junton led her through a doorway into a massive room. "Your son has been a most-welcome guest at our estate these past few days," he continued, seeming eager to change the topic. Junton turned toward his left, profiling a thin curving nose, almost comical in appearance, past which Crella saw Stephon crouched at the hearth. Her son was busy poking at the burning embers with an iron rod, making sparks fly from the disturbance.

The boy loves anything with the capacity to destroy. It was an observation she had made before, but she allowed herself to believe it a positive trait for one who must someday rule.

"I am pleased to hear that, Lord Junton," she said. She hesitated before including his phantom title, as it was somewhat treasonous to refer to him as such, but after all he had done for her and Stephon it was the least she could do to show her appreciation and respect. "It is with regret then, that, as I am sure Stephon has told you, we must be leaving for Westport on the morrow." The date had been pushed back given Alther's injury, but both he and Crella were eager to leave at this point. It was unavoidable, and further delay might upset the king.

Stephon tossed the iron poker carelessly toward a corner, making a clamor and depositing more ash on the already-dirtied stone floor. Crella was appalled by the display, wondering how her son could have forgotten so quickly that he was a guest here. Junton did not seem the least bit offended, however—if anything he appeared pleased. Stephon stood, brushed off clothing that Crella did not recognize as his own, and approached her with an autocratic stride.

"I will not be leaving, Mother." Stephon spoke with all the dignity of a king addressing a servant.

Not wishing to make a scene in front of their host, Crella merely frowned at her son.

"I will leave you two in private to discuss. It has been a pleasure seeing you again, Crella. You and yours are always welcome at our estate." Following his words, Junton exited as promised.

After a moment the two were alone in a room that seemed Stephon was far more comfortable in than was Crella. "What exactly do you mean, Stephon? And you should act with more civility when a guest in someone's home." She spoke with caution in case anyone might be eavesdropping through closed doors.

"I will not be leaving for Westport. The place is a slum not fit for the heir to the Adeltian Throne. You've said so yourself. Cassen has arranged for me—"

"Cassen?" Crella interrupted. "I told you to stay away from that man. He is not to be trusted."

Stephon gave her a conceited snort. "Mother, please. I would hardly call him a man, and believe me when I tell you, the *duchess* is no more immune to my charms than are any of the flippant girls that compete for my affection." The shrewd smirk Stephon wore appalled her. It was true, Stephon was received quite well by the young women at balls and events, but what else could be expected from the only boy with both Adeltian blood and a claim to the throne? As for the prospect of him charming Cassen, the thought revolted her to the point of losing control.

Crella's palm met Stephon's cheek with a crack, and she waited for him to retreat like he always did and submit to her will. But this time he did not. Without moving his head from the way it had been turned from the slap, Stephon slowly raised a pointed finger, pausing dramatically. He still did not look at her while he addressed her, as if his doing so might provoke him to violence.

"Mother, I will forgive you that, your final assault upon me. You are a woman, and as such are given to rash bouts of stupidity and childishness not befitting your advanced age." Now his eyes met hers, and she saw his fury. "But I warn you, should you attempt to strike me again, you will not enjoy the consequences."

Crella was too taken aback to respond. She studied her son, desperate for some sign of the little boy she once knew. She flashed to the memory of the time she had first noticed his behavior changing from pure innocence to questionable morality. Crella had a fondness for bantam wolves, a breed of stunted dog that grew to the size and likeness of a wolf pup and no larger. As a child, she had always had two or three of the long-haired canines in her care, and that had continued until Stephon was a boy of six years. He'd come to her swearing vengeance on one of her pets, promising to skin it for nipping his hand. Crella tried to explain to him, not for the first time, that no animal likes to have its tail yanked, but in looking in Stephon's eyes she knew her words had no effect. She decided it would be best to give away her pets rather than risk the inevitable escalation.

"Cassen has spoken to the king and arranged for me to remain in Eastport as his apprentice. I will learn to do what Alther cannot, manage a city. I will no doubt teach Cassen a great many things as well, but I will not be fool enough to show him all my tricks. Lyell was quick to agree, knowing full and well that left with Alther, I would learn nothing." Stephon paused a moment as if to ponder the depths of his own intellect. "I may have done our kingdom a disservice by not striking him with something more substantial than a vase. I understand your desire to not look a harlot, but continuing to pretend that he is my father is unforgivable."

Crella could not bring herself to comprehend Stephon's comments. How he was able to so nonchalantly accuse her of adultery and speak of murdering his father, she could not understand. She had never before known Stephon to wish to injure Alther and had believed her son had only attacked him in her defense. Cassen, Junton, or both were likely manipulating the boy to best suit their own schemes. *I should never have sent him here.* She wanted to slap him into sense, but she now truly feared his retaliation.

"And on the subject of Red Rivers men, are you aware of what *His Grace*—that disgusting old man—did at the most recent ball? To my half-sister, your *daughter*?" Stephon spat the question as if his mother had somehow been complicit.

Crella had heard of it and was equally disgusted; however, she saw no reason to push her son further down this destructive line of thought. "He merely danced with the girl, as fathers often do with daught—"

"How *dare* you make excuses for that deviant," Stephon interrupted, raging. "Blood relation or not, that is his granddaughter, and he made advances upon her as would any suitor. It is repugnant. I would not blame the Adeltian masses, should they revolt in reaction to a deed so poorly done."

There were ears everywhere, and her son was openly speaking treason—a thing normally best dealt with by turning heel and distancing oneself from the speaker. Crella still could see the face of her servant executed for the same crime, her expression frozen in despair, her eyes forever accusing Crella of being her informer. How much more gruesome a sight would it have been had she seen it in actuality and not only in her imagining? Would she force herself to witness Stephon's impalement?

Crella drove the thoughts off, along with her fears of his potential for reprisal. "You do not know what you are saying. Your words are not your own. You have been made to believe things—"

"I have been made to believe things? Is your hypocrisy boundless?" Stephon now had a dangerous mirth mixed with his fury that threatened assault.

"Your grandfather is *the king*," she said, meeting his fury with her own. *Strike me if you must, but you will hear my words.* "And you will respect and obey him so long as he is as such."

A mischievous and sinister smile spread across Stephon's face. "I would not expect that old man to rule for so long as you might think, Mother. I know a great deal that you do not."

Just as he'd finished his statement, Crella heard a heavy pounding at the door punctuated with authoritative shouting.

TITON SON OF TITON

Titon spent much of the long trek home thinking of the woman, of the crude ring he'd taken from her corpse. He wanted to be rid of it, fearing it carried with it some taint of malfeasance, but he had nothing else to give Red. He focused instead on his plans that he felt would make up for his lack of real jewelry, and as he discussed them aloud, he felt his spirits lifting.

Titon knew that when his father learned of their achievement he would no doubt be proud of them—*both* of them for once. Throughout their trip, Decker had tried to make Titon look good among the men by constantly reminding them all of whose idea it was to descend the cliffs. It was so sloppily done, however, that it had only served to make Titon look like a weakling that needed his little brother to prop him up. Despite that, Titon was eager for Decker to reiterate those same boasts when it came time to recount their tales of victory to their father. The man would have no choice but to acknowledge him for his cunning, and though Titon would not fully admit it to himself, he looked forward to finally winning his father's respect. He also intended to capitalize on that respect.

"With my brother and father's help, it will not take long to finish the house," Titon explained to his new friend.

Titon had already drawn up the plans for the structure in his head. The house itself would be rather unique, not requiring any load-bearing internal walls, nor a central chimney which normally complicated construction of the roof. Titon expected that his father, having built his own home, would doubt it at first, then be forced to recognize its ingenuity as it came together.

"If you need another set of hands," Arron offered.

"I could use your help," said Titon. "But that will be after the main structure is complete. The house may not be difficult to build, but the stove will be. I intend to route the hot smoke through metal piping around the home."

Arron looked at him questioningly.

"I will get more heat from each log burned," Titon explained. "You will see."

The two walked at the rear of the group, as Arron was compelled to stay downwind of the others.

"Just as long as you can still cook atop the damn thing," said Arron. "What was that horrid stew you had planned?"

"Rabbit, carrots, onion stalks, potatoes, chopped parsley, and…tinder berries?"

"It's the berries that seem wrong. They are so sour." Arron had concern on his face. "Your father does not use berries in his stew, does he?"

"No. Maybe mushrooms then."

"That sounds better," replied Arron. "Surely a stew to win any woman's heart." Arron seemed quite willing to humor Titon when it came to the topic of his conquest of Red, though he was likely just happy to have someone to speak to. "My father did far less to steal my mother, and they live together to this day."

The potential for knowing what had worked for Arron's father piqued Titon's interest. He knew little of what really won over women except what he had read in books, which always involved sweeping gestures of chivalry and romance. The men of his clan who had acquired the most favored women did not seem to have followed those methods, however. Everyone knew the story of how his father had stolen his Storm Wolf, and as for Keethro, he was just Keethro. The man could have had his choice of any woman in the clan, and rumors were he did quite a fair amount of choosing before making his final selection. *It is no wonder he chose Red's mother in the end*, thought Titon. Kilandra and Red had their similarities in appearance.

"Tell me how he won her affections, if you know the tale."

Arron looked a little embarrassed. "I am not sure it will really meet your standards. Nor can I be sure that it is all truth."

Titon shrugged. "It cannot hurt to hear it."

"All right. My father claims he went to her home every day and asked to see her, and every day her mother would be the one to answer the door and tell him to go away. He was a tanner's son, same as I, and apparently her mother did not want her daughter with such a man. On the seventh day, her father answered the door instead and told him to piss off or something to that effect. So my father punched him in the face, barged into the home, and left with the girl who then became his wife."

Titon frowned at Arron. All his people's stories of courtship were eerily similar, and none seemed to him to be very realistic. *Perhaps in the case of a tanner's son there would need to be some level of violence involved to find a mate*, Titon admitted. The prospect of having to battle Keethro, however, was as frightening as anything he could imagine, and he did not see it winning him Red's love. His only chance against Keethro was with treachery, and that was not like to impress anyone.

"Well, it is a good story, no doubt. But I think I will stick with my original plan."

"It is no good story! It is the crap my father tells me when I complain how no girl will come near me due to the smell. I will be no tanner once I am out of my father's house, I can tell you that. It is a cruel thing to put your family through."

Titon could not disagree. But every clan needed a tanner, and Arron would no doubt be the one they looked to when the time came, as he had no brothers.

"When I decipher this riddle of courtship, I will share with you all its secrets. It will not matter who your father is or what he does. You will get whichever girl you choose, so long as it is not Red, of course."

Titon took in his surroundings. This would be the last time he would lay eyes on the dark plateaus of the western coast or the sea full of ice. Unable to inhale deeply to enjoy the scent, Titon brushed some of the sea salt that had crystallized on his brow to his palm, dabbed a bit with the tip of his tongue, and determined he preferred the taste to that of the salt traded near his home. *Perhaps I could rig some device that would allow me to farm this salt straight from the air.* Salt was cheap, he knew, but some may pay a premium for this taste of the sea.

"Rika," said Arron.

"Rika?" Titon had to pause for a moment to remember what their topic had been. "That girl with the bird's nest for hair?"

Arron scowled. "The girl with the beautiful bright-red curls of hair, you mean."

"Yes, I meant no insult." Titon did not wish to anger his newfound friend. "A bird's nest is no bad thing. Every bird needs a home."

Arron's scowl grew, making him look mad enough to strike Titon.

"What I meant to say is—"

"Yes, it is a fecking mess, that head-o-hair." Arron interrupted with a chuckle. "And I'll have a mind to tell her to brush the damn thing from time to time, once I have some say in the matter."

Titon laughed in earnest, something he realized had been rare on this trip. "She is the leatherworker's daughter, is she not?"

"Aye, we do a lot of trade with them so I see her often. I tell you, she may not have the finest locks, but what she lacks there she more than makes up for in other areas. The Mountain be thanked. And you of all people could not fault me for liking a *red*-haired girl, no? Even if Red's is hardly so still, she was when you first became enamored, if I have heard you right."

"Yes. I loved her then, I love her more now, and I would love her more again should her hair switch back to the brightest red. She cannot do wrong in my eyes."

"You are not well in the head, I think. You may have slipped on some Dogman entrails and cracked your skull."

"You know what I was thinking?" Titon went on, undaunted. "A bouquet of snow lilies. Oh no, wait, lily petals spread out on the table. I think she would appreciate that. She's very artistic herself."

"So you will build for her a house, filled with the plunder from the greatest raid ever led on the Dogmen, have for her a supper that is like to be even better than the one your mother prefers." Titon heard Arron struggle with the decision of using past or present tense to speak of Titon's mother—everyone did that. "And it will be presented upon a table strewn with the petals from the rarest flower. *Then* you ravage her?"

"Ha, no. Then I give her the metal ring to show my undying devotion to her. Then perhaps after that I can." Titon could not control the size of the smile forming across his face.

"Well, I am no lady, but with such a showing you might even win my heart."

Arron clasped his hands together, placed them to his chest, and stared at Titon affectionately. Titon punched him in the arm and snorted. The two young men walked for a ways in silence while Titon tried to determine if the flower petals should be randomly placed on the table or placed to form a symmetrical pattern.

"Titon," Arron began more seriously, "how long do you intend to live in such a house, though? You have been adamant about our need to move permanently south. Why go through all the trouble just to leave?"

Titon *had* thought of it. There was not much that escaped his constant analysis. "I figure we have another year or two of easy raids on the Dogmen via the cliffs. I only warn of the need to move south so urgently because all things with our people seem to happen slower than planned. And to have an extra year or two alone with Red would be…" Titon trailed off dramatically at the thought, causing Arron to chuckle at his love-struck friend.

❦

Titon had retaken his place at the front with his brother as they neared their home. Passing through other Galatai clan territories on the way, they were already getting a taste of what it was to return as heroes. Word of their conquest spread faster than the pace at which they traveled, so it was no surprise to see a gathering waiting for them when they finally reached their own lands.

What did surprise Titon was who was in attendance, or more precisely, who was not. It was always easy to recognize the outline of his father given his size, but it seemed quite obvious even from far off that he was not present. *You neither see us off nor greet us upon our return, Father?*

Farewells before battle were not a Galatai custom, but a celebration upon victory certainly was. *Perhaps you have a separate ceremony planned just for Decker.* Titon's sardonic thoughts shifted to confusion as he continued to inspect the figures in the distance. The center figure, toward whom the others were turned as if waiting for permission, was clearly that of a woman. With his father absent, Titon would have expected Keethro to be the one the clan would look to for leadership. *Could it be Mother?* The prospect excited him, but he brushed it aside just as quickly as it had come. He must not torment himself with foolish thoughts of her ever improving as did his brother and father.

It soon became evident that it was not his mother. The woman in the center, in addition to having a shape pleasing to the eye, had long dark hair. Beside her was a smaller woman with a similar shape, and around them were sprawled near a hundred of the members of their clan. *Kilandra and Red.*

Titon ignored Kilandra, concentrated instead on his heart's tormentor. The weeks away from Red had only intensified her beauty and perfected her form. What was more, she seemed to stare directly at him with adoring affection.

As he closed distance, Titon saw an unfamiliar expression upon her face. She was infatuated, like a girl looking at her savior who had rescued her from a winter of desperate starvation, a man who single-handedly engineered a raid that went deeper and with more success into Dogman territory than any before him had dared. Titon's chest swelled with pride and burned with the anxiety of being moments away from achieving what had been his goal all along, to have Red's undivided affection. The notion to sweep her off her feet, take her alone into the woods, and have her watch as he built them a shelter in a single night entered his mind. It was stupid, he knew, but he suddenly felt capable of anything.

He tried to envision what he must look like to her, marching back with so many men and provisions in tow, his face purposefully stern, as if their complete and total victory had been a foregone conclusion. *She now sees me as a leader*, he realized, instantly regretting ever having considered a path other than the one that would allow him to take his father's place. The shadow of accomplishment Titon now cast must make even his giant brother who walked beside him seem small. Titon turned his head left to see Decker wearing the very grin Titon had been so careful to avoid. Decker looked doltishly proud, but he was still an obvious conqueror, an obvious leader. Titon then gazed back at Red and felt his own rigid look melt away as he came to realize at whom she truly stared.

ETHEL

"A king for every island. I always wondered how that could even work."

Having a friend near her age had been an incredible relief to Ethel, especially with the rumors now circulating about her and her family. She was able to put most of that from her mind when the two of them were alone together.

Her suspicions that Annora was a mere puppet of Cassen's had been all but quashed, given the sincerity with which she spoke of the man, both favorably and ill. In spite of her candor when speaking of Cassen, there was still the issue of Annora having been well trained, along with possessing a natural inclination not to speak of her life before having left the Spicelands. Ethel found it a difficult task to compel her to share any details regarding her past.

"Sometimes it doesn't," replied Annora. "Why is this road so rounded?"

The road of brick and mortar was actually a pipe that followed the inner side of the city's western walls. The two walked atop it as they spoke.

"It's an aqueduct," said Ethel, mildly annoyed by Annora's conversational parry. "This one brings water from many miles northwest of the city, a place in the mountains where a tributary that feeds the Eos has the freshest, cleanest water of the realm." Annora respectfully nodded to acknowledge what Ethel had said and looked down. *I will have to teach her to look at me as an equal, at least when we are in private.*

"It is like a giant serpent," Annora said quietly.

Ethel had always thought of the wall as shaped like a ribbon, and the pipe as just a thing made to follow, but she could see how a serpent might be a better comparison. The aqueduct seemed to slither beside the wall, alternating westward and northward in kind. "My father was never able to tell me why they were built this way. He says a great deal of stone was wasted, though—that the King's Arm was more properly constructed."

"Why do I not hear any water?"

"No water is flowing now. These were made hundreds of years ago." Ethel kicked a piece of loose mortar as she walked. "My father says they used to carry a stream of water at all times back then, but over time many small leaks developed. As the city's needs grew, it was determined that less water would be wasted if they dammed the flow nearer the source, only opening it for a few hours a day." Ethel forced herself to silence, realizing she rambled details that were not likely of any interest to the girl. *She'll see me like the rest of them do*, Ethel thought to herself, now fearing Annora may have originally only wanted a simple explanation of how they received fresh water, not a lesson and tiring voyage toward the source.

"It must be a great sight when the dam is opened. Is it too far to reach?" Annora sounded genuinely interested, which surprised Ethel.

"I am afraid it is too far to reach on foot, and dangerous as well. But if we have timed it properly, we will reach a spot still within the walls where we can see the start of the daily rush of water." Ethel's mood was once again heightened. "I have often gone there alone just to see it."

Their journey continued in a comfortable silence. A cloud of dust trailed them from the dry dirt they kicked up while walking, but other than that, there was nothing to see but wall and the distant castle. The desolation of this place was in stark contrast to all other areas of the city sheltered within the outer walls. The first King Adellos was the one to have made it unlawful to bring carts or horses over these sections of the piping, due to their tendency to cave. Had Ethel and Annora traveled in any other direction from the castle, they would already be in the middle of an impoverished area, but this corner of the kingdom was only frequented, it seemed, by young highborn looking for mischief, privacy, or both.

"Have you ever actually seen a serpent before?" Ethel asked. She'd been unable to rid herself of serpentine imagery since Annora had mentioned it.

"I have done more than see them. We ate them on the islands."

Ethel looked at Annora with confusion and disgust, and watched as Annora's contentment drained.

"It tastes fine," Annora said in her defense before looking down again.

"Then I should hope to try it some time." Ethel lied as believably as she could. "How did your cooks prepare it?" she asked, feigning interest.

Ethel was pleased to see Annora amused, but did not understand the cause of it.

"My mother cooked it several ways. The best was in bubbling coconut oil."

"Ah, your mother was a cook?"

"On the islands all mothers are many things." Annora spoke quite matter-of-factly. Nonetheless, Ethel was impressed.

"You must have loved her very much."

Annora looked as though she was contemplating whether to simply agree or divulge whatever it was that clearly bothered her—Ethel willed the latter with intensity.

"I grew to neither love nor hate her." Annora let out a breath. "She was a weak woman."

"How so?" Ethel prodded when it seemed Annora would say no more.

"How can you love, let alone pity, a woman who folds to the will of a man so completely that when he tells her north is south, she not only agrees with him, but convinces herself that it is indeed the case?"

Ethel had not expected such candor from Annora on this subject, but she welcomed it. Ethel did not welcome her lingering worry that Alther may possess the very characteristics that Annora described in her mother, however. *He is not so weak as that*, Ethel assured herself. *Not with Mother, at least.* The king may have been a different story, but Ethel could not fault her father for obeying his own.

"She did not object when your father sent you to Adeltia?" She did not distrust Annora's story of being *sold*, at least in some sense, but she could not bring herself to repeat the word.

"By then it did not matter," said Annora, despondent.

Ethel feared that would be the end of the story. It was obviously not a pleasant one. Much to her surprise, Annora continued.

"The kings on our islands not only have many wives, they have many *young* wives. At the age of eleven, when my father saw I'd grown faster than the others, he began preparing me to marry his cousin, the king."

Ethel was able to keep from gasping, more at the revelation that Annora may have been considered some sort of savage royalty at some point than at the potential for incest—if indeed marrying one's father's cousin was considered such on their islands.

"It seemed a great honor at first, and my father and I grew close as he showered me with jewelry to raise my status. I was quite jealous when a close friend of mine married the king before me, becoming his fifteenth wife. She was gone for months celebrating her marriage during which I envied her undeserved luck. But when she returned she was different. She had no great tales of wonderful sights seen on distant islands. She barely spoke at all. She'd become a joyless shell of the girl she once was, and I had no desire to follow in her path. My mother…"

Annora stopped and cleared her throat, causing Ethel to fear for a moment that she meant to spit.

"My mother did nothing to stop my father from forcing me to attend the king's next marriage ceremony. The event attracted the entire island to watch as the king asked his potential brides what made them fit for marriage. The girls before me answered aloud the typical reasons, that they were good cooks, or weavers, or swimmers. When my turn came I asked to tell the king in secret. It was my only chance of escape, as I lacked the courage to have scarred my face, the only other way I could think to avoid this marriage. I watched my father's expression, likely mirroring the king's, turn from pride to dread, as I whispered into the king's ear."

Annora went quiet.

What did you say? Ethel wondered, but she would not press her further, not today. Annora's revelation was more than Ethel had expected. Annora did not seem the type to want pity, and Ethel kept herself from attempting to console her. She decided she'd simply let the rushing water of the aqueduct cheer Annora instead. They were very close now.

As they neared the final bend in the wall that led to their destination, Ethel heard voices. Had she been by herself, it would have been her cue to turn around and leave. They sounded like children at play, however, and with Annora by her side, Ethel did not feel the need to avoid the potential for interaction as was her normal tendency.

"A little farther," a boy said. "At the end you will find a gemstone. You must retrieve it."

Ethel and Annora rounded the bend and saw three boys crouched around the opening in the aqueducts. Ethel quickly recognized one of the boys as Sture. Most Adeltian highborn had an air of arrogance, but Ethel knew Sture to exceed that immodest standard. She also had trouble determining the source of his pretentiousness, as he was quite feeble looking for his age.

"I do not see it," echoed a squeaky voice from inside the tunnel. "I want to come out."

"Derudin will be disappointed if you cannot carry out this simple task. All named students have to complete it in order to progress in their training." Sture looked at the other boys, lifting his shoulders and covering his mouth with his fist as if to stifle laughter.

"What are you doing?" Ethel demanded.

The boys shot to their feet. Two of them made only brief eye contact, but Sture scowled at Ethel with contempt. "What business of yours is it?" The golden insignia of House Ellavium shone against his moleskin coat like a badge of authority.

"It is not safe for your friend to be down there. It will be a rushing river any moment now." Ethel moved toward the opening as she spoke.

"Oh, I know you," Sture said with a growing smile. "You are the bastard girl!"

Ethel ignored his comment and continued toward the lip of the tunnel to yell a warning to whoever was inside, but Sture shoved her back.

"You must come out," Ethel yelled, hoping it would be heard from inside the aqueduct.

"Stay out of this, bastard bitch. I heard you were seducing your own grandfather, you incestuous slut. How about you go—"

Ethel charged Sture and tried to push him out of the way. She may have had five years on the weakling, but he still outweighed her, and her long dress made things difficult. The two fell to the ground, him on top. His look of rage turned to one of amusement, realizing he'd won.

"Does your grandfather ride you like this?" The glee in Sture's empowered voice sickened Ethel, and the smell of leather, sweat, and his minty breath drove her to nausea.

Sture shrieked. Annora had him by his bright blonde hair and pulled him off of Ethel. Annora was a small woman, slightly smaller in frame than Ethel even, but she seemed to have an ox's strength as she handled Sture the way a mother would her young brat.

"Release me," he screamed, but Annora merely signaled to Ethel to continue what she had originally attempted. Ethel sprung to her feet and hurried to the opening.

"Get out of there, it is not safe," she yelled into the dark tunnel. "Come toward my voice!" She thought she heard the pitter-patter of small feet running, but all sound was drowned out by the roar of distant rushing water. The hole was almost the height of a man from the bottom of the aqueduct, and there was no ladder, making it difficult for even a tall, agile boy to get out on his own. Ethel feared she would not be much help either, but she got on her stomach and stretched her arms out nonetheless. "Run to me," she called again, though it was unlikely the person inside could hear her over the water.

She waited, expecting at any moment for a boy's body to wash past her in a flash, unable to grab hold of her hands or, worse yet, pulling her in with him. She tensed her muscles in anticipation, hoping he would not be a heavy one. Then she felt hands grasp her own—tiny hands with spindly wrists—but even so, Ethel was pulled with so great a force that she almost flipped forward.

"Annora, help," she cried, realizing even this small child was too difficult to hoist on her own.

Annora must have flung Sture to the ground before coming to help her, because after the two of them wrestled from the aqueduct what turned out to be a tiny girl with stark-white hair, Sture was covered in dirt and hatred.

"You do not lay hands upon an Adeltian highborn, you servant whore! I will have you flayed for this!"

The little girl was crying, drenched from the waist down, but, from the looks of it, otherwise unharmed.

"She could have been *killed*." Annora's Spicelander accent was unsuppressed by her normally careful articulation.

"My father, Alther, will see that no harm comes to her for helping to save a girl's life." Evoking the king's name rather than just her father's would have been more consequential, but Ethel had no mind to speak his name again after the dinner. "You overstep yourself. You may be highborn, but you are still a conquered people. It would do you well to remember."

It was the simple truth. Ethel had been told by her mother that Adeltians were always a proud people, but that prior to the short and bloody war, their pride had had more justification. All the best had been lost during the fight to save their kingdom. To Ethel, all that seemed to remain of the once noble Adeltians were the dregs and detritus. The irony was not lost on her that the very thing that made their land so rich for farming was now unfortunately foremost in their people. *If only the likes of Sture could have been lost and buried, feeding the crops, so that the worthy could have remained.*

Clearly relieved that they had not been accomplice to murder, Sture's two friends returned to his side, further bolstering his confidence. "Do not assume that your sleeping with the enemy will keep you safe for long. Adeltian traitors will suffer the same fate as the Rivervalian scum when the time comes." Sture spit in their direction, turned on a heel, and left with his friends in tow.

Ethel and Annora shifted their attention to the soaked girl.

"What is your name?" Ethel asked her. "We will take you home."

A few sobs later the girl managed to say, "Eaira," then after a few more, "of House Eddlebrook."

Ethel recognized the house name as Rivervalian. Her parents must have been among the Rivervalians who had come to assume positions of governance that were no longer suitable for Adeltians. Other than Cassen, no Adeltians held positions of governance or power beyond that of a merchant—though merchants were often among the richest in the kingdom. Because so few wished to leave Rivervale, the task of filling those positions left vacant fell on some of the poorer of the noble families, giving Adeltians further cause for feeling superior. It also explained the girl's plain dress.

With Eaira between them, they began to walk her home. Ethel could see in Annora's expression a look of distress, potentially well founded. A servant laying hands upon nobility was not acceptable, and Lyell was always too happy to appease Adeltian nobility.

"You will not be harmed for what happened today. I give you my word," Ethel reassured her. "You saved her life." *Even should I have to marry my grandfather to become queen, I will not let harm befall my only friend.*

DERUDIN

"Derudin, what would you have me do? I cannot imprison a man on the basis of what my First—a man who is known to despise him—sees. Sees with closed eyes, at that." Lyell filled his lungs, letting his breath out in frustration. "No man has contributed to nor profited more from this kingdom than has Cassen. I find it hard to believe that he would be involved in such schemes."

"I am only informing you of what I have seen," Derudin said. "I believe Cassen not just to be involved, but to be one of the architects. I merely ask that you keep that in mind when he speaks with us today."

Meetings always made the king ill-tempered, but this impromptu High Council meeting was something of a different nature. Derudin thought it a good sign that the king was not already raging.

"Yes, yes, I will," said Lyell. "You do know the boy cracked before even having been questioned? He has named several Adeltian nobles, all of which we already knew about, and is claiming he intended to tell us all along—that pompous ass. I do not believe he realizes just how thorough our spies are. No mention of Cassen, however, you will be disappointed to hear. And Crella has thus far been silent." The king motioned for a servant to bring him more wine.

Derudin ran a finger along the joint of the tabletop before him, admiring the way the two narrow pieces, which normally served as console tables on either side of the entryway, came together in combination with Lyell's desk to form a single seamless structure. This work of finery, aside from being a reminder of hundreds years past when skills such as woodworking were as much an art as a profession, had been the centerpiece of High Council meetings ever since the taking of Adeltia. Derudin silently cursed Cassen for having robbed him of the joy of seeing this masterpiece put together as a whole for so long.

As the servant topped off the king's goblet, a commotion was heard from outside the room.

"Let him in." Lyell spoke with annoyance as if he'd anticipated the occurrence.

It was Alther, and he wasted no time storming down the entryway. *How does a father tell his son that he has imprisoned his son and wife?* Derudin had not advised the king on how best to handle this; it was not his area of expertise.

"Where are they?" Alther had come to a stop on the opposite side of the table from Derudin, standing closer to the king than was usual. "If they have been hurt I will hold you accountable."

Alther spoke to his father in a way that seemed to Derudin to be rather uncharacteristic even given the circumstances. Alther had always been ingratiating and compliant when it came to his father. Then again, most men who valued their wellbeing did their best to do the same in the king's presence.

"Yes, I am sure you will. And I am also sure you will expect me to hold *them* accountable for any crimes they may have committed." Lyell's voice was calm but challenging.

"*What crimes?* Crella is no criminal, and she has been accommodating in accepting your request for us to move to Westport."

"It was not a request," corrected Lyell. "And was this before or after Stephon nearly killed you with a vase and she hid him away with her Adeltian friends?"

Derudin could see the look of guilt on Alther's face as he paused to determine his best response. Lyell must have as well.

"Oh, so you knew it was Stephon who attacked you? And you allowed the show of the search for your assailant to go on?" The king's voice rattled with indignation. "I am sure some of your loyal servants were questioned quite thoroughly, and you, no doubt, would expect the same treatment to befall your loving wife and son should *they* be accused of a crime."

"He is my son, and I will handle his punishment. I gave strict instruction that none of the servants were to be mistreated. There was no need for all of this." Alther waved his hand about the room.

Lyell shook his head. "Do you think I would call a meeting of the High Council because your brat of a boy cracked you on the head?"

Alther wore a look of confusion when a door guard indicated that the remaining High Council members had gathered outside the room.

"Send them in." Lyell spoke as if already exhausted.

The first to enter was a man of countless years. Master Larimar had dirty-grey hair that hung from his head and cheeks in wispy patches. He was bent over as he walked, though not using a cane or any instrument to assist his movement, shuffling his feet one after the other with considerable effort. He had the look of a man who was not content unless sitting in a chair, hunched over a book, and even then he was like to be less than affable. He made his way toward the center of the table where a very large, very old book had been placed, already opened.

Beside it sat a small onyx pot with the feathers of two quills protruding from it. As the Master of Records, Larimar was responsible for recording and recalling the events of High Council meetings both present and past, and his influence, as such, was limited to the way in which he framed those writings and recollections. *Enough influence to send a kingdom to ruin if he so desired,* Derudin noted to himself.

The man who followed was an imposing figure. The ornate crest of The Guard was emblazoned upon his ornamental breastplate. Master Warin stood half a head above all others in attendance, save for the king, and easily weighed half again as much. Although he did not appear to have retained the speed and grace of his youth, during which he had held the title of tournament champion for three years, his strength appeared to still be fully intact.

Last to enter was Cassen, who flowed in with his usual elegance in spite of his roundness. His gaze immediately went to Derudin. *Surprised to see me?* thought Derudin, noticing what appeared to be a glimmer of fear in the man's eyes. *I know what you are planning, eunuch.*

There would be no Master of Forces or Master Treasurer present, nor had there ever been when Lyell ruled. He alone managed his military and finances, believing that to assign a single man to oversee the entirety of his army or his treasury would be an invitation for overthrow. Derudin had seen as much happen in kingdoms past and thought it among Lyell's wiser decisions. Nonetheless, when all the men were seated, two chairs remained vacant.

"Due to the short notice of this meeting, Duke Veront and Lord Edwin will not be attending," declared Lyell. He glanced momentarily at both Cassen and Derudin to ensure neither man meant to start a quarrel with the other. "You may proceed, Larimar."

"On this, the twenty-eighth day of the twelfth month of the eight hundred and fifty-second year, an unscheduled meeting of the High Council was called to resolve the issue regarding…" Larimar trailed off to indicate the need for someone to complete his sentence.

"Regarding the arrest of Crella," said Lyell. "Wife of Alther of House Red Rivers, son of the king, and the arrest of Stephon of House Red Rivers, son of Alther, both heirs to the throne and so forth… Both on account of treason."

"*Treason?*" said Alther, demanding explanation. He was now back on his feet, his momentary compliance vanished along with proper High Council decorum.

Master Larimar continued as if the interruption was of no consequence. "Let the record show all members of the Council are in attendance save Duke Veront and Lord Edwin due to—"

"I demand proof of these accusations!" interrupted Alther.

Lyell stared at his son coldly. Derudin's main attention was on

Cassen, searching for signs of guilt, but he currently looked quite pleased. *How can you remain so calm?* Derudin had hoped the arrest of co-conspirators and the threat of Cassen's name being revealed under torture would have shaken the man.

"As you must know, my boy, we have spies placed throughout the kingdom. When so much as a vase is cracked, we know of it. How else do you think I maintain order as a Rivervalian ruling over a city of Adeltians constantly plotting revenge? And revenge for what? Deposing a senseless queen and allowing them to—"

Alther cut off the king, "Striking one's father is no act of *treason*. He is a fool boy, and I will punish him accordingly. His mother too for having first hidden the truth from me. No one was hurt in this, save for me, and I will deal my *own* justice to my *own* wife and child."

Master Warin shifted noisily in his chair.

"Let the record show that one serving girl was drowned," said Larimar as he scratched the words into his book. "*Accidentally* of course. During questioning regarding the attack on Alther, first heir to the throne." Larimar seemed to take particular delight in taunting both Master Warin and Alther with this declaration. How exactly he had come to know such information was a mystery to Derudin.

"Drowned?" The blood had already drained from Alther's face. "*Who?*"

"Must that be recorded?" asked Master Warin. His long brown locks swayed with the motion of his shaking head. "The fool girl inhaled during simple water immersion, and our questioners were unable to expel the fluid from her weak lungs. It was no fault of ours, really."

"I can put a line through it if you wish," Larimar stated, acquiring a deadpan expression. "But once written, a record in the book of histories shall not be redacted."

"Enough of this nonsense," shouted the king. "I will not hear another word of this incident which has no bearing on this meeting. Crella, Stephon, and the Adeltian ingrates they call friends are charged with treason for having colluded to poison the very members of this council and seize control of the city. The evidence of their involvement is irrefutable."

Master Larimar nodded to himself while recording what Lyell had said, adding, "The punishment for which is death by impalement."

"This is lunacy! Crella would never do such a thing. It is unthinkable." Alther's mouth remained slightly agape, and he put his hand to his head as if to help him think.

It was true, the evidence against Crella was more circumstantial than that against her son, who had been seen and heard planning the exact nature of the events that would lead to their subversion. However, it was hard for an unbiased observer, which Derudin believed himself to be, to accept that she had no involvement given the way she concealed her son's attack on Alther and with whom she'd chosen to assist her in the matter. She was also of pure Adeltian blood and had had no say in the man she had married. *Some grudges do not lessen with time… I should know.*

"If I may interject," said Cassen, "I do believe it would be unwise to impale members of the royal family. Especially those of Adeltian blood."

Derudin could not help himself but to shoot a sly glance at the king as if to confirm with him that Cassen's cry for leniency was self-implicating.

"Would imprisonment not suffice our needs without causing hysteria among the masses?" continued Cassen. "Westport is already ripe for rebellion, and our focus should be on questioning all those currently imprisoned to determine who the mastermind behind this treachery truly was, in the event that he has not yet been apprehended."

The king did not have to mirror Derudin's previous glance for Derudin to realize he must have interpreted Cassen's words to mean he had just exonerated himself of all guilt. *Damn this eunuch.*

"I have been lenient with Adeltian highborn for far too long. We will skewer *Lord* Junton and all his minions to demonstrate the price of treason. Crella and the boy will escape such punishment and will instead remain in confinement, so long as they confess and name any others involved yet to be arrested." Lyell's voice carried the confidence of a man who had just arranged a grand compromise, the sagacity of which was incontestable.

Alther growled at the king between clenched teeth, "I will not allow you to sentence my wife and child to a life of imprisonment on the basis of the whisperings of people who are paid to listen and lie." Alther had a fury Derudin had never before seen in the man. He wondered if Alther's newfound defiance was the result of his brush with death or because the fate of his wife and son now hung in the balance.

"I do not remember asking your permission." The king glowered at his son with wide eyes. "Should you find your separation with your traitorous wife too much to bear, I can arrange for you to stay with her. Indefinitely."

"You will regret this," said Alther, pointing at his father. He turned and began to storm down the lengthy entryway, provoking the guards to bar the path.

"Let him go," said the king.

Once the clanging of the doors closing behind Alther died, all that could be heard was the scratching of quill on parchment. The old bookkeep almost wore a grin as he finished the meeting's transcription, and when Derudin fixed his gaze on Cassen, he could see Larimar was not alone in that veiled expression.

CASSEN

Cassen stopped and looked at his reflection in the calm waters below his feet. He barely recognized what he saw.

Staring back at him was a man—a healthy-looking man not unlike those who littered the docks, scurrying about carrying crates that would have slowed an average person to a crawl. He had donned his disguise in a carriage, without the aid of any silvered glass large enough to see himself in full. Trying to distinguish what it was in his appearance that gave him such a feeling of youth and power, he turned his attention to the others dressed in kind. Timeworn muslin vests covered white shirts with long loose sleeves, their trousers were a thick weave of tan cotton, and all had a bandana of some sort protecting heads of thinning hair from the Dawnstar's rays. Perhaps it was his own bandana which covered his short-cropped hair. It was an ugly sight, he had to admit, cut that way with the intention of one day wearing a wig, an idea he'd determined to have been excessive. Then he saw it. *I have a waist*, he noticed with a smirk, checking the surface of the water once more to confirm.

"You simple? I said get in the fecking boat," commanded a gravel-voiced man. Cassen was quick to comply.

Several hours into their southerly voyage, all that could be seen were the specks of other ships to the north. Cassen found himself wishing they had let him row. He grew restless in his seat at the bow.

Cassen's common deckhand attire might have been comfortable if not for the cold. Even as far south as they were, the combination of sea spray, harsh winds, and the onset of winter produced a rather frigid condition. His billowy sleeves, designed to flap in the wind to cool the wearer, were doing their job too well, and the moisture of his damp wooden seat was beginning to creep through to his skin.

"How much longer?" Cassen asked.

None of the men who rowed, assisting the small-sailed skiff in propulsion, turned to face him, and the man at the rudder, wiry, shirtless, and tanned, merely scowled. *A testament to my disguise and a reminder of the importance of power and influence.*

To these men, Cassen was just some lowborn their captain wished to speak to—at best an emissary of someone of wealth. Had they known he was arguably the second most powerful man in the kingdom, he would have expected a more satisfactory response. And perhaps to be offered a drink. He was parched.

The journey dragged on, forcing Cassen to focus on the forward horizon and continuously chew his candied ginger to curtail his creeping nausea. The stare from the man at the stern burned at Cassen's back. His occasional glances rearward had been greeted by increasingly menacing glares.

"You heave into the boat," the man finally said. Cassen turned around to face him, hoping for an explanation. "Or you get thrown over with it when they come." His thick Spicelander accent somehow added to the sincerity of the threat.

When who comes? Cassen knew better than to ask. Sailors were a superstitious lot, and whatever it was this man feared may be attracted by vomit was not like to be something he wished to name aloud. The prospect troubled Cassen—not the idea of sea monsters, but how close he had unknowingly come to being thrown overboard on previous voyages.

After having been resigned to the idea that he'd be making a fool of himself retching into the boat, Cassen saw the merciful outline of a ship in the distance. Five tall, heavily-slanted sails gave it the appearance of the gills of a shark, though its captain would say the boat was far more ill-tempered. Sacarat, or the Satyr, as he was known by some due to his mixed breeding and evil reputation, claimed the *Maiden's Thief* was the fastest in the realm. Though he believed it to be a boast, Cassen did not actually know of any faster.

Having an object in the distance to focus upon helped, but probably not so much as simply knowing the trip was nearing its end. His nausea subsided to the point of him no longer noticing its presence by the time he was climbing the rope netting on the side of the great ship. *No disguise would be needed should anyone who knew me in Adeltia see me climbing as such. Even dressed in my normal clothes, they would insist it was merely someone else making a spectacle.*

He exerted himself as he pushed to climb faster, surprised by his ability. These trips to meet with Sacarat, he had to admit, were as invigorating as they were critically strategic.

"Cass, my rival, how good it is to see you." The man's accent was most peculiar, though Cassen had come to find it comforting. He did not speak like the men of his crew, for they were all Spicerats—a name given by Adeltian merchants. On the sea there was no worse group of men to have board your ship.

"And you, Sacarat."

Cassen was sure never to address him as friend. "A man who calls you a friend that you have not known from childhood is most assuredly your enemy," the Satyr was known to say. Cassen's philosophy was similar but somewhat simpler. *All men are assuredly my enemies*, he reminded himself, yet Cassen found himself trusting this sea scoundrel more than most.

"How do you find the life of piracy treating you as of late?" Cassen asked.

Sacarat crinkled his brow as if offended. He had the look of a man whose frown threatened true danger, a look Cassen imagined all of his people shared. Whereas the Spicerats were typically Spicelanders with mixed breeding from many foreign lands, the Satyr was half Spicerat and half Sacaran, making him mostly Sacaran in truth. Born a bastard prince to Queen Linota of Sacara, his native tongue was that of his native land, as were his loyalties.

"As good as any," replied Sacarat, lifting his frown to move forward and embrace Cassen, along with a few solid strikes on the back.

Cassen took pleasure in seeing the confused looks upon the faces of the men who had brought him, clearly not expecting him to receive such a warm welcome. But they went on with their business with a few shrugs. For a band of sea brigands, the Satyr's crew was impressively disciplined. He may have only been a prince, but on the *Maiden's Thief*, Sacarat was king and his authority unquestioned—not by Cassen and certainly not by any of his crew.

"If anything, it has become too easy," said Sacarat.

"Is that so?"

Though he was a duchess in Adeltia, here Cassen was every bit the duke. All traces of flamboyance and femininity were gone, at least by his own perception. Sacarans were not tolerant of such behavior, and Cassen had known it would be foolish, if not dangerous, to have maintained his normal demeanor upon first meeting the Satyr years prior. That did not mean Sacarat was ignorant to what Cassen was believed to be in Adeltia; he was just convinced it was a façade. Furthermore, he enjoyed teasing Cassen about it—something that a pureblooded Sacaran would never do, but Sacarat was neither pureblooded nor a typical Sacaran. Cassen thought the man may even respect him more because he believed Cassen to have so thoroughly deceived all those in Adeltia.

"I should like to know how stealing both lives and fortunes can be so effortless," Cassen went on. "Does a man facing death not fight with all his strength?"

Sacarat himself was no stranger to the benefits provided by a thick guise of cloth. His own costume was almost farcical, consisting of a wide headband, a gaudy ornamental necklace with matching brass bracers, a woven oxhide sash that left his chest mostly bare, and a heavy sea shawl about his shoulders. It had the desired effect, however. He looked a Spicerat through and through, with the exception of his pronounced nose, a gift from his Sacaran breeding no doubt.

"The crew of the last ship we boarded," said Sacarat as he guided Cassen below decks, "threw us lines. Those of them who were still alive, that is."

They passed through a room with two long tables that served as the ship's galley. Light peeked through small windows as they made their way to the stern.

"Those still alive?" Cassen asked.

It was always shocking to Cassen when he first set foot into the Satyr's quarters. Any doubts that this man was a prince were snuffed upon seeing the ridiculous amount of wealth that had been crammed into the cabin of moderate size. Chests overflowing with gold and silver were stacked atop each other, secured with ropes to the walls as not to tip. A collection of goblets and steins were tightly packed within glass cupboards, brilliant in their gold, silver, and pearl, engraved with the most intricate patterns. And in the corner was a simple cotton hammock. Cassen could not help but feel a certain camaraderie with the man.

The Satyr chuckled. "Their men turned on one another as soon as they saw our sails."

Cassen just looked at him, confused.

"They know by now that we won't leave enough water for them all to survive. Those smart enough have begun to kill each other before they lose their strength."

The mention of water reminded Cassen of his own desperate need. "Why is it you leave them any water at all?"

The Satyr made a sound of disgust. "All this," he waved toward his stacks of gold-laden chests. "It means little. What is gold compared with glory? And who would tell the tales if none lived to return to land?"

"Ah, yes. And tall tales they tell. Some have begun to believe demon ships sail from the Devil's Mouth. It seems there is no other explanation for how the short trip to Westport has become so much more perilous than to my eastern ports." Cassen beamed his thanks as they sat at a small table covered in maps.

"Tell me, how did you take the message which was delivered?" asked Sacarat. "Near as pleased as I, I'll wager, given the smile you wore upon boarding. Or were you merely elated to be once again in my presence?"

"Ah, yes. 'The winds blow north.' Rather cryptic," said Cassen. "I was indeed pleased to hear it, and it is well timed with my own schemes, all of which, of course, serve both our benefits."

"I am sure, I am sure. I believe you in that, but I doubt you can truly grasp what a moment it will be for my people, a moment for which they have waited over one thousand years. It is true—though I find it hard to accept—your people do not even recollect those events past? Ah, but it will make it all the sweeter."

The Satyr spoke of the previous glory of the Sacaran Empire afforded by their total supremacy at sea. It was all but forgotten by the Adeltians and took Cassen a great deal of searching through ancient annals, but he'd finally found some record of the event. It had taken place before the years were recorded as they now were, further lending credence to the Satyr's claim of the time in which it occurred. A great storm was said to have come, so massive that it ripped trees by the roots, heaved rocks from the ground, and pulled fish from the sea. It would stand to reason that such a storm would wipe out any and all ships in its wake, which was said to be all-encompassing. The Sacaran influence would have been all but extinguished.

"That they do not. They have seen what I assume must be your peoples' ships to the south, but they are yet to make the connection, nor to perceive a threat. They are also convinced that your square sails cannot tack into the wind. Which raises the question, how is it that you can predict the direction of the winds, if it is you can?"

"Predict the wind?" The Satyr snorted. "If only I had such powers. I assure you, however, that the sails of our warships, though they do not share the grace of those of the *Maiden's Thief*, will take our armies to the shores of Adeltia no matter the wind's preference. When properly rigged they can cross the wind. Just not so well as I, of course."

Knowing that the Satyr had no claim of controlling or predicting the elements put Cassen's mind at ease. "I suppose you would like to know how it is I intend to help with your conquest so that my rewards, should you see fit to give them, are justified?"

"You have the tongue of a snake, Cass. I like that in you, for a snake's tongue points in two directions, and one knows the truth must lie somewhere in between. But I do not need to know your every plan, just that you have chosen our side, the side of victory. You have given me much in the way of knowledge, but I assure you this: nothing could stop that which is now in motion. An army of a scale your people have never seen will descend on your shores to reclaim our honor. And you will sit atop the throne of your choosing when it is done, as I have no desire to remain a slave to a chair. But we will both command wealth and respect, that much is known, in witness of the now-hiding Gods."

Cassen believed the Satyr's faith and worship of the celestial deities to be genuine, and his swearing by them further evidence of the veracity of their alliance.

"Well then, you need only know that I have efforts in place to improve the ease at which you will achieve conquest. Should any of them succeed, you will face a kingdom led by a fool, and an army already engaged elsewhere, fighting its own people. What's more, the hungry populace should embrace new authority, so long as they are provided with some minor compensations."

"We Sacarans are no strangers to the exchange of food for loyalty. Some say there is no greater loyalty, and offer animal companions as their example. Those we rule are little different after all." Sacarat did not appear to be mocking the masses, but rather stating what he believed to be a universal truth.

"I believe you are right in that. Let us drink, then, to our ruling over many human pets. Is it not a custom among your people to offer refreshment to those aboard your vessel? Even to a rival such as I?" Cassen was thirsty beyond measure at this point, but his priority had been their business, which now seemed settled.

"Yes, of course," bellowed Sacarat. "How poor are my manners! Let us drink!"

TITON SON OF SMALL GRYN

The idea to construct another boat had been discarded in favor of building a raft. Neither he nor Keethro had any experience on real rivers, but it seemed implausible that there would be any sizeable waves, and that a large, flat raft should do nicely. The memory of sleepless nights on the Timid Sea bade them make ample room to lie flat and nap.

They had floated less than a mile on their hasty creation before their inexperience with their materials became evident. The dry horse leather that bound the timbers expanded, making the structure unstable, barely holding together long enough to make shore. They were not too upset at the failure, as they both conceded they had aimed too small to start, with not quite as much room for sleep and storage as would have been preferred. They then spent a day constructing what was, to them, a true work of art: a giant raft one man in width by three in length, bound this time with horse leather that had already soaked. After a strenuous launch and some backslapping, they floated down the river atop their lazy behemoth as if they had tamed a mighty beast.

"How much longer will it be?" Titon growled, doing his best to remain calm. Keethro showed no sign of responding, which only added to Titon's annoyance.

Aside from his current torment, the voyage had been slow but pleasing, and compared to the time spent on the sea, this river rafting experience was one of luxury and leisure. There was usually no wind, but the wind that did come was welcomed to help mitigate the heat. Despite the season, the temperature had risen to an uncomfortable level, at least for Galatai, and they found their stolen coats to be too heavy even for the cooler nights. Deciding to throw them into the water was perhaps the greatest decision they had made, as each man admitted to having thought the other's smell was an irremediable burden that would have to be borne for the duration of the journey.

Of the few people they'd seen on shore during their trip thus far, they'd only been close enough to make contact with one. A young boy with a pole had a line in the water, fishing from the muddy bank. It was not apparent to Titon if the boy spoke a different language, was dumb, or was merely afraid, but his attempt to speak to him as they passed by was met with no success. "Hullo there, boy," Titon had said, sounding as harmless and amicable as possible. "Do you know what city lies down this river?" The boy stared, jaw agape, his wide eyes alternating between Titon and the giant horse hock. "It's just food," Titon had explained before taking a bite of it to demonstrate. That had been enough for the boy, who abandoned his pole and ran. "Goodbye then," Titon called out to the boy's back, unsure of what else he could have done to seem less threatening. "We need to work on your table manners," Keethro had taunted, and Titon decided he'd let Keethro do the sweet talking next time.

"By the Mountain's tits, it takes you long enough to prepare a simple meal," Titon griped in frustration.

The scents that filled Titon's nostrils were those of sizzling fat and onions. With little else to do as they drifted, the men had alternated cooking meals as a form of competition. Titon was confident his skills learned over the years cooking for his wife would have given him a clear advantage, but Keethro had shown a surprising prowess when it came to inventing ways to prepare their unfamiliar game.

They were also no longer alone on their journey. They found the third member of their party, Iron Hips they had dubbed her, on the side of the river, probably left there due to her heft and rough edges. After they took turns washing and scrubbing her with some horsehide, they had a skillet free from rust scale and ready for curing. Keethro had Iron Hips over the fire that burned at the center of their raft, cooking up his latest inspiration. The wet logs that comprised their raft, packed with clay, served as a suitable platform for keeping their small fire going without risk of igniting themselves, and thankfully no rain had threatened since they set off.

"It is no wonder your food tastes good, given our starved state by the time it is prepared," Titon went on. The skill that Keethro had shown with this new skillet was beginning to try Titon's patience. *Damn this Keethro. He is a natural at all things it seems, save archery.*

"Eat some horse jerky if you are so hungry. I am working here," said the chef.

Titon let out a noise of disgust and did not move to eat any jerky. His stomach, twisted in a knot, would not allow him to eat anything other than that which the smells promised.

Life was abundant on this stretch of slow, dark water. Whiskered rodents floated on their backs, diving as soon as they were spotted, lank birds with long curved beaks speared minnows in the river grass near the shore, and schools of small fish broke the surface everywhere. Their well-preserved horsemeat was rarely needed as Titon was able to shoot birds at will, standing steady upon their raft. Just today, he had taken two stout birds with webbed feet and rounded beaks, which supplied the meat for the pending meal. The previous day, Titon had made of the same type of bird a soup flavored with sprigs from a small bush with blue flowers, leaves like short pine needles, and a woody scent. It was a savory bowlful with a generous amount of fat pooled on the top, some of which Keethro had saved. He was using it now to fry the breasts from the two birds, fat side down, for what seemed like a lifetime. Having just added wild onions to the bubbling liquid, the aroma it gave off was intoxicating.

"It must have been a week on this river so far, no?" Titon asked, trying not to lisp with the excess saliva in his mouth.

Keethro moved the breasts each to their own dry piece of wood while he fried some green beans they'd found along the bank. There was also a generous portion of a red berry sauce in a hollowed wooden bowl. These were not the tinder berries they were accustomed to in the North that grew in singleton and had a pungent, somewhat sour taste. These grew in tiny clusters—a sign of danger—but one taste of a tiny burst drupelet, and they knew that these sweet, mildly tart berries were more than edible.

"A week and a day, I believe," said Keethro.

"I must admit, it has been a finer week than I had expected." With ample time for reflection, Titon had become grateful to Keethro for talking him out of marching directly to Strahl.

"It's about to get better." Keethro transferred the cooked beans to the plates with the meat and scraped some salt on top with his knife. He then picked up a breast, dipped it in berry sauce, and took a bite. A devious smile grew on his face as he chewed.

Titon wasted no time doing the same. The thick layer of fatty skin had rendered down to a chewy shell on top of the dark, warm meat, infused with the scent and taste of the wild onions. Titon chewed and swallowed, then found himself dipping the meat again into the berry sauce that he had been prepared to mock, his plans of ridiculing Keethro for serving meat and dessert together forgotten.

Keethro finished chewing some of his green beans, nodding his head in approval of their taste as he asked, "Well?"

"Goat leather," Titon said, barely having time to speak in between bites.

"Ha!" laughed Keethro. He continued to eat with the self-satisfied smirk of a man who had received a compliment beyond expectation.

Amused at his own stubbornness and wearing a grin of his own, Titon went to start on his second breast when their raft lurched to the side, sending much of their stacked firewood into the water.

"A rock?" Keethro stood and looked around for evidence to support his theory.

"Rocks do not hit from the side." Titon knew it must have been a living thing that bumped their raft—a living thing with a weight no less than ten men to have caused such a jolt. "Get your spear."

Titon had his bow at the ready and Keethro a simple spear with a fire-hardened tip. The river that once brimmed with activity had gone barren, the only ripples in the tea-colored water coming from their raft and floating firewood.

Fifteen paces in front of them, directly in their line of travel, they saw what to Titon looked to be no less than a dragon from children's tales, real, alive, and angry. From snout to tail it was easily the length of their raft. It was covered in what appeared to be greenish-black armor with multiple rows of blunted spikes down its neck, back, and tail. Great teeth protruded upward and downward along the sides of its long jaws, smiling death at them.

Titon loosed a shot. The lightweight arrow screamed through the air, striking between the eyes as intended, but bounced off harmlessly, no use against the thick armored skin. The beast disappeared underwater with no hint as to its intended direction. Titon retrieved his own spear, his knife tied to the end, and the two men stood back to back near the center of their raft, poised for action. Titon was sure to not be alone in wishing they had kept the spears from the men they'd recently killed, having discarded them due to their distinctive markings likely identifying them as weapons exclusive to city guards.

"Dawnstar shine light! What was that beast?" Titon was possibly more curious than afraid.

"The river's guardian from the looks of it. The question is how do we kill it or at least scare it off?"

"Same as anything. We poke it with sticks until—"

Both men were knocked to their knees as the beast attacked their vessel, lifting an edge out of the water and ripping a piece of punky wood from the side. Neither had a chance to strike at it, but that problem resolved itself as the beast burst from the water to the rear of the raft, lunging on top. The raft tipped them both toward danger as half their foe's body was planted on the stern, its jaws wide open, ready to snap at anything that came within range. Relieved to see no flames spewing from its mouth, Titon righted himself and prepared to attack in sync with his friend.

Keethro's spear landed in the mouth of the creature and was snapped in half, but the knife point of Titon's spear bit into the creature's shoulder. A dark purple blood oozed out of the wound as the angry beast thrashed about, splashing water with its mighty tail as it withdrew into the river.

"Knife," Titon said.

Keethro complied quickly, tossing him the knife from his belt. Titon heard his friend protest unintelligibly as Titon dove, headfirst, into the water.

The grossly warm water engulfed him as he swam for the bottom. Earlier testing with the long branches had revealed the depth of the river varied, sometimes getting too deep to scratch bottom and with plenty of fallen trees and rocks below on which to get hung up. Titon's attempt to open his eyes was useless, seeing only darkness.

His hands probed around, easily sliding to elbow's length into the slimy decay of the river floor, expecting at any moment to touch the armored back or the toothed snout of their adversary.

With throbbing lungs, Titon made his way to the surface, feeling more vulnerable than he had at the bottom. As he swam to the raft, his foot kicked something solid, but a glance revealed it was a piece of their floating firewood. Keethro hoisted him to safety as soon as he was within arm's length.

"Are you mad?" Keethro demanded of him.

Titon tossed the dark, heavy object he had stuffed in his shirt to the floor of the raft with a clang, smiling after having regained his breath. "I surely would have been, had we lost old Iron Hips."

CRELLA

Crella frowned, not knowing if it was a sadistic joke of Lyell's to have imprisoned her here, in the utmost luxury. Surrounded by opulence, she had been condemned to the very chambers of the former queen, the comforts of which had begun to chafe her.

It was the highest room in the Throne, sprawling and vaster than the size of most nobles' homes, covered from floor to ceiling in pure lavishness. Not a square inch was bereft of cladding in the richest fabric, all some shade of deep red approaching purple. The ceiling was a maze of pleated velvet from which several enormous chandeliers hung. The coving, a lattice of corduroy boning framed in ropes of gold sinew, crowned the upholstered walls, and the carpet that covered the floors was near thick enough to fall upon without injury. It had every amenity afforded to royalty, save those sharp enough to be used to sever an artery, and the balcony—the one from which Lyell had thrown her aunt—was sealed off.

Crella had known nothing about the war that saw her aunt dethroned. She lived with her uncle then, and Calder kept her as insulated from reality as a young princess could be. That her aunt had tumbled from this very room was the first she had learned of the entire incident. Crella's thoughts had immediately gone to those of succession, as she had been trained, and she remembered having been elated that this room would be hers. She had visited it on several occasions throughout her life, though only briefly. It was the queen's prerogative to ensure that all her luxuries were to be shared with others only enough for them to admire and never enough for them to enjoy.

Crella had raised Stephon as similarly to her own upbringing as she could manage, and to this day she still could not understand how or why Stephon had become so troublesome a child. *It must be his father's Northman blood.*

Her current antipathy toward Alther existed only in so much as he was the son of the man who had sentenced her to this hell, and that Alther was so powerless to prevent it. Her only reprieve came in her sleep, when she dreamt of the night she and Alther had uncharacteristically shared. Though it worsened her anguish upon waking to go so violently from the sweetness of those memories to her bitter reality, it did not keep her from wishing for the same dream to come each night, which it often did.

Crella tried to imagine what their life together may have been like, free from Lyell. Earlier on in their marriage, she'd humored Alther by debating what an ideal life would be. Alther envisioned them living far from the cities, in a self-sufficient estate with its own workers, farms, and livestock. She laughed in his face at such a thought, a princess near a farm. Crella detested the countryside and the filth that came with it. The smell of a man, or even a woman, who had been outdoors for just a moment in the Adeltian humidity was enough to make her gag. The thought of living anywhere other than the cool buildings of the Adeltian kingdom with the perpetual breeze provided by wind chimneys was unbearable. She had always described to Alther a life not much different from the one she now lived as idyllic—minus, of course, the imprisonment. Life with Alther on a faraway estate would be infinitely better than her current circumstance—that she had to admit. Provided proper cooling, or perhaps a more amenable climate, such a life could be endured. The North was rife with dangers, but a well-guarded estate must still be safer than the constant threat of impalement by a paranoid king.

But as each day passed, her hope of liberation began to fade, and with it, her memory of that night with Alther and the tea. The image of Alther the near-dauntless lover was replaced with what she had known him to be prior—a meek man, unable to meet her challenges in the smallest of matters, let alone confront his revered father. *I must not delude myself into believing that he will see me freed. He was never that man I dreamt.*

A knock was heard at the door, another mock courtesy that was shown to her.

"You may enter," Crella said, believing it to be the arrival of her third of three daily meals.

She was correct. Her servant placed her tray of food before her, lifting the lids to see the two dishes properly presented. Crella cringed. On one plate there was a pie of sweet cheese with a crumbly crust, baked until beginning to brown on top. It was a decadent dessert, and once a favorite of hers. On the other plate were several overlapping slices of goose liver, covered in a thick cream sauce. Both dishes were so indulgently rich it near turned her stomach. She would have to wait hours to grow hungry enough to touch either. A single spoon rest between the plates. *Do they truly think I would shove a fork into my veins?* But even so, she had to wonder just how long she could continue under such conditions before she might be forced to consider such a thing.

The servant remained, waiting as if she were still his superior.

"Why do you linger?"

"I have a message," he replied. "From friends."

Though he was probably twenty, he looked far younger. He was not the typical stunted boy servant used by Cassen and the like—he was not comely enough for that. His youthful appearance was due only to his weakly nature. This was a man that had willing servitude in his very blood, and it repulsed her.

"I have no friends. Please be gone." Crella thought she dismissed him with all the spurn and sincerity she could muster, though in fairness she desperately wished to know what he would say, if only to be distracted for a moment.

"Junton has been freed, as will you be if you remain strong and do not speak of his or any other's involvement," he whispered. "With you is Peace." And with his message delivered, the servant turned to depart.

It was a ploy, she knew. Just as soon as she would begin to believe his words and he promised her that her freedom was imminent, they would swap him for another servant in an attempt to crush her completely. And in this he was wholly complicit.

Crella snapped. She grabbed her spoon and rushed the servant, grasping him by the hair and pressing hard the angled edge of the spoon's handle to his throat.

"You are *lying*," she snarled at him.

The weakling in her arms did not even struggle nor attempt to speak. He just remained there, quivering in her grip.

"Tell me you lie," she demanded.

"I lie, I lie!" The response came without hesitation.

Crella let the spoon fall to the carpet as she released him. "If they send you again," she promised, "I'll kill you."

The servant nodded tersely and raced out the room, failing to even shut the door behind him.

The final words he had spoken, those of Peace, were the words of her family's people. Some Adeltians, her aunt being the foremost among them, had taken to a sort of faith centered around that of peace and harmony. It was certainly more prevalent among nobility, who knew no hardship and could afford a peaceful existence free from strife, but many commoners as well had adopted the system of belief.

Peace be damned, Crella thought as she looked at the still-open door.

Was it possible the servant had spoken the truth? He'd been so quick to confess to lying, but a man so frail of mind would have said anything she asked in order to be released. *You may have just run off your only prospect of freedom*, she admonished herself.

Crella walked to the door. Lyell would never let her go free. He had too much invested now in her guilt. And yet it was her innocence that ensured her imprisonment. She knew no names, no plans, no schemes of which to confess in attempt to gain some cause for leniency.

A curving stairway was all that could be seen past the doorway. There would be two armored guards that barred the way at the end of those stairs, and her spoon would be of little use against men covered in steel of their own. *But I could distract them*, she thought, *with a thrown object, just long enough to make my way past.* It seemed her only chance.

It was idiocy, she knew, and she squeezed her eyes shut with the strength of her disappointment. How Lyell would love it if she tried to flee; he'd make a spectacle of it as a means of validating her guilt.

Crella closed the door quietly and went to the northern window. She would stand there, alone, for another four hours, staring at the unidentifiable specks that walked below and the forests to the north as the light faded. She'd pick at her food out of boredom before sleeping, then be awoken by a meal with which to break her fast. No Adeltians, nor her docile husband would ever come to rescue her. She was fated to die in this hellish purgatory.

THE BLACKSMITH

There're pavers under here…somewhere, Davin reminded himself as he pulled his empty cart through muddy streets. He could not remember, though, the last time his cart had been laden enough for the wheels to actually make contact with any.

He was on his way to a vendor in the city square to purchase the bitumen necessary for etching the elaborate knives, swords, and axes made for his wealthier patrons. This was one of many stops necessary to acquire all the materials needed for a week's work. It used to be that he could stock up a month's worth of supplies, but money had been hard enough to come by before his second child had arrived and Westport turned to shit. It did not help matters that the younger of his apprentices had spilt the quenching oil for a second time, forcing him to relieve the lad of his duties. The child's family was like to starve, as his mother was too ugly for whoring, but had a hot sword been in that oil at the time, the senseless child could have burned his entire building to the ground—the expense of the lost oil was painful enough.

An ever-growing crowd was gathered in the square, and the angry shouting made Davin wonder. He was pushing through the throng, only wanting to finish his business and be on his way, when he noticed several members of The Guard. They stood arranged around three tall wooden poles, each covered by a black cloth.

Protectors of the King's Injustice, Davin thought to himself. Stories of abuse at the hands of the so-called Protectors of the Realm were rampant, and though some were difficult to believe, commoners such as he did all they could to avoid the possibility of being the object of one such story.

One of the Protectors unfurled a scroll and began to read.

"Here sit three convicted of high treason with attempt upon the life of the king. Junton of House Elderlunds, former Viscount of Edenholme, now stripped of all lands and titles, his wife Beyla, and his accomplice, Stillun of House Verantia." As the man reading from his scroll finished his proclamation, another member drew down the cloth, revealing the bodies of two men and a woman, each sitting atop a pole that pierced them through the rectum. They wore only wounds and filth, as if they had been in the weather and pecked by the birds for some time. Their eyes already devoured by ravens, the corpses peered down with empty sockets, threatening to come alive to pull innocents into their ring of conspiracy.

The crowd let out a gasp and staggered, each individual seeming torn on whether to stay or to flee. The same member of The Guard continued to read.

"For three days shall they remain at each of the three cities, to serve as a reminder to those who seek to undermine the benevolence of their king and ruler, Lyell of House Red Rivers, that the punishment for treason is death. These men were rich before King Lyell deposed the queen who was unfit to rule, and they remained rich thereafter. King Lyell did not conquer for plunder, but for peace. He did not steal from those he had defeated, but merely requested of them to abide by the laws under which prosperity could take root."

Davin could see some in the audience nodding their heads in approval while others shook them in objection. The rest simply looked on in horror. The man who spoke had apparently finished and began to roll up his scroll for safekeeping.

The growing scent of danger seemed to overwhelm even the fetid stench of entrails, and it felt as though he would be committing some misdeed by being the first of the gathering to resume motion. Nonetheless, Davin nudged the man in front of him so that he might continue on his way.

"I don't feel prosperous," came the yell of a man far to the rear.

The crowd stilled in anticipation of a reaction from The Guard, of which there was none. Having ignored the shouter, the lightly armored Protectors continued tidying their things to make an exit.

"Release the princess!"

This time the voice came from very near. Davin turned to examine the man who had shouted. He was in commoner clothing, with the hunched posture typical of a lowborn not wishing to draw attention, but there was something odd about him that Davin was unable to discern.

"Death to the Tyrant!" came a third voice, again alarmingly close to Davin and from a man in similar dress.

The crowd became agitated. When Davin saw the second crier pick up a handful of mud and fling it in the direction of the members of The Guard, he knew it was already past time to leave, but his cart made travel through the dense crowd impossible.

The mud had missed its mark, and it was nevertheless impossible to see just who had thrown it, so The Guard members simply hurried their attempt to exit. Weakness having been sensed, one by one, others began to throw mud of their own. Soon all The Guard were being pelted and covered in wet dirt, causing some to draw their weapons.

Leaving his partially loaded cart would cost him more than he could afford, but remaining seemed equally foolhardy. As he turned away from his possessions, Davin saw the man who had been the third crier, his face consumed with satisfaction. Amidst a throng of mud-flingers, the man's contrast was clearer to see. The commoner clothing he wore was clean— far too clean. Even after a good wash, none of Davin's clothes could have ever looked so crisp and new.

Davin stood, paralyzed, as he bore witness to the invisible hand that guides the masses, deathly afraid that it may see him too.

DECKER

Decker kept his focus on Kilandra. Raiding Dogmen had whetted his appetite for the matured female form, and compared to the women he had seen while in the South, whose faces more closely resembled those of their demonic pets, Kilandra stood a goddess. The clothing she wore—often ridiculed in whisper by the other women—embraced her in much the same way he would like to. The tasteful amounts of flesh peeking through her furs showed her confidence in her complexion, begging to be seen in its entirety. Her shameless self-assurance was most evident in her eyes which, in spite of their grey color, appeared more brilliant than those of any other. Even from this distance he could feel them piercing him, provoking him.

"I challenge you to single combat!" Decker heard what he thought to be the voice of his father, but it came from beside him. "To determine who is best fit to lead our clan!"

Decker's mind was still lost in a fantasy involving Kilandra and him, alone under some furs, when he was pushed with enough force to stumble to a knee. Titon had shoved him with his foot in order to gain his full attention.

Decker's attempt to decipher his brother's words and actions were met with no success. Titon had no need to challenge him as he was already the elder. Furthermore, their father was the head of the clan—not Decker. Any challenge for the right of leadership would need to be directed at the son of Small Gryn.

Managing to peel his attention from Kilandra, Decker faced his brother. Still upon a knee, Decker nearly matched Titon's height. It dawned on Decker that this must be one of Titon's embarrassing charades where he would reenact some obscure scene from a Dogman book, fully expecting everyone to understand and appreciate his jest.

"I yield," Decker said jocularly, hoping for the best.

With lightning-like speed, assisted by the fact that Decker had not put up his defenses, the butt of Titon's axe slammed Decker across the cheek, opening a small cut and demonstrating the sincerity of the challenge.

Decker roiled with a mixture of shock and disgust. Throughout their trip he had done everything he could to help his brother gain the respect of the men. *This is how you reward me?* Decker stood slowly and unhitched the belt that held his knife and throwing axes, letting the assembly fall to the ground. He did the same with the bow on his back.

Titon did nothing slowly. He flung the axe he held to the ground and charged his brother. Titon's shoulder dug into Decker's chest, a blow he could have withstood if not for Titon's heel having been hooked behind his own, sending Decker hard to his back upon the rocky ground. Before he could react, Titon was on top of him where he rained down blows. Decker pointed his elbows upward, defending his face with his bent arms successfully until one of Titon's fists snuck through the side and connected with his jaw. Decker was still reeling from the fall, and Titon's blow had the effect of bringing him into greater focus. He went on the offensive. He bucked Titon off him with ease and connected an upward kick to Titon's stomach which sent him backward.

"Stop this," Decker yelled at his brother as he stood and attempted to back away, but Titon had already begun to again charge. It was a familiar charge, one Decker himself had perfected as a young boy when their father made them train—fueled by blind rage and frustration and utterly ineffective. Instead of sidestepping, which would have allowed Titon to plow face first into the ground, Decker countered Titon's momentum with his own. His greater mass made him the easy victor, and Titon was shoved rearward, off his feet, where he landed badly on his back with Decker on top of him.

Titon had stopped his assault for the moment, and Decker showed him his open palms.

"Stop, Titon. Stop," Decker repeated, but Titon resumed his desperate attack, throwing punch after punch at his brother while still flat on his back. Decker tried to grab Titon's arms to subdue him, but Titon bucked, forcing Decker to fall forward to support himself. Titon turned and sunk his teeth into one of Decker's arms, and Decker responded with the heavy fist of his other arm. He hit Titon square in the face, with more speed than power, but his brother refused to stop. Titon reached for the knife that remained at his belt. Knowing how quick he was with a blade, Decker lost his ability to restrain his attack. He smashed his brother in the face once, again, and a third time with his full fury, letting out a yell along with his frustration.

Silence was all that followed in the wake of his cry—a silence that made Decker feel utterly alone. If there were a hundred onlookers, Decker was no longer aware of a single one. He felt no stares of judgment fall upon him, only the stinging cold of the snowflakes that landed on the back of his wounded scalp.

The realization that Titon had gone limp after his first strike was sickening. His brother lay motionless beneath him, blood pouring from his nose and trickling out his ear. Titon's eyes were open, staring blankly into the distance, his mouth agape but not appearing to be passing breath.

KEETHRO

The amenable nature of their river voyage ended abruptly when the rains came. They had storms just as fierce in the Northluns, but those carried only snow. In the summer months they would receive rain, but those were always gentle and welcomed. The weather in which Keethro and Titon now found themselves was neither.

The thatching they had duplicated from their previous boat had proven inadequate, unable to shelter their bodies or their fire, and with their fire went their spirits. Violent gusts blew a horizontal deluge, spraying them in the face and making safe travel downstream an impossibility. The once calm waters of the river had swollen and rushed with force.

"To shore, before these rapids swallow us." Titon had not so much as finished speaking when Keethro had the long pole in hand, attempting to push them toward the riverbank. Titon paddled with a wide piece of wood that had come loose from the shelter.

With considerable effort, shouts, and cursing, the men were able to land their raft, pulling it partially ashore. "How is it so fecking cold?" Titon bellowed to the sky.

"We need shelter from the wind and rain, a fire is out of the question." A nod from Titon showed he was of like mind. "We can tilt the raft and use brush to fill any gaps between the logs," Keethro added.

Their grunts and heaving produced no results as they tried to lift an edge of the raft. Though they'd once carried it into the water under their own power, the giant they had constructed had become saturated with water and was simply too heavy. The exertion brought Keethro some minor warmth, but he still shook from a dangerous chill.

Titon laughed like a man deranged. "Two Northmen, to die frozen in the heart of the South."

The temperature was not near so cold as they regularly endured in the North, but this combination of wind and rain was an unfamiliar foe. More clothing would do them no good, so long as it was soaked. Some method of shelter was essential before their fingers became useless.

Frantically they built more thatch structures with hearty bracings, cannibalizing their raft for horsehide binding. After a time, they each had a curved shield of fronds and branches large enough that they could sit together, overlapping their sections to keep the wind and rain at bay. They exchanged nods, agreeing that this would do for the time being.

Though they were still drenched, it was much warmer without the wind stripping them of all their heat. They could have been warmer still, had they sat closer, but Keethro knew Titon's pride would only allow so much. Keethro was content to remain where they were, a ways up the riverbank and safe from the churning water. He was convinced they could survive provided the storm did not persist through the night.

But the waters of the river continued to rise. With no cordage to spare to tie it off, their raft would soon be swept away if they did not abandon their shelter and drag it further aground—a task that would cost them what little warmth they'd just gained. The loss of the raft meant little to Keethro so long as they kept their lives, but he knew Titon had grown attached to their creation.

"We should save it," said Titon, confirming Keethro's fears.

This man's stubbornness will be the end of us.

"You stay here while I—"

Just as Titon began to speak, his head jerked backward as if struck in the face.

"What the bloody hell?" he shouted. "Who is out there?" Even Titon's monstrous voice sounded somewhat weak as it was drowned out by the heavy rains.

Before Titon could lower his barrier in search of their attacker, they received a response—a response that could not have come from a mere man. The noise of the rain was accompanied by what sounded like hundreds of rocks plummeting from the sky. Keethro saw in Titon's eyes a strange emotion. It could not be fear, of course—it must have been confusion. But even Keethro, who had no superstitions, felt ill at ease in the presence of whatever power may summon a shower of stones.

"Gods of the River, the Mountain, and the Dawnstar," cried Titon. "It was with no irreverence that we flung our coats into your waters. Know that the urine upon them was not our own, not that that is any excuse. It was a grave error, and we humbly beg your forgiveness."

Keethro had never known Titon to speak directly to his gods, and seeing him do so in desperation was frightening in its own right. Out of instinct Keethro sought the void, clearing his mind so he may think of a way to calm his friend.

"We offer you our raft in sacrifice," Keethro yelled, hoping Titon would accept the idea.

It took only a few moments before the raft was swept away by a sudden rush of water, and Titon's face shone with naked relief. Even

Keethro was awed by the timing of it, but the sound of the rocks falling continued, and several made their way through the thatching.

"Ice," said Titon, first with wonder then with joy. "Gods be merciful, they have turned stone to water!"

Keethro began to laugh, and Titon soon followed. Nothing cheered the man quite like believing he had again escaped certain death. *Merciful and exploitable*, Keethro thought, though it would be some time before he could be fully removed from the disquiet that lingered after seeing the raft be taken just moments after having offered it—to those gods in which he held no belief.

DERUDIN

Two massive hosts of indeterminable origin had formed outside the northern walls of the Adeltian Throne. They stood with discipline, not a single man moving so much as to scratch an itch or shift weight from one leg to the other. The inadequacies of the Throne's defenses were made blatantly apparent with these armies in place. Men with ladders could easily scale the short outer walls of the city, gaining access to turrets that stood in stark contrast to the magnificence of the Throne itself, which extended countless stories above like an enormous gem set upon a dainty ring, ripe for the plucking.

Derudin and his seven disciples stood outside the walls to defend the kingdom. The very city that he and Lyell's hosts had stormed and taken from Queen Adella was now under siege in much the same way.

"Toblin," Derudin commanded. "You must defend our western flank. Draw from the power of the Dawnstar and redirect its fire to the invading army. Set them alight so that we may live."

The Dawnstar shone brightly through the clouds checkering the sky. Although it was the dead of winter, Adeltia did not suffer seasons much, and it was far from cold. Derudin was quite comfortable in his grey robes, but looking at Toblin he could see sweat pouring from his face and soaking through his clothing. *The poor boy fears his own shadow. Let us see how he does against an army.*

Toblin was dressed as impressively as ever. In addition to his royal violet cape, he wore an ornamental breastplate bearing his house name and words. "Everbold," it read at the top; "Fortidia & Audacius," it read below—the ancient tongue for courage and daring. The piece of metal was far too tall for the boy and made him waddle more than usual as he positioned himself to unleash hell upon the invaders.

Toblin closed his eyes, focusing all his efforts on his most important task. The rest of the apprentices waited impatiently as nothing happened—a result they had come to expect. In his quest to set the western host alight, it seemed Toblin was only able to drench himself with enough sweat to quench the fire he was meant to create.

I will give him two minutes, thought Derudin.

Two minutes passed, after which three more of Derudin's least promising students tried a hand, all without so much as smoke coming from the clothing of a single invader.

It was difficult for Derudin to peel himself away from the king in such chaotic times, but conducting these classes had always been a priority of his, even with most of his students having no chance of progress. *Just one would make all my efforts worthwhile*, he thought. Derudin prided himself in being a man of patience, and in the task of finding a successor, he believed he was demonstrating that patience in abundance.

"We are too far away," cried Rexton, the most recent apprentice to have failed.

"Distance is not the problem. Lack of focus is the issue," Derudin explained. "Eaira, do you wish to try?"

The little girl shook her head. Ever since her first demonstration where she had impressed Derudin with her abilities, she had been reluctant to go again. He did not know why, but understanding little girls was not among his gifts. *She has such promise, but greatness can never be forced upon a mage.*

"Sture, Signy, take positions on the western and eastern flanks. Save us from certain death."

The two cousins raced to their positions on the field, eager to show that they could indeed protect the city. Their matching hair of blonde gleamed with brilliant luster in the dawnlight. Their pale skin, however, seemed to be at odds with the exposure, having already turned somewhat pinkish.

Sture was the first to get smoke, but Signy was the first to acquire flame. Within seconds both armies had one member burning and a second smoldering. Sture and Signy retained concentration, continuing to light one soldier after the other until each had all sixteen members of their assigned host consumed in flames.

"Well done," Derudin told them truthfully. "Certainly faster than a man with a longbow could have removed sixteen foes."

Signy appeared quite proud of herself, but Sture was clearly exhilarated with power and let it be known. "A mere bowman is no match for the power of a mage!"

The boy looked close to tears, having finally had a chance to realize his dream of dousing men in fire. *You poor fool*, thought Derudin.

"Is that the conclusion you have drawn from this, Sture?" Derudin asked. "Another demonstration then, perhaps. Toblin, I will need your assistance. Please take this and stand under the bucket."

He gave Toblin a child's bow and an arrow with a large padded tip. The structure to which he directed Toblin supported a giant bucket. Attached to it was a rope that, given a good yank, would rotate the bucket, emptying its contents upon the head of whoever stood beneath.

"Rexton, if you would, please grab hold of the rope. I will need you to pull on it at the first sign of smoke…" Derudin looked at Rexton with utter seriousness. "Toblin's life may depend on it."

Toblin's eyes went wide with fear, and he stopped mid-shuffle to protest.

"Go on, Toblin," Derudin insisted. "I will not allow you to be harmed."

The boy reluctantly obeyed, his fear far from quashed.

"Now, Toblin, I want you to give Sture a moment before you shoot your arrow at him." Derudin looked to Sture with consideration. "He is no doubt very tired from his last exertion."

"I am not tired!" Even if Sture was exhausted, the prospect of having a living target seemed to have revitalized him. "I assume I will not be held responsible when I roast this hog? I am warning you in advance, as my powers are greater than you realize, old man."

Derudin did not show any offense at the way in which he had been addressed. "I am responsible for Toblin's wellbeing. You are merely responsible for setting him on fire. Focus all your energy on Toblin and *only* Toblin. Do not hold back. I will not hear any excuses when you fail the task."

"I will not fail." Having said that, Sture's eyes shot to Toblin with extreme intensity. Toblin immediately began to squirm as if being cooked from the inside, shielding himself with his arms and turning to the side.

"Stand still, Toblin, and face him. Sture will need all the help he can get."

Toblin regained his composure somehow and turned to face Sture, although with his eyes only partially open, as if afraid looking directly upon his attacker may blind him.

Moments later Sture was beginning to show his first signs of frustration, repeatedly clenching his fists. "It is his breastplate," he finally yammered in anger.

"If metal scares you then set his breeches alight, or better yet his hair."

Toblin once again looked as if he were about to be pushed from the top of the Throne, and his eyes began to water with tears.

"No tears, Toblin. He will only use that as another excuse."

"You are shielding him!" Sture was furious now.

"I am afraid not, nor do I know of any such magic. Toblin, you may use your bow."

Toblin seemed to have forgotten about the bow held in his white-knuckle grasp, taking some time to even acknowledge Derudin's words. In a frantic attempt to ready a shot, the arrow fell from his fumbling fingers. He looked to Derudin for permission to pick it up which

Derudin granted with a nod.

"Be quick, Sture," said Derudin. "You are soon to be bested by the most novice bowman in the realm."

Toblin retrieved and nocked the arrow, drawing the bow back with trembling arms. When the arrow finally set sail, it flew in a gentle arc and fell well short of Sture, several paces to the left. It was all Derudin could do not to bury his face in his hand.

"That is enough, Sture," said Derudin. "Had Toblin been a trained bowman, you would now be dead. You may retu—"

Without warning, flames burst from beneath Toblin, and Derudin quickly signaled for Rexton to dump the bucket. The boy did his best to comply, pulling with all his force, but only managed to lift himself. The bucket was too heavy for him to tip. Flames had caught on Toblin's stockings, and he began to scream.

A massive gust of wind sent the structure flying backward, rustling the hair of both boys and snuffing out the flames on Toblin's stockings and the grass he stood upon. In an instant, Derudin had a hold of Sture by the hair and lifted him from the ground.

"You dare defy my explicit instructions? What kind of knave are you?"

Toblin was rolling on the ground, weeping and clutching his leg, and Sture was crying as well, albeit defiantly. "You told me to do it!" he sobbed back at Derudin.

"I told you Toblin and only Toblin, and you lit the dry grass beneath him."

"You said his breeches and his hair, and all I did was burn some straw." His defiance was fading into pure self-pity.

Derudin released the boy in disgust, though in truth he was more disgusted with himself. *I should never have taunted him.*

"Let this be a lesson to all of us in the dangers of magic. Had that gust of wind not come, Toblin could have been badly burned. Toblin, I assume you are all right? Let me have a look."

As he'd expected, Toblin had no actual injury beside that of his pride. His silk stockings had been ruined, but he had not so much as a red mark. Sture and Signy had already suffered worse from the Dawnstar.

"You are fine. Everyone form up. Let us review what we have learned."

The seven apprentices, all who either had faces white from fear, red from tears, or both, slowly reformed their rows of four and three.

"Who can explain why Sture was unable to set Toblin aflame without resorting to burning the grass beneath him?" No one seemed as though they had any intention of proposing a theory, so Derudin allowed them plenty of time to relax and think.

Signy finally spoke up. "His breastplate?"

"Although it would be hopeless to attempt to set a breastplate on fire, that does not explain why Sture was also unable to burn Toblin's breeches or hair." No one else was forthcoming with guesses, so Derudin continued. "Transferring power to candles and inanimate scarecrows is met with no resistance. Transferring power to a living thing is entirely different. Just as all living things have within them some arcane ability, they also carry some arcane contravention. Whereas transference requires focus for proper use, contravention—or resistance—does not. Even the weakest of men and animals are near impossible to use as an efficient target for the transfer of power. The same can be said for anything worn upon their person."

Derudin smiled to his class, attempting to further calm them. "If that were not the case, I am sure some of you would be without living parents by now."

His joke seemed to have had the opposite of the intended effect, as the children began to look sick, scanning their memories for the times they had focused their hatred on their parents and recognizing they might have harmed them. Eaira was the most affected, putting her face in the crook of her elbow.

I should warn them of the exception so that they do not harm anyone by mistake. Derudin knew that lesson was meant to follow today's demonstration, but he feared teaching them now would frighten them—or more specifically, Eaira—from ever practicing magecraft again. He resolved, instead, to teach them in the coming days.

"Couldn't a strong mage set fire to the ground beneath the feet of an army?" asked Sture, back to dreaming up methods of mass carnage.

"Yes, bit by bit you can set the ground alight. But so can an archer with a flaming arrow. It is no great feat. And had Toblin not been standing so still, you would have had great trouble getting his stockings to catch by way of the grass."

Sture scowled with disappointment.

"A great mage can be a powerful force on the battlefield, but his power comes more from utility. He…or she…is not the fountain of death-bringing flame as so often depicted in children's tales." Derudin glanced again at the turrets of the kingdom, focusing on the parts of stone scorched by fires he helped ignite. "And like all great powers, there is often a weakness. An arrow from a longbow can kill a mage just as easily as it can any other man. Remembering that will serve you well."

TALLOS

Pain stabbed through him as Tallos jolted awake. He rolled once again to his stomach, away from the blades of straw that pierced the open wounds of his back. Though sleep was his only escape from the physical pain, that respite came with its own price. The daggers in his flesh that woke him were often less tortuous than the nightmares that caused his tossing.

He had no reason to open his eyes. There was no light to be seen in his crypt of decay. It had not taken long for him to find a root cellar, and it may have been more merciful had the cellar not contained four barrels of vinegar, as he would have long since died of infection. The dankness of the cellar and the warmth of his body had proved the perfect combination for corruption to take in his festering skin. Twice daily, or so he guessed, he would submerge himself in the leftmost barrel, transforming the throbbing pain to that of combustion. Though Tallos preferred the burning, he did not believe he could remain submerged in the powerful vinegar for long without suffering unhealthy consequences. The fumes alone made him light-headed, and he limited the duration of his treatments, always careful to place the lid back on the barrel when done.

The few potatoes and carrots he'd found in the cellar lasted less than a week. Hunger drove him outside, only at night, where he would crawl, naked on his hands and feet, still refusing to open his eyes, in search of food like some blind demon. The biting cold may have killed him if he had become lost and forced to remain on the surface, but he found it easier than expected to navigate through the snow, and never lost feeling in his bare hands or feet.

The world he once called home felt alien to him without the benefit of sight. The sounds and smells of life that had filled the community were no more. The deafening shrieks of roosting ravens disturbed by his presence filled his ears, making the village that he knew sat under a boundless sky seem more like a town within cave. The smell of rotting flesh, burst entrails, and scorched hair was inescapable when outside his vinegary refuge. In vain, Tallos tried to forget the once-welcoming scents that he'd taken for granted in his former life: the bitter smell of rising dough that came from the baker's home in the early morning, the scent of bland soap used by the woman who would wash a barrel of dirty clothes for five coppers or five potatoes—he even found himself nostalgic for the odor of dog manure that had come from the kennels.

Regardless of the fetid bouquets and piercing sounds, regardless of feeling something slither under his foot or creep up his arm while he crawled in search of sustenance, his eyes remained tightly shut. He had no desire to be aided by moonlight while he groped around on the ground, trying to find a body not writhing so horribly with frost fly maggots that it would be too difficult to grasp. When he finally came across a suitable corpse, when his hand made contact with cold human skin, free from slime, he would drag it back to the hole from which he came, instinctively and without need for fumbling about. And into one of the other three barrels of vinegar he placed it, until he at last had all three filled with a body or two, depending on their size.

He found that he much preferred the taste and texture of the pickled flesh he had procured to that of the raw potatoes and carrots. As long as he gathered handfuls of the hair and maggots that floated to the surface, flinging them far from his home, he was able to keep his barrels from giving off too much of a stench. Between the food he had gathered and the seep in the corner, he determined he had enough to last through the winter. The temperature outside decreased each day, but he knew that in his hole it would remain at a constant chill, something that did not bother him any. Even after dips in the vinegar, he did not shiver.

There he remained, content with the fact that, for the moment, he was doing all he could to spite his tormentors, the Mighty Three. And, he assured himself, this was only the beginning.

CASSEN

Cassen knocked three times on the door and waited, not anticipating a response. It had been nearly a week since the High Council meeting. *Certainly long enough for him to stew.* After standing for a minute, Cassen pushed open the unbarred door and stepped inside.

"Alther," he called, almost unable to force out the single word as the reek of alcohol hit him. "I have come to speak with you. Please do not assault me." Cassen was not one to be frightened by a drunken man, especially not after so recently being invigorated by his trip to see the Satyr, but it would do better to keep up appearances.

Cassen crept through the dim anteroom, the only light provided coming from the open door behind him. He continued into the sunken main room, expecting to hear the crunch of glass beneath him as his feet moved into darkness and his eyes strained to adjust. If the stronger smell was any indication, he was getting closer to Alther, or at least his liquor-sodden corpse.

A low growl stopped Cassen where he stood. Lids peeled back as far as possible, he looked in the direction from where the noise had come, wishing, mostly in jest, that he had employed the trick he'd learned from his Sacaran ally: the Satyr's men kept a patch over an eye before storming below decks, allowing them to see in near darkness once removed. Instead, Cassen stood there for a while as the outline of Alther, propped up on a chaise, became known. He had a bottle of Spiceland rum in his hand. *Ah, the joys of bachelordom.*

"Been sampling the spirits?" Cassen inquired.

Alther was alive and awake, but he made no move to respond. Cassen went to the drapes and drew them open, pouring light into the room. Broken glass of various colors littered the ground, built up mostly where the tiled floor met with stone wall, the walls themselves covered with stains where each bottle had hit.

"Don't," Alther groaned.

Cassen pulled the drapes partway closed in compromise. He then found a chair tucked under a desk and placed it in front of Alther—at a healthy distance to avoid the majority of the stench the man produced. Cassen sat and waited, attempting to gauge the severity of Alther's condition.

"If you have come to kick a down dog, I would warn you, they can still bite." Alther's voice carried no humor. "And some carry with them disease."

Alther's ability to analogize seemed a good sign to Cassen. Perhaps he was not as drunk as one would have expected given his surroundings. For all Cassen knew, smashing expensive bottles and sitting in the filth may have been a Rivervalian way of mourning.

"I have not. I have come to offer my condolences, for what they are worth." Cassen spoke with his normal demeanor, that of a concerned duchess.

"I would not put too high a value on them."

"No, I would guess not," Cassen replied.

Other than their brief and recent conversation concerning Crella's sudden lack of need for lady servants—something Cassen hoped had earned him some good favor as he had graciously allowed Alther to back out of the agreement—the two had never spoken outside of social gatherings and council meetings.

"You may leave now if that is all you came here for," said Alther. "Though I doubt it is."

"Do you still have plans to depart for Westport?" Cassen asked.

Alther grunted. "I am afraid my father will have to find some other fool to ruin that city now. It is likely for the better."

On that Cassen could not disagree. Alther's mismanagement of Westport had advanced Cassen's own plans even more rapidly than he had hoped.

"That is most unfortunate."

"Ha. Yes, perhaps for you it is. To have someone more qualified run the city may bite into your own profits." Alther inhaled deeply and let it out in exasperation. "I was a fool to attempt such a task. All the plotting and politics and duplicity required... I have no appetite for it."

No appetite or no aptitude? Cassen mused only to himself. Then he took on a conciliatory tone. "The politics of city management are a dirty business, you are right. Much the same are the politics of adjudication."

The light that hit Alther's face from the side set his scowl afire.

"Lyell is king. He decides who is guilty and who is innocent. It may be dirty, but it is not complex. I warned you not to taunt me with nonsense."

"I make no taunts," Cassen insisted. "Have you considered demanding a trial?" It seemed another good sign that Alther referred to the king as Lyell and not his father.

"On what grounds? There is no basis for demanding such a thing."

"In Rivervalian law there perhaps is not. But we are in the Adeltian Kingdom."

Alther scoffed at the idea. "Should such a spectacle be permitted—and it would not—what evidence could even be produced to show their innocence?"

"Ah yes, what evidence indeed. For under Adeltian law it is not the responsibility of the accused to present evidence of innocence, it is the responsibility of the accuser. To the extent of my influence and abilities, I have inquired as to the legitimacy of the claims made against your wife and son. I regret to inform you that there is in fact ample evidence that Stephon had plotted, and clumsily so, that which he has been accused of. Yes, if it were up to Stephon we would all be drinking from a poisoned chalice, leaving clear his path to ascend to the throne." Cassen smirked. "He is a most ambitious boy, that one you raised."

Cassen noticed the muscles of Alther's jaw flex as the man closed his eyes and ran a hand over his head.

"But the evidence against Crella is sorely lacking," Cassen continued. "She may have referred to Junton as Lord, in deference to his safely stowing her beloved boy, one could argue, but other than that I am afraid there simply is nothing to show that she so much as offered a single utterance in support of, or in acknowledgment of, any such plots."

Alther hurled the bottle of rum at the wall behind Cassen. The glass shattered in all directions, and its dark contents followed. The smell of the oaken barrels in which it had aged and the myriad spices, so artfully balanced, wafted through the air, reminding Cassen of a similar incident in a similar room. *Another drunken duke upon which I step.*

"What difference does any of it make?" Alther shouted. "My father would never allow it. It would undermine his authority. It is absurd to think such a trial could ever happen."

Cassen let out a sigh of resignation. "I suppose you are correct. Forgive me for grasping at threads and opening wounds you'd rather let heal. I have in my heart a special place for Crella, having lived in the same household for that short time when she was so young... She became to me like a sister."

Alther did not respond.

"But you are right," Cassen went on. "Barring, of course, the unlikely event that the king should fall ill—just for a spell—and you were to relieve him... I see no way of it happening."

"You may leave now," said Alther with finality.

Cassen had expected as much. It would take more provocation to stir the meek and honorable Alther to move, even temporarily, against his mighty father. But the behavior Cassen had seen him display at the meeting of the High Council had given him hope that it was still possible. Cassen turned in his chair and began to stand, brushing some life back into his silks with his hands. He had but one more question for Alther, one more means by which to prompt him to action.

"Tell me, how is young Ethel handling all of this?"

ANNORA

Near a month had passed since Annora had come to live with her new acquaintance, a girl she could now honestly call friend. The small room they shared in the dormitories of the Adeltian Academy of High Manners had been transformed from what must have been a fortress of solitude to that of camaraderie. Ethel had confided in Annora, among many things, that she had hoped to gain respect from her fellow students by remaining in the shared housing rather than requesting a separate royal quarters—as was well within her right. But there seemed nothing Ethel could do to gain any acceptance among her peers, an undertaking Annora had come to appreciate as futile. Even the servants responsible for the upkeep of the main building showed Ethel no courtesy, knowing that there would be no repercussions.

Of the activities they partook, Annora most enjoyed Ethel's reading aloud her favored stories. It was not that Annora had grown fond of books; that which she looked forward to the least was being forced by Ethel to read aloud herself, the result of which was a story so broken by interruption that its meaning was lost. Even when Ethel smiled as if Annora had said something correctly, Annora then had to replay the sound in her head repeatedly before recognizing the words. Spicelanders were never meant to read and write, a thing she tried to impress onto Ethel, but the girl was steadfast in her resolve to prove Annora wrong in that.

There had been no reading of late, however. The little light that peered through the mostly drawn curtains was not enough to break the spell of anguish cast on the once-happy room. Since hearing the fate that had befallen her mother and half brother, Ethel had been consumed by bereavement.

"Drink this," Annora said, having brought Ethel some tea, a strong, semi-sweet brew that they normally both enjoyed while breaking their fast.

"You may leave it by the bedside." It was as good as Ethel having refused the drink.

"I will *not*." Annora's accent flared as it always did when she became angry, but her embarrassment only strengthened her determination to stir Ethel from her perpetual grief and slumber. For the past three days she had eaten nothing and drank only sips of water. Annora was afraid not only for Ethel's safety but for her own, should something happen to her. "You will drink this for me and have something to eat so that you do not die and condemn me to the same fate as your mother." Annora felt a twinge of guilt at having said the last bit.

Ethel slowly sat up in her bed and took the cup from Annora's hand. She stared straight ahead, avoiding eye contact and scowling, but at least she appeared as though she'd finally drink more than water.

"Thank you," Annora said in mild apology.

Ethel had spoken to Annora about her mother prior to learning of her imprisonment, but not near so much as her father. "I am afraid you would not like her, my mother, if you were to meet her," Ethel had confessed. "She is very much what you might expect of a highborn lady. She is not a bad woman… She is just very…particular. My father helped me understand that she is not the hateful woman I'd once thought her to be. He is a good man. I know you would love him as I do."

Ethel never spoke of Alther as anything less than a true father, and there was never any mention of some latent longing to know her birth father. Ethel explained how Alther had adopted her as his own and how embarrassing it must have been for him. She was the bastard child of some Adeltian man, and he was a Rivervalian conqueror. He had every right to have her drowned or exiled. Instead he'd suffered every silent ridicule and mocking expression without so much as blinking, and in doing so, gave Ethel the strength to do the same. So when Alther had knocked at their door days prior, and Ethel lashed out at him in anger, Annora knew the seriousness of her dejection.

"Leave me be, you coward," she had screamed at him through the door. "How can you let him destroy our family and do nothing?"

It was all Ethel had to say to stop her father from further pursuing his attempt to console her. He left without another word of his own.

Annora knew Ethel referred not only to the imprisonment of Stephon and her mother, but also of Lyell's advances on Ethel herself. Ethel was convinced that her grandfather planned to marry her, and with Alther powerless to prevent Crella from being jailed, it was obvious he would also be unable to stop such a marriage, should it be Lyell's intention. *A good man perhaps, but what good can such a man accomplish without the strength to act?* It was a sentiment she knew Ethel must share but had never spoken.

"What food is there?" asked Ethel. Annora fetched the nearby tray of all Ethel's favorites and held it out to her. Ethel reached for a rolled pastry with a crumb filling of sugar and nuts. She finished it quickly and went for another.

It was pleasing to see her finally eat, but as Ethel turned to meet her face, Annora saw the tears. Annora put down the tray so she could sit beside her on the bed and hold her as Ethel cried into her chest.

"I should not have spoken to him in that way," Ethel sobbed.

If it drives him to action, it will have been worth it, Annora thought to herself. She did not know how things were done among the ruling parties in the Adeltian Kingdom, but she understood enough from her own land to realize there was little one could do to challenge a king's verdict short of killing him. Voicing this would be of no comfort to her friend. She remained silent and stroked Ethel's hair with her fingers.

"I feel like a prisoner." The words did not sit well with Annora who stopped stroking her hair upon hearing them. *I am a prisoner.* Having recognized her mistake, Ethel looked up at her with an implicit apology.

"Are you not free to leave?" Annora asked her.

"Where would I even go?"

It was a fair question. The thought of a young, pretty highborn girl setting off with a purse full of coin and meeting with anything but ill fortune did not seem rooted in reality. Ethel had none of the experience gained by commoners as they eked out their meager existence, learning to sense, by instinct, signs of potential danger, and to avoid showing the signs of weakness that invited that same danger—neither of which can be taught or defined by words. Without protection it would simply be a matter of time before men would take all that she had. Annora had no answer for her.

"Where would *you* go then?" asked Ethel. "Back to the Spicelands?"

"I do not know. But not there." Annora considered whether she should reveal just how much she had planned. "I would dirty myself and put on the most common clothing I could find. I would cut my hair short like a boy. I would steal as many small items of value as I could and bring them with me to pay for wagon rides and inns. I would search for a safe, honest community, far from the city, where I would be free from the immediate threat of harm. Some place I could work as a farmhand or apprentice for some tradesman."

She did not know how Ethel would react to what she had told her. For a servant to admit to planning to steal and flee would be grounds for severe punishment in any other setting. She could not look at Ethel, though she could tell Ethel stared at her. The thought of toiling in the soil would turn any highborn's stomach. She would not blame Ethel if she resented her for wishing to work in the dirt when she had been given such a comfortable life here at the Throne.

"You must promise to never leave me," said Ethel, deadly serious as she forced Annora to look at her. "And if you do go, you must promise to take me with you."

Annora looked down into her pleading eyes. She knew she could not make such a promise honestly. It would be difficult enough to abscond by herself, let alone with a member of the royal family. But Ethel had been hurt enough these past few days. If a harmless lie would help her, then she would give her that reprieve.

"I promise."

KEETHRO

The cries of gulls reverberated off the clouds.

The birds seemed to have influenced Keethro's dreams, as he had just been walking on the shores of the Timid Sea. It was a most-welcome dream—though he could not remember the last time he'd had it—of his first real voyage as a young boy. His father and uncle had allowed him to accompany them on one of their trips to meet with the sea merchants of the eastern coast. They had expected him to be impressed by the many items the merchants had to trade, and they had to laugh when Keethro ignored the merchants and played at the shore. It was the new landscape that captivated him, and he paid the cold grip of the sea no bother as he chased after the gulls, splashing through the small waves. The elation of having found a new land overwhelmed him, and he had forever longed to see what lay beyond.

Keethro rubbed his eyes free of their waking fog, and saw Titon at the front of the boat. He had both a paddle and a bow clutched in his left hand, and he was able to either paddle or draw and fire an arrow without releasing either. Breathing deeply to take in the warmth of this exotic land, Keethro wondered how it was he had allowed himself to grow so timid with age—to the point of being deathly reluctant to aid his friend on this voyage. *Thank you for making me remember what years of internment with a self-serving woman had robbed me of.* But Keethro was unable to thank Titon, even in thought, without being reminded of the letters, the image of them curling into ash still emblazoned in his mind.

"I am beginning to think the Mighty Three sent the rain merely to bathe us, not humble us," said Titon, seeing Keethro had awoken.

Indeed, it had been many days since they had been able to bathe. After the encounter with the river dragon, both men—even Titon—had decided it would be wisest to avoid unnecessary dips in the murky waters. Being restricted to whore baths with a wet rag had taken its toll on them. Galatai were not acquainted to the amount of sweat one could produce in such damp air.

Your gods took from us Iron Hips, Keethro remembered, picturing the raft being swept away just after offering it in sacrifice. He was still bitter from the loss of their companion, but he knew Titon would have felt her absence just as much, given that he ate the wolf's share, and hungrily so.

"Yes," Keethro said. "I feel…*immaculate*." He got the laughter from Titon he had hoped for. "Something I intend to remedy as soon as we find a city."

They'd wasted no time fashioning a similar, albeit smaller raft. The loss of most of their supplies and the recent flood had them placing more importance in their craft being manageable rather than luxurious.

"Good that you intend to wait that long. I was afraid you might hop onto the first boat with tits aboard that passed us."

The river they'd traveled southwesterly upon fed into another, far larger body of water flowing north to south. It seemed to Keethro more like a narrow sea, but the water was without the taste of salt. "The Eos," both men had agreed in humble veneration when they found themselves upon its mighty waters. They had remained close to the shore to avoid the potential dangers that may lie in its center: odd currents, swells…leviathans. It had been a clear day and they could barely see the far shore. Although daunting, such grandeur gave Keethro hope for the first time that they may actually find a cure for Titon's wife in this faraway land.

"We must be nearing the kingdom of the delta," Keethro guessed aloud. "These are sea birds, I believe. Like the ones on the eastern coast. I would think their presence signifies our approach on the southern seas."

"We can hope so," said Titon. "But it is no matter. We are definitely heading somewhere of great wealth and knowledge."

Keethro supposed it was for the best that they had lost the giant horse hock to the rain. It had given them more of a savage appearance— something they wished to avoid, as they were no longer alone on the water. He had lost count of the many boats and barges that passed, paying them little mind so long as they were not in their way, but one such craft was headed toward them now.

It was an impressive ship with a deck that stood over two men proud of the water's surface. Its sharp bow looked more suited for sea travel, and its sides had been painted white, giving it a finished appearance that was easy to appreciate. The two men looked on in awe of its beauty as it careened toward them.

"We had better move to shore," Keethro thought aloud.

As they began to paddle, the ship continued on its path directly toward them. Three burly men were visible on the bow, waving their hands from one side to the other.

I fear that is not a southern gesture of greeting. It became evident the men were motioning for them to paddle their raft in the opposite direction.

"Keep paddling toward shore," said Titon. Keethro had no cause to object. Their raft did not reverse direction willingly.

The sailor men shouted obscenities at them, and Keethro began to fear for their safety—the safety of the men on the other boat, should they provoke Titon to anger. *God of the Mountain, give Titon restraint*, thought Keethro, having no time to be amused by his inadvertent prayer.

The captain of the other boat must have realized they would not be accommodated in their request, and in turn banked away from shore to avoid the impending collision.

The crafts came dangerously close—so close that the men aboard the other boat saw fit to hurl more than insults. Spit and rotting vegetables made up the majority of the barrage. Keethro watched in horror as pieces flew by Titon's head, smashing upon their raft's deck of lashed timbers. He could not see Titon's expression, but Keethro had known his friend to be incited to violence from less. It would not be long before Titon sent a spear to silence one of their harassers, but rather than look away from the impending debacle, Keethro readied himself to assist Titon in his attack. He'd spent some time earlier in their trip fashioning a throwing weapon not unlike an axe out of a piece of wood and a rusty knife, and Keethro did not mind the opportunity to sink it into something other than the stump he had practiced on.

"Sons of whores," shouted the men. "Fecking dolts!"

Keethro had picked out the man to kill first. It was the shortest, most nimble looking of them. While Titon liked to attack in order of size, Keethro attacked in order of quickness—a combination that had served them well in the past. Keethro could see the ringleader, a large rough-looking fellow missing plenty of teeth, likely due as much to rot as to bar fights. He was winding up to throw something substantial at them. A head of lettuce, dark and wilted, flew from the man's hand, downward, and exploded atop Titon's skull. *A fine throw, but I am afraid it will be your last*, Keethro eulogized, his grip on his makeshift axe tightening in anticipation.

Titon roared with laughter.

"My friend," said Titon, turning to Keethro. He was covered in bits of wet, slimy roughage and grinning. "I believe we are on the wrong side of this river."

DECKER

A thin sheet of ice and snow concealed the stream that ambled past their home. The sheltered water made a different sound, but it was still disturbingly audible. Each of the splashes seemed to bounce between the valley walls, overlapping and endless. To Decker, the unrelenting trickle served as stark reminder that his mother's condition was as perpetual as water's downward flow.

No matter how cold the winters had been in years past, the stream had never fully frozen, making it even more valuable to their family and irritating to Decker. "The Mountain cries for your mother, and his tears cannot be frozen," his father had told him, but during his life Decker had seen little evidence of the three gods his father so revered.

Having already fed his mother her supper, Decker sat beside her in his father's chair. She had fallen silent from her affliction prior to him forming memories of her. All Decker knew was what his father and brother had told him, and all they spoke of was her strength of spirit and her wisdom. He'd gotten better at not allowing his anger to take while visiting her. It was a cruel thing to have so strong a mother and yet be completely without her guidance or acknowledgment. And it was often that Decker wondered, with resentment difficult to repress, that perhaps if she had truly been a mother to him, he might have inherited more of those qualities.

I have made the gravest error a brother can make, Mother. Should Titon's condition not improve, I do not know what I will do.

He did not speak to her with words, the way his father did. He looked at his mother, her long white hair shining with pearl-like luster. To him she looked nothing like a wolf. To him she always seemed some sort of sorceress—from a distant land where magic was plentiful and wyverns roamed the skies. His brother had spoken to him of the more colorful stories he had read, of knights and mages, lightning and fireballs, hydras and dragons. Though he tried to convince Decker, straight faced, that all he told was truth, that such places did exist, Titon would eventually crack a smile, allowing the two to laugh at the notion. In spite of that, Decker still held on to the belief that his mother could be something more, if only to assuage the guilt he felt for only speaking to her with his thoughts. His father encouraged both him and his brother to speak aloud to her, regardless of her condition, but Decker could not. The embarrassment of hearing his own words was too great.

Decker gnashed his teeth and slammed his fist onto the chair's solitary arm. "Why did I not simply let him beat me?" he raged. The thought had not even crossed his mind when Titon had attacked him. Decker had had no chance to think rationally; he'd merely defended himself and with all the restraint he could muster.

Had Titon expected me to let him win? The prospect made the hurt worse, and it was not outside the realm of possibility. He'd been an advocate of his brother's leadership the entire trip, and Titon had responded with begrudging looks. Perhaps it had all been a ploy by his smarter brother to fool the men into believing the fight was justified, despite the lack of precedent. Had Titon merely been too embarrassed to explicitly plan it with him? Or did Titon assume that Decker had anticipated it as a means to finally solidify his right to lead? *What kind of fool am I to not have seen it? And now he will die for my idiocy and aggression.*

Decker remembered where he was, and who sat beside him. *I am sorry, Mother. Titon will recover, and Father will return, as I have promised.* It took all his self-control to prevent his thoughts from wandering toward the outcomes he felt were far more probable.

The two sat in silence as the Dawnstar hid itself behind the mountains. From the stories Decker had heard, she always loved the dawnlight, and there was no shortage of its rays here, in spite of the cold climate. Even in her current condition, she seemed to soak them in, their light making her hair shimmer and her skin glow with health.

A gentle rapping sounded from the door. *They arrive early*, thought Decker, not expecting Ulfor's girls for yet another hour. He kissed his mother on the head, said his silent goodbye, and went to the door.

The figure that greeted him was neither of Ulfor's girls, but it was familiar nonetheless—he had studied it from afar and often. The tight vest Kilandra normally wore had been replaced by a simple fur shawl draped across her shoulders, and Decker could not help but notice the flesh of her breasts so poorly hidden beneath. With some difficulty, he forced his gaze upward, meeting her eyes and finding them just as enticing as the rest of her.

"You must be freezing," Decker said, immediately regretting the clumsy nature of his greeting.

Kilandra laughed politely, putting him at ease. "My mother taught me that to walk amidst the frost with bare skin helps to retain one's youth."

It must be true, he thought, unable to find words with which to respond, too busy wondering how it was that her skin did not rise to bumps from the cold.

"May I come in? Or would you wish to take a walk with me?" Kilandra twisted her body toward the distance, as if anticipating his answer, if not implying what it should be. In any case, he could not bring a woman such as her into his home, not with his mother present—a mother he believed could read his thoughts.

"We'll walk," he said. Decker knew the girls would let themselves in to take care of his mother if he did not answer the door, and there would be no harm in him leaving a bit early.

Kilandra slipped her arm under his as they started out, surprising him more by how fragile it felt than by the action itself. The touch from a beautiful woman seemed unfamiliar to him and sent a burning warmth through his body. Not knowing whether her contact was that of mere friendship or the pursuit of more only increased the sensation. Decker had bedded girls from his clan before, but they had been blushing youths. The ease of which he gained their affection lessened the thrill, as if his success had been a forgone conclusion. And the Dogmen women he had taken had been exhilarating, but when the rush of conquest had gone, he was left with the sight of their imperfections, nearly sapping any gratification. Kilandra had none of these shortcomings. She was composed, she was proud, she was statuesque, and she was *claimed*—by one of the most powerful men in their clan, no less.

Decker peered around to see who may be watching them. *Keethro is a wolf of a man and deadly with an axe,* he reminded himself, unable to shake the feeling that at any moment some cold blade would bite into the length of his spine. It made him shiver and was already beginning to ruin what should have been a rather enjoyable outing.

"It would appear as if we are both cold," she said. Her voice was like winter-chilled honey, melting slowly to reveal its sweetness. She moved her arm to his waist, pulling herself close to him. With his arm heavy bent at the elbow, as to not encircle her, he clasped his hand around her upper arm, tantalizingly close to her breast. "He will not be returning… My husband."

Decker was grateful that she did not speak his name. "My father will assuredly return. What makes you say such a thing about…him?" Decker had no wish to speak the name either.

"We are no longer one, he and I. It has been that way for some time now. He was not the man I once thought he was."

Decker tried to make sense of what he was hearing, continuing to place one foot after the other, crunching the snow with a deliberately shortened stride to stay in step with her. Too preoccupied with the implications of Keethro being forever gone, he gave no second thought to how Keethro and Kilandra had managed to keep such a secret hidden from the gossiping girls of their clan. It was as if Kilandra said exactly what he wished to hear, and he welcomed the words. He dug his thumbnail into his index finger and smiled at what the pain told him. *She is unclaimed and in need of someone to protect her.*

"Your father may return, that is true, but he will return alone. Of this I am sure. And we must accept that it may be a near eternity before that can happen. How far must one travel to find what he seeks? To lands so distant that none of our people have ever gone and come back to speak of them."

"It may be a very long time, but he will return. And not before he has acquired the remedies he seeks." Decker heard his unshakable pride, and thought it justified.

"Yes, no doubt he will." Kilandra kept her eyes forward as she spoke, not looking at Decker, though he glanced at her often. "We will be on our own until then. The elders are wise, but too weak to lead. They have long warned of our need to unite and move south, a thing I also worry is true, yet a new year comes, and we remain divided. I fear we are without the leadership to accomplish such a thing."

"We have just led the greatest of raids upon the Dogmen. You have no reason to fear for your wellbeing." Kilandra did not seem impressed, perhaps because none of her family had been involved in the raid. "I will see to it myself that both you and your young and beautiful daughter are taken care of."

Kilandra tensed at his description of Red. Decker understood the implication, and after a moment of regret, he realized having said so was no blunder at all. Decker was not a fool, nor was he without weaponry when it came to seduction—she had only temporarily disarmed him. He would have to tread carefully though, as he could not expect the tricks that worked on susceptible girls to have the same effects on this more cunning prey.

"I am truly flattered and appreciate your offer. But do you believe that you will be able to continue to launch such successful campaigns without the aid of your brother? How long will it be before the Dogmen poison those lands too, and move yet farther south?"

The mention of his brother brought back all of Decker's anguish and worry. He had looked in on Titon earlier that day, and his condition was unimproved. He still drew breath but was not truly alive. Titon had become like their mother in a sense, but whereas their mother could swallow food and kept her eyes open when awake, albeit gazing blankly into some unseen distance, Titon did none of those things. He would not live for long, and the most they could do to nourish him was sit him up and put honeyed water in his mouth, very little of which seemed to make it down. Even if Titon did survive long enough to awaken, the clan's healers spoke of others who had risen from such states who were never the same. *If I have beaten my brother, the keenest man I have ever known, to the point of becoming simple…* The thought gave Decker such a profound disgust with himself that he nearly heaved.

"You must not blame yourself." Her words were both stern and soothing. "We all saw what happened, and it was no fault of your own."

He started, wondering how she had read his thoughts, but soon realized they must be plastered upon his face. With some effort, he managed to soften his look of self-reproach.

"He gave you no choice. Please…" She slowed her pace and turned to Decker. "You must be strong, if not for yourself, for the rest of us. We *need* you." Her forlorn expression pleaded with him for comfort, and her lips pleaded with him for contact. But he still pictured Titon's helpless face as he lay on the ground, mouth open, staring into nothingness.

"Strength is not what I lack."

"Then you will lead us? You will unite us?" She asked as if expecting him to deny her this most imperative request.

I have failed too many. I will not fail this one. It seemed her wheedling was all he needed to forge an unbreakable resolve. "I will unite our clans, and I will lead them south where we will take lands so rich you will never be cold or hungry."

She smiled softly and returned to his side where they continued their walk. Decker's thoughts returned to gentler things such as the sway of her hips. His arm was around the pronounced curve of her lower back now, and with his hand wrapped around her waist, he could feel her sensuous motion.

"Would you come inside and help me to start a fire? Red is staying with a friend, and it looks as though she has forgotten to put more wood on before she left."

Decker had not noticed they had been walking to her home, but he could not think of a more welcome destination. "I'd be happy to help," he said, trying his best to hide his yearning.

"I have a torch and coat you can borrow on your way back," she said, crushing Decker with the sincerity in her voice. She sounded as if there were no other alternative, and Decker chided himself for believing that there may have been. But as Kilandra moved to go inside, she squeezed herself unnecessarily close between him and the door, brushing against the front of his hips.

A more cunning prey, he reminded himself, his hope renewed.

CASSEN

The faint aroma of citrus and dandelion drifted through the room, soon to be overtaken by more dominant scents. Cassen took pride in his ability to exercise tasteful restraint, and the two solitary candles burning at either end of his grand dining table reminded him of his superiority to most men in that regard. *Tasteful restraint in all things, save my silks.* But Cassen had reason enough for all of his actions, even those contrary to his careful disciplines.

He had arranged for an intimate supper that was to be served shortly. He would be receiving a special guest, one whom he planned to charm with all the contrivances at his disposal. Food, wine, false flattery, these would all be served in careful portions tonight. *Not too much wine*, he reminded himself. It was important that his guest clearly remember the events of the night so that he did not awake the next day thinking it had all been a dream.

"Sir Collin to see you, Duchess." The voice of one of his boy servants heralded the expected arrival.

The man who entered was no knight. He wore the simple brown cloth indicative of servantry, but he was too old to be under Cassen's employ. He looked to be somewhere on the lower end between twenty and thirty years, with the body of a man but the face of a boy. *I could never have male servants of such an age*, Cassen joked to himself. *People might form the wrong impressions.* Cassen's smirk did not reach his face.

"Sir Collin, welcome! And thank you for making the time to see me." The more Cassen studied the man, the less he wanted to do what he had intended, but a little pride was a small price to pay, he resolved. Collin had a face so ordinary it bordered on being offensive. His chin was nonexistent, and his hair was a mess of short, brown ringlets, the strands of which clung together as if they had not been washed in some time. Even for a servant he seemed overly dowdy.

"Please, have a seat." Cassen motioned to the empty chair at the far end of the table. Although not looking entirely comfortable with the situation, the man conceded, sitting across from Cassen separated by a good ten paces. "I assume you had a pleasant trip in spite of the distance. It is a lovely carriage, is it not? I had it sent from Rivervale and often use it myself. The carriages made here are simply inferior. Every pit and rock their wheels encounter do jolt one so. Gives my bones such an ache." Cassen gave his guest no time to respond. "Can I offer you a drink? We have some Rivervalian Red, but the Sacaran Whiteleaf is by far the finer choice. I do believe I am the only one who has access to such a rare specimen, as it comes from ports far to the south with whom we no longer do trade."

The man hesitated before responding. "I am sorry, I am not much of a wine man. Any mead or ale will do, or just some water. But I must ask—"

"Yes, of course," Cassen interrupted. "Fetch some mead for our guest." The servant boy raced to comply.

An honest man, but even honest men crave power. "I can become absolutely parched during the trip from the Throne—no matter how much I drink along the way. But it is not so bad traveling during the winter. I suppose it means little to you with no reference of comparison." Cassen beamed a smile at his guest. "I am sure you would like to know why I have summoned you here, and I assure you, I will explain. But first, let us drink."

The servant was back with a pewter stein overflowing with froth and beaded with condensation. Cassen raised his glass containing a wine of greenish amber. "To new friends."

Collin raised his mug in kind and drank after he saw Cassen do the same. Before either man had returned their drinks to the table a servant was beside each of them with their first dish.

"Lamb ribs with a sweet garlic and rosemary crust. A mint butter sauce accompanies to the side." The servant departed upon completing the description.

"I find it to be so much more pleasing to know exactly what it is I am sinking my teeth into," Cassen said. He plucked from his plate one of the pair of dainty ribs, each artfully leaning against the other, then removed the meat with one scraping bite. *Quite delectable.* He let his satisfaction show on his face.

Collin must have been worried that he was the butt of some joke or trick as he seemed fearful to touch his food. Cassen pretended not to notice. The man would relax soon enough. "So tell me, Collin, where do you come from, and what is it that you do?"

"I am a servant in the main kitchens…Duchess…Cassen." He had some obvious difficulty deciding how to address his host, as most people did.

"Oh, please, you may call me Cassen. I grow so tired of titles and formalities. Do go on. What about your family and origins?"

"My mother was a servant in the same kitchens. Didn't know my father."

"Ah a bastard. Please take no offense. It is an ugly term, and I apologize." Cassen picked up the second rib. "You must try the lamb though. That is unless you are opposed to the eating of meat. It is a most unfortunate affliction that some are stricken with—the aversion to consuming flesh. I do not know how one could survive on mere beans, bread, and roughage."

Collin obeyed and tasted one of the ribs. His eyes went wide, and he wasted little time devouring the second as well.

"We seem to have similar tastes, you and I. I wonder what else we may share in common. Do you know of my story?" Cassen inquired.

Collin was busy chewing and rushed to swallow. "I… There are many stories about you…Cassen."

I must not frighten the man to the point of vomiting and ruining this lovely supper. "I am sure the most entertaining one would have to do with the way I became, well, the way that I am. A *eunuch*, though I do hate the word. I suppose you have similar feelings about the word bastard, after all. Go on, tell me what you have heard."

Collin peered around the room in the fashion of someone who is about to tell a vulgar story not fit for a general audience. He may have just as easily been looking for guards about to rush out of dark corners and arrest him for some accidental misdeed, however.

"They say that your, ehm, *parts* were removed prior to you coming into Duke Calder's service. As an apprentice. I think?"

Collin flinched when the two servants suddenly reappeared with their second course.

"Dragon tails, lightly battered and sizzled until crisp, atop a sweet and fiery vinegar sauce."

"Oh, this is one of my favorites." Cassen immediately removed one of the two curved bodies of fried meat from the other's seemingly coital embrace. He grasped it by the tail and squeezed so that the meat contained in the final section of its thin-shelled armor popped free and into his mouth along with the rest of it. When he was done chewing he explained to Collin, who looked somewhat afraid, "They come from the Eastern Sea and are quite the delicacy."

"I have seen them prepared in the kitchens, but have never had the pleasure." The look on his face confessed that he anticipated no pleasure in eating such a thing.

"Never so much as snuck one? I promise, I will not tell a soul." *It certainly looks as though you have been sneaking something from the kitchens.* "I do insist you try one. I think you will be pleasantly surprised."

"No, I am afraid they are quite strict." Collin lifted one of the shelled creatures and inspected it before taking a bite, though not near as expertly as Cassen as to remove all the meat. Collin's eyebrows rose as he continued to chew.

"See, I would not lie to you."

"They are very good. I would not have guessed. We call them sea bugs. They look quite different with their heads on." Collin seemed truly pleased to have discovered a new edible treat.

Good, you enjoy pleasant surprises.

"Where were we now?" Cassen continued. "Oh yes, my *parts*. I am afraid your story lacks some detail, but I will spare you the embarrassment and tell you myself. Calder, the Duke of Eastport—though it was not quite the city then that it is today," Cassen added with contentment. "He was in need of an assistant, apprentice, or what have you. He wanted, as all do, someone whom he could trust, but he was not a trusting man by nature. Calder was responsible for his niece, Crella, who was quite young then. She lived with him, and as you likely know, her mother died young and her father, the king, not long thereafter of the same affliction. Crella was, and always has been, beautiful—a true symbol of Adeltian elegance. It was imperative to the duke to find someone who could live with him and his niece. Someone to assist him in the difficult duties of running the city, while—and this was most important—posing no danger to her.

"Eunuchs are a rare *breed* I suppose, for lack of a better term, and Calder put out an open request for one such person to become his assistant, a role which lent itself to succession. There were, of course, no highborn eunuchs, so the offer was open to the rest of us. I was a young man of fifteen years at the time, and I was lowborn. The lowest of lowborn. The opportunity for such advancement prior to this announcement was inconceivable."

Cassen took a sip of his wine, taking a moment to revel in his savvy.

"I decided to take matters into my own hands, quite literally in fact. I personally delivered my application, and along with it I included the very *parts* of my being that would have precluded me from applying, had they still been attached."

Cassen watched as Collin lifted his mug of mead and took a long pull. He was pleased to see that he'd managed to finish his other dragon tail during the story, and Cassen finally consumed his own. *Had I served the sausage in peppered gravy as I had wished… Better that I did not.*

"And you must now be wondering why it is that I am telling you all this. Have no fear. I have no desire for you to follow in *those* footsteps. I am merely bringing to light the often forgotten fact—that I *was* a man, both of body and appetite."

The servants returned, replacing their empty plates with their final course.

"A simple cake of cream and strawberry."

Two small pieces of a spongy, spiral-shaped cake were plated, one leaning atop the other. *I wonder if my friend has noticed a theme in tonight's dishes.*

Collin appeared to still be at a loss for words, indicating as much by putting the first piece of his cake in his mouth.

"Your mother was always well cared for, was she not? She never went cold or hungry as servants often do." Servants did not often go cold or hungry—not in the Throne—but Cassen did not think it would prevent the statement from seeming somehow meaningful.

"She never ate like this," Collin joked. He may have found the conversation awkward, but he was clearly enjoying the food. Cassen was sure the man had never had such an incredible meal—even if he had been stealing from the kitchens. *He probably has never had so small a meal either.* It was Cassen's intent to leave his guests, this one most of all, wanting more. *A taste is all you get. Obey me and there is the promise of more.*

"No, few people do. But my point is that both you and your mother have been cared for beyond that of what would be expected for a normal servant. And when your mother went ill, she had the best of the city's menders attend to her, in secret, of course. It was a shame they could not find the cure for her exotic ailment. It brought me sadness to know she had passed."

"You knew my mother?" Collin had a look of disbelief on his face. He had finished his first mug of mead, and a servant, after glancing discretely at Cassen for permission, was refilling it.

"Yes, I knew your mother. She and I were very close prior to my running off to play duke-in-training. It was difficult for us to part, but she understood the reasons. People such as we were could not afford to pass up any opportunity for self-betterment."

Collin drained his mug, likely to help him make sense of the information as well as fill the void left in his belly from such a miniscule supper. Cassen waited patiently for the man to come to the obvious conclusion.

"You knew my mother before I was born?"

Peace forgive me, must I spell it out? "That I did, my *son*." Cassen mellowed his usual femininity to help the fool better conceive that which he was being told.

Horror filled Collin's eyes. "How?" he asked, as if the implication was that he was some spawn of demons.

Cassen resisted the urge to shake his head. "As I just explained, I was not always this way. I was a man much like you." *Very little like you, in all fairness to me.*

Collin slowly seemed to grasp how it may be possible, as if the previous notion of Cassen knowing his mother involved them sipping tea together and gossiping about the most handsome men, both in and out of reach. He looked to his empty mug as if to find some serenity there, and Cassen motioned to the servant to give him another half.

"So you see, Collin, all of this," Cassen gestured toward the table covered in finery, "could one day be yours. I certainly will not be producing any more heirs."

Collin sipped at the small amount of mead left in his mug, eyes staring blankly forward at the table.

"All I need from you in return is the same obedience any father would expect from a son. It should be no great chore for you to be obliged by these requests, knowing full and well that all to be performed is for the betterment of *our* household. The same household you will one day inherit and have to yourself, should you prove to be a son not just by blood, but by way of action." Cassen was every bit the father now, not his usual motherly self. He wondered how it would affect a person to see him transformed in such a way, but what harm would one more layer of manipulation cause?

The entire evening had been a charade, after all. It was no difficult task to find a bastard in the kitchens with a dead or distant mother. The first, unfortunately, had not gone quite to plan and had needed to be disposed of. But it was essential that the man Cassen selected be moved to the point of trusting that his and Cassen's fates were intertwined so thoroughly that it would spur him to commit previously unthinkable crimes. High treason was much to ask from a man with whom you just shared your first supper, but Cassen believed his powers of persuasion to be unmatched, and succeeding tonight would be confirmation enough of that.

The look of worry slid from Collin's face. Cassen knew this expression well. It was that of a man calculating his own fortunes in the event that the heavenly bodies aligned, lifting him from the depths of abjection with their combined pull and placing him atop his rightful throne. "What would you have me do, Father?"

TALLOS

Tallos heard a voice as he drifted between sleep and consciousness.

It was not uncommon for him to be awoken in such a way—his wife talked to him often as he slept. But her pleading words always turned to shrieks of horror as she burned alive in a fire of his own creation. He too felt the burn of those flames, rushing inside in an attempt to save her, his efforts rewarded only with more pain and torment. As he rose from sleep to find himself covered in sweat, what little heat he had from the struggle in his dream would dissipate, leaving him chilled and shivering, no longer aided in warmth by the burn of infection.

He did his best to ignore the phantom voice and rolled to his side to curl into a ball. The skin that covered him from the top of his head to the backs of his heels pulled taut as he did so. It was raised and bumpy, forming peaks and valleys similar to the terrain he knew surrounded him. Now healed, he found he'd lost most sensation, his numb skin serving as a shield against the claw of cold. He imagined he must look much like a monster. His affected skin felt to him how the skin of a dragon was often described, with its scale-like ridges. But he knew he was likely doing himself a false kindness with that comparison.

"Helloooooo?" It was the same voice as before, seeming quite distant, but definitely not imagined.

Tallos lay motionless. He had not considered the fact that he may be found in his hole. Rather, he had envisioned himself emerging with the thaw, reborn into evil and ready to commit atrocities. He also did not know how long he had remained below ground, isolated from all contact, eyes unopened, never speaking, though it seemed it had been long enough that he may have forgotten how to do those things that overworlders would expect of him.

"Anyone out there?" it called again. It was a man's voice and closer than before.

The thought of being discovered was not inviting. No man, nor group of men, would be here looking for survivors out of good will. If scavengers found him underground, naked except for his demon skin, how would they react? If they found the corpses he had preserved in his barrels, mostly stripped of flesh, there would be no way he could explain them. The mystic powers that, for some reason, he believed he would emerge with were not yet realized, his metamorphosis far from complete.

Someone stepped on the door to his cellar. It was a solid door, certainly strong enough to walk upon, but it groaned under the weight of what must be a large man. Such a man would have no trouble killing the weak thing that Tallos had become, and he would have no trouble justifying it either. Panic gripped him. He must not die, murdered by scroungers—it would not serve his purpose. It would please the gods far too much if he were to be destroyed so easily.

Tallos decided to open his eyes, even if perpetual darkness was his only reward. The weak muscles of his eyelids fluttered with the strain, but his lids refused to part, sealed by their own dried excretions. He crawled to the seep and wet his hands to wash them clean.

Whoever was above him scraped at his door. It would not be long before the latch was found and angry men poured inside, looking for anything of value. Tallos searched his mind for any objects that were in the cellar he could use as a weapon but could think of none. He rubbed at his eyes frantically with no effect. They would not open without the threat of torn flesh.

The familiar creak of his cellar door opening froze him in place, just as a devastating pain shot through his head. His eyes felt as if they were exploding, forcing him to bury his head in his arm. He had always been careful just to crack the door before venturing out, and he knew from experience that the pain of catching just a single ray could be excruciating. The agony Tallos now felt was so crippling he feared he would never again be able to see even when his eyes did open.

"Gods be damned!" The shouter sounded shocked, angry, and disgusted.

Tallos had been seen—he must have. He imagined what it must look like, the hunched-over creature hiding guiltily in a corner, three barrels of human remains and a fourth full of vinegar and his own pus. He cowered by the seep, trying to make himself as small as possible so whatever was thrown at him would be less likely to strike. He waited for a spear to hit the wall near his head or pierce through his side, unable to determine which would be worse. Odd noises came from above. They did not sound promising.

One man laughed cruelly, interrupted only by his own fitful coughing. Another man gagged and sounded to also be pouring something on the ground. It was oil, Tallos feared—buckets of it. They intended to burn him to death. Fire was said to kill demons, or was it warlocks? It made no real difference. He knew he would die just the same. But the thought of burning again was far worse than being speared. Tallos decided to call out to them and at least let them know he was human.

"Please, do not harm me," he tried to say, but his open mouth refused to make the sounds it was once capable of. All that came was dry wheezing.

They stomped around above him, two men at least. Messing about with a flint most likely, a whoosh of flame sure to follow. He had to cry out before they set him alight.

"Help me," he attempted. This time all that came was a few squeaks.

"Anybody down there?" called a voice. Why they asked that, he could not tell. Perhaps they wanted to make sure he did not have any living prisoners before they torched him. Someone put a foot on the first step and the wood protested. If they had not seen him yet, they soon would. The second step creaked from the weight of the descending giant.

He tried again to speak, but was overwhelmed instead with the need to cough. From a recent passing sickness, he knew his cough sounded more like the screech of the hellborn. It would do him no good in terms of appearing human. Covering his mouth and fighting to suppress the action, his ability to speak was again prevented.

The man was on the third step, a piece of wood wet with rot that threatened to break even under Tallos's lightened frame. They might believe he rigged it as a trap. His fate would be sealed when the wood split in two.

"Noaaaaa," Tallos finally managed to say, sounding oddly childlike.

"What? Who is down there?"

His mind raced for what he could do or say to delay them killing him. He considered just charging blindly—as he had no other method of charging—toward the man on the stairs in hopes that he'd be killed quickly. But if Tallos wanted to die he could have done that long ago. He would not give up now. The gods would be amused by his pathetic failure.

"Clothing," he said, still unable to recognize the sound of his own voice.

"What's that? Clothing?"

"Please," Tallos said. "Give me clothing."

For several minutes Tallos waited while the man whispered with the others above him, things that Tallos could not make out.

"I am throwing down a shirt and trousers," the man called down.

"No," Tallos said, now having had more time to think. "A robe." His voice was so weak and desperate. "*Please.*"

"Hang on now, little one."

The man must think Tallos a child, and now he worried they might be angry when they saw he was not. They would be even more suspicious if they felt deceived.

It was a good five minutes later before the man called down again. "It is going to be too big for you, but it's all we have."

Tallos heard the sound of some heavy fabric landing at the foot of the stairs, and he wasted no time crawling over, grabbing it with an outstretched arm and dragging it back to his corner where he put it on with nervous energy. He feared at any moment they would come down to peek, seeing him in the process. Relief coursed through him when he felt the hood of the robe and pulled it over his head. *Thank the gods*, he thought, almost bursting to laughter, but he was able to contain himself.

"I am coming up," Tallos said. "Please do not come down here."

Tallos ascended the steps with some difficulty. Walking on just his feet as opposed to crawling felt dangerous; each step played with his equilibrium. He was hunched, feeling the wall with one hand, waving the other in front of himself to avoid collision. The heavy hood kept his eyes sheltered from the worst of the light—he just hoped it was adequate to hide his burnt skin as well. With his hands withdrawn into the sleeves and his hood up, he was as well covered as he could have hoped.

"It is a man," one of them said, alarmed.

"Yes, I am sorry," said Tallos, motioning to his throat. "My voice…"

They seemed to accept his apology, or at least did not perceive him to be of any danger. *Not as yet*, he thought.

"How did you survive down there?" It was the first man, the one who had descended a few of the steps, and his tone was trusting.

"Please, do not go down there. It is piles of shit and piss." In spite of his blindness, weakness, and utter vulnerability, Tallos felt growing power as he believed his deception to be succeeding. "I am ashamed," Tallos said, closing the door behind him, not needing any sight to accomplish the task he had done so many times alone at night.

"Smells like worse than that!" This man's roar was followed by the same cruel laughter from before. His voice gave Tallos no comfort.

With the door closed, the gentle breeze brought the scent of vomit to Tallos. They had apparently been pouring out the contents of their stomachs, not oil.

"What is your name?"

I am Nekasr, he thought to say, half believing it to be true, *and where I go, the world burns.*

"Tallos," he responded. "This was my village."

DERUDIN

"I would advise against a trip to Westport, my king."

Derudin stood obediently beside the seated king. Lyell's grand desk was made evermore monstrous by the scrolls and papers piled upon it. With the tumult following the imprisonment of Crella and Stephon, Lyell had fallen behind in his many self-appointed tasks, namely those of overseeing the kingdom's military and finances, and he angrily studied one such piece of correspondence as Derudin spoke. *It is too much for one man, and he is losing focus.*

The fact that Alther had not gone to Westport as ordered further complicated matters. The city was falling to chaos and members of The Guard had to be stationed in markets to help lower the incidence of theft and murder. Had he the time, Derudin would have sought out Alther in an attempt to advise the man, but between his duties to the king and his classes, he had none to spare.

"But you have not even heard the reasons and necessities for such a trip," said Cassen. He stood before the king wearing his usual simper. "I beg pardon for borrowing from your own title, but would it not be *wise*, my dear Derudin, to first examine all the factors?" As always, it seemed it was Cassen's intent to provoke Derudin to anger.

It will not happen again. Derudin would never forgive himself for once allowing Cassen to agitate him to the point of lashing out. His subsequent absence from the many High Council meetings that Cassen had attended had caused irreparable damage. "What factors are there that will prevent the angry mob from storming the king's litter?" Derudin kept his voice calm.

"I am so glad you have asked. Allow me to explain." Cassen produced a wax-sealed piece of paper. "As you will see, I have been sent by the prince himself to request the king's presence in Westport. It seems Alther has negotiated some more lucrative trade agreements with the Spiceland merchants and wishes to have a banquet feast to celebrate what he is calling the Rebirth of Westport. Quite cleverly done, if I do say so myself."

"You think it clever because it is your own doing. Since when are you Alther's envoy? What do you have to gain from this?" Derudin asked, the king thus far remaining silent.

"I am both offended and flattered that you would think the *Rebirth* was of my own invention. But I assure you, they are Alther's words. I admit I may have used some of my influence with the merchants to help him secure his better contracts, but Alther is not the fool you make him out to be, Derudin. He is an intelligent man—of noble blood, no less."

"Do not twist my words. I implied no such thing. And you are yet to answer my second question." *This silk-covered serpent will be the death of the kingdom if he continues unchecked.*

"The second question?"

"What do you have to gain from this?" Although he felt the anger beginning to boil inside, Derudin's words remained coolly delivered. *Seek the void. Do not let this fool challenge your restraint.*

"Are we not all denizens of the same kingdom? We all have much to gain by not seeing Westport fall to ruin, lest Eastport and the Throne follow."

"Remind me again what good your piece of paper and fraudulent magnanimity will do in the face of a starving, angry horde?"

"Enough bickering," said Lyell, finally looking up from his papers. "I will not pass up the opportunity to reconcile with my son and see him succeed. Partnering with Cassen was perhaps the first intelligent thing he has done since I took Adeltia. We will attend this banquet, but it will be held in the Throne. I would trust my fate to the mob no sooner than I would parley in a blood feud. We will make all the necessary arrangements to ensure all the men of note from Westport are accommodated for the short trip that will be required of them."

"A very fair compromise, my king," said Cassen. "I am sure Alther will be content to hear of it."

Derudin saw no use for further discussion. Once forged, the king's decisions may as well be set in stone.

"I will see to it that Master Warin makes the preparations necessary for security. Thank you for assisting my son, Cassen. It will not be forgotten. If that is all, you may leave."

The king's attention once more on his papers, Cassen shot Derudin a satisfied smile before curtseying and making his exit.

THE WHORE'S BASTARD
Many Years Ago

Head down and shoulders slumped, he struggled to pull his wooden cart, the wheels seeming to catch between every gap of the cobblestones. He felt like an insignificant speck, caught in the shadow of the wall that loomed overhead—a shadow that kept his dirty corner of the city known as the Armpit in darkness well into the afternoon.

When he was younger his mother had told him the story of the wall, blaming it for all the surrounding squalor. "Had Adella finished the wall, we would not live like this," she said, breath reeking of ale. "But she builds her great throne instead, the Castle to End All Coin." He wondered which of her patrons she'd heard that from. His mother was no wordsmith.

Queen Adella received little love from her people. When her brother Adellos II died the kingdom mourned, and soon after she had replaced him, the kingdom wept. But the boy was not fool enough to believe their lot in life would have been any better had the wall spanned across the continent, shielding Adeltia from the threat of northern invasion. Perhaps if his father had been one of the many architects put to death for failing to meet the queen's standards, he would have cause for complaint, but he never knew his father nor did he think he would want to. The Adeltian Throne—that towering object far in the distance and namesake of the kingdom's new capital—did not condemn him… It *called* to him.

He'd not seen his mother since having left her years ago, but in the Armpit he remained. *Better to be an orphan than a whore's bastard,* was what he told himself when his childish longing to see her threatened to take hold.

Passing by the bakers and smiths, fruit vendors and butchers, he hardened his resolve to leave this place entirely, to not be another lifelong victim of the Pit. They all looked so different, these peasant laborers, yet depravity saw them unified. He had no sympathy for this lot, however. Sympathy and compassion were weaknesses he conditioned himself to no longer to feel. These were not people oppressed by an unfinished wall, these were slaves of their own self-pity—his eventual rise above them to be validation of his assertion.

Eating nothing but gruel he was able to save fifty-three coppers—just over half a mark—in the past two months. His belly ached for mutton, but he had not given in, not once since he started saving. With five marks he could buy a cotton shirt and trousers, and with one more he could afford a trim and a bath. Another two would see him into his first pair of shoes, used of course, and a final eighty coppers would get him a ride out of town shared on a wagon. He would take the first job he could get, no matter what it was—*even if it means I must be an architect.*

He came to a sudden halt, sloshing the contents of the many chamber pots in his cart, and attempted to make sense of what he saw. A carriage drawn by two black horses was in front of his employer's shop. The shady fellow was being arrested for some misdeed, no doubt. He was ever trying to cheat him or one of the other boys out of their pay. Self-preservation begged him to return to the abandoned, leaking structure he called home to avoid any guilt by association, but his curiosity would not allow it. He entered the back of the building to empty his pots into the piss wagon, hoping to catch a glimpse of the activity inside.

He was not the only curious boy letting the contents of his pots slowly drain while craning neck in an attempt to spy on the goings-on in their employer's office. Someone of importance was paying him a visit, but to what end he could only guess.

"Who's in there?" he asked the others standing around the wagon.

Strig, the oldest boy sneered. "The Shitlord."

"Who's that?"

Strig just shook his head, laughing to himself. The older ones loved to know something the others did not, and enjoyed making them grovel for answers. Aside from kicking rats, it was about the only modicum of power they were able to wield in this place, and they were not about to give it up.

He thought he had already identified the richest man in the area, the owner of the bar and brothel. The man was often seen strolling the town with one or more of his strongmen in tow, taking what he pleased from vendors who were either afraid of getting their teeth knocked out or of having him send their favorite whore to their wife with a bastard baby in her arms. At any rate, the lack of filth on the man's clothing was impressive, and the boy had made a conscious note to learn all he could about him—a difficult task requiring the suspension of contempt; the very man had been responsible for some of the boy's mother's better beatings. To know there was another far more powerful man in the area—even if just for a visit—made his chest grow hollow with anticipation.

He never saw the Shitlord, which only added to the intrigue, but he later learned that this man who could afford the luxury of massive horses and a leather-lined carriage was indeed the Lord of Shit. It had not occurred to the boy that his employer might have himself been employed by another, let alone that that person could possibly be of any worth. Granted there were like to be several links in the chain of command separating the Shitlord from the boy's toothless boss, the fact remained that the Shitlord was by all accounts exceedingly rich. Far wealthier than the brothel owner, far wealthier than anyone he had ever hoped to see pay a visit to the Armpit. And the man was in charge of transporting, of all things, piss and shit.

Being the clever boy that he was, he eventually came to the realization that the filthier the service, the more profitable it could be, and he resolved never to pass up an opportunity to use that knowledge to better his station in life.

CASSEN

Cassen inhaled deeply the bouquet of excrement, sweat, and blood—not to savor the stench that spoke of his childhood, but to remind himself of how far he had come. How ironic it was that he was on his way to meet a young man not unlike himself in his ambitions, but due to utter stupidity and obliviousness, had managed to descend within the social hierarchy just as rapidly as Cassen had risen.

Cassen was no stranger to the dungeons. He had many contacts within them—among the gaolers as well as the inhabitants. It took far less than lady servants to buy the trust, fleeting that it may be, of these lowborn wardens and malefactors, and it was always worth the cost. He had certainly never promised a prisoner so much as he intended to tonight, but this was no ordinary prisoner.

"Good evening, Vidar," Cassen said with familiarity.

"Ah, the Duchess. Come to rape some of my boys again? Or is it the other way around? I never could tell." Vidar's smile was more disgusting than the smell. "You've turned me into quite the whoremonger."

Cassen wondered how the man managed to amuse himself with the same joke each and every time he came to visit. *Believe whatever you like, so long as you keep your mouth shut as I pay you to.*

"Oh, but you know me so well, my good Vidar. Perhaps you can guess my taste for the night?"

"Well," said the gaoler, stroking his misshapen chin as if truly considering. "I would have to guess you would be in the mood for some choice meat tonight. Perhaps something a bit princely?"

"Whoremonger you may be, but you are good at what you do. I will need an hour with the prince, *undisturbed*." Cassen handed Vidar a golden coin worth fifty marks with a downward wrist and raised pinky.

"I would think a prince might fetch a more handsome sum," said Vidar with a bit of humor. He was at least wise enough not to sound resentful.

"You would be wrong," Cassen replied as he strode passed Vidar dismissively, having snatched the key from his desk. *Show an ounce of weakness to one, and all will take from you a pound.* It was an old Adeltian saying that Cassen thought especially fitting in his current surroundings.

"Interrogators of The Guard already did a number on him," Vidar hollered to Cassen's back. "You may not find him as entertaining as you like."

Cassen needed no escort; he knew where the prince would be. There was a special cell for holding and interrogating nobility, designed to be less physically torturous in exchange for being more mentally so. Vidar had explained to him long ago how they found that those accustomed to the comforts of royalty would crack "too far," as he put it, when placed under the normal methods of deprivation. Once stripped of the belief that they would ever reattain their former glory, they lost the will to live and the care to comply. This had become apparent after Lyell had taken over Adeltia. The attempts on his life implicated many an Adeltian highborn, and Vidar had been present for it all. But in spite of his advanced age, his spindly limbs, and near complete lack of hair, he had the spryness of a far younger man—almost as if he was somehow draining these prisoners of more than just their secrets.

A flutter of excitement passed through Cassen as he imagined for a moment that he was headed to Crella's cell rather than to Stephon's. *What an enthralling time that will be, if and when it comes.* But it was not a realistic goal for the time being. Crella was held in the former queen's chambers at the top of the Throne, and members of The Guard were numerous in that area. It was the most heavily fortified section of the main castle, housing the king himself. Protectors could be difficult and dangerous to bribe, as a small minority of them actually took their vows to heart. It simply was not worth the risk at this time.

Cassen had passed countless empty cells on his way to his final destination. Each was the typical hold, containing no more than a bucket. Stone made the walls and floor, and the bars were of thick, mottled iron. In time he reached a massive door not unlike one that would be found on most frames in the castle. He knocked three times and waited for the reply that was slow to come.

"Enter." The voice did not sound as though it belonged to one confined.

After unlocking the door, Cassen entered and found the cell quite decent indeed. A nobleman would retain some form of dignity after having passed so many horrid cells to finally be placed in such clean, albeit modest, quarters. It would let him know that he was receiving special treatment, giving him the hope of one day being freed. Why else would your gaoler go through the trouble of providing such amenities? In addition to the simple bed and chamber seat, there were luxuries such as books, a bucket of clean water, a bar of soap, a comb, and a tiny razor, too small to easily end one's life with but certainly capable of shaving given enough time—something that would be had in abundance. Stephon's half-eaten supper sat by the door, which appeared to have been a fair plate of food. Cassen made out the remnants of roast chicken, gravy, green beans, and a mug of some frothy beverage that was now empty.

"They told me you would come."

Cassen knew the interrogators would be attempting to goad Stephon into revealing as many names and as much information as possible, but Cassen had nothing to fear. Though he had known about the heavy-handed plot, Cassen had nothing to do with its invention or execution. And it had no chance of success—Cassen had seen to that by implicating some of the conspirators himself. The fact that Stephon had been drawn into it was proof enough that the boy would work well for what Cassen now had in mind. *And I will have little worry of him speaking my name after today, with the banquet so near at hand.*

"And here I am," Cassen said. "I do apologize for the delay."

Stephon lay on his back with a large vellum binding propped upon a pillow on his chest. *The Intricacies of War and Tactics* was a beast of a book, one that Cassen was not himself familiar with, but nobles loved to memorize and quote excerpts from it when arguing about battle tactics and formations with other highborn who had also never seen a battlefield.

Cassen gave a moment's pause to attempt to unravel the mystery of how Stephon knew it was he who had entered the room, but decided the boy likely had no idea, and that with so much time at his disposal, he was able to come up with plenty of cryptic greetings for his few guests and interrogators. Stephon had always had a flair for the dramatic, and Cassen certainly could not fault him for that.

"They said you would free me," said Stephon, his head still completely hidden by the massive book.

"I am sure they said a good many things, most of which, if having struck upon truth, only did so by coincidence. They are toying with you in the hopes that you will tell them everything you know."

"I have already told them everything. Why would they continue to lie?" asked Stephon.

"Perhaps because they have no way of knowing that you have indeed told them *everything*."

"But I have."

Cassen was beginning to worry that Stephon's mind might be too far gone for what he had planned, but there was no harm in continuing his efforts. He had come this far.

"My prince, I have not come to free you, not yet at least. I have come to offer you the greatest gift I can think to give."

Stephon turned the page in his book as if not listening.

"And I do not expect you to believe my offer to be true," Cassen continued. "I will not need from you any promises or trust. I would be a fool to expect them at this point. I only ask that when I bring you proof that my gift is genuine, that you accept it, and remember that it was I who acquired it for you."

Stephon shoved the two sides of the book together, closing it with a solid thud, and hefted it to the side. He sat up in his bed, looking directly at Cassen. He did not look much different than Cassen remembered. He bore no marks or bruises from interrogation, though Cassen had not truly expected to see any. Stephon was the same cleanly shaven, handsome, and arrogant urchin he had always been, and he looked rather annoyed to have been kept down here for so long.

"And what could a lowborn duchess acquire that a prince and heir to the throne could not?"

A key to your cell for one. Cassen had not expected Stephon to have become even more brazen with his time spent in the dungeons, but it was often said that confinement, much like alcohol, allows one's true self to emerge. It was somewhat discomforting to realize Stephon had actually been tempering himself until now.

"There are two men and a fair amount of castle stone that lay between you and the throne, are there not?"

"The king and his son have no claim to the throne. I am the true heir. And I will not be in here forever. I will take what is mine."

What favor can you curry from springing a man from a trap he does not truly believe himself to be within? "Nonetheless, I assume you would be grateful to whomever was able to expedite the process of seeing you from prison and into your rightful throne?"

"That I would. I would reward such a person with a position of high esteem—greater, of course, than that of duke or duchess."

"That is good—"

"But let me be very clear," interrupted Stephon. "As of right now, it is not the king's throne I wish to have. It is his head."

Cassen nearly laughed. He'd heard that Stephon had gone quickly from apologetic to acrimonious as his stay continued, but to hear it firsthand was rather amusing. "Do you speak so boldly with those who question you?"

"Are you not one who is questioning me? I see no difference between you and any of the other fool members of The Guard, and I speak no differently. I have told you already of my plans to destroy the false king and his accomplices, and I tell you again that my plans have not changed. He is a disease upon this great Adeltian Kingdom, and he must be dealt with as such. His taint must be eradicated so that pure Adeltian blood can once again rule. Only then will this kingdom be returned to glory."

Cassen saw no need to point out that Stephon himself was not of pure Adeltian blood, nor that when he was first dragged into this cell, kicking and screaming, he claimed to have only colluded with the Adeltians to such a degree as to thwart them.

"Your Grace, it sounds as if you have given this much thought. I will serve to aid you in every way I can. I realize pleading patience is of no comfort to you. All I can do is beg that you forgive me for the lethargy with which it must seem I perform these tasks. As you know, there are many among even the Adeltians who cower to the false king, and they too seek to hinder me."

"You have wasted enough breath. Go and do as you have promised, and I will see you justly rewarded." With that Stephon propped the heavy book back upon his chest, opened it to a seemingly random page, and looked as if he was again reading.

Cassen eyed the text with amusement. *And to think I did not even get a quote.* "As you command, Your Grace." Cassen curtseyed and exited, shutting and locking the door behind him.

KEETHRO

"This river travel has turned a bit tedious without the risk of collision."

Keethro had to agree with his friend on that account. The pace of life aboard the raft had slowed greatly after paddling to the other shore, unaccosted by leviathans or whirlpools. It had become difficult to remember that they were in a faraway land, surrounded by foreigners who might wish to do them harm. Passing ships on the far shore were too distant to be of interest, and the occasional boat that skimmed ahead of them, pulled by the early morning breeze caught in its sails, did so without incident.

Even the insects had decided their raft was safe enough for harbor, as spiders had begun weaving webs in the gaps between the timbers. Keethro watched as a small frog hopped from log to log, and wondered if the webs would have the strength to hold him.

"These southern men do not look so different from you or me," Keethro said. "Save perhaps for their lack of beards."

"You call that a beard?" snorted Titon.

Without the aid of Kilandra's silvered glass and shears, Keethro had found cropping his beard a rather difficult task. He did his best with his knife, but he could only assume he'd formed a haphazard mess when compared to the close trim he preferred. The water's distorted reflection did little to confirm or deny his hunch, and there was certainly no chance of him asking Titon—not unless laughter and a loss of respect was the response he desired.

Keethro could see he would have no problem blending in among these new people, but that was thanks mainly to how he stood out among Galatai. Titon, on the other hand, still appeared to be very much the foreigner. Oddly enough, in spite of the warm weather, these southern boatmen wore enough fur to look as though they were in the cold of the North. And it would seem the South had its fair share of giant men, seen on passing boats, but none had the massive beard of the archetypal Northlunder who lived among the ice and snow. *Thank the gods Titon was never one to braid his beard*, Keethro thought, annoyed again by his godly reference. *And to hell with the gods, for I know he will not part with the thing.*

"Perhaps it would be wise for you to shear that goat you have upon your face so we can better walk among these Southmen unnoticed."

Titon stroked his prized beard and smiled. "What good would it do me to awaken my wife from her slumber only to have her stab me through the eye and go in search for her real husband?"

As I thought. "Well, you can at least get it cleaned up some." As Keethro spoke, the frog he'd been watching jumped, overshooting what would have been a safe place to land and arriving between two logs with an awaiting web. Keethro found he was satisfied to see his question answered. The web had been damaged, but the frog had not broken through.

"It would feel good to have a woman's hands tending to some grooming…among other things," Keethro added. It was not the proper remark to get the ever-faithful Titon to comply, but it was the best he could do. "And honestly, it is an insult to the Mighty Three for me to be hiding this perfect jaw that they created behind such a mess."

"Bah. A perfect jaw would not yap so much like a woman about grooming and the like." Titon stood and moved to the rear of the boat. "I'm going to have a nap. Wake me if there's trouble."

Keethro meant to respond but was transfixed on the battle before him. A spider far smaller than its prey emerged from where it hid. He had seen instances like these play out where the spider would pluck the creature free, fearing too much damage to its web to be worth the trouble. That was not to be, however. The black spider approached with caution, then began to wrap the frog with silk using its long skeletal legs. The frog, in its helplessness, looked not unlike the Dogmen they slaughtered, but with a burst of strength it struggled, twisting and turning and sending its attacker into retreat. That effort was ultimately without reward. Having only further cocooned itself without managing to break free, the frog lay in wait as the eight-legged assailant returned to finish the task of securing its meal.

Something inside Keethro stirred. He could not help but see the spider as evil, its ensnaring the larger, stronger animal by way of patient insidiousness a method of combat without honor, and Keethro was not without the power to intervene. He picked at the web with a finger, causing the spider to withdraw, and plucked the frog from certain death. He then spent the next hour meticulously pulling and cutting the sticky silk from its skin, each action threatening to cause more harm than good. With its head free from entanglement, the frog ungraciously clamped down on Keethro's finger with surprising force, causing him to laugh. The humor was lost, however, as he worked to free the frog's fragile arms and legs, just managing to do so without dislocating any joints, or so he hoped. Then came the toes and fingers. His neck aching from having been bent over his tiny patient for so long, Keethro fought his discomfort and continued. The rear feet took time, but they were freed with only some minor damage done to the webbing between the toes. The frog's hands were composed of such tiny-boned fingers that there seemed no way to remove the silk without mangling them. The web had more strength than bone, and every pull caused the creature to struggle, biting at Keethro as if he were worse than the spider. And he felt worse, as he tugged in frustration, his own fingers tired and simply too large for such delicate work, removing two of the frog's fingers along with the silk.

"Fecking hell," he cursed aloud. *Had I just freed him the moment he was caught, this would not have happened.* His bitterness was amplified by the fact that the frog still had another hand encased in webbing, his fingers stuck together and useless. Keethro could think of no way to free the hand without mangling it as well.

"Your choice," Keethro said, opening his own hand. The frog hesitated only a moment before jumping off, and a few hops later his dry skin drank in the river as he swam away. Any pride Keethro had hoped to feel from saving the critter was lost having maimed him in the process.

Keethro's pity was short lived. In the distance he could make out what appeared to be a series of boats tied to docks.

"Titon," he called, knowing his friend had risen by the lurch of the raft. "A town."

A place for trade and barter was as welcome a sight as any, as they were in desperate need of resupply. Having been forced to flee Port Phylan in a hurry, each still had a full purse of coinage that had done little but serve as extra weight. Well over three hundred marks remained after over a month of travel.

"Wear your best expression of boyish idiocy, and we will see if we cannot fool these people into thinking we are from these parts," Keethro said. *We will look a pair of vagabonds no matter the case.*

The men navigated their raft expertly enough to not cause any collision when pulling abreast the farthest of five boats tied side by side, forming their own extension of the dock. Most of the boats were dinghies with fixed oars, same as the one to which they tied. It was a fine-looking boat for a dinghy, with a keel and two sets of mounted oars.

"Will they mind us tying off like this?" Keethro would have felt far more comfortable moored directly to a dock, but the few thin docks that existed were completely packed by similar boats, tied beside each other in a series.

"It appears to be the custom," said Titon. "I see no better place to tie off, and you intend for us to act like Southmen. I can stay with the raft while you get us some salt and meat. And a damn pot or skillet."

Keethro was still bitter over the loss of their skillet to the storm, but the lack of a vessel in which to boil water had taken its toll on them both. This river, while mighty, was a far cry from the clear waters of the streams in the mountains. The results of drinking from it directly were not pretty, and required frequent stops to avoid further polluting the waters.

Keethro knew it would be a poor decision to leave Titon alone. "Let's remain together. I have no reason to trust these people yet, especially with a full purse of coins." *And I have a point to prove about that beard.*

Passing by a vendor selling dried fish for two marks per pound, they agreed to purchase some on the way back and proceeded to a shop with plenty of bags and crates of nonperishables in front. Titon already attracted a fair share of sidelong glances, and Keethro knew he was perceptive enough to notice. One does not last as a Galatai clan leader without the ability to sense mistrust and discontent.

Three shopkeeps worked the counter in the store they'd entered, and it appeared they got the grumpiest of the lot. He was an old man with a decent beard—for a Southman—of gnarly white hair, cut short at the chin but long on either side. He wore a perpetual frown that Keethro guessed was not just for the sake of negotiation. "What do you two drifters want?" he asked.

Keethro's eyes went right to the copper pot. "How much for that green piece of rubbish up there? And what is it, some sort of club?"

"Ten marks for the pot. No less." The man's expression did not change.

It was twice what Keethro wanted to pay, but not a bad starting point. "I will do you a favor, old man, and throw it off the docks for you. Three marks."

"Ten marks. No less."

Keethro winced. "Do I look like a prince? How much do you expect a drifter can afford to pay for something he could find on the side of the river?"

"You find me a pot like that on the side of the river, and I will give *you* three marks for it." The man's expression remained, but Keethro was happy to get him into some dialogue.

"How about that rope?" Titon's question sounded more like a demand.

One of the other shopkeeps turned to the third. "Ha, Randal! You owe me a copper. It *can* speak."

Titon glared at the man who just went on about his business, unafraid. *Threats of violence do not seem to carry the same weight out here. Must be lawmen nearby,* Keethro reasoned.

Their shopkeep ignored the others. "Fifteen marks for the full coil, twelve marks for the half."

"Gah," said Titon, making a face of disgust.

"I will just take two pounds of salt then, how much will it be?" *Surely these men will not gouge us on salt.* In the North certain necessities were never haggled over, salt chief among them. Being so common and yet so essential, if a neighbor needed salt, one would give it to him and expect nothing in return. To do otherwise was unheard of.

"Twenty marks."

Keethro scowled at the man, and Titon growled quite audibly.

The shopkeep returned their anger in kind. "I do not know where you two oafs come from, the permafrost by the looks of it," he said, eyeing Titon as if to drive home his point. "But in these parts we have certain customs. You do not cheat a man on salt or fresh water, and if you are accusing me of such, then you can take your business elsewhere. We're all feeling the pinch of the new prices. I buy salt by the lot for nine marks a pound and sell it by the pound just the same to friends and for a hair more to strangers. And you're about as strange as they come."

The man did not appear to be lying, so Keethro put ten marks on the table to diffuse the situation. "Just a pound, then."

With his bag of salt in hand, Keethro said with finality, "And fifteen marks for the full coil *and* the pot."

The shopkeep shook his head, but lacked the genuine anger he had concerning the salt. "You heard my prices."

"Let's go, Titon. We will no doubt find a better price downriver."

The shopkeep frowned as if confused by something but was quick to respond. "Eighteen and they're yours."

"Done," Keethro said, not expecting the man to have come down so far.

On their way back to their modest vessel, they spent another ten marks on dried fish—dried perhaps by southern standards; it was at best lightly smoked. It would do, however, if eaten quickly. Keethro felt rather accomplished having negotiated a fair price for their hardware while also allowing Titon see how much his beard made him look the Northman.

His good feelings vanished when they found their raft floating away from the docks. The boat they had tied to was upriver, the two men aboard laughing while they paddled.

"No more than five boats per mooring," one shouted.

"Not that you could call that bundle of debris a boat!" said the other. Their sleek vessel cut through the water with grace, making the possibility of reprisal out of the question.

"Stay here. I'll get the raft." Keethro dove in before Titon could respond.

After a few minutes of labored swimming, an action he was not adept at, he boarded the raft and attempted to pole back to the docks, finding the river too deep to touch ground. He did his best to paddle with the stick, but it was impossible to tell if he was making any progress.

"It is no use," shouted Titon. "You cannot make it."

Keethro heard the splash of Titon entering the river as he continued to paddle. If anything it seemed he had drifted farther.

Aided by the current, Titon stroked with the arm that carried the pot, holding their newly purchased supplies to his chest with his other. He threw the fish, rope, pot, and salt aboard one by one after reaching the boat and hoisted himself up last.

"The fish is ruined," he said. "The salt we can salvage."

Keethro agreed. He saw no point in mentioning that Titon could have left the supplies on the docks and they then paddle the raft back together. He settled instead for words of comfort. "Damn Southmen."

"I will be happy to drink some boiled water for once though," said Titon, surprisingly unaffected by the confrontation that had cost them five pounds of fish that he was no doubt eager to sample. "Perhaps my next solid shit will put me in a well-enough mood to think about trimming this bush about my face."

Keethro chuckled in approval.

Most of the fish had to be discarded, having already turned to mush, but they saved some and planned to use it as bait before it began to stink too much. The bag of salt sat drying near the fire, and their second pot of water was nearing a boil. Keethro was ready for a nap and had just stretched out on the thin bed of cloth-covered straw at the back of the raft when he caught sight of the most fearsome structure he had ever seen.

"Those are no tits of the Mountain," said Titon, having obviously seen the same thing.

"No." Keethro knew what it must be, but the sheer scale of it made it difficult to believe. "So *that* is a castle."

The rounded turrets of the mighty fortress seemed to reach into the clouds. Massive parapets surrounded the turrets and connecting walls, projecting outward in a way that made imagining they had been built by mortal men even more difficult. Titon looked a dwarf in comparison to such immensity.

"How does such a structure even come to be?" asked Titon with wonder.

"I do not know. It is incredible." But Keethro's true thoughts were much darker. *I fear we may be crushed by those men powerful enough to create such a thing.*

TALLOS

The familiar birdsong of the southern woods filled his ears as Tallos found himself pleasingly surrounded by the crisp winter chill. A light dusting of snow covered the otherwise naked branches of the trees, unmoving in the breeze.

Nothing but sour oak and scraggy pine grew in these parts, and neither tree was of any use other than for timber or firewood. The acorns of the sour oak were not edible, no matter what was done to them. Even tree rats avoided the acrid fruit, eating instead the seeds in the pines' armored cones. In spite of this, Tallos continued forward with anxious steps, a bucket in his hand, and hope in his chest.

Then they saw it. They knew where it was, but each time they came upon it felt like a new discovery. The honey pine had stout, roundish needles. It stood tall among the oaks but short among the other pines. And that was the least of its differences.

Lia was the first to race to the tree. Having been taught to forgo her natural instinct to squat and pee beside it, she instead ran around it in tight circles, waiting for Tallos and Leona to catch up. At the base of the tree, Tallos was happy to notice that their harvesting pail appeared to be undisturbed beneath the simple knee-high roof that sheltered it from the snow and rain. He reached the tree, crouching to allow Lia to lick his face as he petted her. They had been careful not to tap too greedily into its veins, and looking up the trunk, Tallos could confirm it was as healthy as ever. The deep green of its needles contrasted with the bits of light blue from the sky that managed to peek between its countless limbs and fingers, and the scent was pure bliss.

Leona was beside him now, and she took over the responsibility of petting their overjoyed accomplice. Tallos carefully removed the pail, replacing it with the one he carried, and looked inside. A finger's width of thick dark amber pooled at the bottom—a fine harvest. Well pleased, he handed the pail to Leona so she could enjoy the first taste. Her face brightened when she saw how much they had collected. They could have brought it back to town and sold it for a handsome sum, but this was one of their few luxuries, and it had become a tradition for the three of them to share.

Leona dipped a finger into the gooey amber and scooped up a small amount. It stretched and pulled away from the rest, but was almost too thick to drip. She quickly licked the candy from her finger and closed her eyes. Tallos could taste it through her, the deep sweetness that was so much like honey, but both more light and luscious at the same time. To compare it to other tree syrup would be a grave injustice, as it had no green, piney flavor. The wind lifted the long brown strands of her hair, exposing her lean neck and sharp-cornered ears. Her tongue would be even sweeter now, were it possible, and she seemed to read his mind as she leaned forward, eyes still closed, to kiss him. Her lips compressed against his own and began to part.

Tallos's nose smashed into something hard, and he inhaled the scent of unwashed beast.

"Hahaha!" The cry of laughter came from nearby, though it sounded more grating than cruel. "I told you he would pass out soon enough."

Tallos gripped and clawed at the memory of his dream as it was torn from his grasp. The softness of Leona's lips, the curve of her breast…the comfort of being together and safe. He almost preferred the nightmares to these dreams of his fondest memories. How much of them had been glorified and aggrandized, he could no longer say, but what he remembered of his previous life seemed too perfect to have ever been true. To be awakened to his new reality was a painful, jolting process. There was no perfection here, just the stench and ugliness of normalcy.

"Let him be, Kelgun." The pleading voice belonged to John, a man easily over twenty years though certainly not more than thirty. He was no small man—had he been he surely would not be speaking as such to Kelgun—but his demeanor revealed he was no fighting man either. He trotted alongside Tallos on his dapple-grey rouncey, looking as if he were ready to catch him, had Tallos fallen from his seat.

"He falls asleep because he is on the only ambling rouncey in the kingdom," spat Kelgun. "A horse for a boy if ever there was one. I'd have a mind to put a straw bed on it and ride half asleep myself, but someone has to look out for the safety of this damn group." The man turned his head, letting loose a few scratchy coughs. "And I am far too large a man for so tiny a beast."

Sir Kelgun, as he called himself, was no giant, though he would have one believe as such from his self-descriptions. He was middle-aged and rode upon a black destrier—or rather what was left of one. The horse may have been large, but its age made it look unfit for any real use. Nonetheless, atop the massive beast Kelgun did have some semblance of the knight he claimed to be, and in that he needed all the help he could get. His messy beard of wiry black and his menacing stare made him look more a brigand than anything else.

Tallos rubbed the sleep from his eyes and peered about. It seemed the vibrant colors of his dream were also exaggerated beyond that of reality. The needles of the pines and the cloudless sky both looked distinctly grey in contrast with his recent fantasy. He jerked to panicky alertness seeing the deep red upon the top of his right hand. The sleeve of his robe had fallen to the wrist, exposing his grossly raised and colored skin, and he looked to the side to see if John had noticed. John only stared straight ahead, but Tallos could not shake the feeling that the man had seen his secret.

"Tallos, sir? Would you mind if I took my turn?" Dusan, a boy no older than twelve, walked alongside Tallos's mount.

"He's no *sir*, boy," scoffed Kelgun.

"No, of course." Tallos slid from the horse, groaning when his feet made contact with the ground. He tried without much success to stretch the painful knots in his ass and thighs.

"Ha! What's the matter, mage? Can't even handle the peaceful stride of a child's pony? How do I find myself among such a sorry lot?" Kelgun's destrier snorted in what sounded to be approval.

"You are free to leave, just as any are free to join," said Wilkin. "Such is our way."

Wilkin could have been anywhere from sixty to several hundred years of age, there simply was no way of knowing. In any case, he seemed the only respectable member of their party. There was a depth to his eyes that spoke of endless wisdom and a kindness that implied a similar patience. Tallos found it impossible to imagine the man ever having been young. He looked as though he'd been born with his bald head and white, wispy beard.

"Aye, and the sorrier the lot, the more like they are to need protecting." Kelgun unsheathed his sword, and the ringing of the metal was sweet music. His horse may have been old and wearied, but the sword shone with the perfection of a piece of metal that had been crafted and never used except for display. Even then, it would have needed daily oiling, cleaning, and polishing to retain such a luster, yet not once had Tallos seen him tend to it half so much as one might care for an axe.

"I am no mage, as I have told you." Truth be told, Tallos did not mind the charge as it gave him an excuse to remain cloaked.

"No, of course not. That is why you insisted on us fetching you a robe and have since never parted with it. I have smelled much during my days, but you carry with you a stench of feet that might serve one better were they removed at the ankle. It must take a powerful magic to create such an odor, mage." Kelgun laughed alone at his joke.

Tallos had not been afforded an opportunity to bathe since emerging from his vinegary hole, and he imagined Kelgun must be right about his fetid smell. His only hope was to bathe with his robes still on, but that would be certain death given the current cold. Tallos's village had been Wilkin's most northern stop, and Tallos guessed it would take at least another week of southerly travel before it was warm enough to risk such a thing.

"Just do not expect me to assist you by calling the elements, should you start a skirmish," warned Tallos.

"Oh, no. A knight needs no help from the likes of you or any other man who hides his face, pretending to have cryptic powers. I assure you of that. Fairytales do not hold up against the edge of a sword such as mine." Kelgun turned his horse so that he could better face Tallos, causing the beast to sidestep at an impressive pace. "And I never start a fight that I cannot finish. Just ask Sir Stormblade." Kelgun grinned, sheathed his sword, and righted his horse, which had visibly exhausted from the showy maneuver.

Dusan made a disgusted sound in response to Kelgun's boasting, but quietly enough so that only Tallos could hear. The boy then hoisted himself upon the chestnut rouncey and crinkled his nose. *I need a bath, and soon*, thought Tallos, *or even the old tinker may see fit to abandon me.* Tallos walked to the rear of the horse so that he would be downwind of all the travelers.

"C'mere, Lily. Bring me another skin of wine would you?" said Kelgun.

It happened before Tallos had joined, but Dusan had confided in him that his older sister had begun to share Kelgun's bed shortly after he and his sister had joined the group. Lily now acted the part of both wife and squire, washing Kelgun's clothing and fetching him things. Dusan insisted to Tallos that the behavior was coerced, but to Tallos she looked eager enough to please the man. Tallos knew the types of men that the homely daughters of farmers usually wed, and in terms of youth, appearance, and status, Kelgun had them bested by a good margin—even if his knightly title was self-appointed.

Atop her painted pack mule, Lily fell back to ride beside Kelgun so she could hand him a fresh skin of wine, of which there were plenty. He tossed her his empty skin but did so poorly. She leaned back to try to catch it but failed, due to no fault of her own. She had deft hands, Tallos had observed on previous such exchanges, likely from her farm work where it was necessary to toss and catch items during the harvest sort.

"Ahhh. Damn woman. You couldn't catch an arrow to the belly at point blank range. We put the likes of you in at the forefront of a charge to keep the rest of us safe from archers." Tallos saw both John and Dusan's heads shaking, either having heard this before or being simply tired of Kelgun's drunken rambling. "Beats the hell out of a shield. Bolts from a strong bow go right through a shield, they do. But not through a fat man with bumbling hands. No, he learns to catch at the front of the van, and in time he makes it look easy." Kelgun slapped what he must have intended to be Lily's rump as she rode beside him, but struck more her lower back, as her cheeks were mostly molded into the muslin sacks that served as her saddle. She handed him his new skin of wine and went to retrieve the one that had fallen.

Tallos had already picked it off the ground and held it out to her so she did not need to dismount. *Why do I insist on acting kind to these people I intend to see burn?* he wondered.

Tallos was yet to extend his promise to spite the gods since having surfaced. His dreams and memories may have continued to solidify his hatred for the deities he had previously revered, but it did nothing to make him despise his fellow travelers. Any plots he had intended to hatch to slay them in their sleep remained shelled and embryonic. *To slaughter these lambs would simply be sacrilege on too small a scale*, Tallos reasoned in frustration.

"Yes, save your energy, girl. I have a new trick to show you tonight. One that I learned warring and whoring. One that will require more from you than I." Kelgun concluded with his usual laughter.

Lily did not seem to mind the openness with which Kelgun proclaimed his conquest over her, but Dusan was another matter. Tallos could see the boy's left fist clenching the handle of his dagger repeatedly. He did not think Dusan would actually try anything. He was of the age of all thought and no action. Had he been a killer, he surely would have slit the knight's throat in his sleep long ago.

"A village ahead," said Wilkin. Tallos wondered how the old man could see so far as he himself could make out no such features, and Tallos had the eyes of a hawk.

A quarter mile later, Tallos saw the village Wilkin had spoken of, but it was the deep thumping coming from the same direction that drew his main attention.

"What are those sounds?" asked John. The question was directed at Wilkin, but it was Kelgun who pulled his horse to an abrupt stop, causing the beast to snort loudly with a fear of danger shared by its master.

"War drums. We must turn 'round."

DERUDIN

"He is not a statesman," said Lyell. "I should have never assigned him the task of governing so cutthroat a city. I trained him as a boy to hold a sword, and when he became a man I put a pen in his hand. The fault was my own—a fault I will correct."

The king delivered these words with ardor. Since the news of the banquet and possible reconciliation with his son, Lyell's appetite had returned to its normal voraciousness, and his demeanor had improved.

"You plan to relieve him of his duty to Westport?" Derudin asked.

Lyell stood and shifted his weight between his feet. "No, that is still too tight."

The cobbler knelt before the king and began to undo his lacings.

"Simply relieve him? No, of course not. That would be an embarrassment to us both. An elevation is what is necessary."

"You would give him Rivervale?" Aside from replacing Derudin as the king's First, there were no other positions of higher authority that could be given to Alther.

"I said an elevation, not a kingdom." The king let out a sigh of relief as the cobbler removed his shoes. "*Far* too tight," he told the man. "No, there is no such position currently, which is why one must be invented. I intend to put Alther in charge of the military—recruiting, training, preparations, and what have you."

"Master of Forces would not technically be an elevation," Derudin said.

"No, nor would I allow a man to hold such a title. I will still be in charge of the army's movements, mind you."

Derudin saw no need to point out that a position with less authority than a Master of Forces would neither be considered an elevation; the king could assign whatever rank he pleased to his new title. "Master of Steel," Derudin thought aloud.

"Sounds too much like a blacksmith." The king grunted as the cobbler pushed two new shoes on his feet. "The name is not so important. It will be the delivery."

"You will let him know at the banquet then?"

"Assuming all goes well," said Lyell. "Never underestimate your children's capacity for impudence, should you ever have any. But Alther will have reason for good spirits when I let him know he may visit his wife. I may even see her pardoned in time, should it be workable."

"It would call your judgment into question to reverse such a ruling."

"*I* question my own judgment. I have no love for that woman beyond what my eyes appreciate, but The Guard has gotten nothing from her... *Nothing*. She is either innocent or strong beyond belief, and I am not one to think a woman capable of the latter."

"I suppose we could have her guilt expunged by royal decree, removing her of the taint of having to confess as well as any admission on our part that she had never been guilty." There was little a royal decree could not fix, aside from affairs of the heart and conscience, and while Derudin did not necessarily agree that such a plan was in the best interest of the realm, he knew better than to involve himself in a king's personal decisions. Lyell's family was as sacred to him as the Ancient Laws were to Derudin, and he had come to respect that, if only by necessity. It was because of this that he did not press the king on the matter of Ethel, which he believed was the root of much of this continued discord.

The king again stood. "That will do nicely," he said, prompting Derudin and the cobbler to look at him in an attempt to determine to whom he had spoken. "Yes, the shoes are fine as well. Now see them removed and send in the cloth maidens."

That had been Derudin's cue to leave as well. As with most formal dinners and events, it was necessary that the king be adorned in the proper ceremonial garb. This was a rather lengthy procedure that Derudin took no part in—and with good reason.

"Don't wander off too far, Derudin. I intend to leave for the banquet in no more than half of an hour." Lyell looked at the dayglass on his mantle, noting the time for both their benefit.

Derudin nodded and stepped out of the bedchambers and into the study.

There was no sign of the cobbler who had so recently exited through the same door. *The man moves with purpose*, thought Derudin, troubled by the possibility of him perhaps moving with more alacrity than would be justified by simple obedience. In his place, however, a pair of fine-looking cloth maidens made their way down the lengthy hall, stealing Derudin's attention. These two specimens of youth, seen between the halves of the great table Derudin was so fond of, were every bit as admirable. Each wore a matching dress of simple black and white, the diminutive waist set off by a hooped skirt lined with ruffled lace, the neck likewise by shawl-like shoulders, flared and frilled. Like the lacings of a shoe, black trim crisscrossed the front, tied in a bow at the top, the same material worn as collars tight to the skin.

As they bounced past him with springy steps, Derudin's eyes went to the topographical carvings on the walls, though his head was still elsewhere. The maidens, the cobbler, Alther, Cassen…ships with square sails—his thoughts were without rest. The sound of the bedchamber door closing behind the girls echoed through the room, continuing so in his mind long after it had faded.

Derudin inhaled deeply. Mixed with the lingering scent of the two who had passed, the room smelled of conquest and averted disaster. *Sixteen years*, he reminded himself. During that time he and Lyell had overseen the peaceful rule of not one, but two kingdoms—the only two kingdoms of consequence. The decisions made in this room had shaped the realm; the problems they now faced were no greater than any others that together they had resolved.

Derudin walked across the hall and traced his fingers over the deep indentures of the contoured hangings, feeling the detail carved into the crenellations of the Adeltian walls. They had served their purpose, those modest walls, making a populace feel safe while its true fate was determined by those who sat in this room. *I am humble enough to know humility is not among my stronger virtues*, thought Derudin, *but I would be remiss to assume I could have done it all without Lyell.* Indeed, Lyell had overruled Derudin many a time—usually to his own detriment, but on occasion, the king had been so correct that Derudin was left stupefied by his own blindness. *Let the square sails be one such occasion.* The possibility calmed him as he sat in a nearby chair, his drifting mind put to rest.

The bang of the chamber door brought Derudin to rapid attention. The two cloth maidens headed toward him. It did not take a mage's eye to see they were more disheveled than need be, had they merely helped the king to dress. They'd no doubt assisted Lyell in getting out of his current clothing as much as they had getting him into his next set, but as always, they would have performed the latter dutifully. The pair went past Derudin and exited the hall with a giggle.

The king had indeed been properly dressed. He stepped out of his chambers emanating regality. White fur lined the neck of the deep purple cape that flowed down the full length of his body and then some. Layers of finely brocaded fabric, taut around his torso, were visible for the moments when the massive cape saw fit to reveal them. All that was missing was his crown, but Lyell had never been known to wear one. It made Derudin wonder just how long he had dozed. A glance at the dayglass of the room—which would be perfectly synchronized with the one in the king's bedchamber, lest someone be lashed—revealed over an hour had passed.

Noticing where Derudin had looked, the king was amused. "I

apologize. It would seem I do not fit into my finery so well as I once did." He patted his stomach as though he was a husky man, which he was not. "I see you have dressed up as well," he said lightly. "Nonetheless, I hope you will at least enjoy some of the food this evening as I have selected the dishes all myself—favorites of both mine and Alther's." Lyell looked to Derudin with a raised brow. "No need to be such a bore all the time, now is there? To better please your laws and morals, I could always command it so."

"As you wish, my king." Derudin decidedly considered the request an order, not that it truly was. *What harm could there be in one night of indulgence? As commanded, of course.*

"Good. Let them know I will enter now. I assume all is ready?"

"I believe so." Derudin hoped it was the truth. "I will proceed."

The guests would have been gathering for just under an hour now, a customary amount of time to wait for the king. Lyell did not do as some and force his audience to wait without food or drink for hours in the hopes that they would come to associate his arrivals with that of celebration and feast, something Derudin had seen have quite the opposite effect for kings past. But it would certainly be unbecoming to not make his guests wait some amount of time to ensure they all had arrived prior to the king himself.

Derudin was pleased to see the king's escort, comprised of Master Warin and three other members of The Guard, patiently standing outside the study in spite of him not having met them there in advance. Derudin nodded, and they took up their positions flanking the king. Derudin led the entourage from a distance of a good many paces as they descended stairs and walked along the castle's inner wall. He noted the emptiness of the courtyard while allowing the brisk winter air to remove the lingering sluggishness from his doze.

Glancing upward, Derudin saw the monstrosity that was the Throne itself. It did not look any smaller than the day he and Lyell had stormed these walls, taking it as their own. It put him in an odd mood, however, knowing Crella would be directly above where the celebration would be taking place. Should she somehow manage to throw herself from the balcony, it would certainly put a damper on the night's festivities. *I should have seen to the safeguarding of that room myself,* he thought with worry.

As he neared, the sounds of the banquet could be heard. The typical unintelligible roar produced by too many people speaking at once within a single structure, the sound that only grew as each party increased their own volume to be heard over the yelling of the others, already threatened Derudin from a distance. He did not fear the noise, but he found it unsettling to be so completely deprived of a sense—one which he had relied upon heavily over the years to ensure his safety and the safety of those he advised, but it was unavoidable in such circumstance. Music could also be heard, though Lyell was not a champion of overzealous performers who tried to make themselves out to be the very cause for the occasion, insisting on obnoxious displays of table dancing and shouting over the already deafening rumble of those merely trying to hold conversation. Instead, a subdued group of musicians played in a sounding corner to provide some ambiance. Derudin took a moment to silently thank Lyell for this preference.

Nodding at several guards posted at the rear entryway to the banquet hall, ensuring they had noticed him, Derudin then gathered shadows and proceeded inside alone. The sound was not so disarming as were the smells. Derudin was reminded of his promise to partake in the night's feast and began to salivate in wonder of what it would entail. He would chide himself later for his indiscretion, but for now all he could do was scan the room with his nose as much as his eyes for signs of what he'd soon enjoy. From the dais where he stood, home to the one-sided grand table at which the king and his retinue of esteemed guests would sit, Derudin peered downward at the happy patrons. Servants buzzed around the tables, carrying trays overflowing with culinary indulgences. A tanned girl with flowing hair to match carried an enormous salver of pig ribs that looked to have been coated in a sweet glaze and roasted over hot coals to produce a beautiful golden-brown crust that glistened even in the dull candlelight of the room. A similar girl with hair that only fell to her shoulders carried a lighter—though no less tempting—platter of flatbreads, still steaming from the stone ovens and slathered with a garlic butter sauce. She headed directly toward a young male servant with a tray above his head carrying steins of two different styles, one probably filled with mead and the other ale. Their near collision finally drew Derudin's eye to the fact that, while the boys were topless, the girls were also nearly so. Their chests were covered only by the sheerest silk that hung from the neck, billowing as they walked and leaving little to the imagination.

The entire serving crew seemed to all be of the same lineage, looking so similar that they were—at the very least—all from the same region of the Spicelands. It was rare to use all foreign servants for such an event, but it certainly added to the atmosphere in a way. *Rare and potentially dangerous*, thought Derudin. He would have to keep a careful eye on the servants tonight, the females especially, since they were perhaps even more like to be assassins given their *unassuming* nature.

The king himself now walked toward Derudin—directly toward him in fact. Derudin realized it with just enough time to step out of the way. The king, who was no doubt taking in the sights, had nearly trampled Derudin, shrouded in shadows as he was. *I must remain focused tonight,* he admonished himself. *That was unacceptable.*

Derudin had not even completed his task of analyzing all the members of the grand table for potential danger by the time the king was at his place at the center. Already seated to the left of the king's chair were Alther and Cassen. Some Rivervalian nobility filled the seats normally taken by Crella, Stephon, and even Ethel, who was absent for reasons Derudin was not certain of, though he could wager a guess. To the right was a chair left empty for the nonexistent queen, one for Derudin himself, Master Warin, Master Larimar, and several others for whichever Adeltian nobility had lobbied the hardest. Derudin long suspected there was no real precedent for the Master of Records to be seated so prominently, but it was not an argument worth having, especially when it would be made against the sole party controlling the recording and recalling of precedents. Nor could he blame the usually joyless old man for stealing this one harmless bit of pride and luxury for himself, but the fact remained, annoying Derudin: small deceits were always the start of larger ones.

The boisterous rumble began to fade as people were made aware of the king's arrival until nothing could be heard but the soothing sounds of the music. Then the music died down as well, signaling the crier.

"King Lyell of House Red Rivers, ruler of Adeltia and Rivervale!"

The harpist danced her fingers artfully from column to knee, and the music resumed.

Patience was not an esteemed trait of Lyell's, and as such, he wasted no time in addressing his most anticipated guest. "Alther, it's good to see you returned to your agreeable nature. Cassen tells me you have come to some more profitable arrangements with the Spiceland merchants. As you may have noticed, I have seen fit to ensure all our servants tonight are Spicelanders themselves. A reminder to us more so than to them that it is *they* who serve *us*, and that they cannot expect to profit except by our grace. A very…handsome…reminder…"

The king's attention had been captured by one such servant as she filled the plates of some of the Rivervalian guests, and in doing so, bending in such a way that her breasts were made visible as they peeked from beneath the single sheet of silk that hung from her shoulders as a necklace. Even Derudin had trouble averting his eyes from the sight.

All at the table had noticed by now. This would have been the cause of utter embarrassment for previous rulers Derudin had served. But Lyell was not a man who embarrassed easily, especially not over matters that attested to his perpetual virility.

The king erupted into laughter and slammed his palm atop the table after the girl had finally righted herself.

"A fine way to start an evening," cried the king. "I believe I may have felt the Mountain himself shift atop his rocky throne to get a better look. Even Cassen could not tear his eyes from the pair!"

Most everyone joined him in laughter, some out of politeness but most out of true mirth. Cassen merely put his hand to his mouth and simpered, but the king's observation had been correct—not that it was probably anything but a lucky guess. Cassen had indeed been peering; Derudin had noticed after trying to find a more suitable task for his own eyes. He had always had his suspicions that Cassen's lady servants provided more than housekeeping, both to his patrons and to Cassen himself...in ways that did not bear imagining. But the ladies received such ubiquitous praise—and most especially from the wives of the estates—that it had always precluded the assessment.

"Hear, hear!" It was the voice of the elderly Master Larimar, sounding as if he had already drunk his frail frame into stupor. He raised his mug and others joined him.

Everyone looked to be enjoying themselves with the exception of Alther. He did a fine job of appearing merry, but it seemed a façade to Derudin who had known him since birth. Alther had his mug raised in kind and quickly finished its contents.

"Father," he said shortly thereafter. "I offer humble apologies for my misguided actions both concerning recent events at my estate and the management of the once great city of Westport. And knowing that you consider apologies to be worth no more than the hairs upon a woman's lip, I offer you this as well." Alther produced a dusty wine bottle from beneath the table and handed it to his father who sat beside him.

Lyell studied the bottle and frowned. "Rivervale Red, autumn harvest, eight hundred and four?" he said, incredulous. "How did you get such a thing?"

"More important is how I kept it: stored on its back and frigid. You have told us many times wine should be kept much as you like your women. I had been saving it for the birth of my second son. I say we drink it now and celebrate, instead, the Rebirth of Westport."

Derudin cleared his throat in objection. The king pointedly ignored him. *This is a matter of family*, Derudin reminded himself, but it was also just as much a matter of state, should the wine be poisoned. There was a protocol that all food and drink served to the king or any in his company must go through, involving tasters and sniffers trained to detect numerous poisons. Everything was vetted a day in advance of the event to ensure that slow acting poisons were caught, once again prior to being served, and then Derudin was the final layer of defense, his duty to remain vigilant and ensure nothing was slipped into the king's food or drink at the table. It was not a perfect system, but the only perfect defense against poison, Lyell liked to remind him, was to never consume.

"A glass to each of us then. Fathers of a city reborn." Lyell had a tongue for older vintages, especially those of Rivervalian Red, the sweet, full-bodied wine of his people. He handed the bottle to a servant who removed the cork and poured them each a glass, surprisingly free of any sediments. Both men raised their glasses and drank a mouthful.

"Ahhhh, now that is a wine," said Lyell. "The taste and feel of a virgin's lips and the color of her imminent uncorking!"

Servants rotated around the table, offering platters of food to guests individually. Derudin motioned to have a pair of the pig ribs added to his plate and studied the other trenchers en route. Quail, roasted in mustard, honey, thyme, and parsley was the next. The little birds still had their heads intact as some liked to crunch through their fragile skulls and chew the meat off their necks. Derudin opted to pass. Then came a fish of some sort, delicate white meat that looked as if it were poached to perfection in butter, dill, and peppercorns. Derudin had a taste for the bounties of the sea. Having spent so much time on the coast of the Badlands with nothing else to eat, a man might otherwise perish. He motioned for the fish to be added to his plate. Countless other platters passed by with sides such as smashed and buttered turnips, young carrots in molasses, roasted baby cabbage, steamed green flowers, and pease in cream sauce.

"So tell me of these grand plans for Westport. How did you manage to break the will of these Spicelanders?" asked the king.

Alther cleared his throat. "In truth it was much Cassen's doing. I had fallen to new lows recently…" Alther seemed to struggle with his delivery. "But pity does not become a man of noble blood, as I am sure you would agree. I decided to swallow what little was left of my pride and beg Cassen's guidance."

"I hope that is all you swallowed. Cassen never does a favor without asking something in return!" The king could not contain his laughter at his own joke.

Cassen seemed to enjoy the slight more than Alther, for he had the decency to blush and look amused whereas Alther simply looked annoyed. "I will be happy to repay Cassen for the favor he has done for me, but as he has reminded me himself, it would do him no good to see Westport fall to chaos and rebellion, which would no doubt sweep the land 'like a disease,' I believe were his words."

Derudin was none too happy to see Alther appear to be within the clutches of Cassen. *When the favor is called upon to be repaid, will you have the capital to spare?* In the arena of combat, Alther could dice Cassen into a hundred pieces, but in politics he was no match.

"Bah! There is no need for such talk, my boy. Let us focus on the glory that will be, not the gloomy scenarios of utter pessimism."

Derudin's attention was once again embezzled by the bosom of a servant. "Mead or Ale, my master?" She held the tray at head level but the real treasure was beneath. Where they had managed to find so many matching beauties was beyond even Derudin's conceiving. *One would have to kill a Spiceland king and steal his harem*, Derudin thought to himself. His gaze shifted to the jovial king as if to ask him. *No, he would not have.*

It had been so long since Derudin had enjoyed a drink that he could not remember which he preferred—or at least that was his excuse for continuing conversation with the enchantress that stood before him. "Which would my ladyship suggest?" *I envy the Dawnstar himself to have been lucky enough to kiss such lovely skin.*

"Who, my master?" Her voice was thick with both her Spiceland accent and worry that she may be offending someone of extreme rank.

"Nevermind, young thing. I will take the mead." He decided to simply choose the safer option and let her be on her way, and based on the number of steins left on the tray, mead was the favored choice. As he was already looking toward his right, having spoken to the servant, Derudin observed those seated beside him on that less important, but no less interesting, side of the table. Master Warin was already on his seventh pig rib, his beard covered in the sticky glaze, and had no doubt decided it was not worth the trouble of trying to clean until presented with a proper washbasin. Beside him, Master Larimar looked as if he could have been on his seventh stein of mead, as he gazed off into the distance, apparently singing to himself. The room was too loud to tell if he actually sang intelligibly and in time with the music or merely recited paragraphs from his book of records. *Probably the latter, and hopefully nothing best kept secret.*

Master Warin noticed Derudin looking his direction, and his eyes went wide as if he had been caught during a mischief. *What has you so skittish?* Derudin wondered. Warin drew the half-eaten rib away from his mouth, raising it in the air with a smile. "Good, are they not?"

Derudin only then realized he had yet to touch his food. So many years of abstaining had him perhaps more excited by the prospect of it all than the pleasure of the act itself. He found himself content to merely have the food upon his plate. "I am sure it is," he said and raised his stein in Warin's direction. Warin was quick to lift his own in return, having his other hand already upon it, and swilled several gulps. Derudin took a sip of his and nearly spat it out. *How did this pass the poison testers?* It tasted how piss smelled, turned and sour. *Perhaps I am not missing so much as I had feared...or as much as I had hoped.* He looked down at his plate of ribs and fish and pondered if it would even be worth it.

The king burst into raucous laughter. The queen's empty chair between them was no barrier to his booming voice. "Yes," he shouted. "And Edwin had a look upon his face of horror while you smiled, blood pouring from your nose, just happy to have scored your first point!" The king appeared to let the memory wash over him, then poured himself another glass from the vintage bottle. "Your mother near had my skin for that, the Mountain guard her soul."

The king was rare to mention Keldona, his beloved wife and mother of his three children. She died shortly after giving birth to Aileana, younger than Alther by ten years. Derudin had known Keldona well and believed her to have been a good woman. He also believed Lyell's apparent aversion to recollect her memories was out of guilt. He had wanted another child, which she consented to give him, but several months later she fell ill with shakes and fever. Derudin feared she had returned to her cherished ponds too soon after her pregnancy where she loved to observe the polliwogs and butterflies. The air was thick and foul there and believed by many to be the cause of such an ailment.

"Yes, though she would prefer you mention only the Dawnstar," reminded Alther.

"Hah. The religion of women," cried the king. "They do not understand the true nature of men, for if they did, they would know that of the Mighty Three, the Dawnstar is like to be the weakest. You cannot conquer a kingdom without an army so large it flows like the River, and you cannot protect one without walls of the Mountain's stone. And if you retreated once a day, as does the Dawnstar, you'd be labeled a coward."

Keldona had been among those who believed only in the divinity of the Dawnstar, and Edwin and Aileana had come to share the same faith. It was no accident that Edwin now ruled Strahl, his younger sister living there as well, as it was a known safe-haven for the Illumined. Their faith was tolerated in Rivervale, but not without ridicule.

"Wise words, my king," said Cassen slimily. *Has the man ever spoken a word untainted by the filth of deception?*

"And on the subject of women, Alther, my boy, we must speak of Ethel." As the king spoke the words it seemed all in the immediate vicinity stopped their eating, ensuring the sound of their own chewing would not interfere with their overhearing what would come next. Derudin was as eager as any, save perhaps Alther. Lyell made a pacifying gesture with a downward palm to Alther. "Understand, I respect that she is your daught—"

The king stopped mid-sentence without any apparent reason. Derudin studied him and saw that he stared into the distance, transfixed on some point. Following his gaze did Derudin no good, as it appeared to lead to a burning sconce on the far wall.

"Father?" asked Alther. His concern for the king's wellbeing was no farce. Alther looked consumed with worry.

Lyell stood up and turned forward, facing the hundreds of guests in attendance below. His face now showed of discontent as he appeared to take in all he could with his eyes, not looking at all happy with what he saw. The roar of the crowd diminished as some took notice of the glaring king. Then, without warning, the king bent forward, violently spraying a fountain of deep red from his mouth. It covered the table and turned the previously white fur on his cape to a drenched, clumpy mess. The heaving continued for a moment and was followed by convulsions as the king fell face first onto the table. It was then that Derudin realized the red that came from his mouth was as much blood as it was wine.

Out of instinct, Derudin gathered shadows and backed away, thoroughly effective in his effort given everyone's attention had been fixed on the king. There was nothing he could do to defend the king against an unknown attacker, and his priority was to determine if and how he could stop whoever it was that was harming him.

There was not a single person in attendance, however, that did not have the same look of shock upon their face. Master Warin was on his feet, mouth gaping. Cassen looked deceptive as always, but Derudin had to admit, he must have also been somewhat honestly horrified by the sight, given his demeanor. Even Master Larimar seemed to have been sobered by the unexpected scene as he stared at the blood upon the table. But Alther looked worse by far, as would be expected of the king's son. His anxiety was palpable, and in his eyes grew a depth of sadness.

The king's spasm ceased. Alther went to him first, turning his father, still on the table, onto his back and attempting to check for breathing or heartbeat. Gasps could be heard as guests saw the blood-soaked front of the king. The beard he was always so careful to keep flawlessly groomed had the type of beaded drool upon it that made men appear as infirm babies, except that Lyell's was red. Alther's face blanched as he lifted his head from his father's chest.

"Sir Warin," said Cassen who must have forgotten his proper title in the commotion. "Arrest Alther and Derudin at once. Alther's gift must not have been without toxin, and Derudin did nothing to prevent the king's consumption."

Had Derudin not been withdrawn and enshrouded, he would have been the one to feel the clamp of the strong man's hand that grasped the wrist of Alther. Alther had a banquet knife in the other hand, however, and he lashed out at Cassen and screamed.

"You said he would only sicken! He is *dead*!"

Warin's grip on him prevented his lunge at Cassen from landing, and Cassen backed away with a flamboyant show of fear and frailty. Alther seemed to collapse in hopelessness at both the futility of his failed attempt and the loss of his father. Derudin considered it was also possible he too now felt the effects of the poison that had no doubt been present in the wine. Lyell had near finished the bottle, and a look at Alther's glass showed he had only taken the initial gulp during the toast. *A kingdom reborn, and to a grotesque man disguised as a mother, covered in silks tainted with blood and treachery.* If Alther's words were true, whatever was present in the wine meant to "sicken" the king might now kill Alther as well.

"Where is that damn wizard? He was just here," said Master Warin.

Derudin was already on his way out before it was too late. His shroud would not fool eyes that searched with purpose.

"The charlatan has fled." Despite the distance Derudin had placed between him and the room, Cassen's words carried. "Let there be no question as to who was the mastermind behind this murder, then. When you find him, bring him to me…dead or alive."

TITON SON OF SMALL GRYN

"No wonder those river thieves were so eager to trade at the mention of our direction." Titon tore his gaze away from the distant castle just long enough to make eye contact with Keethro. "The city was mere miles away."

"Aye," replied Keethro. "And look at that." He nodded in the direction of the barge on their port side. Larger than any floating structure they had seen thus far, it was comprised of many square sections connected by chains to form a single edifice. Each section was laden with mounds of white crystallized blocks.

"You mean you got cheated by that old bastard?" Titon was amused to see Keethro, who fancied himself an expert negotiator, taken down a notch.

Keethro bared clenched teeth. "Perhaps." He then cupped his hands around his nose and mouth to shout. "Hey there. How much for a pound of salt?"

A few of the men on the barge paused as if they heard but continued on, not caring. Keethro did not give up.

"I have five marks for the first man to throw me a pound. Half a fist will do."

The three grungy men aboard the barge certainly appeared the type to have done some quick business, especially with their employer's goods.

"Eight marks," shouted Keethro with a mix of anger and desperation.

"I'll give ya a full fist for free if you keep yappin' at me like some auction wench," cried one of the men as he finally turned to them. His demeanor changed after seeing the two who did the asking. Titon and Keethro were close enough to board the barge in short order if desired. "It's the king's salt and it's not for sale," explained the man. "Not that I'd care to sell it so low if it were my own. If we so much as lick it we're out a job, so be on your way and don't cause us any trouble."

Titon was a bit disheartened, but Keethro looked relieved. "Perhaps not," he said, exonerating himself of the charge of having been swindled.

The enormity of the castle loomed overhead to their starboard. The closer they had gotten, the larger the structure had become, yet the size of the walls was less impressive than the sheer amount of land they must encompass, spanning as far as the eye could see. A city could fit within with room to spare for farmland it seemed.

"How would you even attack such a thing?" Titon wondered aloud.

"I do not think you would. But we are yet to see how hard it is to get inside. Every giant has a weakness." Keethro smirked.

Keethro was his old self in truth; Titon could see that now. *Should I need to bring down this castle, I brought the right man to help me do so.*

They docked at a crowded pier within sight of a bustling gate that would be their entrance to the kingdom. Atop the gate's two massive turrets flew an identical flag, each larger than a man, depicting a scene not unlike the one it stood upon: a river flowing in front a castle. It seemed an appropriately immense fortification to safeguard the elixirs Titon hoped to find within.

"Let's carry all the supplies we intend to keep. I do not expect this raft will still be here when we return."

Keethro nodded in agreement, and they fashioned packs from their bedding and tied what little they still had to themselves. Their bows, knives, salt, purses, rope, and a green copper pot was easy enough for them to carry between the two of them.

They made their way to the open portcullis, hoping to pass through unobstructed just as the rest of the people appeared to be doing. On the top of the structure behind the parapets, four archers could be seen. At the gate itself were four more guards, a pair on each side, heavily armored in layers of ring mail and each with a halberd of at least two men in length. They all wore matching tabards with many smaller rivers flowing into one larger vein. Titon and Keethro put their heads down and began to walk through as if they had done so every day.

"Ho!" said one of the guards, waving them over to his side of the gate. "Where are you two brigands off to?"

Considering how well Titon's last negotiation with guards had gone, they'd already agreed it would be Keethro who would do the talking. "Same place as all these other fine men and women. Inside for some trading."

"For some trading?" He chuckled. "You don't look like you have anything worth trading."

The other guard did not look so amused. "Rivervale has no need of more vagrants. We got enough of them begging and shitting all over the place as it is."

"We have no need to beg, and we will see that we shit in the proper places," said Keethro.

"No need to beg, eh? That's good to know. What about the big one?

He dumb?"

"I speak," said Titon, "but my friend here has the sharper tongue."

"Well, we don't need any more sharp tongues either. Might be best if you two just went back to wherever you came from. And where would that be?"

"The canyons to the north," said Keethro. They had decided not to mention Strahl or Phylan in case word had spread about any of their recent scuffles. Pretending to be Dogmen was the best they could come up with.

"Yeah? And you didn't meet any conscription parties on the way?"

"Not sure what you mean. We came down the rivers on a raft. We didn't see much of anyone."

"That might explain it then," the guard said gruffly. "Well, it'll be a mark to get in for you. Two marks for the big one, as he's like to use twice the water."

"I don't see anyone else paying to enter," Titon challenged. He did not much care for the demeanor of this guard. It reminded him of another lawman who recently got a bellyful of spear.

"No, they're not. But you see that one there?" The guard pointed to a hunched lady limping her way through the gate. Her clumped hair seemed to somehow have less color than grey, and she had a putrid look about her that promised a foul stench should they get any closer. "She's the queen. And that one there?" The guard pointed to a boy being pulled in a wheeled cart by an old man. His arms flailed around with excitement, his lower half remaining completely still. "That's the prince and heir to the throne."

Now that specific attention had been drawn to the types of people passing through the gates, it seemed odd how few men there were, only those old and decrepit.

"So you see," continued the guard, "I have to let the likes of them through because they're rich and noble, but outsider trash like you pays a fee to enjoy the luxuries of our great city. And now that you mention it, there's an extra fee for carrying weapons, and those bows look mighty deadly."

"Aye, they look good and mean, those bows," chimed in the second guard, now wearing a happy grin.

Keethro placed a hand on Titon's shoulder and addressed the guards meekly. "We barely have two marks between the both of us. Our true intention is to find work inside. We are both talented at several trades, but we've had hard times in the North. We just wish entrance. We're not looking to cause problems."

"Give me what you got, and you can go inside and get good and rich, I'm sure." The quieter guard had a chuckle at the prospect.

Keethro looked to Titon solemnly as if in apology and tossed the guard his entire coin purse. Titon could not believe his eyes as the bag landed with the crunch of many coins into undeserving hands.

The guards laughed openly. "Go on in. And don't try to leave until you've spoken with the conscription officers. They will want to have a word with you." With that, the guards turned their attention to the coin purse, splitting its contents between the two of them.

"How much was in there?" They had walked a ways inside before Titon asked.

"Some two marks or so in copper. I'm going to need to stock up on purses, though. I think we'll have need of that trick again. Just make sure you try and look as angry about it as you did back there."

The atmosphere had changed upon entering the walls. Thick with the smell and noise of too many bodies in too small a place, it threatened to choke Titon's breath. The stench reminded him of the Dogmen kennels, horrid in its own right, but the sounds were perhaps worse. Hundreds if not thousands of voices from close and afar overlapped each other in a growing crescendo of confusion. For a man who'd spent the past decade of his life in the wilderness, beside a gentle stream, with a wife who spoke not a word, it was overwhelming. He figured he'd soon have to shout at Keethro just to be heard as they moved further into the cacophony.

The majesty of the walls had not prepared Titon for the squalor within. Whereas the main road that led to this kingdom, the Eos, was wide and ever flowing, floating graceful hulls in loose formation, these dried mud roads that crossed within were congested with the desultory motion of legs and wheels, both in twos and fours. Those who walked about them now looked to be either starving or suffering from some affliction brought about by the living in filth.

Keethro must have seen it on Titon's face. "Not as you expected?"

"We have seen battles less hellacious than this. Let's find a mender and be out of here as soon as we can. Every guard here reeks of corruption, and they may be the least desperate of this lot."

Just as it seemed the city had declared war upon Titon, it offered an armistice. He and Keethro came upon a section that seemed mostly devoted to food vendors, and Titon realized he was quite hungry in spite of his anxiousness. These vendors had no need for shouting. Long lines formed in front of all their carts, each a similar type of structure with two large wheels on one side and a pair of handles or yoke on the other. Most had small fires going, cooking things that smelled good enough to make Titon forget, for the moment, that they still stood in a cesspit of sweat and feculence from both man and animal.

The vendor that immediately caught both their eyes and which had the longest line served a familiar foe. The head of the very beast, if not quite so large as the one they'd battled, was mounted atop the center cart, displayed at a good height so all could see. "River Dragon Skewers, Two for a Mark," it read.

"I told you it was a dragon," Titon declared, slapping Keethro on the back. "Let us have a taste of this beast."

They had a long time to study the process by which the creature was prepared while waiting. The line snaked back and forth from the leftmost of the vendor's carts, where the monetary transaction in trade for the skewers took place, to the last of its five carts. At the rightmost cart, a tail of the creature was being butchered by a man who appeared well suited for the job, removing the thick, leathery armor with practiced slices to reveal a pink if not purplish flesh. The butcher was a beast unto himself. His head was shaved clean, and two halves of a messy beard clung to either side of his bare chin, the only part of his face not otherwise covered in deep scars. His lower jaw protruded to the extent that his bottom teeth may have been bared if not for his lips being sewn together, done so with crude cordage. The thick muscles of his neck danced to the rhythm of his slicing as he portioned the meat into squares the size of one joint of a finger, stopping only to hack off a new tail from the pile of bodies behind him. The tool for that job fit him almost intimately: a rusted cleaver too large for a normal man to heft with a single hand.

The rest of the workers looked quite similar to each other and nothing like the butcher. They were small and dexterous, completing the remaining tasks of skewering, battering, frying, and salting the meat with alacrity.

The process was engrossing enough to almost distract Titon from the churning anticipation of his stomach. "For such an ugly thing, it looks and smells quite pretty when cooked, does it not?"

"Aye, it does." Keethro seemed equally captivated, albeit by something from a different direction. Titon followed his gaze and saw that behind them in line, a couple of men dressed like the previous guards chortled, each encouraging the other. In front of them, a young pair, a boy and girl, looked extremely uncomfortable. "It is not our fight," Keethro reminded him before he had reason to understand why.

The two men took turns stroking the young girl's hair, then pretending as if they had done nothing. Neither she nor what appeared to have been her brother, given their likeness, could have been more than nine years of age, and seemed helpless to defend themselves against the harassment. The men had upped their antagonism to that of briefly massaging the girl's shoulders and pinching her bottom. She would bat away their hands but did not turn to confront them. It was obvious the boy was torn between allowing his sister to be fondled and facing a foe in which defeat was the only outcome, and the battle for the latter was beginning to win. The look of wistful determination in the boy's eyes reminded Titon of his own son when forced to fight his younger brother in earnest, finally having been provoked to the point of madness during training. *Was I as cruel to Titon as these men are?* He pushed the thought aside and replaced it with thoughts of Titon being victorious in combat against the Dogmen, at last appreciating his training, and coming home to read the letter left for him—all of which should have already taken place by now. He and Decker had no doubt worked together with synergy on their raid, just as when they hunted, and returned home as heroes.

The boy swung around to face his sister's molesters and was met with a foot to his chest, shoving him forcefully to his back and out of line. His sister, who was somehow without tears, jumped after her brother as if their lives depended on it, grabbing him and pulling him to his feet. The people that comprised the line seemed purposefully oblivious to the commotion as the small gap left was consumed, placing those who had been behind the youngsters that much closer to receiving food. The burning hatred in Titon's chest threatened to leap out and engulf the entire crowd. Had this been in the North, he would have given each man a quicker death than was deserved and left them to rot above the ground as he did the Dogmen. *Men such as those deserve to die, and men such as I are charged with ensuring it happens.*

"Be sure to remain within these walls, cowards. The moment you set foot outside their protection I will rip out your throats with my hands." He said the words only in his mind. He could not kill them, not here, and any threat of escalation would result in the men retaliating in the only way they could: later, and against the children.

He stared at them with intensity, though the men were too busy chatting to notice, and the final bend in the line caught Titon by surprise. He and Keethro were at the rightmost cart, the home of the butcher. Titon's attention was again stolen, watching the man work. He was not the lumbering brute one might assume at first glance. His hands were quite deft. They reminded Titon of his own hands, though with shorter, fatter fingers, causing him to wonder with troubled vanity if the butcher's grip might be stronger than his own. As if to answer, one of those hands—thoroughly covered in the slime of raw meat—reached out and grabbed Titon by the neck of his shirt, drawing him in close. Nose to nose, the butcher looked suddenly familiar. What must have appeared to others like aggression, Titon could clearly see was not. The man's every feature was that of a monster except for his eyes. Those eyes peered from behind his mask of scars and spoke to Titon, as his mouth could not, begging him to take heed. They told him to leave this place as soon as he could, and Titon understood. The butcher was a brother, a fellow Galatai, and he was not here of his own volition.

CASSEN

The winding stairway refused to end. This was not Cassen's first time up these steps, but he had never been quite so impatient to ascend them, and, likewise, there had never before seemed to be quite so many. Were it age or anticipation that made the trek now so intolerably sluggish, he could not say, but he would not race up them like some eager boy. Aside from the fact that he would likely not be able to complete the climb at such a pace, not even spurred by his desire, he was more concerned with maintaining his air of dignity. It would not do to be seen breathless. He had waited near a lifetime for this climax, and he would not allow the experience to be sullied by indiscretion.

He recalled how Derudin had looked so recently at the banquet. That slippery trickster had somehow managed to escape capture, but he had not escaped Cassen's eye. Charlatan though he was, he must truly abstain from the pleasures of indulgent food given the way he beamed at and handled that which was served to him. It was as if Derudin were a virgin of a man presented with a sensual goddess to do with as he pleased. *How ironically analogous*, Cassen mused.

Master Warin had served in stark contrast beside the mage, tearing greedily into rib after hurried rib, still leaving bits upon the bone without care. Cassen would not be that man. He would leave no bits on the bone, and he would not race to finish what he'd been so patient to procure. Nor would he suffer the same fate as Derudin—poor old fool that he was—who had not managed to yet dirty a finger by the time Lyell began his theatrics. *Lyell of House Red Rivers, drowned in the red river of his own vomit.* Cassen delighted in the thought of how it would be remembered. He had no hatred for the man, but envy, he found, was often a more spiteful emotion.

But Cassen had envied none more than Alther. That such a fool be rewarded with such a treasure was venom in his veins. The look upon the dullard's face when he realized he'd killed his own father was worth a thousand kingdoms, but it paled in comparison to what lay in wait above. *How ever will he manage to eclipse that expression with one greater when I tell him what I have done with his lovely wife?* It was impossible to imagine.

"Master Cassen…Your Grace…"

After so many years of enjoying people stumbling over his title of duchess, to see them stumbling over how to best address him now was truly splendid. None wished to draw the ire of the next potential queen or king, whatever it was he might come to be.

The man who presently addressed him was one of a pair of low-ranking members of The Guard standing vigil at the steps, and Cassen despised him at first glance. His eyes shone with the gleam of honor and justice—this was one of those who'd barred his path for so long, preventing him from visiting the helpless princess in her tomb of luxury. *Do I truly hate you? Or do I begrudge your incorruptibility?* But Cassen knew that would be little more than begrudging a simple man of his blissful ignorance. This guard was not to be revered. There was no laudability in selflessness. It was a disease that festered in times of abundance, and the tumult that was soon to come would see it culled.

"Sir…?" Cassen asked.

"I am just Harding, Your Grace."

"Well, Harding, see that you and your friend here do not allow *any* interruption of my questioning of the princess. I do not care if I remain there for days upon end and you have to shit in your armor. I do not care if Lyell eats the entrails he spilled on the royal table and comes back to life to demand entry. None will pass these steps until I, myself, have passed them for a second time and in the opposite direction. Is your understanding absolute?"

"Yes, Your Grace. You are not to be disturbed."

"My *questioning* of her is not to be disturbed. The idiots of your order have been interrogating her for how many weeks now? She has yet to admit to anything, and now the king is dead. I will not have my efforts ruined mid-process." With that, Cassen continued the ascent of the final stories of stairs.

"Yes, Your Grace," the guard said quickly, but to Cassen's back.

A few bends later, Cassen stopped to steady himself. He had allowed the previous conversation to excite him more than he'd wished. He took slow, controlled breaths to calm himself. *What physiological quirk is it that makes the area of the heart burn in longing?* Cassen held no belief that the meaty organ served any purpose but to push blood around within one's body, likening any such inclination to belief in deities and magic. But his chest did burn, and toward his left of all places. *An invention of a mind with knowledge of its placement*, he concluded.

With his composure reestablished, he made his way to the top of the stairs, placing his foot upon the landing and pulling his body to his final elevation. Before him stood the door to what he'd craved since having taken the position of Calder's assistant, since having first laid eyes upon her. Visions flooded his mind of entering only to find her cut and bleeding, having found some sharp object with which to end her torment, or hanging from a chandelier that she'd managed to reach by flinging a weighted sheet, but he brushed those notions aside and knocked three times, with the utmost courtesy. He waited a moment, then proceeded inside.

It was the same room he remembered from previous visits, back when King Lyell had requested Cassen find some use for the room. It was Cassen who came up with the idea of having it serve as a prison, an idea that amused the king very much, though he had no one at the time upon which to use it. Cassen, however, had had one such person in mind from the very start.

"Princess Crella," he began. *Or would it technically be Queen Crella until Alther has been formally dispatched?* The thought was amusing—how easily lines of succession could be toyed with to suit the purposes of those who truly held the power.

"Leave it and begone," she responded.

How precious. She thinks me to be a servant. "I am afraid I am not quite what you expect," *not in the least,* "as I have not brought for you any food or water." Surely she must come to recognize his voice, the voice of the Duchess of Eastport.

Crella was at the window gazing downward, dressed in the finery one would expect of a queen retired to a private evening: a long gown, simple and elegant. Cassen had stood there himself and remembered being rather disappointed by the view. From such a height, little could be made of what went on below. The people were all unidentifiable, and thus no more interesting than watching a mound of ants. The window to the south was far more entertaining; one could just begin to make out the structures of Eastport and Westport, which—despite their utilitarian nature—were still quite impressive. *Such a lovely kingdom.*

Where she stood suddenly bothered Cassen. Had she chosen the window to the north in favor of Rivervale as some symbolic gesture? Did she have feelings for Alther in truth—brought to the surface from her imprisonment? *The man must be dealt with, and the sooner the better.* His living only complicated matters.

If she recognized Cassen by now, she made no move to acknowledge it. He studied her. It was regrettable that he so rarely had the chance to these past years. For near two decades he'd had to avert his eyes in order to keep up appearances, but now he could bathe in the sight. What he saw was everything he had remembered from his youth, multiplied—not diminished—by maturity. Though barefoot and resting, her weight tipped forward toward the toe, lifting her heels ever so slightly in such a feminine manner. The arch where her hip became waist was almost lewd in its construction, as if purpose made for his hands to grasp and pull her tight. But for some reason, the graceful curve from her shoulder to the nape of her neck was what he noted most. *Perhaps because she is always turned away from me in disgust.*

"You have no doubt heard the news by now. Even the best-trained servants must have difficulty not letting word of a dead king slip."

Her head turned briefly down and to the side, returning to its previous position thereafter, but not before burning into Cassen's vision the image of her delicate profile.

"Oh, you didn't know? Well, Lyell is dead, though I doubt you cared much for the man. It would seem someone saw fit to poison him after all." Cassen lowered his voice as if speaking only to himself. "Made quite a mess of a lovely banquet too." *Perhaps had it only been his wine that was poisoned, I would have had time to sample the rockfish.* "It was a terrible shame, really."

Cassen gave her ample opportunity to reply, but she made no move to do so.

"I am sure you are wondering who could be responsible for such treachery. Let us go through the list then, shall we? It could not have been *Lord* Junton, he's just been sitting around ever since the whole impalement matter. And it, of course, could not have been Stephon, for he remains in a dungeon—a fine dungeon, mind you, though not in comparison to this one, I am afraid. It was not the daring Master Warin—too busy filling his mouth, nor Master Larimar—content in drowning himself with mead that evening. I suppose that only leaves your dear husband and Derudin."

Cassen studied her for an emotional response, a difficult task given her refusal to face him, and her reflection in the window gave up no details beyond an outline.

"There is an entire kingdom rather upset at your husband and that old man who calls himself a mage. For some reason they think those two had the ambition to collude to usurp."

Cassen walked to the bed. It was a monstrous thing, hip high and covered in all sorts of fabrics, the specifics of which were quite tedious. The game he'd played of pretending to appreciate such things had become so tiresome he ached to reveal. He ran his hand along one of the hardwood posts that supported the canopy above, disgusted by the detail that had gone into its carving. *It will do, though*, he thought.

"You wouldn't be so dimwitted as to believe such a thing, now, would you? You knew your husband better than any; well enough to know he did not have the courage to do as he's been so flatteringly accused." Cassen had not even expected Alther to go through with the plan to sicken the king, not that it truly mattered. "Nor would Derudin, not that you should care about him. That anyone does is proof enough that the realm is populated—even ruled—by superstitious simpletons.

"But no, your loving husband did not so much as lift a finger to free you. I think we both know he lacked the courage to ever oppose his mighty father. After all, he did not even care enough to object when Lyell told him of his plans to take Ethel to bed as his queen."

Excitement flushed Cassen as he saw Crella's fingers bend, not so much to make a fist—she had stopped herself before that—but he had her undivided attention, *that* was not to be doubted. He closed his eyes, enjoying the moment. *That leaves only one person capable of killing such a tyrant, and you know who it is.* Cassen's joy quickly faded. *You know it to be me, and yet again, you will not thank me. You will not acknowledge that I have saved you, once more.* Finding his jaw clenched so tight that his teeth ached, Cassen was forced to open his eyes and remind himself of the power he wielded. *But you will thank me, willingly or not.*

"It reminds me of a story," he said, suddenly at peace again. "Perhaps you know the tale…

"In this very kingdom lived a young princess, many years ago. Her mother and father were stricken with a shared illness, dying at a young age and leaving her an orphan. Luckily for the princess, her mother had a caring brother who volunteered to raise the girl as his own. Perhaps she would have preferred her aunt, but that woman had a kingdom to rule and little time for children. And at any rate, her uncle was much respected.

"He was a robust and powerful man—a *duke*, no less. He took every precaution to ensure the safety of his little princess. He sheltered her from the harshness of the outside world, which he himself never shied from, for he was the adventurous, domineering sort. He did not negotiate with other men; he made demands. Under his command, he saw Eastport rise to be the third richest city in a kingdom of three cities." Cassen had no choice but to snort at that fact. "Perhaps more impressive were his feats in the wilderness. An avid hunter, he would bring back trophies from the far corners of the kingdom. He had heads of wild pigs with curved tusks, elk with great antlers, and fierce cats with giant fangs mounted vainly upon the walls of his estate. The princess despised these trophies, but they were perhaps the least of what she hated of his hunting trips."

"What is it you want?" demanded Crella, not turning from her window.

"For when he returned from these trips, he did so with his blood still fiery from the hunt. He had never married, you see, and had little appetite for whores as there was certainly no conquest to be had there. But what he did have was a beautiful little princess. She could have been no more than—what was it—ten years of age when it began? He would come home putrid, not just from the days of filth that had amassed upon him during his time outdoors, but with the fetid stench of the dead animal he had skinned, gutted, and cleaned with his own hands."

"What do you *want?*" she turned and screamed at him, both her neck and her nostrils flaring in anger.

"What do I want?" he yelled back, no longer using the voice of the duchess. He could see it frightened her as she flinched upon hearing it, his voice free from the cloak of pretense and in all its fury. "I want what you have denied me ever since I set foot inside that estate. You were the pretentious little princess—too good to cast even a sidelong glance my way. And what was I? Some lowborn *shit* who hacked off his own genitals just to climb a bit in status, is that about the measure of it?"

She did not respond.

"*Well?*" he shouted with rage. "But perhaps if you had looked at me, just for a moment, you may have seen a little more. Even if it was just the smallest amount, enough perhaps for you to have acknowledged my mere existence, then maybe that would have been enough."

Cassen began to unwind a solitary sheet of silk that was draped around him as he lowered his voice. "Do you think you were the only one alone in that hell of a home?" He placed the silk on the floor in front of him and began to unwind a second. "I was, what, five years older than you? I was no deviant like your uncle. I saw your beauty but never wanted to steal from you what he so forcefully took." A small pile of silken wraps now formed at his feet, but Crella's eyes remained locked on his own, her unjust antipathy as intense as ever. "A shred of respect was all I wanted… And perhaps from that, a friendship could have even grown. How nice it would have been for both of us to have someone with whom to share secrets with and discuss prospects for the future." Another silk fell to the floor. "But you had no interest in that. I was less to you than a servant—for even a servant you must recognize from time to time in order for them to complete their duties."

The pile of silk in front of him mounted as he spoke, and as it grew, he was liberated from his costume and false frailty. "I was weak at first, I admit it. I should have done what I did long before. But I was likely near as tormented as you were to know what was taking place. I could not stand to sleep in a bed furnished by such a monster, so I slept upon the floor. It was all I had the power to do at first in rebellion and contrition."

So much of his silk had been removed that he felt the cool air on his hips and thighs. "And then came a night when he returned from his hunt, far more poisoned by substance than usual, and I finally saw my chance to save you. I was not a strong man, nor was he a weak one. My chances of success were slim despite his stupor, and slimmer still to escape the act without implication. But for you I did this one and final selfless thing." Crella scowled as though he was lying, prompting his tone to bitter. "I shoved the fool man back down the stone stairs he had climbed to reach your room. Then I followed him with a rock of my own and bashed in his head to ensure the deed was done."

A single layer of silk was all that stood between Cassen and nakedness. He was no specimen to behold, he did not delude himself in that, but for a man of near forty years he was built well. He had the sinewy, thick-hipped look of an older man who had strength beyond that of his stature, and with his true physique nearly revealed, combined with the keys to a kingdom, he felt a god in comparison to what others thought of him.

"I am no champion of the concept of fairness," he continued. "For I have learned that everyone receives exactly that which they have earned—no more and no less." Cassen now removed his final silk, more slowly than all those before it. "But it was not *fair* the way in which you overlooked me and continued to do so even after I had saved you from your vile torturer. It was not *fair* that the night I had finally dispatched him and went to your room to tell you in excitement—expecting, at the very least, a *thank you* or some sobs of relief—but no. It was not *fair* that you did not even have the appreciation to afford me the slightest of nods."

His silk fell, and the pile in front of him now reached well above his knees. Cassen could scarcely contain the elation that jolted through him, threatening to leave his fingertips as bolts of lightning. He saw the horror of realization on her face as she stared, powerless to look away from him. *No, I am not the fool boy you thought I was, nor am I the epicene creature I pretend to be in order to assuage men like your uncle—that prideful halfwit who could barely stand to look upon the genitals I'd presented him, let alone conceive that they might not have been my own.*

"And it will not be *fair,* the way in which I will treat you, until you finally give me the respect that I have for so long deserved."

ETHEL

"This was a bad idea."

Annora did not have to speak the words; her worry showed clearly on her face. And Ethel was of like mind.

The impassioned shouting in the neighboring room was enough to put a chill in even a warrior's spine, not that either of them were equipped with such a thing. Ethel had heard what she thought had been horrid fighting between her mother and father before, but this bellicose quarrelling made her appreciate just how frivolous their skirmishes had been.

"Perhaps we should leave," Ethel suggested.

"I do not even know if that is possible." Annora's eyes went to the door through which they had entered, the same door that hid the source of the commotion.

Upon arriving, they had been ushered into the solar by a male servant who had then, oddly enough, closed the door, sealing them in. The room was large, bright, and nicely furnished, but it was still the domain of a terrifying man. It felt more like a cage for prey than a place of welcome, and the situation had already been uncomfortable enough prior to them overhearing the yelling, given Annora's assertions about Master Warin's character.

"He is a *rapist*," she had insisted.

"The Master of The Guard?"

"I know it with certainty. He debases Ryiah, my friend, with regularity. He is an awful man that I'd sooner see killed than go to for assistance."

"Then Cassen is our only option."

She said the words knowing it was not an option. Cassen was the very perpetrator of the current treachery. He had been at the heart of all her family's conflicts since as long as she could remember. If it were merely his success in Eastport making her father look bad by comparison, she would not have held Cassen in such contempt, but she had long suspected him of purposefully undermining her father's every negotiation with the Spiceland merchants to the extent that Alther's failure had been inevitable. Cassen simply had a way of getting his claws into people and compelling them to do what he wished, and Annora's revelation about Warin and his lady servant was further evidence of how far he would go.

"We cannot go and beg the new tyrant to reverse the very things he has done to put himself into power," Annora had conceded, and in doing so, admitted Warin was their only chance of having justice, poor that it may be.

The door swung open, and through it stomped a woman near the age of Ethel's mother. Though she was not near as stunning, she was still fair by any measure, and that she bore a look of contemptuous disdain only furthered her resemblance to Crella in Ethel's mind.

"Beth," came the pleading voice of Master Warin from far off in the adjacent room. "You are wrong in this." The angry authority with which he spoke made Ethel wonder what he must sound like when he was actually making a demand.

Having heard enough of their earlier ranting to gather that their fight was about Warin's infidelity, it was impossible not to feel pity for this woman—and that had been prior to Ethel hearing her name. *Could this be the Beth my father had hurt so badly?* It only took a moment to realize it could not—this Beth was Adeltian, but it did not stop Ethel's sympathy from growing. This was clearly a woman wronged, pained, and tangled so thoroughly that there was no escaping it. A woman her age could not simply leave her husband, no matter how badly he had despoiled her trust. Unless she had a wealthy family that would take her back in, there would be no breaking from him. *At what age then* can *a woman escape?* It was a question seemingly without an answer and did not bode well for her own growing need to flee.

Warin's wife may have been angry to begin with, but when she saw Ethel and Annora sitting where they were, Ethel feared for their own safety. The woman strode toward them with a hatred so palpable that it threatened to consume the room in hellfire.

Ethel understood. Annora was a lady servant; it was evident in her dress. The clothing Ethel had bought for her served her well in their classes, but when they left the confines of their school dormitories, it was only proper for Annora to return to her normal silken attire. Ethel wanted to curl into a ball and, in doing so, hide her friend from this woman so Annora's youth and exotic beauty would not cause Beth more torment.

"Is this your new whore?" Beth yelled to her husband, still in the other room.

Though Ethel's attention was on the woman before them, she could see from the corner of her eye that Annora was looking downward. It would take an iron will to remain so composed with a threat standing so close, but Annora was a statue of servility.

Then Beth did the unthinkable. In perhaps the most vile of acts Ethel had seen done by a proper woman—and Ethel had seen many, as her mother did her best to be repugnant toward Alther—she spat in Annora's face.

Weight pulled at Ethel's jaw as she gaped, her friend's face bearing all the shame this Beth could transpose to her. Yet Annora remained motionless, not even moving to wipe the spit that now dripped down her forehead, nearing her eye. This was humiliation on an intolerable level, and directed against a target wholly undeserving. Annora, the girl sold by her father against her will into foreign indenture. Annora, the one who had defended both Ethel and Eaira against the mortal tyranny of highborn Sture. Annora, her only friend.

Ethel lunged at the woman, grabbing her by the hair, and pulled with all her might. What Ethel screamed, she could not recall, but it was no doubt among the worst of the obscenities she knew—and she was very well read.

The woman was no dainty victim, however. Her age afforded her a greater strength than did Ethel's, and after her advantage of surprise had been spent, Ethel found herself on her back, the woman atop her, striking, clawing, and shrieking.

"Leave her be, woman!"

Ethel's reluctant curiosity about Warin's voice when making a demand had been satisfied. The weight of it passed through her like a wave, sobering her to instant civility as Beth was pulled from her like a dust mote caught in a rapid inhalation. Beth's eyes were still transfixed on Ethel as Warin chastised her, not realizing Ethel had attacked first, and sent her off to a different part of the home so that he could see to his guests.

"I apologize," said Warin. "My wife is…" He gave a frustrated grunt. "Why are you here?"

Ethel was still shaking from her scuffle and found it difficult to speak.

"We have come for justice," said Annora after wiping her face.

Warin looked immediately exhausted hearing the words, quite the opposite of the reaction Ethel had hoped for. *Here stands the head of the Protectors of the Realm, and he is exasperated by a call for justice?*

"Yes," said Ethel, revitalized by her disbelief. "We believe the wrong man has been arrested for the murder of the king."

Warin shook his head. "No doubt you do. He is your father."

"My *adopted* father." It pained her to refer to him as such, but it strengthened her case for impartiality somewhat. "And he is more than that. He is the most honorable and honest man within these walls. You know it to be true."

"Honor does not preclude murder. Honest men kill all the time," said Warin.

"They don't lie about it," Ethel retorted.

Warin closed his eyes and ran his meaty hand up his brow and through his mess of hair. "I don't determine who is guilty or innocent, girl."

"No," said Ethel. "You just mindlessly obey whatever king has your leash." It was a stupid thing to blurt out, but she would not be patronized by such a man, not if she could help it.

Warin made a disapproving rumble. "Have you and your friend come here just to fight with my wife and insult me, or did you have a purpose for your visit?"

"We demand *justice*," Ethel shouted, unable to control her indignant rage.

"Let me explain something to you, little girl." Warin looked her up and down as if she were to be his next indulgence, and Ethel fought her inclination to shudder. "Like *me*, you also do not determine who is guilty or innocent. Like *me*, you also heed the tug of the king's leash. Unless you have some proof of whoever you think is responsible for Lyell's poisoning, and I am quite sure you do not, then I suggest you go back to your little room and play with your little toys like a good little princess."

"It was Cassen," said Annora. "And I have proof."

Warin's eyes darted to her. "Do you? What proof is that?"

"I was witness to his countless dealings with Adeltian conspirators. They have been plotting to kill the king for as long as I have been in service. My former patron Emrel was deeply—"

"Ahck," interrupted Warin. "You're a *servant*. The whole lot of you are bound to make accusations of the men—the *good* men that you serve. And all so you can be lazy and relieved of service for some short time while the matter resolves. No, I've had enough of the likes of lady servants throwing lies around for their own benefit."

He will not help us. It was evident far sooner, but Ethel had held on to hope until now. Staying longer only invited further trouble. "We are sorry to have disturbed you," she said. "We will be on our way."

Warin grunted and gestured his consent for them to leave. They had reached the door when he spoke again.

"You look so much like your mother," he said.

Ethel did not want to turn around, but she was a mouse and he the cat. If she ran he'd be given to chase. She faced him.

His eyes were all over her. Even had she not known he was predisposed to rape, it would have still felt a violation.

"One final bit of advice, girl. Lay low, as low as you can. Make yourself small and quiet. Things are changing in this kingdom—in the realm. Where the pieces settle may surprise you, and when they do, you'll want to be sure not to be in the poor graces of the new kings and queens."

KEETHRO

Titon's show of restraint with the two vagabonds had shocked Keethro, and now that he saw his friend in the clutches of an equally large and ornery man, Keethro was sure Titon and the beast would come to fatal blows. But Titon merely nodded, almost imperceptibly, and the butcher released him and returned to his work.

Keethro did not wish to ask Titon what it had been about, for fear of sending him into frenzy, but Titon had responded nonetheless. "A warning from an old friend," he said, and Keethro did not press him further.

"Ten skewers for me and six for my friend." It was the next thing Titon had said after several minutes of silence, and it was equally confusing. For all they knew, this meat could taste like goat leather— though it certainly did not smell it. The people behind them in line groaned at the size of the order, knowing it would only delay them from getting theirs that much longer.

"You sure about that?" Keethro asked.

Titon nodded without turning to face him. He had managed to get the eight marks out of his swollen purse without causing too much of a scene, and for that Keethro was thankful.

"This way," said Titon when they'd finally received their meal.

Titon had not yet sampled the meat, which in itself was odd, and now he was leading them back to the line. *Has this city already caused him to part with his sanity?* With the exception of the butcher having used some dark magic on him, it was the only thing that made sense.

Titon pushed his way through the line amid angry, albeit half-hearted objections. Had he been built like a normal man, the crowd would have likely jumped him, but Titon eventually found what he was looking for without any altercation. He handed four of the skewers to the boy and his sister who had been ejected. They took the offering without a word, and hastily retreated from the area before Titon could demand from them some sort of recompense.

Keethro and Titon made their way from the food area, continuing their walk through the sprawling city.

"You are worrying me, my friend. I have never seen you carry food so long without eating." Keethro had also refrained from eating any in case the butcher had somehow communicated a reason to avoid doing so to Titon. His face certainly spoke of danger.

Titon's expression finally changed to that of weak amusement, and he removed three pieces of the meat with a single bite. A smile almost reached his face as he visibly relaxed. Keethro followed suit, and after the two men had chewed and swallowed several more bites they found the breath to speak.

"I had gone far too long without a meal. Do not let me do so again," Keethro said, speaking more for Titon than himself.

"No, I will not. Nor will I allow you to forget our reason for being here. We must find a mender. Perhaps you can work your charms and find us some direction."

My charms will find us the direction, should one actually exist, Keethro mused to himself while finishing the last of his river dragon. He then began to scan his surroundings for a suitable person to approach, feeling oddly optimistic. He considered his ideal candidate. *An honest young woman would be best, preferably a local with a good knowledge of the city and all its wares…but I would settle for an outsider as well, so long as she had a suitably exotic look about her. Long dark hair, skin kissed by the dawnlight, lips that looked hungry for flesh, and large eyes that still had within them the spark of life and innocence, a must. A small waist, ample breasts and buttocks, and her jaw should be well defined. I do not like when a woman's jaw—*

"Hello, my friends!" A small, fidgety man had approached, annoyingly introducing himself as if he'd known them for quite some time. Keethro was none too pleased to have been interrupted while he was so close to determining the exact characteristics of the person who would have no doubt led them to the very elixirs they had come for, as well as provided a very intimate tour of all the city's attractions. This man was quite possibly the opposite in every respect. He looked older than they, though he was attempting to hide his age with a bandana tied about his head, poorly concealing encroaching baldness. He was thick in the gut, but thin in the chest and legs. His skin was light and splotchy, face shaven but not for days, his teeth were a mess of jagged, misshapen spikes, and his eyes were dartingly evasive.

"You are no friend of mine," Keethro growled.

"Oh, but I am. You just do not know it yet! You two strong lads do not appear to be from this region, now are you?" He gave them no opportunity to respond before continuing his speech. "No, I would think not. Probably your first time to the city too, is it? I would guess so. Well then, I am not just your friend—I am perhaps your *best* of friends. I can assist you greatly, oh yes. The patrons of this city pay me and those like me handsomely to see that our new arrivals are well cared for and learn their way around. Why, one could get lost in a city so large as this."

The man's story had the faintest ring of truth to it. His clothing was certainly absurd enough to befit some sort of city greeter or jester. Over a patchwork shirt he wore a short, ragged cape tied tight at the neck; his trousers were a typical hearty weave, but they were almost tight around his womanly legs. Nonetheless, Keethro had no interest in him. He had not yet begun the search for his lady guide, and he could feel her presence. With so many people bustling around she had to be there, her voluptuous curves hidden under some drab garb as to not draw undue attention from the wrong people, and Keethro was anything but the wrong people. When their eyes connected, she would reveal herself to him by pushing back the hood of her robe and letting loose her hair. *I will need only nod to her, and she will come to me. She will embrace me as if we had known each other, yet we will share the thrill of unfamiliarity as we—*

"Then take us to your best mender." Titon's voice was a war hammer that could reverse the path of a charging courser—instead it merely crushed Keethro's hopes. "We seek elixirs, specifically one to cure stupor or slumberskull. My wife was stricken quite suddenly and has remained so for many years. If you can help us, we will reward you."

"Yes, oblivion, eternal sleep, slumberskull. I have heard of this. I do not know the cure for such an ailment, but I can take you to a man who does. And before we go further, please, allow me to introduce myself. I am Tielo, son of no one. And you? If you do not wish to say I will not be offended."

Keethro knew that was a sure way to get Titon to tell him his real name. In fairness, though, they had not discussed using aliases, and improvisation was not one of Titon's strong suits.

"I am Titon son of Small Gryn, and this is my brother in trust, Keethro son of Leif. We come from—"

"We hail from the North," Keethro interrupted. "Though we are wishing to better dress and groom to the customs of this land. Perhaps you could first take us to a barber so that we do not offend your friend with our appearance."

Titon now had a dirty look on his face, making him out to be evermore the northern warrior. They could not pass as Dogmen in their current state, except to the most gullible.

"Oh, he will not be offended in the least," said Tielo. "He sees all kinds of people in his trade and is glad of it. He is a master tincturer— not be confused with a tinker, mind you—and he is not far at all. This way, if you'll follow."

The small man led them through the crowds with speed, although he was able to snake his way through far easier than they. The wake he left was not nearly large enough for Keethro, let alone Titon, and he had to stop often to allow them to catch up. But he'd not lied about the distance; they were there before long. Keethro was disappointed to see this *master* was merely another vendor with his own wheeled cart. It was a large cart, however, with two yokes. And two mighty beasts indeed must have been required to pull such a thing. Whereas the other carts may have had signage that reached two men in height, this cart had shelving filled with wares that reached just as high. The man at the cart, or rather atop it, was himself tall, further aided by the fact that he stood a man above the small crowd gathered below him. Beneath him, various bottles of different colored liquids with both herbs and whole animals suspended within them were displayed and protected behind thick glass. The creatures ranged from ordinary to grotesque, things that Keethro had never seen before. Much of it looked as though it must have come from the sea, as many had fins and flippers or long, flat bodies, yet were not snakes, but nearly all had menacing jaws and large teeth.

The master tincturer, as Tielo had called him, was busy assisting a client. He had disappeared below his deck, but his hand appeared behind a curtain to retrieve a bottle on display. When back atop his cart, he doled out an allotment of the liquid, from what looked to be a suspension containing a hairless rabbit, into a far smaller glass container, corked it, marked it with some ink, and leaned over the railing to hand it to his customer.

"Zhivko," shouted their new companion over the noise of the throng. "It is Tielo. I have brought you customers from afar."

The tall man gave Tielo a bit of a scowl, but his demeanor changed to that of cordiality upon seeing Titon and Keethro. He was an eccentric sort with facial hair that must have required more time in front of silvered glass than did Kilandra's mane. It was a beard of three prongs— two sprouting downward from beneath his nose and a third from his chin, leaving his cheeks bare and giving him a devilish appearance.

"Welcome," he said. "Name your ailment, and I will name the remedy. I have the greatest collection of tinctures in the realm, and though I am not happy to ever part with them, a vial can be had, should you afford the price."

Titon wasted no time. "The ailment is slumberskull, or oblivion I have heard it called here. Would you have a cure for such a thing?"

I should have coached him prior to this meeting, Keethro realized, too late.

"Why of course I would. But the more important question would be, are you certain that is the tincture you require?" The man appeared to look at Titon in an analytical way, squinting at him from multiple directions from atop his cart. "It would appear you do not suffer from such an ailment. Which is well, because the cost is quite prohibitive for such a thing, and you do not look as though you have coin to spare."

"I can afford it," said Titon. Keethro cringed. This negotiation was not headed in the proper direction. "And it is not for me. It is for my wife."

"You must care for her very much to have come all this way from wherever it is you hail. And it is a shame that you may return with nothing, for lack of coin. It saddens me to see cases such as these, but my ingredients cost a small fortune, and I cannot operate a charity, you see." Zhivko appeared to be moving on to the next customer with the intent of showing he had resolved himself to the fact that Titon simply could not afford the remedy.

"Name your price. As sure as the River flows, the Mountain sits, and the Dawnstar rises, I will pay it or find a means to."

"Titon," said Keethro, half growling, half pleading, and fully knowing he'd be powerless to stop Titon set in motion. "Let me assist you."

"It is one hundred marks for such a cure," said Zhivko. The crowd all seemed to gasp quietly at the sum. Keethro saw a smile on one of their faces, though. This was a calculated ploy to fleece a desperate man for all his worth.

"That is outrageous," Keethro cried, trying to steal back some of the momentum. "I have seen similar remedies sold for one-tenth the price!"

"Perhaps, but have any of them worked? I would expect not, else you and your friend would not be here."

It did not matter as Titon was already fumbling through his things trying to locate his coin purse, too eager to pay the full sum. Had this man actually been selling a legitimate remedy, Keethro may have thought it a reasonable price, but the chances of that seemed slim given the amount of pageantry involved in the presentation.

"There he goes," cried Zhivko, pointing a finger with the first honest look on his face, one of desperation. It took Keethro just a moment to understand the meaning: someone had swiped Titon's coin purse and was running away with a fortune that should have belonged to Zhivko himself. Keethro sprinted in the indicated direction and after about twenty paces grabbed the first person he saw that was running in kind.

Tielo curled himself into a ball and cowered after Keethro slammed him onto his back. *You little shit, I should have known.* Coins from Titon's purse were spread out in the dirt around the stunted cutpurse. Keethro expected Titon must have caught up because none of the people around him, desperate though they looked, had made a move to grab for the gold and silver scattered on the ground.

He was only half right.

"Up you go," a man said, "and *slowly.*"

He did not recognize the voice, but it carried the acrimonious authority of what could only be a city guard. Keethro obeyed and saw that he was correct.

Three guards, heavily armored in mail and carrying longswords and stout shields, had their blades drawn and pointed toward his chin.

"This man stole my friend's purse," Keethro said.

The guards snickered and their leader spoke again. "I have no doubt he did. A couple of fools like the two of you would be a fine mark. But that is the least of your worries. Throw down your weapons. You are to come with us on account of avoiding conscription."

"On whose authority?" Titon's voice reverberated through the crowd and the carts and the small structures surrounding them. He sounded a god addressing mortals and a flicker of fear could be seen on the guards' previously cocksure faces. But the sound of a dozen or more other bodies clad in chainmail followed his voice, coming from behind them, and the guards' original demeanors returned.

"On the authority of the fecking king!" With his shout the guard slammed his sword through the ribs of Tielo where he lay on his side, still curled in a ball. Blood spurted from the wound, climbing up the blade, causing the rest of the armored men to erupt in laughter as the helpless thief squirmed and gasped for breath.

CASSEN

Cassen found it strangely difficult to concentrate as he made his way with some speed through the castle. His thoughts were occupied by various concerns, all minor, expected, and being properly dealt with, but their combined weight was cumbrous.

Perhaps foremost among them was Master Warin. Their meeting had gone as well as could have been expected, but Cassen continued to replay the event in his mind in search of hints to the contrary. Without a Master of Forces, the heads of the kingdom's many legions had turned to Warin, making him somewhat of a fulcrum upon which the kingdom now balanced. Luckily, Warin did not seem to fully grasp his own significance. Cassen did not truly require his cooperation either, further negating any cause for concern. *Even should the man defy me, Sacarat will see him and his armies trampled, nonetheless.*

The sound of another's footsteps came from far off, causing Cassen to place his own feet with quiet care. The noisemaker soon came into view: a boy servant approached from the far end of the hall, nearly skipping with carelessness. At the sight of Cassen, however, the boy became rigid and serious. His pace slowed, all gaiety lost. *What is a boy like you even doing here so close to the dungeons?* Cassen wondered. The young servant was unable to conceal his worry as he neared. Shrinking away from Cassen and eventually coming to a stop, he all but cowered against the wall. Only after he had passed the frightened child did Cassen force his face to an expression of geniality, not having realized he'd been wearing such a mask of rancor.

His scowl troubled him. Not only did Cassen believe himself to have mastery over his presented emotions, but more than that, he should have had no cause for displeasure. His every plan of import had been executed without so much as snagging a single fiber of his royal silks. And yet he frowned, and so menacingly as to cause this boy to have nearly pissed himself. *Perhaps he merely feared me raping him*, thought Cassen, but even that innocuous quip irked rather than amused him. Then he remembered what he carried. *No wonder the boy had shied. It is a bit bloodier than your typical sack of potatoes, after all.*

Yet Cassen still could not escape his growing animosity toward Warin and the unfounded worry that came with it.

✤ *Earlier That Day* ✤

"Why should I do this?"

"It is no great task to have a woman transported from one place to another," Cassen explained. "And it is for the good of the realm, therefore making it a task you are duty bound to perform."

"I do not see how having members of The Guard assigned to taking a princess from her rightful home to some faraway land would be for the good of the realm," Warin growled back.

Cassen exhaled theatrically. "No, I do not expect that you would. But might I remind you, Rivervale is not so *far* away—or have you forgotten who last conquered this kingdom? If we do not secure our northern neighbor and appease their masses then it will not be long before King Veront is marching an army upon us, just as he now marches on Strahl."

Cassen did not know how much control he still had over Warin based upon their shared secret of Warin's debasement of his lady servant. With the king dead and the normal order of law on hiatus, the threat of such a truth coming to light was not as great. *So long as he still fears his wife's learning of it*, Cassen thought. He knew Warin had become more agitated with him, especially after his foolish slip-up at the banquet having called the *master* sir. But he would overwhelm Warin with as much detail as possible regarding the true complexity of kingdom management to ensure he did not come to the idiotic conclusion that he himself might be the best fit to fill the void left on the vacant throne.

"Veront is marching on Strahl? *King* Veront?"

"Why yes, my good master. Things happen quite quickly in kingdom politics. Without a vast network of spies and informers one is merely a bystander. Yours must not have been so quick to retrieve such news, I take it?"

"No… No, my spies had not yet informed me of that."

You have no spies, you ignorant fool, just a collection of door guards too dull to listen or report anything happening within. "Well, I am not surprised. I had guessed as much would happen, but I had only confirmed it recently. Should Veront control both Rivervale and Strahl, he will have all the momentum required to then overrun our meager walls and defenses. There are only two ways to prevent such a thing: the western side of the King's Arm magically rises from the ground to protect us—standing strong and tall as it should have long ago—or we take our forces north and seize Rivervale in this most opportune time, while Veront's armies are occupied to the east."

"What keeps Veront from then marching on Adeltia? My wife and home are here."

And a lovely lady servant, let us not forget. "Strahl exists by the grace of Rivervale, and without their imports, Veront will have no food for his army. He will be troubled just marching back to Rivervale, let alone heading south to threaten Adeltia." This was patently false, as Strahl was home to the richest farming of the continent—even their city banners boasted fields of grain—but Cassen was relying on Warin's poor knowledge of such things. *Adeltia will be safe—safely placed into the thankful hands of the Satyr.*

"And the princess?"

Cassen could not help but sigh. For some reason he could not yet grasp, it pained him to think of Crella after their previous encounter. "Crella will remain our captive, but she serves a far greater purpose imprisoned in Rivervale. It will soothe the masses to know a pureblooded Adeltian is within their dungeons—even if her halfblooded Adeltian boy is the one who rules over them."

Warin did not look convinced. "Are you sure it is wise to put that boy upon a throne? He is somewhat…temperamental."

"Did you have anyone else in mind?" Cassen asked coyly.

Warin shook his head. "It just seems odd that we imprison one heir who has so recently poisoned the king, and release a second, who had not so long ago planned to do the same. It is difficult to believe he is the best of choices."

He will not sit the throne for long enough to do any real damage, do not fear. "But he is precisely that. He is the *best* choice, if not a great one. See to it that the necessary arrangements are made to have Crella accompany us when we go north. Let me know the moment the preparations have been completed and we will march." Cassen squinted at Warin to indicate his seriousness. "And she is to be treated with the utmost care. If she is harmed I will hold you, and you alone, accountable. I know you have a penchant for drowning women."

Warin scowled. "No harm will befall her, on that I will stake my life."

So you will, Cassen promised them both in thought.

⊶⊰⊱⊷

The weight of the sack began to make itself felt, and Cassen shifted it to his other hand. Given its solitary content, it was heavier than he would have thought.

"Evening, Vidar." Cassen sauntered past the gaoler without so much as a glance, wondering if he might be bold enough to beg a bribe from he who was now the king—or was it queen—regent.

"Your Grace," Vidar acknowledged with reverence.

Cassen's mood had not grown any cheerier on his way to the depths of the dungeon. The same person who had beleaguered his thoughts for two decades, the girl he had first loved and then grown to hate, desiring her with the spitefulness of a man scorned, the one he thought would now be his plaything and provide him with endless amusement, Crella still yet had some death grip upon his soul.

His subjugation of her had not happened exactly as he had envisioned, but more than that, it simply did not result in the feelings of conquest he had for so long anticipated. Gone was the child who submitted to her overpowering uncle with hopeless despondency, and in her place, a strong, unyielding woman who did not allow him a moment's rest in her determined struggle. He had taken his pleasure of her, but he had not conquered her. After he'd defiled her, so did she him, as she turned and spat in his face. She did not cry. She did not whimper or moan. She fought with every ounce she had within her, and with that she had not been truly beaten. *Not yet, at least,* he told himself.

He could not deny the physical pleasure he'd enjoyed, but he grew increasingly queasy as he recalled the specifics of the act—details he should have been able to indulge in. *It is my failure that sickens me,* he reassured himself. *When she breaks, I will have my peace.* But he could not shake the oddest feeling he had when he pictured her fighting so valiantly. It must have been pity that he felt; he supposed that would be acceptable. For it could not be sympathy nor compassion. He'd cast those off when he was just a child. And he certainly had no affection for the woman—for that cunt who showed him nothing but derision. *I am not that type of man. I do not suffer from those pathetically ordinary conditions had by men of supreme mediocrity.*

Cassen made his way down the familiar stretch that led to the royal cell, not bothering to knock as he unlocked the massive door and swung it open.

Inside he saw young Stephon struggling to heave the same large book as before onto his chest. *A prop book for a prop king.*

Somewhat amused, Cassen allowed Stephon to situate the giant text upon himself before addressing him. "Your Grace, I come bearing a great gift."

Stephon turned a page in his book. "I hope it is more than the worthless air from your lungs that you gifted me with on your last visit."

"No, Your Grace. I have brought exactly that which you have asked." With that, he tossed the sack onto the bed beside Stephon.

Stephon lowered the book and turned tiredly to gaze upon what now lay beside him, as if expecting disappointment. But when he saw it—the dark blood coagulated on the fibers of its hempen weaves—his reaction was like that of a person having just realized he'd been seated next to a venomous snake. He bolted upright in his bed, recoiling away from it.

"What is *this*?" he demanded.

Cassen was amused but kept it to himself. Throwing around bloody bags was not in keeping with his usual demeanor, and he did not wish to draw too much suspicion. *Not that it will matter soon.* "It is the head of the *former* king, as you requested, Your Grace."

"This had better not be some joke or it will be *your* head that is in a sack. Open it."

The impertinence of this young man never ceased to amaze Cassen. *You will make a perfect boy king…for a week perhaps. If not for Sacarat's coming fleet, I would see fit to beat you to death with your grandfather's head and take the throne for myself.* But he did no such thing. Cassen grabbed the bag from the bottom and held it at shoulder level. The head made a sickening thump as it hit the ground, refusing to bounce in Lyell's final act of defiance. It was a grotesque sight: blood caked in the hair and beard, the skin of the face more saggy and loose than Cassen had remembered, but there was no mistaking whose head it was.

Stephon appeared to be speechless for once, just staring at what lay on its cheek in front of him. A grin slowly found its way to his face, as if he were finally realizing the implications.

"And what of Alther?"

"He now has a cell in a dungeon far worse than this one, Your Grace."

"*He* is responsible for this?" Stephon asked in disbelief.

"I am afraid so." Cassen had considered explaining to Stephon his own true part in the murder of the king in order to curry favor with the boy, but had decided against it. If he told him that he was responsible for the murder of his grandfather, the unpredictable brat may have demanded Cassen's head out of some misguided loyalty to the kingdom, the realm, or whatever whim he fancied. He decided instead to allow Stephon to believe as did the rest of the kingdom—that Alther had killed the king. His having brought Stephon the requested gift and handing him the throne would have to be enough.

"And how did he kill him?"

"All evidence indicates the king was poisoned from a bottle of wine given to him by Alther at a recent banquet."

Stephon looked as if he'd just tasted the most sour fruit, having first expected no less than the ripest cherry. "*Poison?*"

"Yes, Your Grace."

"That coward of a man. Poison is the tool of women."

Stephon appeared to wish for affirmation, but given the circumstances, Cassen was uncharacteristically unable to satisfy. The effort of maintaining his usual femininity had become exhausting as of late, making further pageantry that much more burdensome. It was all he could do, in fact, not to act on his former impulse to beat the boy to death. Cassen lowered his eyes so that the antipathy within them would not be seen.

"He is not so brave as you, my king."

Stephon did not reply, causing Cassen to wonder if his cynicism had been detected—a thing difficult to discern with lowered eyes, and looking up now would be an indication of guilt. *You witless fool,* he chided himself. Killing Stephon here and now would cause complications, but it would not be near so dangerous as giving Stephon a reason for animus toward him along with the power to act on it.

"He will suffer for his crime," Stephon said finally and with nothing in his voice to suggest Cassen had offended him. "Of that I assure you. He was no father of mine, and I have known as much for the longest time. He is a disgusting disgrace to the kingdom—not that he ever belonged here."

Stephon stood. *The Intricacies of War and Tactics* lay on the bed awkwardly with its pages folded and crumpling. The book was one of probably no more than two-dozen copies, each worth easily more than most men would earn in a lifetime of common labor. Although he had no love for the text, it still bothered Cassen to see a valuable piece of history so mistreated.

"May I gather your things for you, Your Grace, so that we may see you to your proper place upon the throne?"

"Yes, yes. You do that. I have a kingdom to rule, after all."

"There is one other matter, Your Eminence... It is to do with your mother."

"What of her?"

"She seems to have gone a bit mad during her time spent confined. She is accusing everyone she can think to name of every misdeed and misconduct she can divine. She has been treated with the utmost care, however, I assure you, and not a hair upon her head has fallen to harm." Cassen's stomach turned a bit as he spoke the words, a thing he guessed was due to the potential that Stephon may call for her release.

"She should remain confined. I have no desire to have her second-guessing my every decision in an attempt to undermine my authority. She is likely just as guilty in the king's death as is the vile man she called husband. And I will never forgive her for claiming that man to have been my father. See to it that I do not hear about her again for some time."

Cassen bore a legitimate smile. "As you wish, Your Grace."

TALLOS

John was the first to have joined Wilkin in his travels, the first, at least, of this current group. It was hard to imagine this was the first band of vagrants Wilkin had attracted in what must have been untold years tinkering among lands far and wide. Wilkin did not have to say he had made such journeys, for they were written upon his face. His myriad lines and wrinkles were as visible as the markings on a map of the paths he'd taken, mostly north and south, but spanning the breadth of the continent. An honest face it was, but a face that knew sadness and defeat. How many times had he watched tragedy befall his companions, spared only for being a helpless old man whose skills were more valuable left intact than the entirety of his belongings if stolen? And was he a coward or simply not a fool for allowing such things to happen without throwing himself onto the swords of their attackers, joining his fellow travelers in some desperate rebellion? Or perhaps he'd tried to do as such, just as many times, and was instead impaled by his own impotence, pushed to the side and laughed at by his would-be killers. Time stood still, allowing Tallos to ponder these things whenever he so much as glanced at the man.

"What do you mean war drums?" asked John. This man was less of a puzzle, though not by much. He was not corpulent, but was further so from being chiseled from stone. His finger-length wavy hair and face without a hint of stubble made him seem more like a squire than a tinker's apprentice, and his countenance spoke of his low birth and humility. Yet while some impoverished folk carried with them a hungry, desperate look, warning that they may lash out at any moment to steal whatever opportunity fate put within their grasp, John looked more similar to Wilkin with respect to his incorruptible honor. It seemed to come from a different source, however. Perhaps it was only their extreme difference in stature, John being half again the weight of the average man, Wilkin merely half, but John did not share the feebleness of his mentor—not in appearance. "If there was an army in that tiny village it would be spilling out the sides, and we'd surely see it."

Kelgun shook his head, but only faintly as if to keep his eyes locked on the potential danger that lay ahead, should it reach out and grab him otherwise. "That is worse than an army. Those are the drums of a conscription party."

All had come to a stop save Wilkin. It was not in his nature to halt at the sound of danger, and he continued forward with his two donkeys, one laden with him and the tools of his trade, the other with even more tools and supplies.

"Some knight who's afraid of war," snickered Dusan, who immediately looked as though he regretted having mustered the courage to taunt Kelgun for the first time in earshot.

But Kelgun ignored the boy. "I go no farther. Lily, this way. We head back north."

"She won't," cried Dusan. He looked toward his sister, but she avoided his gaze. She turned her horse to follow Kelgun.

"Ho thur!"

It was the voice of a man not within their party, and it came from some distance. A quick glance around showed Tallos that they had been flanked by mounted men, emerging from the thick forests. Four halberd-wielding men-at-arms wearing tabards painted with what looked to be an upward facing lightning bolt approached them, a pair from each side. They were sturdy men riding upon horses equally muscled. Though somewhat smaller than Kelgun's destrier, their coursers had the statuesque look of youth and power, the striations of their shoulders and legs awash in the gleam of well-groomed dark bay coats. Tallos recalled a book from his youth stating such a breed could gallop at incredible speed for a mile if need be—something he now regretted having hoped to one day see. Their canter carried their riders within easy speaking range of Tallos's party without delay.

"Headed somewhere, young knight?" It was the smallest and seemingly most cocksure of the four mounted men, and his labeling of Kelgun was clear to be no honest compliment. Tallos had no real knowledge of armies and warfare, only what he'd heard from tales of the conquests of valiant knights in great battles, but it was obvious these were paid soldiers, not conscripts. They were probably paid twice and again whatever was handed to surviving conscripts upon victory, and likely had ten times the effectiveness in combat. *Though one must never underestimate the value of arrow fodder.* The phrase of unknown origin was stuck in Tallos's mind, repeating itself.

For once Kelgun had no answer. His expression had gone stern, and he eyed the riders untrustingly.

"Surely you heard the drums and knew their meaning? A man atop a battle-scarred destrier must know a call to arms, no? And be eager to join the battle for the good of the kingdom and the realm?"

"What makes you so sure your side fights for the good of the realm?" asked Kelgun, but his question was met with only a grin.

The remaining halberdiers came to a halt. Wilkin was out of earshot by now, still headed toward the city at his methodical pace. *He will not be throwing himself upon these halberds, it seems.*

"Wherever did you find such an ugly squire?" asked one of the other men.

"The Mountain's tits," cried another. "I believe that boy has tits in kind!" The four men-at-arms erupted in laughter.

"Let her alone!" It was not her noble knight who had come to her defense, but her weakling brother. The men paused a moment in consideration of his request and renewed their laughter.

"Come, all of you," said their leader. "King Veront of Rivervale has need of your services, meager though they may be."

For a man that has seen battle, thought Tallos, *he does not appear to have a proper respect for those whose bodies will shield him from his enemies' arrows.* His dry humor served as little comfort as they were escorted toward the sound of the drums.

KEETHRO

So this is what happens to men who lower their arms.

In the many years he and Titon had fought beside each other, Titon had never dropped his weapons and surrendered. The prospect was as laughable as it was appalling. What danger could be so great as to cause Titon to expect defeat? The man saw a path to victory in the most absurd situations, and no matter how small that opening may be, always somehow managed to squeeze his colossal frame clean through it.

That had not been the case as the several dozen armored guards wielding swords, halberds, spears, and shields closed ranks about them. The weight of the guards' chainmail and weaponry seemed to shake the ground as they marched in step to surround them.

Titon had reached for his knife slowly, and Keethro assumed—as he always did—that Titon intended to kill the largest of them first. But when Titon's hand released the blade into the dirt instead of flicking it toward the skull of one of the guards, Keethro was perhaps more terrified by what this capitulation meant than he had been of his likely imminent death.

Galatai were not taken prisoner. Their battles with the Dogmen had never posed threat of capture. Their only other foe was other Galatai, and they had sacred laws against allowing defeated clansmen to live in dishonor. The prospect of being taken captive had simply not existed. This strange land had changed all of that, and moreover, it seemed to have changed Titon. It was as if he'd grown soft or simply desperate to live in order to find the remedy for his wife and confirm his sons' conquests.

Keethro had found it harder to drop his own knife than it seemed Titon had. He clung to it in confusion until the neck of a guard's spear smashed his wrist, releasing him from both his daze and the hold on his blade.

They were underground now, imprisoned. The conditions were almost comfortable for Keethro, but he imagined Titon must be cramped. They were well fed, and more importantly, they were together.

Twice a day they'd exchange trays with a guard through a slot in the door. Then they'd sit and eat their ample provisions of stale bread, cheese, and dried meats, the only sounds coming from their chews and gulps.

With their pride shattered, there was little of which to speak. For several miserable days they'd sat in near silence. They could certainly not recall stories of past triumph from within a cell, and given that they had just surrendered themselves to this fate, the thought of immediately planning escape was a bit absurd.

"Did we indeed avoid conscription?" It was Titon who broke the quiet.

"I would be better able to answer the question if I knew what this conscription even was." Keethro continued to scratch a trench with the heel of his boot in the floor of hardened sand. "Hopefully we are not in here on account of merely avoiding some ceremonial hand bath."

"The Mighty Three damn them. Why cannot these southern men speak their meaning plainly? It is as if we use a different tongue entirely at times."

It was good to have his friend speaking again, but it also brought with it unexpected thoughts. *There was a time when I wanted to see you like this, crushed and driven into the belly of the earth so that I could take your place. How did I let Kilandra convince me you were anything but a brother?* Somehow the idea of it was more painful than their current confinement, and Keethro was desperate to keep Titon speaking, if only to avoid being left alone with his thoughts.

"They are feeding us well," Keethro said. "My question is *why*? Why are we being so well cared for when there were so many who appeared to be starving in the streets above?" Keethro nursed his wrist as he spoke. It was the type of fracture too small to require bracing lest he suffer embarrassment worse than the injury. It would simply have to mend during continued use.

"That I also do not know. I seem to be growing duller the farther south we travel."

Keethro chuckled. He considered avoiding the topic altogether, but his fear of silence drove him to it. "That *was* a foolish thing you did back there."

Titon grunted in anger. "Who are you to call me foolish for avoiding an unwinnable battle after having yourself turned us from the more obvious path of heading straight for Strahl? Their guards were like to have had lesser armor than these men. They were so covered in steel it was surprising their meager frames could withstand the weight."

Keethro shook his head. "No, I do not mean that. That was an unwinnable battle. You will get no argument from me there. I mean the swindler who would have taken you for all your gold, had the cutpurse not beaten him to it. You realize he was selling a thief's promise?"

"Yes," Titon let out with a pained sigh. It was some time before he continued. "But I would pay all the gold I have and ever will have for even the slightest chance of bringing her back."

"Well, we do not have any gold now, nor do I think we'll have any soon." Keethro made a vague gesture toward their surroundings. "In the case that we do, let me do the dealing so that we can afford the wares of multiple charlatans and increase our odds of finding an elixir that works. Fair enough?"

"Fair enough. If that time ever comes."

"*When* the time comes we'll want to be ready. I recommend we make the best use of this food and drink while we have it to keep our strength up. Some exercise would do us good as well."

Titon leered at Keethro. "I am not sure what kind of exercise you think we have room for in this tiny box, my friend, but I assure you, we have not been in here quite long enough for your charms to have any such effect on me."

For the moment, they did not seem so much prisoners given the way they laughed and ate. *If we can keep our spirits, we may keep our lives*, Keethro thought, though he knew they were just as likely to die in this box of torrid stone and sand.

◈─◈─◈

The many days spent below ground had been monotonous at best. Galatai warriors were not meant to live in cages, and it was obvious to Keethro that it was taking a horrible toll on Titon. They still ate well and managed to retain their strength, but Titon was no longer as eager to do any training. His only exercise consisted of spending a good five minutes of every hour kicking at the door of their cell in an attempt to loosen its iron hinges. He had not yet made any progress, nor did Keethro expect him to break anything but his leg striking such a door.

The past half a day had been different, however. Up until recently there was nothing to be heard outside their enclosure. Keethro had no idea just how deep underground they had been taken, but the previous peace had made it feel quite deep. That had changed when they heard sounds of great rumbling from above, as if some colossal rock was being slid across the naked ground, pulled by a hundred oxen. It might have been a frightening sound, had they not been so utterly bored. Even Keethro found himself thinking like Titon, more willing to face whatever made that noise than to continue in the tedium of this purgatory.

"Those are cheers?" Keethro asked.

"It is wind, no more. Though I like to hear those sounds of the outdoors. It has been far too long since I have heard the trickle of the stream that runs by my home." Having said that, Titon began to kick at the door again, the thud of his foot and the clang of the hinges became all Keethro could hear.

"No, stop. ...Listen."

Titon snorted, kicked once more, then sat down and was quiet for a moment. "The wind I tell you."

"No, it is a massive—"

The sound of approaching footsteps silenced Keethro. This was soon followed by the heavy clanking of their door being unlocked for the first time since they'd been shut inside. Keethro felt his racing heart in his throat.

The sharpened points of spears appeared in the door opening, followed by the guards who held them.

"Out with you!" shouted one.

Keethro shrugged his shoulders at Titon and was the first out the door. His big friend lumbered behind him.

"Where are we going?" Keethro asked.

The half-dozen guards snickered as they continued to direct them forward at spearpoint. Keethro was pleased to see the path slanted upward. He did not think he could stand to be deeper beneath the surface. The leader of the guards finally hinted at their fate. "You go to face the dragons."

Keethro was optimistic about their chances of being able to kill quite a few of the large river beasts, so long as they were on dry land and properly armed, but the glee with which the guard had spoken made him feel as though they would be in for something far worse.

Titon, on the other hand, seemed unaffected. "We have slain dragons before." He spoke with the unimpassioned candor of a man who truly had. Keethro saw no need to remind him that they merely injured a *river* dragon—a beast that regularly found its way on to the plates of these Southmen.

"I don't think you'll be killing any today," said the lead guard, inciting more snickers from his easily impressed underlings.

The small tunnel through which they had been traveling opened wider and taller as they continued. Eventually they came to a pair of great doors. Standing no less than five men in height, they looked to Keethro the type of doors mortal men were only meant to pass through once. Just in front was a motley group of prisoners under the watch of another small force of guards with spears.

Keethro and Titon were prodded until they too were within the group. The men among them ranged from the thin, agile-looking type, to the monstrous—one even larger than Titon. *These men look as if they should be accompanied by a stench,* Keethro thought, wondering why they did not. *Perhaps it is I most in need of a bath.*

The guards had all ceased speaking and stood disciplined and battle ready, their spears pointed at the group of men as if expecting them to turn and run at any moment.

It *had* been cheers they'd heard from their cell, though even now they sounded too numerous to be real, more like an angry storm than so many blaring voices. *I do not believe it is us they cheer for.*

The chains attached to the upper corners of the doors went taut and began to hoist them open with a familiar scraping sound. The moment the doors began to move, the cheers reached crescendo. *Perhaps they are cheering for us after all,* he teased himself, knowing full and well that it must be their horrific death they so eagerly anticipated.

The light that shone through the crack between the doors was blinding, causing all of them to cower behind their own arms. The thick smell of animal dung was quick to follow, assaulting them yet again, though less violently than the light.

Spears at their backs pushed them forward through the still-moving doors to an overwhelming sight. The ground before them sloped up into the arena, which was long and narrow, not much wider in fact than the doors. The doors were halfway under the ground level, and as the group of men were forced upward and out, Keethro saw that the sides of the arena were over three men in height and made of smooth stone that would be impossible to scale. Multiple wooden fences reaching to his shoulder ran lengthwise down the center of the field—a field so long that it would be difficult to sprint across its entire length. All that paled in comparison to the enormity of the crowd, however, the thunder of their ovation serving to remind Keethro of his insignificance.

Keethro was both confused and relieved by the creature he saw inside the arena. A huge boar stood some twenty paces ahead, and he might have been a somewhat menacing foe, had he not been encumbered as he was. Draped around the boar's shoulders was mail barding, a tad long at the knee. Over the top of his mail was a series of overlapping plates as thick and heavy as any armor Keethro had seen. Tied to his tusks and completely blocking his forward vision was a wooden shield with a thick metal facing. The boar carried the weight, but seemed uncompelled to travel for any determined distance, appearing flustered by his blindness.

Keethro looked for something with which to fight and was at first glad to see a fine array of weaponry splayed out on racks at either side. *If they are supplying us so amply with weapons, what is it we will be facing? Certainly not this pig.*

A hush fell over the crowd soon after the doors had swung full open, though it was not apparent why.

"There must be several thousand people here," said Titon, clearly awestruck. Titon was no fan of large gatherings of people, but at least they no longer shouted.

"Perhaps over ten thousand." Keethro was rather sure that his estimate was conservative.

"Then we are to be famous." Keethro did not hear any cynicism in Titon's words.

A single voice sounded throughout the entire arena. Keethro could see it came from a man on his feet, low in the midfield stands. He made grand gestures with his arms as he spoke. "And now for the event you have gathered to see—demonstrated upon some of the most fearsome warriors from the far corners of the realm. In addition to personally having overseen the training of those who are now the most talented swordsmen, spearmen, halberdiers, and archers of the realm, His Majesty King Veront has commissioned the *breeding* of perhaps an even more formidable weapon with which to wage war. Behold, the dragons of Rivervale!"

The crowd erupted again in raucous cheers. Keethro glanced at the other men in their group, confused. *Are these the fearsome warriors?* He decided he would ponder that later and focused on what may lay ahead as identical doors opened at the other end of the field. At first, Keethro could only see some rising smoke, but soon flames crested the gentle slope. Four skinny pillars of fire crept upward, stopping to form a well-spaced row. Keethro was unimpressed as the flames seemed to each be coming from their own wooden contraption that had been wheeled into place. The distance made it difficult to tell how many, but there were at least several men for each contraption, somehow tending to its needs. There was no sign of dragons, however. *Perhaps the flames attract them from the sky?*

One of the guards behind them must have flung the rock that struck the boar on his mailed rump. The beast took off running down the field away from Keethro's group, and after a brief moment of allowing the crowd this amusement, the dragons finally loosed their first attack, stifling all humor.

The flames leapt forward from the wooden structures with incredible speed, arcing only slightly through the air until they reached their target. The enormous shield on the face of the boar served as no protection. The first flaming projectile smashed through both metal and wood, piercing the skull of the animal and protruding out the rear of his shoulder between a gap in the plates. The second came immediately after, impaling the now-turned beast through his upper ribs and pinning him to the ground, puncturing the plate armor cleanly. The third and forth shots missed their marks, if only by a bit, but the obvious intention of showing the savagery with which these new pets of the king could decimate a fully-armored foe had been well demonstrated.

The crowd's fervor reached a new high as the dead boar performed its final throe. These man-sized projectiles spit from the dragon's mouths appeared to be no more than giant arrows. They had thick feathered fletching on their rear and triangular metal points at the tip. The head of the first arrow still burned even after having passed through the boar's head, the flames singeing the hair upon its neck.

The group of men Keethro and Titon were now a part of stared at each other, trying to come to some collective decision without words. Titon seemed the only man among them who did not have fear in his eyes. He looked hungry, in fact, as if he had been just presented a plate of potential heroism upon which to gorge himself. It was inspiring, but Keethro did not believe it would have any effect on their odds of victory.

CASSEN

Stephon was quick to leave his cell, accompanied by an entourage of Protectors to escort him to his royal chambers. *I wonder if he will be happy enough in his grandfather's old quarters or if he will soon insist on taking the chambers atop the Throne.* The thought of young Stephon residing in either was somewhat amusing.

Cassen was at first confused to see Vidar's post abandoned, but as he passed by the final cell he noticed it had a new occupant.

"You may come out now. Your new king and would-be killer is gone."

Cassen thought it wise of the old gaoler to have taken refuge. Knowing Stephon, he might have demanded a sword from one of his escorts and ended Vidar's long and diligent service to the kingdom.

"Thank you, Your Grace."

"Please, I am but a humble duchess now that the kingdom once again belongs to a son of House Red Rivers."

"As you wish, Duchess Cassen."

It was good to see Vidar had remained as humble as when Cassen had first walked in as regent. *I should continue not to bribe this man or he may think me once again a mere duchess in truth.*

Cassen flicked a coin worth fifty marks to the old man just the same. "Tell me, where would our good friend and father of the king currently be staying?"

You are getting soft, Cassen, he mused lightly.

⋘⋙

Cassen had his hand in one of his silken folds, caressing his trophy. The very pocket that had kept hidden items of monumental consequence—slips of paper that could have resulted in Cassen's impalement had they escaped—suddenly seemed inadequate to ensure the safekeeping of the cloth he now fondled. He checked on it regularly to be certain it remained.

The smell of stale water, rust, and excrement was thick in this section of the dungeon, but Cassen ignored it, remembering instead the scent of the woman from whom he had stolen the soft kerchief. The smoothness of the fabric reminded him of her skin. How was it that she had retained such grace over the years, and yet his outward appearance had degraded so visibly? He had been a rather handsome man, he thought...before he'd begun altering his appearance to this thing of his invention. The skin around his abdomen had lost the will to remain firm, hidden under so many folds of silk for so long. But not hers. Her skin was as taut and smooth as any maiden's. It was almost shameful that he should have to handle her so roughly while forcing her to comply, for fear of marring its beauty.

A constant dripping echoed in the lengthy halls of these all-but-empty dungeons. Those few occupants were quiet little mice, staying hidden in their corners as Cassen passed, afraid he'd come to torture them he guessed. The sound itself was torturous—an incessant "splash, splash...splash" that was neither in perfect rhythm nor out of rhythm enough to be truly irregular. He tried to focus instead on the memory of the beautiful sounds made by his Crella but found it was no easy task. What sounds did she make that were pleasant? *What sounds does any woman make that are pleasant?* he wondered as if to imply there were none. But he knew that was not the case. Many of his lady servants had endearing qualities, and plenty of those were their gentle laughs, giggles, and sighs, though none were made while his presence was known. *What did Crella's laughter sound like? Her sighs?* Cassen shook his head in disgust. *Why is it I should care?*

He reminded himself again of the purpose of this trip. Alther. That miserable man who had been gifted—and thus had stolen—that which belonged to Cassen. To think of the man as merely ignorant would be an injustice to those born simple. He was fool beyond compare. Proof of that was the ease with which Cassen had manipulated him into killing his own father. Alther was deserving of the punishment Cassen would soon bestow upon him. What sort of imbecile would seek to incapacitate a king to reverse a ruling? Lyell would have seen through the ploy and punished both Alther and Crella far worse after regaining his health. That Alther had gone through with it was inconceivable, really.

Naïve girls did not bother Cassen so much. They were born into shelter and protected from the brutal realities of the realm. But Alther was no little girl and could not thus avail himself of such an excuse. He had been witness to the way in which things worked in war, in business, and in politics—not that there was much disparity between the three. And yet he remained hopelessly oblivious, far worse than some obtuse princess who at least knew—on some level—that she was living a life of sweet lies.

That notwithstanding, Alther had handed Cassen one of his most bitter failures when he'd refused to be seduced. In spite of what was said of Shal'sezar, the man ran an impressive enterprise, especially so in his variety of stock. Cassen had seen to the selection of the women himself, ensuring their features ran the full gamut of qualities that attracted men. He himself had found them most tempting, to say the least. But none had succeeded in enticing Alther to exchange more than a few words with them. The implication was obvious: Alther was receiving, or taking by force, all that he desired at his own estate. In spitefulness Cassen had resorted to sending a woman, with a swollen belly or infant at her breast, to Alther's door once every few months, when only Crella would be home to receive them. But none had reported achieving more than provoking looks of disgust from Crella, who insisted they must be mistaken before sending them off. Cassen's failure had sickened him then and it sickened him now, and he was unable to decide which would have been worse: Alther invoking a Husband's Right, or Crella having actually grown to enjoy his company.

Cassen stroked the kerchief and felt himself calming. *To see the look upon your face when I give you this trophy, to see your realization of all that I have taken—it will be sweeter than even the taking itself.* Cassen felt a twinge of worry at the prospect that Alther might not be aware of the kerchief Crella kept nestled beside her breast. He brushed the thought from his mind, however. *All those years of marriage—he will know, or I will make him know.* Like the kerchiefs of most noble ladies, it had upon it a unique design that was hers alone. It would not do for a lady to have her kerchief mixed up with another's, after all.

It was not a long walk to where Alther was imprisoned, and Cassen found he was only paces away.

"Who is there?" Then, after a brief pause, "Please, any news of the kingdom?"

Alther must have heard his footsteps. Cassen was usually more cautious in his approach, but he had been lost in thought.

Cassen stopped before coming into Alther's view. He did not answer.

"Please, I must know. Any news of the princess? Crella—is she safe? Who sits the throne? Has there been fighting?"

Cassen heard the desperation in Alther's voice. He dropped all the feminine pretenses of his own and spoke. "There is no fighting, but a fool now sits the throne."

"A fool?" asked Alther sounding of disbelief. "Who is it then? Surely Cassen has taken the throne for himself. He is no fool, but I will kill him. I swear to you on my life—I will kill that vile man for what he has done to me."

Cassen sighed. Unrestrained by theatrics the action actually brought some tranquility. "I do not believe you are in the position to make such oaths."

"Who are you?" Alther demanded. "Show yourself!"

"Oh my, you have become quite brazen now that you have killed a king. A pity it was so late in life."

"I did not kill the king," Alther shouted. "I was tricked by that foul creature Cassen. It was meant to be a poison to merely sicken the man."

It was shameful that Alther had not devised a more believable story by now. All this time alone in a dungeon and all he could think to come up with was the truth. How had the truth served Alther all these years? And still he did not learn.

"I believe you," Cassen told him. "But I am afraid I am the only one who ever will."

"What?" The hopeful panic in Alther's voice almost turned Cassen's stomach. "Please, you must help me. You must tell others. Cassen has sought the throne all this time. It was he who tricked me, and he who had the most to gain."

"But it is not he who sits the throne. You are right, he is no fool. It is none other than your beloved boy. *Stephon* is king." *And a fine king he will surely prove to be.*

"Stephon was released? How?"

Cassen finally walked into view and studied the face of his victim. Alther's expression was that of stunned skepticism, but it only took him a moment before he lunged forward with all his force, sending one arm as far through the bars as possible to grab at him. Cassen avoided the hand with a rearward step, and watched as Alther clawed at the air.

"You miserable heathen bastard," Alther screamed. "I will kill you if I ever leave this cell!"

"Oh, no doubt, you would try. All the more reason to leave you within it. And heathenism is actually a rather—"

"Why?" Alther cried out, interrupting him. It was perhaps the most forlorn and pathetic thing Cassen had ever heard. "Why did you not just kill us both? You could have given me a fake antidote. What purpose is there in my living?" He had stopped grabbing at Cassen and collapsed backward onto the floor where he sat with his head in his hands.

It was at least a reasonable question. Cassen had considered letting Alther die, as it would have simplified things. *I had a very good reason, as you will soon see.* Cassen rubbed Crella's kerchief between his fingers. He felt a pang at the thought of leaving it with Alther, but he knew he could not simply show it to him and keep it. That would indicate weakness.

"Tell me, Alther, what is it that you cherish most in life?"

Cassen had no reason to believe Alther would cooperate in this game other than for the fact that boredom was like to be a more vile tormenter in this place than Cassen himself.

It took Alther a long time to respond, and Cassen waited patiently. But his patience was not rewarded with an answer.

"So you are a man, after all? And not even a eunuch, I'd wager. You tricked Calder—and everyone else."

Alther came to this conclusion faster than Cassen would have guessed, forcing him to wonder how much of Alther's inability to govern came merely from his utter lack of deviousness rather than gross stupidity. In either case, Cassen supposed the order of the revelations would make no huge difference. "How very perceptive of you. And to think I did not even have to drop my silks and show you."

"Everyone assumed Calder had. He was a horrid man with evil in his eyes. I could tell as much just from seeing him once or twice. Crella will not even speak of him. It is as if he never existed to her." He paused. "I fear what she may have suffered under his care."

Cassen was a bit taken aback by both Alther's candor and continued perceptiveness, and as such, declined to respond.

"You were there. You lived with them. Tell me what I fear happened did not occur."

Cassen hesitated for some time before speaking, searching his mind for any reason to not reveal his knowledge to Alther. How nice it would be to finally be recognized by someone who might appreciate the courage required to do what Cassen had done.

"I killed him for it," Cassen said.

Alther, who until now had been pathetic but at least dry eyed, began to weep silently. Cassen watched him cry, still hiding his face with his hands, and wondered why it was that he could not yet take glee in his suffering. He hated Alther more than any other. *This is the undeserving man to whom Crella was gifted, used, and unappreciated*, he reminded himself.

"Thank you," Alther said quietly after steadying himself.

The words almost made no sense to Cassen.

"Though he deserved far worse," Alther continued. "Crella has suffered more than any understand. She is not the monster she seems. She shrouds herself in effrontery for protection, but she is not that which she portrays. I tried to protect her and to show her she was safe. But who was I but the son of the man who conquered her people, a constant reminder of the man whose clutches her aunt killed herself to avoid. And to think my father locked her away in the very place from which her aunt had jumped."

Cassen had nothing to say while watching the tormented man. This was what he had come here to witness.

"And Ethel? She is the result? Crella was not the type to have become pregnant at so young an age otherwise. That appalling man. Thank the Mountain for crushing him before Ethel's birth."

It was I who crushed him, not your feckless mountain god. But the thought had no weight to it.

"Please, see that they are not harmed. I will die in here—that much I know. I will not speak another word against you, not that it matters as none would believe me. But in truth, I will hold you in higher esteem than I hold myself if you do this one thing—not for me—but for two innocents who have known nothing but derision and contempt. I see how your lady servants look to you, and I know you have never mistreated them. They would not act as they do toward you otherwise. You are a father to them. They may not be your daughters by blood, but you would not let harm befall them, nor would you cause it yourself. I only wish my father had shown the same respect for Ethel." Alther rubbed the skin on his forehead with increasing violence. "That pig of a man deserved to die for his behavior. To court one's granddaughter, even if only by marriage…it was an atrocity."

But I do let harm befall my daughters, thought Cassen. *I encourage it. And that is why I stand here and you are confined.*

"My father's death was the only thing that would see Crella freed. I realize that now. I thank you for tricking me into being braver than I truly am. Please, do as I could not. See that Ethel and Crella are cared for, in order that they do not suffer under what is to come for this kingdom—likely nothing but war and bloodshed."

Alther looked at him now. With the exception of Sacarat, Cassen had not been looked upon by another man without seeing the disgust and repulsion present in their eyes. But whereas the Satyr looked at Cassen as an equal, Alther looked at Cassen for what he truly believed himself to be—a man who held the power to do all that he pleased. Alther pleaded to him as a beggar pleads to a king, and something about it revolted Cassen beyond explanation.

Without saying another word Cassen turned and walked away. Alther at least did not degrade himself further by attempting to call out to Cassen any last pleas. *You pathetic, groveling man,* thought Cassen nonetheless.

After Cassen had walked a good distance, he realized he had his hand in his silks where Crella's kerchief still lay. His intention of revealing to Alther that Crella was now his toy had not exactly gone as he'd planned. He fought back the swell of self-accusation as he felt the soft fabric between his fingers and imagined how lovely it must still smell—a scent somewhere between citrus and the onset of autumn, yet impossible to fully discern. *I simply did not wish to part with my token of conquest so soon,* he promised himself. *That is all.*

DECKER

It seemed their entire clan had gathered in the tiny bedroom, awaiting what was known to come. Soon Titon son of Titon would return to life. Soon everyone would see that Decker had not murdered his only brother.

Decker stood at Titon's bedside. Thick white sheets covered his brother. Though no giant to begin with, Titon had come to look scarily weak and sallow during his many days asleep. *We will hunt for tree rats and make another stew of them with tinder berries,* Decker told him without speaking. *We will eat until we nearly burst, and you will regain your strength quickly. I promise.*

He did not believe his sleeping brother could hear his thoughts the way his mother could, but it did no harm. And he must think of things to say in order to keep Titon from hating him. Decker was determined to do everything in his power to ensure he recovered fully, bearing no scars of the wrong that was done him.

Decker had come to recognize what must have driven Titon into his rage; she stood opposite him at the bedside. Even so, Decker hoped his brother would see Red first. It would not do to have him awaken to the sight of the one who had put him into his coma. It was a sickening realization, though, that this would not be the only time Titon had awakened to see her sad, beautiful face after having first been knocked unconscious by Decker. *What sort of man am I? How can I ever be forgiven?* Decker merely hoped that Titon rose healthy this time as he did the last, but without the humiliation that had followed it. It turned Decker's stomach to remember.

Titon's eyelids began to quiver as if struggling to part. Decker imagined the difficulty one must have opening their eyes after so long a sleep. Sometimes he would have to rub his eyes just to speed up the process of rising with the Dawnstar. *Why are you not doing the same? Are you unable to move your arms? If I have caused you a waking sleep I will throw myself from a cliff in shame—but not before ending yours, I swear that to you, brother.*

It was hard to imagine a crueler fate to be suffered by a warrior: to be alive and aware but unable to move the limbs. It was not something Galatai liked to discuss or imagine, and thus none had spoken of it when it came to Titon. Those who suffered such a sickness begged for death from the onset, though no man desired to be the one to have to fulfill that wish. The job often fell to their father. *I will do it, and I will not delay*, thought Decker determinedly.

Growing impatient, Decker glanced at Red. It was a mistake. Seeing her—truly seeing her—for perhaps the first time stirred a slavering desire to devour her. The unrivaled beauty of Kilandra seemed a distant memory. The urge to climb over the bed and have her overwhelmed him, but he would not. *Out of respect for my brother*, he told himself, but he knew it to be false. It was out of fear. The look of shame she would crush him with was all that kept him from acting on his lust. Scorn from such an enchantress would reduce even his father to a quivering boy.

Stay asleep.

Decker looked around the room in a panic, fearful someone had somehow heard his thought. If his mother was near, she might have, but she was not in sight. Still, he could not shake the feeling that he had been heard, nor could he convince himself that the desire was insincere. *If he sleeps long enough, I can have her.* Decker did not have time to resolve the implications of his sudden selfishness.

Gasps from the crowd signaled Titon's activity. Decker watched as one eye finally opened, followed by the other.

Red veins crawled through the whites of Titon's eyes so thick that there was hardly any white left within them. Even the dark blue of his irises seemed to have turned purple. Titon's eyes rolled slowly away from Decker, allowing him to breathe a sigh of relief. They went to Red, but as they fixed on her they did not soften. The bulging veins seemed to come alive with anger and writhe within their spherical prisons.

It was he that heard me.

Titon's eyes turned with a sudden fury, locking upon Decker, and while he had looked angry with Red, Titon now also showed the hurt of a brother betrayed. Decker tried to speak, finding it impossible to force out any words. As Titon's eyes grew wider and he shrunk backward into his pillow, Decker attempted to gesture with his hands that he meant him no harm, but the hands he raised were curled into fists. Titon squirmed in his bed and grasped for something at his side, a knife. With all his force, Decker tried to back away, but his efforts were in vain. There were too many people gathered, all so eager to see Titon's awakening, and they pushed him closer to the bedside—closer to the hand that held the blade.

The knifepoint turned toward him and began creeping toward his guts. *This time I will let him stab me*, thought Decker, attempting to be still, but as the sharp tip made contact with his shirt his hands did not obey. He lashed out at his brother, hammering him with three blows. Decker heard their mother cry out in sobbing desperation somewhere in the back. Titon was not stopped, however, and the knife pierced Decker's shirt and began to press into his skin, threatening to break through. Decker hit him harder, again three times. The sound of the successive impacts of his fists against his brother's face was awful—a palpable "thwack, thwack, thwack" as if he were beating a corpse. But the knife kept pressing, splitting his skin and about to disembowel him. Decker panicked and hit his brother again, holding nothing back. The "thwack, thwack, thwack" was so loud it reverberated in his ears. Then he heard the booming voice of another Titon call out his name.

"What sort of coward attacks his helpless brother as he sleeps?" His father held his mighty axe—the axe that Decker had seen take the heads of those in their clan who had been condemned to die for unforgivable actions. And now he was one of them, and his father's axe swung down to remove his own head. With a face bent in rage, his father's mouth opened wide and screeched, "Ahht, ahht, ahhhht!"

⊷⊶

"Ahht, ahht, ahhhht!"

Decker jolted upright and opened his eyes as wide as he could, willing them to adjust. His heart raced, and he was further unsettled when he did not recognize his surroundings.

"Ahht, ahht, ahhhht!"

He breathed deeply as his senses returned and placed his hands upon his face. He did not remember much of what he had dreamt, only that he was glad to now be awake. He was in Kilandra's home—or was it still Keethro's? His hands continued up his face, stretching his skin and finally running through his long, tangled hair. In either case, he had been sleeping in Kilandra's bed. He confirmed as much by looking to his right to see her still sleeping beside him. Her coverings were thick, but he could still make out her form beneath. It was enough for him to want to wake her with an assault—one she would no doubt enjoy. He had learned quickly that she wished to be pushed rather than lead…contrary to what one may have guessed given her extreme confidence and sensuality. And she wished to be pushed much further than most. It had worked out well, as Decker would not be led in such things—no matter how lovely the leader.

He would have indulged in the act if not for the foul mood his dreams had placed him in. And that damn jay was making itself known far too early as well. Kilandra had no trouble sleeping through the racket, but he had been woken by it nearly every day of the past week. He was also starved near to death.

"Ahht, ahht, ahhhht!"

The River drown you, damn bird! He reached for the mug filled with wine. Chilled by the cold of the winter morning, it was actually quite refreshing.

He swished it around in his mouth for a while and swallowed it down.

Rolling out of bed and standing to stretch, he found he erected quite a fort in his underclothes thanks to the Dawnstar's calling. He looked once again at the graceful shape made by her body under the coverings and sucked at his upper lip. *Another time. Soon though*, he promised himself.

Like most of the homes of their clansmen, this home had a large root cellar outdoors and a smaller one that could be accessed while still indoors. Decker planned to break his fast on some cheese and eggs, both of which had caught his eye in the small cellar the previous night when he'd fetched the wine. He put on a shirt to help stave off the cold and closed the door behind him, softly as to not wake his sleeping paramour.

The wood beneath his bare feet nipped at him, reminding him that he should have put on some socks, but he was too hungry now. He made his way to the main room where the iron-topped stove resided, but did not feel as much heat coming from it as he'd hoped.

"Dammit, Red," he muttered under his breath. She should have placed more wood inside when she returned home last night. The girl had become a true nuisance to him. As would be expected, he did not feel comfortable in the presence of both her and her mother, and in fairness, he did not find himself comfortable in Red's presence even when the two were alone, given how he could not look upon her without being reminded of his brother. He was already accustomed to avoiding the girl. He'd done no different in the past, rejecting every request from her friends for him to pursue her in order to avoid tormenting Titon. *A whole lot of good it had done.* He wished he never had to see her again, but given the circumstances, that was not likely.

There was still a bit of coal with embers, and it was not long before the several logs he placed inside were surrounded by flames. He put his hand over the skillet that sat atop the stove. It would soon be suitably warm to cook his eggs, and he made his way toward the cellar.

The front door burst open, causing Decker to ready himself for battle out of instinct, but it was merely Red. He did not know where she had been and did not really care, but she had an urgency about her that let him know he would soon find out. Before she spoke, her eyes went downward and darted up again to meet his own. He did not need to look down himself to realize that the Dawnstar still beckoned. He hoped his scraggy beard might hide the majority of his newfound color.

Red spoke quickly, ignoring the embarrassment of the situation. "It's Titon. He is awake and well." She was dressed in heavy furs suitable for walking in the frigid temperatures of the northern winter. They may have hidden her body, but they did not succeed in covering the youth and beauty of her face, now framed with dark hair showing only glimmers of crimson. Despite her somewhat cheerful voice, she wore a troubled expression. "But... Just come and see."

Decker dressed as quickly as he could and met her outside. During the short walk to where Titon stayed, Red was reluctant to speak.

"How is it that you were with him so early? Is that where you have been staying?"

Red took long enough to answer, and did so only with a nod. She seemed uncomfortable around him as well, which he supposed was rather understandable. It did not soften his feelings toward her, however. *Perhaps you should simply stay away from him. You have caused enough harm as it is.*

It did not take them long to reach their destination, though the thick snow on the ground fought their every step. Upon entering the home, Decker had a sickening feeling in his gut. It felt as though he'd been here more recently than he had, and the air tasted of disease.

Relief flooded him when he saw Titon awake and sitting up in bed, his lower body covered by grey sheets that gave Decker unexplained comfort. With the exception of some darkness underneath, Titon's blue eyes looked alert and healthy, accented only by their distinctive flecks of silver.

"Maybe you should wait outside," he told Red. It was not a request.

"The healer says it is best for him to see everyone that he knew," she started, "…but I will wait outside for now."

He knew? Red's words made him wonder, but Decker made his way to the side of the bed.

"How are you, brother?"

Titon frowned at him, not in anger, but confusion. "Brother?" Titon turned to the healer. "This one is my brother?"

The healer nodded to him, then spoke to Decker. "He has lost most of his memories. He does not yet remember his name or anyone who has come to see him since he has woken. Though it has only been you and the girl so far."

Decker moved his attention to the healer. It was difficult to see his brother looking so bewildered. Titon was the one who had an answer for every question, a solution to every problem. That Red had told him Titon was well already had Decker feverish. "How long until his memories return?" he demanded.

"There is no way to tell," said the old man. "It could be a few days or they may never return. All we can do now is speak to him about his past and hope he remembers by and by."

Decker gnashed his teeth and looked once again at Titon. Not only did his brother look upon him as though he was a stranger, but Titon's vacant, befuddled stare now made him look to be one as well.

"You lied to me," Decker growled at Red as he stormed out of the room.

"What? He is awake and the healer says—"

"He is not *well*," he yelled at her with all his rage. She deserved it. She had caused this. She had been the problem ever since they were young. She stole Titon's confidence, and she had forced Decker to steal his mind, his memories, and everything that he was. "And he is *not* my brother!"

❦

"Pack your belongings," Decker ordered Kilandra as he burst into the bedroom. He had with him his own bag of things. He had already said his goodbyes to his mother. If things went his way, he would not be gone for long, nor would he return for long before again heading out.

"What is going on? Is there something wrong?" Kilandra sat up in the bed, covering herself with the blanket. For a woman who dressed so scantily, she was modest with her nudity in casual settings, and it was successful in its intended effect of making him want her more.

"Someone must take charge and unite the clans—is not that what you always have said? The time has come."

"What is it you intend to do?"

"Pack your things. We can discuss it on the way."

"On the way where?"

"East, north, west, south, and then east again. The longer we delay the more like we are to be caught in a blizzard. I wish to leave well before noon. We should be in Joarr's territory in time to eat our second meal." Decker already grew impatient with her questioning him. "He is a good friend to my father. He will join me and others will follow."

Kilandra looked at him with disbelief. "And you expect me to have packed everything I need within an hour?"

"No, I expect you to have packed enough of what you need within the lesser half of an hour. Now hurry."

"What about Red?"

"Red will be fine on her own. She is not coming with us."

"This is absurd—"

Decker slammed his fist through the side of her tall clothes chest. "Yes," he yelled at her. "It *is*! But I remind you again, this was *your* plan. If there is a man to do such a thing it is me and no other. The only question that remains is whether it will be you or perhaps some other woman by my side as I do it. Now pack your things and meet me outside in no more than half an hour. I have some things that must be dealt with before I leave."

With that, Decker left her looking stunned, bitter, and above all beautiful with her coverings still clutched to her naked chest. *If we had more time I would have given her a more convincing argument*, he thought. But she would do as he said, he was quite sure of it. And he would finally be rid of Red as well. Together they would unite the clans during the winter and march south in the spring—to what end he did not know as this plan was not truly his own. But he would have glory or he would have death. He had no choice now. Living a common life was no longer an option with his brother lost. *I will bring destruction to the South to lessen that which I have brought my home. I will conquer their lands—just as he wished—in honor of my dead brother, who would have known far better how to do it.*

KEETHRO

Half of the men Keethro and Titon had entered the arena with immediately took flight. Some of them did not see or simply ignored the weapons, but the majority snatched whatever sword or mace was most readily available. Whether they wished to attempt to reach the dragons before they had reloaded or merely to more quickly end their anxiety, Keethro could not tell. He only knew that in spite of being hardened by war, even his own anxiousness was nearly unbearable. "We all feel a crippling fear when faced with death," Titon used to say to his warriors prior to a battle against a fellow clan. "But fear is like a beautiful woman. Cower from it, and it will know you to be unworthy. Embrace it with confidence, and you will become its master." Fine words to rally your troops, Keethro had always thought, but he did not believe Titon to have ever truly been afraid.

Two men took a different tack and bolted back toward the open arena doors, but the guards were ready for them. One caught a spear through the eye and the other was impaled in the abdomen. The guards took turns spitting on the still-living coward as he squirmed and screamed, and the audience close enough to have seen laughed at the man's agony.

Keethro turned his attention to Titon, who walked at his usual pace to the racks of weaponry and selected a large metal-faced shield not unlike the one that had been fixed to the boar.

"You're sure you want that slowing you down? You saw what those arrows did to it." Keethro did not expect his words to change Titon's mind.

"Trust me," he said and handed Keethro a small axe suitable for throwing.

A svelte man with a tan complexion led the charge downfield, far ahead of the others. Red strips of cloth tied above his biceps streamed behind him as he ran. He'd snatched a sword not unlike his own frame, thin and gracefully curved, and it gleamed as it caught the Dawnstar's ample rays. Well behind him was the giant, lumbering forward without a weapon. He had three others close on his heels, and they seemed determined to keep the big one between themselves and the fire-spitting dragons. A final man lagged behind that group, his light skin and long hair of bright blonde making him stand out more than any. In each hand he had a longsword, both of which he occasionally swung around with exceptional deftness. Keethro realized the man's display was not for show, but rather for familiarizing himself with the weapons. *I will have to keep an eye on that one, should they make us eventually fight each other,* thought Keethro. He purposefully turned his mind from the prospect of having to face Titon.

The svelte man had nearly crossed half the field by the time the next arrow was launched. He must have had a good view of the men firing the contraptions as he anticipated the shot and dropped to his stomach. The arrow flew over his head, nearly touching his long dark hair that trailed out behind him. A second arrow flew, aimed at a far larger target. It struck the giant high in the chest, going through him to impale two of his followers, and ripped the arm off the third at the shoulder. The three impaled men fell backward and lay motionless while the fourth ran in circles, screaming and fountaining blood from his wound.

Keethro realized he had been paying too much attention to the field and not enough to his selection of weapons, but Titon had for him two more small axes.

"We move," said Titon as he hefted his shield onto one arm and tested his grip on its straps, then lifting a two-handed axe in his opposite fist.

Keethro was ready to break into a run, but Titon began jogging downfield with his shield in front of him. Keethro followed, and the final person from their group, a sturdy-built middle-aged man, did the same. He had selected a spiked buckler and longsword for his weaponry and held them as if he might know how to use them.

The svelte one on his belly had not yet risen. Keethro suspected he had hoped all four dragons would have fired at once, allowing him to close the remaining distance before they could reload. The remaining two refused to fire, however, and he too refused to move from his relatively safe position. The impasse gave Keethro, Titon, and their assumed ally time to make up some distance on the field.

They had made it a little more than a quarter of the way downfield by the time all four dragons were again ready to strike. With the two yet to fire still trained on the unmoving man, the other two were free to fire on the remaining targets. One fired at the frantic man with one arm and missed. *A foolish mistake,* thought Keethro, as there was no need to waste shots on a man who was of no danger. But it showed their enemy to be supremely confident that their victory was assured, which in itself was disheartening.

The other dragon launched an arrow at the blonde-haired warrior who was now midfield. The man dodged right with blinding speed, but the arrow clipped one of his swords and ripped it from his hand, forcing him to stop and retrieve it with caution. The two dragons aimed at the prone man both fired as he began to slither forward like a snake. One arrow went high, and the other went low, first hitting the ground, then bouncing over his head.

"Faster," said Titon. They still did not run, but their speed considerably improved. Their companion followed in kind.

The svelte man leapt from the ground and charged at full speed toward the dragons and their keepers. One was quick to reload, however, and fired. He twisted his body and spun to the side, nearly successful in his attempt, but the arrow's tip made contact with his waist and cut him deeply. Blood poured from the man, but no entrails had spilled. His charge continued, accompanied with a scream of defiance. He managed to come within a few paces of the dragons when an arrow flew clean through his right breast, silencing him and sending him to his back.

Keethro felt his heart thumping, but he was not winded. They'd come to within a hundred paces of the blonde-haired warrior who was himself now a mere hundred paces from the dragons. His mane danced behind him as he moved with increasing speed. One fired, missing him completely. It puzzled Keethro until he glanced behind to where the arrow had landed and saw the one-armed man had been killed. *What gall*, he thought, but he then saw the source of their confidence.

Four warhorses galloped through the far doors, prompting the man who had been running with Keethro and Titon to stop midfield by one of the fences. *A strange man who fears horses but not dragons*, thought Keethro.

Three of the horses rode past the fiery contraptions, their riders each carrying a massive ball and chain. The horses were covered in black armor that glistened as if wet, and the men atop were armored in kind, looking like greedy reapers. The effect was lost only somewhat as the fourth horse reared, frightened perhaps by the flames, and began trampling the nearest dragon's crew with its unseated rider still caught in a stirrup.

The weapons of the horsemen may have been daunting, but Keethro soon noticed their long chains made them ill suited for joint attacks. The third horseman was forced to break from the other two as they charged the dual-wielding warrior from either side. The warrior dove and rolled at just the right moment toward one of the horses, avoiding the spiked balls of death while managing to slice the exposed ankle of one of the beasts. The horse fell forward, digging a trench in the hard-packed sand with its body.

The horseman that broke away came at Keethro and Titon. With the best-balanced of his axes in hand, Keethro stopped to throw. When the rider was at twenty paces he sent the axe with all his force, and it flew through the air with enough rancor to split steel. The axe blade found the vertical slit in the man's helmet and forced its way through. His body went limp and fell backward on the horse as it galloped past.

When the single remaining horseman circled for a second attack on the blonde-haired warrior, Keethro made a silent wager that the rider would be the one to die. But before the two made contact, fire leapt forth from one of the dragons. The arrow caught the warrior in the lower back and passed through, just barely missing the horseman, who then stopped and began cursing at the dragon's keepers. Keethro took the opportunity to better their odds and heaved his axe. He watched as it curved through the air, an impressive distance even for a man without an injured wrist. The axe head glanced off the side of the man's helmet and buried into the neck of the horse. The animal whinnied and rose high on its hind legs, causing the rider to slip. The horse then collapsed lifeless to its side, completely crushing its rider in the process.

Titon continued forward and reached the horse that the blonde warrior had maimed, motioning for Keethro to catch up. *Good, a living shield*, thought Keethro as he sprinted to oblige. The horse's front legs were both badly broken. Red-stained bones protruded as it pushed through the sand, trying frantically to right itself. With one slice from his mighty axe, Titon took the head off the unconscious rider, and with another, Titon brought an end to the horse's suffering, eliciting a collective gasp from the audience.

Titon slammed the side of his axe against his mammoth shield as if to provoke the three dragons that remained, and the crowd broke again into cheer. It made little difference to Keethro that they may now have the crowd on their side. *It will not change how this ends.*

Keethro caught up to Titon and remained behind him. They now had fewer than a hundred paces between them and the dragons. A glance to the rear revealed the thick swordsman farther behind—again moving forward, albeit slightly crouched as if to jump and roll at any moment.

As close as they now were, Keethro could tell exactly what the men were doing with their arrow-hurling contraptions. The devices themselves looked to be enormous bows placed on their sides and mounted upon wheels. With the exception of the dragon farthest left which had acquired two extra crew from the broken dragon, three men in light armor worked each device. One readied the arrows, one tensioned the bow with a lever, and the third aimed and fired. Keethro was sickened to see all three dragons were now ready to fire, two of which pointed at him and Titon, the other at the lagging swordsman.

"Stand tall and thin," Titon instructed as he himself turned to his side, crossing one leg in front of the other while continuing his sidelong advance. Keethro stayed behind him and did the same, though he saw no point in trying to make themselves smaller targets. *The machines skewered a pig at over three hundred paces. They will have no difficulty hitting the side of a giant soon to be at fifty.*

The swordsman behind them must have felt the same and broke into a sprint, not straight forward, but alternating diagonally left and right. A deep "thwunk" sounded as the dragon aimed at him fired. Keethro watched out of the corner of his eye as the flaming bolt caught the spike of the man's buckler held to the side. The impact spun him—so violently that he slammed into the ground and began the horrid, moaning inhalations of the unconscious and gravely injured.

Titon continued his methodical advance as they closed to fifty paces. The five men of the recently fired dragon yelled at each other while frantically struggling to re-arm their machine—their extra members seeming only to add to their hysteria.

"They will not miss," Keethro said to Titon.

"I am hoping they do not."

He's lost all sense. But Keethro saw no better option than to trust him. He supposed it would not be so bad to die upon the same dragon arrow that impaled the mighty Titon.

The dreaded sound of the dragon's release was heard. Keethro braced himself for death as he watched the trail of flame scream toward them. The tip of the arrow that should have punctured Titon's shield instead scraped against the surface with a spray of sparks. Titon had angled the face sharply, deflecting the arrow's glancing blow, but the force of impact was so great that it smashed his shield into his body and staggered him. The crowd erupted into a frenzy of ovation, but there was no time to celebrate. Keethro saw the fearful determination of the crew of the only dragon ready to fire. He also saw what they were planning.

"They are aiming—"

He did not have time to finish. Titon squatted just as the machine fired low. The impact with his shield was similar to the previous one, though this time it knocked him to his ass. The arrow deflected downward into the ground, spraying clumps of sand into Keethro's eyes as he remained standing and dumbfounded. Titon righted himself, threw down both his shield and heavy axe, and charged, letting out a war cry so fierce that each of the eleven men manning the dragons visibly balked.

Keethro wasted no time. He sprinted as well, blinking his eyes free of grit. His target was the five-man crew that was closest to being ready to fire another arrow. Despite their extra members, they had neglected to light the tip of their projectile, and the less-impressive arrow was placed into the waiting machine, ready to be fired. Keethro let his final axe fly at the man responsible for aiming the wooden beast. The axe handle slammed the intended target on the top of the head, dazing him. The other men fought to fire the weapon, but with the semi-lucid man vying to do the same, they botched the attack, firing with the machine pointed at an awkward angle and missed completely. Keethro only had a moment to congratulate himself for achieving such a throw while half-blinded and running at full speed. He turned his attention to the next group of men who were trying to finish loading, but Titon was already on top of them as they fumbled with the heavy arrow.

Keethro jumped over the machine that last fired, and its crew scattered and ran—only to find that the giant doors behind them had been closed after the crazed warhorse had run back inside with rider still in tow. He grabbed the first man he could, who shrieked—not unlike a Dogman—as Keethro grappled with him to remove his helmet, then used it to cave in his head. Titon launched an assault on the other men and managed to grab two at once. With one in each hand, he raised them in the air by their throats, choking them until their windpipes caved. Keethro continued to give chase to the men one by one, still using the helmet to end them, while Titon had decided to use a giant dragon arrow as a spear.

The only ones screaming more loudly than the men they killed were those in the stands. The sound was like nothing Keethro had heard before, and knowing that it was in celebration of his victory felt not much different than when he was with a woman. To have gone from almost certain death—a death that was so eagerly anticipated and cheered for by a horde of bloodthirsty strangers—to winning the support of those very masses that had craved his humiliating defeat... It was something that even the thrill of victory in a battle against incredible odds simply could not compare.

Three men had managed to escape the lower ground between the dragons and the doors and ran to midfield. Keethro expected them to arm themselves with the weapons that had been dropped, but they did no such thing. They merely continued to run, and Keethro spat in the dirt in disgust. "Titon," he called. "Over here."

Titon finished his kill by cranking the neck of a man under his arm so savagely that his head would have surely come off if not for the unbroken skin. He came to Keethro and appeared delighted when he saw what he had in mind.

"I watched them do it. You arm it like this." Keethro demonstrated on one of the machines and Titon quickly followed suit on another. The spearmen on the other side of the field must have remained, not allowing the dragons' keepers to escape into the safety of the lower ground. It took Keethro and Titon some time to impale all three men—eight shots in total—and it was as enjoyable for them as it must have been for the onlookers who celebrated each success.

The cheers slowly morphed into a chant. It was difficult to make out what they said as it echoed and reverberated, but Keethro soon heard it clear.

"Northman! Northman! Northman!" sounded the chant of countless voices. *It is not Northmen they say, it is Northman.* But Keethro was not about to pity himself. It was good just to be alive, and more importantly, to have been with Titon as he achieved his glory. *You deserve it, my friend.*

The chanting stopped with a suddenness that foreboded danger, and Keethro scanned the inner arena for the coming foe. Neither pair of great doors had opened, however, and a look toward the sky revealed no flying menace. In the lowest seats of the midfield, however, a single man draped in a large cape stood—a different one than had done the earlier announcing. With a single raised finger, this ruling man had brought the entire arena to silence, and he remained motionless, waiting for Keethro and Titon's attention. Keethro's elation was snuffed as he recalled his thoughts about the men powerful enough to create such monstrous castle walls, and he feared being crushed by such a man more now than ever.

ALTHER

Drip...drip, drip...drip, drip. That erratic sound was all that could be heard since Cassen's strange and quiet departure. He'd looked almost morose to Alther, a look that Alther might have been able to take pleasure in under other circumstances, seeing that pompous man in mourning, but certainly not after he'd just begged the man to protect his wife and daughter.

Back and forth Alther rocked on the floor—not out of some madness that had taken him, but because the motion was the best he could do to soothe his mind. And nonetheless, back and forth his mind went, replaying Cassen's words and expressions, attempting to decipher their true meaning. When that failed, Alther then resorted to assigning blame to those most responsible for this tragic state.

The dungeons had not been so quiet his entire stay, a duration that he had lost all reckoning of. Sometime before Cassen's visit a man had been dragged into a cell, screaming and fighting. The man was irate, if not gripped in full by lunacy, and he yelled endlessly for hours approaching on days. His voice filled the vaults, echoing off the wet walls and gliding with freedom through the bars of every cell, preventing Alther from being able to think or sleep. Finally, some men clad in coin purses or chainmail, probably the latter, came to silence him. How Alther missed that man, whose insanity would now be so welcome a diversion.

All that was left to do was throw names and scenarios haplessly around in his mind, none of which were any good, neither past nor present. His father and Cassen were the two that plagued him most, aside, of course, from himself. Alther could not deny that he had a hand, either in action or deliberate inaction, in every event that had led to this: a meaningless existence that would stretch for eternity in this cell. Ethel's life would be in peril just by her close association to him as her stepfather, and his wife remained imprisoned for all he knew. "The Mighty Three hate a coward, boy." It was a lesson his father had tried to drill into both him and Edwin. A lesson learned far too late, in Alther's case.

Even if Stephon did release Crella, Alther knew their angry, fickle son might send her right back to confinement once she overstepped his new authority as king. *Angry and fickle*, thought Alther. *Those words are a kindness to the boy.* How was it that he and Crella had raised such a charming young woman and such a cold, detached boy right beside her? Again, it seemed to come down to Alther's own contribution: half the boy's blood. Ethel, the product of incest, had better breeding than the one Alther had sired.

Something grabbed hold of Alther, a distant sound. A sweet, alluring aberration from the monotonous dripping. He strained to listen, cupping his hands around his ear and pressing hard against the iron bars.

There were men approaching, many men. Heavy men by the sound of it. Alther thought he could feel their steps through the ground, the vibrations traveling up the bars to tingle the ridges of his hands. It would be foolish and gravely disappointing to hope they were here for him, but perhaps they might have come at least for someone in a nearby cell, or better yet, to usher in a new arrival. Maybe the person would be housed in a cell farther down than Alther. It was yet to happen, but it would be a treat: to actually see another prisoner, to put a face to the man before he began his childlike pleas for lawful justice. It was too much to ask for, Alther knew, but he could not shake the hope that the man brought might be crazy like that other one, requiring not just jailing, but confinement in chains to a cell wall, a perch from which he would sing to Alther for a few blissful hours.

Alther's spirits lifted further as he heard pieces of some sort of disagreement brewing down the end of the long hall.

"...I assure you I had no idea... I was merely doing my job..."

The voice had worry in it...grave worry...mortal worry. But it was not the voice of a prisoner; Alther could tell that much from the sound of it. It was an older man's voice, a familiar one. Alther had heard it before and while down here, he believed. It never spoke many words, but the words had always been spoken with some level of authority or humor. Alther wished he had been more attentive when they'd first brought him here. He'd been so consumed with anguish that he had not even made note of those he passed—not prisoners, not gaolers, not guards.

"Your Grace, I beg you...for over thirty years I've served..."

Your Grace? Is the king here? Could it be Stephon?

"Your Gr—"

The man's pleas were cut short by pained grunts, but little else could be heard over the sound of moving chainmail.

The men came now, marching down the hall, bringing with them answers and more entertainment. Alther buzzed with excitement, tainted only ever so slightly with the concern that their visit could somehow worsen his current situation. It was hard to fathom.

"Your kerchief," demanded one of the men. Alther knew that voice without question.

Stephon was the first to step into view, wiping his foil clean of what could only be blood, mentioning something to one of his many followers about a scabbard of exotic leather.

To see his face was enough to crush Alther, to put him on his knees. Stephon had not always been contemptible—that realization swept Alther as he saw him. He had been no worse than any other boy in his younger years, and father and son had enjoyed their time spent together. His memories with Stephon play-fencing with wooden rapiers and building shelters in the forest gardens of Adeltia were far better than any he could remember sharing with his own father. *How had I forgotten? And has Stephon remembered as well?* It was suddenly conceivable that all Stephon had needed was the authority that he'd always craved, and after having it, could have become a fair man, if not a bit overzealous with the pursuit of his own form of justice.

"Father, I have come to free you." It was all Stephon would need say to give Alther a chance at redemption. Stephon would have his throne and Alther would have his wife and daughter. Truth be told, it would be little different than when his father yet lived—a thought that sobered Alther.

"Alther, *get up.*"

How many times Stephon had given him the command, Alther could not determine, but his son looked far from happy having to repeat himself. Alther stood and instinctively stepped back from the bars.

"How does it feel to be a prisoner?" asked Stephon.

He looked healthy in spite of his time spent imprisoned. *The boy has a certain fortitude to him,* Alther thought with pride. To know his son had endured the dungeons without withering to the decrepit, rocking man he himself had become was a relief on some level. *I should have come to visit him.* He'd had his reasons for not doing so—it would have only angered him more, it would have hurt his chances of ever being freed, and so on, but Alther always had reasons to justify his inactivity. *Now I know how much he must have craved a familiar face.*

"I know the feeling well," continued Stephon. "I spent a good many nights in such confinement. Much longer than you have…thus far."

Alther looked at the men surrounding his boy. Seven men, heavy clad in plate and mail, but no helms. Their expressions ranged from deadly serious: those who looked to be members of The Guard, to smirks: those who looked to be recently appointed Adeltian knights, and the Adeltian knights outnumbered those of The Guard.

"I am sorry, Stephon, I never meant to wrong you. Your imprisonment was your grandfather's doing. I specifically—"

"You were specifically happy enough to let me rot in a cell. Do not hide behind your father's cape. You may find it is no longer an effective tactic now that you've killed him."

"I did not mean to kill him."

Stephon snorted. "You Red Rivers are all the same. You fail to hold yourselves accountable for your actions. What you did to Lyell was cowardly, but I'd expect no different from you. You blather endlessly about justice and honor, yet you only fancy one or the other when it serves your purposes. Tell me, Alther, where was the *honor* in ravaging Adeltia? In slaughtering the men, violating the women, and throwing the queen from her tower? What crime did she commit? How was *justice* served there?"

Alther had no response, and again, it was he who was responsible. Had Crella and her aunt found him to be a worthy groom, there would have been no war. But Alther was also stunned to silence by the change in his son. This was not the slack-jawed Stephon who had been dragged down the king's study.

"But I have not come here to condemn you for your father's crimes. If there is one thing I have learned from you—one thing that I have found to be so deplorable, so vile, that I have taken note of it in you, so that I should never make the mistake of mirroring it—it is this: that there may be no worse a quality in a man than the utter passivity you possess." Stephon let his words linger for a moment. "In truth, I do not feel as though I have ever even had such a tendency within myself. I am a man of action, most *unlike* you." Stephon stepped forward and put a hand on a bar. "Which brings me to a more important issue…

"As I have already promised, I am not here to condemn you for the actions of your father. You say you never meant to wrong me. Well, I find that to be as contemptible a lie as any a man has ever spoken. And I wish for you to confess."

Alther searched the depths of his mind, something he was already well acquainted with, given his setting. Of the many things he had found to hate himself for, he had not uncovered any dishonesty toward his son. There was the time he kept the truth about the baker's son's parentage from Stephon, but surely that could not be what he spoke of.

"I honestly do not know what you want me to confess. I failed you as a father, by being so weak a man, that I admit, but I—"

"As a *father*? How can you remain so audacious from within a cell?"

Alther could only look at him, stupefied.

"You were *never* a father to me, because you are *not my father*. I've heard as much from your own mouth."

Stephon had cried out similar things before, in anger, but Alther had never thought he meant it literally. It was hard to believe he did now. This all seemed some sort of show for him to gain the respect of his Adeltian cohorts. Stephon had always preferred the ways and traditions of his mother's kingdom.

"Stephon, I know—with certainty—that you are my son. I see the best and worst of myself within you, and I blame myself—"

"I warn you," said Stephon with a raised finger. "Do not take that tone. Lies, it seems, are all you can spout. You *pity* me? The king? No. You grovel to me. You do as I say, as I command, and you hope that I do not take offense to the way in which you have done so."

Humility. The one thing his father had unintentionally taught Alther was the very thing his son lacked so thoroughly that it threatened to destroy a kingdom. Lyell had insisted the boy be trained in the Rivervalian custom—with swords of true steel, the swords that saw Alther battered and bruised as a child. In this solitary thing, Alther had refused his father with uncharacteristic courage, not wanting his son to endure the pain that he had. Stephon had been trained as an Adeltian fencer instead, learning the dances of civilized combat that resulted in little more than bruised egos, and in Stephon's case, not even that, for he was exceptional at the sport.

Looking at the smirks on the faces of the Adeltian knights—not fencers, for even Adeltians knew their military could not be composed of dancing men with weapons intended only for dueling or practice—Alther decided to take another tack.

"Have you thought this through, Stephon? If you are not my son, you have no claim to the throne. My sister, Aileana, would be the rightful heir."

Stephon laughed at him, stepping backward and spreading his hands to either side. "Look around you." He motioned toward one of the stern-looking members of The Guard. "To you, this man may look an impartial member of The Guard, a Protector of the Realm. But he is an *Adeltian* man, same as the others. Tell me, who do you think here has any impulse to follow the lineage of some murderous foreign people? Do you see any Rivervalian men in power before you?"

Alther sought the void, but it was far from grasp. "I see but one," he said. "And he is an unwitting boy I should have drowned long ago."

Stephon smirked. "Cut out his tongue. We wouldn't want him saying anything so clever at his sentencing."

TITON SON OF SMALL GRYN

The crowd remained deathly silent as the lone man stood and spoke. To Titon, the man was only significant in that he had forestalled his much deserved ovation. On its own, each voice from the stands was of no consequence, yet when combined, those meager cries joined to create a solitary behemoth of sound that was like nothing Titon had before experienced. He longed to have them chanting for him again, and the opportunity soon presented itself.

The clang of coiling chains and the rumble of the giant doors on ancient hinges filled him with hope—hope for more bloodshed and glory. He picked up a pair of the projectiles shot from the dragons. Titon had dubbed them dragon's tongues, having developed a fondness for them as he'd let them soar through the air to obliterate the last of the dragons' former masters. Leaving the dragons behind was like parting with a lover, but he and Keethro quickly put distance between themselves and the doors, not knowing what beast may come charging out.

Titon was not impressed with what he saw. A row of ten guards marched forward in formation. Like the guards who escorted them from their cell to the arena, these men too bore spears, but that was both the beginning and the end of their similarities. Golden plate, adorned in resplendent gems of blue, red, and royal purple, covered the men in an ostentatious display. Jagged spikes long as swords projected from their spaulders. Perhaps they would have looked menacing to a lesser man. To Titon they looked as though they were dressed for some sort of comical performance rather than for battle. *What kind of fool places gems upon a man's armor?* Their golden scales of plate overlapped in countless ways at the joints, allowing them to move gracefully in spite of their rigidity, but the plate itself appeared to have no real thickness to it. With a bare fist Titon could likely cave in the breastplate and the chest of one of these flimsy men whose eyes did not even hunger for battle, and he found himself growing impatient to test his theory.

"I am Titon son of Small Gryn—the *Northman*. And I am insulted by this latest challenge!"

With that, he dropped one of his dragon's tongues and grasped the other with both hands above his head. He hurled the giant arrow with all his spite at the largest of the men. As predicted, it sliced through his breastplate as if it were made of cloth, felling him backward where he struggled for a few moments before going limp. The other guards did not so much as flinch. They had not even lowered their spears, which were still planted in the ground pointing straight up. The crowd, however, burst once again into a cheer which filled Titon with the feeling of empowerment he'd craved.

Just as soon as the crowd had resumed its roars they again were silenced, and with it went Titon's elation.

"Titon," he heard Keethro growl as if angry, but Titon knew of no reason for his friend to be upset with him.

Keethro signaled with a tilted head and glance for Titon to look toward the midfield. Titon did not wish to turn from the remaining men who were close enough to throw spears of their own, but it was possible Keethro was alerting him to a more pressing threat.

There was no danger midfield, just the same solitary man in the stands, propped up by his enormous cape. This time, however, Titon heard him speak.

"Northman," he addressed Titon calmly, "the men before you are not there for battle but as an escort to your royal quarters. You have proven yourself to be a great warrior—a warrior that could no doubt benefit this kingdom. I will speak with you and your friend on the matter when the Dawnstar rises on the morrow. In witness of the Mighty Three, you have my word no harm shall befall you."

The man spoke so solemnly that it was difficult to believe he could be heard at such a distance in this setting. Yet the crowd remained deathly quiet when he spoke, and despite the weight of his words, the wind seemed to carry them dutifully out of reverence for the speaker.

The nine remaining guards flipped their spears and jabbed them into the ground each at their right heel, signifying they had no intent of using them.

The man had mentioned Titon's own gods. Titon had not expected nor even considered the fact that these southern strangers may worship the same gods as he, and he feared it may be some trick. The Dogmen certainly did not worship the Mighty Three. They had books that made mention, but as best he could tell, the Dogmen had some odd beliefs with no named gods among them.

Titon looked toward Keethro who nodded his desire to comply with the man's request. Wondering what treasures this leader of a kingdom might bestow upon them for their services, Titon remembered their purpose for having traveled south in the first place. *How is it that I am so easily distracted by glory when my wife requires a remedy?*

Titon nodded his head deeply with respect to the standing man. He did not wish to comply, but he saw no better alternative.

❦

Titon and Keethro ate well that night. The caped man had not lied about their quarters being royal; Titon had never seen such extravagance. The fabric that covered the table was as soft as a woman's skin, but only half as soft as the linens that covered the beds. The beds themselves were sturdy and rose far off the ground, but they lacked firmness to an extent that they were uncomfortable to lie upon. There was even some sort of plush fabric underfoot, the purpose of which was lost on Titon as it quickly became filthy from his boots. What was most remarkable, however, were the levers that when turned produced a seemingly endless flow of what tasted to be fresh water, cold as from the mountains. Titon had begun to bathe himself with the water from the small one in the kitchen when Keethro called for him to come see something.

"Look at this," Keethro marveled. He threw a lever and a fountain of warm water sprung from a hole in the ceiling.

"These people seem to have no restraint when it comes to luxury. Any man can place a barrel of water above his head and open a hole to let it shower him, but would it not be easier to simply jump in the river?"

"Perhaps, but when you have an army of servants eager to fetch barrels and it is cold outside…"

Titon saw the logic in that but wondered how weak such men must be who did not know what it was like to build a fire next to a river in the dead of winter, break through the ice, and spend what time you could scrubbing before jumping out to warm yourself by the flames. Only the Galatai women were afforded the comfort of lukewarm water during the cold season, and that was only if they had a man who wished to enjoy them clean. Titon imagined one of his boys might be fetching water and heating it for some lucky girl, as he had for their mother. *How all the girls must be fighting over them, now that they have returned with plunder and triumph.*

When they had finished bathing and dressing themselves in foreign cloth, it was time to eat and past time to drink. Serving women brought them ale and long, thin loaves of bread after instructing them to sit at the table that was not in the kitchen.

"I must admit, this silly floor feels good on my feet," said Keethro.

Titon broke the bread with his fingers revealing perfectly white and delicate innards within the chewy crust. With cold butter spread atop, it was without question the best he had ever tasted.

"Bah. Don't get used to it. Every man in the South must think himself a king. Did you see the throne they have for shitting? How can a man need such a thing?"

"Need…want…it was a comfortable shit I had, I tell you that."

Titon must have washed down his meal with half a normal man's weight of the stuff the Southmen called ale, yet he felt no effect. The food was both odd and delicious. Titon had a fondness for trying new tastes, and he was not disappointed. The first real dish brought to them was a bowl of minced meat, formed into balls, fried, and covered in a sauce of onions, cream, and butter. Despite the rich, almost sweet sauce, the tender spheres of what must have been beef retained a crunchy exterior and a strong, meaty flavor. Titon decided it would be his favorite dish of the night and in that he had been correct, but the following dishes were also delectable. The next looked like a plate of nothing more than wet leaves, but inside was a whole fish, swimming in a bath of herbs and butter. It was trout, said the servants, and though it looked far too large to be such, Titon enjoyed it nonetheless. The last was the oddest of all and was again from the river. River guardians they were called, and the armored creatures looked as though they might come alive at any moment and claw at the men in defense of the assault now being waged upon them. They had one enormous claw and another that was so tiny it was likely no use at all, and the servants demonstrated how to break their shells to get at the flesh. Their armor was perhaps more formidable than that worn by the golden guards of the arena, but Titon found it was worthwhile to break through in order to taste the sweet meat inside, best eaten drenched in butter.

"It must have taken a dozen cows to produce the butter needed for this feast," Titon said to his friend. But Keethro was lost to him by now, having been affected by the ale.

"You saw her did you not? The River drown me, she was a goddess in plain women's dress."

"The River need not drown you—you are accomplishing that yourself, my friend." Titon had not noticed the girl Keethro spoke of. His focus was on that which the servants brought.

"You are a man ruled by your belly," Elise had told Titon once. "I should not fear you being stolen by a fair maiden so much as I would an old crone who has mastered the art of the skillet." But she had nothing to fear. She was a fine cook and as fair as any maiden. *Tomorrow I will demand a king give me your remedy, Ellie. Tomorrow will be a great day.*

When the two serving girls returned with a final course, both men were forced to refuse. Titon had for them a question instead. "Tell us, what is the name of the man who rules this kingdom?"

The girls looked nervously at each other as if unsure of how best to answer. Keethro must have spoken earlier of the shorter of the two. Though she had a pretty face, the taller one suffered from a bit of a hunch and flat bottom, and Titon knew Keethro was inclined to judge his women based more on the appearance of their backside than their front—especially so when drunken. And even Titon could not deny the shorter girl's near perfection in that regard.

"King Veront is the ruler of Rivervale, m'lord," said the taller.

Keethro found something about her response hilarious, most likely the way she had addressed Titon, and began laughing himself silly.

"What kind of man is he?" Titon asked over his friend's laughter.

Again the girls exchanged glances. This time it was the shorter of the two who spoke. "It is not our place to judge the king. Please forgive us."

"Do not judge him then. Just tell me what others say of him."

The shorter girl responded after some delay. "He is known to be honest and ruthless, m'lord."

"And he worships the River, the Mountain, and the Dawnstar like any other man?"

"Nearly all in Rivervale worship the Mighty Three. In Strahl they worship the Only One, but those beliefs are not shared by us, nor our king. We must be going now, our absence will be noticed. With your permission…"

"Aye, go on," Titon said.

Keethro still laughed so hard he probably had not realized he'd just missed his last opportunity to lure the shorter one into bed. The girls appeared to have had an honest fear of reprimand, and it must have carried a weight greater than reduced pay or rations.

"This is a strange land we have found ourselves in, Keethro."

Keethro's laughter subsided, and he began to look around the room, craning his neck as if to peer around the corners. "Where has she gone? She will be back, no?"

"No, my drunken fool of a friend, I fear she has gone for the evening. It is perhaps better this way. You would have embarrassed yourself with a poor performance, and the tales would have traveled far and wide. It would ruin your chances with countless such southern women. Better that you sleep well tonight, eh?"

"She was like no other, though. You saw her, didn't you? She was a goddess in Jane's woman's dress."

Keethro appeared to be getting worse rather than better based upon his slurred and senseless speech. "To bed with you. Tomorrow we go before this King Veront as champions of the arena. He will grant me a remedy for Ellie and perhaps a true princess for you—his own daughter, I would wager. Tomorrow will be a great day indeed."

Keethro nodded and stumbled into his own quarters, leaving Titon to enjoy his first good night of rest in as long as he could remember. With the thinnest sheet he could find among the bed linens as his only covering, Titon laid upon the floor. Nondescript thoughts of pleasantness turned to dream as he drifted to sleep.

"M'lord."

With reluctance, Titon came to realize the voice was not dreamt. He sat up and saw in his doorway the lovely silhouette of the shorter serving girl.

"What are you doing here?" he asked, not angrily.

"The king requested that I come and give you comfort," she said. She did not move from the doorway. As Titon's eyes reacquainted themselves with a more wakeful state, he could see some sort of light fabric hung from her loosely. It was a far different attire than she had worn when serving the meal, if he remembered correctly.

"You may tell him I am quite comfortable, and thank him for his hospitality."

The girl turned to the side as if to leave, but stopped. Her hand went to her face, but Titon's eyes went to the new shape that presented itself. *Perhaps Keethro was right in his assessment*, thought Titon, not wishing to remember how long it had been since he'd lain with a woman. *She is perhaps a goddess, now in matching dress.* He thought he heard her lament.

"What is the matter?" he asked.

"The king does not ask us to do things lightly. If I disobey..."

"You have seen to my comfort as best you could. You're not disobeying," Titon insisted, to himself as much as to her.

"He will not see it that way." She shook her head. "And he may not trust you if you refuse."

Titon could not help but groan in his displeasure, which seemed to frighten her.

"I will go," she said, turning and making a hasty exit.

"Wait," he called to her, remembering she only knew him as a beast who had just brutally slain over half a dozen men in the arena. Galatai women were no strangers to the realities of combat, but the thought of this southern innocent having borne witness to his slaughter gave Titon a sickening feeling.

He threw off his linen and went after her, catching her with both hands by her waist. It had seemed the least threatening place to grab her, yet at the same time, suggested otherwise. Titon released one hand and walked her back to the room, her stride shy but willing. He guided her to the bed where she lay on her back, staring at him with a maiden's trepidation.

Titon again groaned, this time under his breath as not to scare her. She was not to blame for this quandary, and he had no desire to see her distressed. He pulled the bedsheets over her, hiding her from more than just the threat of cold. She looked at him with confusion.

"He won't know the difference," Titon told her as he got back onto the floor, wondering if sleep would even be possible at this point.

"He'll know." There was desperation in her voice.

"There's no way for him to know," he assured her. The honesty in his words must have put her to ease, as she did not protest further. Fighting the images in his mind and an unfamiliar self-doubt, Titon did his best to fall asleep.

TALLOS

Nekasr does not fear death, Tallos reminded himself, *and around him the world burns.*

The town Tallos and his group had been escorted to reeked of contagious despair. The only grins of the many people milling around belonged to the few men in armor. It reminded Tallos of a leper town he'd once visited for trade. The men who ran the lucrative business of housing the afflicted relatives of those with means laughed and joked among themselves while the infirm sat in despondency, awaiting death.

Even so, it did not do for him to be so troubled. *It was foolish to have scarred myself,* thought Tallos. *The gods must have laughed to see it done, knowing the complications it would cause.*

It seemed a reasonable enough thing to blame his worry upon. Had he looked like any other man, being conscripted into an army might even serve his purposes. His intention, after all, was to wreak havoc—a task he had yet to begin—and a war seemed as good a place to start as any.

"Mighty Three be damned," cried the man at the dais. "I have not smelled a stench so foul since praying at your sister's bush!" The many papers piled in front of him and his authoritative demeanor made him out to be the one in charge. "I am a master provisioner, yet you must think me an alchemist to have brought me this lot. Am I to turn shit to steel and find a place for them in an army?"

The man to whom he spoke was the quietest of the four horsemen, relegated to see Tallos and his five companions to the town after their supplies and mounts had been reappropriated. He just shrugged and turned his horse around, leaving Tallos and the rest with the boisterous provisioner.

Surrounding him and his dais was what remained of a village. It had not been destroyed, but it certainly was no longer what it once must have been. Every home and building had some combination of piles of clothing, chests, and metal cookware just outside the front door, which Tallos guessed had previously belonged inside. Hundreds of men were arranged in a queue that extended down the full length of the main road, filing slowly into a large central building. The women were in clusters outside various houses. *What must they do with the children?* Tallos wondered if new parents were exempt from this treatment and how such an army would eat if they did this to every farming village. But it was the castoffs that awakened his fire, reminding him of how he had found his own home similarly ravaged.

"I'll take a look at the girl first," said the provisioner. "Over here, you little tart."

Lily looked first to Kelgun who refused to meet her glance, then she reluctantly walked to the dais.

"Nope, don't look at him. I'm your master now. Turn around, would ya? There ya go. Hmmm…" The man appeared to be truly considering his options. "Well, you and your old lover or father or both are in luck. You're too ugly for entertainment. You're a washwoman if I've ever seen one. Head that way." He pointed to a home with the largest cluster of women at it.

"Do something," Dusan demanded of Kelgun, and too loudly.

"What's he going to do, boy?" asked the amused provisioner.

Lily limped off, keeping her head down, and made no backward glances. Tallos purposefully avoided looking toward Dusan. *And around him the world burns*, he said again to himself.

The provisioner turned his attention to John. "I bet it's you that stinks. You big ones always turn ripe before the rest of them." Tallos found it a bit hypocritical considering the source, who easily bested John in girth. "I should know," cried the man, with a laugh and slap of his belly. *Perhaps not.* "What is it you do, big boy?"

John did not appear to wish to meet eyes with the man, not that any should want to. The provisioner's patchy beard did little to hide his saggy jowls, and his left eye was either lazy or trained to look elsewhere.

"I am a tinker's apprentice, m'lord."

"Haha! Wrong on both counts I'd wager. I'm no lord and you're certainly no tinker's apprentice. You know how many times I've heard that one? You damn fools think you can just say tinker and avoid service to the kingdom?"

"He is my apprentice." It was Wilkin's old weakened voice. Not even he had been spared from this process. The men-at-arms had forced him to leave his donkeys and supplies at the entrance to the village, and without them he looked little different from any other decrepit man.

"Oh is he now? And I assume you are a master tinker, traveled 'round the realm six by seven times by now, eh? Oddly enough, when I look at the two of you, I see an overgrown boy and his grandfather who both think they've got half again as many brains as they actually do. No, I don't believe my recruiters would be foolish enough to bring me a real tinker, do you? But even if you can tinker, you can surely read and write, no?"

Wilkin stared at the man a moment and then nodded, resigned to accept his ignorance.

"Okay, old man. You are assigned to notes and queries. I warn you though, if you get there and they find out you lied about writing in order to get out of harder duties, they'll chop off your fingers. And if you can't read, they'll gouge out your eyes. You still remember how to read and write knowing all that?"

Again Wilkin stared at him, then nodded.

"Ha! Well don't you come crying to me when they do, not that you could manage without any eyes, I suppose. That way." He pointed toward a lonely home with one guard at the door about a hundred paces away. Wilkin shook his head in disbelief and began to shuffle to where he had been directed.

"Okay, big boy. You look like you can lift a shield. Infantry division is that way."

John just stood there, dumbfounded.

"Go on now, no need to play stupid—that won't help either. You can be dim or simple and still raise a shield."

"You are a fool," blurted John. "You have just sent the realm's best tinker to copy letters. Do you know the fate to which one is condemned who wrongs a tinker?"

The provisioner glared at John with more contempt than anger. "Guards," he called while keeping his eyes firmly fixed upon his challenger. "I think we've got a malcontent. Find a home for him."

Two mailed men with differing tabards, one showing a keep before a river and the other a series of branching rivers that Tallos had previously mistaken for lightning, seized John by the arms and dragged him to a metal cage in plain sight from where Tallos and the rest stood. John did not struggle as the men hoisted him up and sealed him inside the birdcage-like contraption. Tallos wondered how long it would be before John's look of defiance changed to diffidence as the thirst set in.

"Gepner." The deep, angry voice came from behind, and all turned to see what sort of man may have made such a sound.

"What is it, Otis?" The provisioner did not appear to be pleased by the interruption.

"They said there was a girl." The man that approached was a brute. He dwarfed the guards and the mounted men who had captured Tallos's party, weighing near double that of the largest, and he wore a type of armor not shared by any of his fellow conscription officers. A cascade of spade-shaped pieces of water-hardened leather overlapped each other to form a hard yet pliant suit that shifted with his motion as he strode forward. His face was also well armored, albeit by overlapping scars. He had a sword of the finest steel in hand and was flipping it around as if it were weightless, not threateningly, but rather like a boy who'd acquired a new trinket. Tallos knew that sword—the one whose blade always shone with brilliance no matter how it was abused. A glance toward Kelgun revealed he'd recognized it as well. His face spoke his sour contempt.

Otis stopped a few paces before the provisioner and sheathed the sword. "Where is she?"

If Gepner was afraid of this giant, he did not show it. "You would not care for her. She's ugly. Ugly and too old for your tastes."

"I'll be the judge of that. Now where is she?"

Gepner flicked his head at a young assistant who took off with haste. "You are making my job as provisioner very difficult," complained Gepner. "You ruined the last two. They won't so much as speak now, let alone do any washing."

Otis let loose a gravelly laugh with his hands clasped over his enormous gut. "Battles are won with armies, not washwomen. And I was promised the flesh of war."

"The war has not even begun."

"For me it has," insisted Otis.

Lily had a look of hope in her eyes as Gepner's assistant brought her back. That hope died, though, when she saw Otis staring at her.

Otis made a vile noise in the back of his throat and shot a blob of phlegm toward Lily's knees. Clearly appalled, she tried to avoid it, but it struck the side of her roughspun trousers.

"I told you she—"

"She'll do," Otis interrupted. "The recruits are busy eating. Come, girl. Let us speak in private." He walked forward with a hungry smirk and grabbed Lily by the back of the neck, his fingers nearly touching at the front of her throat.

"No!" Dusan had managed to sound even younger than he was in his desperate objection.

Otis turned to face him with mirth. "What's this? This your little sweetheart, boy? Or do you merely wish to take her place?"

"She's my sister! Let her go!" Dusan rushed forward but stopped prior to getting too close to his mammoth foe.

Otis chuckled and rubbed his bald head with a meaty hand. "Tell you what." With that same hand he took hold of Lily again by the waist and hoisted her above his head. Her struggle came to an abrupt stop as if he'd threatened to break her neck with his other hand. "Get me to drop her, and you can do with her as you like."

Dusan looked to Otis as if to question his sincerity and was met with a raised brow of enticement.

"We don't have time for this." Gepner's protest was made irrelevant as Dusan bolted forward. No doubt expecting to be met with a kick, he then dodged to the side. Otis nearly dropped Lily as he laughed so heartily, watching Dusan jump into the muddy slush to avoid a blow that never came.

Dusan was quick to his feet, however, and leapt forward, landing a kick to Otis's stomach. Their difference in weight was so extreme that the force sent Dusan backward. Otis already looked to be boring of the game, but Dusan resumed his attack. Risking a potentially fatal kick from the giant, Dusan stood in front of him and punched Otis square in the jaw, difficult as it was for him to reach. Otis merely shook his head, prompting Dusan to hit him again, this time with a windmilled shot to the nose. The strike caught Otis's attention, and he shoved the boy backward violently with a foot. Dusan landed on his back, his head slamming onto the only hard patch of ground in sight.

"Do I now have your permission to skewer your ugly sister, boy?"

Otis's taunt seemed to crush the already defeated Dusan. He staggered to his feet with sulking shoulders, looking downward. Otis snorted amusedly and turned his attention to Gepner. It was the opening Dusan must have been hoping for, as he sprinted forward, flinging mud at Otis's face and grabbing the hilt of the giant's sword with both hands. The ring of steel sounded as the blade was pulled upward, to the tip, then rung out again as Otis grabbed Dusan's hands and shoved the blade back into its sheath.

Dusan backed away, the apprehension on his face shared by all those in attendance. Lily had fallen to the mucky ground.

Gepner laughed openly. "You dropped her. The boy bested you."

Otis's angry stare gave place to a solemn look. "I am a man of my word. You can do with your sister as you like." Dusan just stared dumbly, not believing the words. "Tomorrow, after I've split her in half."

This time when Dusan screamed and charged, Otis put a boot in his belly. Dusan spun and fell to his stomach. With his foot, Otis shoved Dusan's face deep into the mud. He then wiped the mud off his own face.

"If there is one thing I hate," said Otis, "it's a man who doesn't respect fair play."

Gepner shook his head, but looked as though he'd expected no less from Otis. "Hurry it up, Otis. The line grows, and I have work to do."

Dusan's arms flailed, alternating between trying to push himself upward and grabbing at Otis's boot. It would not be long before he suffocated, provided Otis wasn't already crushing his skull with his weight.

"Release him." The voice came from behind, and Tallos knew the speaker, though he did not know him to be the valiant type.

Otis did not even look at Kelgun. Instead, he spoke to Gepner. "Where did you find this lot?"

Gepner ignored the question. "Kill the boy if you want, but I need the men," he reminded Otis.

"You need numbers. *I* need men. Men who will follow orders, not those who think they're the ones who ought to be giving them. But I have a way of teaching even the most dimwitted their place." With that Otis turned to Kelgun. "This your little runt?"

"No," said Kelgun. "But that's my sword."

Otis lifted his foot from Dusan who rolled to his back and fought for breath. Then he unsheathed the blade. "This? It's a little light."

"I can show you how to use it, if you like." Somehow Kelgun, the same man who was fearful of the now silent war drums, did not look intimidated. Tallos could tell he was still rather intoxicated, but he hid it better than usual.

"You think a sword makes a man?" Otis flung the weapon toward Kelgun where it jabbed to the hilt into the brown slush. "Have your toothpick."

Otis pulled a plank of wood from the base of the provisioner's dais, eliciting some curses of protest.

Otis came at Kelgun with his wooden plank, swinging it over his head. Kelgun, his sword in hand, blocked the blow, but only just. Otis repeated the attack, and each time Kelgun blocked, it came that much closer to slamming into Kelgun's head as splinters flew in all directions. Kelgun had circled while moving rearward, and was near the dais once again.

"Fight, you coward," taunted Otis, and Kelgun obliged with some downward slashes of his own. They were blindingly fast, but Otis managed to block each one, none of which seemed to have much power behind them. Then came Kelgun's true attack, a strike that appeared no different than those before it, but was artfully redirected to swing wide and hit from the side. The tactic worked, striking Otis on the ribs, but the slashing cut was no match for the thick hardened leather and left little more than a scratch on the surface.

Spear him with the point, thought Tallos, and as if by command, Kelgun thrust his blade at what looked to be a weak point in Otis's armor, where the shoulder met the breast. Otis turned away from the attack, allowing the blade to scratch along his armored chest. Kelgun flicked his wrist as he withdrew, catching Otis's cheek and opening a small wound.

Otis retaliated with fury. With both hands he swung the wooden plank sideways at Kelgun's head, a move Kelgun looked happy enough to block with his blade, close to the hilt. The wood broke on impact, and the top half continued its motion to connect with Kelgun's head.

Otis was on top of him in an instant, striking the dazed knight with repeated blows with the half of the plank that remained. One such strike hit Kelgun's wrist, causing him to drop his sword, and Otis kicked him in the gut so hard Tallos could feel the impact. Otis followed up, putting a foot on Kelgun's chest as he lay on his back.

"Do you yield?" Otis demanded response by pushing the sharp splintered plank into his throat.

Kelgun made no sound.

"You yield," Otis answered for him, then hocked another impressive glob of phlegm on Kelgun's face. Otis turned to Gepner. "Infantry for this one, right?"

"I would think so."

Otis retrieved Kelgun's sword from the ground, flung it free of dirt, and sheathed it. "Your job is easier than you claim it to be," he said to Gepner as he returned to the dais and threw the broken plank near where it had come from. He then went to Lily, who sat speechless in the mud, grabbed her by the hair and proceeded to drag her behind him. Neither Kelgun nor Dusan moved to protest this time.

"All right," said Gepner as if nothing out of the ordinary had occurred. "What's next here?" His eyes went to Tallos, who had managed to forget about his own quandary amidst the chaos. "I suppose you'll tell me you're a monk and that—Mountain's tits! I was wrong."

Tallos had moved up to the front of the dais obediently, and by the way Gepner had begun to contort his face, he knew it was his stench that had hit the man.

"What sort of monk are you? You must pay homage to the gods of rotting flesh."

Tallos had not come up with a plan that would allow him to remain in his robes, if even such a possibility existed. But in any case, he knew that he must rid himself of the stench.

"Please, allow me to jump in the river and bathe myself with stationed guard. It would be a kindness to the others in the camp." There were plenty of fires going inside warm-looking buildings that would allow him to dry without disrobing. "I am not a fighting man, but I can read and write." It was the only station he thought may allow him to retain his robes during service.

"Step back, you. *Farther.*"

Tallos complied, as did the small group of people behind him.

"You don't think I know what you are? We've had men like you rot an entire legion of infantry before. Remove your robe, plague bearer."

It was exactly what he had sought to avoid, but if this man thought him pestilent, perhaps that would explain the appearance of his skin, and he would be cast out completely. He stopped himself before praying to the gods for assistance—he'd gotten better at that, at least.

Tallos was not moving quickly enough for the provisioner, however. "Guards, force his fecking robe off," he commanded.

Tallos raised his hands to show it would not be necessary and untied the cords at the neck and waist. Then, looking as feeble as he could to assist in their presumption, he pushed off his garment at the hood and shoulders, allowing it to fall to the ground and reveal him in stark nakedness.

A wave of gasps and muffled shrieks passed through all those near. Tallos thought he recognized the gasp of Dusan. *Why does it hurt to be judged by one I sought to see dead?* He had no time to contemplate such things, however, as the situation continued to worsen.

"Kill him," shouted one of the guards to his side. "He's no monk nor plague bearer. He is a necromancer, a practicer of dark arts."

"Do *not* kill him," shouted Gepner as the guards began closing in on Tallos, swords raised. "Cut down a demon and he will only return that much stronger, you fools! Seize him, and put him in chains. …He must be burned alive."

TITON SON OF SMALL GRYN

Titon filled his lungs through his nose, enjoying the rich oaken scent emanating from the magnificent doors in front of him. They were not nearly the size of those found in the arena, but they far surpassed them in prominence due to their elaborate carvings. The scene depicted a great battle. Armored men laid siege to a castle with weapons of war Titon could have never imagined. Massive contraptions hurled boulders at the turrets along the walls, shattering them to pieces and sending men falling to their death. The drawbridge of the castle gate was raised, exposing an empty moat, but a makeshift bridge had been formed with piles of dead bodies over which several dozen men wheeled an enormous roofed log. The thing was at the gate, smashing through the drawbridge and portcullis, shards of wood flying in all directions. Other men had ladders across the moat and alongside the walls, crossing and climbing only to have rocks dropped upon them or their ladder thrust backward with long poles. Some had made it to the top of the walls where they advanced on the hordes of archers raining endless volleys of arrows down on those who had not yet crossed the moat.

Titon wondered how long it took to create such a carving, and if it could even be accomplished by a single man in a lifetime. More so, he wondered how war could be waged on such a scale. *It must be utter chaos*, he thought, remembering how difficult it had been just to get his raiding parties of never more than fifty to attack with any coordination or order.

He and Keethro had been escorted to those doors by golden-armored guards similar to those that had led them from the arena. Titon noticed the scene upon their tabard was identical to the one that flew over the gatehouses: the river flowing before a massive keep. They wore the same gaudy armor with spikes and gems. Even the pommels, hilts, and cross-guards of the longswords these men carried were covered in gold. *At least they had the sense to keep the blades bare*, he thought with a combination of disgust and humor.

A guard knocked four times, aided by the thick metal ring on his finger, a large black jewel held in a wolf's jaws, and the doors soon opened. At the end of the lengthy room, Titon saw a massive throne, near two men in height, sat upon a raised dais another man's height above the floor. The steps leading up to the seat were so large they would be cumbersome to climb and a fair defense against a charging attacker. But the throne was empty. Below it, the king was seated at the head of a great table. He wore no cape today, covered instead by tanned leather, skillfully tooled to reveal an intricate pattern. Short hair of light brown, heavily receding at the forehead, revealed him to be older than Titon. This was further evidenced by the deep lines on his face, caused by years of intense thought or disappointment. Perhaps both.

The doors had already closed behind them when Titon realized he had done little but analyze the appearance of this man, so eager he was to determine the likelihood of procuring his wife's remedy. He glanced around the room now, and noticed a row of more gold-plated guards on raised platforms to the left and right of the table. Including the six that had served as escorts, there must have been well over three-dozen guards present in the room, all armed with spears, swords, or maces.

"The man you killed in the arena was one of my best guards and a good friend." It was the king who spoke. He stared at Titon and Keethro coldly with his elbows upon the table, hands in loose fists coming together at the knuckles, his chin resting upon his thumbs.

"I killed many men in the arena. But you must forgive me, king. I did not know there was one you liked most." Titon did his best not to sound threatening.

"I am afraid there is little a king *must* do, and of those things none of them are demanded by his subjects." Though he was easy enough to hear, the man spoke quietly as if he had no reason to do otherwise. It was obvious to Titon the power this man must wield, and the calmness with which he spoke seemed to affirm that assessment.

Titon swallowed down the sour taste in his mouth in an attempt to be rid of his pride as well. "I apologize. I am not from these parts, and I have not spoken to many kings in my time. We are not so formal where I come from."

"Hmph… No, indeed you are not. *Savages.* That is what they call your kind here in Rivervale. But you and your friend here did not fight like foolish savages in the arena, now did you? You made quite a mockery of my well-trained troops, in fact. You relieved them of their mighty dragons and tamed them for yourselves."

Titon ignored the part about the combat in favor of the bit about his friend. "This is Keethro son of Leif, and I could not have succeeded without him. We have fought countless battles against our own people and the weakling Dogmen."

"And you are Titon was it? Son of Small Gryn? The Northman?"

"Aye. Though it was your people who named me Northman."

"Tell me, Titon, are you just a common man back in your home? Or are you a leader? And the son of those who were leaders before you?"

Titon hesitated, finding the question inexplicably embarrassing. "I am a leader of a Galatai clan. So was my father. So was his father. A very small clan compared to the might of this kingdom."

"Yes, I figured as much. And there are many such small clans? In the Northluns, I assume?"

"Aye, the Northluns are home to perhaps a hundred clans."

"And enough men to fill, say, the arena seats?"

Titon thought for a bit. "I do not know. I would guess not near that many. Maybe half. And half of those men would be boys, truth be told."

"And why is it that you and your friend have come to visit Rivervale? Surely you are not here just to enjoy the offerings of our food vendors."

For a man who looked so completely bored and uninterested, he had no lack of questions. Hopefully his response to Titon's next answer would be equally as casual and result in their reward and dismissal. "No, we have not. We have come in search of a remedy for my wife—one I am sure a kingdom as great as yours has within it. After we have the elixir to end my wife's waking slumber, we will return to our homes. With tales of your legendary charity." Titon was satisfied in his delivery of his precomposed words.

Though he stood at the far end of the table which was near four men in length, Titon could still make out the tiniest of smirks form on the king's face, and he could not recall having said anything comical. It was troubling to see a man who appeared to be the embodiment of apathy suddenly amused. Titon also found it a bit odd that there was such a long table in between them, one that could easily sit several dozen men, and yet this ruler of a vast kingdom had no advisors.

"My charity? You think I would wish to have every starving Northman headed south to infest my city in hope of free meals?" His tone had not changed despite the challenge in his question.

"No, I guess you would not. Your legendary riches, is what I meant to say." Titon could see Keethro shifting uncomfortably beside him, which furthered his own discomfort.

"Hmmm, my riches. But then I may have thousands of barbarians attacking my farms, climbing my walls, and pillaging my lands—united in the hope of securing those riches for themselves."

Now it was Titon who shifted uncomfortably. "Forgive me. I am a fighting man, and no master of words. I only mean to praise your kingdom. We to the north are of no threat to your might. I promise you that."

"Hmph… No, I would think not. But if you were a threat, it would be foolish of you to admit as such, would it not?"

Titon gave up speaking and merely frowned, though not in anger—not completely. This was not a battle in which he was equipped to engage.

"I do not suppose you know the name of my house. Your serving girls mentioned you did not even know my *given* name. There are kings that would behead a man for less." He locked eyes with Titon and allowed the words to echo in the hall before continuing.

"I am King Veront of House Bywater, ruler of Rivervale. I come from a long line of proud men—proud and *weak* men—all of whom served under *great* men. It had seemed our house name was a bit of a curse, condemning Bywaters to bystanders, forever observing and assisting those men of mightier currents. My father, Duke Vanert was his name, though I don't suppose you would have heard of him either, served the eminent King Leofwin. Dutifully, I might add." Veront paused to sip from his goblet and reposition himself in his chair, leaning back into it more casually. "I had him killed, my father. He had a penchant for whoring, which was as much to my mother's displeasure as it was to mine. Any woman who can be paid to spread her legs can be paid a little more to spy—to go through your papers and things and steal bits of information one would not think to hide. It is a degrading transaction, and more so to the man in most cases. For a man of supposed power to need to pay a woman to join him in bed... No, my father's pride was feigned. He knew he would never rise to greatness. It was a kindness I did to him. And a kindness to the kingdom.

"I succeeded my father and served Leofwin for a time and then his son Lyell." Veront leaned forward in his chair and further beetled a brow that had already been signifying stern judgment. "But they are now both dead, and it is I, a Bywater, who bears the burden of ensuring the prosperity of this kingdom. I did not rise to power by stroke of luck, and I certainly did not find my rightful seat by way of charity—that thing that is mislabeled when a person does another a good deed, and the beneficiary is foolish enough to believe nothing will be expected in return. So if you have come to me today expecting charity, I would advise you to seek it elsewhere."

We came to you at blade point, thought Titon. He did not enjoy the cold countenance of this King Veront, but at least he was straightforward and blunt, if not a bit long-winded.

"Fair enough, king. Let us know what we can do to repay our debt. I wish to earn my wife's remedy, not have it gifted. I see no reason for us not to be friends and to forge an alliance between our people. If that is what you would like as well."

"Hmph." This time his disinterested grunt seemed to have a bit of gaiety in it. "You owe me a great debt already, which I do not think you realize. In addition to potentially discrediting the effectiveness of my dragons and killing my favored guard, you have been leading raids on vassals of the Rivervalian kingdom. Those Dogmen you spoke of earlier, who is it you think they pay their levies to?"

Titon was not sure of what these levies were, but he had gathered the Dogmen were allies to this kingdom. Nonetheless, he could not bring himself to apologize. "The Dogmen are the vilest of men. They torture and starve wolves to the point of madness. They feed their demon-dogs the flesh of man. The men among them run and hide when we come to steal their gold and the souls of their women. And they have no respect for or devotion to the Mighty Three. They do not deserve to live."

"We will have to work on your manners. It is very impolite to leave a king's question unanswered." In spite of his words, the king lessened his frown. "They owe levies to Rivervale—not that they pay them with any regularity. I wonder, in fact, if they have a greater fear of your raids or the incursions of my tax collectors."

Titon had no need to wonder. "They store their gold beneath their floors and inside hidden rooms. Little good it does them when we come and tear their homes apart."

"Information I will have to pass along to my collectors. But no, I find it hard to blame you for the killing of the men of Fourpaw Canyon. I have no fondness for them myself, nor their religion. And it is a wise thing to part a fool from his money, for a fool with money is a dangerous thing. Nonetheless, you have clearly profited from plunder that was owed to this kingdom, and for that you are further indebted."

Much of the gold Titon had collected from the Dogmen over the years had recently been captured by Veront's guards, but he did not think it wise to complain of that.

"I do not wish for you to think of me as an unjust king," Veront went on. "I do all that I can to ensure proper justice be dealt to all those, even those whom I call friend. I am sure as a leader you have done no less."

Titon nodded his head in solemn agreement.

"And since having left the arena you have been given royal treatment. I understand you enjoyed more than just food and housing last night. Am I correct?" Veront raised a brow, but with no humor.

As Titon nodded again, he noticed Keethro turn to look at him, no doubt with incredulity. *I will have to explain to him later*, thought Titon.

"So since you ask of me an elixir, one that would bring your wife from slumber, and yet you have taken from me Fourpaw plunder, the glory of my dragons, and a golden guard, I would say you would first owe me a great deal. Would you disagree?"

"To be fair, King Veront," interjected Keethro, "we did our best to show your dragons in good light by demonstrating their abilities on the cowards who first crewed them. I do not believe they were disparaged in any way."

King Veront looked at Keethro as if he was an impudent child. "Do you not? And who do you think will crew those dragons in the war but the same cowards you so easily unnerved? Do you think we selected the worst crews among them to be those to first demonstrate their grandeur? You painted a picture in my men's minds of exactly what may happen to them when they march into battle, and not a pretty one." He returned his focus to Titon. "Which is exactly what I need you to remedy. You have inspired the people of Rivervale who believe you to be a fearsome warrior and leader. I plan to use that to treat the very disease of uncertainty that you have spread among my armies. What I ask of you in return for your wife's cure is your fealty. Serve me, not as a normal man, but as a leader of men. Pledge to me your undying loyalty, and I will give you an army of men that you will march to the east, to a city by the name of Strahl. When you have stormed the walls of its meager castle, raised my banners, and returned with the body of its former ruler, you will have your elixir."

Titon had no love for Strahl given he and Keethro's encounter with the city's guards. The idea of earning Elise's remedy by way of glory in war was as great a prospect as any for which he could have hoped. He had a sudden respect for this king who sat before him. This man appreciated Titon for what he truly was and did not seek to humiliate him by means of some menial service to the kingdom. *I will take Strahl, and gladly so. It will look little different than the scene upon the doors.*

"I accept."

"Good," said King Veront, suddenly impassioned. "Titon son of Small Gryn, in witness of the Gods of the River, the Mountain, and the Dawnstar, do you pledge your fealty to me and agree to obey my every command until I have relieved you of service?"

Titon would have preferred to have had some other conditions in place, but he knew better than to vex a king with minutiae. "In witness of the Mighty Three, I do. I am yours to command until you command otherwise."

"Very well. Let it be known then that you are now Sir Titon son of Small Gryn, a knight of Rivervale." Titon had no choice but to grin at Keethro, and in doing so saw the frowns on the guards to his side. He was a knight. How funny it would be to tell those back at home. "You will soon command a force of three thousand men and lay siege to Strahl." Veront gestured with his head to one of the guards in the rear. "Give him your sword."

Though Titon preferred axes, the sword placed in his hands was well balanced, and he imagined he could wield it with some effectiveness. It certainly responded quickly to the slightest force from his wrist, and he was already becoming eager to test it on flesh.

"As you recall, you took from me a golden guard. His name was

Timmons, and in addition to being a fine man, I considered him a friend. Your first command, and the one by which you will prove your loyalty, is to take the life of your friend here, this Keethro. His blood upon your blade shall equal us in this debt that cannot be repaid by the simple sacking of a city."

The words staggered Titon. He looked to the floor and frowned, committing himself to deep thought as if to decipher the true meaning of what had just been said. Surely this king did not expect from him what had just been asked. From the corner of his eye, he could see the butts of the spears of some of the knights on the raised platform twisting as they readjusted their grips in anticipation of his rebellion. Titon puzzled over his options, attempting to find some escape.

Titon did not yet raise his eyes. "Keethro is a brother. He is not merely a friend. I will need his help if I am to take a castle with only three thousand men, especially so if they are as cowardly as the ones we faced in the arena."

"You are correct. The men who crewed the dragons were cowards. All the men of worth had already been conscripted to serve stations of greater import. I have doubled my army to nearly twenty thousand of the finest swordsmen, spearmen, halberdiers, and archers, and our cavalry is unmatched. I would not waste three thousand of my forces in a task I thought could not be accomplished. You will find a way if your oaths to the Mighty Three are sincere and if you truly seek a remedy for your wife."

Two of the nearest guards seized Keethro by either arm. Titon looked at his friend, begging him to reveal a solution, but Keethro must have had none, for he did not speak. He just looked at Titon with worry and disbelief. Titon surveyed the room, seeing no less than he had before: over three-dozen guards. Their armor may have been for show, but their weapons were not. It would not be possible to escape from here alive if he disobeyed the king.

The butcher warned me, thought Titon, remembering the man's grim yet urgent expression. *Perhaps if we had left immediately, we could have both escaped with our lives.*

Titon closed his eyes, squeezing his eyelids together with force. This kingdom had the elixir he had been searching for. One of them must live so there would be a chance that it could reach Elise. If they both were to die, she would be the third casualty.

"Then I would request an axe," Titon said. "I will not kill my brother with a foreign weapon. Let him have the honor of dying by the blade of our people."

"Very well." The king motioned to the same guard to retrieve an axe from the wall. Titon had noticed it hanging there and had hoped for another, but it would do.

The guard traded him weapons. It was a large axe, made to be swung by an equally large man and with two hands. Titon clutched the weapon with violence, its brittle leathern bindings creaking under the strain. He and Keethro had laughed in the face of death countless times—to have their partnership severed in such a way was beyond disgraceful.

He looked to his friend for the last time. Keethro appeared baffled. Not even he could negotiate the waters of the river that had flooded them both. *I will see you again, under the Mountain, my brother, should I still be granted access after this.*

Titon raised the axe partially above his head, feeling not its weight, but the yoke of sadness that came to rest upon his shoulders. To strike a man in the left of the neck and slice downward at an angle was as humane a death as could be had. But as Titon peeked from the left corner of his eye to gauge the distance of the king, he had no intention of giving that man a humane death. *Forgive me, Ellie, but I will not be commanded to kill a brother. And if the Mighty Three condemn me for this, then they were never worth my devotion.*

DERUDIN

He had never had a vision before—gazings, yes, but never a vision.

It was no small feat to gaze. With one's eyes shut, focusing so intently on a well-known place, near or distant, the present happenings were possible to reveal. Mages all had their own tricks. Some imagined themselves as an object in the room, a vase or a wandering rodent. Others gazed while bathing in the power of the Dawnstar, and some did not shut their eyes at all. Derudin's master had gazed with the aid of silvered glass. Standing across from it, Erober would look into his reflection's eyes, seeing them stare into his own eyes, already staring into its eyes, and so forth. Derudin's method was to focus on the element with which he had the strongest bond: that which can be trapped in mouth, but not grasped with hand, that which dries your eyes yet brings the rain. Knowing that the gods' breath connected him to all places he would ever hope to gaze was his special key to unlocking the doors of distance. It was the wind that carried voices, after all, and when he melded with it, he could float like a breeze to wherever he wished, so long as he knew the place. While some mages had all their senses intact when gazing, Derudin could only hear. His gazings involved no sight at all, a thing Erober taunted him to redress. "Without sight in your gazings, how can you expect to ever have a vision?" It had formed a rift between them, miniscule, but ever present—Derudin's first failing. *My first of many.*

Visions were a different thing entirely. To have a vision was to see into the future—a future always clouded by the ambiguity of time. Any man who has been forced to wait for his freedom or to see a loved one could tell you that time is a greater obstacle than any distance. And so it was with visions—for Derudin at least. No matter how he tried, he could never peer beyond the present.

As he awoke from this, his first vision, he was startled by the clarity of it. Perhaps it was just the combination of having all of his senses, where he was used to merely having one, but the events he had witnessed were explicit. And so was their meaning, he believed.

At the center of his vision was a man—a good man, for in his vision

Derudin had the power to see within him. His short brown hair was unkempt and drenched with the sweat of fear, and his beard was drenched in tears. This man did not cry for himself, however. He cried for those he had failed, and he feared only for their safety. He had already come to realize his own life was forfeit.

Above him stood what could have only been a cruel man. Derudin could not look into his soul, but the contempt in the man's eyes was plain enough to see. This man had condemned the other to die and wished for it to happen in a manner that would disgrace the sufferer and elevate himself.

The tearful man was lowered slowly into a muddy pit filled with his own pigs. Thousands of the hungry animals squealed and grunted as they climbed atop each other in the filth to be the first to get a bite of their master. The blood running down his naked legs and dribbling off his toes sent the swine into frenzy. Eventually, one pushed itself off the back of another, grabbed hold of the man's foot, and yanked him from his perch. On the ground he fought to stand, and somehow managed to, in spite of the many hungry mouths removing the meat from his legs in massive bites, each of which could be heard as blunted teeth crushed through wet flesh.

Though Derudin had no embodiment, the dying man could see him. He looked at Derudin with desperation and pleaded for help, but Derudin felt he could do nothing. Still the man stood as his legs were stripped bare, and his stomach was ripped open, spilling his entrails. It was then that Derudin realized he had the power to intervene. The clouds above darkened and lightning rained down upon the animals. Some were struck dead where they stood while the others fled in mass exodus.

The disemboweled man fell to the ground, sending up a puff of dry dust from earth that had so recently been a sopping pit. The stench that flooded Derudin was that of death—not the death of this man, but the death of the kingdom that would follow.

A boisterous cackle resounded in Derudin's head, threatening to shatter his skull. He looked up to smite the vile noisemaker, fully expecting it to be Cassen, but the body he saw was far too thin. The confusion of it broke his concentration, and thus his vision ended.

Derudin threw off his single sheet and stood beside his bed while he gathered himself. The poor conditions of this home where he'd chosen to stay were at first a comfort, reminding him of simpler times, but now he felt the impotence of being a man stripped of all political power. He had grown accustomed to having his servant bring him words from the town square so that he could remain informed on the happenings of the kingdom. But more so, he had grown accustomed to having some influence over those happenings, and as of this moment, he had neither knowledge nor sway.

He tried to focus and remember what he had seen while asleep, but it felt as though it was slipping from his grasp. *This is not right*, he thought. *A vision should gain clarity with time, not be lost.* Derudin found himself wishing for his former mentor. *How would Erober instruct me?* Derudin flinched as he remembered. *Perhaps I was too soft on my students…*

One thing remained clear from what he had seen: he must save Alther.

∞⟨⟩∞

Derudin was bombarded with blows. A knee struck his thigh, an elbow his ribs, and someone's forehead bashed him in the back of the skull. It defied his imagining that people should require lessons on how best to walk without smashing into each other.

The crowd he now plodded amongst was the worst of the kingdom's people, Westportians. He counted himself lucky to have made his hideaway home in Westport, however, else he would have never made it in time for the event.

Derudin's trip to the town square had been quite revealing, and he chided himself for not having checked in regularly. Everything he had learned on his painful voyage to the square had been from overhearing common gossip. Cassen had apparently ceded power to the formerly imprisoned Stephon in a move that Derudin did not yet understand. *Why would that greedy man give up the very power he had lied, killed, and self-mutilated to attain?* It made no sense, but he had little time to think. Stephon was on his way here, if he hadn't already arrived. It was said the new king had a major announcement, and he had chosen to deliver it to Westport first of all.

Talk among the people of Westport was not favorable of the fledgling king. Derudin had trouble conceiving of a reason why Stephon would even wish to set foot in this hole of a city. *If he has come to raise the levies as he once advised…* Derudin could only imagine the carnage that would follow should Stephon try something so foolish and in person, no less. Derudin would be lucky to escape alive himself. Gathering shadows does one little good when being trampled by a thousand angry feet.

Derudin flowed with the crowd around what he believed would be the final corner between him and a proper view of the square's dais. He could already begin to smell the remnants of the pieces that had fallen off and out of those three Adeltians impaled for treason. There were some smells that simply refused to part, no matter what was done in attempt to remove them—not that much had been done in this city.

Although flanked on either side by several dozen members of The Guard, Stephon's golden ringlets were the first thing Derudin saw. Every time Derudin laid eyes upon the boy it was as if he had grown another two inches. *Or perhaps his childish temperament merely shrinks him in memory,* thought Derudin. The boy stood proud, aided further still by the brilliant Adeltian crown upon his head. *I wonder which of these peasants will be wearing that crown tonight…or melting it down.*

"Subjects of the Adeltian Kingdom," cried Stephon, "As you all know, I have been wrongfully imprisoned for some time." Derudin was forced to admit, Stephon's overconfidence served him well upon a stage, but he could not help but think that the kingdom would have been better off even in the hands of Cassen. Everything Derudin had seen of this boy was the embodiment of privileged ignorance.

"But I am not angry for having been tortured as such… No, I thank my tormentors. For they have opened my eyes to what it means to suffer. Good people of Westport, I have shared in your misery. I have had nothing but stale bread, moldy cheese, and sour wine with which to wash it down. I know what it is to be in want."

The crowd gave a collective but muffled snigger at the remark. *How many of them would kill for such a meal*, Derudin wondered, but none of those in attendance moved yet toward aggression. Derudin guessed they were all too entertained by the spectacle.

Stephon either did not notice or chose to ignore it. "You may all wonder what it was that I had wished for most while locked away. Exoneration? Vindication? Freedom?"

Derudin shook his head and wondered how long this travesty of a speech might continue.

"I will tell you what I longed for, as I believe it is the very thing you good people desire as well: *vengeance*." Unbelievably, Derudin saw many around him, even the squat old woman in front of him whom he was pressed against, nod in earnest agreement.

"But in order to have proper vengeance, one must know who it was that truly wronged them. Why is it that we Adeltians have been made to suffer for so long? Do we even remember when it began? It started before my birth, and yet I have come to know its origin from my studies and the recollections of other good Adeltians. Adeltians who stood in defiance of the powers that tried to subdue our greatness. Was Westport not the greatest city of the realm prior to the invasion of the Rivervalian scum?"

Now there were even some shouts of agreement from within the crowd, prompting Derudin to rub his brow. *What do you think you will accomplish with this riling speech, boy? These people will be angrier and yet just as hungry. And you are the very product of the Rivervalian invasion.*

But Stephon seemed to have read his thoughts. "You may be wondering how it is that I can stand atop this platform and speak to you in such a way, given my parentage. And that is among the many reasons I have come today, and *first* to Westport, the still-beating heart of this great kingdom." Stephon signaled to some of the men behind him and a path was cleared. Onto the platform was wheeled a gallows, suspended from which was a cage holding a solitary occupant. Derudin felt as though a mighty fist had struck him and stole his breath.

"We have all been told a terrible lie—I most of all. That lie has cast a shadow upon this kingdom for so long that most of us no longer realized we were beneath it. Just before my imprisonment, however, I confirmed the truth—a truth so damning that those who shared in its knowledge were falsely accused of treason and impaled. The smell that still festers from their brutal display here, that is not from their rotten remains, but from the fetid injustice that was dealt to them."

Alther slouched in the cage, which was too narrow for sitting and too short for standing. His hands clung to the bars only enough to support the weight of his upper body. He made no move to communicate with the crowd, to beg for forgiveness, or to plead his innocence. Alther was a man defeated and many times betrayed—that much was clear for any fool to see. He did not deserve the punishment that was being served to him, and it would only be a matter of time before this crowd recognized that and stormed the stage to see him freed.

"This man you see caged, this scum from the bottom of the Eos, he and his kind are the reason we have suffered. It was his father who broke treaty with our beloved queen of Peace and threw her from her tower. And like his father, this man sought to subjugate all of Adeltia with lies and treachery." With a flourish of his regal cape, Stephon took a step forward and raised his voice in anger. "I ask you, what lie could be worse than telling a *true* prince of Adeltia that half his blood was of Rivervalian descent? As I stand before you and beside this monster, I ask that you look unto us both to see if there is any resemblance."

For all his powers, this was something Derudin had not foreseen. Some gasps could be heard among the crowd, but Derudin could not believe they would accept Stephon's assertion. Stephon had his mother's hair, but he shared his father's mouth and jaw. It did not help matters that Alther's face was now shrouded by an overgrown beard, hiding those similarities.

Speak up, Alther. It is your only chance, Derudin pleaded. But Alther made no move to comply. Instead he looked as though he had endured his final blow and had died within his cage. Derudin looked to the skies in search of clouds, but there were none. *What good would a few lightning bolts do now, in any case?* It was a diversionary tactic, not a mortal one, and the energy of these angry people was greater than he could hope to channel or disperse.

"I will now tell you the truth," continued Stephon. "My mother, the beautiful Princess Crella—she is a whore." Now there were full-bodied gasps. The woman in front of Derudin nearly smashed his chin with the back of her head as she recoiled. Even Alther was stirred to some motion and raised his head. "None of us have wished to admit this, me perhaps least of all, for I love my mother. I love her for being pure Adeltian, and I even love her for her indecency. But I will forever hate her for her cowardice. In fear for her own safety and reputation, she saw fit to allow this horrid lie to persist. We all knew what she was when she had her first bastard at as young an age as one can carry a child, and I will admit to you, in fairness, that I too am a bastard. I do not know who my father was. My mother shared beds with many men. My father could very well be Kevos of House Gangsong, Sir Stormblade." Alther's head was turning back and forth in solemn disbelief—Sir Stormblade had perished well over a year before Stephon's birth. "It would explain how the man fought so bravely, knowing his pregnant princess would be raped if he did not defeat the invaders. How many hundreds did Sir Stormblade dispatch with his two foils before he died upon the banks of the Eos?" Stephon's flair for rewriting history seemed to have no bounds. Sir Kevos was a berserker who used two swords, not foils. Derudin could not wait for this to be over.

"But I tell you this: I know whose son I am not, for if you cut my veins you will see blood as pure as your own. I am not this vile man's son. I am the one true heir to the Adeltian throne. I am King Stephon of House Eldaren, your bastard king. And my first gift to you is *vengeance!*" With that, Stephon went behind the gallows and kicked it as if to push it off the stage in one final gesture. The heavy structure barely moved, and he motioned to the members of The Guard to help. The crowd clamored forward, looking hungry for a piece of the meal that was finally being served.

Alther's wheeled prison was shoved over the edge, somehow rolling on top of the densely packed mass of people without tipping. Those directly around the cage lucky enough not be crushed by the base jumped upward, trying to grab the bottom.

As the people continued to press forward, Derudin, it seemed, was the only one moving back. He watched as Alther scanned the crowd, probably looking for someone who might help him—not that any could at this point, not without an army. Alther's eyes found Derudin's among the masses and their gazes locked. *I cannot help you*, thought Derudin. He feared the look of disappointment that would surely spread on Alther's face. But Alther's countenance only hardened. Alther, the rightful king, mouthed one final request to Derudin, "Save Ethel."

In truth, the words could have been anything. Derudin was no mouth reader and Alther's speech had no sound. His mouth simply opened and closed with a cadence that matched Derudin's assumption.

At the moment Derudin believed himself to understand the meaning and went to nod his understanding, one man climbed another and grabbed the bottom of Alther's cage. The weight tipped the structure forward, sending Alther and his metal coffin onto the top of the crowd. Hundreds of hands reached upward toward him, those close enough poking through his cage, scratching and clawing. Alther, brought back to life by the assault, screamed and struggled, but with little room to move in the cage his efforts were all but futile.

Derudin was filled with a rage unbecoming of a man beholden to the Ancient Laws. He drew from the power of the Dawnstar's early rays and focused them onto the platform upon which Stephon stood. Derudin only had line of sight on the front of the platform, however, and an ember soon formed. The structure did not erupt in flames. It merely smoldered at the point Derudin had focused. He poured in more energy, and the damp wood began to be eaten away as it smoked and turned to ash.

Several guards had noticed and alerted Stephon to the fire, pointing at the disintegrating wood. Stephon merely frowned, removed his cape, and threw it over the wood. Then he began to scrutinize the crowd.

You damn fool, Derudin chastised himself as he pulled the hood of his coat further over his head. *What did you think would happen?* Derudin at least had not been foolish enough to dress in his usual robes. His disguise made him look more an old farmhand than anything else—a very old farmhand. He began to weave his way backward in the crowd diagonally, as moving straight backward may surely single him out.

Stephon was laughing now, his attention caught by something more interesting than an errant fire. "He's now a eunuch," Stephon cried with glee. Derudin could only bury his face to hide his disgust. "Let it be known," continued the young king, yelling over the tumult of the crowd, "that there will be no penalty for the killing of any such Rivervalians. Slay them all, and together we will see this kingdom bask in the glory of purity and Peace."

Derudin's thoughts went to little Eaira. The girl would be in peril the moment word spread to the Throne. He could still hear Alther's screams as he turned the bend that put him out of sight of the platform. They would be no kinder to a young girl, Derudin knew.

ANNORA

"My lady, we must leave," Annora pleaded.

Ethel had already been in a terrible state after learning her father had been imprisoned for the murder of the king, but the latest news from Westport had seen her to stupor. Ethel walked to and fro, hastily putting her things into a heavy chest. Tears pulsed down the well-carved streams on her cheeks, yet she did not sob or whimper. She moved mindlessly, but she was at least moving. *I should not have told her.*

"Ethel, listen to me. We cannot bring this thing. We can take only what is light and valuable. Things we can conceal, above all. If we are to leave the city, you must not appear to be who you are. Listen, *please.*"

I should leave her. The thought pained her, but it was an unassailable truth. *Even in her right mind she will only slow me and draw attention. She will never survive outside these walls.* Annora felt her anger surging.

Ethel would not break from her trance. She was now packing some of her ball gowns and silk slippers. Annora wanted to hit her—and she did.

The blow surprised them both. Annora had simply endured all she could of this foolish girl, but if truth be told, she was equally mad at herself for having considered leaving her. Ethel was as close to a sister and friend as she had known since being sent from her islands, and leaving her to die at the hands of the first drunken fool who decided to kill her, having forgotten that Alther was her father only by marriage, was unacceptable.

"He is dead," said Ethel, showing some sign of clear headedness.

"We should do as he would wish and leave here. It is not safe for either of us. Anyone who is not pure Adeltian may be murdered without consequence. We must leave."

"Eaira."

It was a name Annora had hoped would not come from Ethel's

mouth. They had both become close with the girl ever since her rescue. Eaira was not unlike Ethel; Adeltians wanted nothing to do with her, and the few Rivervalian families that lived near her all had children old enough to have been left behind in Rivervale or no children at all. That was the problem, however. She lived in the estates purposefully set aside for Rivervalian nobility. They would be the first to be raided once the news from Westport flooded the city.

"She and her parents have no doubt left already," Annora said.

"And what if they have not? What if she is hiding in a cabinet after just hearing her parents be killed?"

There are not like to be any cabinets left unopened by those ransacking her estate, Annora thought, but telling Ethel that would do no more than further upset her. *This is idiocy.*

"Grab your jewelry and coins. If we leave now we may get to her before the masses learn of your brother's decree. But if we see they are already there…"

Ethel nodded her agreement and raced to gather her things.

They came here often to fetch their young companion for walks in the gardens, but this time Annora noticed the way to the Rivervalian estates was strangely quiet. The two guards normally stationed at the entry were nowhere to be seen. That was perhaps for the best since they may have hassled them about Ethel being dressed as a servant, but Annora feared the implications of their absence.

Annora had heard of the happenings in Westport as gossip between some of the other servants in the laundry. The woman who spoke it was the sister of a courier, so it was possible that word had not yet spread among the city. The apparent abandonment of these estates was no great indicator, as many of these families probably left immediately after the king was killed.

"They have fled. We should turn back," Annora said.

Ethel shushed her.

Now within the private walls of the community, Annora strained to listen for sounds of danger while creeping down the wide cobbled street, fully exposed by the light of the evening Dawnstar. The structures on either side of the road were so massive that each could have been an inn, yet they housed single families and their servants. Eaira's was the fifth such home on their left. Ethel had told Annora that many of the families here were actually the poorest of the Rivervalian nobility. They could not afford such manors in their own cities, but Lyell had enticed them here with some of the better properties. It was yet another source of discontent among Adeltians.

"The front doors are closed," observed Ethel as they passed a few homes. It was indeed a good sign that they were perhaps the first to come here. Those who would come to pillage after hearing Stephon's unthinkable decree would surely not have the courtesy to close the doors behind them. It seemed to Annora that Ethel was the only member of her family with any sense. Lyell was a tyrant and Alther a coward. She reminded herself that Ethel was not related to either, however, and wondered if the rumors of Stephon's parentage could be true. The son of Sir Stormblade—even Ethel loved to recount the tales of that brave knight.

Annora concentrated on the thick curtains in the windows of each estate they passed, looking for movement. Had they always been drawn closed in every home? She could not recall.

A shiver crawled up Annora's back as she heard Ethel gasp. She saw it too; the front door of Eaira's home was cracked open. *Perhaps her family left in a hurry, as they should have*, Annora hoped.

Annora led the way, trampling through flowers they were normally so careful to avoid by using the steps further down the road. *Better to get Ethel used to doing things differently.* Annora knew they would be faced with discomforts and challenges far worse than destroying some flowerbeds if they were to make it outside the city.

The light of the Dawnstar seemed to shy away from the partly opened door. Annora had no belief in the Mighty Three, or any gods, but the warning here was clear: inside is darkness…and death. It made her pause, and Ethel went past her and opened the door.

There was no ominous creek of hinges. There were no foul smells, and no trails of blood. There was nothing, and it was odd enough in itself. They had always been greeted at this door by a servant or Lady Janette, Eaira's mother. She was an ordinary woman with a pleasant smile. Annora felt as though she had a thankful nature, but she was probably grateful that Eaira had found some friends, even if they were almost twice her age.

"Eaira," Ethel called out in a loud whisper as the two of them made their way through the anteroom. Then they saw their first signs of a struggle.

Furniture in the main room had been overturned erratically. Annora pictured someone running through and pulling things onto their path to slow a pursuer. Ethel continued the search, leading Annora down the hall that would bring them to Eaira's room. But Ethel froze when she rounded the corner.

There were four bodies. A man and a woman both lay with blood pooled around their heads. Each had suffered a gory blow. The man's ear had been completely destroyed by the impact, and the woman had been struck in the face. It was clear to Annora who she was. *I am sorry Lady Janette*, she thought, *you did not deserve this.* She assumed the well-dressed man near her was her husband, but they had never met him.

Eager to finish the search and leave, Annora pushed past. She did her best to step over the puddles, but it was impossible. Blood pulled at her shoe as she lifted her foot from its viscous grasp. She urged on Ethel, who had a look of shock on her face, but to her credit she followed in her footsteps.

The other two bodies were just as gruesome, but there was no blood. Annora recognized them as the guards normally stationed at the entry to the estates. Both men lay on their backs, killed in some horrific way. In the center of each man's chest was a crater the size of a large fist, the flesh, cloth, and leather surrounding which was blackened and scorched. The acrid smell of burning reminded Annora of the ship that had brought her to this land where some of the men and women being transported were branded. The screams she heard were only those of her memories. Surrounding her now was a deathly silence, broken only by the sound of their own clothing rustling as they lurked.

They reached the second room along the corridor and peeked in together.

"Eaira," Ethel cried out again, in a desperate whisper. "It's Eth—"

A figure charged out of the darkness of a closet in the room. It struck Ethel in the stomach with all its force, but Ethel did not budge.

"Eaira!" Ethel had apparently lost control over her volume in her elation. The little girl merely clung to her waist, burying her face into Ethel's belly.

"Ethel?"

The unfamiliar voice was not unfriendly, but it did not belong to a little girl, which was all Annora was hoping to hear. It was the voice of an old man, and although it seemed to come from within the room, Annora could see no sign of anyone.

At the same moment, a crashing noise came from the anteroom. It was followed by a mass of heavy footfalls that suffocated the life out of Annora's newly hopeful spirits. *Looters.*

Before there was time to think or move, the men made their way down the hall, some shouting orders, others shouting reports of what they saw. Annora's presence was among those reports.

Four men with an unmistakable crest on their armor were upon them, and there were more spreading throughout the house. They were members of The Guard, and Annora was not surprised to see that they were among the first to turn to pillage and plunder despite their vows to the realm and humanity. But she soon saw she was wrong to have guessed that.

"Found her," yelled one of the men. "Along with some others."

How it was that they had been sent to search for Ethel so quickly and had known exactly where to go made no sense.

The men were in heavier armor than usual. Their ceremonial placards now rested upon chainmail in place of their usual cloth. Each man had a sword at their belt as well as a heavy, blunted dagger of some sort.

"Who are the others?" asked a man still farther back.

"Looks to be two servants."

"Leave them and bring the girl, then. The young king is quick to anger. We must not make him wait."

The man obeyed the command and moved to grab Eaira from Ethel's clutches, but both were wrapped so tightly around the other he did not succeed in his effort.

"Let her go, you damn washwoman," he snarled.

A second man stepped in to assist the one now yanking on Ethel's hair in his effort to separate her from Eaira.

"That is no servant, you knave," said the second man. "That is Crella's bastard…her first one…Ethel."

"Bring them all and be quick with it, lest we all be impaled on account of torpor. And mind your fecking tongue about the bastard business or I'll tear it out myself."

Annora did not know whether she should be relieved or devastated that the three of them would remain together, if only for the time being. She had always considered herself a captive of these people, but there was a sickening difference between being a well-fed servant and being escorted by armored guard to see the new king, feared even by his own men. *The realm would be better off without these kings*, thought Annora, *the apparent source of all suffering. Given the chance, I would see them all dead.*

KEETHRO

Keethro looked at Titon. It was Titon to be sure, with a raised and glintless axe in hand, yet he had trouble recognizing the giant that now stood before him. The expression he wore was a familiar one. Keethro had seen it countless times—mostly on the faces of Dogmen, just before they shit themselves. He had seen it most recently on the face of the butcher as he diced up the tails of river dragons. But he had never seen it on Titon. It was the look of defeat, and it put a ball of writhing maggots in Keethro's throat to witness it. He did not know if the revulsion he now felt was owed more to this King Veront, the breaker of men, or to Titon, the man Keethro foolishly thought could not be broken.

"Don't miss," Keethro advised his executioner. Titon nodded solemnly in response.

So this is what it is to know you will die, Keethro thought. He wondered if perhaps it would be worth it to try and yank one of the guards that held him into the path of the blade as it swung. Would another man's suffering or death comfort him in his own? Or would Titon's warrior's instinct follow his motion, resulting only in an equally fatal, but more torturous death? Keethro decided it would make little difference.

For some reason it felt as though he had forever to ponder his fate and reflect on his mistakes. *I was a fool to come here, knowing that such an end would be in store. In that, Kilandra was right. But I have not failed her, nor have I failed myself. It is my daughter whom I have failed*, he concluded. To have let Red be shaped and molded by that spiteful woman he called wife was beyond shameful. Images of his daughter consumed his thoughts: her birth, her first words, and the first time she'd cursed at him the same way in which her mother did. *She was not the seed of this man before me. It simply could not be. That was a lie I told myself to ease the guilt of never truly being a father. If you Mighty Three should exist, and I do not believe you do, take me to your hell. Let me feel the wrath of the Dawnstar's flames so that Red may grow to be a better woman than her mother. Do that, and I will be in your debt.*

"Wait."

The distant voice could have come from the Mountain himself, for it seemed to have no origin. Keethro was adrift in his thoughts. Titon was frozen, however, as if he, too, had heard it.

"I needed only know that you would do it. Your friend's death will not undo the death of mine."

It was the king. Expecting Titon would look relieved, Keethro was surprised to see nothing but boiling hatred. Titon closed his eyes, and his expression mellowed for the moment.

"He will be confined to the prisons until you return from Strahl victorious. Three thousand men is a significant portion of my army, and I must be sure to have more than just your word to bring them back." Veront motioned for the guards to fulfill his implicit command, and they wasted no time walking Keethro back down the hall, toward the massive doors that had given him and Titon entry to this place of misery.

"How long of a march is it to Strahl?" Titon had found his voice in time for Keethro to hear a few last bits of their conversation.

"Two weeks in good weather."

"Then expect me back and with the heads of the men you desire in no more than a moon."

At least now Keethro had a timeframe, albeit a hopelessly optimistic one typical of Titon. In the off chance that he actually returned and King Veront honored his words, Keethro could not imagine a scenario where he and Titon could again consider each other brothers. Not after what had just transpired.

The more Keethro thought about it, the more it infuriated him. Titon had nodded in acknowledgment to Veront's implication that Titon had been with a woman the previous night. Was it the shorter serving girl? The very one that Keethro had confided in Titon his affection for? *No wonder you were so eager to see your drunken friend to sleep*, thought Keethro. It was becoming more and more apparent that the legend that was Titon son of Small Gryn, paragon of virtue, fearless leader, and faithful husband, was no more than a myth. The Titon Keethro knew and loved would have never considered chopping him down as commanded. *Perhaps* Sir *Titon now requires an audience of thousands for his heroics.*

DECKER

There was a heaving boulder where his belly should have been, and it pulled him down, pinning him to the hard bottom of his seat. *How is it that asking a fellow Galatai for a formal alliance can cause more apprehension than an actual battle?* Decker wondered if it was because he had only seen battle against Dogmen, but upon further reflection decided it would cause him less anxiety to raise axes against this man, rather than continue at his current task.

Decker was seated in one of eighteen chairs that surrounded a circular table. Behind every chair, hung high on the wall, was a two-handed axe not unlike his father's. To his right sat Kilandra, adorned in her usual furs. Her clothing that he'd once found to be so tasteful and refined was fast becoming an annoyance, as were some of her mannerisms. He could not help but wonder if he would have been better served by her remaining at home.

Directly across from Decker, seated in the only chair that differed from the rest with its high back, was Ivgar son of Kaun.

"I can have some pickled milk fetched for you if the mead is too strong." Ivgar distinctly reminded Decker of another giant man as he spoke those words, but where Titon had long auburn hair and a wild beard, this man had a mane of dull grey and the hair upon his face was cropped short. He stared at Decker with cold blue eyes that questioned his very competence.

Decker downed the contents of his mug and placed it gingerly back upon the table, returning Ivgar's stare. "I have not come here to drain you of all your winter mead. I am here to offer—"

"You offer an *alliance*," said Ivgar, cutting him off. "You've said as much already. And how many clans have agreed to join you so far?"

Decker took his time before answering, letting this man know he was not pleased with having been interrupted. "Six of the eight clans I've visited have already agreed." He was stretching the truth, but it seemed necessary. Of the leaders who had not refused outright, only Joarr and two others had given him a definitive yes. "And with even half our people, I can achieve this conquest that is long overdue. Yours is a strong clan. You do not want to be remembered as one who did not share in the glory."

Ivgar was unmoved. "Long overdue? How can a boy of what—fifteen, sixteen years—judge anything to be long overdue?"

At least he believes me to be older than I am. "I do not claim to have come by this idea myself. Winters grow longer and harsher each year. Some may disagree, but our elders do not. We cannot remain in the North forever."

Ivgar furrowed his brow. The skin on his face was like beaten metal, scarred and pocked by battle and the elements. Decker found himself wondering who would be the victor if the two did battle. A man of his age would no doubt have learned many tricks that might give him the advantage over Decker's youthful speed.

"We cannot, can we? Perhaps it was your harlot here who told you it was wise to come into a man's home and tell him what he can and cannot do."

Decker's anger surged—and worsened still as he felt Kilandra place her hand atop his wrist as if to calm him. He inhaled deeply through flared nostrils and summoned what little restraint he had left before speaking. "My words are honest truth, not some petty insult." Decker glared at the clan leader. *We may have an answer as to who is the greater warrior after all.*

Ivgar merely grunted. "The winters grow longer, do they? One would think your family would remember the last winter that was truly bad. It nearly killed your brother from what I understand."

My brother is dead, thought Decker, but he did not think Ivgar meant to anger him given his apologetic tone.

"My clan has done quite well for itself in spite of these increasingly grim winters you speak of," continued Ivgar. "And we have more goats to be affected by such conditions."

Decker watched the sand cascade down the spiraling dayglass that rest at the center of the table. Such a piece might be worth more than all of what they had brought back from their epic raid. He did not believe this man to be lying about his prosperity. It was known that the clans farther north, just below the permafrost, had more flatland for grazing when the thaws came. Decker's father liked to say that he had no wish to be a herdsman, but that boast was never made during the winter.

"Our people were united once. You know this, no?"

Decker did not move to answer, as he had none.

"Perhaps, then, you require a lesson in history that your father neglected to teach. Many years ago—many *hundreds* of years—our clans were united. And united they went south and conquered kingdoms—kingdoms with armies mind you, nothing like the Dogmen whelps you have faced. They brought back riches and stories of grandeur: farms and rivers as wide as seas, deer fat as pigs, and eternal summer." The man's face hardened. "But they also brought back with them the ways of the southern kings." Ivgar paused to drink from his cup as if recounting the story pained him. "You truly know nothing of this?"

Decker looked to Kilandra for an explanation, but she shook her head at him dismissively.

"Our own leader, Vloki was his name, built for himself a throne and began to demand that clansmen pay him a share of their belongings in return for his protection. *His* protection. Tell me, how can one man claim to be the power that protects when it is the other men and their sons who do the fighting—the same as those he pretends to safeguard?

"It was those of my blood who were first to rebel, and others soon followed. My ancestors took the tyrant's head and tore down his throne. And in its place they built the modest fort that you now sit within."

Decker had never heard these stories of their people's past before. What he knew of their history did not extend so far back. All he knew of were valiant battles fought in the previous hundred years between clans for pride and lands. He had never thought to question why, although they fought over bordering lands, none of the clans had ever sought to truly conquer another. The revelation of this sordid history of Galatai acting like southern oppressors was disturbing in its own right, but the idea that he was now thought by some to be attempting to become the next Galatai tyrant was appalling. His brother had often made Decker feel young and stupid, but this was something worse. Ivgar might as well have been a thousand years old and speaking to Decker, an infant.

"We are Galatai, *men of the glacier*," Ivgar went on. "We belong in the North and nowhere else. Harsh winters will come, as they have before, and harsh winters we will endure. But my clansmen have no want to go south. Nothing good has ever come of it."

Decker's stare had not moved from the dayglass, and he fought a sudden urge to shatter it into a thousand pieces. The support he had acquired from Joarr and the others to the east meant little now.

Decker swallowed hard, tasting defeat for the first time in as long as he could remember. "I have much to think about," he said. *And many to question.* "I apologize for coming here in this way. Thank you for your wisdom…and mead." As Decker stood, Ivgar did as well—an unexpected show of respect.

"I knew your father's father." Ivgar stared at Decker as if he was both sad and angry. "He was a great man."

Ivgar's praising a man Decker had never known meant little to him. *My* father *is a great man.* But even as he formed the thoughts, he was pestered by the fact that he had never heard these stories from the man—not of Small Gryn nor of a Galatai history tainted by tyranny.

Decker nodded at Ivgar and signaled for Kilandra to follow him as he moved to leave.

Kilandra avoided Decker's gaze and cleared her throat. "I will stay for a few moments and discuss matters pertaining to—"

Decker saw no need to allow Kilandra to finish. She had done this before with all the clan leaders save Joarr. Decker thought nothing of it at first, but the smirks of the men outside the halls when he exited alone had worn his patience thin. He did not think Kilandra so brazen as to actually do anything illicit behind his back; however, staying behind—no matter her purpose—was disrespectful and undermined his position as a leader. He grabbed her by the wrist and pulled her from the chair as though she were a child.

"What did you hope to accomplish by that?" Kilandra demanded of him as soon as they were out of earshot of the men stationed outside the fort. "Should you ever lay a hand upon me like that again..." Her face was full of fire.

"You have embarrassed us both enough with your flirting. You will remain by my side always or not at all. I will not have you crippling my leadership with your insistence on being alone with every man of power we come across."

"How dare you accuse me—"

"I have not accused you of anything," growled Decker. "I have merely revealed a shameful truth. And why is it that I had no knowledge of the things Ivgar spoke of? Why have people of your age not seen fit to tell us?"

"People of *my age?* Perhaps you have no knowledge of it because you are a naïve little boy."

"Perhaps I am just a stupid boy—the one you seduced and convinced to set out on this task of uniting our clans only to look like a fool. How could you allow me to enter a man's home and ask him to form again a union that his family is so proud of destroying?"

"I was not aware that the mighty Decker son of Titon needed permission to do anything, let alone from a woman. There are a great many things your father has hidden from you, and you will not blame me for your own ignorance."

I envied Keethro in his having her... Now I am beginning to envy him in his having left. "You are right. I might be better served by a woman closer to my own age and ignorance. I believe your daughter may also agree."

Kilandra's hand shot out like the string of a dry-fired bow and cracked against Decker's face with similar violence. Had she hit someone her own weight with such a blow, it would have knocked the person to the ground, but Decker merely let it sting his cheek with the indifference of the Mountain himself.

"I would strongly advise you reconsider any pursuit of my daughter lest you anger the Mighty Three with your incest. There is a *great deal* that your father has kept from you." With that, she turned and left.

As the large flakes of new snow fell around him, Decker remained a statue of thought, trying to deduce her meaning. He might have believed she was implying that Red had become like a daughter to him now that he and Kilandra had shared a bed…which in some ways Red had. But Kilandra's having stressed that his father had withheld knowledge could only mean that Titon himself was somehow involved.

It is impossible, thought Decker. *He would never betray Mother.*

Titon was more than a father to Decker. He was the embodiment of what a man should be. His honor and virtue was unquestioned. Had a man accused Decker's father of such a thing, he'd likely have died where he stood.

Kilandra may have been gone from sight, but her venom remained. It flowed through Decker's veins, eating at the very foundation of his beliefs. His father would have been a young man then, but it still would have been after Decker's brother had been born. Surely his father had already formed the unbreakable union with Elise that Decker had always known them to have. *Red.* Her very name clawed at him. Such bright red hair she had as a child, a trait not shared by either parent. But the man whose honor was now in question did, and it was so obvious Kilandra had no need to even point it out.

It was a lie. It had to be. But awash in a sea of snow and in an unfriendly land, Decker had no one to turn to for reassurance. In times like these, Decker would look to his brother for logic and answers. Titon would no doubt be able to determine if Kilandra spoke truth or lie. He would have read some trick in a book to test for blood relation or come up with some such method himself. There was no riddle Titon could not solve. But that was before Decker had smashed the life from him, robbing Titon of all his joy and their clan of all his gifts.

Decker wondered what his father might be doing now. *Have you found Mother's remedy yet, Father? Or are you enjoying the comforts of the South while we freeze? Or worse yet, are you busy making me more bastard sisters?* An image of his father and Keethro with blushing southern maidens entered Decker's mind, a pillar of disquiet that would not be moved no matter how he tried to be rid of it.

Could you have picked no better man to accompany you on a mission of mischief, Father? Kilandra had done little but speak ill of Keethro, and it made Decker wonder why his father could even consider the man friend. But maybe Keethro and his father were more alike than Decker realized. It was a sickening thought.

How is it that you left us without so much as saying goodbye, and before even learning if we had been successful? His father should have known how important it was for Decker and Titon to have finally proven their worth in his eyes, but especially so for Titon. *How could you show such contempt for your firstborn? Were you jealous of his intellect? Or was Titon's love for Red the source of your scorn, the potential incest a constant reminder of your infidelity?* His older brother would have been devastated by their father's departure had Decker not first cost him all memories. Decker knew, in spite of Titon's private grumblings, he loved their father more than he dare admit. *And more than he should have, in light of what I now know of the man.*

The wind howled at him like an angry wolf and threw spears of frozen malice at his face. Beneath the noise of the wind, however, Decker heard a far more bothersome sound. The ceaseless trickle of the stream that never froze seemed to follow him wherever he went and became more noticeable always in his times of suffering. It strung a harp with his nerves and plucked a song of provocation. *If this stream that you love is truly formed from the tears of your mountain god, Father, then I will seek out its source and stab him in the eye.*

CRELLA

You will do this, she ordered herself, *and your torment will soon be over.*

Her every muscle ached as she stood on her perch several feet off the floor, her whole body tensed. A vile moisture began to gather on her skin, threatening to turn to droplets of sweat. *You must not remain here another night.*

The memories of her life spent at her uncle's estate were mostly shrouded in darkness. She had no misgivings about her feelings toward the man—she'd always known she hated him—but she had refused to remind herself of why. That Cassen had reawakened her burning abhorrence for all men of power only served to strengthen her need to be gone from this place.

You should have run long ago, she scolded herself. *You should have taken Ethel far from this kingdom.* The thought of her daughter having to persist without her was sickening. There was pride to be had in the strong woman Ethel had become, in the face of her hardships, but the scorn her peers showed Ethel would not be shared by the kingdom's new ruler. How long would it be before Cassen tired of Crella and moved on to her daughter? Lyell seemed a saint now by comparison.

Crella squeezed her eyes closed, willing the memory of the night Cassen had spoken of to return with more clarity, no matter how painful. *Was Stephon truly the first miscreant of my creation?* she wondered. *Or am I to blame for Cassen as well?* She did not recall the night of her uncle's death quite the same as Cassen had recounted. She did not remember having escaped that night without torture, only that she had awoken to find Calder dead at the bottom of the steps in the morning.

Her legs wobbled, but she kept herself from toppling. There was no reason for it to be so difficult to remain standing where she was, upon this trunk she'd dragged toward the door. Crella breathed deeply and steadied herself. She would see this done, and properly. They had been so careful to clear the room of all the implements that could be used to end a life. There was no crystal, no silvered glass, no lacings or ribbon. How ironic it was that the thing she had found was the very item that almost killed her husband. Huge porcelain vases yet remained, and Crella had broken one to find it produced edges sharp as any glass. And with a piece of cloth wrapped around it to serve as a handle, she had fashioned a rather viable weapon.

Should it be a servant or Cassen, it does not matter. Whoever passes through this door next will die. From upon her trunk she would have height and momentum to her advantage as she plunged her makeshift blade into the neck of that unlucky man. *Let it be Cassen*, she thought. Her chance of success attacking Cassen was far less than her latest weakly servant, but still she hoped for it to be her tormentor who next arrived. She shuddered thinking of his repulsive touch. *I will make him a eunuch in truth.*

But revenge was not her only goal; it was escape. She'd forgone her bath to have enough water to wash the blood from the clothes of her victim—the clothes she would then don herself. The likelihood of walking past the guards unnoticed was not good, but there was a chance. Guards paid servants little notice, and they did their best to avoid eye contact with men of high station. They would not notice she'd escaped for hours, giving her enough time—she hoped—to find Ethel and flee north.

A droplet of sweat fell from her nose and splashed on her foot. It would be so easy to step down and bathe herself in the cool, inviting water, to wash the filth from her body. It would be easier still to use her porcelain blade to cut her thigh as she rest there, and drift peacefully to sleep. *I will do no such thing*, she resolved, readjusting her grip on her weapon. *They have not beaten me.*

Crella caught her breath and cocked her head. She strained to hear. Her pulse quickened and her head began to throb as she heard the sound of approaching footsteps. It was no servant.

CASSEN

Lyell was a fool not to have used this room more often. The throne room had the musty smell of disuse, and it was a shame, considering its magnificence. *How long will it be before the smell is gone and replaced by the delicate scents of my Sacaran tallow?* Cassen mused, more so about whether he would choose to rule from Rivervale or Adeltia—a decision impossible to make, as he did not yet know what Rivervale had to offer. He made a point now to take in all he could see, nearly all of which was illustrious, but the horizontal drapes that tempered the dawnlight of the ceiling glass were a clear detraction and would need to be discarded. He had come to appreciate most other things of antiquity, but the clothing, the curtains, the linens— essentially all the fabric-based extravagance surrounding his false life— had required feigned interest.

He would light no tallow candles today, however. That duty apparently had been bestowed upon Sture, Stephon's newest friend and ally.

"And now, Your Grace, I will boil the wine inside the chalice."

Sture gave an impressive performance if truth be told. Derudin had taught the little brat well in his class of magicianry—to call it magic would be an insult to children who believed in such things. Sture had wheeled a large platform just inside the doors of the room. Upon it sat many candles and a metal chalice. It was a good twenty paces from where the lad stood at the foot of the throne, and he had already pretended to light each candle using nothing but his mind or some such nonsense. Cassen did not have the patience to endure the entire farced explanation, choosing instead to envision Sacarat's men storming this very room while Stephon hoped in vain to be defended by this boy's incantations.

Cassen's lack of faith did not prevent the chalice from emitting some sort of gurgling noise, however, accompanied by an impressive amount of steam plumed above. Clearly there was some heat source beneath the platform, but he would not ruin Stephon's delight. *Better to have him bright eyed and gleeful. He will be less likely to destroy himself or the kingdom in what little time he has left to rule.* After witnessing Stephon's sacrifice of Alther firsthand, Cassen had been forced to consider the possibility that Stephon might actually be able to manage such a thing before the Satyr made landfall—which would be a terrible shame.

Sture had ingratiated himself with Stephon by recovering Derudin's diary. It was written in some archaic scribble that only Sture could decipher. Cassen's doubts as to whether he truly translated the contents were somewhat squelched when the words he'd read were things Sture would be unlikely to have concocted—Derudin had not written so positively about Sture himself.

"Impressive, I must say. I would prefer to see your talents demonstrated upon a less willing object, however. If you can boil wine could you not also boil the blood of a man?" Stephon motioned for one of his two guards at the far door to step forward, and he did…reluctantly.

A fine question. I should like to see how Sture navigates these troublesome waters. Stephon's challenge was a clever one, though it probably could have been accomplished without besoiling the trust of his guard. *Ahh, the ignorance of youth.*

Sture turned to face Stephon with a look of concern. "There are…limitations…when it comes to such things."

Cassen could not help but chuckle from where he stood at the side of Stephon's throne.

His mockery did not go unnoticed by Sture whose disposition darkened in anger. "Living things have natural defenses against magic. Defenses that are in place regardless of training. Derudin had a word for it…"

"Yes, if only you could think of the word," Cassen said, "that would explain it all away." Cassen had already shown his hand with his laughter, he might as well let his thoughts be heard.

Sture ignored him and addressed the king. "There must be ways around them. Derudin mentions exceptions in his diary but does not specify. With time and subjects to test on… I am not without ideas."

"Let's put your best theory to the test, then. Why not? What will it take? Bat wings? The blood of a virgin?" Stephon seemed to wish to join in the ridicule, a small hedge considering his unabashed interest in the subject.

Sture was not offended. "No, nothing like that. May I try on the guard? Or perhaps your advisor?"

It was not at all what Cassen had expected. Sture's eagerness to test his theories was unsettling, and being named gave him an embarrassing rush of nerves.

"Very well," said Stephon. "You may try on the guard. But please, I wish to see this magic put to a proper use. I already have servants that can light candles and boil things."

Sture was filled with honest delight as he bounded toward the guard who looked as though he were ready to relieve himself in his armor.

Should he kill this guard, even with some trickery, I may be forced to admire this impudent boy.

A knock on the great metal doors reverberated throughout the throne room, much to Cassen's displeasure.

"Enter." Stephon sounded equally annoyed.

The doors parted and some very familiar young women were escorted inside. Annora was the first to catch Cassen's eye. She was accompanied by Ethel and some frazzled little girl. Ethel was dressed in servants' clothes, which meant she had either been enjoying a game of play-the-pauper or she had planned to flee the kingdom. *Not an unwise decision.* That Annora looked guilty enough to have been attempting to escape with her was another issue.

"Your Grace," said the leader of the half-dozen-man escort. He was a humorless looking member of The Guard, the type Cassen despised. "These two were found with the girl you sent us after. I believe one of them is your sister."

"*Half*-sister," growled the young king. So far it seemed only Stephon's blood had come to boil. *Perhaps this guard is a mage as well,* thought Cassen, amused.

"I beg forgiveness, Your Grace. We believe this to be her servant, though they refused to speak. We thought it best to not mistreat them."

"Leave us."

"Yes, Your Grace, but I am duty bound to remind you that we have not yet searched them for weaponry. If you would like us to do so now or at least to remain—"

"If they manage to kill my two guards, mage, and eunuch, I'll simply slap whatever weapons they have from their dainty hands and beat them to obedience myself. Now, *leave us.*"

The doors opened and closed once more, allowing the six escorts to escape.

"You three, approach," commanded Stephon.

The girls walked slowly toward the throne, the smaller one clinging tightly to Ethel's skirts. Ethel looked regal even in her peasant attire, which did little to hide her figure, and Annora was every bit as captivating as Cassen remembered, though she would not meet his gaze. *How can such dark eyes burn with such brilliant flame?*

"King Stephon, Your Grace, I know this Spiceland servant. Under your—" Sture interrupted himself with a clearing of the throat. "Under the Rivervalian tyrant's rule, she thought it acceptable to lay hands upon me. The Spiceland cunt does not know her place. I beg you, let me test my powers upon her so that we do not waste a trained guard."

Stephon looked disinterested in what Sture had to say and showed the boy his open palm to delay his untimely request. "Do you know what it is that previous kings lacked?"

Cassen had to remind himself that he was indeed more than a mere observer of the events unfolding before him when he realized that he was the one to whom the question had been posed. "No doubt a great many things, Your Grace."

Stephon scowled with the annoyance of a child deprived of a toy. "If you intend to remain as my First, I would advise you to answer my questions precisely or not at all." Cassen moved to respond but was cut off. "What they lacked," continued Stephon, "was broadmindedness and creativity—things I happen to have in abundance."

Just a few more days—a week at most, Cassen reminded himself. *And all you will have in abundance will be ignominy.*

"Sture, read again the passage from Derudin's book concerning Eaira."

Stephon's command clearly irked the boy, but he obeyed and retrieved the book from the foot of the throne. After some page flipping he found the spot he had been searching for and frowned. "I still believe these words to be written in error—"

"Read them."

"Yes, Your Grace." Sture shot a look of contempt toward Eaira before he began—little good it did considering her face remained buried in Ethel's side. "Perhaps my most promising student is a young girl by the name of Eaira. Although her true capacity for conductance remains untested, her focus and continence is as impressive as any I have before witnessed. A drop of water boiled within a bucket and a pinpoint of melted glass have been all that she has been willing to share, yet I suspect her capable of far more in time." Sture shook his head. "The girl has not so much as lit a candle in class. Derudin has written lies upon these pages knowing the book would be found."

"Cassen, my First, what are your thoughts as to the benefits of magic to the kingdom?" Stephon asked as if he already knew the answer, and he did. Cassen had revealed to him his belief that Derudin was a fraud.

"Your Grace, everything I have seen of magic has been no more than parlor tricks." Sture scoffed audibly at Cassen's reply. "I am yet to bear witness to anything that could not be explained by natural phenomena."

"There is little wisdom in such conventional thinking, unless you think it wise to trust the old men that came before you. I have always wondered why it is that those in power did not simply demand more from the ones who call themselves mages. Tonight I shall do just that, however. Sture, I grant you your wish. You will prove to me and my eunuch that your powers are more than tricks. Please, demonstrate your worst upon this Spiceland woman who has wronged you."

"You will do no such thing!" Ethel had found her voice. "You sit upon the throne you stole from Father, who loved you in spite of your lack of character. You killed the only good man in the entire kingdom. I had once thought our grandfather the least fit man imaginable to rule, but that was only because I never considered you a man. You are a foolish little boy. I only pray that you realize it before you die, when someone with enough courage finally kills you as they all wish to."

Stephon sucked at his teeth and made a pained face as though he'd bitten into a lemon. "My dear half-sister, I am not the 'little boy' you once knew." His voice surprisingly had no anger in it. "While you were sipping tea and dancing with your fellow debutantes, I was trapped in a prison cell. I did not rot in that cell, however. I rebelled. I honed my mind with the whetstone of wisdom provided to me in the form of ancient writings. Any fool can read a book. We all know you have many girlish novels that serve in the place of friends. But a book is not a friend. A book is a tool. And all tools are useless in the hands of those who do not know how to use them."

The young king stroked his narrow chin as if it had hair upon it. "A passage comes to mind—though I admit I cannot remember the name of the text. A king's greatest enemy wears no armor and carries no sword. She is the one that calls him son, the one that calls him brother, and the one that sleeps beside him. She undermines his every action with appeals for clemency and compassion, and she is the kiss that invites the collapse of his kingdom."

That Stephon was able to quote so relevant a passage was markedly impressive to Cassen—compassion was, after all, a horrible weakness, the acknowledgment of which was astute. *Perhaps the boy did read a few words while confined.*

"But there really is no need for you to fear, Ethel, if you allow me to explain my full intent. Derudin believes the little whelp clutching to you to be a powerful mage, and I mean to put that to trial as well. Guards, seize the servant and the little girl and bring them forward."

The two guards executed their command, both looking relieved to no longer be the bodies of interest. One grabbed Annora's upper arm, and the other attempted to pry Eaira from Ethel's clothing. The little girl put up a powerful fight as she clung to her surrogate mother, but Cassen's focus was on Ethel herself. The hatred in her eyes was transparent, and he was not surprised when she bolted forward as soon as Eaira's small hands lost their grip.

Ethel was no great threat, but she sprinted toward where Stephon sat with the ferocity of a wild animal protecting her young. Sture cowered as she neared him, though he was not her target. The shine of a blade caught Cassen's eye as she came within a few paces of the throne, and Cassen stepped in front of his king, grasped her wrist that held the weapon, and easily broke her momentum.

"I will kill you if you hurt either one of them," shrieked Ethel. She fought Cassen's grip with all her vigor, but she was no match. Cassen was confronted with an inexplicable feeling of disgust as he recalled how her mother had fought so similarly.

Stephon had a good bout of laughter at the spectacle as his two guards hurried toward Ethel in their heavy armor. Cassen removed the knife from her hand himself, not trusting the two idiots to be up to the task without harming her. They each took an arm and dragged her back down the few steps she had climbed that lead to the throne.

"Saved by a eunuch. I do appreciate the gesture, Cassen, but in the future, when a woman charges me, just allow it. It would have entertained me to see if she even followed through with her pathetic attack or merely cried at my feet."

"I would have killed you," Ethel yelled in defiance, and she did not stop there. Her threats and screeching acrimony continued as she thrashed violently while the guards held her.

The young king rubbed his temples in protest. "Peace's mercy. Please take her away. Lock her in the throne chambers so that we may proceed here."

The guards returned shortly after dragging Ethel off, her shrieks completely deadened by the thick doors of the room tucked behind the throne. Eaira had attempted to clutch on to Annora the same way she had been to Ethel, but Annora had made the girl hold her hand instead. The spite in Annora's eyes must have been mostly for Stephon, but the fraction of it that was for Cassen was enough to make him feel almost guilty. *You haven't anything to fear, my little Spiceland runaway. This charade will be over soon enough.*

It was Eaira that Stephon now addressed. "Little girl, please listen to what I have to say as it is incredibly important. Come here first so that I may speak to you without raising my voice."

The girl looked to Annora who nodded slightly. She had no choice after all; Ethel's attack had demonstrated the futility of rebellion. Eaira walked with caution toward the throne, looking back to ensure Annora was still there. When she was a few paces away, Stephon resumed.

"Your friend over there is going to need your help in a moment. This boy that you know, Sture, has accused her of a crime and will be attempting to punish her for it. You have my permission to stop him—if you can—using whatever magic or powers that are at your disposal. Do you understand?"

The girl gave no indication that she did. Instead, tears welled in her eyes.

"This is rather silly," said Stephon. "I am inclined to believe you were right about Derudin's writings, Sture. In any case, you may go ahead and perform whatever dark arts upon her you wish in order to have your revenge."

A most sincere smile stretched across Sture's face.

"Your Grace," Cassen interjected. "It may be wise to conduct this test on someone who might actually be able to otherwise defend themselves. It is no great feat to kill a weakling girl, even if performed by a weakling boy." Sture looked at Cassen with contempt.

"Perhaps my quote should be amended to include 'she is the one without genitals who pleads for mercy.' As my First you owe allegiance to me before this little trollop you call daughter. And I wish to see her die to magic."

"Oh, you misunderstand me," Cassen said, doing his best to hide his growing anger. "Her fate is of no consequence to me, but harming a daughter of the Spicelands will only complicate our dealings with their people. This girl was to be the wife of a king before I purchased her. Her death will not go unnoticed."

"I do not *misunderstand* anything," said Stephon. "Should Sture fail to kill her, she may yet be wife to a king, or at least share his bed for a spell, for I might wish to sample her Spiceland treasures. Then, I may very well cut the skin from her frame and write upon it a letter of apology to the primitives of the Spicelands for having debased her. And should they take issue with my sincere apology, I will send a fleet of warships to the shores of their little islands and take by force that which those before me have so generously bartered for."

"Apologies, Your Grace. I see you have thought this through far more than I have, and I yield to your wisdom." There was no reason to explain to Stephon that he had no fleet of warships—that the many ships that crowded the port cities' docks, many of which were armed with defunct catapults in an attempt to scare off Spicerats, were actually owned by Spiceland and Adeltian merchants.

"As you should. Sture, please continue. And be quick about it."

Sture motioned for the guards to seize Annora's arms, and after they did so, he moved forward and placed his hand upon the center of her chest. *If this knave is merely using this opportunity to touch his first breast, he will certainly regret it.* Stephon would not be overjoyed if all this effort caused the victim nothing more than embarrassment.

And just as Cassen had suspected, nothing much happened. He watched Annora's eyes intently since all he could now see of Sture was his back. She still had within her all her strength and defiance. A boy's hand upon her chest was not enough to unnerve her, nor apparently was the threat of some gruesome death by magic. Cassen found himself admiring her just as he had the night she had recounted her tale of defending herself against Emrel—the man Cassen had given her to for the express purpose of being violated. Cassen quickly pushed that thought aside.

Her expression began to change, albeit slowly. Her defiance melted away, replaced with confusion. She was not the only one confused, though. The guards holding her exchanged troubled looks when what appeared to be smoke began to rise from between Sture and her. *What sort of device did that boy slip into his hand? Will it be enough to truly harm her or just produce some smoke?* Cassen wondered. *And why should I care?* Cassen reminded himself that he would gladly sacrifice a hundred of the girls he had been calling daughters in exchange for the consummate victory that was so close at hand.

Cassen turned his attention to the king he would soon depose with the help of the Satyr. Stephon gripped the large wooden arms of his throne tightly and leaned forward, sniffing the air. The smoke was no illusion. Cassen could smell it as well. Stephon's look of hunger irritated Cassen, but he found a way to comfort himself. *Let the idiot believe he has the power of true magic at his disposal. It will make his defeat all the sweeter.*

A whimper turned Cassen's attention back to the scene in front of him. It was not the little girl as he had hoped. Eaira had her face hidden in her hands, and she certainly did not look to invoking any magic of her own to save her friend.

It was Annora who had made the sound, and as Cassen looked upon her he felt something inside him revolt. Bile made its way up his throat and into his mouth, but he swallowed it down and hardened his resolve. *She is a piece of property, paid for and imported from a faraway land. Nothing more.*

Annora struggled, her moist eyes glistening in agony, but the guards held her firmly. The smell of charred flesh hit Cassen just as she began to scream. Her cries filled the room as she writhed like a helpless animal caught in a toothed trap.

Again, Cassen looked to Stephon, searching for any indication that he might stop this demonstration short of Sture killing her with whatever instrument he held. Stephon had mentioned his desire to bed Annora— perhaps his fondness went deep enough to wish to spare her. But Stephon's delight was plain to see. To him, this was validation of his curiosity, and he showed no sign of wishing for this triumphant moment to end.

Cassen closed his eyes as his rage built, but it did nothing to stifle Annora's wails, which grew louder and more desperate still.

"Enough!"

A man's strong voice echoed throughout the room. Cassen opened his eyes in search of who had yelled, but he saw no new occupants. His attention went to his hand as he noticed he was gripping something quite tightly. It was Ethel's knife, plunged through the top of Stephon's hand, pinning him to his wooden throne. Stephon's head turned slowly in utter disbelief to face his wound. The boy king was awash with incredulity as his gaze shifted from his bleeding hand to the man who had attacked him, probably wondering what demon had possessed the docile duchess he had so kindly made his First.

All of Cassen's careful planning had been undone with a single thrust—and of his own action, no less.

What have I done?

TALLOS

The Dawnstar stood low in the darkened sky, taunting Tallos with its presence. He paid it no mind, instead inhaling the sweet-smelling air, enjoying it for the first time since having gone underground. The scent that flooded his nostrils and chest brought back the memory of the day he had first approached Leona as she struggled to wash her family's clothing in the cold. *Some small respite it is that I should die enjoying the same perfume of early winter snow and chimney smoke.*

But he was not merely to die. A bonfire had been built for the sole purpose of his destruction. After the men had determined fire to be the only suitable means of snuffing out his existence, a healthy debate had begun over how best to accomplish the task. The typical execution by burning was achieved by simply starting a fire under the prisoner staked above a mass of wood. The dissenters argued that they had seen such burnings take place before, and that the stake often weakened and broke before the flames had consumed the body. Their fear was that Tallos might simply fall to freedom prior to his body being devoured fully by fire and turned to ash—the only way to be sure he'd truly been dispatched. The plan that was settled upon was to first build a massive blaze, chain him to a stake, and hoist him, not above, but directly into the center of the conflagration.

It was perhaps a more humane method, but it made no difference to Tallos. His recollection of the pain he'd endured when setting his own home alight had not faded so much as the scars that it had left. And those scars were as clear and gruesome to his own eyes as they were to the many who stared at him.

It was no mystery to him why they thought him a demon—it was, after all, exactly what he had intended to become. But his failure in that task was now utterly complete. The fact that he'd eaten human flesh meant little. He imagined most would have done the same if faced with starvation. The taste was far from unpleasant, and it was made easier for him, able to eat in the comfort of darkness.

There was, however, a mystery that Tallos now pondered. As he sat naked, cold, and in chains, kept alive only by the heat of the fire that would soon kill him, he could not help but wonder how this camp existed as it did. Of the hundred or so men here, he counted no more than a dozen who were those in charge of conscription. The rest all complied with the orders of these few men, their new masters, as if there was no alternative. The men of the village had even been armed with swords and shields and received instructions on their proper use. Should they choose to, the armed villagers could easily overwhelm the few who had originally forced them into this fate worse than slavery—for slaves were not marched into death with the same haste that Otis promised his conscripts, giving these men even more cause to fight.

"Otis, make sure your miserable recruits are alert in case we have need of their blades." Gepner had remained in command and had been barking orders ever since Tallos was deemed a demon. "Erik, go get the scribes from notes and queries, all of them. Half of them probably can't write worth a damn, and I want what takes place here kept record of."

The skinny man that ran to fetch the scribes shared little in common with the Erik Tallos had known. He tried to remember his large, red-speckled friend, but every image formed in his mind was of Erik clutching his neck, blood spurting from between his fingers. *How much of Erik's death was my fault, and not the gods'?* Little difference it made now, but little differences seemed to be what consumed his thoughts—and what likely consumed all men's thoughts before dying, Tallos imagined.

When the wind shifted, the heat of the bonfire became more than Tallos wanted or needed for warmth, awakening his deadened skin in anticipation of the torture that awaited him. Tallos reminded himself that he had lost everything, and with nothing left to lose, he no longer had need of fear. But the crackling pyre with flames reaching overhead made clinging to this notion rather difficult.

The many village men with shields and swords were lined up next to the bonfire. Otis stood in front with a look of reproach. Tallos's ordeal had kept Otis from his intended time with Lily, Gepner having ordered him and his conscripts to keep vigil over the captured demon. Though Otis stood a fortress in his water-hardened leather, Kelgun had shown the man to be mortal. Twenty or so recruits would be more than enough to topple him and find a seam in his armor or smash his helmless head.

The four mounted men-at-arms were in their own group, chatting amongst themselves, butts still in their saddles. Occasionally they would all glance at Tallos and laugh or frown. These men presented the biggest threat should the villagers rebel. Their long-pointed halberds were the perfect weapons for dispatching unarmored foes from a distance. If the villagers were to acquire the weapons for themselves, however, they would serve equally well for countering the mounted men, pulling them down with the hooked side or merely impaling their charging horses with the sharpened tip.

A slow procession of old men with quill jars and parchment followed the man called Erik back to his place at Gepner's side. Tallos found he was relieved to see Wilkin was among them and unharmed. Another group of villagers, mostly women and children, streamed in from the opposite direction. Tallos thought he saw Dusan and Lily among them, but he could not be sure. He scanned the infantry in hopes of finding John but saw no sign of him. Tallos had seen him removed from the gibbet far sooner than expected and hoped he would have gone directly into infantry without further punishment. *The more friendly faces, the better my chances of escape.* Tallos realized he had no intention of dying without a fight.

It seemed the time had come. The two mailed men who had cast aside their weapons in order to fashion Tallos's crossed stake had completed the task. They spoke quietly to each other, glancing nervously toward Tallos.

Gepner approached. "Stop your gossiping and break the demon's chains near the ground."

"Shouldn't we stake him first?" asked one of the stake's proud constructors.

"Just do as I ask," Gepner spat, then looked to Tallos smugly. "There's been a change in plan. Otis, have a few of your recruits wheel over the gibbet."

Tallos did not need any more reason to hate this provisioner. His loathing had grown by bounds when Gepner had begun to pray to the Mighty Three shortly after passing judgment on Tallos. *Finally I find one deserving of my wrath, but I have little means by which to make him feel it.* Tallos's fate rested solely in the hands of the villagers. With the hundred or so that had just joined the onlookers they were easily two hundred strong, whereas there were only nine of those who commanded them present.

Tallos stood and faced them. "Men and women of the Fourpaws," he began, "I am not the demon these men have judged me to be."

"Let me shut him up," growled Otis. "I want to see a man burn, not hear a boring speech."

"No," said Gepner. "Let the demon speak. All can see what he is. We have no reason to fear his words."

Otis grunted his disapproval.

"I am a Fourpaw man, the same as you. My village was destroyed by a small raiding party of Northmen."

The two men responsible for Tallos's staking began to bang away at the chains that were anchored into the earth. The noise made it difficult to be heard so he was forced to shout.

"They killed my friends, my wife, and my dog. Everyone I knew was murdered or worse. Everything I ever built or owned was burned to the ground."

"Then why do you still live?" It was Otis who challenged him. And the question singed Tallos as much as any fire.

"Because I was a *coward*. Just like all of you. I thought to fight, but I hesitated. And then, when the fighting started, I ran." Tallos had decided to take some liberties with his story, but the sentiment remained. "Had we all raised arms together against the few men who came to destroy us, we would have suffered losses, but we would have won. And those of us who died would not have died in vain. These men who hold you captive are no better than the Northmen that attack us. They come and demand from us our money, our service, our lives, and they offer nothing in return."

Tallos had expected to see some nodding in the crowd, but they were all motionless. "Do not make the same mistake that our village did and allow so few to destroy so many. You men with the swords—protect your wives and children. Sir Kelgun, show these men what courage is, and lead them against these oppressors!"

The clanging of the men working on his chains stopped. Tallos looked at the group of unarmed women and children, trying to gauge if his words had had the intended effect, expecting at any moment for just one of them to raise a cry causing all others to follow in rebellion. Lily and her brother Dusan were close enough that he could tell for certain it was them. The boy stared at Tallos with sad eyes, but Lily only looked down. Tallos looked at the other faces surrounding them, but they were all much the same. That was to be expected; they were the meek ones— too weak even for arrow fodder.

Tallos looked to the center where the scribes stood. All of them wrote busily save Wilkin. He thought he saw the old man nod at him. Was it a nod of respect or apology? It was impossible to tell. In any case, the scribes would be of no use. Their quills carried no power here.

Tallos turned his attention to the armed villagers. They were motionless as well, save for some fidgeting. It would only take one man to charge Otis and the others would assist him in felling the giant. How many of their friends had they already seen maimed in training? And how many would survive an actual battle? Kelgun had shown courage earlier, and now with the potential aid of so many others there was little reason for him not to attempt one last time, perhaps earning his title of sir in truth. But when Tallos looked at him all he saw was a beaten man whose scorn was directed now at Tallos instead of his captors. *I should not have called him by name. That was foolish.* Tallos searched instead for John. That was a man with true honor, even if he was no swordsman, but he was nowhere to be seen among the many faces.

A deep laughter came forth. Otis had his arms crossed upon his belly and each hearty guffaw pushed them up and down again. He did not even seem to care that he had his back to the mass of armed men that Tallos had just dared to kill him. Nor was it Tallos he truly laughed at. The man knew battle, and he knew the men that waged it bravely. Behind him were no such men; even Tallos could see that now.

"These men fight for Rivervale, not for darkness," said Gepner. "Put the demon in the cage, and let us see this done with already."

Tallos tried to imagine what he must look like addressing this crowd of people. Lit by the flames that would soon consume him, covered by self-inflicted scars of a horrific nature, and completely naked, he had just pleaded with them. He wanted to burst into laughter as the two men who had severed his chains grasped him by either arm, but his hatred presided and would not allow it. The fire that he was about to be thrown upon paled in comparison to the one that built within. He loathed the weakness of these people, and loathed himself for having once shared that weakness.

He flexed the muscles of his arms, slowly building tension between the two that held him. His stay underground had withered him and each man to his side was easily stronger than him, but he did not let it impede his struggle. He pulled harder still, fueled by his hatred, he aimed to crush these two men together, but they were simply too strong. They only pulled his arms further outward, painfully so, and attempted to hoist him into the gibbet that had arrived. Tallos grabbed them by their tabards, holding as tightly as he could, and fought to remain uncaged.

"By the light of the Dawnstar's crack," one yelled. "Someone help us."

Otis moved forward with a look of pleasure. His slow, confident stride brought him face to face with Tallos. "Do you think I fear you? I know you are just a man. Now be good, and let them coop you..." Otis put both his hands behind Tallos's skull, lacing his fingers together. "Or I'll be forced to hurt you."

Otis was moments away from driving his head into Tallos's face, but that was not what bothered Tallos most. The leather-clad behemoth's breath stank of rotten meat, completely replacing the pleasant scent of smoke and snow. *Was it one such as you that raped Leona?* The thought of this smirking pig having his way with her was more than he could bear. Tallos inhaled the putrid air, allowing it to fill him with rancor. He would let his wrath be heard one final time.

He was too late. Otis was no patient man, and his bald, sweaty crown was already on its way to smash out Tallos's teeth. Tallos began to scream in rage, hopeful that he would be heard before being knocked asleep, or at least that he may awake to the sight of some of his teeth embedded in his attacker's forehead.

A torrent of flame shot from Tallos's mouth, the force of which sent

Otis flying backward. Tallos did not wait to see the hulking body hit the ground before first turning to the guard on his left and then to his right, howling flame at them as they each were ripped from his grasp. He dropped the scraps of their tabards from his hands and marched to his next victim, not scrutinizing the absurdity of these events he must be dreaming, only eager to exact his vengeance.

Gepner was a coward of a man. Tallos already knew as much. The hefty provisioner pushed Erik to the ground as he turned to run from Tallos, but in doing so tripped over himself and tumbled.

"Mountain's mercy," he cried. "Please, spare me."

Tallos grabbed Gepner by the loose mail on his shoulders and pulled him to his feet. "I will show you the same mercy the Mountain showed my village."

Smoke began to rise from under Gepner's mail, and he shrieked with horror. Fire burst from his chest, setting his beard alight. Tallos released him, allowing him to run and fan the flames. Tallos then slammed his foot on Erik as he wriggled on the ground beside him, reaching for a blade. The thin bones of the man's wrist snapped, and he whimpered. Tallos put him out of his misery with expedience, willing his head to combust. Erik's eyes first reddened, then blackened, then burst.

Tallos turned to where the horsemen had been, but they were nowhere to be seen. He focused his attention instead to the armed men of the village, the beast of retribution still hungering inside him. *They deserve to die for their cowardice.*

Pandemonium had spread. Men and women scattered in all directions, but mostly away from Tallos. A man in plain clothes and with a sword in hand ran past him—one of the cravens. Curious, Tallos allowed him to continue on his course and was not surprised when he saw his destination was a fair-looking woman. She was dressed much the same as most women of the Fourpaw villages, much the same as Leona had dressed. Her long hair must have been knocked loose during the commotion, as she would have no doubt worn it in the more modest and customary folded tail when in the presence of strange men. It flowed in the soft breeze as had Leona's, and when the man embraced her, Tallos felt the pang of anger. He had not forsaken his gods to save cowards from the very fate he had suffered himself.

Tallos blew hellfire from his lungs, engulfing the couple from many paces away. He did not pity this man who had allowed his village to be despoiled and then refused to answer Tallos's call for insurrection. And he did not pity this woman, a weakling creature, her path never decided by her own actions but by others, namely the one she called husband—a man likely to have been chosen for her by her parents.

I am Nekasr, and around me the world burns.

As the woman was consumed by flame, Tallos's thoughts betrayed him. The face that disappeared into the red death became Leona's.

I will not be deterred by illusion, he told himself, and continued his assault.

His storm of fury hid her from sight, but it did nothing to stifle her soft yet audible lament—anguish that sounded no different than those times he'd been unable to ease Leona's suffering, when she'd lost her younger sister and when Lia had run off.

As the woman's cries persisted, Tallos's will to commit this first of many atrocities persisted in kind. The gods he loathed would have no choice but to notice an act so vile as this. When he allowed his flames to cease, all that would remain would be their two bodies, charred to black, together in their final embrace.

The thought suddenly repulsed him. This man had at least made it to his wife in time to shield her. *Where was I when Leona needed me? On a fool's errand, one she'd warned me not to take.* This man may have been too timid to fight, but at least he had run to be with her in death. *He is a hero compared to me.*

Tallos hardened his resolve, refusing to stop what he had begun. It was too late to, in any case. But his creeping doubt made him finally question what it was he was becoming. Seemingly boundless power rushed through him, making him feel invincible—godlike. The realization stifled him.

Tallos inhaled, trying to suck the hellfire back within himself, back where it belonged. He could almost hear the gods laughing at him, mocking him. This act of killing a defenseless couple had not made him feel as though he had provoked the gods—he felt more as though he had become their instrument.

As the blinding light went dark, so did the world. Tallos was thankful he could not yet see, but he would not run from what he had done; he would stay and look upon it. In his mind, he could still hear the woman's lamentation. It sounded of grief and emotional despair, not physical suffering, and it confirmed for him, albeit far too late, that killing the meek did not suit his cause. Forsaking the laws espoused in the names of the gods would not draw their ire—those laws were spurious decrees that the gods themselves broke with their every breath. *I must find a more deserving recipient of my wrath.*

It was worse than he had expected. As his vision returned he saw movement—he had not killed them. Lia's sad eyes assailed him from his memories. Knowing that he would have to end their suffering just as he had ended hers struck him with weight, but he would not neglect his duty, nor would he delay it.

He turned from them and walked toward where he knew a weapon sharp enough to see the task done quickly would rest. He saw only dark shapes, his eyes still fearful of allowing in more light, but he made out the mound that was his aim. As Tallos neared Otis's corpse, he saw another figure knelt beside him. Tallos willed his eyes to adjust, but the kneeling man jumped back before he could be identified.

"Stand back, mage."

The man had the gleaming weapon raised, threatening to swing down. The voice was strong, so much so that Tallos might have mistaken him for a brave man, had he not recognized it.

"The sword, Kelgun." Tallos extended his open hand. As his sight returned, he saw the fear on Kelgun's broken face, one eye swollen shut and his cheek scabbed over. The knight reluctantly surrendered his blade, presenting it to Tallos hilt first. Under other circumstances it may have amused Tallos, but there was no humor to be had in the task to come.

With downcast eyes, Tallos walked back to his scene of foul carnage. He suppressed emotion as the snow gave way to the bare earth exposed by his flames, knowing their bodies, blackened and writhing, would soon follow.

Their death will not have been for nothing, decided Tallos. *This will serve as my lesson and eternal reminder.* Tallos still felt the power surge within himself, its source unknown but seeming somehow external. He would ponder that later. He owed these two victims something: to name for them who would receive his retribution in their stead.

That the woman remained able to weep so elegantly confused him. She did not sound as though she were near death, and when Tallos's eyes found her, nor did she look it. Though her husband still hid her with his body, Tallos saw her face. Nowhere near as beautiful as Leona, she still had a presence. Or perhaps it was merely that they were both unscathed that was so exalting. The oval of melted snow, dirt steaming from the heat but not dry enough to have scorched, encircled them, yet not a strand of hair nor bit of their cloth had been charred.

"We watched the Northmen slaughter them both." It was Mile's voice, Tallos's uncle, that entered his thoughts unexpectedly. The way this man sheltered his woman—frightened and trembling himself— brought to mind a story Mile had told Tallos to frighten him from ever entering the northern woods. He described how he had witnessed his own father, the one whom he'd always looked to as a man of courage, turn into a quivering fool once dragged from his home, just clinging to his wife rather than fighting to protect her. "Your mother and I were lucky to have escaped with our lives," he'd said. "You don't ever want to see a Northman."

How exactly these two had survived his inferno was less puzzling than his own confusion as to whom he should destroy. Perhaps it was because the possibility of revenge against his true enemy had seemed so hopeless before, but that was no longer the case.

He stood, naked and empowered, before the two innocents he'd somehow saved from fiery death at his own hand, before a town he'd liberated from conscription, before the unseen minions of the gods—those monsters to the north who had stolen from him everything, and he bellowed in his agony and hatred.

"Northmen! It is your turn to cower in fear. I am Tallos, and I will see your world burn before me."

ANNORA

A porcelain vase, probably worth a small kingdom, exploded against the wall near where she dressed. Annora tried to pay it no mind and continued changing. The dress she had grabbed was the least gaudy that could be quickly found, and yet the green bodice was sewn with gold thread and covered in gems, the skirts plumed out in a ridiculous manner, and the lacings were a series of short individual ties, impossible for her to do up on her own. Another crash came from just outside her closet followed by the holler of a man gone mad.

"Warin, you incompetent blackguard! I will have you dragged behind the *Maiden's Thief!*" That Cassen had somehow lost his feminine inflection was frightening enough, but the man had become incensed after finding blood at the entrance of these royal chambers that were otherwise empty. He paced back and forth, alone in the room of purple and red—made redder still by his anger—destroying everything with the capacity to shatter while cursing Warin's name.

These were not the first threats of murder she'd recently heard. Annora could not recall with exactness what had occurred in the throne room—just that the blinding pain in her chest had lessened, the guards released her, and Stephon had begun promising death to Cassen with high-pitched shrieks. Then she was led away and up countless stairs by a man with an iron grip, more relieved that her chest no longer felt like burning death than she was to be alive.

It was Cassen who had led her up those many steps, and it must have been he who'd saved her as well. Knowing that, she chanced speaking with the belief that he had no intention of harming her. *Not tonight, at least.*

"We should go." She made her plea while still within her closet.

She heard another object smash into a wall and braved an exit.

"Please, they will be looking for us both, and we will be imprisoned or worse."

Annora was growing tired of having to convince Adeltian nobility to flee their own kingdom. It was only then that she realized Ethel and Eaira were in equally grave danger.

"Where are Ethel and Eaira? We must not leave without them."

"Oh, must we not?" Cassen laughed like a madman. His new voice did not match his feminine appearance. Though she always thought him to be hiding something, she had grown accustomed to him being the way that he was. "You would throw your life away for some highborn brats? Girls you just met a few weeks ago?"

She ignored his boorish questions. "Was it you who yelled and saved me?" She wanted to be sure.

Cassen merely shook his head as if it pained him to recall the event.

Why did you do it? Annora feared the answer to that question. Cassen now a man, eunuch or not, allowed for explanations better left unsought.

She began to remember more clearly what had happened in the throne room. Stephon had struggled to free his hand while shouting orders for the guards to seize Cassen where he stood, but the guards refused to obey. "Why did you not just kill him?"

"We have wasted enough time here," he said dismissively. "Come."

Her chest still sent pangs of agony through her body with every motion, but it did not bleed. The crumpled servant's cloth that lay on the floor in the closet caught her eye, parts scorched through, and her desire for protection overruled her reservations about Cassen's motives.

"Help me with my lacings, and I will not slow you further."

⧈⊶⧈

Cassen had found some stately men's garb in a separate closet of the room Annora now realized was the queen's royal chambers, but why he had taken her there remained a mystery. It seemed an unnecessary risk to have climbed to the top of the very castle they needed to escape. But the castle had been strangely empty when they crept out, and now outside its walls, her immediate safety remained her primary concern. Cassen's plan to take a boat to meet friends of his was better than any she could have concocted should she be left alone.

He looked a different person entirely with his new vestment. It was the typical dress of an Adeltian nobleman, something Cassen would never have been seen in as a duchess. His gaunt face made more sense now that he was stripped of his surplus of silks and showed himself to be built no different to most men. The brown cotton trousers were ill-fitting, but the long woolen coat covered the areas where it was more noticeable.

Finally afforded some time to think, Annora realized that that place at the top of the stairs, that opulent red room of anger and anxiety, was supposed to have been where Ethel's mother was kept.

Ethel and Eaira.

"Will he kill them?"

Cassen did not look at her as they scurried down the paved road, leading to where, she did not know. "We must hurry," he said as his pace quickened.

We should go back and get them. The thought was brave and stupid, and Annora could not help but be thankful that the responsibility of that final decision no longer fell on her.

"They need only to survive a few more days—a week at most," said Cassen.

"How is that?"

Cassen brought them around a bend, the change in direction giving him the apparent justification to ignore yet another of her questions. *Cassen the duchess would not have been so rude.*

He led her into a building with a dirt floor and the sweet scent of straw mixed with the thick pungency of horse.

"I hope you can ride," he said.

The idea seemed idiotic. "I have never ridden a horse in my life."

"Then I hope you can learn quickly."

They passed by stall after stall, most empty but some with horses inside that Cassen by some means judged as not fitting their needs. They all looked and sounded the same, blowing and snorting, the meaning of which Annora could not interpret.

"Are these even your horses?" she asked him.

Cassen selected a horse with a dark coat and white stripe on its face and busied himself fumbling with the clasps of the saddle. The animal was thinner than the ones that pulled their carriages and looked to have a knack for speed that frightened Annora.

"Why of course. And I would expect you recognize your own palfrey as well, my dear daughter. Or we may need to see you to a mender and cancel our early morning sail. Now grab some straw and make yourself known."

Annora attempted to feed Cassen's horse and the one near it that he had indicated would be her own. His horse was eager to take the hay from her hands, but the other was agitated and would not eat.

"I do not see myself learning to ride anytime before the guards are upon us." *Especially in the dark.* It had already been an hour or more since the throne room, and the Dawnstar had retired. Annora was thankful and a bit surprised that none of the people they had seen roaming were armored. She would have expected Stephon to have put every man at his disposal to work searching for them.

"No, you may be correct. You will ride with me."

It was not long before they made their way out of the Adeltian Throne, though not as she had pictured, and making far more noise than was comfortable. The clatter of the horses' feet on the pavers was louder than she recalled from her carriage rides.

"Someone will hear us," she worried aloud.

"I hope they do. A pair of horses that make no sound would be sure to draw attention."

Frowning at Cassen's back did little good, but she did it just the same. They must have made quite a sight in addition to their racket. She was seated behind him, forced to clasp her arms around his waist to avoid tumbling off the beast's rump. The skirts of her ridiculous dress hung to either side as they traveled at what felt like a dangerous gait, though the bored expression of the horse that tailed them, reins tied to their saddle, led her to admit it may just be an issue of perception.

"Isn't this the way to Eastport?"

"It is." He answered as if her question required no further explanation.

"Are you not concerned that you will be recognized?"

"Would you rec—well I suppose *you* might. But the men of the docks are not my lady daughters, and none have seen me in men's dress save when I go there in disguise. Any that know me well enough to recognize me will also know to fear me."

"I still think Westport would be the safer option."

Cassen snorted. "I do not think you have spent enough time in Westport to make such an appraisal. The city has lacked proper management since—"

He quieted with a quickness that was worrying. Cassen was always eager to belittle his rival city. *He must have heard something.*

"Are we in danger?" she whispered after waiting in silence as long as she could bear.

"No. No more than we have ever been." He sounded reticent. *It must have to do with having to leave his great city behind.* It made her wonder what land they would even sail to from Eastport. She certainly had no wish to return to the Spicelands and hoped instead Cassen intended to sail up the eastern shore to Midport or Strahl.

In spite of Cassen's half-hearted assurance, Annora scanned for possible threats—roadblocks or places for guards to lay ambush—but there was little to see. "Where are all the guards? And the people?"

They had only passed a handful of people on the road, empty carriages for the most part, and not a single patrolling guard.

"You might find people are reluctant to leave their homes when a king declares murder to be legal." It was a fair point, but only answered half the question.

"And the guards?"

Cassen grunted in disgust. "It would seem our good friend Master Warin has seen fit to take his prestigious Protectors north with the armies—ahead of schedule."

When in the queen's chambers, Cassen had cursed the man as if Warin had betrayed him, but it seemed an odd place to discover such a thing. *There is more to this story than you are revealing*, she thought. *Had you even any intention of preventing Warin from raping Ryiah, or did you merely use it to leverage the man?*

She chanced pressing him further. "What business does The Guard have in the North?"

"The realm is vast and filled with humanity, all of whom require protection." He made no effort to sound sincere.

"What was your part in it?"

Cassen turned momentarily to give her a sidelong glance. The furrow in his brow was clear to see. "I do not claim to be a better man than Warin. I am merely better at hiding my malevolence."

Annora pondered the accuracy of his statement. How many people truly believed Cassen to be a better man than Warin? And just how heinous was Cassen if he thought himself good at masking it?

Their journey continued in silence for what felt like hours, interrupted only once to switch horses. The feisty palfrey had calmed, though, and seemed happy enough to bear their weight.

"Remember," said Cassen, "when we get to the docks, you are my daughter. That should not be too difficult a task, considering. Just follow my lead. We will secure our own small boat with sail."

"And who will pilot this boat? You cannot simply *ride* a sea vessel." All children played in small boats in the Spicelands, and Annora was no exception. None of her boats had been with sail, but she had seen enough to know sailing was no easy endeavor.

"I have some experience with rigging, but I will require your assistance."

Had someone told her that she and Cassen would be sailing...and that he would be manning the boat... It was too absurd a notion to even humor. But he was not the duchess anymore, and she was not a lady servant. He was an Adeltian noble and she his highborn child. She just hoped the darkness would be enough to hide the improbable nature of that claim given their difference in appearance.

The second half of the trip was quiet but went by faster than the first. Annora found herself looking forward to spending some time on the water, if only to be away from this kingdom.

The smell of wet wood and the salty tang of ocean snuck up on her, and the time for riding was done. Cassen tied off their horses and led her toward the mass of boats rocking gently in the water.

"Remember, you are my highborn daughter."

Annora nodded. *I would be better served reminding myself that I am under the care of a man that cannot be trusted.*

Annora felt the uneven planks of the docks through the soles of her soft shoes. Memories of having first set foot on docks such as these came to her, and they were not pleasant. After enduring a lengthy voyage in the company of the most sordid men she had ever encountered, under constant threat of debasement, there was little relief to be had landing in Adeltia, not knowing if worse was yet to come.

"Probably shouldn't be sneaking up on people such as me under the cover of night."

A man with thick hair covering his arms barred their path. In one hand he had a long slender blade, already stained with blood.

"We do not wish for trouble. My daughter and I require a boat for the day."

"Heh, you don't want any trouble, you just want a boat? Clearly you don't have much experience with the damn things then." The man stuck his knife through the eye of a large fish, gutted and stripped of meat on one side. "And perhaps you haven't noticed, the day's over."

"So it is, however, I will gladly pay for both today and tomorrow should I find a suitable vessel. Do you know of anyone willing to hire out a boat? One with a sail?"

"Aye, I know plenty, just none that do business at night." The scrutinizing look this man gave them made Annora uneasy. "What are you two up to anyhow?"

"Looking for a boat," said Cassen tersely. "One with a sail," he repeated.

The fisherman snorted mock amusement before answering. "I know a guy. How about you and your daughter here just wait a bit. I'll fetch a friend of mine who has a nice little sloop."

"Yes, please do. We will await your return."

"Father, what is wrong with *his* boat?" Annora asked before the man had time to leave, her Spiceland accent faint, but present. She walked down the docks a few steps peering at the boat in the darkness.

"Oh no, you wouldn't like my skiff. There's no ballast in 'er, and she's prone to tip. I'm a fisherman, no sailor, and my boat's much the same. My friend has just what you need. You two just wait a bit, and I'll be back before you know it."

Annora found and held eye contact with the fisherman and sauntered to Cassen's side, wrapping both her arms around one of his. "I have a better idea," she said, still gazing at the man. "How about my *father* pays for two nights on your boat, as he's promised. …The first night is his, and the second night will be yours." She moved one of her hands along Cassen's arm to ensure her meaning was understood.

She could feel the man's filthy eyes accost her from head to toe and back up again. It was all she could do to maintain her composure and not reveal her repulsion.

"I get the first night," said the fisherman. He did not have to lick his lips; his body spoke the action for him.

"Out of the question." Cassen sounded as adamant as he had in the throne room.

"All right, all right. The second. Just be careful with the damn boat. Do you even know how to sail?" In spite of speaking to Cassen, the man's eyes were still on Annora.

Cassen merely grunted with discontent at the man. "What provisions are on board? Is there any wine?"

"It's a fishing vessel not an inn. There's some rum and water in the bow storage, but that's all I've got. And don't drink it all either."

Annora remained at Cassen's arm as he stepped forward and pressed a large silver coin onto the cutting board next to the fish. "You'll get the other upon our return."

❦

Cassen had been scowling since they set off from the docks by oar, and his disposition had not changed in spite of the good distance now between them and the docks.

"That was a foolish and unnecessary thing you did." He finally broke the silence with words no different from his look.

Annora, already angry, just ignored him. *The fool does not even know how his own city works.*

"You were to be my daughter—no more."

"I was not aware I was acting anything more. I thought I played the part rather well, considering the father."

"Are you not aware that whoring outside of an authorized brothel is not permitted? That there is a reward for reporting those who do so to avoid the taxes? Where do you think that man would have gone had your little ploy failed?" Cassen had stopped rowing. He apparently needed all his strength to chastise her.

"To the same place he was already headed. And certainly not to report us to some authority for a pittance of a reward."

"Is that right?"

"*Yes, it is right.*" Her accent flared, but she was too heated to care. "He'd go to a brothel owner who would have exacted a more severe penalty upon us both and paid him a fraction of the contents of your purse instead."

Cassen let loose a round of insolent laughter clearly intended to belittle her. "And how did you come to that conclusion?"

The laundry was the best place for talk and gossip, and none of the women with choice stories had been born as washwomen. Anna, Shellie, and Jeanne, aside from being the more interesting of the women, all admitted—rather proudly—to working in brothels when they were younger. Most of their tales were a bit tall, but oftentimes pieces of their differing lies overlapped where there was truth, lending itself to believability. Annora knew exactly how the brothels operated, and how they differed between Eastport and Westport. It was a common topic, as many of the prettier servant girls contemplated running off with the idea of building enough coin with a quick bit of degradation to afford a true escape from servitude. The older women were quick to encourage the idea—to those they disliked. To the others, they warned of the true dangers involved and the certainty of never escaping until both your value and coin were gone.

"The man was lying." It was as definite a fact as any Annora had ever known, and she had no desire to explain her reasoning in further detail.

Cassen just chuckled to himself.

Annora turned her back to him, but there was no way to be rid of him on so small a craft. It was about three men in length—three very short men. There was no cabin, and Cassen was nearer the bow of the boat, looking rearward as he rowed. *He is probably too afraid to raise sail and was lying about having any experience.*

A brutal wave struck her, not of water but of hunger. It must have been over half a day since she'd eaten, and her desperation spurred her to action. Leaving her seat at the stern she passed Cassen, handing him the two lines that controlled the rudder.

"Steering too much responsibility for my lady daughter?"

"You can do nothing as well as I. Where are these friends of yours if they even exist? We have been headed straight south if I am not mistaken. You may wish to correct our course when we raise sail, *captain.*"

Annora had every hatch in the front of the boat open and was rummaging through with anger, throwing old rope, broken chunks of punky wood, and heavy pieces of anchors on to the deck behind her. "Nothing but flotsam in this damn boat!"

"Let me know if you find anything to eat. I have a king's hunger."

Cassen was the only one amused by his quip as Annora had had quite enough mention of kings for one lifetime. "We will be lucky enough to find fresh water."

Annora brought a glass jug sealed with a rotten cork back where Cassen could see and shook its contents in front of him. "This is the rum I believe we are commanded not to finish." *Probably more spit than rum.*

"I will have that man flayed for insolence upon our return."

Yes, insolence…because lying would be too serious a charge. "Upon our return?" He might be returning one day, but Annora had no plans to.

"Just keep looking, dammit. Food would be nice, but we need water."

"I *have* looked. There is no food or water." She knew she could not blame Cassen for this particular problem as it was her idea to take this man's boat, but there was no reason for their continued slow travel.

"Perhaps if you raised sail we could meet up with your friends before we die of thirst?"

Cassen let his oars hang over the water and the boat continued to drift forward. She could not help but notice his arms were somewhat muscled and lean. He did not have the brawny frame of a blacksmith or swordsman, but neither was he the maidenly eunuch that all had known him to be. It only served to bring a scowl to her face as Annora thought how easy it would have been for him to have rid the kingdom of its budding tyrant when he'd had the chance.

"I will man the rudder," said Cassen as he moved to free the boom. "You stay at the mast and be ready to raise the main when I tell you. Do you know how to fix a line to a cleat?"

She stared at him with the implication of having been insulted. She would loop the line around with a twist the way she thought she'd seen it done and hope for the best before she allowed him to give her a lesson. His patronizing air had already taken its toll.

Annora took hold of the line to raise the sail and noted the gentle breeze. It was scarcely enough to ruffle her hair, and she wished for stronger wind to move them with speed.

"Raise it full and tie it off," said Cassen.

The sail went to the top of the mast with little effort and the loops and twists around the cleat seemed to be holding. She knotted the loose end just in case. The wind caught the sail, lifting it along with Annora's spirits while Cassen adjusted a line attached to the boom.

The vessel continued to pick up speed, but Annora soon heard a sound like rushing water that was somehow distant. When she glanced at Cassen he had the same confused look upon his face that she was feeling.

"Lower the sail," he commanded.

She made her disappointment known as she moved to undo her knots and loops. *If this is some trick to make me look foolish…*

"Hurry!" There was panic in his voice, and the sound grew louder. The line went taut on the cleat, making it impossible for her to undo her knot. "Hold on," he cried and Annora went belly to deck and saw Cassen did the same. A massive gust of wind struck them, and she readied herself for a swim. The realization that it would be impossible for the two of them to right this boat if it toppled gripped her with fear.

The boat began to list. Annora held on to the mast as it tilted more and more. Anything beyond the midpoint between vertical and horizontal would result in capsize given that the vessel was not built for sailing. But the boat continued to lurch to the side, passing the point that she had feared and continuing to tip further still. Cassen's eyes were wide and frightened—the sea was feared by all men, and he was no exception. This boat may not even float when flipped, which would force them to cling to whatever small pieces of trash they could find, their limbs dangling dangerously into the dark waters for whatever lay below to grab hold of. They leaned so sharply it took all her strength to hold on and keep from falling into the water. She considered letting go on purpose, thinking it might help to right the boat. As she contemplated the effect such a decision would have, the choice was made for her. Rather than capsizing, the boat began to roll back to rightness, and the winds died down.

After a few moments they were at a healthy list and traveling with a good southerly speed. Annora breathed deeply and willed herself to relax. She turned her attention to Cassen whose white face began to flood pink with embarrassment. The brush with death had stripped her of her acrimony, and she decided not to taunt him, though it was well within her right.

"It looks like the rum and water were not the only things our fisherman friend lied about," he said.

It was as good a concession as she could have hoped to get from him. This boat had a fine ballast after all, and as they continued due south—to where, she still could not guess—she believed they would have more need of it.

KEETHRO

A month at the very least. I will eat. I will sleep. I will endure.

Those had been Keethro's initial thoughts, and they were sobering in their own right. This sentencing meant Keethro must remain in the purgatory that was Rivervale's underground prison for much longer than he had before—and alone. As his mind had rattled off scenarios, he'd begun to fear he may end up in the arena, forced to fight impossible odds yet again and without his everfount of luck and courage that was Titon. He now found himself wishing those fears had come true.

A blanket of darkness engulfed him as he descended—far deeper below the surface than he had on his previous dungeon visit. Had he been lucky enough to have been slated for more battles in the arena, Keethro would no doubt have remained in the upper levels of this underworld through which he was being dragged. Instead, his voyage continued downward, and as he plummeted, so did his hope of ever surfacing.

A man should not know how it feels to wear a corset, and yet Keethro imagined he must; his ribs felt increasingly restricted by the small tunnels that shrunk in around him. That which he breathed had a consistency more like phlegm than air in its thickness, and the act of filling his lungs became a burdensome task that required conscious thought. There was surely a rotten stench, though he had long since begun breathing through his mouth out of some instinctive reflex. His sense of smell was not the only one lacking. All sounds were dampened, all sights seemed blurred, and he felt as though he was floating—or rather sinking—ever downward, no longer needing to walk. *Perhaps I am dead.* The thought was his only comfort.

"I said, what's yer *fecking* name?"

It was not the sound of the man's voice that brought Keethro out of his stupor so much as the spit that licked his eyes. In front of him was a man that looked more like the type of creature only children feared might exist. The troll-man looked down his long hooked nose at Keethro, begging him *not* to answer so that he could exact some punishment.

"Keethro."

The hair upon the many moles of the man's face danced as he let out a gravelly cackle, sending more filth in Keethro's direction. "Take a finger!"

It was then Keethro realized it was not merely he and this disgusting man that attended this convergence; there were guards as well. Somewhere along the way, the golden guards who had held Keethro by his arms must have simply transformed into these demons of the underworld, for the thought of those prestigious men having met with the likes of these who now gripped him was too hilarious a notion to conceive. They were men, but it was as if they had been bred for the explicit purpose of being wardens of such a place. Their comically imbalanced features would have been a source of ridicule in the light of the Dawnstar, but down here it only seemed to empower them with belonging.

Keethro was also not the only prisoner. He had been brought down with a boy, it seemed, though all new arrivals must look like boys in this place. The man was probably no younger than twenty. He squirmed as his own pair of disfigured guards held him. A third grabbed the wrist of his right hand and placed the man's entire pinky into the jaws of some enormous pliers. The guard began to apply pressure—the tool so large that it required him using both his arms. A series of crunches echoed through Keethro's skull as the man's finger was consumed, one bone at a time. Somehow the victim of the torture had remained in a silent horror until the instrument was removed, at which point he screamed like a child, unrestrained by pride.

"Now's the fun part," said the troll-man when the shrieks finally died down. "We get to see if yer friend returns the favor. What's yer name?" The question was directed toward the man who had just lost a finger.

It took a few moments for the man to compose himself, but when he did, his first action was to give Keethro a vengeful stare. Keethro felt his own right pinky tingle as the man's lips began to part. A lifetime of training had gone into the coordination of that small digit which was the last to make contact with his throwing axes. It may not seem like an exceedingly important finger to most men, but the thought of losing that finger now seemed to Keethro somehow worse than the loss of an arm.

"One hundred…fifty-eight."

Keethro's heart fell to his stomach and sweat oozed from his every pore, threatening to make his guards lose their grip. He could already feel the cold metal, still wet with the other man's blood, clamping down on his pinky. He would try to offer his left, he decided sickly. Perhaps they would not care from which hand the finger came.

The troll-man appeared as though he had seen a sight more disgusting than himself. "That's unfortunate," he said, still speaking to the young prisoner. "Ye'll learn to be less forgiving down here in yer new home." When he turned back to Keethro his face lit up again in spite of the darkness. "Remember yer name yet?"

Keethro looked toward the one who would no doubt suffer the loss of another finger should Keethro answer incorrectly. The man's left hand was moving slightly, three fingers curling back as if he were pointing downward. His face still had the same vengeful look upon it, however.

Does he mean one further along or one less? He did not want to hear the man shriek again, if only because it was distressing. "One hundred and fifty-seven." Keethro answered.

The frown of Keethro's fellow prisoner melted.

"Let's go," said the troll-man, the disappointment clear in his voice.

They were led deeper into the dankness. Keethro began to wonder if all directions traveled in this place truly led downward or if the amalgam of hopelessness and despair merely made it seem so. Every step felt as though it was further separating him from his former reality. *I will never see the Dawnstar again,* he realized.

The ceiling, the walls, and the floor were all the same rusty color like dried blood. The rock foundation of the castle had ended long ago, and they were in a series of tunnels dug into hard-packed clay. The sound of barking animals could be heard not far off. *Do they see the light of the torches or do they bark like this always?*

The source of the noise was eventually revealed. And they were animals. Horrid creatures. Inside a single giant cage were at least a hundred men. The structure may have been large, but the conditions were cramped. The cage spanned thirty paces by three paces, and its top was less than head height. Most of the men's hands—or what was left of them—grasped the thick wires of the cage so they could lean forward and support their weight. Others were piled into groups, all clustered and sitting uncomfortably close to one another. But all of them seemed to be barking, yelling, or hooting in some way, save those that sat mute and grinning in the laps of other men.

"Quiet," yelled the troll-man, and the men were silenced. "I've brought you more flesh, not that you deserve it, and I must explain to them the rules." A smile crept across the long face of the hunched underground monster, and some chuckles could be heard amongst the captives. "Number one: no eating each other unless I say so. Number two: no fighting unless I say so. As for raping…well, boys will be boys."

Grotesque giggling and hooting was the response to the last bit.

"And for each rule you break, I take a finger."

Keethro surveyed the caged men, all of whom seemed to be staring right back at him as opposed to one hundred fifty-eight. Keethro must have been the only man to still have ten fingers. Those missing their digits mostly had useless flaps of scarred skin that had taken their place, dangling over the crossed wires of the rust-riddled cage.

"Now it's time that we see this new meat properly—"

The gaoler stopped speaking just as Keethro felt a faint wetness brush his cheek. The bulk of whatever it was had hit the gaoler, his face now covered in the dark, wet spatter. It looked at first as though it was blood—and that may have been partly true—but the stench that soon wafted indicated it was primarily excrement. A maniacal laughter followed, coming from a seemingly crazed man, squatting over his stumpy palm, eager to fling another handful once his bowels would comply.

"Bring him to me," shouted the now irate troll-man. Those in the cage were quick to obey. The shit-flinger had no time for a second throw and was smashed against the front of the metal enclosure. Keethro felt his guards release him as they rushed to tend to their more urgent calling.

Run. The thought came to him, and yet he knew that he would not. He could not hope to navigate the maze of tunnels and would no doubt encounter too many guards along the way. He did not fear death so much as he feared the punishment for attempting escape.

The troll-man bared his rotten teeth as he saw that his assailant had no more fingers left to take. Even the guards that were holding the man's stubbed hands through the holes of the cage appeared to fear the building rage of their leader, and they cowered as far from him as they could while still maintaining their grasp on the prisoner. The angry gaoler unsheathed his knife and plunged it through the cage into the eye of the man, finally ceasing his laughter.

"Eat," said the troll-man, wiping his knife on his trousers.

Men who had previously been sitting, particularly those who were the largest, rushed to the corpse. A mound of dirty bodies collected, all clawing and pushing each other in an attempt to get a bite. The sound of joints popping resounded through the dense air, and some men exited the fray with a calf or forearm to take back to their awaiting companions.

Keethro forced down the push of vomit. It would be beyond foolish to waste the contents of his stomach. Surviving a month here would require everything he had, though he was realizing he never would have been sent here, had Veront ever had any intention of honoring his deal with Titon.

Keethro's face must have betrayed his dread. He stood alone, with no guards holding him, and the troll-man looked at him, slimy teeth exposed by his joyous grin.

You should have killed me, Titon.

TITON SON OF SMALL GRYN

"He is going to kill you."

Titon was more concerned at the moment with river dragons than any threat posed to him by a man. He and his men had come to the first of the several rivers they would have to cross on their way to Strahl, all of which Titon and Keethro had forded on their way south, albeit farther upstream. Titon was among his soldiers, all kneeling at the bank to fill their skins and bellies with water far cleaner than that of the Eos.

"You're a Galatai clansman, are you not?" continued the man. He spoke quietly and did not look toward Titon, but there was little doubt that other men near them could hear. "Veront hates our kind. Anything he's told you is a lie."

Titon finished drinking and fought his impulse to back away from the water's edge. Any dragons below would no doubt be well aware of the turbulence caused by so many men splashing water on their faces and breaking the surface with their lips to swill some greedy gulps. *There's safety in the horde*, Titon told himself and turned toward the speaker. The man was the size of a Galatai, but he lacked a certain hardness in his demeanor. And it was difficult to imagine why any man, let alone someone truly from the North, would wish to have so little hair upon his face.

"I'm only half," said the man. "My mother was from Fourpaw, and my father was a raider."

"That is not possible." Titon did not feel the need to explain further.

"I do not lie to you. He left her alive and returned several days after. They raised me alone in the remnants of their village and later joined another community. He cut his hair and—"

"Then what are you doing here?" Though something about the man seemed honest—his utter pitifulness perhaps—Titon was not about to believe this farfetched story.

"He may have shaved his face, but he was still Galatai. What do you think happened when Veront's collectors came and demanded a portion of all his coin?"

Titon's grunt of agreement was involuntary. "My business with Veront is none of your concern."

"It is. I am a part of this hopeless attack. Not even Veront expects it to succeed. My friend is a cupbearer and overhears many things. It is just a diversion—"

"I've heard enough," Titon growled at him. "And I command you, keep silent." Titon left before the man could blurt any more nonsense, wishing to himself that he'd picked a different place at the bank to drink.

Titon returned to his two officers in their quickly erected tent, a pair of sirs, one possibly the most boring man he'd ever met, and the other probably the most irritating.

"What did the scouts report?" Titon asked, doing his best to not let his disdain for either man show.

"Nothing out of the ordinary." Sir Aleric of House something or other, Titon had already forgotten, seemed to take pleasure in ensuring Titon had as little information as possible. As the previous commander of two of the three legions now under Titon's control, the man was not artful in hiding his resentment.

"Where are they? I'd like to speak with them myself." Titon directed the question to Sir Edgar, the tight-lipped officer in chainmail and leather, in hopes he'd be more likely to divulge a satisfactory answer. Edgar deferred to Aleric with a head gesture.

"I sent them off already. Scouts serve no purpose at camp."

Titon inhaled and sought the void. *Scouts serve no purpose when their commander gets no information from them.* He'd been civil with Aleric until now, and he meant to maintain his southern comportment for as long as possible—*just as Keethro would advise me with his throat clearing and looks of worry.* "The next time they return, be sure they do not set off until I speak with them. Understood?"

Aleric snorted his understanding accompanied with a barely perceptible shake of his head. *In the North, we move our heads in the other direction to indicate agreement,* Titon thought with mounting acrimony.

Titon turned his attention to the table they stood at. "If I understand this map correctly, we can continue a bit north of east and we'll pass north of Strahl…"

"We have no reason to pass north of Strahl," Aleric explained as if to a child. "I realize maps are not common where you come from. However, as you should be able to see, there is a river to their west and an ocean to their east. Northmen may be able to drink from the sea, but Rivervalians cannot."

The void never seemed so far from reach. "If we were, *however*, to pass north of Strahl, would we be able to get between them and the coast, or do their walls extend to sea? On the map it does not appear—"

"Of course their walls do not extend into the sea," interrupted Aleric. "What kind of question is that?"

"Then I intend for our army to pass north and attack from the east."

Aleric's attention had been stolen by a man who had entered their tent and was whispering something in his ear.

"What is it?" Titon demanded.

Aleric held up a finger as the man finished his message, then nodded and the man left. Titon tried to make note of the messenger's appearance, but all these southern men looked much the same in their near-matching clothes. "It's nothing. You were saying?"

Titon was done negotiating. "We head just north of east. That is my command."

Aleric let out an exasperated breath. "Veront will not be pleased by the extra time it takes."

"Then we will march longer and faster and with less delay. Pack up now. We leave immediately."

The repacking of the tent always somehow took longer than the setting up, and Titon made a note that they would not raise the structure for future stops unless it was truly needed to protect the maps from rain. After the meeting, Titon had noticed Aleric pull Edgar to the side to discuss something in private, but he had no time to be irked by their southern gossip. He instead surveyed the men, all three thousand of them. It was a great many men, to be sure, but they did not move with a unity of purpose. He'd be surprised if a third of these men had even trained beside each other, let alone seen combat.

Aleric appeared to be holding up the process of resuming the march, as he'd sent two of their lead men off on some random errand.

"What is this?" Titon demanded. "We should already be on our way."

"There is urgent business that requires our attention." Aleric did not even face Titon as he spoke. *He must not have been present at the arena*, thought Titon. There was no other explanation for how this man, who wore the same thin plate as the golden guards, excepting that his was dyed a deep green, could feel so secure snubbing Titon.

"What business?" That Titon had not been first made aware of the issue was frustrating enough, but Aleric's display of insubordination in front of the men undermined Titon's ability to lead.

It was Edgar who responded. "A traitor."

The men returned with a third at spearpoint. It was the halfbreed who had spoken to Titon at the riverbank.

"This man has been heard speaking treason," Aleric announced for all to hear. "The punishment is death by drawing." He then turned to Titon with half a smirk, an implicit challenge for Titon to overrule him.

Titon ignored him and looked at the halfbreed. Men were busy binding his feet together while others attached a rope to his wrists, already bound behind his back. The man did not struggle or beg for his life. He did not even look to Titon for aid. *He is Galatai*, thought Titon. *I can see that now.*

They grabbed their captive under his arms and carried him to one of only three horses had by their army. It was Titon's horse, and he didn't think they meant for the man to ride the beast in Titon's stead—Titon having only used the horse to haul his gear thus far. The thought of walking beside a horse that was dragging a brother—even a half-brother who knew nothing of his people—was unacceptable. Titon finally looked to Aleric and noticed the man was truly eager to see what Titon would do.

"Stop," Titon commanded the men, though their work had essentially been completed. They stepped away from the prisoner as Titon approached. "Kneel." The man obeyed, falling hard to his knees, his hands behind his back, tied to the rope that lay slack on the ground.

"He is a traitor," Aleric called out, as if to remind Titon that assisting him would be an offense in itself.

Titon ignored him, speaking instead to his three legions of hushed soldiers. "I am your commander now. I, alone, will determine who is innocent and who is guilty when charged with a crime." Titon looked at the rope on the hardened earth. He would have to sharpen his axe after slicing it where it lay on account of the rocks that would ruin his edge.

"Halfbreed," Titon said, acknowledging him as Galatai, if only in part. "You are charged with treason. Do you deny these charges?"

The man did not look up. He merely shook his head.

"Then may you rest at the foot of the Mountain." Titon's axe swung down, taking the man's head off cleanly and without making contact with the ground. *I promised Ellie I would slay every man, woman, and child in my way.* It was more an explanation than an apology. He did not pity this tactless man. He'd left Titon no choice.

As the blood pooled on the cold earth near Titon's feet, he addressed his men.

"*I* am your commander now," he repeated. He searched the crowd of men hoping to find the one who had whispered to Aleric. "And whoever is next to fail to report *directly* to me on any contention, no matter how small, will suffer the same fate as this man."

DECKER

One foot, then the other. Only death can defeat me.

Decker was in agony, but he was far from broken. Battles such as these were the ones in which he excelled. He had long since tired of fighting interminable wars, the outcome of which there was nothing he could do to influence or hasten. Word from his clan had been that none of Titon's memories had returned, Decker's father was somewhere in the South—his time of return as uncertain as Decker's faith in his motives—and Decker had been awaiting in vain the waking of his mother for a lifetime.

But this was different. This battle could be fought with strength of body and strength of will. This battle would be soon won or soon lost. And in this battle, Decker could use all his fury and rage, both of which he had in dangerous abundance.

The taunts of his enemy came unrelenting. Under the heavy layer of ice the stream trickled with the same song of challenge that it had had for each of the many risings and fallings of the Dawnstar since Decker had departed. The cold lanced him through his thick layers of furs and skins, and the wind ripped at his face as though his beard was not there. Canyons of dried blood ran along lips too painful to move, but with no water, no food, and no one to speak to, it was of little consequence. Chewing snow was no longer an option as doing so had already covered his mouth in unbearable sores, and breaking through the ice of the stream for a drink was no longer possible, as it had become too thick—not that he would allow himself to do such a thing, in any case.

"One day you will rest under the foot of the Mountain, but for now you work in the rays of the Dawnstar and wash in the water of the River." Those words from his father were always more a command than an encouragement, but now they incited Decker to anger. Why it was acceptable to wash oneself in the river when pissing in it was considered sacrilege made no sense. Why a man would wish to be buried under the foot of a god was also puzzling. The thought of being covered with dirt did not seem a pleasant way to rest for eternity. The trust his father placed in his gods was contradictory in many ways, though that was not what bothered Decker the most. *How can you show your precious Three such unfaltering faith, yet betray Mother so shamelessly? And what kind of man can do such a thing, then preach honor to his sons as if he were the very embodiment of integrity?*

The impact made when his boots parted enough snow to hit rock or ice sent bolts of pain through his already aching head. As each step brought him farther forward, so did it bring him farther skyward. Breaths came easy at this height, but the act was like cold fire in his lungs and did not seem to satisfy his thirst for air as it should have. It was difficult to believe that this trek, up what appeared to be a solitary mountain, had never been attempted before. And if it had, why were there no legends of the endeavor? Perhaps there were. There were, after all, so many things that Decker had not been taught about his people and their past. And the things he had been told seemed evermore the types of foolish stories recited to children to pacify them to contentedness.

Only death can defeat me.

Decker could not remember, in truth, but he hoped that his trick for ensuring victory had been his own invention and not a lesson of his father's. Decker had not always been the largest and strongest man yet to be a man; there was a time well recollected when he was just a large boy. Axe combat became more dangerous to practice as boys grew, gaining the strength to devastate even with the soft wood of their practice weapons. It was among the reasons his father had made Decker and his brother train when they were younger than most. Before even that time, their father had taken them to see other boys fight. One in particular caught Decker's eye—and the eyes of all others as well—for he was the best with axe by far. He was a bit smaller than average for his age, though not so much as Titon, and he bested boys far larger and with more experience. Everyone had concluded that the boy had a knack for axes, that natural talent was the cause for his supremacy. Only Decker saw the truth. The boy, Grenspur was his name, was no more gifted than any of the others, truth be told. The difference was his willingness to commit. The boy simply was not afraid to be struck and thus never flinched, never hesitated, and almost never lost. Decker had applied that important principle to his own combat when his training had begun, and after a time he began to reap the rewards. But where Grenspur was small and weak, Decker was a force of nature. It became habit for Decker to ignore all fear of pain or defeat, and as it became rarer for him to suffer either, it became that much easier. Eventually there were none that could contest him, not even his elder brother who was vexingly nimble. Grenspur was not so lucky. Word that the boy had been maimed during practice spread with sadness through their clan, but the news did not deter Decker. *Better to be killed by your better than to lose to your lesser*, he reasoned.

And so it would be with the stream.

Only death can defeat me.

The first signs of weakness began to show, and they were not in Decker. As the climb steepened, the stream thinned, and the incessant trickle changed in tone. The sound that now came from the water beneath his feet was lighter, faster, and more desperate. *You are cracking,* thought Decker, but the smile that began to form on his face had to be abandoned lest he split his two lips to four.

Driven by the first form of encouragement he'd had since setting out, Decker tried to pick up his pace. Upon commanding his legs to move faster, however, he found they did not comply. Each step required picking up a heavy boot, solid with ice, and plowing it through a mass of snow past his knees in depth. The action was performed with as much quickness as the conditions would allow, but even his arms seemed to drag him downward, having become absurdly heavy. Decker found himself wondering if he could have even gone faster if he had been fully rested. His answer came to him when he realized his pace was slowing.

Decker grunted with foul humor. *This is what you wanted. A test greater than would seem possible—where failure meant death.* He refused to consider that perhaps death was his true goal from the beginning, pulling the thought from its root and burning it like the uninvited weed it was. *Yes a fire. A fire would be nice.*

He tripped forward, face first into the snow. It felt much the same as when his brother managed to hit him square in the nose with a ball of snow, a feat he managed more often than one might imagine. When Decker connected with such a throw it would knock the wind from his target—Decker knew the feeling well since his father's throw delivered the same force of impact. His brother, however, had such incredible accuracy coupled with an innate ability to predict the direction in which one would attempt to dodge, that he could throw at his target's head and rarely miss. *My brother has an eagle's aim and the instincts of a wolf. ...Had,* he reminded himself, *before I took it all away from him.*

The image of Titon looking at him as he'd sat up in the healer's bed came to Decker, unwanted. They were strangers now. And why? Because of their father's weakness. *Titon attacked me over love for our half-sister—a love mistaken for lust.* The thought was reviling. Had their father told them the truth, it would not have brought any more shame to their mother—it merely would have prevented the tragedy that had resulted.

Decker pushed himself to his feet, fueled with a new madness. He picked up the deadened block that was his left foot and placed it in front of his right.

Only death can defeat me.

He had never before entertained the notion of fighting his father. Titon son of Small Gryn had never given him a reason for any resentment beyond what a child temporarily feels for a parent when disciplined. But now it seemed justified, if not obligatory. The pillar of integrity that stood the same height as Decker needed to be felled. The hypocrisy could not be allowed to stand any longer.

Decker's eyes betrayed him. A dull grey was visible in the distance, blanketed on either side by the monotony of white. Nothing existed here that was not covered with snow, especially not this time of year, yet the beautiful earthen rock became clearer as he approached, warming him from afar. Mounds of the same round stones Galatai liked to place in the fire when out at hunt, either to boil water in a skin or just to keep with them while they slept, bade him come rest inside the grotto they formed. His feet lightened as he moved, no longer plowing through snow, and he entered the unlikely haven. He felt the dry heat of stones as he lay upon them, his cheek pressed to one which served as the softest pillow. *Am I dead?* He did not fear the thought, he merely wondered, as he drifted off into utter tranquility.

⛉

Decker awoke to pain in his feet. A thousand knives stabbed at his toes—toes that he would be happy to trade for a drink. His thirst overwhelmed his thoughts, and he stumbled to stand and search of something to quench it.

The sound was gone. Had he conquered the stream or merely lost it? He did not know, but he did not care to find out until first finding water. It was all around him. He could feel its weight in the air. His hope was that this cave might have a seep he could drink from. Warm as he was, he had no desire to melt snow in his hands if he didn't have to.

The yellow light of early evening flooded through the grotto, and he was pleased to see there was much for him to explore inside. Heading away from the small entrance and deeper within, Decker had to focus not to topple on the loose rocks as his feet were of little use.

A horrid sight confronted him as he rounded a bend. Before him stretched a lake of solid ice enshrouded by mist. It was massive in size, but more so, it was astonishing to see such a vast open space within the side of a mountain. He had no desire to be astonished, however, only quenched, and he threw a rock in dejection as he turned to leave. He had been in ice caves before. They were so dangerous only fools entered them without rope and hooks—and those fools rarely exited.

He stopped moving when he heard the sound. Hope and doubt fought within him as he knew it could not be true. The splash he heard must have been a product of his forlorn mind.

After hobbling to the edge of the lake he plunged his hand through the mist, feeling its warmth as he realized what he'd truly found. *A steam pool.* His hand broke the smooth surface of the tepid water, and he brought a handful to his mouth. It tasted as sweet as any he'd ever drunk, and he wasted no time putting his face directly in it.

His stomach ached with the mass of water he'd consumed, but it was pain filled with relief. Decker rolled to his back, letting his head dip into the water. It was inviting, and he was in need of washing. The cave would provide him with enough warmth to dry before redressing, and he was soon stripped naked and wading.

Had the pool been moderate in size it may have felt wrong cleaning himself in it, but it was so massive it seemed incorruptible by the filth of a single man. The emerald water was clear as glass, and he continued deeper until he swam, no longer able to touch the rock floor. It was a great reprieve for his feet to no longer bear his weight. His frostbite was painful, but he had endured worse.

Diving to the bottom he opened his eyes. He did not believe fish would live in such a pool, but his hunger drove him in search of whatever food there may be, shelled creatures in particular. Clinging to the bottom were bunches of black mollusks as he'd hoped. They were similar to the ones he and his brother dove for in the mud-bottom lakes during summer, but these had far narrower shells and it was not long before he found they also had a sweeter taste. Titon had taught him the trick to eating them raw which involved first removing the brown sack found inside. *Titon would have been in awe of this place.*

The thought drove Decker back underwater where tears could not trouble him. He swam to what looked to be the deepest part and continued as his ears throbbed with pain. The glint of metal caught his eye and he swam farther still, releasing the pressure in his ears with yet another technique learned from his older brother. He could only imagine what might lay at the bottom of a pool in a cave so far north—perhaps he was the first person ever to swim in this lake. Tales were told of dragons that lived in caves, protecting vast fortunes of precious metals and gems.

The thought of returning home with a bounty of gems amused him, if only for the jealous anger it would incite in Kilandra upon him gifting them to his mother. It was possible he could infuriate her further if he gave them instead to a young girl who he would then lay with, but the idea of seduction for the purpose of scheming turned his stomach. He had no desire to become the very thing he loathed in Kilandra. Keethro's sister had warned him before he set off with the woman, but Decker had not heeded her words. "You need fear Kilandra worse than my brother's return. The woman is vile poison wrapped in a flower. Do not trust her." And in any case, there were no girls, young or otherwise, that he truly cared for in their clan. *Save Red.* The thought almost made him inhale water, but then he saw what had caused the glimmer.

It was a blade, the thick curved edge of what must be an axe. He grasped it and pulled until it came free from its rocky prison, then clenched the hard metal above the handle in his teeth and swam to the surface.

Wading to shore in the shallows, he had time to inspect the weapon. In spite of having been underwater for what must have been some great length of time, it showed no signs of rust. There was no binding to have decayed as the helve, with room enough for three hands, was carved from the rough stem of a great antler. Decker sliced the air with it as he left the water, impressed with its balance. It was the metal that was most captivating, however. It was odd enough that the blade and neck were a single piece that ran through the length of the handle, but it glowed with such brilliance that it seemed to radiate heat, filling him with warmth and vigor. It had little flex, yet remained near as light as an axe more fit to be thrown.

Breaking from his trance, Decker realized he had been out of the water for some time now. *How long have I been swinging this blade?* It was long enough to become dry, except for his hair, but not long enough for his arms to tire. He dressed himself, eying the resting axe as he did so, wishing to find something less fleeting than air to test his new toy upon. *The River himself, should he find the courage to face me.*

After a walk around the perimeter of the pool, ensuring there were no other secrets hidden within, Decker left the refuge of the cave with a renewed zeal, eager to recover the sound of the stream and follow it to its source. The task proved difficult as the wind had picked up, masking the sound of any water. Hanging low in the sky, the Dawnstar burned deep red, an angry red Decker would soon share in mood if he could not find what he sought. He kicked clear the snow on the ground and placed his ear to the ice.

There you are, my nemesis, and weaker than ever. He tried to determine from where the water flowed, but what he heard made little sense. The trickle seemed to lead in the direction of the cave from which he'd come. What was more, the sound grew ever fainter. A gust of wind knocked a pile of snow atop him, but he remained motionless as it helped him to hear. The stream sounded as if it was dying, its pitch gaining as its intensity lessened.

Do not hide from me you coward! His silent taunt had no effect. The sound was gone, and in its place, just beneath the howling warning of an oncoming storm, was the creaking of newly forming ice.

CASSEN

He studied Annora as she lay on the deck of the bow, chest rising and falling near in rhythm with the motion of the boat on the swell. Though she was not the Adeltian model of beauty that was Crella, she was every bit as stunning. The many diaphanous layers of her skirts had become damp from the spray and clung to her, outlining her sensuous hips and breasts separated by so slender a waist. How tempting it had been for him, surrounded by such youthful beauty, and always forbidden to indulge, having all the power yet keeping constant abstinence. Calling them daughters was his own ill-humor, for they were truly his pets, his toys, his trinkets—delicacies to be consumed at a later date. And yet as he looked at her now, all he felt was fear... Fear that men such as he would be the first they encountered as the wind carried them southward.

Cassen scanned the horizon but saw nothing. They had lost sight of shore soon after raising sail, and that was just more than a day ago. The lack of fresh water was making itself felt like a toddler tugging a mother's dress—and Cassen had no tolerance for toddlers. It seemed neither hot nor cold, yet the humidity forced him to sweat, the ocean continued to cover him with life-sapping salt, and the Dawnstar burnt him with vengeful wrath. Annora was fairing better due to her islander complexion and lack of predisposition to swelter, but even she would be crazed with thirst in a day or two. His own tongue felt as if it was twice its normal size, and he had given up trying to produce any moisture in his mouth.

The solitary swig of the cheap rum he'd finished hours ago had been the best drink to ever cross his lips. A mouthful of seawater would feel so nice, salty though it may be, and he could spit it out after. But he knew better. Daemun's draught, it was called, though most sailors called it demon's or deadman's out of ignorance, making the same mistake they did when naming the abandoned keep far to the west. The story of Lord Daemun was a dark one—one Cassen would rather not recollect, even if he believed it to be mere fabler's fantasy. Still, it helped turn his stomach to the idea of drinking from the sea, and for that he was grateful.

How did you arrive here, you damn fool? He knew, for he had asked himself more than once already. It seemed he had made mistake after mistake ever since the death of Lyell. *Ever since you murdered him.*

Yes, he must not forget that he was now a killer of kings. It gave him strength, having done what most men would tremble at the thought of. Kings were near gods with bottomless purses that afforded them vast amounts of spies and information. Everyone was an informer for the king. When questioned by such authority there were few who would dare lie, except perhaps when posed questions that condemned themselves or their closest kin. And yet Cassen had disposed of such a god-like man the way one might toss aside a worn kerchief.

His fingers stopped their chronic stroking of Crella's fabric as the action met his conscious thought. His mistakes were too grievous to rank, but of all of them, allowing her to fall into Warin's clutches was the worst. *He is a known rapist.* It was the most reviling thought—that Warin might be having his way with her this very moment, and Cassen punished himself by remaining focused upon it. *Is there a more contemptible man in all the realm?* Cassen could certainly think of none. His loathing of Alther had paled in comparison to Warin, for at least Alther was not completely blind to his own ignorance. Warin, on the other hand, was a knife too dull for butter, convinced he was sharp enough for shaving. The memory of when he first confronted Warin about his lady servant returned. Warin had denied the charge in its entirety, claiming he'd never so much as touched her, but he quickly changed his defense. *How long will you be able to pretend your acts with either of them were consensual when I return with the Satyr's army and string a harp with your entrails?*

Cassen's thoughts of revenge were enough to calm him, along with the realization that Crella had been Warin's captive for much longer than since he'd taken her north with him. More importantly, marching with an army and his fellow Guard members would not afford him the privacy to do any of the things Cassen feared. Warin would need to maintain his guise of virtue.

Cassen pressed Crella's kerchief deep into his pocket, resolved not to think of her anymore. He forced himself instead to ponder one of his more recent missteps. The fisherman… *How is it that you were outwitted by a lowly docksman, a man so transparent that Annora was able to read and manipulate him with ease?* He looked at her once more, his beautiful and oddly strong daughter. *We are even now, I suppose*, he thought, then scanned the horizon for salvation.

Eyes can play tricks on a person at sea, so Cassen closed them for a count before taking a second look in the same direction. Five white spokes protruded from the horizon, same as he had seen before, the same he saw every time the *Maiden's Thief* first came into view. The sight was almost enough to send him to tears, but he laughed instead. "Never leave a mortal enemy who yet draws breath,"—it was a tenet he lived by and had broken having left Stephon struggling with the knife in his hand. It would have been easy to put the boy to death and assure the Satyr's victory, but Cassen wanted Stephon alive for what was to come. The five glorious specks in the distance, gradually becoming triangles, reassured him that he had made the correct decision.

I will let her sleep, he thought, though the desire to wake her was overwhelming. No doubt Annora would be cheered by the knowledge of their rescue, but she would need all her strength just to handle the stares of the men aboard that vessel. Cassen had never seen the Satyr interact with women but was confident his foreign ally would respect Annora, given whom she belonged to.

With a turn of the rudder they were headed east, and slowly at that. Cassen fumbled with the lines on the boom in an attempt to get more speed, concerned only with putting their vessel in the direct path of the Satyr's boat as quickly as possible. The sudden urge to vomit came to him, and not from seasickness. Cassen did not need to close his eyes to verify what he saw on the horizon this time, for the massive square sails of the second ship were plain to recognize. The warship was not only closer than the Satyr's ship—it was headed directly toward them.

"Wake," Cassen said, his voice too scratchy for his panic to show. "Annora, there is trouble."

She roused like a painting come to life, though Cassen had no time to appreciate the sight. How simpler things would be if she were an ugly toad as he guessed a true daughter of his making would be.

"What could be more trouble than dying of thirst?" She was rubbing her eyes and stretching, her long hair falling down her back. *We should cut that hair*, he thought, but shoved the idea aside like the rubbish it was. Desperation was the last thing they needed to show if they were to survive this ordeal.

"A boat!" Her glee was sickening as she pointed toward the warship now only several miles off. "But they are not your friends?"

"Friends of friends, but not the type I'd want to meet. My friends are there," he said, pointing to the south with his head.

Annora studied the distant sails for a moment. "Your friends' ship looks more menacing than the one that approaches."

That it may be, but not to us. "We need to discuss how to best handle this encounter."

⚬⊰⊱⚬

Cassen steered the vessel directly toward the oncoming ship. Satisfied with their trajectory and minutes away from contact, he reached over the side of the skiff and scooped a handful of seawater into his mouth. *I will have death or fresh water soon, the success of which depends on the slickness of my tongue,* he reasoned.

Though he was determined to not be outwitted by another seaman, some serious hurdles remained in Cassen's way. All the logic in the realm may do little good to convince these war-hungry men that Annora was not a mermaid sans tail, sent to them by the gods to do with as they pleased. What was worse, they may not understand a word of his common tongue—Sacarans had their own language.

"Throw a ladder, and be quick about it," Cassen shouted.

Men with barbed spears attached to ropes lined the bow's railings three men's height above. Cassen and Annora would be hauled upon the ship one way or the other, and Cassen preferred the method that did not require puncture wounds.

Annora climbed first, as they had discussed, and Cassen followed, allowing their skiff to drift off. As greedy hands pulled Annora over the rail, Cassen struggled to remain tranquil—anger he could show, but all panic must be repressed. As he himself was hoisted over the rails, that became difficult.

Of the hundreds that must be aboard, they were greeted by no fewer than ten, two of whose strong arms had pulled Cassen over with the force of malice. They stared at Cassen and Annora—mostly at Annora—while mumbling amongst each other in words that had no meaning. They looked amused. Eager smiles crossed most of their faces, faces covered with dark unkempt beards grown from weeks at sea. All stood Cassen's height or shorter, none of them large men, but all looked to possess a seafarer's wiry strength.

Cassen tried to appear to pay them no mind as he brushed his clothing with his hands. "Fetch water and see our course corrected," Cassen commanded. "I will have words—"

Annora let out a yelp, and Cassen glanced upward just in time to see that one of the men had squeezed her breast. It was the second time in so many days that one who meant her harm had accosted her in such a way, though this olive-skinned assailer smelling of acrid sweat appeared a far greater menace than had the Adeltian boy.

Cassen turned to another man, this one having the look of authority. "Take that man's hand and feed it to the fish, and I will see that the Satyr does not take your own." Cassen had no need to fake his disdain, but was purposeful in his self-assuredness. It was a risk calling Sacarat by his informal name as it might be considered slander, but Cassen had already weighed it in his mind.

The man inspected Cassen intently, but did not speak. *He does not comprehend my words.* Cassen widened his eyes, incredulous. "Chop...off...his...*hand*." He repressed the urge to mime a chopping motion as it seemed beneath a man of Cassen's station—whatever station it was he was pretending to have.

The presumed captain did not break his stare. It penetrated Cassen not unlike Duke Calder's had, but this was a man who hunted men, not animals. These Sacarans were a people who had waited a full millennium to kill, humiliate, and subjugate Adeltians such as Cassen—not be ordered around by them. Cassen returned the man's stolid glare with one of his own, not even contemplating letting his gaze wander from the man's black eyes.

"Amavaeo elmanuus," the man finally said. No action took place until he turned from Cassen to his men, at which point clamor ensued.

And now we die.

❦

Cassen searched the waves for some discernable pattern, but the rollers and breakers seemed to come and go without purpose. *Much like the actions of men,* he thought. To be at the mercy of such randomness was disquieting, and his hand crept toward his waist. He let his fingers rest atop the fabric tucked beneath his belt, content to know it was still safe.

The porthole that he peered out of was a vertical slit, barely a finger in width. Such quarters seemed ill-fit for a captain of such a colossal ship, but Cassen reminded himself this was a warship—there would be no luxury in having a larger window through which flaming projectiles may come.

"Will we reach it soon?" asked Annora. She sat on the edge of a hammock in the room, still unwilling, it seemed, to allow herself to be at ease.

"I cannot see the ship from here, but I would assume so." His words did not appear to comfort her. "How is your burn?"

"It will heal," she said, chagrinned. "So long as no more men grab at it."

Given what had just happened to the last man, Cassen did not expect she need worry for the time being.

"What kinds of friends are these people anyhow?"

"Sacarans," Cassen replied.

"*Sacarans?*"

The name of the people had not gone completely from Adeltian vernacular, but had come instead to be fictional in nature. Mothers used threat of being shipped to Sacara to frighten their brats, no longer believing such a place existed.

"Our friends in Adeltia will know them well in the coming days. This ship is one of hundreds carrying armies to their shores. And Adeltia's mighty king has but one good hand to defend his people." Cassen finished with a smirk.

"These people are degenerate savages. I now see why you get along with them."

"Oh, you have become quite the Adeltian princess. You would no doubt say the same thing if we had run into a ship full of Spiceland sailors."

Annora scowled at the accusation. "I would," she said in defiance.

Cassen snorted. "Well, you will soon have the chance. The men aboard this ship are Sacaran, but those aboard my friend's ship are mostly Spicelanders. Spicerats to be more precise."

"You cannot be serious…"

"But I am. They are not so bad as you have been led to believe listening to the gossip of the women in the laundry. Well, at least not when seen from a different perspective."

"Being friend to a murderer or tyrant does not make that murderer or tyrant decent."

"You are right in that," said Cassen. "But a person with no tyrants as friends is like to be a slave. Better to befriend ruthlessness than call it master."

Annora exhaled and shook her head.

"And that should be the last we hear of the word 'friend' lest we offend our new host. He is not fond of it." *Good that I remembered.*

"I hope your *acquaintance* speaks our tongue as opposed to just barely understanding it."

"Ah, he speaks it well, though it is his second known language. The captain of this vessel is like to speak it also, but Sacaran pride does not allow one to do something poorly. I do not think they intended to ever use the common tongue for any reason other than to know what it was those they were soon to conquer screamed in the throes of death."

Annora hid her face from him. *She worries for her friends. Perhaps she is right to.* "They have promised not to harm the nobility. They know there are some I have a vested interest in." The sentiment did not have its intended effect.

Minutes later as they sat in silence, a knock was heard at the door.

"Time for you to meet my good rival, Sacarat," said Cassen to Annora. "Though I do not think you will be very fond of him."

ETHEL

"Is it not beautiful, Sister?"

A fire of hatred burned in her belly commensurate with the mass of flames before her. Spine straight and muscles taut, Ethel stood beside her half-brother. The nearest blaze cast a flickering light on Stephon's face in the evening twilight. "That fool Veront calls them *dragons*," he scoffed. "The man has no flair for words, but what would one expect from a man with Rivervalian blood."

To the left of Stephon was an old man in loose cottons. He might have been tall, if not for his stoop, and he might have been handsome, before the decades had put bags under his eyes and stripped the color from his hair. *How can such an unremarkable man create such weapons of destruction?* Ethel wondered.

The three of them were atop a small turret overlooking the waters to the south of Eastport. Along the shore, Stephon had two dozen menacing structures facing the water, each armed with a flaming arrow near two men in length. A pivoting arm on either side of the structures had been rotated back under tension, and held in the hand of each arm was a rope that would no doubt propel the arrow, although how far Ethel could not guess.

"My spies…well they are mine now…discovered he was constructing similar weapons over a month ago, and my engineers have seen their simplistic design improved upon—*greatly*. Dysar here calls them ballistae, a name I am inclined to allow persist. Would you like to see them fire, my sister?"

He was so adamant now about calling her *sister*. For half a day she had been locked in the room behind the throne, unable to hear a sliver of what went on outside. For hours she'd alternated between pounding the doors and searching for a means of prying them open herself, fearing for the lives of Annora and Eaira and eventually her own as the notion that she had been left there to rot seemed more possible. Stephon had already proven he was capable of worse.

Stephon himself had come to free her from the prison, and in a *gracious* attempt to smooth matters over, decreed her his full-blooded sister. "Our mother is a whore and our fathers no doubt different men, but that does not mean we should not be brother and sister," he'd said.

The bandage on his right hand had worried her and, glancing at it now, it still did. If Annora was the one responsible for his injury, she would be suffering if not dead. Ethel had demanded to know what he'd done with her two friends to which he responded, "I set them free before Sture could harm either one. I did it for you, my sister." She did not believe him in the slightest, but she feared he might be keeping them imprisoned with the intent of worse, should Ethel cause him trouble. She did not care to guess why Stephon had come to want her friendship—if that even was the case, but she would humor him as best she could until she found a means to free Annora and Eaira, assuming they were still alive. The days that had passed since then felt like an eternity, and with eyes upon her at all times, Ethel was no closer to learning of either of their whereabouts.

Ethel nodded her consent, pleasing Stephon as his brow jumped.

"All of them," Stephon shouted down to the men. "You will fire all of them on my command." Stephon raised an upward pointing finger atop an outstretched arm.

Lightning strike him where he stands, Ethel prayed, willing it to actually occur. *Let it take me as well if it must—I do not care.* She closed her eyes and pictured a bolt leaping from the dark clouds above, making contact with the tip of that well-kept finger. The hair of her neck and arms stood on end as the moist air surrounding her seemed to brim with energy.

A violent crack sounded, followed immediately by screams of agony.

"Peace's mercy. Silence his cries," shouted Stephon.

Upon opening her eyes Ethel saw a man below impaled through the shoulder by a massive shard of wood. An arm had snapped off one of the closer ballistae, finding a new body in which to embed itself.

"I told them, only use heartwood for the arms. That wood is clearly of two tones." Dysar's somber disappointment was evident in his voice.

"Should we kill him, Your Grace?" came a distraught voice from below.

"No, you damn fool. Put a hand on his mouth and send him to a mender. We will be under siege in a day or less," said Stephon. Then with a lowered voice, "There is no need to be killing our own."

"Under siege?" Ethel asked, wondering what game Stephon might be playing.

Stephon shook his head and snubbed her. "Consider that preparation for war, men. Some of us will be maimed and die, but the others must continue the defense. Adeltia will not fall into the hands of foreigners. Not under my rule. Now *fire*!"

An uncoordinated volley of flame leapt from the structures, streaking through the air with unimaginable speed. The fiery trails traveled so far Ethel thought she may lose sight of them, and when she did, it was difficult to tell if it was due to distance or the water having snuffed their flames.

Stephon wore a satisfied scowl as Ethel turned to look at him.

"You have done the kingdom a great service, Dysar. If I come to need a First, you will be atop the list."

Dysar appeared deep in thought, stroking the shaved skin of his chin. "I had expected more range… The arrows were over fletched. Must remedy that."

"Well do so quickly," said Stephon. "We do not know when or where these attacks will come from, and we must see the machines spread along the coast."

"What attacks?" Ethel placed her hand upon Stephon's arm to prevent the possibility of him ignoring her, but the contact with him reminded her of whom she touched. Though he'd assured her otherwise, this boy-turned-man was the one responsible for seeing their father, *her* father, tortured and killed. The guards and servants she'd overheard speaking of its brutality—hushed to silence upon their noticing her—recounted details almost too gruesome to be believed.

"It may come as a surprise to girls who sit within their provided comforts, sipping tea and oblivious to what goes on beyond the walls, but there are those who would wish to harm us. Those who would like to see our kingdom destroyed."

You needn't look outside the walls, she thought. *One such person stands before you.* "What do you mean? Speak plainly so my woman's ears can make sense of it. If we are in danger, why are you playing with these…things…on the water? Shouldn't we be guarding the walls?"

Stephon exhaled a mighty breath. "Oh, my sweet sister, these *are* the walls…" Stephon swept his hand in front of himself toward the ballistae. "And the shoreline is the battlefield. We are to be attacked by sea. By whom, I do not know, only that their fleet is massive."

Dysar was making his way off the tower, but turned for a final word. "The ballistae are deadly accurate. We should be able to set ship to fire at near five hundred paces…provided the winds comply." A strong breeze seemed to answer in defiance, pulling at his dark brown cottons as he disappeared down the stairway.

"I only learned about it the moment after you threw your tantrum in the throne room," continued Stephon. "You would not have waited for so long in there if not for my urgent need to make preparations to save the kingdom."

Perhaps he did not have time to torture Annora and Eaira in earnest, then. The thought gave her some hope.

"And where is our army?" she asked.

Stephon ran his left hand over his face and spoke with stifled anger. "Master Warin, it seems, has taken it upon himself to march north on Rivervale without my consent. I have made arrangements for his disposal, but there is no need to rush. I would as soon let him take Rivervale first. I always wanted some land in the North."

He is without sense. "You expect a handful of your wooden archers to repel a fleet without an army to defend them? What if they land ashore elsewhere and march upon us?"

She saw a flash of uncertainty upon his face. "My dear sister, I think it is time for you to return to your sanctuary in the Throne. I cannot discuss every detail of our preparations only to have them fall upon a woman's stone ears. You need only know that I will protect you from harm."

Stephon called down to the guards to come escort Ethel. She had no desire to remain in his company, but she also felt inclined to stay and watch the horizon for danger. She knew the southern border was vast and could not be guarded by these few ballistae even if Stephon spread them in time. Ethel scanned the edge of the sea, unsure of whether she truly wished to see something—unsure of whether she actually wanted to see this kingdom destroyed as she'd so recently wished.

"There," she said faintly, unsure if she'd even spoken audibly.

Stephon ignored her, yelling something to Dysar who had reached the bottom of the turret.

"Look there," Ethel said at Stephon, now with urgency, pointing toward the sea.

A dark square could be seen in the distance against a sky lit yellow by the setting Dawnstar.

"Is that one of ours?" she asked.

"They come," yelled Stephon, a bit frantic. "Dysar, get your men ready to fire. You there, guard, run and fetch the boy Sture and his cousin or sister—that girl that looks just like him."

The guard ran to obey.

"We only have a hundred bolts constructed," Dysar said from below, his frail voice almost lost to the wind. "I warned against loosing a whole voll—"

"Then make *more*," Stephon screamed at him. Dysar bowed and shuffled off at a hurried pace.

Stephon regained his composure and turned to Ethel with a king's self-assurance. "It seems you will bear witness to my making of history after all."

❦

An hour had passed, and the Dawnstar touched the western shore. Shadowing the southern skyline was a fleet the likes of which Ethel had never believed existed. There were hundreds—too many to count without losing track, but at least two hundred ships each as large as any she'd seen formed a single row, pushing hard on their shores.

"How long until we can send our first volley?" Stephon had no fear in his voice now. He was a child anticipating the greatest prize one of his ilk could hope for: unfettered glory.

Dysar was a different matter. The man had become pale and sweaty once the ship count rose above fifty and he had declined in appearance ever since. "By my estimate we have another five minutes before they are within range, and then only another five at most before they begin to land the shores. It takes us twenty seconds to load and another ten to properly aim. Given we have twenty three machines—"

"Spare me the arithmetic. Just see that your men load with the haste that is required. We fire in five minutes when they are in range."

"That is the other issue, Your Grace," continued Dysar. "They span a mile or more in breadth, and we only managed to push the ballistae a mile in kind. If they spread farther apart we will not have the ability to hit them."

"They will only spread as they are fleeing in fright. When their crews see the ships to either side go up in flame they will retreat." Stephon gave Dysar a reassuring smile. "Do not fear, old man. We have Peace on our side."

"Yes, of course," replied Dysar. "With you is Peace."

Stephon seemed satisfied with the man's response, but Ethel did not see the sincerity in it, only desperation.

"Sture, how long until you and your sister can set ships ablaze?" Stephon addressed the two young ones he'd summoned. Ethel made no effort to conceal her hatred for Sture as she glowered at him, but he was transfixed on the ships.

"We have never attempted at such a distance," said Sture. "It will be difficult without seeing in detail the thing we are to burn."

"It will not be so hard, Your Grace." Signy turned red as she spoke, but her words were confident. "Not if we picture and focus on the tiniest of threads upon their sails. Knowing they are there will be enough. The Dawnstar is still in full view. I have lit a candle at over a hundred paces under similar conditions."

"A stationary candle that you had studied beforehand," said Sture, clearly not pleased to have been contradicted. "We do not even know what these sails are made of."

"I was hoping you could ignite the wood of the bow," said Stephon.

Sture looked to Signy as if to let her dig her own grave. "Wood does not catch so quickly, nor does damp wood tend to remain lit," she admitted.

"Very well. Light their sails then, but be quick."

The young pair went quiet and stared off, Sture to the east and Signy to the west.

Ethel focused on the ships herself. They looked enormous now that they were within a mile, and her brother's confidence seemed more misplaced by the moment. Stephon at least had the sense to have a horse for each of them at the bottom of the tower, should things go sour. *Where will I ride it though?* She could follow Stephon and hope he had another plan, but that seemed naïve. This was like to be a disaster, and her muscles already twitched, begging her to run. *I will ride to the Throne, enter the dungeons, bribe the gaolers with gold—if they even remain—and see my friends and mother freed*, Ethel decided. *From there we will ride north to Rivervale.* It was a plan so audacious it was a wonder Stephon himself had not concocted it, but Ethel was committed and determined.

Flames engulfed one of the ships far to the east.

"Well done, Sture. Another," said Stephon.

"It was not him," said Dysar. "A ballista fired early and with luck. We should commence firing only after another minute."

"Another minute be damned. Fire at will!"

Stephon's order to fire was repeated down the ballista line in both directions, and a volley went forth. A flock of burning arrows the shape of flying geese soared through the sky. Flames sprung from the foremost sails of a ship to the west, leaping quickly with the wind from one sail to another, but the fiery birds had not yet reached the vessel.

"Cotton canvas," cried Signy, much louder than needed. "The sails are simple cotton canvas!" Then much quieter and abashed, "...It helps to know."

The arrows began to land. More than half struck water and disappeared, but the others tore into sails and prows, spreading fire quickly around the perimeter of the ships.

"They use tar on their hulls. I was counting on that." Dysar had passion in his voice, but his face still spoke of doom.

Sails continued to ignite on ships east and west that had not been struck by flaming arrows. Sture and Signy were silent as they focused on one ship then the next, turning the dark silhouettes of their sails to vivid infernos.

"Reload, damn you. Quickly!" Stephon turned to Ethel with a satisfied grin. "Do you see what happens to my enemies? What king has ever put the power of magic to such brilliant use? And to save a kingdom, at that. None shall dare offend us after this display, and Peace will triumph over the realm."

"Are those oars? My old eyes..." Dysar's voice now matched his unchanged expression.

Ethel became flushed with waves of hot panic. The boats had slowed, but the vast majority continued forward. The fire on those whose sails burned did not spread to the rest of the ship.

"Should we perhaps mount up and leave, Your Grace...my brother?" Ethel could not mask the alarm in her voice. "We are not of much use... Just to be safe..."

"Ha. It is no wonder our kingdom fell the last time a woman led. Your kind lacks resolution." Stephon no longer looked at her. He was focused instead on the sight before him. "Why have we not fired a second volley?"

As the words left his mouth the machines began to fire their second round of attack, although only one or two at a time.

"Faster, damn you," yelled Stephon.

The first few shots all hit their marks, but a gust of wind came from the north as the rest were fired, causing most to drift past their targets and land harmlessly in the water behind.

Ethel pressed her damp hands into the cool stone of the parapet. *If I flee to my horse, Stephon will have me stopped, and then his pride will never allow him to leave. I must convince him to retreat—after the next failed volley.*

"Peace, see this wind settled," said Stephon in frustration. "Did you not teach your men how to account for a bit of breeze?"

Dysar need not respond as the wind howled to the point of all of them having to brace themselves against it.

"All the sails are afire, Your Grace," yelled Sture over the wind. "May we go?"

Stephon looked at the boy as if Sture had just kicked him in the shin. "Go where?" he demanded. "You may go home to speak of victory after every last invader has been burned. Set their tar-laden hulls aflame. Now!"

Signy was already staring hard at the closest ship that had not yet been struck in the prow by ballista, but she did not appear to be having success. Sture gazed forward toward the ships. Seeming neither confident nor concentrated, he appeared to be attempting to incinerate his fears more than their enemies' hulls.

"This gale may cause some misfires, Your Grace, but it is fanning their fires and slowing their approach." Dysar's voice was difficult to hear now over the keening wind.

"The North keep its abominable storms. We have no need of them," responded Stephon.

The ships were so close now that Ethel could somewhat make out what was happening upon them. On those with hulls engulfed in flames, men poured overboard, on others, oars stroked in tandem, and on all she saw smaller vessels being shoved over the railings. The men in the water fought to right those small boats in the sea and clamored into them by the dozen.

"They are launching skiffs, Your Grace. We should get you to safety," shouted Dysar.

Perhaps Dysar's words of reason will have more effect than my own.

"Then shoot their skiffs!" Stephon cupped his hands around his mouth, repeating, "Shoot their skiffs," to the men below, none of who appeared to hear him.

He will not leave. He is mad. In spite of the cold ripping wind, Ethel felt nothing but heat. Every other sensation had become numbed, yet something frozen and painful lanced her repeatedly in the back.

She turned to look behind her, but there was nothing—nothing but the same lancing pain upon her face. *Rain,* she realized. *A fitting end for us both, to be slain in a frigid rainstorm.*

The sea was littered now with bodies and small boats, spewing from the ships like a disturbed colony of insects. Signy's face was impossible to see as it was covered by her flapping hair, but Sture wept. His tears fell forward rather than downward, carried by the wind along with the growing number of other droplets to extinguish the flames that had been their only hope of victory.

As Ethel's chance of escape diminished, so did her missteps seem evermore distinct. Stephon's failings were her own. Her retreat into her books and her music, her inability to face her peers, to force them to respect her, it was all somehow to blame for the man her brother had become. *I have become the worst of both my parents,* she thought, *and in no way was I a sister. I could have shown him another path, yet I only scorned him as our mother did our father.*

The fluttering noise of thick fabric ceased as the large banner atop their turret pulled free. It tumbled through the air, the sigil clearly visible: the proud Adeltian Throne jutting through the clouds.

Ethel heard cries from below and looked to see if attackers had flanked them upon land. But the men had their arms raised and were cheering. The surf now moved away from shore rather than toward it, splashing waves over the bows of skiffs so close Ethel thought she could see the anger on the attackers' faces. *Anger or fear?* The waves battered the small boats so relentlessly that many began to capsize. A great warship in the distance had turned to the east, listing so severely it threatened to tip, and others followed suit.

"The storm is preventing their landfall," yelled Dysar. "It is too strong."

The squall intensified as if incited by Dysar's words, and Ethel bent at the knees to ensure a strong gust would not blow her over the stone wall. Stephon's vindictive laughter cut through the roar of the wind, interrupted only by the crack of firing ballistae.

THE BEGUILED

As he approached the halfway point of his journey, just before his path looped back toward where he'd come, he was greeted by a familiar sight. There was no motion by the patch of birch trees, nor any disturbance in the snow at their base. This trap was empty, as were the many before, but Titon was well aware that he had within his clutches another kind of prey.

His nostrils flared, though he was not in need of breath, and his skin went hot, threatening to break sweat, though he was not warm. He did not know with certainty who trailed him, but could wager a guess. Had he been followed by any other, he'd simply have been flattered and amused, but for *her* to be at his heels put a fire in his chest—a fire he could not pretend was purely anger.

She had made her choice, and by all accounts she'd chosen well. Their friendship undiminished, Titon and Keethro had waged a tacit war, a war of two fronts, and each had scored a victory. Just as Titon had won the respect of the men, his fearless aggression having placed him above all others, Keethro had won the affection of the women with more subtle tactics. But whereas the battle for leadership required the swaying of many, the other struggle had always been over just one.

She was a most alluring contradiction in her design. The other women called her wanton names, and she dressed and walked—her stride was itself a sinful act—as if they were deserved. Yet among the men, raucous and coarse, none had ever claimed to have bedded her, save perhaps in boastful jest. Brazen though she seemed from afar, she turned coquettish and bashful when in private, increasing desire while thwarting its fulfillment. Youthful though she was, she had the fullness of a nursing mother—a fullness impossible not to notice given the way in which it was displayed. Yet unlike the other girls who bathed in the river with carelessness, making a peek easy enough for restive eyes, Kilandra was never seen exposed.

Without need of speaking, she called his name.

Rage was all that kept him from turning. Why she had chosen to come to him now was enough to drive him to madness. Two years prior she would have come an angel, but now her furs of white hid a fiendish succubus. Had she planned this? To wait for Elise's belly to have swollen? Had she heard it gossiped that he no longer stole the souls of Dogmen women, furthering his lustful agony?

But the more he mulled her intentions, the less they seemed to matter, and before he knew it, he was upon her. Flesh on flesh, with a ferocity that had built for years, he assaulted her, and as though she had always felt the same, she answered. Naked upon her white furs, the two embraced, exchanging with their lips a lifetime of longing, now acknowledged, and an unspoken agreement to a lifetime of secrecy that would be theirs alone.

As his trespass became irreversible, she suddenly refused him, giving way to a one-sided skirmish. Her initial savagery was impressive as she screamed and bit, but the duration of her struggle betrayed its insincerity. Nonetheless, her having yielded spurred him to heightened passion, and he consumed her with his every sense: her soft skin, given as if for the first time to gooseflesh; her taste, ripened yet virgin; and her eyes, stripped of their usual defiance.

Elation upon guilt and relief upon dread, he looked at her in the finality of his act, studying her expression of ecstasy. That he was a leader meant nothing—that he was her master meant all. But as he enjoyed his newfound glory, his ultimate conquest, so did his prize change. Her body shrunk beneath him, replaced by the slight frame of a woman svelte and lithesome. Her dark hair, first losing its cobalt luster, went grey and then white. But in the throes of euphoria, he did not notice, nor did it matter, as he realized his most coveted triumph.

❦

His eyes would not yet open, but he could sense he was in darkness. This was a place he had never before awoken in—Keethro was at least sure of that much. These unfamiliar and potentially threatening surroundings did not allow him the presence of mind to be properly disturbed by the illusion he'd just experienced...dreamt through the eyes of another.

It felt more as if he had slipped from a womb than merely been roused to consciousness. Moisture clung to his skin, and an uncomfortable heat blanketed him near completely. One part of him, however, was cold, exposed, erect...and damp—a dampness not fully explained by an erotic dream envisioned to completion.

No stranger to awakening to physical intercourse, his priority was regaining his sight without looking foolish, and he made no move to hide his turgidity. The quiet stillness he was in felt somehow contrived. It was as if he was the object of hushed observation.

How odd it was, to find he was somewhat relieved by the repugnant sight before him. Keethro's memories returned to him, with a suddenness that was to be expected. Chief among them was the fear that he would have awoken to an act of violation far worse than it appeared he had suffered. It was odd as well, that which he felt toward the man who now looked at him, sickly thin and hunched, toothlessly beaming as if he'd committed a proud mischief. Those were not the only eyes upon

Keethro. As he'd guessed, his molestation had been the focal point of the underground community. The light of the solitary sconce outside their cage glimmered in those eager eyes, all awaiting Keethro's response.

Pity—that was what he felt toward the skinny creature who had profaned him. He taunted Keethro, licking his gums and lips, savoring what remained of their encounter, and apparently taking pleasure in something he saw in Keethro's expression. The vile thing sat upon the lap of his large keeper, another beast similar to the guards in that he seemed at home in this place as he stroked what remained of the hair on the head of his pet. A notion crossed Keethro's mind that perhaps he had misplaced master and servant as he watched them interact, those gentle strokes denoting more pride than ownership, but it made no difference. Keethro would kill them both—that much was certain, and he would do so with less malice than he would have previously imagined.

The two rightmost fingers of his axe hand twitched and cramped in rebellion—they were the true price he'd pay for his mortal needs of sleep and dignity. Before having drifted to troubling dreams, Keethro had surveyed the mangled fingers of all the men, finding none who had lost any on their left before their right. In doing so, Keethro had resigned himself to the inevitable loss of some of his most important digits, and the reality that he would never throw an axe again with any mastery. It was a small price to pay, he reasoned, should he be able to some day escape and have his revenge on the man who put him here.

The bigger man died quickly, but Keethro was surprised by the strength and rage of the smaller, who defended first his companion and then himself. He died regardless, though his neck was so small and wiry it proved impossible to break cleanly, forcing Keethro to kill him gruesomely by bashing his head against the clay ground. Smashing the life from him gave Keethro time to ponder and gain clarity. There was a strange sadness that came with destroying these two creatures who'd found a home, if not a happiness, in this horrid place. Keethro came to realize that if anything, he thanked them. Two fingers was less than he'd expected to lose in teaching the others the result of interfering with his slumber, the sodden taint on his honor now all but expunged by his revenge. "I am a heavy sleeper," he admitted to the corpse, ensuring it was dead with a final thud against the ground, "and I value my rest."

I have no hatred to spare for these two, Keethro realized as he returned to his corner to close his eyes, no longer having to fear being disturbed by his fellow prisoners. It would likely be several hours before the guards would come and notice the bodies. *All my hatred has been promised, in full, to my faithful friend. The one responsible for my being here. The one I was a fool to have ever considered a brother.*

TITON SON OF SMALL GRYN

"All halt."

Titon looked rearward toward the man who had issued the unwanted command. Aleric had already dismounted and was busy directing his underlings on where to erect the tent. The legions of men marching behind were forced to come to a disorderly stop, some obviously not wishing to disobey Titon's previous order to follow only his instructions, but unable to continue forward without trampling those who had faltered. The worst part of it was they did all of this within eyesight of their enemy—an enemy that would no doubt be bolstered by their lack of discipline.

Titon's horse seemed to be equally disappointed as Titon tugged at the reins and walked him back to where Aleric and Edgar stood.

"We should advance a thousand or so more paces to where the gate's path runs to the sea." Titon spoke with as much cordiality as possible. Pretending Aleric was a neighbor's child that he could not discipline helped in that regard. "The ground is slightly lower there, and I do not want them sneaking any messages or supplies through during the night."

"The higher ground is better." Aleric did not turn to Titon as he spoke.

Sir Edgar did not appear to share his colleague's scorn. He looked at Titon worriedly and said nothing.

"It would be foolish to charge the gate at an angle." Titon went on, hoping reason might finally win over this malcontent. "We'll remain in range of their bows for a longer—"

"They've already begun to raise the tent." Aleric interrupted while sitting down to remove his boots, still not facing Titon.

Titon tore his death stare away from Aleric's back and turned it to his true enemy. The castle he saw was no less impressive than it had been as they marched north of it to reach the sea, then south to reach—almost reach—its eastern gate. Then he looked toward his troops, those that would need to storm that gate.

Three thousand men… It no longer seems like so many.

The horde before him was separating into three legions of equal size, each slowly forming its own rough rectangle with its back to the sea. To Titon they looked a force capable of storming a castle in their number, but they lacked the implements he'd seen carved on the doors of Veront's throne room. They had no boulder-hurling contraptions, no ladders, no rams. Veront had not even spared any of his dragons from the arena. *The only thing on that door we might hope to reproduce is the pile of bodies that spanned the moat.*

But he would not be deterred. The nightmares from his fitful sleep had redoubled his cause for urgency, the image of Keethro's head having been the one he'd recently cleaved from the halfbreed's shoulders still fresh in his mind. The castle that sat behind him may have looked majestic, enveloped by the setting Dawnstar, but it was an infant in comparison to the behemoth that guarded Rivervale and had no moat. If they formed a mound of bodies, they would use it instead to climb the walls—a thing Titon hoped to avoid by breeching the gate.

When the men had settled into formation, Titon addressed them.

"Tomorrow we take the small fort you see in the distance." Titon paced in front of them, speaking with enough strength to be heard by all. "Though most of you look to be no strangers to combat…" The lie was almost too much for him to say without a grimace. "…For some this will be your first battle. Those of you who have not witnessed the horrors of war, I tell you now, it is more gruesome than you imagine. Turn to your left and right. Expect to see the heads of those men roll upon the ground, their arms ripped from their bodies, and their entrails spilled and trampled by your own feet. That will help you tomorrow when what you see is worse."

"Hmph." Titon did not need to look to know the smug and disapproving grunt had come from Aleric who stood behind him. Titon's speech after executing the halfbreed clearly had not worked as hoped to stop this man from being a blister in the boot. Aleric had continued to bemoan Titon's decision to march past Strahl to the coastline—loudly so. And each time Titon would try to remind Aleric that it was he who commanded them, Aleric would have some retort about Veront being their true commander. *This man is a liability without benefit*, Titon thought, but he continued as if he had not heard the sound.

Titon let his hard gaze sweep all three legions, hoping each man would feel it. "Listen to the words I speak now, and obey the commands I yell tomorrow. Doing otherwise would be a grievous mistake."

The son of Small Gryn had marched his men without compassion for nine days at half again normal pace and at half ration. He suspected they'd hated him for it, but returning to Rivervale with haste to ensure their deal remained fresh in King Veront's mind had become an even more pressing concern after the halfbreed's warning. *I hope you are enjoying the large portions of the Rivervale prisons, Keethro,* Titon thought upon finishing each of his own half-sized meals. Only in these last few days had Titon allowed them to switch to double rations and slow their pace, and the thankfulness was written on the faces of all his men.

Only victory matters, Titon reminded himself, in preparation for the action he feared he may come to regret. The parting Dawnstar bathed the two crescents of his weapon in amber and violet as he raised it above his head. "And on the battlefield," he yelled, "no mistakes are forgiven." With a fluid motion Titon turned and swung his blade downward, first connecting with the plate on Aleric's shoulder and continuing until the man was split to the ass in two. His halves fell to either side, each still in their plate containers, with the exception of his intestines, which spilled between.

Sir Edgar had a panicked look but calmed when Titon nodded to him as only one man can do to another in acknowledgment of their mutual accord.

"If you are upwind of this, the smell of war," Titon went on, "be sure to come and give your nostrils their fill before you retire. If you are too far to see what it is this man last ate, come and let your eyes share in his feast. Look upon it until you grow weary from the mundaneness of it. If such things give you pause tomorrow, your enemy will cut you down the moment you hesitate." *I found a purpose for you after all, Sir Aleric.*

His thoughts went to the pheasant killed by one of their scouts, which had been herbed and salted and would soon be roasted over oak coals. The man with the lucky arrow had said it was a tradition in Rivervale to offer your leader game before a battle, as it brought greater chance of victory. Tonight, Titon planned to amend that tradition to include sharing it with the man who'd killed it. His speech would only require a few more minutes, and he had a hunger in his belly that not even the stink of Aleric's bowels could expunge. "But let there be no mistake," he continued. "Tomorrow you will be afraid, as will I. We all feel the grip of fear when faced with death. But fear is like a beautiful woman…"

◦⊰⊱◦

"Looks to be four, maybe five thousand infantry with a cavalcade of several hundred," said Randir.

It was the same as Titon had estimated. Just as Titon had roused his men, his enemy had also stirred to action in the predawn glow.

"And what are they doing outside the protection of the walls?" Titon asked.

Randir did not need pause to think. "Lord Edwin is Illumined. They will avoid killing—even their sworn enemies—whenever possible. He is showing you the brunt of his army in the hopes that you will know that victory is hopeless and leave."

Titon's face contorted in disgust. "But I could have ten thousand men hiding in the mountains to the north, and he would have just shown his forces for nothing."

Randir was unmoved. "He could also have ten thousand men hiding behind his walls."

"If he were truly wishing to avoid battle at all costs then he would need show all fifteen thousand, no?"

Randir shrugged as if to concede with some reluctance.

Titon had not noticed Randir until the conclusion of his rallying speech the previous night. Randir was the third survivor from the arena, knocked unconscious by the dragon's wrath but otherwise unharmed. It was his frame that caught Titon's attention as he scanned his soldiers— the man was built much like Keethro, if not a bit shorter, and Titon made the connection upon seeing the buckler on his arm. Titon invited him to share the pheasant and found he was a good source of honest knowledge, nothing at all like Sir Edgar who seemed to know little more than his own name and title.

"You appear to respect the man," Titon prodded.

"I have no love for Edwin, but respect, yes. He has done a great thing for the people of Strahl, the Illumined."

Titon found Randir's praise a bit disconcerting. "You speak as if you were one of them."

"I was never fool enough to consider myself Illumined. I may find their values laudable, but I do not share their beliefs. My wife is among them, however."

"Your *wife*?" Titon made no attempt to mask his shock. "She lives within those walls? Am I wise to turn my back on you during combat knowing this?"

Randir scowled with vehemence. "I owe you my life for what happened in the arena. On my honor as a knight, I will help you take this city, though I do not feel we stand a chance. If we do not succeed, another army will. This is just a fraction of Veront's forces, and he will take Strahl in time."

And he is a knight as well... Titon could not help but believe the man, given how sincerely offended he was at the implication of treachery. And it would be foolish for him to tell Titon all of this, should he truly plan to betray him. "And if we do succeed?"

"Then I'd only ask that I am given temporary leave to protect my wife and her home from that which follows."

He knows war. "You will have it. I will accompany you myself and ensure her safety. You have my word as a Galatai warrior." *My word as a knight means little,* thought Titon, recalling the events that followed his swearing allegiance to the king.

Randir nodded with reverence.

"They may have numbers, but now that they are outside their walls we have range," Titon explained. "I see no spears or halberds above their heads. Their swords and shields will not fare well against row upon row of spear." *I hope.* The first to draw blood was often the first to win, and Titon's experience with throwing weapons had taught him that the first to draw blood was often, if not always, the one with greater range.

"We have the ocean to our backs. It will make retreat very difficult should things go wrong," said Randir.

"Aye, the ocean is where I want it. But I am not familiar with this southern word you speak...*retreat?*"

Randir gave Titon a good-humored snort in response.

"And we will soon have another thing behind us with the Dawnstar's rising," Titon added. "With an ocean and a god backing us, I find it hard to believe we could manage to be defeated, even with the whimpering boys we have been given. And also, our men know we do not have the rations to return to Rivervale."

Sir Edgar approached, clearing his throat as he came.

"The men are ready?" Titon asked the new arrival.

"Aye," said Edgar.

"What is that?" Titon pointed to the distance. A solitary man was on horseback, pulling a large wagon of some sort. He stopped midway between the armies and began to erect a structure. "It does not look to be a weapon."

"No. It's a parley table." Sir Edgar had found his voice, ugly thing that it was. "And I'd remind you, King Veront gave you command over the army, not the power to bargain with his enemies. There is no reason to send men to parley. It's like to be a trap at any rate."

Titon heard the words but looked to Randir for perhaps more sage advice.

"He is right," said Randir with a nod. "The Illumined are not without honor, but Lord Edwin would not hesitate to kill you with duplicity if it meant saving lives. What is the weight of a lie and one life measured against the lives of thousands?"

It had only taken a minute for the man to finish constructing the table, complete with what looked to be three chairs on either side, though it was difficult to tell given the distance and low light. The hunched man mounted his horse and rode back, disappearing into the mass of soldiers outside the walls no sooner than three mounted men appeared from the mob, making their way toward the table.

The men on horseback glimmered as the first rays peeked over the distant ocean edge. All three bore full plate, sans helm, polished and undyed. Such plain armor would likely not just be for show, but Titon was eager to see if the suits actually had dints and scratches from use, or if they were as pristine as they appeared from a distance.

"Is that their Lord Edwin?" asked Titon.

"That looks to be him there in the middle with the yellow cape and flowing mane," said Randir.

"What can you tell me of the man? Is he a swordsman? Just a politician?"

"He is a trained swordsman, a fine one at that, but he is most known for his horsemanship," replied Randir.

"His horsemanship? You get on the beast, and it takes you some place. Where is the skill in that?"

"It is not so simple. The man has control of a horse as a normal man controls himself. He can jump them, stand atop them, lean off the side and pick up a rose…" Titon was far from impressed. The man sounded a jester. "And he can spear a man through the eye of his choosing at a full gallop." *A dangerous jester.*

"Then I will fight him when he is dismounted if possible, or just kill his horse."

Randir did not look convinced.

"I know you slept through most of the arena," Titon said, grinning at his new friend, "but men fall hard from injured horses."

"Aye," Randir admitted with another snort. "I was awake for that part."

Titon arched his back and stretched out his arms. *It will be good to put these double rations to some use other than walking and gossip.* "Anything else I should know about the man I intend to kill?"

Randir chewed his lip as if pained.

"Out with it," Titon commanded.

"There are rumors that the man is…foppish."

The word was not one Titon was familiar with; however, it certainly did not sound threatening.

"Very well. You two remain here and await my command. Make sure the men are poised to charge." Titon's stunt with Aleric must have made an impression, as neither man moved to object.

The three men of Strahl were seated at the table as Titon strode up to them. Each had a shield resting on the back of his chair and a sword sheathed at his side. Titon imagined he must not have looked quite as they'd expected from a leader of a Rivervalian army, on foot, covered in soft leathers, a two-handed axe in his hands. Their perplexed glares supported his theory.

Titon pulled out the center seat on his side and plopped himself down, sitting wide-legged and leaning backwards as if with friends. "They tell me you wish to speak with me."

"What sort of foolishness is this? Who are you, and why has your leader not come to meet with us?" It was the man in the middle, Lord

Edwin—vexed as a woman shushed. He had a large frame but with not much meat on it from the look of his gaunt cheeks. As the wind blew his strands of wavy brown into his eyes he was forced to whip his head to the side to clear his view. *This boy must wash his hair more than a woman the way it flutters in the breeze.*

"I am Sir Titon son of Small Gryn, and my leader is busy doing whatever it is kings do."

"Who leads this army? You are clearly some brute sent to try and intimidate us. And let me tell you—it shan't work. We Illumined have no fear of death. The Dawnstar guide us in this life and reward us in the next." The men to his side nodded their compliance.

The mention of the Dawnstar was a bit puzzling as this man claimed to be *Illumined*, but these Southmen made little sense. "I have told you once, and I will tell you a second time. I, alone, command the army before you flying the banners of Rivervale—the army that will see yours defeated."

"You do not even know your sigils, foreigner," scoffed Edwin. "Those you fly are Bywater banners, and Veront is no true king."

Titon shook his head with a disbelieving grimace. *There is a battle to be fought, and these men would rather discuss banners.*

"Where I am from we do not suffer these *parleys* prior to battle—we come to fight, not to blabber. But I lead a southern army now, and I will play your games…to a point. I offer you the chance to surrender. Your women will suffer less if our men are not fervent from battle. You have my word as one who knows war."

Lord Edwin shot upright, sending his seat and shield flying behind him. Titon remained unmoved. "You vile shit," Edwin spat. "How dare you make demands of our great city and threaten its civilians—and with what? Your mere three legions? May the Light blind you for your arrogance so that you do not have to witness the crushing defeat you will no doubt suffer on this day. Who do you think you are to spit on the Dawnstar and not be burned?"

Titon was not one to stand for being accused of blasphemy, but this man did not have what it took to truly anger him. His boyishness made him seem like a child throwing a tantrum as opposed to a man deserving of Titon's true wrath.

"I do not spit on the Dawnstar, nor do I piss in the River…and even I quake before the Mountain. Who am I? Remember the name this time because it is the name of the man who will send you to your grave. I am Titon, and I will have this city."

Edwin was signaling to his companions to get up and leave when he froze in place. "*Titon* you said?" His head cocked at an angle. "The same Titon who killed two of our patrols in cold blood?"

"Aye, I killed two of your miserable guards, but—"

The man unsheathed his sword with alacrity, the sound of it ringing in the air as he interrupted. "I hereby arrest you on account of murder. Throw down your weapon and come—"

Titon did not enjoy being interrupted and returned the favor. He grabbed a middle leg of the table and flipped it forward, pushing it into the three men like a giant shield while keeping hold of it. In the same motion he used his free hand to retrieve the axe from beside him and swung it under the repurposed table. His blade found its way into a joint of the first man's armor, cutting through his knee without pause and continuing into the leg of their leader. The blade struck metal there, hard metal, but the force was sufficient to crumple the leg sideways.

The three men's horses were gone before the two that had been crippled fell to the ground. The third man slashed at Titon with his sword, hitting only wood. Titon rushed the man with his table and slammed him with enough force to lift him from his feet, sending him to fall hard on his back. The man with the severed leg was shrilling death as he writhed on the ground, no threat, but Edwin had sword in hand, supporting himself with his other arm and one good knee, and lunged at Titon with a desperate cut. The attack came from the rear and was aimed at Titon's exposed calf, but he stepped out of reach for a moment, then returned to kick Edwin's hand, releasing the sword from his grip.

He had courage, this Edwin, as he crawled forward without any noises of injury and tried to grapple a foot. Titon would have grabbed a lesser man by the hair and sliced off his head with a slow sawing motion of his axe blade. Instead, he rewarded the man's courage with a quick death. A swing of his axe parted the man's head from his body. *I have need of this*, Titon reminded himself, retrieving the head and tying it to his belt by the hair.

Leaving the two injured men where they lay and not even looking back at his own army, Titon picked up his makeshift shield and charged forward—toward five thousand men clamoring to get back inside the walls of their castle.

THE GAZER

A medley of snow and pine leaf swirled past her, held hostage and forced south by an angry wind. This storm that now blew was domineering in its own right and would only grow fiercer with her coaxing. The trees bent knee, both in reverence, and to dodge its fury, the clanspeople took shelter in their homes, and the Dawnstar seemed eager to retreat for the day. Even to her, this storm was a meddlesome beast. Left to its own devices it would likely cost her her secondborn son, delaying his stubborn progress through the northern snow. She closed her eyes and gazed at him, confirming as she'd suspected. Decker may have been aided by the warmth of rare metal, but he could not endure a full week of blizzard, were it permitted to continue.

Elise shifted sight to her eldest son. Titon was much changed, but much the same, choosing to weather the storm with his nose in a book. He'd spent the past two weeks regaining both strength and wisdom, encouraged mostly by his pungent friend the tanner's son. It was in the tanner's home where Titon now read, though he had already begun the construction of his own self-inspired shelter. Elise did not lament that he now visited her less frequently and for little duration. For a young man ever in search of knowledge, a lifeless, unfamiliar mother did not provide much toward that aim.

With some reluctance, she turned her gaze to her other Titon—the one she had earlier watched chase an army into and out from its own castle walls. Ripe with conquest, he shared in the spoils of war with his men: pilfered food, drink, and cheer, but not in pilfered pleasure…as she half wished he might. Her faithful husband's devotion was as unyielding as his axe, and witnessing it time and again only cut her deeper. *You must never know my reasons,* she said to him in her thoughts, apologizing for both a decade of deceit and a century to come.

She tore her gaze away from him now, convinced that the strengthened winds would not cause him any danger, and focused on her task. The dark gale ripped through her as she stood beside their now-frozen stream, alone and safe from prying eyes. She could not call a storm, nor could she add to its total strength, but she could hasten it...shape it...guide it—into something far more fleeting and intense. She felt the energy of it flow through her, a sensation neither elating nor unpleasant, as she pulled it from its northern source. Decker was too near the origin to be greatly affected by the concentration of power, a week's worth of rage condensed into a day of wrath, but those south of her would feel it true.

So fixated was she on her effort, she did not realize until it was too late that she had begun to weep. Tearless and silent, she poured out her sorrow so that it may be carried away with the snow and pine. It seemed a lifetime since she had last expressed an emotion, and in truth, doing so brought her no relief. She hardened herself, redoubling her focus and thwarting the weakness she knew accompanied lack of restraint. *You are the only one to blame,* she scolded herself, then swallowed hard one final time, burying the entirety of her anguish back within—back where it belonged. She was a stone, once again, and so she vowed remain.

FROM THE AUTHOR

You are a brave reader to have invested so much of your time in an unproven book by an unknown author. Thank you!

This book has attracted plenty of negative attention: claims that it is sexist, muddled, morbid, etc. This series is not intended for everyone, but it would be a shame to have detractors prevent the smaller portion of fantasy readers who might actually enjoy it from giving it a chance. Reviews are greatly appreciated, not only because they give potential readers info, but because they feed the algorithmic beasts which determine success and failure—being controversial used to be a good thing, now it just lowers your all-important average rating. Against the advice of those smarter and more successful, I read them all, and they help justify the immense amount of time spent on this not-nearly-enough-to-live-on endeavor of writing epic fantasy.

Sign up for the newsletter to be notified of the sequels:

Book 1: The Axe and the Throne
Book 2: Tides of the Realm
Book 3: *Title Pending*

www.MDIreman.com

Made in the USA
Columbia, SC
23 March 2020

89819083R00295